N

GOLDEN STATE BRIDES

TWO-IN-ONE COLLECTION

Keli Gwyn
Erica Vetsch

D1113443

BARBOUR
PUBLISHING

Published by Barbour Publishing, Inc., P.O. Box 719, Uhrichsville, Ohio 44683, www.barbourbooks.com

Our mission is to publish and distribute inspirational products offering exceptional value and biblical encouragement to the masses.

 Member of the
Evangelical Christian
Publishers Association

Printed in the United States of America.

A Bride Opens Shop in El Dorado, California

by Keli Gwyn

Dedication

To my awesome husband, Carl Gwyn
I spend countless hours time-warped to the 1800s,
but when I return to reality, there you are—
loving me, supporting me, and encouraging me.
Thank you for being my best friend,
my plotting partner, and president of my fan club.
I admire you, respect you,
and love you with all my heart.
In my book, you're a hero,
and I'm ever so grateful you're mine!

Chapter 1

April 1870
The Sierra Foothills of California

The stagecoach lurched to a stop, throwing Elenora and Matilda Watkins against a damask-covered sidewall.

Elenora clutched her nine-year-old daughter to her side. "Are you all right, Tildy?"

"Oh Mama. You don't have to be so skittery." Tildy shrugged out of the protective embrace, scooted across the bench seat, and shoved the leather window shade aside. "I want to see what's going on." She peeked out, whirled around with wide eyes and an enormous grin, and let the dust shield fall with a *thwap*. "It's an outlaw, and he's pointing a gun at the driver."

Where did her daughter get those wild notions of hers? Elenora shot Tildy a reassuring smile and leaned over the center jump seat to have a look. "Lord, help us."

A shudder ripped through her. The horrid man atop the big black horse was, in fact, aiming a gun at the coachman, but he was aiming a look of sheer evil at *her*. One of his eyes bored into her while the other seemed to roam. His sneer made her skin crawl.

How could this be happening? They'd ridden all the way from Omaha on that snorting beast of a train and made the line changes in Ogden and Sacramento City without incident. Why did something have to go wrong on the final five miles between Shingle Springs and El Dorado?

The outlaw's deep voice boomed. "Hand it over."

"I tells ya. I ain't carryin' no gold." The driver spat a stream of tobacco juice in the dirt. "If I was I'd have someone ridin' shotgun, wouldn't I?"

"If you're haulin' any valuables, I'll find 'em. Get down here, and show me what's inside, and then we'll take a look in the boot."

Elenora bristled. Under no circumstances would that scoundrel harm her daughter. He'd have to kill her first. She put Tildy on her right, positioned herself so she could see the men, and tipped her hat to block their view of her.

Resting a hand on her midsection, her thoughts flew to the twenty-five hundred dollars hidden beneath her corset. What would she do if the money were taken? She needed it to secure the partnership and provide for Tildy.

"Mama?" For once in her life Tildy had the presence of mind to whisper. "Do you think he'll shoot us?"

Elenora drew a fortifying breath. She must be strong for Tildy's sake, even though her mouth was as dry as the dust caking the stagecoach walls. "Don't you fret. We'll say a little prayer." She clasped Tildy's slender hands in hers. "Almighty God, watch over us, I beseech Thee. Our lives are in Thy hands. Amen." Hopefully she'd sounded convincing. The Lord hadn't seemed to pay her any mind lately.

If only she'd gathered the gumption to break free of Pa's controlling ways sooner, she'd have a gun and know how to use it. But instead of being able to protect herself and Tildy from this menace, they were at his mercy. Part of her longed to leap from the coach and give the overgrown cornstalk of a man with his flowing blond hair a piece of her mind, but that would be foolhardy—and she was no fool.

Since the seasoned driver had challenged the younger man,

he must have a plan, one involving that rifle she'd seen him stow under his seat or the pistol slung at his side.

If only there were something she could do to help. All she could think of was flirting with the outlaw in order to distract him, a thought so loathsome it soured her stomach. But if that would keep Tildy from harm's way, she'd do her best. Jake had made it clear he found her unappealing, but nothing about her had ever pleased her late husband. Surely a man depraved enough to threaten a woman and child at gunpoint wouldn't be as particular.

Elenora pinched her cheeks to add color to them and grasped the handle of the tiny door.

"Mama?" Tildy spoke in hushed tones, but her words spilled out in a torrent. "Are you gonna take on an outlaw?"

She should have known Tildy would embrace the exciting elements of their dilemma. "I'll do what I can to help the driver. I need you to stay inside. And don't make a sound."

"I can watch, can't I?"

"If you'll keep yourself out of sight." *Please, let Tildy mind me.*

Elenora flung open the door. She braced herself with a hand on one side of the opening, lifted her skirt enough to show her ankle the way she'd seen saloon girls back East do, and hooked her boot heel over the small stirrup-like step mounted beneath the door. Although every fiber of her being protested at the prospect of behaving in such wanton fashion, she produced the most alluring smile she could. "Don't tell me a big, strong man like you is interested in a trunk full of frocks and bonnets, which is all you'll find back there."

The vile man trained his good eye on her. "Well, now. This is getting more interesting by the minute." He slid from his saddle, pulled a cigar from his coat pocket, and bit off the end, which he sent flying with a noisy puff. "Come on out, missy, and let me have a good look at you."

If she could keep his attention on her, the coachman would be better able to locate his rifle and get into position. From his post up on the seat, he ought to have a clear shot.

Summoning every ounce of courage she possessed, Elenora addressed the leering man in front of her with a sickeningly sweet tone like the ones she'd heard silk-clad strumpets use when potential customers walked by. "It's such a long way down. Won't you be a gentleman and help a lady out?"

The words tasted bitter, but the possibility of him touching her was far worse. Only for Tildy would she attempt such a ploy.

Elenora held out her gloved hand and batted her eyes. Her stomach lurched. Losing her meal wasn't an option. All she needed was to distract him for a few more seconds and give the driver time to—

Shots rang in the distance, and horses' hooves pounded the ground. "Aaaiieeee!"

The shriek sent shivers racing along the length of her spine. Did the awful man have accomplices?

He wheeled around. "What the—" He sounded as surprised as she.

His huge horse reared with an angry snort, and Elenora started. The outlaw threw his cigar in the dirt, shoved his gun in his holster, snarled something at the frightened animal, and mounted it in one fluid motion. And then, in a flash of black, the horrid man fled.

"Yee-haw!" Another ear-piercing scream heralded the approach of two more riders with dirty bandanas over their mouths and dusty cowboy hats jerked low, waving guns in the air.

Had things just gone from gray to black? Distracting one man had been risky, but taking on two was more than she could handle. Since they were bouncing on the backs of their horses and the coach was stopped, the driver would have the advantage. Tildy's life and hers were in his hands now.

She ducked inside the coach, pulled the door closed, and dropped onto the seat beside Tildy, who craned her neck to see what was going on outside.

"What's happening, Mama?"

"We'll be fine, sweetheart. There are more men coming, but I'm sure they don't mean us any harm." Thankfully, years of schooling her emotions while she worked alongside Pa enabled her to keep her voice level. No sense alarming Tildy. Not that she seemed worried. Her fascination with hair-raising adventures knew no bounds. She sat in her rumpled green dress with her bonnet hanging by its strings and her bright blue eyes sparkling.

Laughter rang out as the two riders reined in their mounts beside the coach. "We sure showed him, didn't we, Timmy?" one of them shouted. "Had him high-tailin' like cats afire."

The stage shifted as the driver climbed from his perch. "What are you two scalawags up to? You done run off trouble this time, but I don't take kindly to you terrorizing my passengers ever' other week or so."

Tildy poked her head through the window.

"Matilda Anne, what do you think you're doing?"

"Watching."

Her daughter had no fear, which was more than Elenora could say for herself. Rude customers she could handle, but men brandishing firearms were another matter. She'd never forget the sight of the robber Pa had shot lying motionless with blood pooling around him on the shop floor. "Get back inside. We can see well enough from here."

Tildy plunked herself on the leather seat, folded her arms,

and gave a quick nod. "We're safe now. These are the good guys."

"We don't know that for sure."

The driver waved the back of a hand at the mounted men. "You two scoot on home before I report your antics to Sheriff Henderson." Since he didn't sound the least bit concerned, perhaps Tildy was right.

With a whoop, the rowdies took off. Elenora released the breath she hadn't realized she'd been holding.

The driver yanked open the door, pulled off his hat, and wiped a shirtsleeve across his weathered forehead. The musty scents of tobacco and sweat filled the coach. "Sorry about the ruckus, ma'am. That gunman"—he cast a glance in the direction the black horse had gone—"could've ruined our day. Sure am glad you and the young'un didn't make a fuss."

Tildy let loose with a most unladylike snort of disgust. She perched on the edge of the seat, twirling a dark brown braid around her finger. "I'm not a young'un. I'm going on ten, and I know all about outlaws. I read the wanted posters at the sheriff's office." She hunched over and lowered her voice. "Makes Mama scowl something fierce when she catches me."

"Ya don't say. You must be a smart young lady then."

"That robber." Tildy jabbed a thumb over her shoulder. "Have you seen his face on a poster?"

The burly man buried a hand in his mop of salt-and-pepper hair and scratched his scalp. "Can't say as I have, little miss. Must not be from around here."

"Do you think he would have killed us if those other men hadn't come up shooting and hollering?"

Elenora rubbed Tildy's back. "I think you've said enough, dear. We don't want to keep this man from his duty. Besides, Mr. Rutledge is expecting us."

The driver shook his head, and his flowing beard swayed.

"Got yourself a gabby one, don't ya? You ain't got no reason to worry though. I'm right handy with a gun." He patted the holster slung at his side. "But it were timely the way them Talbot twins come riding up when they did. Couldn't have planned a better day for one of their mock holdups."

"You know those boys?" Elenora asked.

"Yup. Tommy and Timmy. They turned thirteen last month and think they're full-fledged men now, but they still got some growin' up to do. They live in El Dorado, same as your Mr. Rutledge."

Tildy snickered. "He's not *our* Mr. Rutledge. Mama's just going to work with him in his shop." A mischievous glint shone in her eyes. "Course if he's real nice, maybe Mama will like him, and he could be—"

"We're not far from El Dorado, are we, sir?"

The driver jammed his sweat-stained hat on his head. "No ma'am. Couple more miles is all. I'll have you there faster than you can say Rutledge Mercantile." He chuckled as he headed for his seat.

With a call from the driver to his team, they were underway. Tildy scrambled around the folded end of the jump seat and planted herself on the rear-facing bench as far from Elenora as possible in the confines of the tiny passenger compartment.

The stagecoach, which had seemed little more than a torture chamber on wheels earlier, now struck Elenora as cozy. Thank the Almighty they were unharmed. She shuddered to think what terrible fate might have befallen them if the twins hadn't ridden up when they did.

Perhaps the Lord had actually heard her prayer after all. Mama had always said He was ever present, protecting His flock at all times. If only her faith were as strong as Mama's had been. But after an arranged marriage to a man with a mean mouth followed by his funeral and years under Pa's thumb, Elenora couldn't help but wonder if God cared about her happiness. He certainly didn't seem to be the comforting presence Mama had found Him.

Not that Elenora had forsaken her faith. She'd prayed about the move West, but when answers weren't forthcoming, she took charge of the situation. For years she'd done what Pa expected of her, but she'd finally found the courage to break free of his tightfisted hold and lead her own life.

In less than an hour she'd be a partner in a successful mercantile. Pa might not have been willing to make her a partner in his, but Mr. Rutledge had chosen her from all the candidates who'd answered his advertisement for a partner. Although being accosted en route to her new home didn't paint a promising picture, she'd dealt with railroaders in Omaha. She could do this. She would simply stand tall, face the future with her feet planted firmly beneath her, and rely on the one person she could trust. Herself.

Tildy's boots scraped the wooden floor as she swung her legs. "I can't wait to get there. I just know Mr. Rutledge will like me. What did Mrs. Rutledge say again?" Only her spirited daughter could make such a smooth shift from their perilous situation to the adventure awaiting them in El Dorado.

"You know the answer, sweetheart. It hasn't changed."

"Say it anyways, one more time. *Please?*"

Elenora shook her head and smiled. How could she deny Tildy's request? Her poor girl had been cooped up for days. "She said her son has a soft spot for little girls, and she's sure he'll let you help him in the shop from time to time."

"I hope he sells candy."

"Since there's a grocer in town, he may not. We'll know soon enough."

"There were grocers in Omaha, but Grandpa still had candy in his mercantile." Tildy rubbed her stomach. She sat quietly for a moment and then creased her forehead. "Do you think Mr. Rutledge will be. . .friendlier than Grandpa?"

"His mother said he has blue eyes that twinkle when he smiles and a laugh that bounces off the rafters, so what do you think?"

"I think he sounds wonderful. And I know I'm going to like him." Tildy stood, rolled up the supple leather covering the glassless side window, and secured it with the straps. The landscape sped by in a blur of sprawling oaks and shrubs with reddish-brown bark and pale green oval leaves—*manzanita* the conductor had called them. A hint of a breeze carried the earthy scent from clumps of California bunchgrass sprinkled over the hillsides.

Tildy leaned out. Elenora opened her mouth to issue a warning but bit back the words. What was a little dust after the fine black particles that had rained on them the past week? They already smelled of grease and soot. She attempted to smooth the wrinkles in the sturdy poplin of her skirt, glanced at her once-white gloves, and sighed.

Hopefully Mr. Rutledge was an understanding man and wouldn't think less of her for arriving in such a state. And please, let him be all Tildy hoped he'd be. She needed to see that there were men in this world who would treat her kindly. Jake's razor-sharp tongue had left scars, and Pa didn't know how to be anything but gruff. If Maude Rutledge had been truthful, her son would be a decided improvement. There was one way to find out. Tildy could speak with him first.

Elenora patted her midriff, the fat envelope crinkling beneath the layers of fabric. Lord willing, Mr. Rutledge would prove to be a fair business partner, too, who would welcome her ideas for the shop and allow her equal say in how her inheritance from Jake's parents was spent.

Since Mr. Rutledge had agreed to take her as his partner and was said to be fond of children, she had hope. Something she'd not felt in a long time.

The stagecoach rumbled into El Dorado, and Miles Rutledge glanced up in time to see it rush by the windows at the front of his shop at half past two. Confound it! He was late. He'd been occupied helping the last customer and lost track of time. How could he have let this happen? His new partner was on that coach, and he wasn't there to greet him.

Miles shed his white apron, tossed it on the counter, and grabbed his short frock coat and hat. "I'm off, Sammy," he called to his clerk. In his haste, Miles let the door bang shut, rattling its glass center.

With long strides, he covered the block between his business and the Wells Fargo office, shrugging into his coat as he went. He'd planned to change his collar and comb his hair. From what Mother said, Watkins valued order. Being tardy and looking less than his best didn't make for a good first impression.

A young girl stood beside the coach craning her neck. Watkins's daughter, no doubt. He drew near and beheld a sunny smile that could brighten the darkest day. "You're Mr. Rutledge, aren't you?"

"Yes, I am."

"I'm Tildy. I got permission to talk to you as long as I promised not to be pesky." Her wide grin revealed a pair of dimples.

He scanned the area. A petite woman stood a few feet away,

a violin case cradled in her arms like a baby, watching them intently while the driver unloaded what must be her luggage. She took a step toward Miles and the girl, making no attempt to hide her interest in their conversation, although she kept much of her face hidden beneath her wide-brimmed hat. Not another busybody. El Dorado had its fair share already.

"We've come such a long ways," the girl continued, "and I'm awfully glad we're here. I hated sitting on a train six whole days, but I liked riding in the stagecoach. A real live outlaw tried to hold us up. That was the best thing." She beamed.

"An outlaw? Around here?" He addressed the driver, who thumped the last of the woman's three trunks on the wooden walkway. "What happened, Wally?"

The stocky man straightened and rubbed his back. "For once the Talbot twins done something right. Showed up before the scoundrel could fire a shot and ran him off."

Miles nodded. "I'm glad no one was hurt. Any idea who he was?"

"None. Ain't seen an outlaw in these parts in a long while. This one was a tall, skinny fellow on a large black horse. Since he beat a path north like a cougar was on his tail, I don't expect any more trouble. I got to pick up a party in Placerville, but you oughtta have a word with the sheriff."

"I'll do that."

The woman turned to Wally and spoke in a clear, refined voice. "You don't think we're in danger then?"

"No ma'am. I hear tell the papers back East are full of stories about outlaws and Injuns attackin' travelers, but them things are more likely to happen in open country. Not here where folks has settled."

"Good." She exhaled audibly and lowered her case to her side.

Miles rarely saw a woman with a violin. Did she actually play? Before he could steal a glance at her neck to look for the telltale mark, she spoke with Wally, who patted her trunks, pointed to the hotel, and nodded. She turned, revealing the right side of her face, and Miles took in her regal profile. What was she doing in a small town in the Sierra Foothills? Women of her bearing generally gravitated to Sacramento City or San Francisco.

"Do you sell candy?"

Miles started. He'd forgotten about the girl. He leaned forward with his hands on his knees. "Yes, Miss Watkins, I sell some candy."

She giggled. "I'm not even ten yet. That's not old enough to be *Miss* Watkins. I'm just Tildy. My real name's Matilda." She made a face. "It was my grandmother's name, but I can't stand it. Mama calls me Tildy, but Grandpa calls me Matilda, even though I asked him not to."

Miles glanced down the wide main street. Where was the girl's father? And why had she referred to her mother? Was she still pining for her mama perhaps? He'd heard about people who refused to accept the deaths of loved ones and spoke of them as if they were still alive.

"Mama said your first name is Miles. I like it. My teacher told us about a famous man named Miles Standish. He was one of the Pilgrims on the Mayflower. Do you know about him?"

"I've heard of him. But I'm not named after him. Like you, Tildy, I'm named after a grandparent, my mother's father."

He fought to stay focused on the child's chatter, all the while trying to make sense of the references to her mother. The woman from the coach must be waiting for someone, because she hadn't gone away. Instead she'd moved closer and was sure to hear every word he and the girl said. He must locate Watkins.

"Mama told me you live with your mother."

"She lives with me, yes. You'll meet her shortly. Right now I want to meet your papa. Where is he?"

Tildy stared at him, her mouth gaping wide enough to catch a swarm of flies. She shook herself. "He died a long time ago, when I was a little girl."

"I beg your pardon. Did you say your father has passed on?" He knew about loss. But what this girl said made no sense.

"Uh-huh. But I'll tell you a secret." She beckoned him with a crooked finger, and he drew near. With her hand cupped around his ear, she whispered, "I'm not sad. I just wish Mama could find a nice man who could make her eyes shine like Grandpa's do when he looks at his new wife. I don't like her being sad."

So *Mrs.* Watkins had misled him, had she? What exactly did the E. F. on her stationary stand for then? Exploitative Female? Had she seen her chance to invest in a successful business and taken it, heedless of his response?

Tildy's breath warmed his cheek. "But she said I'd like you, and she's right."

He straightened and forced a smile. It wasn't Tildy's fault her mother had turned out to be a scheming interloper. The woman might have considered her child's feelings instead of her own aspirations though. He disliked the thought of disappointing the girl, but he had no plans to take a woman as his business partner, especially one he couldn't trust. If there was one thing he'd learned from his late wife, it was to be wary of women who would say whatever it took to get their way.

He lifted his eyes to the cloudless sky and uttered a silent prayer. *Lord, surely this can't be Your plan for me, can it? I want to follow Your leading, but I can't bear to have another woman use me for her own ends the way Irene did.*

"Where is your mother?"

A puzzled look pinched Tildy's face. "Mr. Rutledge, she's right there." She pointed at the dignified woman beside the trunks, who took a sudden interest in her handbag.

Elenora busied herself looking in her reticule. Her nerves were tighter than the strings on her violin. Mr. Rutledge didn't sound any too pleased at the prospect of meeting her. But at least he'd been kind to Tildy. Not once had he shown the slightest impatience, and yet something wasn't right. She'd made it clear in her letters that Jake had died.

"Mama, I didn't prattle, did I?"

Tildy stood at Mr. Rutledge's side, gazing at him with adoration. As Elenora expected, Tildy had taken to him like a weary traveler to a way station. After the treatment she'd endured from the men in her life, any kindness would have won her over. But would Mr. Rutledge continue to be as tolerant when he realized she could talk from now until Christmas with little encouragement?

Elenora gave him a more thorough appraisal. As men went, he was pleasing. He cut a fine figure in his frock coat and derby. His dark brown hair looked recently trimmed. Mrs. Rutledge had said he was tall, but Elenora hadn't realized just how tall. She barely came to his chin, one strong and round as a chin should be, not blunt and square like hers. With that unmistakable reddish mark below his jawline on the left side, he must be a violinist, too, although his mother hadn't said he played.

"You did fine, Tildy." Elenora raised her gaze to meet Mr. Rutledge's. Vivid blue eyes flashed as he looked down his aristocratic nose at her. He advanced and stood so close she fought the urge to step back. This stranger seemed anything but the easygoing, jovial man his mother's comments had led her to expect. Tildy squeezed between them, and he widened the gap. Elenora could have kissed her daughter then and there.

"Mama, this is Mr. Miles Rutledge. Mr. Rutledge, may I introduce my mother, Mrs. Elenora Watkins?" Tildy had spoken slowly and politely, which had to be an effort considering she was all atwitter.

Elenora extended a gloved hand. "I'm pleased to make your acquaintance, Mr. Rutledge."

He grasped her hand and gave it a perfunctory shake. The look in his eyes made her want to flinch. What was it she saw in their depths? Displeasure? Disgust? Or was it anger?

"Mama, you were right. He is a nice man. And I think he's handsome, don't you? I know you were afraid he'd be—"

"Yes Tildy, he's, um, a fine-looking man." She attempted a smile, but it felt strained. Why was he glaring at her? "Did you find out if he sells candy?"

"Your daughter did ask, *Mrs.* Watkins. She's honest about what she wants."

"She can be outspoken at times, but she means well. And I've told her whispering is impolite. Did she say something amiss?"

His carefully combed mustache concealed a portion of his mouth, but the small lines at the corners indicated his lips were pursed. "Not at all. Tildy is forthcoming, unlike some people."

Elenora fingered the silk violets at her throat. Mama had always said the tiny purple blossoms stood for modesty and served as a reminder to show no impropriety in appearance, behavior, or manner. Much of the time Elenora maintained rigid control, but this man vexed her. What did he mean by those inexplicable lines he'd dropped into their discourse?

She lowered her violin to her side and passed a hand over her rumpled dress. "Mr. Rutledge, I suggest we retire to your mercantile where you and I can share a private conversation. Would there be someplace for Tildy to wait? Someplace safe?"

"She could look around the shop while we discuss things in my back room. Sammy—he's my clerk—would look after her."

"Thank you. I guess I'm a little nervous after our encounter on the stagecoach."

"As Wally said, that was a rare occurrence. El Dorado is a civilized place, a fact I recall having Mother mention in one of the letters I had her draft. Our sheriff rarely has cause to pull his gun."

"She said many things, that being one of them." But were they true? The town might be a safer place than Elenora had first thought, but was Mr. Rutledge really the kind, amiable man his mother had led her to expect? She'd best find out.

Tildy tugged on Elenora's sleeve and lifted eyes full of concern. "Is everything all right?"

She brushed a hand across Tildy's cheek. "I'm sure it will be, sweetheart, as soon as Mr. Rutledge and I have an opportunity to. . .come to an understanding."

"Shall we go?" he asked.

She lifted her gaze to meet his. "By all means." His glacial look chilled her to the core, and she broke eye contact. Hopefully she hadn't revealed any of the emotions threatening to twist her insides into a tangled mess.

He pointed out his shop, and she swept down the rutted road toward it—and her uncertain future. Why had she dared hope things would work out well? She knew better.

Chapter 2

The bell on the door of Rutledge Mercantile tinkled as Elenora marched inside, with Tildy in front and Mr. Rutledge behind. Housed in the bottom of an impressive two-story rock-sided building with a brick front, the shop was much larger than Pa's place.

Elenora's bootheels thudded on the even, well-maintained wooden floor. She ran a hand over the smooth top of an oak display case that had been polished to a glossy sheen. Such workmanship. And not a fingerprint could be seen on the cases' glass fronts. Mr. Rutledge obviously took pride in his business.

He carried pots and pans of every size and shape, crockery for any use possible, and enough washboards to supply a town twice the size of El Dorado. However, the meager selection of fabrics in serviceable colors would need supplementing. It was so like a man to overlook the finer things.

She paused before shelves where candles lay in straight rows, like soldiers standing at attention, and fought the urge to smile. A thick sweet scent drew her forward, where she found small bags of pipe tobacco, again arranged with military precision. What she could do with a bit of fabric, some ribbon, and artful arranging.

"Look, Mama. He has toys." Tildy darted over two rows and dropped to her knees in front of a case housing an iron bank, two wooden tops, and a bowl of marbles.

Mr. Rutledge sauntered up to Tildy and tapped her on the shoulder. "I think you forgot something."

She followed his hand to where he gestured. "Oh! The candy. And look. You have my favorite. Peppermint sticks. Do you like them, too?"

"I'm partial to lemon drops myself. Always have a few in my pocket." With a tilt of his head, he beckoned her, and she tripped along at his side. They reached the jars lining the front edge of the counter, and he paused with his hand over one. "May I, Mrs. Watkins?"

She opened her mouth to refuse, but one look at Tildy's eager countenance, and she just couldn't. "I suppose so."

Tildy accepted the red-and-white-striped sweet with one of her sunny smiles. She popped the candy in her mouth but pulled it out quickly, her cheeks bright pink. "Thank you, Mr. Rutledge."

He tugged one of her braids, and she giggled. "You're most welcome."

Elenora pressed a hand to her chest and felt a swell of pride. Tildy might be prone to chatter, but she could charm most people she met with her enthusiasm and candor. She had Mr. Rutledge eager to do her bidding after a mere ten minutes. How sad that neither Jake nor Pa had warmed to her as many did.

"Let me get Sammy so he can meet you lovely ladies." Mr. Rutledge grinned at Tildy, but his expression hardened when he looked at Elenora.

She tilted her chin a mite higher and straightened. Was she seeing things, or had her gesture caused one side of his mouth to quirk in a smile? She couldn't be sure because he executed an about-face, made his way to a heavy burgundy curtain hanging in a doorway at the back of the large room, and disappeared behind it.

Moments later, he reappeared with a young man crowned with a shock of curly hair several shades lighter than Mr.

Rutledge's rich nut brown. After completing the introductions, he ushered her to the brocade curtain, pushed it aside, and followed her into his back room.

She scanned the scene before her. Boxes and crates, many open and rummaged through, occupied much of the floor space and were tucked haphazardly on rows of floor-to-ceiling shelves filling half the room. The shop was well kept, but this. . .

Mr. Rutledge took such care with his appearance. Every hair was in place, his white shirt crisply pressed, and his boots recently polished, but clearly his exacting nature didn't apply to all aspects of his life. His mother hadn't exaggerated when she'd written that he could use help establishing order.

He spun the desk chair around, removed the mountain of papers in it, and waved his free hand at the leather surface now visible. "Be my guest."

She took the proffered seat. Because the rolltop desk beside her held mounds of invoices, catalogs, and advertisements, she set her violin at her feet.

His mother had said bookkeeping was not her son's forte. It would seem Mrs. Rutledge possessed the gift of understatement. How anyone could conduct a business amidst such chaos, Elenora couldn't fathom. She was organized, though, and could soon have the back room put to rights.

Mr. Rutledge grabbed a bentwood chair and placed it in front of her, but he didn't sit. Instead he strode a few paces away, wheeled around, and held his fisted hands at his sides.

"You're a woman."

"You're observant."

He inhaled deeply, his nostrils flaring. "You're going to continue your game, are you?"

"Game? What game? I don't understand."

He stalked toward her one slow step at a time, his fists

planted on his waist, until he towered over her. "I rarely get upset, Mrs. Watkins, but your charade is. . .is. . .contemptible."

She leaped to her feet, her chest heaving, and stared into icy-blue eyes. Mere inches from him, she heard his labored breathing and saw his jaw flex. What could she have done to drive him to such an ungentlemanly outburst? Perhaps allowing Tildy to meet him first had been a mistake, but she had to see how he reacted to her daughter, to see if he were a patient man. "I'm sorry if you think I used you ill."

"You're sorry? Is that all you have to say for yourself? No explanation? Just 'I'm sorry'?"

The smell of sandalwood shaving soap tickled her nose. "I didn't think you'd mind, and I n–needed to know if you could get along with her." Oh bother. Why did her voice have to tremble? She must be strong. Hadn't she vowed never to let another man run roughshod over her?

He cast his eyes toward the shop. "*Her?* As in Tildy?"

"Yes, Tildy. Who else?"

"What's *she* got to do with it?"

"Everything. As I said in my letters, she's used to visiting me while I'm working. I had to be sure you would honestly welcome her, not merely tolerate her."

Twin furrows creased his broad forehead, reminding her of the endless stretch of rails she'd traveled to reach him. He paced, not an easy task given the many obstacles in his path.

Dust motes danced in the shaft of sunlight streaming through one of the back windows. Birdsong drew her eye to shrubs and trees across the alley from the shop. Beyond them stood a white clapboard house. According to what his mother had written, that would be his house.

He returned to stand before her. His anger had faded, easing the tightness in his fine features. Yes. Very fine features indeed.

"Ah-ha!"

"What?"

"You're blushing, Mrs. Watkins."

Was she? Her hands flew to her warm cheeks.

"I can understand your embarrassment. A woman doesn't like to admit her failings."

"I beg your pardon. What *are* you talking about?"

"You thought you could use your daughter to smooth the way. That I'd be so taken with Tildy I'd overlook your deception."

Her mouth fell open, and she snapped it shut with such force her teeth clacked together. "Mr. Rutledge, I do believe you're overreacting. You strike me as a reasonable man. Won't you allow me to explain?"

He held out a hand. "By all means."

She sat, snatched one of the many fliers littering the desktop, and fanned herself. "It's warm for spring, isn't it?"

"Midsixties, which is normal for this time of year."

"It was in the forties when we left Omaha."

He crossed his arms and tapped a foot. "I'm waiting."

She moistened her lips and took a deep breath. "I love my daughter and didn't have the heart to restrain her. She's been eager to meet you. I wanted to see if you could endure her chatter. Not everyone can." Pa certainly had no tolerance for it, and his new wife even less.

Mr. Rutledge seated himself in the bentwood chair. "Tildy is a remarkable girl. But you still haven't answered my question. Why did you portray yourself as a man?"

She laughed. "A man? Whatever gave you that idea?"

"The letters came from E. F. Watkins."

"That's correct. I learned long ago to use my initials in correspondence. Some men don't welcome women into their enclave. I was delighted to discover you weren't one of them."

He leaned back, raising the front chair legs off the floor. The man surely wasn't thinking straight, or perhaps he didn't consider her worth impressing, because a gentleman would never tilt back like that in a lady's presence. "Then, you admit to—let's soften the term—misleading me?"

"My, but you're persistent. To be honest, I have no earthly idea how you could have mistaken me for a man when I clearly stated I'm a widow and gave you my full name in the first letter."

"Elenora."

How lovely it sounded rolling off his tongue. Almost musical. "Yes. Elenora Francine Watkins."

"I, um, didn't know until Tildy said it."

"How could you not have known? Unless you—"

"Didn't read the letters." He ran a finger beneath his collar. "Mother offered to pen my replies, but whenever I asked to see your letters. . . She produced an envelope on occasion, but the letters themselves. . . She relayed the key facts."

"Surely she—" No. Mrs. Rutledge had obviously kept the information from her son. But why? It made no sense.

The legs of his chair banged against the floor. "I think it's time we paid my mother a visit."

"Moth–er!" Mr. Rutledge called.

A tall gray-haired woman hobbled into the entry of his two-story white house. A dusting of flour covered her ample front, and she smelled of cinnamon. "Good afternoon and welcome. You must be Mrs. Watkins. I'm Maude Rutledge." She wiped her hands on her apron, extended one to Elenora, and clasped hers firmly.

"Yes, she's *Mrs.* Watkins. A fact you neglected to mention."

Mrs. Rutledge swatted him on the arm. "Calm yourself, Miles. I'm sure they heard you bellow all the way down to the livery."

"I'd like to hear your explanation. Now, if you don't mind."

"Tut-tut, son. I taught you better manners than that." She turned to Elenora. "Where is your daughter, Mrs. Watkins?"

She opened her mouth to answer, but he beat her to it.

"With Sammy. So 'fess up. Why did you deliberately withhold information from me? Or do you think I'm blind and wouldn't notice that an attractive woman showed up instead of a man?"

Elenora feigned interest in the braided rug. Did Mr. Rutledge realize what he'd said? Perhaps not in his agitated state. She couldn't recall the last time a man had said she was attractive. She wasn't, of course, but it was nice to hear him say so.

"I never once said she was a man. I wouldn't lie to you. I'm a God-fearing woman. Since the other candidates were men, you assumed she was a widower."

"And you allowed me to labor under that assumption for months. Now I understand why you were never able to locate her letters when I asked for them. But why did you do it? You may have worked in the shop, but it is my business."

Mrs. Rutledge shook her head and turned to Elenora. "You must be tired after your journey. I've got tea ready, if you'd care to join us. I'm moving slowly today—the rheumatism, you know. I'll toddle along to the kitchen and meet you two shortly."

Mr. Rutledge huffed. "It's not like you to ignore me, Mother. We need to talk about this."

"Don't pay him any mind, Mrs. Watkins. He's really an affable fellow when he doesn't have a thorn in his pride. We'll talk later, son." She shuffled toward a door to their left.

"Fine. I can wait. This way, Mrs. Watkins." He indicated a door on their right.

Elenora entered the parlor. With windows on two walls, the room was drenched in light. She took a seat on a floral-patterned settee, and he established himself in a large leather wing chair. Feminine touches abounded. A vase with sunny daffodils on the table. Antimacassars on the chair backs. A framed sampler over the mantel.

Mrs. Rutledge obviously had some influence in her son's home, but she'd gone too far meddling in his business the way she had. How could she have allowed her son to believe his new partner was a man? And for what reason? She'd better have some answers, or he wouldn't be the only one grilling her.

The second hand on the grandfather clock made three revolutions. With each swing of the pendulum, the tightness in Elenora's neck and shoulders intensified. She could take the oppressive silence no longer. "I see you have a piano. Do you play?"

"Mother does."

Working with this man would prove difficult, unless his mother was right. Once he dealt with his shock, perhaps he'd relax, as he had with Tildy.

With things strained as they were, Elenora chose not to ask if he played violin. If he did, surely he'd know where to find the nearest orchestra. But she had to say something to ease the tension. "Thank you for showing my daughter such kindness. I hadn't dared hope for such a welcome on her behalf."

"Contrary to what you may be thinking, I'm not a complete boor."

He had no idea what she was thinking, which was a good thing since her thoughts continued to follow lines rarely traveled. What was it about him that was so arresting? The graceful slope of his cheekbones? His sapphire eyes? Or the way his broad shoulders filled his tailored frock coat?

The second hand completed two more journeys. The clock chimed three times, and Mrs. Rutledge entered, a tea tray in her hands. Her son stood and took it from her. "You should have let me carry this."

"I can still get around, although I'm not as spry as I once was. That's why I'm relieved you're here to take my place in the shop, Mrs. Watkins. Miles needs someone with more vigor than I possess—and someone who isn't terrified to enter that mess he calls a back room." She smiled and poured the tea.

He took the cup she handed him. "I've been patient. Now, tell me why you kept Mrs. Watkins's. . .gender a mystery."

Mrs. Rutledge fluttered a hand in his direction. "I didn't think it was of consequence. She has sterling qualifications and is willing to make a tidy investment in the business. You said she sounded like the ideal person for the job. Are you going to tell me now she's not?"

Elenora's hand shook, forcing her to set down her cup. What would she do if Mr. Rutledge refused to take her as his partner? Was he like Pa? Because if that were the case. . .

"I can find no fault with her on those counts, but I cannot—indeed I *will not*—have a woman as my partner." His firm declaration contrasted with the confusion he'd shown earlier. And why wouldn't he look at her?

"Miles David Rutledge, I can't believe what I'm hearing." Color flooded Mrs. Rutledge's softly wrinkled face, and her breathing grew labored. "Are you telling me that you, who chose to set up shop in the forward-thinking state of California, are closed-minded? Why, just last week you said you wouldn't be surprised to see Susan B. Anthony, Elizabeth Cady Stanton, and the other suffragists succeed in getting women the right to vote."

He added milk to his tea, his spoon clinking against the fine china as he stirred. "I said I expect to see it in my lifetime, yes, but I don't think the world is ready yet. I'm certainly not prepared for a woman to have her name on the door of my shop, even one as capable as Mrs. Watkins. I can imagine the ribbing I'd get from my friends."

Elenora squared her shoulders. Being discounted simply because she was a woman was bad enough, but being talked about as if she weren't there fluffed her feathers. "You needn't concern yourself, Mr. Rutledge, for I have no intention of being your partner. You've made it clear I'm not welcome."

Mrs. Rutledge's gaze shifted from her son to Elenora. "You don't mean to say you've come all this way and changed your mind, do you? Miles was just caught off guard. He may not take kindly to surprises, but my son's a reasonable man. Give him time."

Elenora studied him briefly. Although she had no doubt of his mother's sincerity, Mr. Rutledge looked anything but approachable as he stared into the distance with his mouth clamped shut and his brows drawn together.

"While I appreciate your concern, Mrs. Rutledge, I'm unwilling to take that chance. I have a daughter to think about and a future to plan."

The color drained from the older woman's face, rendering her pallid—and far less intimidating. "What will you do?"

"I have, as I see it, three options. I could return to Omaha, but since that would not be in my daughter's best interest, I refuse to do so. I'm aware men still outnumber women here in California and could place a matrimonial advertisement as some have." Was it her imagination, or had Mr. Rutledge flinched? She shook off the thought and continued.

"However, since my primary concern is Tildy's happiness, I'm left with one choice, one that appeals to me but may unsettle you, Mr. Rutledge."

"And that would be?" He eyed her with apparent curiosity—and a welcome touch of concern.

Good. Let him squirm. The thought might be ungracious, but she didn't care. He'd find out she was not a woman willing to be easily dismissed. After dealing with Pa's high-handed ways for thirty years, it was time she exerted herself and took a risk. She'd lived among rowdy railroad men, so she wouldn't let one unsuccessful outlaw frighten her away. She would simply see to it that Tildy was always close at hand.

"I did my research before I headed west and know women are able to own businesses here, so. . .I'll open my own."

Mrs. Rutledge choked on her tea and coughed into her handkerchief. Conversation ceased until she could speak. "Where do you intend to set up shop, my dear?"

"Since Tildy has her heart set on living in El Dorado, and since you've both extolled its virtues, I shall remain here. I saw a vacant building as the coach came into town—right across the street from your son's, as a matter of fact."

Mr. Rutledge uttered a couple of unintelligible syllables and trained his wide blue eyes on her. The shock evident on his face gave Elenora a surge of confidence.

A full five seconds passed before he responded. "And what type of business do you intend to run?"

She gave him one of her most proper drawing-room smiles. "Why, a mercantile of course."

Chapter 3

His mother's eyes brightened. "Your own mercantile, Mrs. Watkins? What an. . .interesting idea. With your experience you're sure to make a success of it. Wouldn't you agree, son?"

Miles debated how to answer. He'd be a fool to encourage Mrs. Watkins, and yet he admired her pluck. A knowledgeable and determined competitor like her could spell trouble for him, though. "You kept your father's books, so surely you're aware I have far more than twenty-five hundred dollars invested in the mercantile."

"Indeed. Pa has over four times that in his, and your shop is even larger, but I daresay it wasn't as grand at first as it is now. I'll start small and build my business."

Mother leaned forward. "You said in your letters you have a knack for buying. Tell me. What will you carry? I'd love to see new fabrics. Miles has had some of his over a year and can't be convinced to add more until those sell."

"Mother! I thought you were on my side."

She acted as though she hadn't heard him and kept her attention on Mrs. Watkins. "Some lighter weights would be nice. With temperatures climbing to over one hundred in the summer, lawn, batiste, or dotted Swiss would be good choices."

"Fabric definitely, in a variety of colors. And notions. Buttons, ribbon, and the like. I want to carry some books. I saw several ladies on the train with their noses buried in one called *Little Women*. Since women appreciate beauty, I'll sell items that will be both functional as well as attractive."

Mrs. Watkins had struck him as rather serious, but excitement shone in her chocolate-brown eyes when the talk turned to her proposed business. When he'd met her at the stagecoach, he'd been too shocked to notice more than the fact that she was good-looking. Even in her present rumpled state, she would turn the head of any man. But there was more to her than thick brown tresses and a flawless complexion. She was a woman possessed of intelligence, ambition, and drive. A powerful combination.

Had he been too quick to dismiss her?

No. He couldn't have a woman as his partner, especially one who seemed every bit as strong-minded as Irene and who had already shown she had ideas of her own—ideas that differed from his. A man would understand that a junior partner could offer suggestions, but he wouldn't expect them to be taken. A forceful woman, on the other hand, would do or say whatever it took to get her way. Irene certainly had, and her choices had robbed him of his happiness.

"Son, where is your head? Are you woolgathering?"

He rubbed his temple. "Go on. I'm listening."

"I asked if you'd be willing to loan Mrs. Watkins some of your catalogs so she can start preparing her orders."

"You want *me* to help *her* set up shop? Across the street from mine?"

Mother gave him her most schoolmarmish scowl, the one he'd dreaded as a boy. "It's the least you can do after refusing to honor your agreement, don't you think?"

He massaged the back of his neck in an attempt to ease the tightness between his shoulders. Mother had never deceived him prior to this, and for the life of him, he couldn't figure out why she had this time. She'd been aboveboard in her dealings with Father. They'd been a wonderful team, and Miles wanted what they'd had. But instead she'd kept things from him the way Irene used to.

Well, he wouldn't give up as easily this time. He'd press Mother for information later. For now he'd do his best to see if Mrs. Watkins was serious about opening a shop. She didn't seem like the kind of woman to rush into something.

"I'm beginning to get the picture. You planned this all along, didn't you, Mother of mine? You've dropped not-so-subtle hints about wanting me to change things in the Mercantile, but I never thought you'd go to such lengths to set a fire under me."

He shifted his attention to the determined widow. "And tell me, Mrs. Watkins. Is opening a shop your attempt to get even with me for not handing you the key to mine?"

She stood and pulled herself to her full height, her lips pursed and eyes flashing, every bit the affronted female ready to fling her fury his way. "Mr. Rutledge! How can you say such a thing? I would never stoop to revenge. You are forcing me to take action. If there's any place to lay the blame, it's at your own feet, along with your mother's, don't you think?"

He shot out of his seat and returned her penetrating gaze, one that would have downed a weaker man. "After your impulsive declaration, I don't know what to think." A truth that galled him.

Mother clutched the arms of her chair and rose with effort. "I think you should return to the shop, gather the catalogs, and escort Mrs. Watkins and her daughter to the hotel."

Get her out of his house and leave him to sort out his thoughts? A capital idea. "Where are you staying? I thought I heard you tell Wally to have your trunks delivered to the Oriental Hotel."

"If that's the large white one half a block from your shop, beside the tall oak tree, yes."

They reached the entry. Mother stood by his side and took

his arm. "No doubt you've had your fill of restaurant fare after your travels. Miles and I would be delighted to have you and Matilda join us for a home-cooked meal, wouldn't we, son?" She squeezed his arm none too gently.

He'd be rude to refuse. Besides, over supper he might be able to dissuade Mrs. Watkins from moving forward with her ill-conceived plan. Although he'd hate to see the woman lose her life savings, what with a child to provide for, she was doomed to fail. Her pitiful excuse of a shop would stand no chance against his well-established one. The townspeople were loyal to him and would be wary of an outsider.

"Yes, the two of you may join us. I know Mother's been eager to meet your charming daughter. And now, Mrs. Watkins, since I'm sure you'd like to freshen up after your travels, I'll see you and Tildy to the hotel."

If Mrs. Watkins were to lift that chin of hers any higher, she'd get a crick in her neck. "I will definitely avail myself of their services, sir."

From the firm set of her lips, he could see she was riled. All he'd done was suggest she might like to bathe. He was certain she'd like to rid herself of the layers of grime and locomotive odor. If their situations were reversed, he would.

Mother released her grip on his arm, tossed him a scowl, and addressed Mrs. Watkins with an apologetic tone. "I'm sure Miles meant to be helpful and didn't realize he'd been rather forward to mention such a thing. Traveling does take a toll on a body, but the hotel has all the amenities."

He'd bungled things again, had he? It wasn't like him to tickle his tonsils with his toes. He dealt with female customers all the time, but he'd behaved like a blunderbuss ever since meeting the petite widow with the backbone of steel. Despite her intention to fight for his customers, she intrigued him. He'd get a chance to find out more about her at supper.

"As delightful as it would be to partake of your cooking and your company, my daughter and I will dine at the hotel restaurant."

"We'll have you over another time, dear."

"Thank you, Mrs. Rutledge, for your gracious welcome. And now I'll get Tildy, and we'll make our way to the hotel." Mrs. Watkins smiled at Mother. "Mr. Rutledge." She gave him the briefest of nods and swept through the door he held open for her.

He stood at the window until she disappeared beyond the hedge surrounding the yard.

Mother rested a hand on his shoulder. "This wasn't one of your better days, son. You've got your work cut out for you. She's got a good head on her shoulders and will do everything in her power to succeed."

Mrs. Watkins could try, but she'd find out what he was made of soon enough. He'd spent fifteen years building the mercantile into the thriving business it was today, and he wouldn't let anyone threaten its survival. Especially a headstrong woman like her.

"It's so dirty, Mama."

Tildy ran a hand over a simple pine display case and held up a dust-covered palm to Elenora. The sun slanted through the large plate glass window at the front of the shop—her shop—throwing shadows over the littered floor.

"It may be dirty, but at least we're clean now." Never had a bath felt as good as the one she'd taken after Tildy finished hers the day before. They still smelled of lavender, thanks to the bar of French-milled soap she'd tucked in one of their trunks at the last minute.

"How long do you think it will be before you can open up?"

"I'll have the place clean in two shakes, but it's going to take time to get merchandise." If she'd known she would be going into business for herself, she would have begun ordering catalogs months before. As it was, she didn't know quite how to proceed since Mr. Rutledge had ignored his mother's request to loan his.

"Good morning."

Elenora spun around. Mrs. Rutledge stood in the open doorway of the rectangular room with her son behind her clutching a crate in his arms.

"Good morning. Won't you come in?"

They entered. Mrs. Rutledge sidestepped piles of debris left from the last tenant, but Mr. Rutledge remained rooted in place, his well-formed brows drawn. Evidently he was here against his will.

"You're looking lovely this morning, Mrs. Watkins. And this must be your daughter."

"Yes. My dear, this is Mrs. Rutledge."

Tildy greeted the older woman and smiled. She swept her gaze over Tildy, her penetrating blue eyes reminding Elenora of her son's. "Welcome, Matilda."

"Oh, please call me Tildy. I don't like being called Matilda."

Mrs. Rutledge looked down her long nose at Tildy, whose smile faded. "You're rather outspoken for a young girl, aren't you? Matilda is a perfectly respectable name. Since it's yours, that's what I will call you."

"Don't mind her, Tildy." Mr. Rutledge thumped the crate on the floor and joined them. "Mother doesn't believe in using nicknames. That's why she gave me a name that can't be shortened." He leaned over and spoke in an exaggerated whisper. "She may seem strict, but there's a soft spot inside. You'd never suspect it to look at her, but I'm almost certain there's a piece of candy in her pocket."

Tildy gave him a halfhearted smile. Apparently encouraged to have an ally, she refrained from voicing the retort Elenora had feared. Mr. Rutledge certainly had a way with Tildy.

"I'll not have you revealing all my secrets, son." Mrs. Rutledge pulled a peppermint stick from the very pocket he'd mentioned and slipped it to Tildy. "For later."

Her eyes as big as wagon wheels, Tildy glanced from Mrs. Rutledge to her son and back again. "Thank you," she squeaked.

He smiled warmly at her, but he appraised Elenora with a cool stare. "You managed to talk Steele into renting to you, I see. He's known as one of the most ruthless businessmen for miles. Charges far more than the place is worth. Did you agree to his terms?"

The weasel of a man had driven a hard bargain, but what choice did she have? His building was the only one available, and it did have furnished living quarters above, although the former resident had left them in a deplorable condition. The rooms would need a thorough scrubbing before they'd be habitable.

It hadn't been easy, but she'd negotiated a reduction in the first month's rent in exchange for cleaning the place. Despite her best efforts though, Mr. Steele wouldn't agree to offer her a long-term lease. If she were late with her rent by even one day, he reserved the right to evict her. She'd just see to it she was never late. "I negotiated a fair contract."

Mrs. Rutledge scowled at her son and turned to Elenora, gracing her with a smile. "I'm sure you managed things quite well. And I'm happy to tell you that Miles has agreed to loan you some catalogs after all. I figured you'd need them."

He inclined his head toward the crate by the door. "I'll let you use them. But only for twenty-four hours. That should give you time to copy addresses and write a few orders. After that it's up to you."

One day? She'd have to drop everything and stay up all night, and even then she wouldn't have nearly enough time to get the information she needed. Hopefully she could locate vendors in Sacramento City who carried wares from several suppliers and had some goods on hand. With the train coming as far up as Shingle Springs, shipments shouldn't take too long to reach her. She would visit the livery tomorrow and do some investigating.

"Thank you, Mr. Rutledge. You're too kind."

"If it weren't for Mother I'd have left you to fend for yourself. I'm not in the habit of assisting my competitors."

Mrs. Rutledge chuckled. "Son, you've never had a competitor, but it's high time you did. Having Mrs. Watkins here will make your life more interesting."

Elenora got the distinct impression Mrs. Rutledge found their situation amusing, although it was anything but. A rocky road loomed ahead, and her son was the biggest boulder in the path.

Chapter 4

Elenora stood beneath the wide wooden awning over the front of her shop two weeks later, surveying the sign hanging in the window.

The carpenter leaned against one of the sturdy beams supporting the shade structure. "Are ye happy with the placement, ma'am, or shall I shorten the chains?"

"It's fine, Mr. MacDougall. Thank you for everything."

"All in a day's work, lass. I'll gather me things and be on me way."

The ruddy Scot went inside the shop. She read the sign aloud. "Watkins General Merchandise. Established 1870."

Every time she thought about being a proprietor, her heart sang. Her place was but a quarter the size of Mr. Rutledge's and not nearly as impressive as his, or even Pa's, but it was hers. And no one could tell her how to run it.

The red-haired gentleman bid her good day, tipped his hat, and sauntered down the walkway. She should take advantage of Tildy's absence to visit the blacksmith and check on her special order, but she couldn't stop admiring the sign. Seeing her name on it made everything real.

"You look like a cat that just slurped a bowl of cream."

"Oh! Mrs. Rutledge. I didn't hear you coming."

"I don't tromp the sidewalks like that daughter of yours. I thought you might have heard my old joints clicking though." She peered through the large window. "Where is Matilda?"

Elenora glanced at Rutledge Mercantile. "Across the street

talking with your son. Again. I don't want her to be a pest, but I knew it would be easier for Mr. MacDougall to work if she weren't here wearing out his ears."

Mrs. Rutledge chuckled. "Miles doesn't mind. Her visits are the high point of his day." She shifted her gaze to the sign. "Quite satisfactory."

"I've always dreamed of seeing my name on the door in gilt-edged letters, but that will have to wait until I'm generating a profit and can afford to have the sign maker over from Placerville. Everything here costs a good deal more than I'm used to." She held out a hand toward the front door. "Would you like to come inside? I've added stools since you were here last, so you could get off your feet."

"You think of everything. I'd love to see what's new."

They entered the shop. Mrs. Rutledge eased herself onto one of the seats. Elenora slipped behind the single row of glass-front display cases running the length of the narrow shop and removed a piece of porcelain. "An ambitious vendor up from Sacramento City showed me this. Isn't it beautiful?" She set the vanity tray before Mrs. Rutledge, who ran a finger over the flowers painted on the fine white china.

"Violets. How fitting. Yours look lovely with the orchid calico you're wearing."

"I almost asked Mr. MacDougall to put some on the corners of my sign, but I fear I pushed him to the limits of his creativity with the curlicues I asked him to add around the edge."

"They're a nice touch. What's that I smell? Lavender?"

"The vendor had received a shipment of European soaps. I have Pears glycerin bars, too, but I passed on the ones from Wrights." She wrinkled her nose. "I'll leave it to your son to carry theirs. Men may like the strong coal tar smell, but I prefer something more delicate."

"I agree. May I see the lavender one?" Elenora removed a bar from the display case and handed the fragrant soap to Mrs. Rutledge, who took a whiff. "Mmm. I'll take it." She opened the reticule hanging from her wrist and produced a coin.

Elenora waved a hand. "Consider it a gift."

"You're as bad as Miles with those peppermint sticks he slips Matilda. You'll not stay in business long if you give away your wares."

"But I'll have a loyal customer, I hope." She smiled. "My shipment of fabric and notions is due the end of the week. If all goes well, I'll have enough merchandise to open next Monday. Then I'll see if the townspeople are willing to stop in. I know they've been your son's loyal customers." How she hoped they'd pay her a visit. Surely curiosity would draw some of them.

"That may be, but Miles is known for stocking the basics. He may make all the frills and frippery comments he likes, but women prefer pretty things. They'll be glad you're offering alternatives. One does tire of biscuits and craves a doughnut or cruller at times, even if we know better." Mrs. Rutledge patted her waistline.

She'd stopped by every couple of days. Her interest seemed genuine, but why was she eager to support her son's competitor? Elenora could keep quiet no longer. In spite of her hammering heart, she came from behind the counter and perched on a stool. "May I ask you a question? It's somewhat personal."

"You want to know why I didn't tell Miles about you." Mrs. Rutledge shifted, and her stool creaked. "As a rule I don't stick my nose in others' affairs, but when it comes to my son I've been known to make an exception. I'm not one to mince words either, so I'll be blunt. Miles fell apart when Irene died. They'd been married less than three years when he lost. . .everything that mattered to him."

A wave of what could only be called grief washed over Mrs. Rutledge's face. She gazed at the counter for what felt like hours before continuing.

"For the next three years my dear boy poured himself into his business. His letters during that time nearly tore my heart out. Not that he complained, although I almost wish he would have. But Miles is not prone to moping. A more genial, good-natured man you'll never meet."

She was right to a certain extent. Look how her son joked with Tildy. He was friendly with everyone, although Elenora thought he tended to be more guarded with her, even to the point of being testy at times. Perhaps her perceptions were colored by his rejection of her as his partner. She must try to view him in a more favorable light, since they were to be in frequent contact. "He wrote? So you lived elsewhere?"

"My husband, Mark—God rest his soul—was a tailor in New York City, and I worked alongside him. When arthritis bent his fingers five years ago, we decided to come west. Mark and I wanted see if we could bring back some of Miles's zest for life. He's better, but I've been searching for ways to restore him to the man he was. I thought having a partner would help. And quite frankly, you were the best suited. Alas, he's decided to do without, until his second-choice candidate is available this fall."

"But you knew I was a woman and chose not to tell him."

Mrs. Rutledge eased herself from the stool, picked up the soap, and averted her eyes. "Indeed you are. And a busy woman with a shop you're getting ready to open, so I'd best be about my business. Good day." She left without another word.

Elenora resisted the urge to slide the back of the case closed with such force that it would rattle the glass front, although the temptation to do so was great.

Mrs. Rutledge could be frustrating at times, but she must

have her reasons for evading the question. Patience would more likely produce the answer than pestering, so the best course of action would be to wait for a more opportune time to inquire.

Elenora pressed a hand to the spray of tiny silk flowers at her throat. *Modesty. Decorum. Control.*

Miles flew down the walkway the following morning and burst through the barbershop's open door.

Abe Fitzsimmons rested his clasped hands on his round middle. "Why, I do declare, Miles Rutledge. You're later than a snowstorm in July. And what kept you? Or is it *who?*"

Miles hung his jacket on a peg and folded his long form into the barber chair. "Business."

"You been comin' here every Tuesday at eleven o'clock sharp for goin' on fifteen years, and you waltz in ten—that's right— ten full minutes late, and all you can say is 'business.' Hank, Will, what do you think? Do I refuse to cut Beau Brummel's hair until he spills the beans?"

Miles grinned. "You two side with Abe, and I'll charge you double for your strings."

A grin planted itself on Will Dupree's tanned face and grew until it reached from ear to ear, and he burst out laughing. "Th– th–then I'll. . ." He struggled to catch his breath. "I'll go across the street to Mrs. Watkins's place."

"And I call you my friend?" Miles lifted his gaze to the ceiling of Abe's sandalwood-scented shop and shook his head. He should have known they'd have their fun with him. He supposed he had it coming, seeing as how he was the reason the spunky woman had chosen to go into business in the first place. A chuckle rumbled low in Miles's chest and escaped.

Hank Henderson twirled his ever-present ring of keys around his finger, the mass of metal jingling with each revolution. "I heard tell she was seen with a violin, so likely she'll carry strings—and rosin, too. For a lower price." The sheriff tossed his key ring in the air, caught it, and continued in a voice that held not a hint of a smile. "Which reminds me. I think we should invite her to our practice tonight. We could use a second fiddler—to help Miles out."

"A pretty lady in a den of foxes sure would liven things up." The gray-haired barber paused in his efforts to whip up a good lather and pointed the shaving brush at Miles. "Unless you're afraid of the *competition*."

Will hooted and slapped his side.

Miles feigned irritation. "Can't a man have a trim. . .and some peace? If you keep this up, old Abe here's likely to laugh at a crucial moment, and I don't want to leave bleeding and bandaged."

"You heard him, gents. This is serious. I have a masterpiece to work. Miles has to look his best, or the unattached females who've been fawnin' over him are likely to take their business to *Watkins Wonder Wares*."

Hank took a seat in one of the chairs along the wall opposite the large oval mirror. "And the wives will drag their husbands along."

"I carry most of the things she does. And my selections are more serviceable. What self-respecting man needs a sterling silver shoehorn with flowers on the handle?"

Abe unfolded his razor and ran it along the strop with a rhythmic *whop whop*. "But you like flowers, Miles. Have a garden full of them as I recall."

Will dropped into one of the chairs and draped his legs over the side. "We don't mean any harm, my good man, but it does make a fellow curious why you'd rather have her as your rival instead of your partner. Many men would balk at the idea of giving the position to a female, but I didn't take you as one of them, not with your Eastern education and all."

Miles leaned forward so Abe could drape a white sheet over him. "How would you like to have a woman working alongside you, Will, telling you how to run your farm?"

"Pearl does work with me. . .and tells me what she thinks. She's had some right fine ideas, too. She told me I ought to get the horse I've been hankering after. He arrives next week."

Abe pushed Miles back against the chair. "Well, I perform my handiwork alone, and if you value your face"—he brandished the shining razor—"you'll sit still."

Hank asked Will about his new horse. Miles closed his eyes and hoped Abe concentrated fully on the shave.

Minutes later a gentle breeze from the open door fluttered the cloth covering Miles. He inhaled deeply, relishing the woodsy smell of the shaving soap. Will had a point. The right woman could be an asset. Pearl proved that. But the wrong one could threaten to crush a man's spirit.

Miles's stomach clenched. Irene had acted interested in him and his business before they wed. As eager as he'd been to marry and have a family, he'd overlooked her tendency to talk about balls, teas, and such things. It hadn't taken long to see that all she cared about was her social calendar. Even the arrival of their precious little girl hadn't been enough to keep her home. She'd been at a soiree when the fire had—

No! He didn't need another woman to complicate his life, especially one certain to tell him how to run his shop. Mother did more than enough of that. But he didn't need a competitor either.

Like as not, though, Mrs. Watkins wouldn't last long.

Women were fickle creatures. Irene had spent the first three months of their marriage playing the role of an adoring wife, but she'd soon grown bored. From then on she'd spent more time with her friends than with him. From what he could see, she'd viewed their marriage as a means to an end. She was happy as long as he kept her reticule filled with cash and served as an escort when she required one. He'd dismissed his doubts and rushed into the marriage, and his haste had cost him dearly. He wouldn't make that mistake again.

Abe wiped the last of the shaving soap from Miles's face, spun the chair toward the back of the shop, and began the cut. The shears clicked as he worked.

Miles did his best to appear interested as Hank described the capture of a bank robber he'd been party to in his days as a deputy up in Auburn. Although they'd all heard the story a hundred times, that never stopped him.

"And one day I'll round up another as ruthless as Baby Face Cain, or my name's not Hank Henderson."

Miles spoke, careful not to move his head as Abe made his finishing touches. "That reminds me. Tildy said someone tried to hold up the stage on their way into town, but the Talbot twins ran him off. You hear about that, Hank?"

"When Wally was here a few days back, he mentioned the skinny feller and his big black horse, but I haven't heard a word since. I figure him for a vagrant who's moved on."

"I told Tildy not to expect to see him again, but she's got a hankerin' for adventure." Miles chuckled.

Abe reached for his hand mirror. "That mite's wearin' a rut between her ma's shop and yours. I seen her go back and forth two, three times a day. Wouldn't have her workin' as your spy, would you?"

Miles grabbed the mirror, pointed it at the barber, and

issued a playful reproach. "Why Abe Fitzsimmons, in all the years I've known you, I've never heard such nonsense come out of your mouth. I don't need a spy. Mother keeps me well informed about what's happening in town—especially the goings-on across the street from the Mercantile. But Tildy did say her mama asks about my shipments."

Footfalls on the walkway came closer and stopped. Abe's next customer no doubt.

Miles examined the cut. "Good for another week. And now I'll leave you three to your chin wagging, but let me assure you the woman in question poses no threat. She'll make her noble attempt, lose her money, and take the next train back to Omaha in no time. You'll see."

A familiar female voice replied. "Is that so?"

Miles shifted the mirror so he could see the woman behind him, who wore a pretty purple dress and a sour expression, and groaned inwardly.

Mrs. Watkins.

Chapter 5

W ill and Hank leaped to their feet. Miles yanked off the sheet covering him and flung it in the barber's chair. He stood and faced Mrs. Watkins.

No one said a word for the better part of a minute. Time seemed to stand still as she stared at him, her face free of emotion. Irene would have tossed out a sharp retort and stormed off. But Mrs. Watkins stood there unblinking, unmoving.

Abe picked up the sheet and folded it slowly and precisely.

Hank found his voice first and made a feeble attempt to ease the tension. He cleared his throat. "Fancy you stopping by, ma'am. We were just talking about you."

"So I gathered."

A red flush spread over Hank's neck. "Earlier, I mean. W—we were talking about you and your violin."

She shifted her gaze to him, a flicker of surprise the first sign of her feelings. "My violin, Sheriff Henderson? Whatever for?"

"The fellows and I—" Hank clutched his Stetson. "Begging your pardon, Mrs. Watkins. I don't believe you've met Mr. Fitzsimmons and Mr. Dupree. Let me do this up proper." He completed the introductions, despite his obvious discomfort. The chink in Hank's armor was womenfolk. The longtime bachelor turned to mush when a member of the fairer sex paid him attention.

As if she sensed Hank's discomfort, Mrs. Watkins thanked him for his service and gave him a rare smile, warm but without any sign of attraction. He released the death grip on his hat.

She shifted her attention to the portly barber. "I'm pleased to make your acquaintance, Mr. Fitzsimmons."

"Abe, ma'am. Just plain ol' Abe. It's what everyone calls me. Fitzsimmons is enough to tangle a tongue."

"Abe then. And Mr. Dupree." She nodded at Will. "It's a pleasure to meet you. Your wife stopped by my shop one day when I had the door ajar. She's a fine lady."

Will grinned. "That she is. Pearl told me you'd spoken."

"Now that we've attended to the niceties, Mrs. Watkins," Hank continued, "what I wanted to say was that if you'd like to join us tonight for our informal music practice, we'd welcome you. We meet here at Abe's at half past seven every Tuesday."

Mrs. Watkins looked from one man to the next with the exception of Miles, understandably wary. It wasn't every day a group of men extended a woman such an offer. If she thought the others shared the dim view of her prospects she'd heard him express, she had every right to doubt their sincerity.

"What do you play?" she asked Hank.

"I play the cello, Abe the viola, Will one of those newfangled banjos, and Miles the fiddle."

Her eyebrows went north, and Miles pressed his lips together to keep from smiling.

She kept her gaze on Hank. "A *fiddle,* you say. Do you play folk music then?"

"Yes, ma'am," Abe volunteered, "and have a right fine time of it. Whenever you want to join us for some toe-tappin' fun, mosey on over."

"While I appreciate the offer, I must decline. I shall be busy with my shop, for contrary to what some believe"—she pinned Miles with a direct gaze—"I intend to make a success of it. And now I must bid you gentlemen good day, but if you could stop by my shop, Mr. Rutledge, I'd appreciate it." She turned with a swish of her skirts and left.

Miles grabbed his coat and shoved in his arms. "Thanks for the shave and cut, Abe. And Will, that hayfork you wanted arrived."

He strode down the walkway until he caught up with Mrs. Watkins and fell in step beside her. She said nothing and acted as though she weren't aware of his presence. A sidelong glance gave him a glimpse of her mouth, which was set in a firm line. Not that he could blame her for being upset with him. Once again he'd tasted boot leather. He'd have to rein in that tongue of his, which was getting him in more trouble these days than it had in ages. This time, at least, he hadn't intended her to hear him.

But he wouldn't be ignored. "Mrs. Watkins, I'd like to know why you wanted to see me."

She stopped so quickly he had to take two steps back. "I didn't mean to eavesdrop, Mr. Rutledge. I should have announced myself."

This was more like it. She shouldn't have listened to a private conversation. But he shouldn't have been so outspoken either. "I'm the one who owes you an apology. I told you the day you arrived I'm not a boor, but I've done little to prove that."

Mrs. Watkins lifted wide eyes to him, but the flash of fire from before had changed to surprise or curiosity. She really was an attractive woman, despite her serious mien. If only she'd smile more often.

"Your mother and I have come up with a plan, and I'd like to tell you about it. Might we go somewhere private?"

"Sure. We can go to my shop. . .or yours."

"Yours is fine. I wanted another opportunity to look at your nice selection of fabrics." One corner of her mouth lifted in a too-brief smile, revealing dimples like her daughter's.

Had Mrs. Watkins just teased him? He pondered that all the way to his back room, where he offered her his rolling leather desk chair and took the bentwood himself.

Her gaze swept the room. And there it was again. That hint of a smile. He hadn't imagined it. He'd give a silver dollar for her thoughts.

She got right to the point. "It's about Tildy."

"Is she all right?"

Mrs. Watkins straightened the blotter on his desktop. "She's fine. She's with your mother."

"At the house?"

"She's invited Tildy to stay with her while I'm working. I'd intended to let you know sooner, but the livery wagon arrived, and I had to show the men where to put the crates. Then I sneaked a peek at the goods. Before I knew it two hours had passed." She lined up a lead pencil with the edge of the blotter, picked up his wax seal press, and turned it over to view his initials. "I came to see you at the Mercantile, but Sammy said you get your hair cut Tuesday mornings."

"Why was it so urgent? I don't have a problem with Mother entertaining. She knows that."

Mrs. Watkins replaced the press and focused on him. "Your mother didn't invite her for a visit. She's offered to watch Tildy for me while I work, at least until the new school term starts in the fall."

"Since you have your own shop, I thought she'd stay with you."

"I did, too, but she wants to play games or talk, and I have work to do. She gets bored, and your mother noticed that when she stopped by this morning. She said she could use Tildy's help with her chores. She'll teach her how to cook, sew, and the like, which I can't. It's your house though, so I thought it only fair to let you know about our arrangement before I finalize things."

Mother had managed to get the lively girl under his roof for the better part of each day, had she? What next? "You're asking *my* permission?"

"Permission? No. But I would appreciate your support of the plan. Tildy is perceptive, and I wouldn't want her to feel unwelcome."

"There's no danger of that. She's welcome in my shop and my home."

Mrs. Watkins reached toward his sleeve as though she were going to touch him but jerked her hand back, her cheeks tinged a becoming shade of pink. "Thank you, Mr. Rutledge. I know you're doing it for Tildy's sake, but I'm grateful all the same."

He fixed his eyes on her slender fingers resting on the arm of the chair. The sudden desire to place his hand over them took him by surprise. He mustn't let Mrs. Watkins wile her way into his good graces with a display of gratitude. Mustn't forget that she had declared herself his adversary when she decided to set up shop directly across the street from his and was doing everything in her power to succeed.

She wouldn't, of course, but in the future he'd keep those thoughts to himself.

After several seconds she rose, swept to the curtain, and paused. "There's one more thing."

More? "Yes?"

"Your mother invited me to have dinner at your place each day, so I can spend time with Tildy. I was hesitant to accept the offer because it could be a bit awkward, what with us being competitors and all, but she insisted. Unless you object, I'll be joining you. . .starting today."

He clenched his teeth. That was not what he needed. Two strong women conspiring against him. A man's home was supposed to be his sanctuary, and yet his was being invaded by the woman intent on besting him—aided and abetted by his own mother. But what could he do about it? To refuse would cast him in a bad light and prove to Mrs. Watkins that she was getting to him. "Suit yourself."

She left. And so did his appetite.

Elenora rounded the corner half an hour later and trooped up Church Street. Although she was eager to see Tildy, the thought of facing Mr. Rutledge caused a swarm of butterflies to perform acrobatics in her stomach. He hadn't voiced his objection to having her at his table, but he didn't need to. His scowl had spoken for him.

If his mother hadn't made such an irresistible offer, she wouldn't be in this situation. But Mrs. Rutledge was right. How could a woman run a shop and get dinner? Besides—Elenora chuckled—she was a terrible cook. Pa's housekeeper had flatly refused to have her in the kitchen, which suited her just fine since, as far as she was concerned, cooking was as appealing as mucking out a horse's stall.

Tildy dashed down the hill toward Elenora. "I was watching for you. Oh, Mama, I like Mrs. Rutledge. She's not nearly as scary as I thought. She's kinda strict, and I have to mind her, but she doesn't snap at me or tell me to be quiet all the time like Grandpa did. And she lets me help her."

"That's wonderful, darling." Although she missed having Tildy around, knowing her girl was happy with the new arrangements did Elenora's heart good.

Gravel crunched beneath their heels as Tildy preceded Elenora up the path to the cheery white house, which sat amidst a profusion of flowers. Due to her agitated state of mind on her previous visit, Elenora hadn't noticed the riot of multicolored blooms filling the spacious yard. Mrs. Rutledge certainly had a way with plants.

The door flew open, and Mr. Rutledge stood on the threshold. Apparently he'd changed his collar since she'd last seen him, because the stray hairs and damp swipe from shaving cream she'd noticed earlier were gone. Rarely had she seen a man take such care with his appearance. His moustache arched in a perfect curve over his upper lip and was meticulously trimmed. Most men she'd waited on through the years weren't as exacting about such things, but she rather liked the fact that Mr. Rutledge was. He was the picture of a finely groomed gentleman.

"What's this I hear about you keeping my mother company, Tildy girl?"

"She's watching me while Mama works. And she's teaching me things, too. I got to open the jar of peaches, make the butter all pretty with one of her molds, and set the table. Grandpa's housekeeper called me a nuisance and wouldn't let me do anything like that."

"I'm sure Mother appreciates your help. A good partner is hard to find."

Elenora didn't dare bite her tongue because she could cause serious damage to hers if she did so in her current state of mind. "How nice that your mother appreciates a good partner when she sees one. Not everyone does."

He shifted his focus to Elenora. "True, but she knew what she was getting in advance."

Before she could come up with a retort, he held out an arm to Tildy. "Shall we see what smells so good?"

Elenora followed them into the dining room to the left of the entryway. A magnificent oak sideboard and matching china cabinet with etched glass doors graced two walls. Sunlight streamed in the two windows, colliding with the crystal chandelier and splashing shimmering streaks of color across the walls.

"There you are." Mrs. Rutledge stood in the doorway to the kitchen. "I'm so glad you agreed to join us, Mrs. Watkins. And you're home right on time, son. You must've smelled the food, as usual."

"I did. And it smells delicious." He kissed her cheek.

Mr. Rutledge seated Tildy on one side of the rectangular table and Elenora across from her. "I'll help Mother carry things in, and we'll be ready."

Elenora ran a finger around the gold-edged rim of the dinner plate. The quality and clarity of the bright white porcelain surpassed any she'd ever used. This had to have been a recent purchase because the pattern was Haviland's Moss Rose, one that had just been released. She'd processed a special order for it at the request of one of Pa's customers in Omaha. Mrs. Rutledge must have admired it as well, likely because of her interest in flowers. "Do be careful when you're handling these dishes, Tildy. They're much fancier than the ones you're used to."

Mr. Rutledge returned bearing a large tureen with steam wafting from it. "There's no need to worry. We use these dishes every day, so I ordered extra place settings."

How nice it must be to surround oneself with such fine things. Pa's shop had provided them with a decent place to live, but his furnishings weren't nearly as lavish as those Mr. Rutledge had. He'd obviously done well for himself.

She would work hard and see that some of the townspeople's money flowed her way. In time she'd have a home as lovely as this one. What fun it would be to write Pa and tell him about her success. He might regret his decision to cast her aside then.

The loaf of golden-brown bread Mrs. Rutledge carried made Elenora's mouth water. The older woman surveyed the table. "If you'll bring in the peaches, son, we'll be all set." She eased herself into the chair on Elenora's right.

He returned with the fruit and took his place at the head of the table opposite his mother. "Let's give thanks."

He and Mrs. Rutledge extended their hands toward Elenora and Tildy. Her daughter shot her a silent plea for direction. Elenora nodded and followed the lead of their host and hostess. She had no trouble accepting the hand Mrs. Rutledge offered, but taking her son's was another matter. All she could think of was that lame excuse for a handshake he'd given her at the stagecoach. Propriety demanded she comply, but she certainly didn't want to.

Mr. Rutledge's deep, rich voice filled the room. "Dear Lord, thank You for the food we're about to receive, and bless the hands that prepared it. Be with our guests as they settle in and learn about life in the West. In Your precious name, amen."

The moment the prayer ended, Mr. Rutledge released her. She put her hand in her lap and wiped it on her skirt. Even so she could still feel the warmth that had emanated from him.

He ladled meaty stew and passed bowls to his mother and Elenora. He handed one to Tildy, who had her lips so tightly pressed together her eyes squinted. "What's the matter? Don't you like stew?"

She nodded enthusiastically.

"Then what is it?"

She dug her teeth into her lower lip.

"It's all right," Elenora said. "Mr. Rutledge asked you a question, so you may answer."

Tildy's breath whooshed out. "Oh good, 'cause I thought I was going to pop. Mama said I was supposed to be seen and not heard, but it's powerful hard for me not to talk."

Mr. Rutledge's mustache twitched as though he was holding

back laughter. "What are you itching to say?"

"You do things real different than we do."

"You're not used to joining hands for the blessing? We've always done it that way, so I didn't think to say anything."

Tildy slathered her slice of warm bread with butter, her face scrunched in obvious concentration. What was going on in that active mind of hers? Whatever it was would no doubt tumble from her mouth shortly. With luck it wouldn't be something inappropriate, as had been the case more often than Elenora liked to remember. Her daughter's frankness had embarrassed her many a time.

With careful movements, Tildy rested her knife on the edge of her plate. "I like the hand-holding part, even though we've never done that. It's the way you talk to God."

Mrs. Rutledge inhaled sharply. "Why child, I understood you and your mother attend services regularly. Don't you pray?"

"Oh, yes. Mama does, before every meal, just like you. Other times, too. But she uses Thee's and Thou's and other fancy words like 'beseech' and 'transgressions.' Mr. Rutledge talked to Him like He was a friend."

"And speaking of transgressions. . ." Elenora pressed a finger to her lips.

"But Mama, you said I—"

"Could answer a question, not give a speech, dear."

Mrs. Rutledge shook her head. Not a good sign. No telling what she thought of Tildy's upbringing. "For years I had to keep Tildy quiet. Once Jake— Once things changed, I didn't have the heart to silence her. She's used to considerable freedom at the table."

Mrs. Rutledge passed the bread to Elenora. "No harm done. While I'm not of a mind to allow children to prattle, I can't fault her for being curious." She smiled at Tildy. "If you have questions about prayer, Matilda, you may talk with me later. I'd be happy to tell you what I know."

"Yes ma'am." Tildy cast a sideways glance at Mr. Rutledge, who gave her a sympathetic smile in return. He certainly had a knack for knowing exactly what she needed. What a pity he didn't have a family. He'd make a fine father.

The rest of the meal passed without incident. Mr. Rutledge regaled them with the history of the area.

"Mud Springs?" Elenora paused with her spoon in the air. "What an unusual name. Why did the settlers choose it? Because the springs were muddy?"

"Precisely. It's said the spring turned brown when the miners used it to water their stock. The name was changed to El Dorado in '55 shortly after I arrived because we realized the earlier one was unlikely to entice people to settle here."

Elenora scooped a peach slice. "A wise decision. I doubt I'd have been as eager to come here if that was the name."

His meal finished, Mr. Rutledge laid his napkin on the table. "Why did you come?"

"Because you advertised for a partner and accepted my offer. Why do you think?"

"I think you want something, but I'm not sure what. Or perhaps you wanted to get away from something. . .or someone."

"Son, I don't think now is the time for this." Mrs. Rutledge pursed her lips and inclined her head toward Tildy. "Little pitchers needn't be filled with sour milk."

Elenora pushed the last bit of peach around her dish. What did he expect her to say? That she couldn't spend another day with Pa scrutinizing her every move? That since he'd given her position to his new stepson, she refused to stay where she wasn't wanted? That she'd scream if she had to listen to Pa's new wife scold Tildy one more time?

Mr. Rutledge had no right to know why she'd come or what she was thinking. He didn't want her as a partner in his shop any more than her own father did.

Well, she'd show Mr. Rutledge she was a woman with a backbone and brains. Her shop would attract so many of his customers that cobwebs would cover his cash drawer. He'd come crawling back, begging her forgiveness and ruining the knees of his finely tailored trousers in the process.

She smiled at the thought. Yes. Mr. Miles Rutledge would rue the day he'd scorned her.

The following Monday Elenora opened her shop to customers. She enjoyed a steady flow all morning. Most made a small purchase. That wasn't the start she'd hoped for, but her cases and shelves held precious little. It would take time to expand the business.

She returned bolts of fabric to the shelves. The women who'd been in seemed glad to see new colors and designs, but Elenora had only sold one piece. Hopefully those women who'd gone home to ask their husbands' permission to make a purchase would be back soon.

The bell on the door sent out its cheery ring, and she looked up to find Will Dupree's wife in the shop. "Good morning, Mrs. Watkins. It's a fine day for your opening, isn't it? Have you had a chance to step out for some air?"

"I've been busy, but Tildy and I are joining the Rutledges for dinner, so I'll get a brief stroll. I do miss the long walks I used to take."

"I can't imagine being inside all day. May's milder temperatures make me eager to be outdoors tending my garden. My hands fairly itch to feel the soil. Will says the good Lord must have intended me to be a farmer's wife."

Elenora brought her hands together with a clap. "Oh! You might like my new tools." She led the way to the back of her shop where she'd planted upturned shovels, rakes, and hoes in barrels, and pulled out a spade.

Mrs. Dupree cast a skeptical glance at the display. "I'm sure they're fine, but Will has all of these."

"Yes, but his were designed by men, for men. These are for women. See how they're smaller?"

Mrs. Dupree examined a shovel, and her face lit up. "How clever. I must have one of these—and a hoe, too."

"I suppose you need to ask your husband."

"Will gives me pin money. Besides, what man doesn't believe in having the best tools for the job?"

Elenora concluded the sale and carried the implements to the door. "I appreciate your business, but what will your husband think of you supporting his friend's competitor?"

"Miles has enjoyed his comfortable position in El Dorado for fifteen years. It's time we had some choices without having to make the trek to Placerville. From what I've heard, many of the women feel the same way, even if the men are more resistant to the idea of a female proprietor."

"The women have been complimentary, yes, but their handbags weren't much lighter when they left. I have to remind myself it takes time to build a following."

"But you will. You must." Mrs. Dupree grinned, revealing deep dimples in her round face. "Miles needs to see that a woman can run a mercantile as well as a man. Wouldn't you agree?"

Elenora wished she could believe all would go well. But wishing was for children, not sensible adults. "I never intended to open my own place. I thought— My plans changed, though. I'm determined to work hard and provide a secure future for Tildy."

Mrs. Dupree grew serious. "I think you're doing a fine job. I saw your daughter at Miles's place, and she seems content. She told him a story, and his laughter filled the shop."

"They do get on well." She could find no fault in his treatment of Tildy. Tildy had put him on a pedestal the day they met, and he seemed to enjoy her company.

Elenora opened the door and followed Mrs. Dupree onto the walkway. They stood in the shade of the wide wooden awning in front of Elenora's shop. "At first I was concerned about the amount of time Tildy spends over there, but Mrs. Rutledge assures me her son welcomes Tildy's visits. He doesn't seem to mind her chatter."

"Miles likes children. My daughter remembers the day he got a shipment of gumdrops and gave her one of every flavor. I doubt your daughter is any trouble at all, but if she were, he'd let you know."

"Yes, I'm sure he would." He'd certainly let her know *she* was a thorn in his side. To his credit, though, he didn't seem upset that his mother had invited her to share the noon meal with them each day. "How old is your daughter?"

"Constance is nine, the same age as yours, I understand. She's been after me to have you over so she can play with Tildy." Mrs. Dupree smiled. "I'd welcome the opportunity to get to know you better, too. I'm usually so busy on the farm that I don't get to spend much time with a friend. Would you like to come to our place for supper Wednesday?"

Warmth filled Elenora. A friend? How long had it been since she'd had one? Years. And a playmate for Tildy as well. "We'd be delighted. Although Tildy's happy spending time with

Mrs. Rutledge, I know she'd love to meet another girl."

Elenora carried the tools to Mrs. Dupree's wagon and laid them in the bed. "Thank you again for your business, your invitation. . .and your support."

"We women must stick together." Mrs. Dupree gave another of her heartwarming smiles, climbed aboard the seat, and took the reins. She leaned toward Elenora, tilted her head in the direction of Rutledge Mercantile, and spoke in hushed tones. "Not to spoil your morning, but Miles is on his way over, and he looks none too happy."

Chapter 6

Miles doffed his hat to Pearl Dupree and followed Mrs. Watkins into her shop. He shut the door with more force than he'd intended, and the bell clanged.

"Just what do you think you're doing throwing business my way? I don't need your help."

Her bodice rose and fell. "Mr. Rutledge, kindly remember I'm a lady and don't appreciate men barking at me. If you'll take a seat, we can discuss this as two businesspeople." She motioned toward some stools.

"I wasn't barking."

"No?" One brow lifted, and she pressed her lips together. Pretty pink lips that twitched.

"You're laughing at me."

"Only on the inside. To do otherwise would be improper."

"What is it you find so amusing?" Women could be so hard to figure out. All the more reason he didn't need a female partner. Although he understood Mother most of the time, Irene had skirted around things. She'd avoided giving him direct answers if keeping him guessing would further her plans. He'd rarely known where he stood with her.

"Why does it matter?"

"Why must you be so. . .so. . .female?"

She planted herself on one of the stools and made a show of smoothing her skirt and fluffing her lacy collar. What next? A fan to flit before her dancing eyes? When Mrs. Watkins dropped her guardedness, she could be almost charming. He forced a cough into his closed hand.

The light left her eyes, and she stared into his. For a small woman, she put on an impressive show of force. "I believe you came to lodge another complaint against me, Mr. Rutledge. What have I done this time?"

How refreshing. A woman who didn't keep him guessing. He seated himself on the stool next to hers and hooked his heels on the bottom rung. "Mr. Willow bought a spade from me this morning."

"Good. A sale is always welcome, is it not?"

"He came here first. Why didn't you show him yours? I know you have them, because Pearl just left with one."

Mrs. Watkins stood. "Come with me, please." As she passed, the scent of rose water made him smile. She liked roses, did she?

He followed her to the rear of the shop, where barrels sat on either side of a doorway leading to her back room. What lay beyond that flowery curtain? Order, no doubt.

"Here." She held out a shovel, blade up.

He spun the tool around and held it in working position. "What's wrong with this? Looks like a child's plaything. Is the manufacturer scrimping on materials?" The head was two-thirds the normal size, and the handle, with its smaller grip, was too short.

She shook her head. "You are so. . .male." She pulled the shovel from his hands, jammed it in the barrel, and flounced back to her stool.

In the space of a few strides, he faced her once more. He stared down at her, and she stared right back, her eyes dark and her lips tight.

"I've missed something. Enlighten me."

"Mrs. Dupree wanted the shovel and hoe because they were designed with her in mind. Don't you see?"

He scratched his head.

Mrs. Watkins gave him the same long-suffering look she used on Tildy when the adventure-loving girl talked about outlaws and such. "My mother used to get a sore back after working in the garden because the tools were large and heavy. I hired Mr. MacDougall to make the shorter handles and the smithy to fashion smaller blades. Woman-sized."

Miles smiled as understanding dawned. "You don't carry man-sized models, so—"

"I sent Mr. Willow to your shop."

"I don't need you to send customers my way. I'm perfectly capable of running my business without your help."

She opened her mouth to speak but closed it. With a hop, she left the stool, walked to her front window, and gazed at his shop. He joined her, and she produced a weak smile. "I'm well aware you don't need my help."

Tildy was right. Her mother *was* sad. Not an "I didn't make a sale sad," but a bone-deep sadness that had stolen the smile from her and left tightness in its place.

"I never intended to be standing here in my own place across the street from yours. I don't wish you ill, Mr. Rutledge. I've done my best not to carry the same things you do, which isn't easy, since you have a shop brimming with merchandise."

"Indeed I do. I've been at this a long time and have the loyalty of the townspeople." The sooner she accepted the truth, the better. If she boarded the next train out of town, she'd have a chance of escaping with some of her money. If not, she stood to lose it all in her valiant attempt to compete with him. Those were the facts, pure and simple.

Mrs. Watkins shifted her attention to her shop with its scanty wares. "You've proven yourself, but I have a long way to go. I've got to make this work so I can support Tildy."

"I understand. I have a living to make, too."

Her gaze bore into him, a probing look that reached a part of him long undisturbed. A part he wasn't ready to reveal to a woman he'd known such a short time. Even if she did have the warmest brown eyes he'd ever seen.

Elenora smothered the last bite of beef with smooth brown gravy and savored the rich taste. "Thank you for another delicious dinner, Mrs. Rutledge. Sharing your noondays is a blessing to me."

"And me," Tildy added. "Mama's cooking is so bad that Grandpa said she was as much use in the kitchen as a broken axle on a wagon. She burned the toast this morning and broke the fried eggs when she flipped them."

Mrs. Rutledge scowled. "Matilda, is that any way to talk about your mother?"

Tildy lowered her head. "Sorry, Mama."

"It's fine, dear. You're right. I have a good deal to learn."

Mr. Rutledge lifted Tildy's chin with a finger. "I hear you helped Mother fix dinner. That true?"

Sunshine replaced the clouds. "I got to roll the beef balls and coat them with flour. I wanted to chop the onion, but she said she didn't want to see me cry."

Mrs. Rutledge rose. "I plan to make hash tomorrow, so you may dice the potatoes. . .provided you'll still your tongue and concentrate on the task." She gathered the empty plates and trundled off.

Tildy swiveled her head, watching openmouthed until Mrs. Rutledge disappeared into her kitchen. "Mama! Did you hear that? She's going to let me do it. I know I can. And I'll be all kinds of careful. I'll mind her, and I *will* keep quiet. I can be if I put my mind to it and swallow all the things that want to pop out."

Mr. Rutledge shifted his eyes from Tildy to Elenora.

"My daughter embraces life full force and can be rather excitable, but I know she'll be a help."

Tildy huffed. "Excitable, exuberant, and expressive. Those are Mama's favorite words for me. She doesn't know how hard I try to hold things inside, but it's not easy."

Mr. Rutledge laid his napkin on the table. "I think those are admirable qualities. You have all of them and more. I'd say you're pretty, playful, and precocious."

"Pretty? I like that, Mr. Rutledge, but what does precocious mean?"

Elenora felt his gaze on her but focused on Tildy rather than stealing a glance at him. "He means you know a lot for a girl your age."

Tildy rested her elbows on the table and propped her chin in her hands. "I know something you don't, Mama."

"And what would that be?"

"I know Mr. Rutledge plays the fiddle."

"Yes. I've heard. Sheriff Henderson told me when I dropped by the barbershop last week. He invited me to join their practice, but Mr. Rutledge and his friends play folk music, not classical pieces as I do."

"You could learn," he said.

The challenge in his voice did not escape Elenora's notice. The thought of standing in a barn filled with farm animals, foul smells, and men who imbibed too freely held no appeal. Concert halls with plush seats and cultured audiences were more to her liking. "While you and your friends may enjoy folk music, I've not developed a fondness for it myself."

One side of his mouth lifted in a lopsided grin, and his expressive blue eyes actually twinkled, just as his mother had described. The sight was so unexpected and delightful she had to hide her own grin behind her napkin.

"Mama loves playing her violin. She wanted me to learn, but I tried once and made such horrible screeching sounds I hurt my own ears and made Grandpa mad. I'd love to hear you fiddle. Will you play for us sometime?"

"I'd be happy to play for you, Tildy, but I'm afraid your mother might not appreciate my talent as a fiddler. I'm sure she's an accomplished musician." His words were polite enough, but the dance his mustache performed did little to hide his amusement. To think she'd hoped he played classical violin. His response wasn't surprising though. The folk musicians back East hadn't shared her passion for the composers' works either. If only she'd been allowed to join the orchestra, how much fun she could have had.

"She can read those funny-looking notes and play all of them. But she plays boring things she calls concertos and arias. I got to hear fiddling with Grandpa one time, and I liked it lots better."

"Tildy dear, that's quite enough."

Mr. Rutledge chuckled with undisguised mirth. "What do you ladies say to a walk through the garden?"

"Oh, Mama! You have to see it. Mrs. Rutledge lets me go out there and have tea parties. There's all sorts of flowers and a bench and a birdbath and—"

"You've convinced me." Elenora seized the opportunity to put an end to the conversation. Clearly she and Mr. Rutledge had different tastes in music, and she had no interest in hearing any more about the folksy tunes he and his friends favored.

Minutes later she stood before a row of shrubs bearing pink

roses with a hint of purple and inhaled their fragrance. "The scent is a bit fruity." Tildy had dashed off around the back of the house in pursuit of an elusive butterfly, but Mr. Rutledge waited at Elenora's side. "They're lovely. I'll have to ask your mother what kind they are."

"She wouldn't be able to tell you."

He didn't appear to be teasing. Instead he watched her intently, causing a tingling at the back of her neck. Her cheeks warmed, and yet she couldn't pull her gaze from his handsome face. "And you can?"

"Surprised?"

Completely. She'd never met a man with an appreciation of flowers. Mr. Rutledge wasn't exactly what she'd first thought. "Just curious. What kind are they?"

"Old Blush. Not much good as a cut flower, but they make a fine hedge."

She moved to a trellis covered with a climbing bush and examined a mass of pink roses. "And these?"

"A family that moved here from Texas gave me that cutting. It's called Seven Sisters."

She touched each rose in the cluster. "Why aren't there seven?"

"That's for the colors. There are supposed to be seven, from cream to dark pink."

She pressed her nose to the blooms. They were pretty with their ruffled petals but lacked much of a scent.

Mr. Rutledge gave her another searching look. "Do you have any?"

"What? Roses?"

"Sisters."

She moved down the stone-edged path, and he walked by her side. "No." Only a baby brother who had stolen Pa's heart—and broken it when he died. She'd never been enough for Pa because she was only a girl.

Mama had loved her, though, even if Pa didn't seem to. But she had an opportunity to make him proud of her now. "My parents didn't think they could have children. They were married five years before I was born. Mama called me her special surprise."

"You're definitely full of surprises, Mrs. Watkins. When I saw you at the stagecoach clutching your violin and hiding underneath that big hat of yours, I didn't expect to have you at my dinner table. And I certainly didn't expect you to go into business across the street from mine."

"Well, I didn't expect you to turn me down the minute we met. But you did me a favor. Running a shop and being my own boss agrees with me. I have plenty of ideas to attract customers, so you'll have to work hard to keep those you have."

"I doubt that. The novelty will wear off soon enough, and the townspeople will revert to old habits." He stopped before a shrub as tall as she was, cupped a light pink bloom, and pulled it toward her. "Try this one."

She buried her nose in the flower and inhaled deeply. "Mmm. What a wonderful fragrance. It's so strong I can almost taste it. Sweet, like the satisfaction I'll savor when you're fighting to keep your doors open."

He smiled. "It's called Autumn Damask. Goes back before the turn of the century. This variety is known for the double bloom and having what some say is the finest perfume of all roses. Smells as good as success, which is what I'll have when you're forced to admit failure and close up shop."

They continued down the path. "How do the flowers fare in the heat? I've been told it can get quite hot here in the Foothills, although I'm prepared to handle all the heat that comes my way, from the sun or other sources."

"Roses, like established businesses, are hardier than you might think, but I plant those varieties requiring shade under the oaks. There's a bench over there, too." He pulled out his pocket watch. "We have a few minutes. Would you like to try it out?"

Sitting in a flower garden surrounded by roses and the man who tended them? The man who wanted nothing better than to see her admit defeat and return to Nebraska? "I don't think—"

"Mama!" Tildy darted over to them. "Look what I found." She held out cupped hands.

Elenora stepped back. "It's some kind of critter, isn't it?"

"Yes. A pretty one with long wings you can see through." She opened her hands slightly to reveal a huge green bug.

"How. . .lovely. That pest must be able to fly pretty fast."

"Let me have a look." Mr. Rutledge peered at the ugly thing crawling inside the cave Tildy had created. "A lacewing fly. But your mama's mistaken about this, among other things. It isn't a pest. This insect's larvae eat aphids that like to plague my roses. Sometimes larger creatures prey on small ones. It's a fact of life."

Tildy smirked. "Mama doesn't like crawly things, but I do."

That was true, but pesky men who thought themselves better than her were worse. And Mr. Rutledge was being particularly pesky at present.

Footfalls sounded on the path. Mrs. Rutledge hobbled over to them, still clad in her apron. She held out a dish towel. "Matilda, those dishes aren't going to dry themselves."

"If you leave them out long enough—" Tildy scrunched her face. "Yes ma'am. See you later, Mama." She hugged Elenora.

Mrs. Rutledge patted her son's arm. "Don't mind us. We have an appointment with a dishpan."

"And we have one with a bench." He nodded toward the

one nearby. "Shall we?"

Mrs. Rutledge put a hand on Tildy's back. "Enjoy your-selves." They headed toward the house, but Tildy stole a glance over her shoulder.

Given no choice but to acquiesce, Elenora settled on the small bench as far to one side as possible. Mr. Rutledge joined her, removed his derby, and placed it on his knee. He was so close the scent of his woodsy shaving soap—the same one the barber had slathered on him—warred with that of the roses nearby.

She gazed at the oak canopy. A jaybird squawked and took flight. That's what she should do. Get away. Why she'd even agreed to take a stroll with Mr. Rutledge was a puzzle. The man unsettled her. She could deal with his occasional outbursts. She'd endured Pa's for years, and Mr. Rutledge's paled in comparison. But this. . . What did he want?

"You have another shipment due tomorrow, I hear."

He wanted to pry, did he? Well, two could play that game. She'd made her inquiries at the livery, too. "As do you."

"Large one?"

"Biggest yet."

"More gewgaws and trinkets?"

She pressed a finger to her lips lest she spout the words she ached to hurl at him. *Patience, Elenora.*

"What did I do this time?"

That was a switch. Apparently he realized he might have offended her. "My wares are not mere trifles, Mr. Rutledge. They're items intended to enhance people's lives. To brighten their homes and bring cheer."

"A silver pocketknife with flowers on the handle can do all that?" He reached in his pocket and produced a wooden-handled version. "This one works just as well and costs less."

"May I?" She held out her hand. He placed one of his

beneath it, laid the knife on her upturned palm, and closed her fingers over it. Heat raced up her arm, and it was all she could do not to shiver. "Th–thank you."

He released her hand. She grasped the knife and held it up. "Does this. . ." After taking a breath to restore her sense of composure, she tried again. "Does this look like something a woman would pull from her reticule? It's big and heavy."

"A woman doesn't need a knife."

She returned his, careful not to have any contact with him. "What if she needed to cut the twine on a package or open an envelope? She'd require the proper tool, wouldn't she? One designed for smaller hands."

Mischief glinted in his expressive eyes. She lowered hers.

"And I suppose the tortoiseshell hair combs, nail file with the ivory grip, and ostrich feather fan in your display cases are *tools*, too?"

If she had a fan of any kind right now, she'd be sorely tempted to swat him with it—or hide behind it so he couldn't see how he affected her. And why did he? Because he'd taken note of her stock? Because having him tease her was more enjoyable than it ought to be? Or both?

"Mrs. Watkins?"

"Hmm?"

"I know my collar's clean since I changed it before dinner, but I've rarely had anyone study it so intently."

She forced herself to meet his gaze, but that was a mistake. Every feature captivated her. His firm chin. His sculpted cheekbones. His broad brow. But those eyes of his were the most dangerous. She could feel him delving deeper and deeper and didn't know how to stop him. But she must. Men cared about one thing. Themselves. "I admire a man who takes pains with his appearance."

He grinned, revealing straight white teeth. He must use plenty of tooth powder.

Yes. Think about tooth powder. Don't think about how winsome he looks when he smiles.

"You're tactful, Mrs. Watkins. Mother says I'm a dandy."

Her chin quivered as she tried in vain to suppress a laugh. "I'm s–sorry." Her battle lost, she hid behind her hand in an attempt to control herself.

"You have a lovely laugh. Tildy misses it, you know."

The sound died in Elenora's throat. "She told you that?"

"She tells me many things. That I don't have enough toys in my shop. That her grandpa smokes a pipe and used to blow smoke rings for her to chase. That she wants a friend her age."

There was a subject she could grab hold of and use to pull her from dangerous territory. "Your friend Mrs. Dupree invited Tildy and me to supper tomorrow so the girls can get acquainted."

"Constance is a sweet girl, and Pearl's a rare find, as Will often says. You'll like them." Mr. Rutledge checked his watch again. "I need to go."

"I do, too." She stood, and he followed suit. She'd started down the path but hadn't gotten far when he stopped in front of the Damask rosebush.

"One moment, please." He produced his knife, cut one of the pink buds, and handed it to her. "A single rose for the woman who's single-handedly opened my eyes to new possibilities."

Her breath hitched in her throat. Who would have thought Mr. Rutledge could say something so sweet? "Thank you."

He snapped the blade back into its sheath and shoved the knife in his pocket. "Don't get used to free gifts, Mrs. Watkins. You'll have to earn everything you get from here on out because I'm running a successful business, and no headstrong woman is going to change that."

Sweet? Had she really been so easily fooled? He wasn't being kind. He was threatening her. Well, he'd met his match. "And I won't let a pigheaded man send me packing. I'm here to stay, so you'd better get used to the idea."

"We'll see about that. I have to get back. You can stay or go, but I'll be at the mercantile today, tomorrow, and a year from now." He left, his long strides carrying him across the yard until he shoved his way through the hedge across from the mercantile and disappeared.

She stared at the rose. Although she longed to drop it on his doorstep and crush it under her bootheel, she couldn't bring herself to do it. He'd given her the beautiful bloom, and she'd keep it to remind herself not to fall prey to his ploys ever again.

Chapter 7

Will Dupree entered Rutledge Mercantile on a sunny Saturday and clapped a hand on Miles's shoulder. "That's some scowl you're wearing, my good man. What's ailing you?"

Miles turned from the window. "Who said anything was?"

"Wouldn't be the steady stream coming and going at Watkins General Merchandise the past two weeks, would it?"

Most days Will's teasing didn't bother Miles, but he wanted no part of it this morning. The widow with the warm brown eyes wouldn't leave his thoughts. Every day but Sunday she sat at his table, took his hand, and bowed in prayer. And then he spent the next hour listening to her carry on about how well things were going.

She'd had a few good days, sure, but that wouldn't last. Before she knew it folks would return to the mercantile, and she'd be forced to watch them fill his place. But would he be allowed to gush like she was now? No. He'd have to behave like a gentleman and keep his thoughts to himself or suffer Mother's disapproval. Why did she encourage Mrs. Watkins anyhow?

He dipped a cloth in the furniture polish. The strong scents of linseed oil and turpentine cleared his head but didn't lift his spirits. "Did you need something or just come to stir up trouble?"

Will held up his hands. "Whoa! She must really be getting to you."

Miles slammed the tin on the display case and rubbed

the oak top with vigor. "I haven't the slightest interest in Mrs. Watkins or her business."

"The fact that your place is empty, you've got Sammy out front washing windows, and I catch you glaring at her shop means nothing then?"

"Don't you have crops to tend?"

Will propped his elbows on a nearby case, leaned back, and surveyed the mercantile. "Seems to me having a woman like her around here could be good for business. The ladies would come for her fancy wares and bring their menfolk."

"The men wouldn't buy any more than they ever did."

"Hank walked out of her place with a mustache cup, and Tiny bought some pricey English cologne."

Miles froze in midswipe. "Tiny? Scent would be wasted on him. Nothing could mask the smell of his forge. It's in his skin."

"He's been wanting a wife."

The hairs on the back of Miles's neck stood on end. "*He's* interested in Mrs. Watkins?"

"She's easy on the eyes. Hardworking, too."

Miles slapped the cloth on the counter and jammed the lid on the polish. The thought of Tiny Briggs courting Mrs. Watkins soured his stomach. Not that he wanted her for himself. Oh no! He'd had a weak moment when he handed her the rose and spouted that line of sentimental claptrap. She'd gone doe-eyed, and he'd seen the light. Never again would he fall for a woman who used her feminine wiles to get what she wanted. He'd made that mistake with Irene, but he was older and wiser now. "She's small. He's a giant."

Will chuckled. "Three times her size at least, but why do you care?"

"I don't. I just hope he realizes she doesn't have a biddable bone in her body."

"That doesn't put you off. The whole town knows she's at your table for dinner every day."

"Just keeping tabs on the competition." Miles glanced across the street. Another customer leaving with a parcel and a smile. He must do something about this situation. But what?

Elenora occupied a pew in the small church the next day. She bowed her head and did her best to keep her mind on the minister's closing prayer.

"And we thank You for this lovely spring day. Be with us as we go about our business, and keep us ever mindful of Your precepts. Amen."

Business. Perhaps God did care about hers. She'd been doing well. Her sales had picked up. True, more was going out than coming in, but that was to be expected.

Her inheritance from Jake's parents had seemed a great sum back in Omaha, but prices in California were higher. How quickly the first two thousand dollars had gone. She had to arrange her few goods carefully so the shop didn't look half empty.

Mrs. Rutledge coaxed a postlude from the old pianoforte. The room filled with the buzz of many conversations.

"Mrs. Watkins." Elenora beheld a snowy-haired woman with eagerness in her eyes. "Was that a livery wagon I saw at your place yesterday?"

Elenora nodded. "I received a shipment of women's hats and wicker baskets." Items that would fill several shelves, provided she left enough space between them.

"I could use a new bonnet. I'll stop by soon, dear." The woman excused herself.

"Mama, can I go outside with Constance?"

She corrected Tildy with a kind but firm tone. "You *may*, but please don't muss your dress."

Elenora made her way to the back of the church where Reverend Parks stood in the doorway bidding congregants farewell. Unlike her minister in Omaha, he wore no special collar or robes. Just a frock coat and bib-front shirt like Mr. Rutledge.

The minister smiled. "Mrs. Watkins, isn't it?"

"Elenora Watkins, yes, Reverend. And the young girl with the brown braids and blue dress with Constance Dupree is my daughter, Tildy."

"We've met. I gather she's not one to remain a stranger for long."

"She's outgoing. She did mind her manners, didn't she?"

"You needn't worry." Tildy spied him and waved. He waved back. "She complimented me on my prayers. It seems she finds mine as pleasing as those of Miles Rutledge. She said I talk to the Lord—what were her words?" He squinted. " 'Friendly-like.' "

"That sounds like Tildy. I've been working with her on exercising discretion in her speech, but she's young yet."

He chuckled. "I find her honesty refreshing. To my way of thinking, she has a better understanding of prayer than some adults. God wants us to feel free to come to Him."

"Your sermon was interesting. I've never heard one like it. You have a way of making the scriptures understandable."

"Then I've done what I set out to do. And I thank you for your kind words."

Elenora warmed at his graciousness. He was far easier to talk with than her minister in Omaha. Perhaps because Mr. Parks was younger, about ten years older than Mr. Rutledge's thirty-five, it would appear. The reverend's russet hair held a hint of gray. "I've enjoyed the elders' messages, but it's been lovely to have you with us today. How many other churches do you serve?"

"Four in all. Most months I spend two Sundays at the main church in Placerville, one at Georgetown, and the last split between Diamond Springs and here."

"Two services in one day?"

"Diamond Springs is only two miles east on the main road." He held out a hand toward the Sierra Nevada Mountains, which stretched their majestic peaks to the azure sky.

"I've not been up the hill yet. My shop keeps me busy."

"I hear things are going well."

She shrugged. "For now, but that could change."

"If you've given your plans to the Lord, you can rest in Him. Have faith, Mrs. Watkins."

Mr. Rutledge approached, gave her a cursory nod, and smiled at the minister. Why did everyone else get a warm greeting while she got cold water tossed her way?

"You've met my competition, have you, Mr. Parks?"

Elenora couldn't believe her ears. Mr. Rutledge might have been short with her on occasion, but she'd never seen him show disrespect toward others. "I've met *Reverend* Parks."

"He doesn't use the title, Mrs. Watkins." Mr. Rutledge said it matter-of-factly, but his comment still rankled.

"Miles is right. Some people resist a man of the cloth. I learned years ago that it's easier to build bridges when I don't insist on formalities."

Mr. Rutledge's expression hadn't changed. Apparently he'd intended to educate her, not pass judgment. "I've never thought of that, Mr. Parks, but I can see your point. My father made me wait on any man wearing a minister's collar whenever one came in his shop. Pa said he didn't want any reminders of the God who took Mama from us."

Mr. Parks gave her such a compassionate look that her respect for him grew. "Your father didn't share your faith?"

She shook her head and blinked to clear the sudden moisture. "Mama took me to church when I was young. After I lost her, I went by myself. I knew that's what she'd have wanted."

Mr. Parks directed his attention to Mr. Rutledge. "A mother's love is a blessing. Wouldn't you agree, my friend?"

Mr. Rutledge chuckled. "Most days, but mine has become rather meddlesome of late."

Elenora peered at him through her lashes. How could he joke about his mother's interference, and with the minister no less?

A smile tugged at Mr. Parks's lips. "I heard about a surprise dealt you two. Instead of being partners, you're competitors? But friendly ones, I trust?"

Mr. Rutledge didn't answer. She searched for a suitable response. "We. . .that is to say I. . .don't wish him ill. There's business enough for the both of us, as I've told him."

Mr. Parks looked from her to Mr. Rutledge and back. "El Dorado's not a big town. I'm sure he's feeling the effects."

The smile on Mr. Rutledge's face evaporated, replaced by something she had trouble identifying. "I'll weather the storm. No doubt it'll pass quickly."

"Huh!" Elenora clutched her Bible to keep from forming fists. "You, Mr. Rutledge, are in for a surprise. My business is doing better every day."

"For the time being."

Mr. Parks spoke, his soft voice filled with concern. "I sense some friction between you."

She let out a ragged breath. How disappointed Mama would be if she knew her daughter had lashed out in front of a minister of the Gospel. "I'm sorry. It's just that Mr. Rutledge seems determined to discount my abilities." She couldn't bring herself to look at him and focused on Mr. Parks instead.

"I'd say the opposite is true. If you posed no threat, would Miles be concerned?"

She ventured a gaze at Mr. Rutledge. It appeared the gentle rebuke had affected him also. He'd uncrossed his arms, and his forehead was no longer furrowed. "I'm concerned, Mrs. Watkins, but not about *my* business. To show you I don't harbor ill will either, I invite you and Tildy to join us for dinner at my house. Mr. Parks will be there, along with the Duprees."

Mr. Rutledge was concerned about her business, was he? Did he doubt her abilities that much? She had half a mind to decline his offer, but she'd enjoy visiting with Pearl, and Tildy would love to have time with Constance.

She'd just have to ignore her host as best she could.

Two hours later Tildy stood in front of Mr. Rutledge's house and gave her friend a hug. "Good-bye, Constance." The young girl climbed aboard the wagon, and Tildy waved until Will turned his team onto the main road and the Duprees disappeared from view. She skipped over to Elenora. "Mrs. Rutledge said Constance can visit me one day this week. I can't wait."

"Constance is a delightful girl. I'm sure you two will have a wonderful time."

"They're a fine family," Mr. Parks said. "Will and Pearl's wedding ceremony was the first I performed in this church. Hard to believe that was thirteen years ago, isn't it, Miles?"

"Sure is. I'll never forget the day Will first set eyes on Pearl. His chin hit the floor so hard I expected to see a bruise."

Tildy sidled up to Mr. Rutledge. "Have you ever been in love?"

Elenora cringed. "Tildy, dearest, that's a personal question." One that produced a pained look on his face. He'd never mentioned his late wife, but he must have loved her very much. Elenora's heart went out to him.

He rallied quickly and eased the awkward silence. "I was, once. She passed away, like your papa."

Tildy's face fell. "Oh, that's sad. Do you still miss her?"

"It was a long time ago."

Eight years, from what Mrs. Rutledge had said. Why had he never remarried? Surely a handsome and successful man like Mr. Rutledge would have his pick of the eligible women. "I think it's time we were leaving, sweetheart. We could take that walk I talked about."

"If you'll wait for me to gather my things," Mr. Parks said, "I could join you two. I'm heading back to Diamond Springs. An orchardist and his mother who attend our Sunday meetings invited me to stay with them."

"It's kind of you to offer, but I had my heart set on a leisurely stroll through the countryside."

"It won't be leisurely," Tildy muttered. "Mama doesn't know how to slow down."

"We'll have a good time. You'll see."

Elenora thanked Mr. Rutledge for the dinner invitation, bid the minister farewell, and took Tildy's hand. The lush green landscape beckoned. Birds called from the arms of plentiful oaks, and a breeze tossed strands of hair that had escaped Elenora's chignon.

How could it be that a full month had gone by in which she'd not gone on a single walk or even once played her violin? The shop took most of her time. Then there were the mornings and evenings when she had to see to meals, laundry, ironing, and the many tasks Pa's housekeeper had taken care of. Poor Tildy must feel neglected.

They'd gone but twenty feet when Mr. Parks called Elenora's name. "Yes?"

"Since you're unfamiliar with the terrain, Miles would like to accompany you."

"He would?"

Chapter 8

M iles addressed Mr. Parks in a low voice. "I would?"

"I know a gentleman like you wouldn't want anything to happen to two lovely ladies who don't know the lay of the land, so I felt certain you'd want to join them."

Put like that, how could he refuse? "Of course."

"Are you coming?" Tildy bounded up to him. "Please say you will. The walk would be heaps more fun if you came."

Mr. Parks grinned. "It's settled then. Have a good time." He headed into the house.

Tildy skipped down the street toward her mother, a cloud of dust billowing about her ankles.

Miles followed and stopped beside Mrs. Watkins. "It seems you have a tour guide." Judging by her tight smile, the idea was as unwelcome to her as it was to him.

She nodded. "Is he always so. . .helpful?"

"He's persuasive."

"I don't need a guide, but since it seems we have no choice, I think it only fair to tell you I intend to take a long walk."

"I understand."

They reached South Street, the alley that ran between his house and the mercantile, and she paused.

"Did you have a destination in mind?" he asked.

She dipped her chin. "Perhaps I was a bit hasty. I've seen what lies to the west, so I thought I'd go east, since I don't know what's out that way."

"East it is." He led them down the alley and stopped when

they reached the intersection in view of the Wells Fargo office across Main.

Mrs. Watkins held out a hand to the south. "Where does this road lead?"

"It's the major route through the Mother Lode. Goes to Amador and Calaveras Counties and towns like Jackson and Angels Camp."

Tildy bounced up and down, her braids swinging wildly. "I know about Calaveras County. Jim Smiley's frog jumped there."

He smiled at the animated girl. "You've read Mark Twain's story about Dan'l Webster, have you?"

"Lots of times. I'd like to see a frog-jumping contest. Do you have them around here?"

"Nothing as grand as that, but we had a pie social shortly before you arrived in town, and our next concert will be in June."

Mrs. Watkins wheeled around. "A concert? Where?"

"It's held above my shop in Rutledge Hall."

"Who's performing?"

"The Mud Springs Musical Society."

Her shoulders drooped. "Oh, I thought it might have been a classical performance, not fiddling and such."

What did she have against fiddling? "Have you ever played folk music?"

Her brows rose. "Certainly not."

"Why not?"

"I'm a lady and don't have a fondness for smelly barns and coarse men who've overindulged in strong spirits. I prefer concert halls and gentlemen in tailcoats. I realize things are different here and that I may have to be content playing for my own pleasure."

"I think you're in for some surprises. California is no

longer the Wild West. Over in Placerville the hotels have running water, the streets are lit with gaslights, and they have a Philharmonic Society."

She brightened for a moment, and then the light in her dark eyes faded. "But this isn't Placerville."

"No, but we do all right. Would you like to see a gold mine? The Union and Church Mine sites are two miles southeast of town near Deadman Creek."

Tildy squealed. "I would. Deadman Creek sounds spooky."

Mrs. Watkins's reaction was less enthusiastic. "I suppose."

"Do you think we'll find any gold?" Tildy asked.

"The only gold we're likely to see today are the fancy baubles in your mother's shop. She has a rather impressive selection of them."

Mrs. Watkins planted a fist at her waist. "Are you poking fun at me?"

He grinned. "I'm trying. Is it working?"

"Perhaps." She smiled.

He'd have to tease her more often. She had a lovely smile.

They'd walked for half an hour when Miles led Mrs. Watkins and Tildy off the main road down a path lined with oaks, an occasional evergreen, and a profusion of wildflowers. Clusters of bunchgrass waved in the gentle breeze, and frogs croaked in the distance.

"Wait a minute, Mr. Rutledge. Tildy's fallen behind."

"Is she all right?"

"Just tired, I suspect."

Mrs. Watkins obviously enjoyed walking and showed no signs of fatigue, but Tildy dragged her feet. She gave a halfhearted smile when she reached them.

He lifted her chin so he could see her face beneath the wide brim of her bonnet. "You look like a wilted blossom."

"I didn't know we'd be going so far. I'll wear out my boots with all this walking." She stuck out her lower lip.

"I have an idea." He squatted with his back to her. "Hop on. You can ride piggyback."

He waited, but when she didn't climb up, he glanced over his shoulder. She stood frozen in place, a look of apparent disbelief on her face, while Mrs. Watkins brushed her cheek as though she was wiping away a tear. What had he said to elicit such responses?

Tildy roused first. "I've never had a piggyback ride before. Papa didn't play with me. He didn't even want me around. He mostly just hollered."

"Then it's high time you had a ride." It was a good thing Jake Watkins was no longer among the living, because Miles would've been sorely tempted to throttle the man. How could he have mistreated this wonderful girl? And if he'd mistreated a child, what had his wife endured?

Mrs. Watkins mouthed "thank you." She patted Tildy's shoulder. "Looks like your boots are spared."

Tildy clambered on Miles's back, and he shifted the wisp of a girl into position. He reveled in the feel of her slender arms looped around his shoulders. May hadn't gotten big enough to carry this way, although he'd dreamed of the day she would be. Would his daughter have been as bright and fun-loving as Tildy? Pain gripped his heart, squeezing so hard he ached, as he had the day he returned home to news of the fire.

Tildy broke in on his thoughts, rescuing him from bitter remembrances. "What are you waiting for, Mr. Rutledge? Let's get going."

He took a few quick strides, bouncing her about, and she giggled. He laughed along with her.

The gratitude on Mrs. Watkins's face made him feel like a king. She turned and, with her hand shading her eyes, surveyed the landscape. "The trail's clearly visible, so I'll go first."

"It's flat here but gets steep near the mines. Tildy and I will be right behind you."

His eager rider leaned forward. "This is fun. You're so tall I can see a long ways. How much farther?"

"We're over halfway."

She shifted from side to side but soon settled down and rode in silence.

A good ten minutes passed, and yet she hadn't said a word. "You asleep back there, Tildy girl?"

"I'm doing what Mr. Parks said. There's a time to keep silent and a time to talk. I was being quiet so I could watch for wild animals. Some men on the train said there are grizzly bears in California."

"There used to be, but most of them have been killed."

"A time to kill, and a time to heal. Mr. Parks said that, too. But I think killing the bears is mean."

"People are scared of them. They're big and powerful. But if one were after you or your mama, I'd take care of you."

Tildy craned her neck to look at him. "Even shoot a gun?"

"Even shoot a gun."

Mrs. Watkins came to an abrupt stop. "Do you have one?"

He nearly stumbled to avoid running into her. "Not with me. I hadn't exactly planned on this outing."

"No, of course not. Are we in danger?"

The woman had turned worrying into an art form. "Not from grizzlies, but you could get a blister."

Tildy chuckled. "Mama's a fraidycat. She doesn't like to

think about guns and outlaws and such."

"What I don't like, sweetheart, is the harm they do. But I'd protect you."

Miles shifted Tildy to a more comfortable position. "How? Shoot the bandit with one of your piercing looks?"

"Huh! You think *my* looks are piercing? You ought to get a glimpse of your own." Her smile went into hiding, and determination filled her eyes. "I'd pull out a gun if I had one and knew how to use it."

"You don't?"

"Pa wouldn't hear of it. He said it wasn't ladylike. But I—" Mrs. Watkins clamped her mouth shut.

He wouldn't have envisioned her as a woman willing to wield a firearm, but if she chose to learn, he was sure she'd rope in some poor sap to teach her. He wouldn't take that on. Mother had done well, but Irene's lesson had been a disaster.

Tildy leaned to one side. "Grandpa wanted me to behave like a lady, too, and didn't like it when I—"

"Hush, my dear. Those days are behind us." Mrs. Watkins grimaced as though memories of her father brought pain. "Why don't we think of something pleasant?"

"I have an idea." Miles set Tildy down and pointed to a nearby plant. "Do you see those little yellow flowers on the long stems? They're called fiddlenecks. You could pick some for your mama."

Mrs. Watkins's laughter rang out. "Are you teasing me again?"

"*Me?* Tease *you?* Not this time."

"Oh Mr. Rutledge, you made Mama laugh. Do it again."

He would if he could. The woman was far too serious. "A time to weep, and a time to laugh. I think you're right, Tildy. It's your mama's time to laugh. She has a lovely one."

A becoming flush heightened Mrs. Watkins's color. She studied him for several seconds before shifting her gaze to the valley. "I th–think it's time to explore a mine. Isn't that what I see down there?"

It appeared the solemn widow who kept her laugh under lock and key wasn't immune to him after all. Interesting.

Mr. Rutledge stood beside Elenora as she peered into the main shaft of Union Mine. "This isn't at all what I expected. It's not even next to that creek you mentioned, the one with the gruesome name."

He rested a hand on the opening carved in the rock face and stood behind her. She did her best to ignore his presence, although his looming form made doing so difficult.

She gazed into the mouth of the tunnel. "I had no idea there were huge mines like this. I've always pictured a man stooped over a gold pan at the water's edge."

"It was like that in the early days when the loose gold was panned, but the easy pickings were gone by the end of '49. Nowadays the ore has to be dug or washed out of the hillsides."

"Can we go inside?" Tildy asked.

"Since the mine's been inactive the last couple of years, I wouldn't take the chance."

Elenora examined a glittering chunk of quartz. "Does that mean the miners got all the gold that was here?"

"The Church Mine over yonder is still active. Wouldn't surprise me if this one were worked again someday though. If there's gold to be found, someone will mine it."

Tildy slipped her hand in Mr. Rutledge's. "Can we see Deadman Creek now?"

"Certainly. We'll show your mama it's not eerie at all."

Elenora heard the murmur of water rushing over rocks in the distance. She trailed after Tildy and Mr. Rutledge, stood at the top of the bank, and surveyed the scene below.

He was right. This creek was much like those she'd seen back East. Trees and bushes lined the two banks, which sloped toward the meandering trickle of water in the center of the bed. Maybe she had let the name get to her. Tildy loved talking about stagecoach hold-ups, shootouts, and such. But she hadn't seen a man shot before her eyes.

Elenora shuddered as she recalled the day Pa had defended his shop against the robber who'd held her at gunpoint. She'd been spared, but her skin grew clammy whenever she thought of how close she'd come to being killed.

Treading carefully, she made her way down the slope until she was at the water's edge. Mr. Rutledge ambled over and stood beside her. She took a quick step to the side. If she let him get too close, her heart skittered and her mind went down a perturbing path, filling with thoughts of him. His kindness toward Tildy. The kisses he planted on his mother's cheek when he returned home for dinner each day. And that appealing cleft between his well-formed brows.

He spoke in a low, deep voice she found oddly reassuring. "See. Just a harmless creek."

"So it is." Even though her heart seemed determined to beat in double time, she'd learned her lesson in the garden. No way would he take her in again, even though he seemed sincere. He'd appeared to be in earnest before, and look what had happened. She must put some distance between them. "Where did Tildy go?"

"She darted after a dragonfly. I'll find her."

He disappeared beyond a rise, and Elenora breathed easier.

She rested a hand on a tree trunk, closed her eyes, and listened to the sounds she loved. The burbling of the creek. The strains of birdsong. The whisper of leaves stirred by a gentle breeze.

A branch snapped, and her heart lodged in her throat. That wasn't a rabbit or squirrel. The creature moving in the undergrowth on the opposite side of the creek was much larger. Through a break in the shrubs, she spied something large and black. A grizzly bear?

Had Mr. Rutledge been wrong? He said most of them had been killed.

Most. But not all?

She stood rooted to the spot. Alone. With no gun. Not that a revolver would be any match against such a big creature. The blood rushed in her ears, and her mouth went dry.

She'd always heard one's life passed before one's eyes at such a time, but hers didn't. All she could think of was Tildy. What would she do with no mother or father to care for her? Who would raise her daughter? Not Pa. Tildy would be miserable with him and his wife.

Lord. Help!

Heavy breathing followed. And then a whicker.

She caught a glimpse of a horse through an opening in the thicket. A black horse. A large black horse.

It couldn't be. The huge horse wasn't to be feared, but if it belonged to that vile man who'd tried to rob the stagecoach, she faced danger of a different kind. It must belong to someone, because she was sure she'd seen a fender and stirrup. Who else would be lurking in the bushes but someone bent on evil?

A full minute dragged by, each second an eternity. She remained as still as the angel statue Pa had ordered for Mama's grave. Elenora needed angels to watch over her, or Dead*man* Creek would need a new name.

Try as she might, she couldn't see who was with the horse, although someone was obviously leading the animal away, because all she could now see was the tail. No one said anything, but her skin turned to gooseflesh. The person leading the horse had to be the outlaw. She was sure of it.

"Mrs. Watkins."

She jumped, spun around, and glared at Mr. Rutledge. "How dare you scare me like that?"

"You're letting the place get to you."

"I saw something. Over there. Through the bushes." She jabbed a finger at the small break in the mazanita.

"I don't see anything."

She stared at the spot, but all she saw were red-brown shrubs with their muted green leaves. Had she imagined it? "You didn't hear it? There was a horse. A black horse."

"A horse, you say? I'm sure I'd have noticed that. I think your mind is playing tricks on you. Happens sometimes when people dwell on their fears."

"I know what I saw, and I think that was the same horse the outlaw rode."

"There are plenty of black horses around here. I own two that Will stables for me."

"Since you're here, it obviously wasn't one of yours, now was it?" She stomped up the bank, her fists clenched at her sides. "You said you'd protect me—us. See if I trust you again. I'll do it myself."

He caught up to her. "I'd protect you if there were anything to protect you from. But I can't fight what isn't there."

"Fine. Don't believe me. I have to find Tildy and make sure she's all right."

"She is. Listen." Sounds of Tildy's laughter rang out, and Elenora heaved an audible sigh.

"Look, Mama." Tildy bounded up to her and held out a bouquet. "Mr. Rutledge is teaching me about wildflowers. These are sun cups, this is an Indian paintbrush, and my favorites are the pussytoes."

Elenora struggled to slow her galloping heart. She mustn't let on about what she'd seen. More talk about the outlaw would only serve to fuel Tildy's vivid imagination. "He does know a great deal about flowers, doesn't he?"

One side of his mouth lifted in a crooked smile. "Is it wrong for a man to appreciate a thing of beauty?" His gaze lingered on her, roving over her face as though drinking in every detail, and she gulped. With him studying her like that, she had a hard time remembering she was irritated with him. His slow perusal made it hard to think at all.

"Why are your cheeks red, Mama?"

Elenora fanned herself. "Because it's warm. I'll help you look for more wildflowers. Perhaps we can find one he doesn't know."

"I think he'll know them all. He's real smart."

"That may be, but I'm going on a hunt. Come on." She would find one he couldn't name if she had to search until suppertime.

Elenora and Tildy scoured the landscape for new varieties. Elenora remained alert, looking and listening, but it seemed the horse was nowhere around. Perhaps she'd been hasty to assume it was the outlaw's, but a saddled horse with no rider wouldn't have been wandering around on its own. The owner must have been leading the animal. Considering the densely packed manzanita in that area, such a move made sense. It also explained why he hadn't seen her. Had he been in the saddle instead of on foot, he would have.

Since the horse was headed in the opposite direction, the

danger had likely passed. Even so, her heart refused to return to a sedate pace. Between the encounter at the creek and the way Mr. Rutledge had startled her afterward, it could be some time before it did.

Despite her scare, she wasn't going to let her one day of rest go to waste. She would savor what was left of her time outdoors. Right now that meant searching for wildflowers with her daughter.

After several attempts Elenora still hadn't been able to unearth a single specimen that stumped him.

"Do you know what these are, Mr. Rutledge?" Tildy held up flowers with yellow centers and scalloped white edges.

"Those are just the flower for your fastidious mama. Tidy tips."

Elenora tried to look away, but he was far too attractive with his face lit up like that. "Now I know you're teasing me."

"I don't think he is, Mama. That's not his teasing smile. It's his happy smile. See how his eyes are sparkly? They crinkle around the edges when he's teasing, and his mustache gets jumpy."

"Looks like you've got me figured out, Tildy. Seems to be taking your mama longer."

Tildy scampered off on one side of the narrow trail. Elenora resisted the urge to linger. Being alone with him when he was displaying his charming side wreaked havoc with her ability to remain aloof. "I'm not giving up. There's got to be something you can't identify."

"Be my guest." He waved a hand over the lush landscape.

She tromped between ankle-high clumps of bunchgrass and an occasional manzanita bush. They must be getting close to town by now. She had little time left to locate another species.

Wait. What was that in the distance? She hadn't seen a

flower like it before. Hefting her skirts to her boot tops, she plowed through the undergrowth in pursuit of her prey. The fabric rustled as she walked, and startled insects flitted away.

"Stop, Mrs. Watkins!"

"Ha!" She tossed the reply over her shoulder and pressed on. "Are you afraid I've found one you don't know, Mr. Rutledge?"

"Don't take another step!"

Chapter 9

Footfalls thundered behind Elenora. And then she was airborne.

Mr. Rutledge had wrapped his large hands around her waist and lifted her several feet off the ground. She held on to her hat to keep branches of a sprawling oak from snatching it.

He set her down a ways from where she'd been but didn't loosen his hold. She spun around and pressed her palms to his chest. Instead of pushing him away as she should have, she froze. His breath came in noisy puffs.

"What's wrong? Why did you grab me?"

Once his breathing slowed, he spoke. "You were headed straight for some poison oak."

Relief washed over her. "Is that all? For a minute I thought you were going to tell me you'd seen the horse."

"I wasn't thinking about that. Only about you."

No man had ever looked at her with such a mixture of concern and. . .interest. His eyes traveled over her face the way they had earlier, settling on her lips for an eternity before he met her gaze. He was attracted to *her*—a plain-looking widow who had a child to care for and a shop in direct competition with his? Her heart skipped along a bumpy path.

"You're a beautiful woman. A touch on the stubborn side, but beautiful." He leaned toward her, his warm breath brushing her cheek.

She broke free of his hold and stepped back. "Mr. Rutledge, please. You're being far too friendly for. . .a competitor."

He dropped his hands, hanging them limply at his sides. His mouth gaped for an instant before he snapped it shut and pressed his lips into a firm line. "Don't worry. It won't happen again."

Tildy rushed up. "What's wrong? Did you see a grizzly?"

Mr. Rutledge smiled, but it didn't reach his eyes, which conveyed something else. Disappointment perhaps? Well, he'd have to deal with that, because she wasn't about to encourage his advances. He intended to force her out of business, and she couldn't forget that. Even if he was more handsome than a man had a right to be and caused her heart to do things of its own accord.

"No bear. Not even a frog. But your mama was headed for some poison oak."

Tildy scrunched her face, clearly puzzled. "Don't you mean poison ivy?"

"You have that back East, but out here we have poison oak. It's as dangerous and can make a person mighty uncomfortable. Let me show you." He led them to the shrub and used a stick to lift a cluster of shiny, dark green, scalloped leaflets. "See how there are three leaves, just like poison ivy? Remember the old saying, 'Leaves of three, let it be.' Steer clear of it, or you could itch something fierce.

"You need to keep an eye out for rattlers, too. They have the distinctive rattling sound, diamonds on their backs, and triangular-shaped heads. If you give them a wide berth, they generally won't strike. You'd do well to keep this in mind, because a bite can make a body quite sick."

Tildy nodded. "I will."

"That goes for you, too, Mrs. Watkins, since you plan to do a fair amount of walking."

His patronizing tone grated on her. Why was it that every time he paid her a compliment or seemed to admire her as a woman, he spoiled everything moments later? "I may not have recognized poison oak, but I've heard about rattlesnakes. I'm an educated woman, not a child."

"Then why did you keep going when I called?"

"I thought you were teasing me again. Besides"—she lifted her chin and gave him her smuggest of smiles—"I was sure I'd found a flower that would stump you."

He had the nerve to laugh in her face. "Not only stubborn, but competitive, too. Don't you know when to admit defeat?" His double meaning wasn't lost on her.

"I'll do no such a thing. Not now. Not later. You'll just have to accept the fact that my business is going to succeed." He had no idea how resourceful she could be—but he would soon enough. She'd rack her brain until she came up with plenty of ways to keep the customers on the north side of the street and leave him stewing in an empty shop on the south.

"And now I'll show you the flower I was after." She marched in the direction of the bloom she'd spotted, careful to avoid the poison oak.

When they reached the plant, she held the flower, and a sly smile spread across his face. "What a fitting choice. A snapdragon."

She didn't dignify that with a response.

Why was he happiest when he was teasing or taunting her? Perhaps because if he took a serious look at the situation, he'd have to admit she was a force to be reckoned with. And that truth would wipe the smile from his face.

Elenora stood in her shop the next day and tore her gaze from Rutledge Mercantile. She mustn't think about the owner or how he'd come so close to—

"It's hard to choose between the yellow and the green. I'd love a dress from each, but Papa said one will do."

She shook herself from her reverie, spun the bolt of buttery lawn, and held the length of fabric in front of Jane Abbott. "I've heard it gets warm here, so this lightweight material would be a good choice. Take a peek in the looking glass and see how nice it looks with your creamy complexion and lovely blond hair."

The young woman examined her reflection and turned to her friend Lucy Lyle, the doctor's daughter. "What do you think?"

"I agree. Now hurry and make your purchase. I know you want to get over to Rutledge Mercantile and see *him*."

Miss Abbott giggled. "Lucy, you shouldn't say such things. Besides, I don't even know if he's taken notice of me. I've got the notion he still thinks of me as a pesky young schoolgirl. But I'm a lady now."

She turned to Elenora. "You've seen him many times. Do you think he's handsome?"

"Who? Mr. Rutledge?"

Miss Abbott's giggles turned into unbridled laughter. When she finally contained herself, she shook her head, causing her mass of honey-colored curls to bounce. "Not Mr. Rutledge. He's *old*. Besides, he hasn't shown any woman attention since his wife died back when I was a girl in short skirts. I'm talking about his clerk, Sammy."

"Oh."

"So, do you?"

Elenora cut the cloth. How could she have been so foolish? She couldn't bear it if the garrulous girl were to let Mr. Rutledge know about her slip. She chose her words carefully. "It's what you think that's important. He's treated my daughter well, and that's what matters to me."

"Well, I think he's the finest man in all of El Dorado County. Maybe even the whole state of California."

Miss Lyle glanced at the watch pinned to her bodice. "If we don't get over there soon, you won't have time to talk to him. You know Mr. Rutledge locks the door at noon straight up. We've only got fifteen minutes."

Elenora wrapped the fabric in brown paper and tied the package with string. "Thank you for your patronage, Miss Abbott."

"I'll be back for the green batiste as soon as I can talk Papa into it." She stopped at the door. "And Mrs. Watkins, not a word to Sammy, please."

"Not a one."

The young women made their way across the street, and Elenora busied herself putting away the bolts of fabric. She must figure out how to draw more business her way. While sales had been brisk at first, they'd slowed the past few days. The mercantile, however, no longer resembled a ghost town. She'd seen seven people enter in the last half hour. From what Miss Abbott and Miss Lyle had said, Mr. Rutledge had received a large shipment with a number of new items.

She must do something to entice the townspeople into her place, but her next orders weren't due to arrive for days—and would contain considerably less than his. Had he been right? Was the novelty of a new business in town wearing off?

"Lord, Mr. Parks says we can trust Thee with our concerns, big and small. I ask Thee to uphold my shop so I can provide for Tildy."

Miles knelt before the case housing men's accessories later that afternoon, took a pair of black suspenders from those draped over Tildy's arm, and added them to the display.

"Mama has braces that are silky and have flowers on them."

"I know." Some woman would no doubt get them as a gift for her husband, and he'd have to wear the showy things.

"You like flowers. Why don't you buy them?"

"White dress suspenders like these are fine for me." He reached for the two pairs she held, added them to the case, and stood. "Isn't it time you get back to the house and help Mother with our supper?"

"I wish we could eat with you all the time. Mama burned the bacon this morning, and it stunk real bad." Tildy pinched her nose and shuddered.

"Since it doesn't look like you're starving, she must be doing something right."

"Your mother cooks good food, so you don't need a wife who can, right?"

"I don't need a wife, no." He strode to the back room with Tildy his shadow.

"Don't you get lonesome sometimes?"

He shoved the curtain aside. "Do I look lonesome?"

"Mrs. Rutledge told Mama you like little girls, and I like you. I wish—"

"Time to run along, Tildy. I'm sure Mother is waiting for you."

The corners of her mouth turned down. "Yes, sir." She trudged to the back door, cast him a sorrowful glance, and left.

Where had Tildy gotten the idea that her mama should marry him? Certainly not from her mother. Could it have been from his? Mother might throw Mrs. Watkins in his path at every turn, but surely she wouldn't involve a child in her matchmaking scheme. Would she?

"Mr. Rutledge?" Sammy pulled back the drape and poked

his head inside. "The shop's filled up. I could use your help."

"On my way." He glanced in the mirror, smoothed a stray hair, and followed Sammy out.

"There you are, Mr. Rutledge." A stoop-shouldered woman smelling of camphor tottered to him, her cane tapping on the wooden floor. "Would you be a dear boy and get me another bottle of that liniment I favor?"

"Certainly, Miss Crowley." He hastened to the case up front filled with assorted medicines. His eyes drifted across the street. Mrs. Watkins stood behind her counter putting away bolts of fabric. As had been the case the past four days, his shop was full, and hers was empty.

With the concert coming up, the ladies were eager to see the new fabrics he'd ordered. And he'd splurged for the more expensive stockings Irene had favored. He'd sold four pairs just that morning following hushed transactions with women eager to sample the quality.

A lone wagon waited in front of Mrs. Watkins's place, its occupants nowhere to be seen. The team seemed restless.

A distant rumble rattled the panes in the mercantile's five front windows.

"Yaaaaaw!"

Miles rushed to the door and threw it open. Two riders sped toward town in a cloud of dust.

The Talbot twins, of course. Didn't those boys know better than to race down Main Street? Someone could get hurt.

In a flash they reached the row of shops and sped past.

The horses hitched to the wagon across the street whinnied and reared. The heavy conveyance slammed into the pillars supporting the awning over Mrs. Watkins' shop.

Miles shouted a warning.

A thunderous crash followed.

He watched dumbfounded as the sturdy awning smashed into the massive sheet of plate glass. The trim boards around the window pulled away from the surrounding bricks, a few of which broke free and bounced down the pile of rubble on the walkway. The door with its glass center was ripped from its hinges. The frame broke into pieces that looked like a giant's toothpicks.

With speed he didn't know he possessed, he raced across the street and stopped short at the mound in front of the gaping hole that used to be the front of her shop. "Elenora!"

He flung boards and bricks aside.

"Mrs. Watkins? Can you hear me?"

There was no answer.

He hefted a large section of the massive awning aside, scaled the mountain of debris, and leaped into her shop.

Chapter 10

Mrs. Watkins stood next to the row of display cases in her shop clutching a jagged piece of wood to her chest, a vacant look on her ashen face.

"Thank the Lord you're all right." Miles swept his gaze over the mass of broken boards and the shattered glass, which glistened in the afternoon sun. Apparently nothing had hit her, although several pieces had come close.

She lifted wide eyes to him. "M–m–my sign."

"You can have another one made."

"But my name. It's gone." She laid the fragment on the counter and traced the letters with a trembling finger—*STAB*.

Stab? He pressed a hand to his temple and struggled to remember the wording. "Watkins General Merchandise." Nothing there. But wait. The bottom had read "Established 1870." *Stab*.

Mrs. Watkins looked as though she'd been stabbed, as if one of the glass shards had pierced her heart. A chill settled around his own.

"I always wanted my name on the door, but Pa. . ." Her wobbly smile and glazed expression made a knotty mess of his insides.

She laughed, a high-pitched cackle like the one he'd heard in a Shakespearean play in New York. The hairs on the back of his neck stood at attention.

With no warning she gripped the edge of the counter and shook violently, her eerie laugh giving way to ragged breaths. She was in a state of shock.

He pulled her into his arms, wrapping them tightly around

her and nestling her to him. She smelled of roses and—he sniffed her hair—burned bacon. A smile tugged at his lips. He hadn't held a woman so close in eight years. She was a mere slip of a thing, strong and yet soft. "It's all right, Ellie. I'm here. I'll take care of you."

She buried her face against his chest. He continued to offer assurances, comforting her as best he could, although his words struck him as woefully inadequate platitudes. What could he possibly say to soothe her in the face of such a disaster?

At length she shivered, and he rubbed her arms. The mild friction burned his palms, and he flinched. She tensed.

"I'm b–better. I didn't mean to. . ." She pulled away and looked into his face. Hers still bore a pallor that accentuated the deep flush on her cheeks. "What's this?" A featherlight touch brushed his forehead. "You've been hurt. Let me see your hands."

He held them out, powerless to do anything but follow her lead. She took them in hers and turned them over. "You're bleeding."

Cuts and scrapes covered his palms, but all he could feel was warmth flowing from her, up his arms, and into his soul. He glanced at her bloodstained sleeves. "I ruined your dress."

"Don't think a thing of it. That's the least of my concerns."

"I'm sorry about your shop."

She focused on his hands, still cradled in hers, and prattled, which was unlike her. "Oh dear. Look at these. You have some serious scratches. They need to be treated right away. You wouldn't want to risk an infection. I'll get—"

"I'm fine." He didn't even remember getting cut. All he'd been able to think about was reaching Ellie as quickly as he could. When he'd called her name and she didn't respond, he'd pictured her beneath the rubble, hurt. . .or worse, and terror had gripped him.

"Soap, water, and a soft cloth. That's what we need." She let go of him and teetered toward her back room.

He reached out to steady her, but she shook free. "I'll tend to your hands and then see about cleaning up the place and covering the opening with some blankets or something."

"You can't stay here." He motioned toward the rubble. "The front of the building's gone. Anyone could get in. And there's a storm brewing."

She spun around, and her dark eyes bored into him. "I can and I will. This"—she made a sweep of her hand—"is all I have. I'm not leaving, so you're not going to have the satisfaction of seeing me give up and run home to my pa. I'll just have to figure out a way to protect myself and my daughter." She blinked several times, but he saw no sign of tears.

An idea occurred to him. Not that Ellie would welcome it, but he could try. "You have other options."

"You're mistaken, Mr. Rutledge. You know as well as I this is the only space available, and I'm grateful to have it. Mr. Steele wasn't fond of the idea of renting it to a—to me."

"Move your wares into my place."

"*Your* place? I think not. I'll get those things." She raised her square chin and marched to the back of the shop, all signs of her unsteadiness gone. Good thing she was no longer looking at him, because he couldn't hide his smile. What an enchanting little bastion of bravado she was. He shadowed her, stopping at the entry to her backroom.

She held the floral curtain aside. "If you'll sit at the table, I'll be right back and see to your hands."

"That's not necessary. I can take care of myself."

"So can I." She followed her declaration with a too-sweet smile.

How he'd love to kiss that saucy smirk off her pink lips. On second thought, the smirk could stay. It showed an ability to face adversity with her characteristic courage, which he found most appealing. He'd like to kiss her because—

Lord, what am I thinking? Forgive me for having such foolish thoughts at a time like this. Ellie needs my help. Be with her, and—

"Mrs. Watkins! Miles!"

The shout roused him. Hank had scaled the mound and entered through the huge hole at the front of Ellie's shop. Sammy, Abe, and several others faced the building and stared at the devastation with mouths agape. The window, door, and awning were gone, but the brick front had survived the impact. Even so, the damage was significant. Ellie couldn't stay here, and the sooner she accepted that fact, the better.

Miles hastened to put the townspeople's fears to rest. "She's fine. Shaken, but fine."

Hank glowered. "Wait till I get my hands on the Talbots. They've gone too far this time."

"Mama!" Tildy appeared around the corner by the mercantile and raced across the street. "Mama, where are you?" Her head bobbed as she scanned the interior of the shop with terror-filled eyes.

"She's all right, Tildy girl. No, don't climb over that yourself. Sammy, help her please."

Once Tildy was inside the shop, she flew past Miles and threw herself at Ellie. "Oh, Mama! You're alive."

"I'm sorry you were scared, sweetheart, but I wasn't hurt." Ellie rubbed Tildy's back and looked over her head at the crowd in front of her shop, her gaze passing from one person to the next. "Thank you all for coming, but we'll be fine. I'll be back in business before you know it."

Although she spoke with assurance, Miles stood close enough to note the tremor in her lower lip. Ellie had to put her feelings aside for her daughter's sake and was doing an admirable job of it, but he'd never forget those first moments when she was near collapse and took refuge in his arms. He'd see to it she didn't face this crisis alone.

Hank stepped forward. "With all due respect, ma'am, this is a serious situation. You'll need help. I'm sure I speak for the rest of the townsfolk when I say we'll be here for you."

Voices rose in agreement.

"I don't—" She looked at Tildy and back at Hank. "Yes, Sheriff, I suppose I will need help. Once I've had time to appraise the situation, I'll be grateful to accept that offer."

Miles stationed himself between Hank and Ellie. "Sammy, run over to the mercantile and grab all the tarpaulins I have. We can get a temporary covering up before dark."

"Mr. Rutledge."

"Yes, Mrs. Watkins?"

"Before you do anything, we need to care for your hands."

How like a woman to fuss over nothing. "Not now. There's work to be done."

"Rutledge," Tiny, the smithy called. "Your mother's coming."

Miles stood on one side of the pile, Mother on the other, a hand clasped to her heaving bosom. "How's Elenora?"

"I'm here, Mrs. Rutledge." She appeared at his side, her arm around Tildy. "Nothing hit me, not even any of the glass, but your son hurt his hands when he tore through the rubble. I've got things ready to tend them."

"You've got more than enough to deal with. I can see to Miles. . .unless you'd rather I take Tildy and leave you to bandage him."

She smiled at Mother. "Thank you, Mrs. Rutledge." She cupped Tildy's cheek. "I need you to go with her, sweetheart, so I can make things safe for you here. I'll come as soon as I can."

Tildy trudged alongside Mother and paused at the corner to cast a woeful glance at her mama's shop before disappearing from view.

Hank chuckled. "We'll leave you to your, um, nursemaid, Miles, and be back with our tools shortly. Come on, men."

Miles whipped around to face Ellie, but she was gone.

Elenora drummed her nails on the table in her back room. The audacity of the man. If Mr. Rutledge thought she'd surrender control of the situation to him, he was in for a surprise. She might have made a spectacle of herself clinging to him like one of his roses to a trellis, but she wasn't the type of woman who wilted in the face of adversity. The sooner she made that clear, the better.

Footfalls heralded his approach. She sucked in a breath and steeled herself for the confrontation. He paused when he reached the curtain. "Ellie?"

Ellie? How dare he call her that? She shoved the curtain aside. "Mr. Rutledge, I realize one is prone to say or do things in the midst of a crisis that are uncustomary, but being that the moment has passed, kindly address me as Mrs. Watkins."

"I thought—"

"You thought incorrectly. I may have availed myself of your steadying presence, but that doesn't alter things between us. I'm a lady, a businesswoman, and a person due respect."

"I do respect you, more than you know. Most women would have dissolved in a puddle of tears, but you didn't."

"And I have no intention of doing so." Never had she seen such compassion in his expressive eyes, but she mustn't let herself be swayed. He was her competitor, and given his earlier attempts to woo her with kind words, which had been followed by cutting remarks, he couldn't be trusted.

"If you'll take a seat, I'll have a look at your hands." Although the prospect caused ripples in her stomach, she owed him that much. He had come to her aid after all. If he hadn't been there, she might have given way to the flood of feeling that had overtaken her. He'd kept her from drowning in a sea of self-pity.

"You don't need to do this."

"How will you help hang those tarpaulins if I don't?"

His smile lacked the warmth she'd come to expect. "You have a point."

They sat. She forced her hands not to tremble as she took one of his and wiped his palm with the moist cloth. "I'm afraid you won't be able to play your fiddle for a few days."

"I'll manage." He winced when she dabbed the deepest of the cuts.

"I'm sorry. I didn't mean to hurt you."

"You'll take my customers without a thought but not my offer of help?"

She rinsed out the cloth. "Why should I? You've made it clear you resent me being in business and are counting the days until I close my door. When I have one to close that is." She gave a dry laugh.

"Besting you in business is one thing, but taking advantage of your misfortune is another. I'd help anyone in town who found themselves in a similar situation. You can't operate your business the way it is. I'm offering you a temporary solution, that's all. I can clear some of my cases, and—"

"I appreciate your offer, but I'll find another solution to my dilemma." One that didn't involve accepting her competitor's charity.

Elenora shifted in the rocking chair she'd lugged downstairs to her back room and tucked the quilt around her. Thankfully the temperatures in early May didn't dip too low at night.

She listened for voices but heard only the steady creak of the chair as she rocked and the rhythmic drumming of rain on the metal roof. Hopefully no one else would pass in front of the shop as those intoxicated men with their colorful language had.

Why hadn't she accepted Mr. Rutledge's offer to watch her place? He'd be here with his gun. The iron skillet resting at her feet could do serious damage but would be no match against an armed intruder.

Come now, Elenora. Don't think about such things.

The chime on the mantel clock in her little parlor above sounded twelve times. Five more hours until dawn. And then what?

Mr. Rutledge was right. She couldn't do business with her shop in such a state. Repairs would take time. Several days or even a week. But they couldn't begin tomorrow, what with a storm raging and her landlord out of town.

She grabbed the skillet and padded to the front of the shop. Slivers of moonlight crept between the tarpaulins the men had draped over the gaping hole. Cool night air seeped in, causing her to shiver. The sweet scent of potpourri stopped her. A splintered board had landed close to Mama's crystal bowl, but thankfully the keepsake hadn't been broken.

Mama. With her voice as soft as a kitten's underbelly. She'd always had the right words to make things better. What would she say if she were here now?

Pray.

Elenora plunked her skillet on the display case and lifted

her face heavenward, but no words came. How could she pray? She'd asked God to uphold her business mere hours before the thunderous crash. Evidently He hadn't heard her—or didn't want her to succeed.

Why should it surprise her that God didn't care about her dreams? No man ever had. Pa had never gotten over his disappointment that she was a girl. Even though she'd loved working in his shop, he'd refused to make her his partner. He'd offered the position to Jake Watkins instead and insisted she marry him. Jake, with his cruel tongue. When he left for the war and she took his place, Pa still refused to consider her anything but his clerk.

Then she'd come to El Dorado filled with excitement, and Mr. Rutledge had rejected her.

But he *had* apologized. He'd even said he respected her and didn't want to see her fail. Did he mean that though? Or would he use her setback to his advantage?

If she were to accept the offer to operate out of his shop while the repairs were underway, he'd learn her ways of doing things. Not only that, but she'd have to pay additional rent. With the tremendous sum Mr. Steele charged, she couldn't afford to line Mr. Rutledge's pockets as well. She must figure out how to survive until she could open her doors again.

Heavy thudding on the walkway signaled the approach of a large person. An image of the outlaw filled her mind. He was in the area. She knew it. Mr. Rutledge could pooh-pooh her encounter at Deadman Creek all he wanted, but that horse belonged to the menacing man who'd been intent on robbing the coach, and no one could convince her otherwise.

Please. Let him pass by. The footfalls ceased in front of her shop, and the tarpaulins rustled.

Elenora grabbed the skillet, raised it over her shoulder, and waited, her heart slamming against her ribs.

Chapter 11

"No, Ellie! Don't!"

The cry came too late.

She completed her swing and struck something big and black. And soft.

Moisture sprayed her, and she grimaced.

"Mr. Rutledge! Are you all right?" Where had the blow landed, and how badly had she hurt him?

"I'm fine." He stepped though the tarpaulin and let it go. A gust of wind sent it flapping, flinging water over them both. "What a violent rainstorm, a real duck drencher as Abe would say."

"I didn't hit you? I felt blood."

"You didn't draw blood, but it wasn't for lack of trying. What you felt was water." He pulled off his hat and shook himself, sending a shower of drops splashing at their feet.

"I hit something."

"You did, but not me. Thankfully you've got a light burning in the back, so I saw you and your skillet in shadow. You destroyed my umbrella though." He held up a mangled mess of black silk serge and bent ribbing. "It's a good thing I carry a sturdy male model and not one of the lightweight frilly feminine things you sell."

"You scared me half to death, and now you have the audacity to insult my wares? Have you no consideration?"

"I battled the elements to check on you in the middle of the night, and you took a swing at me. Have you no appreciation?"

She rested the frying pan on the nearest stool and took

several calming breaths, giving her time to form a reply, one that didn't sound snappish. She should be grateful, but he'd given her a terrible fright. "Thank you for coming over, but as you can see, I was fully prepared to protect myself."

He laughed. "With an iron skillet? Do you really think you're going to stop an armed man with that?"

"If I hadn't lit the lamp and you hadn't seen the blow coming, you wouldn't be laughing. You'd be nursing a fierce headache."

"A concussion is more like it. You could have knocked me out cold."

She smiled. "Perhaps I'd have knocked some sense into you."

"What's that supposed to mean?"

"That it's about time you realize I'm far more capable than you give me credit for."

His voice held amusement, and even though she couldn't see his eyes in the dark, they were no doubt twinkling. "Oh, you're capable all right. Capable of driving a man to distraction. Seriously, though. How am I supposed to rest knowing all that's shielding you and Tildy are some tarpaulins? Anyone could slip inside."

"Why should that concern you? Didn't you say I have nothing to fear?"

"I said this is no longer the Wild West, but there are still unsavory characters around."

She knew that, but it did her good to hear him admit it. "That's exactly why I'm going to get a gun. I'll not spend one more night like this."

"Does that mean you'll be over to buy one tomorrow?"

"Hah! Buy a gun from you and pay retail? Never. I'll do my research before I make my purchase. . .wholesale. Until then I'll find another solution."

"Does that mean you're considering my offer?" How odd. He sounded almost eager.

"What that means is that I'm exploring all my options." And moving her wares into his shop was most definitely *not* one of them.

Miles stood in front of Ellie's shop shortly after nine the next morning, the Scottish carpenter at his side. The rain had eased, but he and MacDougall were buffeted by winds from the west as they sent the heavy black clouds scudding toward the peaks to the east.

"She's a lucky lass. The stick frame did its job, keeping the brick facade in place."

"I'm relieved to hear that, since she's adamant about staying in the building, despite the damage. I thought it looked secure, but I value your opinion."

"As do I, Mr. MacDougall."

Miles spun around. Where had Ellie come from? "I didn't expect to see you up and about already after your vigil." He'd snatched three hours' sleep after his, but she must be operating on even less.

"I can't afford to waste the day dozing. I've got work to do."

Mr. MacDougall tipped his hat. "Good morning, ma'am." Additional color flooded his ruddy face. "Begging your pardon. I can't say it's a good one from where ye stand, although ye were spared worse trouble. As I've told Miles, yer place is structurally sound."

"Do you have an idea how long it will take to get everything fixed?" she asked.

"The repairs themselves will only take a few days, but

ye'll have a wait for supplies. The glass for the door can be had in Placerville, but a sheet that size"—he pointed to where the window had been—"will have to be shipped from San Francisco. Then there's the lumber. The boards for the awning won't pose much of a problem since they're pine, but the fir for the window and doorframes will take longer. They're cut from clear-grained sapwood free of knots, so it's a special order."

"Would you be willing to take the job?"

"I'm the man for the awning, but ye'll need a cabinetmaker to build the frames and a glazier to install the glass."

Her shoulders drooped, as did the corners of her mouth. "From what you say I won't be able to open again for weeks. I can't close up shop that long. I'll have to come up with a plan. In the meantime would you draw up a list of what I need to order?"

"I'll get right on it. And I'll be back to secure the tarpaulins with boards later."

Ellie concluded her business with the carpenter and bid him farewell. She surveyed the makeshift covering protecting her shop, and sadness filled her eyes. "I hadn't realized how much work was involved, and I dare not think of the expense."

"Isn't Steele going to cover the cost?" Miles asked.

"Of course, but. . ."

"Don't tell me. He expects you to front the money."

She tilted her chin in that defiant gesture of hers. "It makes sense. He can't transact business here while he's in San Francisco."

"He's been known to go back on his word. I don't trust him. Since he wasn't keen on renting to you in the first place, you'd be wise to let me supervise the repairs. He and I don't see eye to eye on everything, but I can deal with his kind."

She rested her gloved hand on Miles's arm, and he resisted

the urge to smile. "You've done more than enough already. It's come to my attention you stayed up all night watching my place from yours. I appreciate that, but I'll see to things from here on out."

Her dismissal felt like a kick in the gut. He had a burning desire to protect her and Tildy. After all, they had no one else to look out for them. But some women were too independent for their own good and didn't know when to let a man step in. "I'm available if you'd like my help, Ellie."

She withdrew her hand and pinned him with a piercing look. "What I'd like, *Mr. Rutledge*, is for you to honor my requests. I have several people to see, so I'll be on my way. Good day."

The next three hours crawled. Miles fought his fatigue, but the lack of customers in town after the storm gave him too much time to think. In his muddle-headed state, his thoughts were poor company. A certain woman with a wagonload of independence continued to invade them. Why couldn't he put Ellie out of his mind?

Because he cared, whether he wanted to or not, and felt powerless to do anything about it. How could he, when she'd made it clear she didn't want his help?

Miles locked up the mercantile and trudged up the hill to his house. Perhaps Ellie would be in a more receptive frame of mind and dinner would be a pleasant affair.

"Son, is that you?"

He entered the kitchen and found Mother and Tildy putting the meal on the small table in the corner. "Why aren't we eating in the dining room?"

"Mama's not coming, so we're going to have a cozy time, just the three of us. I've never had you two all to myself. It'll be special, won't it, Mr. Rutledge?"

"Yes, Tildy." He looked over her head at Mother. "Where is she?"

"Elenora is dining at the hotel restaurant."

"With someone?"

Tildy set a pan of cornbread on the table. "With Sheriff Henderson."

Ellie was having dinner with Hank? He hadn't dined with a woman once in the ten years he'd been in El Dorado. What could it mean? Was he sweet on her?

Elenora took the seat the sheriff held for her and waited while he pushed her chair closer to the table. He sat opposite her, his neck ablaze. The poor man. He looked more uncomfortable than a saloon girl in a church service. The sooner she got down to the business at hand, the better.

"Sheriff, I'm obliged you agreed to meet with me. I've a number of questions related to the security of my shop. Given your expertise, I value your thoughts on the matter. My primary concern is having the place watched at night. I've come up with a plan."

She launched into her explanation, pausing when the waiter took their orders. The sheriff listened intently, and his color slowly returned to normal. "So what do you think?"

"The Talbot twins caused the trouble in the first place, ma'am, so I don't reckon you should pay them to stand guard. I think they owe it to you. Those fellers have a history of trouble-making and need to learn a lesson."

"I'm aware of their reputation. They like to give me heart failure when they rode up to the stagecoach that day. But I think giving them the opportunity to make reparations will be good for them, without pay as you said. Unless you have serious reservations."

He rubbed his chin. "Watching your place might teach them a thing or two. I could have a talk with them if you'd like and let them know they'll be dealing with me if they let you down. Sometimes the badge comes in handy for making a point." He patted his.

"I'd prefer to talk to them first. I plan to pay them and their mother a visit this afternoon. I've another proposition for them, if they prove themselves worthy. One that would put a little money in their pockets. But if I need your help, I'll avail myself of it. What I'd like now is for you to educate me about handguns. I intend to purchase one and would like to make a wise decision."

To his credit Sheriff Henderson showed no surprise. She'd tapped into a subject he knew a great deal about, and he visibly relaxed. He spent their entire mealtime giving her a thorough understanding of her options.

The waiter removed their plates, and she made her final request. "I'll need an instructor. Would you be willing to teach me how to shoot?"

His speech grew halting, and his neck flamed once again. "I'm not. . . I'm afraid I can't do that."

"I thought you'd be the best choice. But perhaps you don't believe a woman should own—"

"That's not it. You have every right to own a gun. Anyone with a business should be able to protect it. But I w–wouldn't make the best teacher for you."

True. With his trouble talking to women, he wouldn't. "I understand. Is there someone you'd recommend? Someone as skilled as yourself?"

Her compliment caused the color to spread to the shy sheriff's cheeks. "We have a real marksman, but I'm not sure he'd be willing to instruct you, either. I might have to persuade him."

Minutes later Elenora paused beneath the hotel's enclosed balcony. She used her most professional tone and made sure the others nearby could hear her, hopefully forestalling any gossip. "Thank you, Sheriff. You've been most helpful. I appreciate you taking time to discuss the situation with my shop." She extended a hand as a man would, and he shook it.

"All in a day's work, Mrs. Watkins." He doffed his hat and took off down the walkway.

As painful as their meeting had been for him, she'd learned a great deal and couldn't wait to move forward with her plans. If the Lord chose to bless them, she wouldn't mind.

That afternoon Miles left the mercantile, sauntered down the walkway, and paused at the door to the sheriff's office. Hank sat with his feet on the corner of his desk and his hands clasped behind his head, staring at the ceiling. Recounting his time with Ellie, no doubt.

Miles pasted on a smile and went inside. "Howdy."

Hank dropped his feet to the floor with a jangle of spurs, crossed his arms over his chest, and grinned. "Howdy yourself. I expected to see you long before this. I've been back the better part of two hours. What took you so long?"

"Been busy. But I wanted to see if you've had a chance to talk with the Talbot twins about the damage they caused."

"The Talbots, you say? Can't fool me, Miles. You heard I dined with Mrs. Watkins and want to grill me—after you skewer me, that is."

He should have known he couldn't keep his real reason for

coming from his friend. Hank knew him too well. "How'd it go?"

"The lady and I had a fine time. Her head isn't filled with fluff like some women. I can see why she's turned yours."

"She's done no such thing."

"You can rest easy. My bachelorhood's not in danger. In fact, I steered her your way."

"My way? Why?"

"I'll leave it to her to tell you."

Even though he tried to pry it out of Hank, his friend said nothing more.

Miles marched down Main Street toward Ellie's place but stopped outside the grocer's. When was the last time that many women had been in the shop at one time? Had Mr. Olds received another shipment of Belgian chocolate?

Ellie was at the center of the group, looking lovelier than he'd ever seen her. Her radiant smile could chase away the dark clouds looming over the Sierras.

This was no run on foreign confections. No doubt the gaggle of gabby women was discussing her plight and his thwarted attempts to come to her aid. He could imagine the laughter that must have filled the place when she told them how close she'd come to bashing him over the head with her frying pan.

He wanted to know what Ellie and Hank had discussed and ask if she'd like him to deliver some firewood since her place would be chillier than usual, but he wouldn't set foot inside Olds' shop and subject himself to another rebuff in full view of others. He'd talk with her later.

The door to the grocer's gave a squeak, and hurried foot-steps followed. "Mr. Rutledge." Ellie caught up to him, a basket of groceries over her arm. "Would you have a minute?"

He had the rest of the day. "I can spare one. Why?"

"I thought you might like to know why I wasn't at dinner."

He stopped. "It's none of my business."

"I invited Sheriff Henderson to share a meal. I wanted his advice on how to protect my shop. You watched it for me last night, but I needed to find another solution. I've arranged for some young men to guard the place. And I've placed an order for a gun."

Her words were simple enough to follow, but he couldn't determine what shone from her bright eyes. If he were pressed to identify it, he'd say eagerness. "But you don't even know how to shoot."

"I intend to learn. Sheriff Henderson recommended a man who could teach me."

"Him?"

She shook her head. "You."

Chapter 12

Elenora stood on the porch of a small farmhouse later that afternoon and prepared to take her leave. "Thank you for agreeing to my plan, Mrs. Talbot."

"If my boys give you any trouble, be sure and let me know."

"I don't expect any." As she'd hoped, the twins' mother had agreed to let her sons stand guard over the shop until the repairs were completed. She hadn't scoffed at the possibility of the outlaw returning, not since her sons had seen a man skulking about near Union Mine a few weeks after the attempted holdup, around the same time Elenora had spied the big black horse at the creek.

She returned to town at a brisk pace. How quickly the weather had changed. Wet and cold the night before. Dry and warm today. Moisture gathered under her snug collar. Her wardrobe had served her well in Omaha, but she must see about having lighter-weight dresses made. She certainly had enough fabric, which was sitting in her shop behind the temporary covering Mr. MacDougall had fashioned for her with oiled tarpaulins and boards. No dust or moisture could get in, but neither could customers.

If her plan to go door-to-door as traveling salesmen did was successful, she would still bring in some income, which was vital. A month with no revenue, coupled with the money she must advance for the repairs, would take a sizeable chunk of her remaining funds. There were also three shipments due with invoices requiring payment.

But at least she had help to watch her place now. Although Sheriff Henderson had questioned her choice of asking Tommy and Timmy to stand guard, he'd agreed they were strong and knew how to handle a gun.

She'd know how to fire one soon, but first she had to schedule her lesson. If only Mr. Rutledge hadn't insisted on using his revolver. She'd prefer to wait for hers to arrive and use it, but if she wanted him to teach her, she'd have to use his .44 caliber Colt with its eight-inch barrel. Although it grated on her to admit it, he had a point. If she were teaching someone to play the violin, she would demonstrate the fingerings on her own instrument.

In no time she reached the mercantile. She opened the door, and a cheery chime announced her arrival.

Sammy greeted her. "It's a shame about your shop. What are you going to do?"

"I'll make the best of the situation."

"But you can't do business without a storefront."

The young man was cut from the same cloth as his employer. "Not in the traditional sense." She lifted her chin. "But I'm not a traditional woman."

Sammy quirked a smile. "No ma'am. Was there something I could help you with?"

"I'm here to speak with Mr. Rutledge."

"He's down at Abe's. What with all the excitement, he didn't get his haircut this morning."

No doubt he was talking about her. Oh well. She'd see him later. Right now she'd find out the cost of renting a delivery wagon. She excused herself and left the shop in such a hurry the bell clanged. Her bootheels clicked a rapid staccato on the wooden walkway as she made her way to the livery.

Abe popped out of his place. "You're just the lady I wanted to see. I been hearin' news about you and want to make sure my ears are working right."

Leave it to him to waylay her. The word *hurry* wasn't in his vocabulary. She should have crossed the street so he wouldn't have the opportunity to stop her. The livery would be closing soon. "Of course." She smiled and stepped inside. "What did you hear?"

"Word is you aim to get yourself a gun and learn to shoot."

She flicked her gaze from Abe to Mr. Rutledge, whose tall frame filled the barber chair, to the sheriff, who stood in the corner of the small shop. "That's true. I've asked Mr. Rutledge to teach me. From what I've heard he's the best shot in town."

The jovial barber grinned. "Sure is. He has a passel of ribbons to prove it, too, don't you, Miles?"

"I have a few. So, Mrs. Watkins, does this mean you're willing to accept my terms?" He pulled off the sheet covering him, stood, and grabbed his frock coat. His expressive eyes bored into her as though he were searching for something.

"I am." She did her best to paint a picture of sincerity.

Her efforts seemed to have an effect. He ceased his intense scrutiny and donned his jacket. "All right then. I'll ask Sammy to close up Saturday, and I'll meet you at Will and Pearl's place. Now if you'll excuse me, I have a business to run." He tipped his hat and left.

Abe stood at her side, and they watched Mr. Rutledge's retreating form. "He doesn't seem very enthusiastic about teaching me, does he? I don't understand. His mother said he insisted she learn to shoot when she started working in the mercantile."

"Don't mind him. He's probably worried that you'll outshoot him is all."

The sheriff joined them. "Abe's right. Miles will come around once he sees how eager you are to learn."

She hoped Mr. Rutledge's friends were right, but she had

her doubts. It seemed she possessed a knack for getting him riled up.

Miles leaned against the fence around Will's paddock. "Looks like you're keeping my horses in good shape."

"Don't I always? But you didn't come out early to check on your team. What has you scowling? Seems to me you'd be in fine spirits. It isn't every day a lady you find attractive asks for a shooting lesson."

Ellie was that, but he wasn't about to let a pretty woman turn his head. He'd been down that road, and it was a dead end filled with nothing but heartache. "For the record, she didn't intend to seek me out. Hank put her up to it."

Will's new mare nuzzled his arm. He produced an apple. "Here you go, girl." He fed her the fruit and patted her neck. "You know what your trouble is, Miles? You don't realize when you've been given a gift."

"Being forced to teach Mrs. Watkins isn't what I'd consider a gift. More like a burden."

"Don't think Tiny would see it that way. Or MacDougall. Or—"

"They don't know her the way I do. She's headstrong and stubborn."

"And you're not?" Will strode toward the barn. "If I were in your shoes, my good man, I'd thank Hank for recommending me and enjoy the experience."

Miles fell in step. "I guess it's better than teaching Mother, even if Mrs. Watkins is outspoken."

"She's not like Irene."

"Leave her out of it."

Will threw up his hands in mock surrender. "No need to get testy."

Miles gritted his teeth. *Lord, it's been eight years. Why, after all this time, does the mention of her name set me off? Help me put the past in the past—and keep it there.*

They reached the barn, and Will slid the large door to the side, seemingly oblivious to the screech of rollers in need of oil. He grabbed a crate, filled it with tin cans, and carried it outside, where he plunked it down. Miles followed, looked down the road, and saw Mrs. Watkins approaching with Tildy skipping along at her side. He felt a hand on his shoulder.

"She's a wonderful mother. Can't fault her on that."

"No." Will was right. If anything, Ellie erred on the protective side. "But she's opinionated. Her way is the only way. And when it comes to handling a gun, there's no room for discussion. She has to do what I say, or she could get hurt."

"From what Hank told me, she agreed to use your gun even though she wanted to wait for hers to arrive. That sounds to me like someone who's willing to compromise. Maybe you're just looking for trouble because you didn't see it coming before."

Miles clenched his teeth to keep from singeing Will's ears. Will meant well, but he had a wonderful marriage to a woman who loved him. He didn't know what it was like to have a wife who challenged him at every turn and made his life miserable. Strong-willed women needed to learn their place, or accidents could happen.

"Mrs. Watkins has a good head on her shoulders. She won't do anything foolish. If you can look at what's in front of you instead of what's behind, I think you'll be a lot happier."

"I don't need a lecture."

"What you need is some fun in your life. And here's somebody who can add it."

Tildy sped toward Miles with her arms open wide. He caught her, spun her around, and set the breathless girl on her feet.

"Oh, Mr. Rutledge, isn't it the best day ever? We get to eat supper here, Mama got candy for me to share with Constance and her brothers, and I get to play in the new tree house with them."

"It's a wonderful day, Tildy girl."

Will inclined his head toward a large oak beyond the farmhouse. "Constance is waiting for you at the rope swing." He turned to Ellie, whose warm brown eyes shone with obvious anticipation. "Welcome. I've got everything set for you and Miles. I told the neighbors you'd be practicing in the back field, and the children know to stay near the house."

"Thank you. I'll speak with Pearl, and then I'll be ready, Mr. Rutledge." The light in her eyes dimmed. She gave him a curt nod and departed.

Miles grunted. Why did she brighten when speaking with Will but close up tighter than a poppy at sunset when addressing him?

No sooner was she out of earshot than Will jabbed him with an elbow. "Relax, my good man, and she will, too. Some of my best courting was done while teaching Pearl to shoot."

"I'm not courting."

"You could. It's high time you find someone."

First Mother, and now Will. He respected Ellie's ability and wanted to protect her, but that didn't mean he wanted to court her. This was a shooting lesson and nothing more. He just wanted to make it through the lesson without incident and go home.

Elenora closed her hand around the soft cotton balls Pearl passed her. They would help deaden the sound of the shots, but they could also come in handy if Mr. Rutledge snapped at her. She peered at him through the kitchen window of the Dupree farmhouse. From the depth of the creases on his broad forehead, it was clear he wasn't looking forward to their lesson nearly as much as she.

"Don't worry. It's not that bad. You might even find you enjoy it."

Elenora roused herself from her musings. "I want to learn. Pa wouldn't let me handle his gun, although I would've felt much safer if I'd known how to shoot when. . ." She rested her trembling hands on the window ledge.

Pearl screwed the zinc lid on the Mason jar filled with fluffy white spheres and padded to Elenora's side. "You don't have to talk about it if you'd rather not, but I remind the children it's easier to let go of bad memories if we tell them to someone."

She'd said the same thing to Tildy. As hard as it was to think about that horrid day, the images persisted. "A customer came in the shop one afternoon when Pa was in the back room. Something about the man troubled me. He. . . Well, he leered at me. It made my skin crawl. Then he took out his gun and demanded all the money in the till. He aimed the revolver at my heart, and I was so scared I couldn't move. I could tell from the strong odor of liquor and his slurred speech he'd been drinking. He pulled back the hammer, and I was sure I was as good as dead."

"That's awful. What happened?"

"Pa shot him. I've only seen two people die. Jake and. . .that man. Jake died as a result of a wound that got infected and went in his sleep, but the robber. . . Pa shot him in the chest. I've never seen so much blood at one time. The sight made me so sick I thought I'd lose my breakfast." She shuddered.

"Are you all right?"

"I'll be fine. I just need a bit of fresh air."

Elenora hurried to the porch, where she gripped the railing. Several moments passed as she attempted to banish the images.

Pearl joined Elenora, stood by her side, and waited in companionable silence.

Elenora looked into the distance and continued her tale. "Pa refused to let me handle a gun, even after that horrid experience. He said it wasn't ladylike. I felt so helpless, but I didn't have a choice. Until I received the money from Jake's parents, I was dependent on Pa."

"But you'll be able to protect yourself now. Have you picked out a gun yet?"

The tightness in her chest eased, and her breath came easier. "I found a model just right for me. It should be here next week. That's why I'm so eager to learn how to handle a gun."

Pearl leaned back against the railing and lowered her voice. "I hope the lesson goes well and Miles isn't too. . .intense."

"Is there something I should know?"

"He had a bad experience in the past. I'm not one to speak ill of those who've passed on, but his late wife, Irene, wasn't as cooperative as she might have been. So if he seems short, it might not have anything to do with you." She fidgeted with a button on her bodice. "I hope you don't think poorly of me for telling you."

"I'm glad you did. It helps."

"Ready, Mrs. Watkins?" Mr. Rutledge called.

"Coming." Elenora smiled and hoped it looked genuine. The scowl he wore didn't bode well. Perhaps if she presented a pleasant manner, the lesson would be tolerable.

He clutched a crate in his hands and motioned her to follow with a tilt of his head.

She fell in step beside him. "Thank you for doing this."

"I want to be clear about my expectations. You're to do

everything I say. If you refuse to follow my instructions and put either of us in danger, the lesson's over. Do you understand?"

"Is it really necessary for you to be so heavy-handed? You might find it easier to get people to do your bidding if you used honey instead of vinegar." She lifted her head and her hem and took off at a brisk pace.

Miles plunked the crate beneath a sheltering oak at the southernmost point of the Dupree farm with such force the cans clanged together. He straightened and found Ellie surveying him, that determined chin of hers tilted. Teaching another headstrong woman to shoot ranked up there with pulling weeds.

She smiled. Granted, her attempt to appear cheerful looked forced, but she was obviously trying to be agreeable. It wasn't her fault Hank had talked her into this. He would have done anything to avoid spending time in the company of an attractive woman, especially when he'd have to do a fair amount of the talking. No doubt she'd carried their dinner conversation, which is why he'd been able to make it through the meal.

"When did you plan to get started?" Ellie's smile had dimmed, replaced by her let's-get-to-business look. Perhaps things would be more bearable than he'd first thought, since she did seem eager to learn.

"We'll start by setting up the targets. They sit on this plank Will's nailed between the two uprights."

She helped him position the tin cans, some of which bore holes from previous practices. At least she was determined and would no doubt work hard to hit one as often as possible. Irene had only managed to do so once before she'd declared the lesson over and demanded he take her home. Even Mother had done better than that. But then, she'd respected him and done as he asked. If Irene had done the same, May wouldn't have been in that woman's home the night the fire broke out, and he wouldn't have lost his family.

"All done." Ellie brushed her hands down her sides.

"It's time to get in position. Stand here." He scraped a line in the dirt about twenty-five feet from the row of cans. The dust he raised clung to the moisture coating the back of his neck.

"So far?"

"This is close, actually. My revolver's an Army model Colt and has a much greater range than this. I usually stand fifty feet back. Since you'd be using a gun inside your shop though, you wouldn't even be this far from the intru—from your target."

He pulled the gun from its holster, and she moved to the side. "That's far enough," he said when she was several feet away. "Let me warn you, it's going to be loud and there'll be some smoke." He fired, knocking off a can with each of his five shots.

"You're quite good. I didn't expect you to know so much about this. You're not like those rough men I saw in Omaha. You're. . .nice."

Nice? What did she mean by that? He was as much a man as Hank. "Just because I grow flowers doesn't mean I'm weak."

He hadn't meant to sound so defensive, but for some reason, her opinion mattered more than he would have thought.

"You're not. I shouldn't have been surprised. You're good at whatever you undertake."

"Not everything. I can't figure you out."

She put her hand to the flowers at her throat, her mouth open in a look of disbelief. "Me? I'm not hard to understand. I just want to run a successful business, provide for my daughter, and prove that I'm—"

"As capable as any man, especially one with a shop across

the street from yours."

She smiled again, although this one brought a light to her eyes. "I wouldn't have put it exactly like that."

"But I'm right, aren't I?"

She rubbed her hands together. "When do I get to shoot?"

He chuckled. The lesson was going much better than he'd expected. Unlike Irene, Ellie wanted to be here and seemed to enjoy his company. He was certainly enjoying hers. "Not yet. I want you to get used to holding the gun first, see how it feels in your hands. Since it's empty, you'll be safe." He rotated the cylinder so she could see. "It might be heavier than you think, so hold it tightly."

"How?"

"It'd be easiest if I help you. May I?"

"Oh. You mean. . ." Her face flushed. "Why yes, I suppose that would be necessary."

He positioned her right hand on the grip, her left underneath, supporting it. "You'll keep your index finger beside the trigger guard until you're actually ready to shoot."

"Now what?"

"You need to learn how to aim. I'll show you." He stood behind her and placed his hands over hers. "Hold your arms out at shoulder level."

She did. He caught a whiff of a pleasing floral perfume. Her hair brushed his cheek as he checked her position. Having her so close sent his pulse rate into double time. He forced his thoughts back to the lesson.

"Good. Next you pull the hammer back like so. And whatever you do, keep your fingers out of the way when the gun's cocked. See the sight on the rear, here?" He pointed it out.

"The notch?"

"Yes. You'll line up that blade sight on the front so it's in the middle of the notch. Now, point the gun at the center of whatever you're aiming at, in this case a can."

"It's hard to focus."

True. He was having the devil of a time doing so. Taking a breath, he concentrated on the instructions he gave her. "Try closing one eye. Once you have your target sighted, you'll put your finger on the trigger."

"And pull it, right?"

"No. I'll show you why. Let me have the gun."

He released the hammer and shoved the revolver in his holster. Ellie had given him the perfect opportunity to have some of that fun Will had talked about and teach her an important lesson at the same time. Giving her no warning, he grabbed her hand and jerked her to him. She lost her balance and fell against his chest, just as he'd planned.

She lifted wide eyes. "What did you do that for?"

"Two reasons. First, to demonstrate how pulling the trigger suddenly or with a jerky movement could throw off your aim. And second"—he lowered his voice—"because I rather like having you in my arms."

She gazed at him, her face flooded with more feeling than he'd ever seen. Surprise. Hesitation. And could that be anticipation? Clearly she was torn. He drank in the sight, which warmed him more than the summer sun slanting from the west.

"Now take a deep breath."

She did and held it, apparently waiting to see what he'd do next.

"Perfect. After you've done that you'll *squeeze* the trigger, easing it back nice and slow." He took his time wrapping his arms around her and hugging her to him until her cheek rested against his chest. "Nice, wouldn't you agree?"

She pushed away from him. "I. . . We. . . Mr. Rutledge, I

think it would be best if we resume the lesson."

"Of course." She'd let him hold her, if only for a moment. It felt good to have her in his arms, just as it had when she'd taken refuge there before. But he wanted more. Would she let him kiss her? "I need to tell you about the recoil."

"Recoil?" Confusion caused her lovely face to scrunch the same way Tildy's did on occasion. "Sheriff Henderson told me about the process, but he didn't mention that."

"Once you've fired the shot, the force will make your arms fly up"—with a finger under her chin, he lifted it—"and back." He tilted her head with his thumb.

"And then?" She stood still, her eyes locked with his, and swallowed. Her parted lips quivered. So did she.

"You could find that your head is spinning and you're dazed." She looked as though both were true. He leaned toward her and paused, but she offered him no encouragement. Not even a slight tilt of her head.

What am I doing? Ellie doesn't even like me that much.

Chapter 13

Elenora broke eye contact, stepped back, and willed her heart to cease its wild dance. Why had she allowed Mr. Rutledge to take her in his arms like that? His actions had illustrated his points, but he might think she welcomed his advances. And that was definitely not the case. She was here to learn to fire a gun so she could protect her business, and that was all.

He pulled his gun from the holster. "Are you ready to shoot?"

"I want to watch you one more time first. I looked at the cans before. This time I'll keep my eye on you."

His mustache twitched, as though he were resisting the urge to smile.

She mentally kicked herself. "That didn't come out the way I meant."

"You watch me all the time. Why should this be any different?"

"I don't. Well, maybe now and then. Since your shop is across from mine, I can't help but see you—it." She resisted the urge to wince.

He grinned. "Before you feast your eyes, I have to reload."

Although she enjoyed his teasing, she did her best to appear unaffected. "Sheriff Henderson and I did talk about this. It sounds like a time-consuming process."

"It's not that bad. Takes a strong hand though, so I'll take care of it."

That was fine with her. She had no desire to deal with the black powder. Thankfully, she wouldn't have to.

She watched intently as he went through the process, from biting open the first paper cartridge to fitting the percussion caps at the back of each chamber. "Why did you leave one of the chambers empty?"

"I keep the first one empty so the gun won't go off unexpectedly. Since I put mine under my cash drawer loaded and ready to use, I don't want any accidents."

"That's why you had five shots instead of six then?"

"Exactly." He finished his task and moved into position. "You wanted to watch me shoot once more?"

"I want to see that recoil you talked about."

"I'll fire one more round, and then it's your turn." He sent the five cans flying and turned to her, his brows raised, as if he expected a response—or a compliment.

She could see why Sheriff Henderson had recommended Mr. Rutledge, but she wasn't going to gush just because he was an excellent marksman. "I've got the idea now."

While he reloaded, she held an imaginary gun, took aim, and pretended to shoot.

He held his revolver out to her. "Ready, Ellie?"

"No one's ever called me Ellie before. I really wish you wouldn't. It's not proper."

He laughed, a warm, rich sound that melted her resolve. No matter how hard she tried to resist his charm, he would disarm her, and she'd forget why he'd riled her.

"I'll try to remember, but I'm afraid I may have formed a new habit."

Crinkles appeared around his eyes, and his mustache twitched. His teasing smile. She should have known. She couldn't keep herself from smiling in return.

"From that grin of yours, I'd say you're ready to give it a go. Am I right?"

"Yes!" Reining in her excitement wasn't easy. For years she'd admired the handguns in the shop down the street from Pa's, but he wouldn't even allow her to hold his.

She took the Colt, which was every bit as heavy as the sheriff's model, and got into position. Mr. Rutledge stepped to the side a few feet from her. "Aren't you going to be with me the first time?"

"I can't. The sound and smoke right behind you would be too much. You have to do this on your own."

As much as she longed to show him she could handle this, she didn't want to get hurt. "Do you think I'm ready?"

"Tell me about the steps as you walk through each of them, but don't pull the hammer or squeeze the trigger yet."

She did as he asked, and he nodded.

"I'd say you're as ready as you can be, Ellie."

"All right then, *Mr.* Rutledge. I'll need time to get the feel of things, so you mustn't tease me if I miss."

"Of course not."

She cocked the hammer, took aim, and fired her first shot.

"Oh!" The force caused her to stumble backward.

He rushed toward her. "Are you—"

"I'm fine. The gun flew up farther than I expected, that's all."

"Has a kick like a mule, doesn't it?"

"Quite." She groaned. "I didn't hit anything."

He chuckled. "Not a can, but I think you scared that tree back there."

She huffed. "Really! You gave me your word."

His mustache did its little dance. "Sorry. I couldn't resist."

"I'm going to hit one, you know. It might take a few shots though."

"I brought plenty of ammunition. Fire away."

She fired sixteen shots before she hit her first can, but he deserved some credit for not laughing again. His pointers did help.

Nearly two hours had passed by the time they finished. Elenora wiped the back of her hand over her forehead. "I never did get them all."

"Don't worry. You got three out of five and were close on the other two that last round, which is fine. If you had to shoot in the shop, you'd be far closer to a much larger target."

"I'd hoped to do better."

"Once you put in some practice, you'll get more consistent."

"Indeed I will. But right now I need to rest." She rubbed her right arm.

"You're likely to be sore for a while."

He gathered the cans, carried the crate to where she leaned against the trunk of a tall ponderosa pine, and set it down. Resting a hand beside her head, he looked into her face. His gaze traveled from her eyes to her lips and lingered there. She swallowed.

"You know, Ellie, this turned out better than I expected. I'd be willing to give you another lesson or two." He reached a hand toward her cheek, where she felt wisps of hair against her sticky skin, and brushed them aside.

She warmed at his touch, but as much as she wanted to give way to the feelings coursing through her, she couldn't. He'd rejected her and was now her rival. "While I appreciate the offer, that won't be necessary. You've taught me what I need to know. Pearl said I could practice whenever I'd like, and I will."

He hefted the crate, and the cans clattered. "What will you use? Will's gun? He got that antique from his father. Or perhaps you'd hoped to borrow my later model?"

She smiled, a syrupy smile with a topping of smug. "Neither. I'll use my own once it arrives."

"Yes. I can imagine what you chose. A fancy ivory-handled derringer with curlicues and whatnot engraved on its shiny silver barrel. The kind of gun a woman would call *cute*."

"My gun will suit me just fine." Wait until he saw it.

The following Thursday Elenora returned from her round of visits, hastened to the Wells Fargo office, and rushed inside to the agent's counter. "Good afternoon, Mr. McCormick. Did Wally leave my package?"

"He did. Here you go."

She placed the parcel in her basket and scurried down the walkway, averting her eyes as she passed others. The sooner she reached her shop, the sooner she could admire her gun. All she had to do was make it past the Oriental Hotel, turn the corner, and—

"Elenora."

She located Pearl waving at her from across the street. Her friend darted over. "Is that it?"

"Yes. Would you like to come to my place and see it?"

"By all means."

Moments later they stood at the table in Elenora's back room, the revolver resting on its bed of brown velour in the box before them. She rubbed a finger over the soft fabric. "I like how the case has a section to hold a box of cartridges."

"I'm sure you're eager to try out your gun. When can we expect you?"

"I finished my calls early, so I'd like to come out now if that's all right. I should be able to get in a good hour of practice before I have to pick up Tildy."

"Certainly. I got the saddle soap Will's waiting for, so we can walk together."

They ambled down the road toward the Dupree farm. Although Elenora couldn't wait to fire her gun for the first time, she treasured the time with Pearl. Having a friend with whom to share her joys and struggles was wonderful.

The conversation shifted from talk of Elenora's gun to her business.

"Your plan seems to be working well. Mrs. Talbot is singing your praises."

Elenora laughed. "She's far too kind. All I did was come up with the idea of selling my wares door-to-door until I can open my shop again."

"You employed her sons, the same young men who caused the accident. You've been in town long enough to hear the rumors. Many people believe them to be nothing but mischief-makers and wanted to see them punished. Including Miles. How do you feel about that?"

"I was angry with the twins at first, but I realized they were just having fun. They were shocked when they saw the damage they caused, and they're paying me back by guarding my place without pay to make up for it. I can sleep at night thanks to them."

Pearl shifted her basket from one arm to the other. "But they're making your deliveries and being paid for that. At least that's what Will heard at the feed store yesterday."

How quickly news spread in a small town. "I needed some-one, and they've been quite reliable. Not only that, but I owe them, too. There are those who seem to forget that Tommy and Timmy saved Tildy and me from that outlaw the day we came into town."

"Yes, but that wasn't their intention. They were up to another of their pranks. I don't mean to question your decision, Elenora, but they've earned their reputation as troublemakers.

Miles and the others may be right. They could use a firm hand."

"Mrs. Talbot is doing her best. It's not easy for a widow to raise a child alone. I, at least, have a girl. She has two sons on the verge of manhood. They're full of energy and ideas but don't have a way to put them to good use. She believes they took the townspeople's label to heart and use it as an excuse for their wild behavior. I think if they have a purpose and are treated with respect, they'll mend their ways. She agrees."

Pearl smiled. "You certainly have experience with a bright, adventurous child."

"That I do. I wish Mr. Rutledge and some of the others would trust my judgment in this. Sheriff Henderson saw things my way after I explained my reasons."

"Our esteemed sheriff certainly seems to be your advocate. There wouldn't be something between you two, would there?"

Elenora laughed. "Our shy sheriff? No. He's been helpful, but he's not—"

"Miles. And don't give me that innocent look. I saw the way the two of you were acting after your lesson. He couldn't take his eyes off you, and you flushed whenever you caught a glimpse of him. Something happened out in the back field, didn't it?"

She let Pearl's question go unanswered until the silence grew as thick as the crowns of the trees overhead providing them with welcome shade. Talking about personal matters wasn't something Elenora was used to, but perhaps that's what friends did. "He was a gentleman, but I think he wanted to. . ."

"Kiss you?"

Heat seared her cheeks. "I didn't let him. I've got a business to run. I can't let my feelings get in the way."

"So, you do have feelings for him then?"

"I don't know. Some days I feel drawn to him, but others

I wonder why. He and I seem to rub each other's fur the wrong way at times."

They'd reached the edge of the Duprees' property. Pearl stopped, set her basket down, and leaned against the slat fence surrounding her garden. "Miles is a good man, but he's been hurt, as I suspect you have. The Lord can work healing, but it takes time. I suggest you pray and give the situation to God."

"All right, but I don't know what good it will do."

"You don't think him capable of change?"

"He can change things if He wants, but He doesn't seem to care much about me these days. I asked Him to protect my shop, but. . ." She blinked rapidly.

"He told me you didn't want his help."

Understanding dawned. "I didn't mean Mr. Rutledge. I was talking about God."

Pearl rested a hand on Elenora's arm. "The Lord cares deeply about you. He doesn't always answer our prayers the way we'd like, but that's because He knows better than we do what we need."

What she needed was to get away before a traitorous tear could escape. "Yes, of course. And now I really must get started with my practice if I'm to make it back to town in time."

"I'll pray for you."

"Thank you." Perhaps the Lord would be more inclined to listen to a sweet person like Pearl than He would a strong-minded one like her.

That night Elenora stood at her parlor window, which overlooked Main Street. Although it was nearly ten, the lamps continued to burn in Rutledge Hall, causing a faint glow around the iron shutters over the front windows. They were closed, despite the warm evening.

How much practice did the Mud Springs Musical Society need? They'd met three extra times the past week. That ought to be more than enough rehearsal time for a group of folk musicians who did more improvising than memorizing. She let the curtains flutter from her fingers.

The floorboards creaked as she crept downstairs into her shop. Over a week had passed since the awning had come crashing through the front, and yet the repairs hadn't even begun. Getting the supplies took forever.

In the meantime dust had managed to find its way past the tarpaulins, coating the display cases and the sheets she'd spread over her wares. But that was a temporary state. Things would be put to rights soon, and she'd be open for business once again.

She must survive this setback and succeed because there was no going back. Pa had made that clear when he took Clayton as his partner—a stepson with no training instead of his own daughter. And after all the years she'd worked alongside him learning everything there was to know about running a mercantile. It wasn't fair. She slammed a fist on the counter.

"Ouch!" She cradled her hand to her chest.

She'd just have to figure out how to bring in more income until she could reopen. Traipsing over the township took time. While she enjoyed getting to know the women, she could only visit a handful each day. Each of them wanted to offer her something to eat before she discussed her wares, requiring her to spend a minimum of an hour at each house. She'd sampled a wider variety of desserts the past week than she'd had in the last five years combined.

If only there were some way to make better use of her time.

She snapped her fingers. "That's it!" She knew just what she'd do. Tomorrow couldn't come soon enough.

The strong scent of marigolds and buzz of bees stopped Elenora. She paused and drank in the sight and sounds before stepping from Mrs. Sanders's Main Street home. What a productive day this had been. The older woman had ordered several yards of fabric, notions aplenty, and a fancy trunk with brass fittings in which to pack her new wardrobe for her upcoming trip to visit her sister in San Francisco.

While that order was worth the time it took to meet with a customer individually, Elenora marveled at the success of her group presentations, or Shopping Socials as she called them. A number of women had practically tripped over one another in their rush to schedule a gathering in their homes since she'd offered to play her violin for them.

Rather than serving one dessert to her, as had been the case before, they now offered a variety to their guests. She no longer had to eat four or more a day, which was a good thing. Despite all the walking she was doing as she traveled from house to house, the steady succession of sweets had begun to tax her waistbands.

The most rewarding aspect of the events was the fellowship. Getting to know the women of El Dorado and understand their needs would enable her to stock items better suited to them. While that would serve her financially, seeing their excitement as they envisioned the changes they could make in their homes, wardrobes, and lives excited her. They wanted to be as cultured as women in the more settled parts of the country, and she could use her experience to enlighten them.

"Mrs. Watkins!" Tommy waved at her from his perch on the railing in front of the saloon across the street, the ever-present length of rope he used to practice tying knots clutched in his hand. The sooner she could get him away from there, the better. She beckoned, and he leaped down and charged across the street, startling Dr. Lyle's team in the process.

"Mr. Talbot, you must watch what you're doing." She gave the doctor an apologetic smile as he passed, pulled a list from her reticule, and handed it to Tommy. "I've got seven orders for you to deliver, but they're a bit spread out, I'm afraid. Do you think you'll have time to get them done before five?"

"I reckon so, but I can always roust Timmy if we need him."

"I'd prefer to let him sleep, since he's pulling the second shift tonight."

Tommy grinned. "Good idea. 'Sides, he's not much good with the lady customers. His face glowed red as a horseshoe fresh out of the smithy's fire when Miss Abbott asked why them silk stockings wasn't in her delivery."

Elenora cringed. How many of those passing by had heard him? She spoke softly and hoped he'd follow suit. "I realize you're more comfortable discussing such matters than your brother, but a gentleman doesn't mention a woman's intimate articles. If you have to tell me such things, at least keep your voice down."

The spirited young man hid beneath the brim of his dusty felt hat. "Yes'm."

Tommy and Tildy were much alike, both struggling to tame their tongues. Mr. Rutledge could use some help in that area as well. At dinner yesterday he'd made one of his frivolities versus necessities comments, saying he'd built his business on the latter and found carrying the former a waste of time and money. What fun it had been to remind him of the conniption he'd had when the shipment with his expensive sandalwood shaving soap from England was late the week before.

"Are you laughing at me?"

Oh dear. She'd tried to suppress the snigger, but thinking about Mr. Rutledge's tendency to open his mouth before his mind was engaged tickled her. "I'm sorry. It had nothing to do with you. I was thinking of something else. I'll leave you to get those items to the customers and have an early supper for you when you get back—such as it is."

"Your grub ain't that bad. Ma's pot roast can be tough as shoe leather, too. Um. That didn't come out right. I mean—"

"There's no harm done. I know what you meant. I got busy and forgot to add water, that's all. At least only the bottom burned."

They shared a laugh, and she set out for the post office. She'd taken three steps when Tommy called her.

"What is it?"

"If you want me to get to those deliveries, you'll have to let me in the shop."

"Of course." She reached in her handbag, pulled out a key, and gave it to him. "This is my only spare. You and Timmy will have to share it."

His jaw hung to his knees as he stared at the key she'd placed on his palm. "You mean for us to keep this?"

"Yes. That way you can come and go as you need."

His voice came out raspy. "Ain't no one ever trusted us like you. Most folks call us trouble times two."

"I've heard. But are you?"

He shook his head, and his long blond locks slapped his cheeks. "No ma'am. And we'll take right good care of this. You won't be sorry."

She smiled. "I'm counting on that."

Tommy clomped down the walkway, the key clutched in his fist, whistling a lively tune.

The jangle of spurs drew Elenora's attention. "I thought that was you, Sheriff."

He stood beside her and watched until Tommy passed her boarded-up shop and rounded the corner of the hotel on his way to the back entrance of her place. "Can't say as I've ever seen Tommy strut quite like that."

The young man did have a pronounced swagger. "I gave him a key to the shop."

"I thought that's what I saw. There's some would say you're being foolhardy."

"But you're not one of them, I hope."

Sheriff Henderson pulled a large ring of keys from his pocket. "A man feels mighty important when he's packing metal." He laughed at his own joke and sobered. "I hope you've not misplaced your trust, but I got a feeling you know what you're doing."

"Why, Sheriff, you said you're not good with words, but those suit me just fine."

A flush crept up his neck, and she wished she'd not attempted to tease him. He didn't take it as well as— Oh, bother! Why must she think of Mr. Rutledge at every turn?

She excused herself and hurried to the shoemaker's before he closed for the dinner hour. Tildy's old boots pinched her toes, and Elenora was eager to get the new pair the cobbler had made. Her dear girl was convinced the side laces on the stiff leather boots would make her look more grown up. The decorative tassels at the tops, however, would come as a surprise. Elenora couldn't wait to see the grin on Tildy's face when she saw them. Times might be tough now, but things would improve. One small splurge wouldn't hurt. Besides, she'd been such a good sport about staying with Mrs. Rutledge each day that she deserved a reward.

Elenora left the shoemaker's with a brown paper parcel. She strolled down the walkway but came to a stop when Pearl Dupree walked out of Rutledge Mercantile. "What are you doing in town in the middle of the day? I thought you'd be busy working in your garden."

Pearl beamed. "Will and I are celebrating our wedding anniversary. He said I shouldn't have to cook today, so he's taking me to dinner at the Oriental Hotel. Isn't that sweet?"

"Happy anniversary." Elenora looked around. "Are the children with you?"

"We'll take them with us to the concert tonight, of course, but they're home right now. We rarely leave them, but Paul's old enough to mind the others, and Constance can get a simple meal, so it's just Will and me. I feel as excited as I did when he was courting me."

"Have a wonderful time. I won't keep you since I'd like to make it to the livery before I grab a quick bite of dinner myself and practice the pieces I'm playing at my next social."

A dull ache filled Elenora's chest. She'd never been courted or had a man make her feel special. Not unless she counted the day Mr. Rutledge have given her the rose. No. They weren't exactly friends, so that didn't count.

Chapter 14

Miles donned his hat and coat shortly before noon on that long-awaited Saturday. Only seven more hours until the concert. He stood before his shop and smiled.

Ellie marched toward the livery wearing her purple dress, the one that made her dark eyes shine. He waited for a rider to pass and crossed Main, dodging a muddy patch left from the light rain earlier that morning. The musty, dusty smell of damp earth filled the air. What he'd like was a whiff of her perfume, the one she'd worn during their shooting lesson. No doubt the stuff was from Europe and she'd paid way too much for it, but the fragrance rivaled that of his best roses.

It wasn't likely she'd let him get close enough to drink in the scent though. She'd kept her distance ever since the shooting lesson. Dinner without her wasn't the same, and she'd missed several the past week. She should schedule her house calls so she didn't have to give up her time with Tildy. They only saw each other a few minutes in the morning and again at night. Didn't she want to be with her daughter? He'd give anything in the world if he could be with his again. But May was gone.

No. He wouldn't think about that. He couldn't. Eight years wasn't long enough to ease the stabbing pain that pierced his heart whenever he recalled the day he'd come home and learned of the tragedy. If only Irene had put May first, but her friends were all that mattered to her.

By the time Miles reached the livery, he'd managed to return his thoughts to the present. Eager to see Ellie again, he went inside and heard her say his name.

"—to tell Mr. Rutledge yourself. I hadn't planned to see him today."

Silas, the owner of the livery, darted his eyes to Miles and back to her.

"He's behind me, isn't he?" Silas nodded. She turned slowly and frowned.

What had he done this time? He hadn't even opened his mouth yet. "Good morning, Mrs. Watkins."

"Mr. Rutledge." She gave him a halfhearted smile but said nothing more.

"Are you still upset because I spoke my mind about the twins? If that's it, time will tell."

"Quite true. You'll see that they can be trusted."

Silas sauntered across the livery, folded his arms over his chest, and stood beside Miles. "I suppose you're checking on your shipment. I asked the good lady to tell you it's due 'round three." He leaned close and spoke through the side of his mouth in an exaggerated whisper Ellie was sure to hear. "The air seems on the chilly side today. You two on the outs again?"

The tight-lipped liveryman was the last person he'd have expected to ask such a question. Perhaps this was his way of letting them know what the busybodies were saying.

Miles assumed a light tone. If Ellie would go along with him, they could dispel the rumors. "We put on a good show. You know there are those who aren't happy unless there's some new morsel to pass on. Truth is, my friend and I were about to go to my house for dinner, where Tildy has a surprise waiting for her mama. Weren't we, Mrs. Watkins?"

Would she call him on his ploy? He gave her a genuine smile.

She studied him for a moment, her gaze so intense she could

have blazed holes in the wall behind him.

And then she laughed. Not a dignified laugh befitting a lady, but an honest-to-goodness get-some-fresh-air-in-your-lungs laugh that, while puzzling, was as welcome as a breeze on a midsummer's day. She recovered, dabbed her eyes with the back of her hand, and closed the distance between them. "Yes, *my friend*, I'm dining at your place today. Shall we be going?"

He held out his arm, and, wonder of wonders, she rested her small hand on it without a moment's hesitation and looked at him with eagerness on her upturned face.

No sooner had they left the livery than she pulled her hand away and swatted his arm playfully. "You are a most exasperating man, Mr. Rutledge."

"You can be quite exasperating yourself, Ellie."

She stopped, and he waited for her rebuke. When she faced him, she wore the sweetest smile he'd ever seen. Not her sterile businesswoman smile, her loving mother smile, or her syrupy smile. This was a warm-from-the-oven apple-pie smile. He could almost smell the cinnamon.

"My friend." She chuckled. "You called me that, you know?"

He nodded. Speaking would spoil the moment, so he waited.

She looked at him. Really looked—as though she were seeing neither a business rival nor stubborn cynic, but the man beneath. He swallowed, and his collar felt tight.

"You're the first man who's ever considered me his friend. So. . .I suppose. . .all things considered. . ." A becoming blush crept into her cheeks.

Please. Don't let her stop now.

"Pa calls me Nora, and I don't care for it one bit. But Ellie? Well, it does have a nice ring to it. Although. . .it's not proper for you to use it. You do know that?"

"Yes, Ellie."

She gave him one more searching gaze and started down the walkway. He kept pace with her and rejoiced when she turned up Church Street toward his house.

"Mother will be glad to see you. She's missed you."

"I've been busy, but one of her delicious meals eaten with delightful company would be just the thing. I don't get nearly enough time with Tildy these days, which grieves me. However, this turn of events won't last forever, and I'll be able to reopen my shop."

The sun broke through the clouds, bathing her in light. She stopped, closed her eyes, and smiled. He took advantage of the opportunity to admire her lovely face. Ellie relaxed was a rare sight, one he'd like to see more often. All too soon she started walking again.

"How are your house calls working out?"

"I'm getting to know the townspeople. I've learned that Mrs. Pratt wants a floor covering to coordinate with her green and gold wallpaper, that Mrs. Barton collects decorative ink-stands, and that Miss Crowley—" She shook her head. "Why am I telling you? You care about their practical needs, not their decor or collections."

"I know they buy more soap flakes and stove polish than carpets and curios."

She clenched the spray of silk flowers at her throat in a choke hold. He'd sent her smile into hiding and groaned inwardly. When would he learn to curb his wayward tongue? Could he recapture the moment? "But there's more to life than work, right?"

"Yes, Mr. Rutledge, there is. I wondered when you'd realize that. Or did you say that just to mollify me?"

"You should know by now I'm not one to tread carefully when words are involved. I generally say what I mean."

They reached the hedge in front of his house, and she paused. "Then tell me. Did you order the Haviland china because you wanted it or because your mother did?"

"The china? I liked it. Why?"

"It's what I'd consider a luxury. So you see, Mr. Rutledge"—she smiled once again—"there's hope for you yet."

"Is there?" He brushed the back of a hand over her cheek.

She tensed. "Oh dear. I didn't mean to mislead you. Being friends is one thing, but I'm not looking for anything else. If I gave you that impression, I'm sorry."

Friends. He tried to say it, but the word stuck in his craw.

Tildy stood before the full-length mirror in Elenora's bedroom and turned in a circle, her head swiveling so she could see herself at every angle. She ran a hand over the wide sash at her waist. "Look how the skirt sways when I move and the tassels on my new boots dance. Don't I look like a princess?"

"A very pretty princess."

The peach taffeta fell in soft folds and ended just below her knees in two rows of quilled flounces. The large bow trailing down her back had quilled edges as well. Mrs. Rutledge must have spent hours pinning and pressing the small folds. Her son had said Tildy had a surprise, but Elenora never expected something so grand. The gifted gown was the finest Tildy had ever owned.

"And you're a queen, Mama. Mr. Rutledge's eyes will sparkle when he sees you. Green is his favorite color."

"My dear, where *do* you get your ideas? He will have one thing on his mind. His music. Here. Let me put these on your braids."

Tildy stood with her back to Elenora as she tied the ribbons into bows. "I do find it odd that the townspeople dress up for a folk music gathering." Perhaps this concert constituted culture in El Dorado. Pearl had assured her the emerald silk was a good choice.

"Mrs. Rutledge called it the social event of the season. There's a big secret, too, but she wouldn't tell me anything else, no matter how many times I asked. Mr. Rutledge neither."

"Mrs. Sanders mentioned it when I was at her place this morning. She said the Musical Society chooses a special number to perform at their spring concert and everyone tries to figure out what it is. That's why they kept the doors and windows of Rutledge Hall closed during their practices." The citizens of El Dorado were certainly making a great deal of fuss about some simple folk tunes. At least the event was in a meeting hall instead of a barn.

The clock in her parlor chimed the quarter hour. Tildy dashed from the room and returned moments later, her cheeks flushed with excitement. "Hurry, Mama! They're letting people inside. We need to go so we can get good seats. I want to be able to see Mr. Rutledge."

Elenora had seen more than enough of him recently. Ever since their meeting at the livery, he'd hovered around her like a bee buzzing around his rosebushes. She appreciated his show of friendship, but his words earlier that day, although offered in jest, had stung. She could hear him now. "I know you're not looking forward to tonight, but you may find you've been wrong about a great many things and have to eat your words for a change. And that, Ellie, is something I'd like to see." His laugh echoed in her memory.

She would attend this so-called concert, but as for eating words, there'd better be some water available, because he'd need a nice big glass of it to wash his down.

Tildy tugged on Elenora's hand and pulled her down South Street behind the mercantile. Gathering her skirts, Elenora mounted the staircase that hugged the back wall of the rock-sided building, which extended well beyond the smaller ones on either side.

When they reached the top and entered Rutledge Hall, her jaw went slack. Several seconds passed before she regained her composure. Although this was a small-town affair, the guests wore fashions as fine as any she'd seen in the East.

While the spacious room lacked the plush velvet-covered chairs she was accustomed to, there was an air of elegance nonetheless. Long wooden benches with varnished seats gleamed in the warm light cast by evenly spaced lamps that lined three walls. The emerald brocade curtain at the front of the raised stage area complemented the foliage in the Daisy wallpaper by William Morris, which she'd seen in one of the catalogs Mr. Rutledge loaned her. That explained the dog-eared page. The assortment of meadow flowers on the pale gold background reminded her of the walk they'd taken when he whisked her through the air and gazed at her with such rapt—

"Mama." Tildy yanked on her sleeve. "He's over there talking to Mr. and Mrs. Dupree. Doesn't he look good?"

Elenora followed the direction of Tildy's inclined head and had to keep from gaping a second time. Mr. Rutledge was the picture of a cultured gentleman in his formal black tailcoat and white satin cravat. He was by far the most handsome man in the room, but she'd never heard of anyone fiddling in finery.

He looked up, saw her, and appeared to stop midsentence. Will Dupree looked her way, smiled, and gave Miles a playful shove in her direction.

"He's coming."

"Yes, sweetheart. I see that."

He wended his way around clusters of well-dressed towns-people and reached the entry, where Tildy and Elenora stood beside the curtained stage that filled the back wall of the rectangular room. Elenora endeavored to appear unaffected.

"Welcome to Rutledge Hall, ladies. I've reserved seats for you next to Mother." He held out a hand to a vacant spot in the front row.

"Oh! You didn't need to do that." Her voice came out breathy. Mr. Rutledge was always well kempt, but seeing him in this fine setting looking every bit the dapper gentleman had her grasping at her usual composure.

"I wanted to make sure Tildy had a good view."

"Tildy? Yes, of course. Thank you." And here she thought he'd saved it for her. But why would he when she'd made it clear they were friends and nothing more? Apparently he wanted to show her that he honored her wishes. She should be happy, but hollowness filled her instead.

"This place is lots fancier than I expected. Mama said it might be—"

"I said it might not be quite like the venues she's been to before."

He grinned. "No, but it is a step above a barn."

Tildy giggled. "It smells a lot better than one. Are all those flowers yours?" She pointed at a huge floral arrangement gracing the base of the stage and filling the room with a rich perfume.

"They are."

"My dear, we should take our seats."

"Allow me." He held out his arm to Tildy, who took it and beamed.

Once seated, Elenora smoothed her skirts. Mr. Rutledge leaned over so close his mustache brushed her cheek, and she shivered. He whispered, and with the noise level in the room, she strained to hear him. "I hope you enjoy the performance, Ellie."

He straightened, bowed, and slipped behind the curtain.

The crowd seemed to take his departure as a sign. Conversation ceased, and they filled the benches. Once the rustling of fabric ended, the room grew so quiet she could hear the pocket watch of the man behind her ticking.

All eyes were riveted on the doorway to the right of the stage. Will Dupree entered with Mrs. Rutledge and escorted her to the seat on the opposite side of Tildy amidst a polite round of applause.

When the room had once again grown silent, the conductor, Mr. Morton, stepped through the curtain and addressed the assembly. "Ladies and gentlemen, please join me in acknowledging our esteemed host, Mr. Miles Rutledge, who graciously allows us use of the hall." Enthusiastic applause followed the introduction.

He welcomed everyone and slipped behind the heavy draperies. A hush fell over the room as the curtains opened. Elenora's skin tingled. This was no gathering of fiddlers. The Mud Springs Musical Society was an *orchestra*.

All this time Mr. Rutledge had allowed her to believe he was a simple fiddler. He'd had fun at her expense.

Tildy tugged on Elenora's sleeve. She held a finger to her lips as she leaned toward her daughter.

"Mama," she whispered, "it's not going to be fiddling, is it?" The corners of her mouth drooped.

"I don't believe so, dearest, but I do think we're in for a treat. Let's watch and see." She worked to sound cheerful for

Tildy's sake, but the thickness in her throat made getting the words out difficult. Mr. Rutledge knew how much she loved classical music, and yet he'd deprived her of the anticipation. A punch in the stomach would have caused less pain.

How could he have allowed her to labor under a false impression for so long? He might look like a gentleman, but his behavior was unfitting of one. Just wait until this concert was over. She'd let him know exactly what she thought of his deception.

Sheriff Hank Henderson rose and stepped forward. "Our first number will be 'Contented Peace,' an aria by Johann Sebastian Bach." He bowed, returned to his chair, and rested his cello between his knees.

Mr. Morton stepped onto his platform and raised his baton. The orchestra began, and Elenora closed her eyes so she could focus on the music instead of a certain musician whose silence had led her to say things that cast her in a poor light. She struggled to remember what she'd said to Abe, Will, and the sheriff. They'd done nothing amiss and didn't deserve her wrath. Whatever she'd said to Mr. Rutledge, though, was deserved and paled in comparison with what he'd hear later this evening when she could get a moment alone with him.

When she opened her eyes, she scowled at him, and he met her gaze. Then he did the unthinkable. He winked at her in a totally ungentlemanly display, and her blood boiled. He'd known all along what he intended to do and was enjoying himself. Well, he'd find out she wasn't a woman to cross.

Three short selections followed the aria, another piece by Bach and two by Handel. In spite of her pique, she had to admit the performance was as polished as any she'd heard back East. She'd wanted no part of the folk group Abe and the others had invited her to, but to be a full-fledged member of this orchestra would suit her just fine. Although there were no women among their number, she could be the first.

When Mr. Morton stepped forward to introduce the finale, he had everyone's full attention. "Ladies and gentleman, as is the tradition at the Mud Springs Musical Society's summer concert, we've prepared a special selection for your listening pleasure. I know there's been intense speculation, but every member of the Society pledged to keep the name of the work in strict confidence. It's my pleasure to announce that we will be performing *The Four Seasons* by Antonio Vivaldi. Our featured soloist for the entire work will soon be revealed. Please enjoy our rendition."

Elenora inhaled sharply.

Tildy pulled on her sleeve again. "What is it, Mama?"

"It's an incredible piece. There will be four concertos of three movements each. The first concerto is called 'Spring.' One violinist is pitted against the entire orchestra in a magnificent solo. It takes a talented musician to play that part. You might like this."

Her eyes were riveted on the stage. Who was to perform the solo? The orchestra had begun, and yet not one of the violinists had risen. The solo began thirty seconds into the piece. One of the men would have to stand soon.

A full fifteen seconds of the first movement elapsed before the soloist arose. When he did, she gasped. "It's him!" Heat rushed to her cheeks, and she clamped a hand over her mouth. A couple of people snickered.

When Mr. Rutledge reached his first rest about a minute into the number, Tildy tapped Elenora on the shoulder. Elenora leaned over, her eyes never leaving him.

"He's good, isn't he, Mama?"

She was careful to keep her voice low. "Yes, quite good." He was an incredibly gifted violinist, although that truth rankled.

Why was this solo always given to a man? She'd spent weeks practicing these concertos back in Omaha and was sure she'd been better than anyone else who'd auditioned for the part, and yet the conductor had chosen Mr. Lent. The banker had done a passable job, but her instructor agreed her performance was superior. Even so, she'd been denied admittance to the orchestra.

Had she arrived in El Dorado earlier and learned about the Society, she might be the one up front receiving the admiring glances. Unless, of course, Mr. Morton was as closed-minded as his chosen soloist. She intended to find out.

Although Mr. Rutledge had made a fool of her, she rarely had the opportunity to hear her favorite piece performed and wasn't about to let him rob her of the pleasure. She would enjoy the music—even if the featured musician was a shameless trickster.

The over forty minutes it took for *The Four Seasons* to be performed passed all too quickly. Elenora savored every movement, every measure, every note as the music transported her to another plane.

Try as she might, she couldn't help but admire Mr. Rutledge. He was exceedingly handsome tonight with his fine features relaxed and his brilliant blue eyes shining with obvious joy. Better than that, though, was his execution of the famous composition. His skill as a violinist rivaled her own. Clearly he felt the music to the depths of his soul. She'd never seen anyone move as fluidly as he did, resting much of his weight on the balls of his feet and swaying from side to side with grace befitting a ballet dancer.

After he'd taken his final bow and the thunderous applause finally subsided at the conclusion of the concert, Tildy rushed up to him. Mrs. Rutledge smiled at her son and turned to Elenora. "Miles practiced for months and couldn't have been more prepared, but my dear boy was so anxious he couldn't eat supper. I do believe he's outdone himself."

"He's an accomplished violinist."

His mother beamed. "This was the most ambitious undertaking the Society has attempted. They'll have to go a long way to top tonight's performance. And now if you'll excuse me, I want to congratulate the musicians."

Elenora longed to leave, but courtesy demanded she stay for the refreshments. Perhaps if she were to engage in conversation with her customers and new friends, she could avoid speaking with Mr. Rutledge tonight while her emotions were awhirl. She needed time to think before she confronted him, or she could have trouble keeping her tongue in check.

Miles wanted nothing more than to talk with Ellie, but she seemed to be avoiding him. Although she hadn't taken her eyes off him during his solo, she hadn't looked his way since. He longed to hear her impression of the concert. Hopefully tonight had served to change her opinion of El Dorado. The town might be small, but the citizens were every bit as talented as those back East.

He positioned himself near the door so she couldn't slip out unnoticed. At length she tore Tildy away from her friend Constance and prepared to leave.

When Ellie neared, he ended his conversation with the grocer, stepped into her path, and assumed his most gentlemanly tone. "Mrs. Watkins, might I escort you and Tildy home?"

She scanned the hall where small clusters of people still visited. "That's not necessary. Besides, you'll need to lock up once everyone leaves."

"I'll be back before they notice I've gone. Shall we, Tildy?"

She took his extended hand. Ellie pressed her lips together and frowned, but she didn't protest, which he took as a good sign.

He kept Tildy talking until they stood at the back of Ellie's shop. She groped in her reticule for the key, let herself in, and busied herself lighting candles while he waited outside the open door with Tildy. He gave her a hug, speaking beside her ear as he did. "Good night, Tildy girl. And now, I'd like a few minutes with your mother—alone."

She whispered. "Are you going to kiss her?"

He'd like to—very much—but whether or not she'd be receptive remained to be seen. "I'm going to ask her about the concert."

Ellie appeared in the doorway, the flickering candlelight making it impossible to read her expression. "It's way past your bedtime, sweetheart, so please bid Mr. Rutledge good night."

"I already did, so I'll get ready for bed." She took the candle from Ellie and headed up the stairs.

"Hmm. She usually begs me to stay up a little longer. Thank you for seeing us home." She reached for the doorknob, but he caught her hand.

"Ellie, please. Don't go just yet."

The light from the candle she'd left on the table illuminated a portion of her face, which still gave no indication what she was thinking. He raised her hand and pressed it to his lips. She jerked free.

"Mr. Rutledge! How dare you, especially after what you did to me."

"What did I do?"

"I came to town, and you accused me of deceiving you when I'd done no such thing. But you knowingly misled me.

All this time you allowed me to believe you were a fiddler and that the Mud Springs Musical Society was a folk music group. Not only that, but you winked at me."

She had seen him. He'd regretted his impulsive action and hoped she'd missed it. "You're right. I did deceive you. And it was wrong of me."

"Why did you do it?"

"I didn't like your high-and-mighty attitude. You marched into town and belittled our music, so I thought I'd show you how wrong you were."

She clapped a hand to her chest. "Me? I was honest about how I felt. You weren't."

He rested a hand on her forearm. "I made a poor choice, and I admit that. But I'm trying to apologize. Can you find it in your heart to forgive me?"

She pressed her lips into a tight line. "Why should I?"

"Because you know I'm telling the truth. And because friends forgive one another."

Her expression softened. "Friends do. But are we really friends?"

"You're mine. And I'd like to be yours, if you'll stop fighting me at every turn."

"I don't."

"You do, but I don't think I'm your real adversary."

Her eyes roved over his face. "Who is then?"

"You are. You're so eager to prove you can succeed, but no one is asking for proof."

Several seconds went by before she replied, "You certainly proved how prideful I can be. I was rather outspoken, and I'm sorry about that."

"Apology accepted." He smiled.

She reached up, and her fingertips grazed the red spot

below his chin. "A violinist's badge of honor."

He'd never thought of it like that, but he liked the way she said it. He took her hand in his, placed a kiss on her upturned palm, and closed her fingers over it.

She cradled her fisted hand to her chest. "The Musical Society played well, and your Vivaldi solo was one of the best I've ever heard."

"Thank you. That means a great deal, coming from you."

"You have talent, but I'm not about to fawn all over you—or stop trying to best you."

He chuckled. "I should hope not."

"I'm glad we're in agreement on that. Good night, Mr. Rutledge." She gave him a saucy smile, went inside, and closed the door.

Will was right. She wasn't like Irene, who'd turned his head with her self-serving flattery. Ellie's praise, though slow in coming, was genuine. He strolled back to the hall feeling ten feet tall.

Chapter 15

The rustle of skirts and thudding of bootheels caught Elenora's attention the following Monday. She spun around and found a group of women ambling along the walkway in her direction.

"You're just the woman we wanted to see," Mrs. Olds said. "I was helping Miss Crowley with her grocery order this morning, and she said you were seen talking to Mr. Morton after the concert. Several other women saw the same. Word is you're thinking of gaining admittance to the Musical Society."

Elenora did her best to appear unruffled. "I spoke with several people that evening, including the conductor. I congratulated him on the performance."

Jane Abbott stepped to the front of the group. "My mother said she heard you ask when you could meet with him. *Please,* say you did."

"I don't think I should—" She looked from one woman to the next, all wearing expectant expressions. "Yes. I set up a time to discuss my music with him."

Pearl smiled. "You'll be the first woman admitted to the Society."

"I have no idea whether or not Mr. Morton will allow me to audition."

A stout woman with an expression as sweet as molasses pushed up her spectacles and grinned. "He will."

Elenora didn't know what to say, so she shrugged.

"I know," the woman continued, "because after the concert

he told me about your request. He was hesitant to meet with you, but I convinced him times are changing and said the members of the Society had best prepare themselves for it. He waffled a bit, but I can be quite persuasive."

"He told you? Why?"

Several women chuckled, but Pearl explained. "This dear woman is Mrs. Morton. She's been up in Grass Valley helping her niece with a new baby but arrived home in time for the concert."

"Oh!" Elenora's scalp tingled, and her skin turned to gooseflesh. "Are you saying he's actually decided to let me audition? That's wonderful."

Miss Abbott bobbed her head so enthusiastically her golden curls bounced. "It's high time the men of El Dorado realized how capable we women are. I, for one, can't wait to see the look on Mr. Rutledge's face when you walk into the hall for practice Thursday. He'll have to eat those words of his."

"Hush, Jane." Lucy Lyle frowned at her friend. "It's impolite to repeat hearsay."

"It's not hearsay. I heard him with my own ears talking to Mr. Dupree. He said"—Miss Abbott smoothed her hair in a gesture just like Mr. Rutledge's and lowered her voice—" 'I have plans of my own, and, willful woman though she is, I've no doubt she'll see things my way once I have my say.' "

Miss Abbott's impression caused several of the women to laugh, but Elenora forced a smile. So he thought she was willful, did he? Well, he'd not seen anything yet. She'd convince Mr. Morton of her ability, saunter into the next Musical Society rehearsal, and show Mr. Rutledge what she was made of.

At precisely eleven o'clock Tuesday, Miles entered the barbershop.

"You're right on time." Abe held out a hand to the black leather chair, and Miles sank into it.

He closed his eyes and inhaled the rich woodsy fragrance that greeted him every morning when he performed his ablutions. Nothing smelled quite as good as his favorite shaving soap, and nothing left him feeling as well groomed as a close shave. If folks didn't already think him a dandy, he would come to Abe for his every day. No one knew how to trim a mustache as well as his friend.

The weekly half hour with Abe relaxed Miles like nothing else. Not that he was tense. Far from it. Things had changed the night of the concert. He'd pulled a few bricks out of the wall Ellie hid behind. She'd even reached out and touched him, caressing the red mark below his chin with her fingertips. He heaved a contented sigh.

The barber draped a sheet over Miles. "You look plumb tuckered out. I reckoned you would've recovered by now. It's been three days."

He opened his eyes. "Recovered? What do you mean? I don't think I could've enjoyed the concert more."

Abe grabbed the shaving mug and brush, and whipped up a frothy mass of soap bubbles. "Then what I'm seein' is a man at peace, that it?"

Was he? Will had said something similar yesterday. Maybe his friends were right. The world appeared brighter than it had in a long while. Colors seemed more vivid than usual, scents stronger, and Mother's cooking tastier. Even the lather on his face felt better than he remembered. Normally he didn't notice, but things were different. He was different.

"What you're seeing is a man who knows what he wants and is aiming to get it."

Abe grinned. "And what would that be? No. Let me guess.

You're hankerin' to perform a duet with Mrs. Watkins. Talk in town is she spent an hour at the Morton place last evening, so you just might get your wish."

Miles couldn't believe what he was hearing. If he weren't afraid of getting a mouthful of soap, he would protest. Asking Ellie to join their informal Tuesday night folk music practices was one thing. Those sessions were about having fun. But the Musical Society was a different matter entirely. The members worked hard and presented a polished performance. No woman he knew had the experience or training required to warrant membership. From what he'd heard, Ellie was no different. She'd been denied admittance to the orchestra in Omaha, and yet she was trying to join theirs.

Hopefully Mr. Morton had been tactful when he explained the situation to her. She could get testy when she didn't get her way. And she wouldn't this time. She'd proven she had the skills needed to run a business, but until she measured up to the skills of the other musicians, she wouldn't earn the right to perform with them. El Dorado might be small, but the Society had achieved notoriety as one of the best groups in the area.

Abe reached for his razor, sharpened it, and fixed probing gray eyes on Miles. "That scowl tells me you ain't happy with the idea."

"Are you?"

"Don't rightly know. I suppose I'd have to hear her play first. But one thing I do know is that she loves the music. I can't say as I've ever seen anyone as taken with one of our performances as she was. Perhaps her comin' from the East and all, she appreciates the composers' works more than most."

Miles blew out a breath, sending bits of white foam flying. "That's an unfair comparison, and you know it. The people here are as cultured in their own way."

"Say what you will, but it seems to me they take more of a likin' to your fiddlin' than they did your Vivaldi solo. The hall was full, but twice as many show up when we play at a folk dance."

"She liked it."

Abe raised his shaggy brows. "Liked? The woman was as drawn to you as a horse thief to a prize filly. Every time I glanced her way, Ellie-nora was starin' at you with those doe-eyes of hers. 'Course maybe it weren't just the music had her in a trance."

That comment didn't deserve a response. Not that Miles could come up with one anyhow. Abe was right. Even though Ellie was usually mindful of propriety, her gaze had rested on him the entire time. Not that he minded her staring at him. Her obvious pleasure had pushed him to new heights. He'd never performed the piece with the finesse he had that night.

When he'd walked her home and placed that kiss on her palm, she'd looked completely undone, although she recovered quickly enough.

And then she'd said words that meant far more than her praise of his performance. *I'm not about to fawn all over you—or stop trying to best you.* Delivered with that spirit of hers, he'd seen her in a new light. She might be a determined woman who could be stubborn at times, but she wasn't obstinate like Irene. And Ellie certainly wasn't deceptive. He knew where he stood with her, which was why he'd decided to offer her a partnership after all.

"You want me to dine with you? At the hotel?" Elenora was taken aback by the unexpected request and the eagerness that shone in Mr. Rutledge's expressive eyes. Hopefully her face revealed only mild curiosity, but she feared she looked as shocked as she felt. "Why can't we go to your place as usual?"

He rested a hand on the hitching post in front of the bank. "Folks have been talking, and I want to put an end to it."

Although the women had agreed to be discreet and not let anyone else know of her plan to audition, he must have found out about her meeting with Mr. Morton.

Mr. Rutledge inclined his head toward the sheriff's office and beckoned her with a crooked finger. She drew near, and he leaned close. "If you agree to dine with me, the rumors about you and Hank will—"

"My relationship with Sheriff Henderson is purely professional, and you know it." She stepped back and studied him. He appeared affronted, but his moustache twitched. Why, he was teasing. And here she'd been afraid he was going to grill her on her intentions regarding the Musical Society, when that didn't seem to be the case at all. Perhaps he'd come around, as Mr. Morton and several of the other men had.

She tossed out a playful retort. "What's the *real* reason for your invitation? Perhaps you've thought of some other derogatory terms with which to malign my merchandise and want to try them out. I don't think you've used 'fribble' or 'folderol.'"

He grinned. "Now Ellie, give me some credit. I do care about your reputation." He sobered. "The truth is, my appreciation of your business acumen has grown. You've employed some innovative techniques lately, and I've an offer I'd like you to consider."

She couldn't believe what she was hearing. "You *are* a mystery. But since I want to know what you're after—and since I have a fondness for the hotel's peach and pecan pie—I'll accept your invitation."

Ten minutes later Elenora sat in the hotel's lobby as they

waited for a table in the restaurant. Mr. Rutledge occupied the other end of the floral settee. Tantalizing scents caused her mouth to water, but more than a meal she wanted answers. He'd said nothing since requesting a table, and her curiosity was eating at her. She glanced around the lobby, saw no one, and slid closer to him.

He arched a brow but remained silent.

"Why the change of heart? Until today you've had nothing good to say about my methods of doing business while my shop's being repaired. And now you're full of praise."

"When I first heard you were out visiting the womenfolk, I thought you were making social calls, and I had trouble with that. I knew a woman once who spent too much of her time doing so, to the detriment of others. The fellows down at the livery set me straight though. You've come up with a way to bring in business in spite of your shop being closed. Many people would've wrung their hands and bemoaned their fate, but you didn't. You're a competent businesswoman with new ideas, and I admire that."

She'd been clutching her reticule, but it slipped from her hand, sending a coin rolling over the floor. The shiny disc spun in smaller and smaller circles, the scratching sound of metal on wood increasing with each revolution until it fell over with a *plop*. He retrieved the silver dollar, took her hand in his, and placed the coin on her palm. Even though she wore gloves, his warmth penetrated the thin fabric. She should have ended the contact, but she couldn't stop staring at his large fingers wrapped around hers, fingers that bore scars from his scramble over the rubble that had been the front of her shop.

He released her. "I've startled you."

"Startled" didn't come close. "Stunned" would be a more accurate description. His impassioned speech was totally unexpected.

She lifted her head, not sure what she'd see in his eyes. Not sure what she wanted to see. "What, exactly, are you trying to say?"

"I didn't make a good first impression. I'd like to start over. Will you give me another chance?" His words and apologetic tone were in harmony.

"Are you asking me to be your partner after all?"

"I think we'd make a good team. You work as hard as I do, and you said yourself I could use help with my bookkeeping and back room." His voice held not a hint of humor. She'd rarely seen him as serious.

She attempted a smile but was unable to keep it in place for more than two seconds. For months she'd dreamed of being part owner of his thriving business, but so much had changed since she'd arrived in town. She had her own place and was her own boss. No one could tell her what to do.

Although her doors hadn't been open long, she'd been doing well before the accident. Even now she'd managed to find a way to make sales. Each day presented challenges, but she enjoyed them. Was she willing to give all that up in exchange for the security she'd have if she accepted his offer?

The cleft between his brows deepened as he drew them together. He'd obviously taken a risk in asking her and deserved an honest answer. "I don't know. The repairs on my shop will begin soon, and I'll be able to open my doors again. I know you want to help, but. . ." He did. That was clear. But why? She needed time to sort things out. "This is so sudden."

His words spilled out in a rush, nearly tumbling over one another Tildy-style. "You don't have to make a decision right away, but if you accept my offer I could have your wares moved to my shop whenever you're ready. You wouldn't have to spend your days tromping from house to house holding your socials. I'm sure you'd rather be here in town where you're close to Tildy."

What did he mean by bringing Tildy into the discussion? He had no idea what it was like to be a woman raising a child on her own. To worry about meeting that child's needs. To lie awake at night fighting tears because you knew you were falling short.

Elenora leaped to her feet, and he followed suit. "Due to circumstances beyond my control I've had to conduct business at my customers' homes, true, but I'm a good mother. I'm also a widowed businesswoman doing my best to provide for my daughter."

"I'm sorry, Ellie. I should have chosen my words more carefully. I want to—"

"I haven't neglected Tildy. She enjoys the things your mother is teaching her during the day, and I spend time with her every evening. She's happier here than she's ever been in her life. If you don't believe me, ask her."

Elenora's chest rose and fell rapidly. She wanted nothing more than to walk away and leave him with only his condemnation for company, but he'd just follow her to his place.

"I didn't mean to imply that you're lacking as a mother." He had the good sense to look sorry for his accusation. "I can see how much you love Tildy. I thought you'd like to be closer to her, which you would be if you worked in my shop."

My shop. That's what Pa had always said, too, even after all the years and hard work she'd poured into his place. And that's what Mr. Rutledge would say if she were foolish enough to accept his offer. She'd be a junior partner, but he'd have the final say. Now that she'd tasted independence, she wasn't about to give it up. Certainly not for a man like Mr. Rutledge, who felt free to speak his own mind, even when it concerned *her* business.

She didn't need time. One seemingly heartfelt apology

wasn't enough to sway her. Not after all the disparaging remarks he'd made the past two months. Perhaps this ploy was his way of eliminating the competition. If he was so concerned, she must be doing something right.

And she'd keep on doing it—right after she dined with him and got as much information out of him about his precious shop and how he ran it as she could.

The following evening Miles sat in Rutledge Hall with his violin between his knees, the neck toward the floor, and adjusted the bridge. He held up the instrument to check the orientation. Hank entered, greeted several men on his way over to Miles, and watched while he repeated the process two more times until he was satisfied. After he checked the pitch of the strings, he glanced at his friend. Hank leaned against the wall wearing a grin. "What?"

"What do you mean, what?"

"I've seen that look before. You know something I don't."

"I know a good many things. I'm the sheriff, and, as such, I'm a keeper of secrets."

Miles laid his violin in its case and stood. He had four inches on Hank, which would force him to look up, giving Miles the advantage. Hank might not say what was on his mind, but he flushed when he was uncomfortable, and Miles intended to use whatever means he could to find out what Hank was hiding. Right now Hank's neck was the color of the velvet on which Miles's violin rested. "I assume this has to do with Mrs. Watkins. She agreed to go to dinner with me yesterday at the hotel."

"So I heard. How'd things go?" Hank pulled his pocket

watch out of his waistcoat and checked the time.

"She's considering my offer."

"Do you think you can work with her? She's got a mind of her own."

"She's bright, works hard, and knows all there is to know about running a mercantile. No one's ever shown as much interest in my business as she did. One question led to another, and before I knew it I needed to get back to the mercantile."

"I hope things work out for you." Hank glanced at the door. "Mr. Morton should be here by now."

Something wasn't right. Punctuality wasn't one of Hank's virtues, so why was he concerned about their conductor being a few minutes later than usual?

Two sets of footfalls made their way up the wooden staircase, one heavy and one light. Almost sounded like—

A soft peal of laughter drifted through the open door. Female laughter.

Miles looked at Hank, who'd moved to his spot and taken a sudden interest in his cello.

Ellie stepped inside, her violin case in her hand. Mr. Morton followed and made his way to the platform. The room grew silent as one man after another noticed her arrival. They turned en masse and looked at Miles, several of them sporting silly grins.

He crossed the room and stood before her. "I heard you'd spoken with Mr. Morton, but I didn't expect to see you here."

Her rigid posture and raised chin reminded him of their first meeting when he'd acted in haste, and she'd decided to open her own place. She'd struck the same pose that day.

"Why not? Because I'm a woman, one with a business to oversee and a daughter to care for? One who should stay home where she belongs and not intrude on the sacred domain reserved for men?"

"That's not it." If she believed his surprise stemmed from his earlier opposition to her on those grounds, she'd never accept his offer of a partnership. "When I heard you weren't admitted to the orchestra in Omaha, I thought. . ." Judging by the challenge in her eyes and the warning on several of the musicians' faces, he'd better not say what he thought.

"You thought what? That I'm undeserving of membership in this fine organization because I lack the talent?"

He said nothing. Words would only make things worse, because none of those that came to mind could tactfully convey his concern about her ability.

She held his gaze for several seconds. A shadow crossed her face, so fleeting he wondered if he'd imagined it, and she thrust that determined chin of hers higher yet. "Your silence speaks for itself. But it's your turn to be surprised, Mr. Rutledge, because Mr. Morton doesn't share your opinion."

Chapter 16

A shiver shimmied up Elenora's spine, and she smiled in anticipation of her initial performance before the Society. In a few short minutes Mr. Rutledge would get his comeuppance. Although he was a gifted musician, he had no right assuming her skills were lacking.

He scanned the faces of those in the room and rested his eyes on her. "They knew, didn't they? And no one told me. Why?"

"I thought you'd have heard by now. There aren't many secrets in El Dorado. Everyone knows I enjoy playing and have been providing the entertainment at my socials. You don't think the women have come just to buy my wares, do you?" She laughed, but he didn't look amused.

Mr. Morton joined them. "Judging by the shocked look on your face when you saw Mrs. Watkins, Miles, it would appear your friends have had some fun at your expense."

"So you admitted her?"

"She auditioned for me. Based on her talent, I welcomed her without reservation."

"You made the decision on your own? I would have thought you'd consult us."

"She's agreed to perform the same selection for all of you that she did for me. When you hear her, I think you'll understand why I was eager to have her as a member." He raised his voice. "Gentlemen, kindly take your seats and prepare to play the fourth movement of *The Four Seasons*. Mrs. Watkins will be joining us."

"*The Four Seasons?* That's a fine choice, Mrs. Watkins, one that will test any musician." The storm clouds darkening Mr. Rutledge's countenance parted, and a smile lit his face. When he beamed like that, he looked warm, friendly—and more handsome than any man she'd ever met. But this glimpse of him at his best would be brief, since she was about to perform a portion of the lengthy solo that had earned him a chorus of compliments at the concert.

He followed her up the steps to the stage and stood where he had during the final number at the concert. She waited off to the side while the rest of the orchestra took their seats and located their music. A frisson of excitement shook her. Any minute now Mr. Rutledge would be forced to eat another course of his hasty words. Although it shouldn't, that thought brought her immense satisfaction.

Mr. Morton mounted his platform. "Miles, kindly take your seat. Mrs. Watkins is performing the solo."

"But that was my so—"

A chorus of sniggers, chuckles, and one belly laugh ensued. Mr. Rutledge's face contorted, whether in anger or pain she couldn't be sure. And then, to her amazement, a rosy flush flooded his cheeks. He slunk to a vacant chair in the front row, dropped into it, and fumbled through the music on his stand.

His apparent humiliation touched a deep chord. She couldn't begin to count the number of times Pa had put her in her place in front of customers. *His* customers, as he'd insisted on calling them. She remembered the sinking feeling in her stomach and the bitter taste in her mouth.

Perhaps her decision to play the piece that had afforded Mr. Rutledge the admiration of the townspeople was a mistake. It was one thing to compete with him in business, but to upstage him musically as well could be considered unkind. A man didn't appreciate being bested, especially by a woman. And certainly not in front of his peers.

But why should she concern herself with his feelings when he'd disregarded hers? He poked fun at her wares and her way of doing business whenever he wanted. She'd even caught him talking about her behind her back.

She had every right to perform the piece. And she wouldn't let him keep her from it. She'd do her best, and he would have to admit she had talent. She swept to the front of the stage, tucked her violin under her chin, and watched Mr. Morton's baton.

Miles stood before the mirror in his back room the next morning, combed his hair, and grabbed his hat. He shoved the curtain aside and headed for the front door, addressing his clerk as he passed. "I won't be gone long, Sammy." At least he hoped he wouldn't.

"Pardon me for saying so, sir, but you don't seem to be yourself this morning."

Miles paused with his hand on the doorknob. "What do you mean?"

"Your waistcoat. You buttoned it crooked."

"So I did." He fixed his mistake, one he couldn't recall having made since he was a boy in short pants. *Focus, Rutledge. You can't let a woman get to you like this.*

He left his shop and waited for a farmer with a load of feed to rumble past. Early though it was, El Dorado was a hive of activity as folks tried to get as much done as possible before the heat of the day. He had a task of his own to perform, one he couldn't put off, not if he wanted Ellie to accept his offer.

Stepping lightly so as not to stir up dust that would cling to his clothes, he crossed the wide street, made his way around the corner of the Oriental Hotel at the end of the block, and approached the back door of Ellie's shop.

She emerged and flung a tub of dishwater his way. He jumped back.

"I'm sorry. I didn't see you. I got your boots, didn't I?"

She had. He'd need to condition the leather as soon as he got back. "No harm done."

"Tildy's not here."

"I know. I didn't come to see her."

Ellie held out a hand toward the open door. "Won't you come in then?" She leaned the tub against the wall and wiped her hands on an apron smeared with jam—blackberry, judging by the deep purple stain seeping into the white fabric. A single braid hung down her back, and if the number of loose hairs was an indication, she'd yet to complete her morning routine. Even though she didn't seem to be a woman focused on appearances like Irene, who'd spent hours primping, Ellie was usually well put together. He'd never seen her look as homey—or as appealing.

He followed her into her back room. An unmistakable scent filled the air, the same one he'd smelled in Mother's kitchen earlier. "You didn't burn the bacon."

"You do have a way with words, don't you?"

"Sorry." What a fool he was. He'd come to make peace. Instead he'd been downright rude. She studied him with such intensity he felt like an insect being eyed by a hungry bird. It was all he could do not to squirm.

Her expression softened. "Since I owe you an apology, I'll accept yours."

"What do you have to apologize for? I'm the one with the

habit of tasting boot blacking."

"You may speak before thinking at times, but I know you mean well, whereas I set out to put you in your place last night. I was wrong to do it, and I hope you can forgive me."

Women. After all the years he'd spent waiting on them, he still couldn't figure them out. Especially the one before him, a woman who could make him madder than a yellow jacket one minute and send his heart soaring the next.

When Ellie had drawn her bow across the strings for the final note of her stunning performance and turned to face the members of Musical Society with her head held high, ready to take their feedback with courage befitting a man, his chest had swelled so much his waistcoast buttons had been in danger of popping off. Rarely had Irene affected him the way Ellie did last night.

Whatever she took on she gave her all, be it raising a daughter on her own, running a business, or performing a challenging solo. If she were to accept his offer of a partnership, he'd reap the benefits—in many ways. "You had every right to audition. The only excuse for my behavior is that I was caught off guard."

"I was surprised, too. You generally know what's going on in town."

"Seems my friends were out to teach me a lesson. One I needed to learn."

A bud of a smile curved her mouth, growing until it bloomed into one so warm and welcoming he wanted to plant a kiss on those lovely lips of hers. She stared at his. Was she inviting him to—

"You may—"

"Really?" He hadn't meant to sound so eager.

"What?" She looked into his eyes, and her smile evaporated as quickly as the dishwater she'd tossed out. "Oh!" She looked away and fanned her cheeks. Although he couldn't see them, he guessed they'd taken on a pretty pink tinge.

He turned her around and let his hands linger on her upper arms. She stared at the top button of his waistcoat. Good thing Sammy had pointed out the need to refasten it. Wouldn't do for her to know how flustered he'd been when he dressed. Not that she'd have any idea why. For all she knew he was angry with her for joining the Musical Society. He had to make her understand. "Ellie, please look at me."

She did as he asked, but what he saw wasn't amusement or confusion. He got a glimpse of something much deeper. It was as though she'd opened a window to her soul, allowing him to see into her heart. The burning need for someone to appreciate her and show her some tenderness was so startling, so intense, that he dropped his hands to his sides and took a step back.

For a moment she stood rooted to the spot, her attention fixed on his boots. Then she whirled around and removed empty crates from the chairs and table, stacking them willy-nilly. "What I was going to say is that you may have a seat, but I realized my back room is in a terrible state. Since I haven't been able to open my shop to customers and have been busy packing orders for the Tal—for my employees to deliver, I've let things go. I'll have the place cleared up forthwith."

She reached over her head and attempted to add one more of the slatted pine boxes to the unwieldy stack. It teetered precariously.

"Careful!"

Before he could right the crates, the tower toppled, sending the containers crashing to the floor and Ellie reeling backward. He reached for her, but she caught her heel and landed on the floor with a thump, where she sat with her boots peeking from beneath her splayed skirt and a stunned look on her face.

He dropped to his knees beside her and rested a hand on

her back. "Are you all right?"

Rather than answering, she giggled. Softly at first and then louder and louder until she erupted in peals of laughter, an undignified display so unlike her and so refreshing he couldn't help but laugh along with her. At length she resumed a measure of control, although her lips still twitched.

"Let me help you." He stood, extended a hand, which she took without a moment's hesitation, and pulled her to her feet.

She straightened her dress, reached behind her to brush off the dust, and scrunched her face. "Oooh!"

"You hit hard. You're going to be sore. I suggest sitting on a pillow for a few days."

She swatted his arm, merriment dancing in her warm brown eyes. "Mr. Rutledge, a gentleman doesn't mention such things."

"Nor does a lady howl, although I quite enjoyed the spectacle." He awaited the rebuke or retort sure to come.

"You can be quite pleasant company when you choose to be, can't you?"

Her voice held no edge, but he'd proceed with caution anyhow. "Does that mean you're considering my offer?"

"Not seriously, although I'm glad you finally realize I'm a worthy opponent."

She was that. He had to find a way to get her working for him instead of against him. If she accepted his offer and wasn't under the pressure she faced now, perhaps she'd relax more often. When she did, she was a lot of fun. "You'd make a worthy partner, too."

"But I'd have limited say. Here"—she pointed a finger at the floor—"I'm in charge."

"In charge of what? You're in a building so badly damaged you can't even use it."

"I'm making progress. Let me show you." She pulled aside

the curtain, beckoned him to follow her into the shop, and extended a hand toward the front, which was still covered in tarpaulins. The woodsy scent of freshly cut lumber overtook the smell of bacon. He located the source, a pile of boards behind her display cases.

"The pine for the awning and the fir for the trim were delivered several days ago. The plate glass arrived yesterday, but it was broken in two, although no one knows when or how that happened. I'll have to wait for a new sheet to be shipped from San Francisco. It's unfortunate, but I sent Mr. Steele a telegram, and he agreed to visit the factory to see if they'll rush the order."

Miles squatted and ran a hand over the smooth strips of fir. "How long does MacDougall think it will take to get you up and running again?"

"Another three weeks."

He stood and rested a hand on the dusty countertop. "You could be selling your wares in my shop tomorrow."

"I'll be fine. I've a number of socials scheduled, and I'm using the time to make plans for my reopening. I aim to have some surprises for my customers."

"New merchandise?"

"That. . .among other things."

She gave him a sly smile—and an idea. If he could get her to himself for a few days, away from her business, he'd be able to show her how much he'd changed. Once she saw that he valued her opinions, she'd be more likely to accept his offer. He'd much rather see her bent over the books in his back room than behind the counter in her shop waiting on customers she'd lured away from him.

"If you want to get more wares, I know just how you can do it. Join me on a buying trip to Sacramento City next week."

"Please, Mama. Just one more time."

Elenora pinched the string between her thumbs and first fingers in the two places Tildy had pointed out with her chin, reached around her hands, and opened it to reveal a new pattern. "What do you call this game again?"

Tildy took a turn, creating another in a sequence of transformations that had her captivated. "Cat's cradle. Timmy taught me, and he showed me his arrowheads. He said they're real ones from the Miwok Indians who live around here. He's pretty smart for a boy, even if he doesn't say much."

Mrs. Rutledge set a stack of plates on the kitchen table beside the silverware and condiments and patted Tildy's shoulder. "You've gotten him talking, which is commendable. Mrs. Talbot said he's let Tommy do most of the talking since they were tykes."

Tildy held out the string configuration to her. "Would you like to take a turn?"

"I've had more than enough already. Besides, I need to make the gravy. Perhaps you can talk Miles into playing with you. It should be easy, since you've got him wound around your little finger."

The grandfather clock in the parlor chimed twelve times, and Mrs. Rutledge paused with a cup of flour over the drippings in the skillet. "Matilda, would you dash over to the shop and hurry him along? I'd like to get dinner over with quickly, since he said he'd tend to the rug beating for me after the meal. You might enjoy watching him. He creates quite a cloud of dust."

"Yes ma'am." She skipped out of the room with the string still stretched over her hands.

The tantalizing scents of beef and cooked onions caused Elenora's stomach to rumble—rather loudly. Papa's new wife used to frown when she heard such an unladylike noise. Elenora pressed a hand to her midsection in an attempt to put an end to the embarrassing sound. "Excuse me."

Mrs. Rutledge whisked the mixture in the iron skillet. She didn't seem at all offended by the growling, which finally subsided. In fact, she chuckled. "Sounds like you're ready for dinner. All that walking you're doing works up an appetite. It can be draining in this heat, though, even for someone who enjoys it. If you were to take Miles up on his offer, you wouldn't have to be out in the sun. Have you made a decision?"

Forthright. That description fit his mother like a glove. If she could speak her mind. . . "I can't. He's been complimentary of late, but for weeks he did nothing but question my way of doing things."

"He did. But you have to admit, your methods are unorthodox."

"*Unorthodox?* Last week you called them innovative." Whose side was she on? Her son's, of course. Elenora pressed her lips together and stared out the window.

"My dear, you needn't take offense. I'm not out to criticize you. I know my son. He can be slow to embrace change, but the fact that he's made you the offer again proves he's teachable." Her voice had risen. She paused. When she spoke her tone was soft and pleading. "Can't you give him a chance?"

"I'll set the table." Elenora rose, carried the dishes into the dining room, and arranged the place settings. She put the mustard at Mr. Rutledge's place. He fancied the spicy spread on his pot roast. If she agreed to be his partner, he'd have even more spice in his life. But how would he take to having someone around who insisted on having a say in the business? Not well, from all she'd seen.

The idea of being his partner caused her empty stomach to roil. Mama had talked about asking the Lord to give her a sense of peace so she'd know what He wanted her to do. Elenora smiled. If that were true and God led using such means, the answer was clear. The only thing that stopped the swirling in her belly was the thought of standing in her own shop, opening her new door, and welcoming her customers inside to look at the wonderful merchandise she had for sale.

And she knew how to get it. She would go on the buying trip and let Mr. Rutledge introduce her to the vendors. Not having to locate them on her own would speed things up nicely, and she'd be able to reopen with new goods sure to draw people into her place.

She returned to the kitchen for the butter dish. "If you're sure about working in the mercantile in his place while watching Tildy for me, I'll travel to Sacramento City with him."

Mrs. Rutledge smiled. "I'm glad to hear that. You won't regret it."

No, but when Mr. Rutledge found out she wasn't accepting his offer, he would.

Chapter 17

Miles sat before a vendor's desk four days later with Ellie at his side. The businessman's ebony hair held enough grease to lubricate every hinge in Sacramento City. Even the hand he'd offered when they'd arrived felt slick.

"I'm afraid you misunderstood, Mr. Beadle. I'm serving as Mrs. Watkins's escort today and making the introductions. She has a shop of her own, but she's not ready to place any orders yet. Should she choose to place one with you, we'll return tomorrow."

"Indeed? Do forgive me, ma'am. I'm unaccustomed to dealing with members of the weaker sex." He dipped a bow before Ellie. The broad smile on his gaunt face when he arose was at odds with the conspiratorial wink he shot Miles.

"Good day, sir. Shall we go, Mr. Rutledge?" Elenora made a show of wiping her feet on the worn rug at the door of the small smoke-filled office and marched down the wooden walkway. Her gloved fists swung in time with each clomp of her heels. He matched her lengthy strides.

Once they were out of earshot of passersby, she spoke her mind. "Weaker sex! How dare he say such a thing? Doesn't he know women here have rights and can conduct business on their own behalf? If he thinks for one minute that I—"

"Calm yourself, Ellie. Mr. Beadle might not be as enlightened as some, but you can't expect the world to change overnight. Look how long it took me to come around."

She stopped, and he followed suit. Her eyes flitted from side to side as they roved over his face. He wished he could keep his as impassive as hers. It wouldn't do for her to see how much he was enjoying her outburst. She looked like a banty hen with her feathers fluffed.

He couldn't fault her for being upset. Mr. Beadle had been out of line, but she had to learn to lower her expectations. While California was more progressive than other parts of the country, it would take men time to grow accustomed to seeing women hold positions unheard of in days gone by. He was just getting used to the idea himself, although it did have hidden benefits. Making the rounds of Sacramento City's wholesale houses was decidedly more agreeable with an attractive woman like Ellie at his side.

Her assessment complete, she met his gaze. "I see from the telltale twitch of your lips that you're enjoying this, but I fail to see any humor in the situation. While you have made progress, I wouldn't exactly say you've been a model of broad-mindedness."

"That's balderdash! Whose idea was it to make this trip in the first place? And who's been taking a businesswoman around to meet as many vendors as possible, in spite of the looks I'm getting from most of the men? I'd say I'm being quite progressive—and downright charitable."

Her chin dropped, leaving her mouth parted, and he had the strongest urge to kiss her. Had they been alone, he might have tried it just to see how she'd react.

"*Progressive? Charitable?* That's exactly what I mean. Implying I need your charity because I'm a woman doesn't exactly qualify as progressive thinking in my mind."

"All right. Perhaps my word choices weren't the best. How about big-hearted or kind? Would one of those work for you?"

She stared at him so long he could have grown a beard, but when she spoke her tone was as warm as the sun-baked roadway beside them. "Thank you for making the effort to understand. I know it's only a matter of semantics, but it's important to me. Shall we go? I'd like to make as many stops as possible before supper." She gathered her skirts and crossed the dusty street.

What a spunky little thing she was. All the more reason he needed her to join forces with him. If she didn't, she'd continue to draw business away from the mercantile. He couldn't afford to let that happen. Besides, working with her could be more fun than he'd first thought.

When Ellie reached Marchand and Babineaux Wholesalers, she rested her hand on Miles's as he reached for the door-knob, and he froze. She wasn't in the habit of touching him, although he liked it when she did. "I think things might go more smoothly if you were to start the conversation and wait a while to tell them I'm representing myself. I'd like to see how they respond under normal circumstances."

"I'll do that." She never ceased to amaze him. A minute ago she'd been so angry with Mr. Beadle her dark eyes smoldered, but she'd obviously thought better of her approach.

They entered an ornately furnished room filled with the rich scents of éclairs and that highfalutin café au lait Marchand was partial to. The portly Frenchman jumped up, brushed crumbs from his paisley waistcoat, and shoved his arms in his swallowtail coat.

Would this trussed-up gent and his showy ways appeal to Ellie? So far not one vendor had enticed her to place an order. Would Marchand handle her barrage of questions with his usual aplomb and succeed where other valiant men had failed?

"*Bonjour, Madame et Monsieur.* If you please, have a seat." Marchand pulled out one of the Rococo Revival chairs in front of his massive desk. Miles stifled a groan. Some might like the silk tufted cushions and oval backs, but of all the chairs in all the vendors' offices in Sacramento City, these had to be the most uncomfortable. He'd take a plush American-made wing-back armchair over these any day.

True to her word, Ellie remained quiet while Marchand conversed with Miles. Only those who knew her as he did would understand what an effort she put forth. Her placid face revealed nothing, but her bright eyes belied her apparent calm. Now to let her have her fun. He'd have his, too. Ellie in her element was a sight to behold.

"Mr. Marchand, allow me to introduce my business associate. Mrs. Watkins owns a shop up our way, and she has some questions for you."

The Frenchman appeared more self-possessed than many of his peers. Aside from a momentary widening of the eyes, he gave no other indication of surprise. She gave the suave salesman a fleeting smile and proceeded to subject him to the rigorous examination his counterparts had endured.

When Ellie conducted business she was the picture of self-control. He could see why her father had let her do much of the buying for his shop. Miles had seen men who didn't fare as well against wily wholesalers as she did. She'd be quite an asset once she agreed to be his partner. As hard as it was for him to take his eyes off her, though, she could become a distraction—albeit a pleasant one.

Her intense tone drew his attention to the conversation. "As I said, Mr. Marchand, I have no interest in your regular matches. The white phosphorous is a known cause of phossy jaw, which is potentially fatal, as I'm sure you're well aware. I want a quote on safety matches made with red phosphorous. The fact that you offer an extra box of the other free of charge if one buys a dozen doesn't interest me. Why would I want more of an inferior product?"

He couldn't agree more. Ellie was not only bright. She was also well informed. Although the wholesaler did his best to counter her sound arguments, she stood firm.

Miles spent the next half hour listening to her grill the Frenchman. What a remarkable woman she was. Why had it taken him so long to see it? At least he had.

Now to invite her to dine with him at a fancy Sacramento City restaurant and convince her of the benefits of joining forces over a leisurely meal.

Elenora arrived at the port breathless and stood in the shade of the railroad depot. The bustle of the city was unlike anything she'd ever seen. Boats jostled for position on the Sacramento River. Passengers debarked from the *Yosemite* while workmen unloaded freight from the massive flat-bottomed riverboat. Railroad workers issued continued warnings to the throng to hurry and clear the area because a train was due to arrive on the tracks that paralleled the riverfront. A group of travelers made their way to the horse-drawn trolley car waiting at the street beyond the depot.

The engine of the side-wheel steamer thrummed, as though the vessel were eager to be on its way. Freight men plunked crates on carts that clunked over the wooden planks of the loading dock as workers rushed the cargo to waiting wagons. The buzz of countless conversations was sprinkled with laughter and an occasional shout.

How was she to find her new friend in this crowd? She should have suggested a less populated meeting spot, but the good-natured mercantile owner from Marysville had insisted she see the heart of the city, as he called it. It shouldn't be too hard to locate him, though. Not many men wore a bright red cravat as he did. Although it made his round cheeks appear redder than they really were, he didn't seem to care about such things. He was far more interested in others than himself and had put her at ease the moment she'd met him.

"Sweets for my charming new friend who's made my visit to this great city sweeter."

She wheeled around. "Oh Mr. Grayson. I didn't hear you."

"Who can hear anything in this hubbub?" He handed her a box from the California Candy Factory. "They're made right here in Sacramento City."

"Thank you. That's kind of you, but I shouldn't accept a gift from a gentleman I've known such a short time. It's not proper." Not that she minded. His fatherly gesture touched her. Pa didn't do such things, although she'd often wished he had. Each year for her birthday and Christmas, he'd told her she could pick out something from his shop. Just once she would have loved him to surprise her as Mr. Grayson had.

"Don't think of it as a gift. You can call it a product sample, and you accepted a number of those today." He swept a hand toward the dock. "Didn't I tell you the port was a sight to behold? A body can feel the excitement in the air. It gets my blood flowing every time, and at my age that's a good thing." He chuckled.

He wasn't *that* old. If she were to guess, she'd say he was about Pa's age. But Mr. Grayson was nothing like Pa. The complete opposite, in fact. Mr. Grayson was stout, had a full head of salt-and-pepper hair, and showered compliments on her. "I can't believe how much freight they've unloaded. It's no wonder there are so many wholesalers in the city."

"And you've seen a good many of them the past couple of days, haven't you?"

"I have, and it's been such fun. I can't wait until my shipments arrive. My reopening will be a grand event."

He gave her one of his jolly grins. "Undoubtedly. Knowing your customers' interests and tastes as you do, you're sure to have chosen items they'll want. I expect to see your business thriving when I make my way up the hill."

"You're going to visit my shop?" What a nice surprise. She'd be able to show him how well she was doing.

"Yes, my dear lady. I've been impressed by what I've seen already. That's why I have a proposition for you, which I'll share over supper, if you'll agree to dine with me again."

Elenora glanced around the railroad car the following afternoon. Since only two stops remained, the final one being the terminus where they would catch the stage, few passengers occupied the plush velvet seats. Mr. Rutledge, who sat opposite her, leaned forward. One of his legs bounced rapidly, and he pressed a palm to his knee as though he wanted to stop the motion. She knew what was coming but dreaded giving him an answer he wouldn't want to hear.

"Have you made up your mind?"

She focused on the oak-covered hills rushing past the open windows, which allowed the stench from the smoke and a shower of fine black particles to drift inside. The task before her was equally unappealing. Although she felt certain of her decision, turning him down after he'd helped her numerous times and shown such kindness to Tildy seemed a bit heartless.

Elenora recalled the moment he'd rushed to her aid when the awning collapsed, and she bit back a sigh. She'd been eager to accept his offer when she arrived in El Dorado, but much had changed since then. She had options now and couldn't let feelings of obligation sway her. Turning to Mr. Rutledge, she worked to sound grateful but firm.

"I appreciate all you've done for me. The introductions you made were a great help. I've considered your renewed offer of a partnership, but—"

"That man talked you out of it, didn't he?"

His clipped words and tight features told a different story than his slumped shoulders. His offer had been sincere, and he was disappointed. While the sight gave her a moment's pause, she couldn't forget how easily he'd dismissed her when he'd first met her or how many times he'd poked fun at her wares and ways of doing things. She mustn't show any hesitation.

"His name is Mr. Grayson, and no, he didn't try to talk me out of it. He made an offer of his own. A very attractive one."

Mr. Rutledge's knee ceased its bouncing, and he sat upright. "He's too old for you."

Did he seriously think Mr. Grayson had a romantic interest in her? A smile begged for release, so she pressed a hand to her mouth and averted her eyes. When she'd restored her composure, she lifted her gaze. "He made a business proposal. As I told you, I'm not looking for anything else."

"But he took you out to eat—twice."

When the maître d' had led her to the table where Mr. Grayson waited for her last night, she'd passed Mr. Rutledge. At the time she hadn't understood why he was so curt when she greeted him. Apparently he was either jealous—which was preposterous—or he felt it his duty to protect her, as he had in the past. "Men discuss business over meals all the time."

"He's the reason I didn't see you yesterday and why you turned down my invitation to join me for supper the day before, isn't he?"

"I'd already accepted his invitation, yes. We met right after you'd left to go to the saddler, and I became engrossed in our conversation. He asked me to join him for supper so we could continue our discussion."

"You'd just met him, and yet you agreed to have supper with him? How do you know you can trust him? Men can be. . . unsavory characters. You can't let fine clothes or fancy talk fool you."

She could no longer contain her smile. "Your concern does you credit, but I consider myself a good judge of character. I'm aware of the dangers a woman alone faces, which is why I was careful to be circumspect. All our interactions were in full view of others."

"He held your hand."

She'd not been aware that Mr. Rutledge was in the hotel lobby last night when Mr. Grayson made his departure. Not that it mattered. She had nothing to hide. "I offered him my hand, but being that he's older and somewhat set in his ways, I don't think he realized I intended him merely to shake it as you men do when you part."

The kindly man had stared at her gloved hand for an instant before he'd clasped it and given it a squeeze. He'd released her posthaste, bowed, and gone his way. "I have a tendency to fly in the face of convention on that particular point of etiquette in my effort to be taken seriously as a businesswoman. But you, of all people, should be able to understand."

Her attempt at humor fell flat. He didn't laugh or grin. His moustache didn't even twitch. "What, may I ask, did he propose?"

"That's a rather personal question, but since it affects you. . ." She took a steadying breath. "He's made a tentative offer of a partnership—a full partnership—in his mercantile up in Marysville."

"How can he afford to do that? You have your expertise and your wares, I understand, but a junior partnership is all that qualifies you for."

"Mr. Grayson has no family left. His daughter and her little one were on their way out West after the war, but they fell ill along the way and never made it. He'd planned to teach her everything he knew and leave the business to her. Now that some time has passed, he's decided to find someone else."

"Why you?" He cringed. "Forgive me. That didn't come out the way I meant."

"It's all right." She'd asked herself the same question many times over the past two days. All she could think of was that perhaps the Lord really had heard her prayers. "He overheard me talking with one of the wholesalers and was intrigued by my way of doing things."

"I see." He paused and cast his eyes upward as though he were considering his words before he uttered them. "His offer is quite generous. Have you given him an answer?"

"He wants me to take some time to think about it and will pay me a visit in a few weeks. In the meantime, I'm going to continue to work hard and—" What a ninny she was. She'd come far too close to telling Mr. Rutledge her plans. She'd lain awake last night thinking up ideas and hadn't been able to sleep until well after midnight. Mr. Grayson was sure to be impressed when he saw how well she was doing.

"And force me to do the same."

The train rounded a bend, sending the cardboard box beside her sliding. She caught the package before it tumbled off the seat, set it in her lap, and removed the top. Thankfully the doll was fine. She ran a finger over the smooth porcelain face and rosebud lips. "Tildy's never been one to play with dolls much, but I couldn't resist this one. It looks a lot like she did as a baby."

"Babies are beautiful, aren't they?"

His voice caught, and she found him gazing at the doll with a wistful expression. Had he hoped to have children? "They are. Tildy's a blessing, even if she is a handful at times."

"I bought May a Grenier papier mâché doll on a buying trip like this one, but I wasn't able to give it to her. When I got home"—he spoke so softly she had to strain to hear him over the clanking of the train's wheels as they ate up the miles of track—"my precious little girl was gone forever. Both she and Irene were taken from me at the same time."

He'd lost a child! Why hadn't he said anything before? She longed to reach out to him, but touching him would be improper. Words would have to suffice. "Oh Mr. Rutledge, I'm so sorry."

He gazed out the window, his features taut. A tremor in his upper body evidenced his struggle for control.

With a hiss of the brakes, the train came to a stop in Latrobe. The other passengers disembarked, leaving them alone for the final two miles of the ride before their transfer to the stagecoach at the end station in Shingle Springs. The conductor peeked in, doffed his cap, and moved on.

Although Elenora was desperate to find out what had happened to Mr. Rutledge's wife and daughter, she remained silent. . .until the need to offer comfort was more than she could bear. With no one around, she needn't worry about prying eyes. She reached for his hand resting on the plush velvet seat and placed her gloved one atop it.

When he tensed, she pulled away. He jumped up, grabbed their luggage from the overhead rack, set it in the aisle, and returned to his seat opposite her. Billowing steam and the chugging of the engine signaled their departure.

He fixed his piercing blue eyes on her, and his brittle tone chilled her to the core. "I can't match Grayson's offer, Ellie, but I won't stand by and let you steal my customers. I have a living to make, too."

Even though he'd used his special name for her, his pronouncement held not one speck of his usual good nature. She missed it.

Chapter 18

Miles dropped his carpetbag on his four-poster bed, reached inside, and grabbed one of his white shirts. He wadded it into a ball and slammed it into the wicker laundry basket. Five more followed, each hurled with gusto. He was about to send a pair of trousers sailing when a sound stopped him.

Mother stood in the doorway, that all-knowing look she was famous for on her face. "I don't suppose I need to ask how things went."

His chest tightened. He forced himself to take a deep breath, but what he really wanted to do was punch something. Hard. "That stubborn woman turned me down."

She sat on the edge of the bed, picked up the stack of soiled collars, and flipped through them. "Sixteen? That's four a day, which is excessive even for you. Were you that eager to impress her?"

"How could I impress her when she spent most of the time keeping company with another man?"

"Another man? That doesn't sound like Elenora. What happened?"

"She met a man as old as Abe, and he's out to take her away from here."

Mother patted the spot beside her, and he plunked himself down with such force she caught hold of a corner post until the waves subsided. "I haven't seen you this riled up since the day Abe got to talking and trimmed off too much over your right ear. You'd really warmed to the idea of having her as your partner, hadn't you?"

"Why does she have to be so hardheaded? If she weren't set on proving herself, she'd see that what she has here is more than enough. I can't give her everything Grayson promised, but from what she'd said in her letters, she thought forming a partnership with me was a good idea. Now she wants more."

"What exactly did this Mr. Grayson offer her?"

"An equal partnership and the possibility of inheriting his business someday."

Mother reached for his hand the way Ellie had after he'd told her about May. How he'd ached for her to lace her fingers with his as Mother was. But Ellie had pulled away quickly. Far too quickly for his liking. All he'd been able to think about was taking her into his arms and kissing her until she breathed his given name. He'd needed to put some distance between them.

Much as he wanted to read more into her gesture, he had to face facts. She'd reacted out of sympathy, not because she had feelings for him. She didn't want to work with him. It was clear she intended to best him and wouldn't be satisfied until she succeeded—or ran off to be Grayson's *partner*.

"His business? What business is that?"

"He owns a mercantile in Marysville, and he's scouring the Gold Country in search of a partner. From what she said, he's decided she'd make a good one."

"Hmm. I wonder why he's considering a woman. It seems more likely he'd be looking for a man. Did you ask her about that?"

He gave a dry laugh. "I'm not the best one to bring that up. She did say something about his daughter and grandchild not surviving the trip west and him having no one to inherit his shop. Maybe he's so lonely he'll investigate any possibility."

"It sounds more like he's in need of a family and thinks she and Tildy would make a good one. Considering the strained relations Elenora has with her father, I can see how she and this man would be drawn to one another. So, what are you going to do about it?"

"What can I do? Ellie's one of the most determined women I've ever met. When she makes up her mind about something, there's no stopping her."

Mother squeezed his hand. "That's nothing new. She's been out to best you since she set up shop. What's really troubling you? The fact that you have feelings for her, or the fact that she doesn't return them?"

He jumped up and pitched three pairs of trousers into the basket, one right after another. "I don't have feelings for her."

"There are those who might believe you, son, but I know you. And I know you have what it takes to convince her to stay—if you really want her to."

He did. Desperately. He just needed to figure out how.

Elenora stood inside her shop a week after the trip to Sacramento City and listened to the symphony of construction sounds out front. Never in her life would she have imagined being so excited about the rasp of saws slicing through wood or the clanging of hammers on nails, but today they were as welcome as one of Handel's arrangements. Why, if people wouldn't think her addlepated, she would grab her violin and serenade the workers with "The Hallelujah Chorus."

And the smell. She inhaled deeply. No perfume was as pleasing as the scent of freshly cut lumber.

After four weeks the work was finally underway. Only three more days and she'd be able to throw open her new door and invite her customers inside. With everything she had planned, her reopening should be a grand affair.

"Ye look happy, Mrs. Watkins." The carpenter handed the cabinet-maker a piece of the fir that would frame the sheet of plate glass, which had arrived the day before with not so much as a scratch. Sawdust clung to Mr. MacDougall's red hair and bushy beard.

"I am."

"With Tommy and Timmy's help we'll have ye back in business before ye can say, 'my heart's in the Highlands.'"

She laughed. "Your heart may be in Scotland, but mine's right here in El Dorado, and it's so full it feels like it's about to pop, as Tildy would say."

"I haven't seen the lassie around. I thought she'd want to watch the goings-on."

Tommy looked up from where he knelt on the walkway with a saw in hand. "She was walking toward the livery with Mr. Rutledge a ways back. I heard him say he had a surprise for her."

Elenora stepped though the opening where her door would soon be hung and glanced down the street. "I thought she was with his mother." She caught the carpenter's eye. "If you don't need me, I'll head over there and see if they're expecting anything for me today."

"We men have things well in hand."

She entered the livery moments later. The blend of animal scents, hay, and leather didn't bother a farmer's wife like Pearl, but the combination never failed to make Elenora queasy. Or perhaps her queasiness stemmed from the fact that she must face Mr. Rutledge again. Ever since their conversation on the train, things between them had been strained. He brightened when he chatted with Tildy, but the rest of the time he seemed distant, which wasn't like him.

"Mama!" Tildy dashed up to her. "Guess what? Mr. Rutledge is going to the Independence Day celebration in Placerville, and he said he'd be happy to take us. There's a parade and a horse race and games for the children and—"

"That sounds like fun, sweetheart, but I've already made plans to join the Duprees for a picnic at their place."

A cloud passed over Tildy's face, sending her sunny disposition into hiding. "It won't be as much fun if he's not there."

"You'll have a good time with your friends. And I happen to know that Mr. Dupree bought some firecrackers."

Her eyes wide, Tildy stared. "You've never let me anywhere near fireworks."

Mr. Rutledge joined them. "Fireworks? Where?"

"At Constance's," Tildy said. "Her pa's going to set them off on the Fourth of July. Mama said we're going there—not to Placerville with you."

"What is Will thinking? They're dangerous and could cause a fire. I refuse to sell the blasted things."

Elenora pulled Tildy to her side. She'd never heard him use such a strong word. While she didn't like the idea of firecrackers being set off, he seemed to have strong feelings about them. "Mr. Rutledge, please watch your language."

"Where did he get them? From you?"

"Do you honestly think I'd sell them? If so, you've misjudged me." Again. "Will had them sent up from Sacramento City, and Pearl said he takes every precaution. He'll light them in his cleared field, and we'll all stand back with buckets of water in case they're needed."

Tildy shrugged out of Elenora's embrace and sidled up to Mr. Rutledge. "I wish you were going to be there. I'll miss you."

"Well now, I'm sure I could wheedle an invitation out of Mrs. Dupree if I told her Mother would take a bowl of her potato salad. And I could give you that riding lesson you've been wanting."

Tildy jumped up and down, setting some of the horses to shifting in their stalls. He placed a hand on her shoulder to settle her down.

"Do you really mean it? You're going to teach me? That's the best surprise ever. Oh Mama, I'm going to be a real Western girl. Isn't that exciting?"

Elenora didn't take kindly to being put on the spot. They'd talked about the possibility of riding lessons over dinner several days ago, but as far as she was concerned, they hadn't reached a decision. "I told you I'd think about it, dearest. As Mr. Rutledge pointed out, you'd need a saddle, but I can't afford one just now."

"Mrs. Watkins, Tildy, I have something to show you, if you'll follow me."

Elenora trod carefully through the straw. She didn't relish the idea of stepping in. . .*stuff.* They stopped before a stand covered with a blanket, and she drew in a short breath. Only one thing would be under that. "You got her—"

He whisked off the throw.

"—a saddle?"

Tildy squealed, threw herself at him, and wrapped her arms around his waist. He pulled her to him and closed his eyes as though he wanted to savor every second of the embrace. When she drew back, he released her and smiled.

"Thank you, Mr. Rutledge. This is the best present anyone's ever given me." She made for the saddle and ran her hands over it. "Isn't it beautiful, Mama?" She pressed her cheek to the seat and inhaled. "And it smells so good."

"Yes, dear. It's quite nice, isn't it? Why don't you have a good look at it while Mr. Rutledge and I talk for a minute."

She gestured toward the front of the livery, and he followed her.

"What is it, Ellie? You don't sound very happy."

"I realize this must have been why you made the trip to the saddlery when we were in the city, but I wish you'd have told me what you planned. Why didn't you?"

"I wanted it to be a surprise."

"Oh, it was. But it's far too generous a gift."

He waved a hand dismissively. "I can afford it. You haven't driven me to the poor house yet."

Elenora cast a glance at Tildy, who explored every inch of the saddle, a cute girl-sized one—Western, just like she'd wanted. He certainly knew how to please her, even though his gift was far too extravagant. "It's not only the money. I don't want her to get too attached."

"To me you mean?"

"It'll make it harder for her to leave, and I can't bear to see her hurt."

He rested a hand on her arm. Sincerity coated his every word. "I'd never do anything to hurt her. I care for her—deeply."

"I know you do. But if I accept Mr. Grayson's offer. . . The closer she gets to people here, the more difficult it will be for her to say good-bye."

"She'll have a hard time leaving, no matter what, because she loves it here—even if you don't."

Is that what he thought? "I may not be as vocal about my opinions as Tildy, but I'm happy here."

"I'm not convinced. If you were happy, I wouldn't expect to see you jump at the first opportunity to leave. Of course, accepting Grayson's offer would be easier than running a place of your own when you have a thriving business like mine standing in your way of success."

"You think I'm taking the easy way out because I don't think I can make it here? Well, you're wrong about that." And she'd show him how wrong he was. Wait until he saw what she had planned for her reopening.

The following Monday Elenora flitted from one customer to the next. Many of those she'd visited during the weeks her shop was closed had come to help her celebrate her first day back in business.

"Good morning, Mrs. Barton. Thank you for stopping by."

"I wouldn't miss this. Never once has Mr. Rutledge offered muffins and coffee to his customers. And I want an opportunity to win one of those photographs of Mark Twain you're giving away. I've read his collection of short stories many times and am eager to get a copy of his latest work." She reached for his recently released book, *Innocents Abroad*, which occupied a small table at the front of the shop. "However did you manage to get autographed copies when he's living clear across the country in New York?"

"A merchant doesn't reveal all her secrets." Elenora glanced at Mrs. Rutledge, who had volunteered to serve the refreshments, and the two exchanged a smile. "The drawing tickets are at the counter. Tildy will be happy to help you. And remember, you get one just for coming in and a second because you're purchasing the book."

The next two hours flew as she assisted one customer after another. At eleven Mrs. Rutledge and Tildy left to see to dinner, leaving Elenora on her own. If she'd known what a success her first morning would be, she would have asked Tommy and Timmy to help. They knew her wares quite well now. However, since other women would need to get home, too, she should be able to handle things on her own.

By a quarter after eleven, the shop had cleared, and she could finally put away the bolts of fabric she'd not had time to tend to earlier. Her back was to the door when the bell chimed. She spun around. "Good morning, Abe. How may I help you?"

"I heard tell you have some new shavin' soaps from across the pond. I thought I'd take a look-see—or whiff, I should say."

She slid open the back of the display case and brought out three bars. One by one he passed them under his nose and inhaled deeply. From the spicy citrus to the pungent bay rum, every one brought a smile.

"I'll take one of each." He pinched his trousers above the knees, hitched them up, and squatted before the case. "Now, Ellie-nora, let me have a peek at that razor."

She pulled out the box and removed the cover. Abe straightened, took one look, and gasped. "I can't believe my eyes. That's a William Revitt with ivory scales. May I?"

"By all means." She'd looked forward to showing him the straightedge, but his reaction surpassed her expectations.

The barber rubbed his hands together, smiled, and picked up the razor. With practiced ease, he extended the blade and examined the elegant tool from every angle. "This has wonderful balance. And would you look at the detailed engraving on both ends of the handle? How much you askin'? Not that it matters. I got to have this."

She told him the price. Although it was steep, he didn't falter. She would make a tidy profit on the sale.

The day wasn't even half over, and her cash drawer was bulging. If things kept up like this, she'd have to stow some of the money elsewhere until she could get to the bank.

Miles peered out the window of his shop at the one directly across the street. Several more people entered, accepted the treats Ellie had used to tempt them inside, and made purchases. If things kept up like this, he'd have little to take to the bank.

The bell on the door rang, and he abandoned his post, where he'd spent far too much time keeping an eye on Ellie's place. "Morning, Mr. Colby. What can I do for you today?"

"I came for my pipe tobacco. You have it in stock, I hope."

"Right here." Miles reached in the case and pulled out a drawstring bag.

"You giving anything away?"

"I beg your pardon."

"She is." He jabbed his thumb at Ellie's shop. "I aim to win one of those fancy photographs of Mark Twain she's got. They're not like the little ones with the funny name I'm used to seeing either. Them pictures she has are as big as a slice of bread. You know what I'm talking about?"

"They're called cabinet cards, and they're over twice as large as a *carte de visite*."

"That's right. He's done signed 'em, too, just like those books of his she's selling. Don't know how she pulled it off, him being back in Buffalo and all."

"Buffalo?" Miles's heart plunged into his boots, which he'd had time to polish that morning, thanks to a certain shopkeeper drawing away his business with her ploys.

"Yes sirree. He got hisself a bride in February. Married her in Elmira and settled in Buffalo not far from my niece. She said in her last letter she's seen the two of 'em in town. Didn't you tell me once you have an uncle in those parts? Perhaps he's seen 'em, too."

"Could be." There was no perhaps about it. Uncle Marcus had no doubt taken the photograph of Twain in his studio—and asked him to sign the books. How could Mother have done this to her own son? Seeing her over at Ellie's serving as hostess earlier was bad enough, but helping her lure his customers away was quite another matter. He'd have a talk with Mother later.

He led Mr. Colby to the counter and told him the price of the smoking tobacco.

"Don't suppose you're offering a discount?"

"Why would I be? That's the price I've charged you for years."

Colby reached in his waistcoat pocket and pulled out a wooden disc that had been painted green. "Got this over to her place. She calls it a Tildy Token. Every time I go in and spend at least fifty cents, she'll give me one. When I get ten, she'll give me ten percent off one purchase."

"*What?* How can she do that?"

"I reckon she can do whatever she wants. So, you going to offer me a discount or not?"

He couldn't let Ellie steal his customers, but he wasn't so desperate that he'd follow suit. "I tell you what. If you'll buy a second bag of tobacco, I'll give you a box of safety matches—free of charge."

Colby grinned, revealing tobacco-stained teeth. "Well, now. I figured a sharp, young man like you would come 'round to my way of thinking."

Miles completed the transaction and ran his thumb and forefinger over his moustache. Ellie was going to be more trouble than he'd first thought. She was out to prove to that Grayson character she had what it took to be a valuable partner. Miles understood her goal and tactics. He admired her for them even. But she might put more of a dent in his profits than he'd anticipated.

She couldn't afford to cut her profits for long, though. He had reserves, which she didn't. He could survive the war, but would she?

And what would she think of his way of winning customers back to the mercantile?

Chapter 19

That's a lovely flower," Elenora remarked.

Mrs. Pratt was known for being free with her information. Perhaps the elderly woman would reveal where she'd gotten the gorgeous mauve bloom. Her husband was bedridden, so he couldn't have given it to her.

"Isn't it? Mr. Rutledge is giving a rose to every woman who visits the mercantile today. He said this one's called a Great Western. I chose it for both its color and rich perfume." She buried her nose in the flower and inhaled deeply.

He was giving away roses? To any woman who entered his shop? That explained why fewer women had stopped by her place that morning than during the first three days she'd been open. "How generous of him."

"And those of us who make a purchase receive a gift. Just look at this lovely creation." She pulled a handkerchief from the reticule on her wrist, a simple white version like those he sold, although Mrs. Pratt's had been embellished. Apparently Mr. Rutledge had begun to see the value of offering some of the finer things. That could pose a problem.

"He said his mother added the lace edge and embroidered the rose. Her work is exquisite, don't you think?"

"She's quite talented, yes." So Mrs. Rutledge was helping her son now? Well, that should come as no surprise. When she'd volunteered to contact her brother about getting Mark Twain's books autographed, Mr. Grayson hadn't made his offer. Now that she knew about him, she must have decided to shift her support to her son.

"If you paid him a visit, he'd have to give you a rose, too, wouldn't he?"

He had given her one. It lay upstairs between parchment sheets in her Bible, a reminder not to give in to him, no matter how charming he might appear.

When he'd handed her the rose that day in his garden and said those sweet words about how she'd opened his eyes to new possibilities, she'd come far too close to giving in to the pleasure of the moment. But then he'd spoiled the mood by saying she'd have to earn everything else she got.

As hurt as she'd been at the time, the message was one she mustn't forget. Mr. Rutledge might claim to be her friend—and indeed he had been kind to her on numerous occasions—but he was out to best her in business. Her task was clear. She must make use of every means possible to keep the customers on her side of the street if she were to show Mr. Grayson she was the best candidate for partner.

She couldn't afford to give way to sentimentality. Even if Mr. Rutledge did have the ability to make her forget herself at times.

Elenora ran a finger around the bowl, gathered the last bit of deviled egg filling, and popped it in her mouth. She'd added enough mustard to give it a nice tang. She put the filled eggs in the cut glass serving tray and placed them next to the bowl of coleslaw in her wicker basket. "Come Tildy. It's time to go."

They set off for their Fourth of July picnic at the Duprees' farm and arrived to a warm welcome. The children dashed off to play, and Elenora followed Pearl inside.

Her cheery kitchen smelled of fried chicken. White eyelet curtains framed the open windows, but there wasn't even a hint of a breeze to stir the air. Elenora took a seat at the kitchen table, pulled out her fan, and did her best to create enough of a breeze to bring some relief. "I can't believe you spent time over a stove in this heat, although we'll all enjoy the chicken. I boiled the eggs last night after the sun finally set."

"The first summer's the hardest, but you'll acclimate. Will chose a picnic spot under a cluster of oaks where we'll have plenty of shade. But enough about the weather. We only have a few minutes before we leave, and I want to hear what happened in Sacramento City. Will said Miles asked you to be his partner after all, but from what I can see, you're more intent on competing with him than ever."

"I met the sweetest man. He's about my father's age, but he's much different. He heard me talking with one of the vendors and struck up a conversation. We spent the rest of that day and the next together. He's considering making me a full partner in his mercantile up in Marysville."

Pearl covered the platter of fried chicken with a dishcloth and took a seat beside Elenora. "I've heard the scuttlebutt, so I know about the offer. I don't mean to pry, but is this man romantically interested in you? There are those who believe that may be the case."

Elenora laughed. "It sounds like you may have been talking to Mr. Rutledge. I think Mr. Grayson sees me more as a daughter. He lost his and has no one to leave his business to. He left his mercantile in the hands of his clerk and has been traveling throughout the Gold Country seeking just the right person. From what he's said, I could be the one. He's going to come up here and visit my shop, so I'm doing everything I can to build the business."

"I can understand how attractive his offer is, but I wouldn't want to see you rush into anything. I suggest you pray about it and listen for the Lord's leading."

"I'll pray, but I've never really heard from God the way some do, although I wish I did. It would make things clearer."

"He speaks in a number of ways. You could ask Him to communicate with you in one you'd recognize. And now if I can ask you to make the lemonade, I'll slip into the dining room and get a tablecloth."

Elenora grabbed a plump lemon, cut it in half, and mashed it onto the juicer. The clean scent of the fruit chased away the odor of fried chicken, and a refreshing mist from the rind settled on her. She gave a good squeeze, and a stream of juice shot into her eyes. She closed them, groped for a dish towel, and swiped at her moist face.

Heavy footfalls sounded as someone crossed the room. "I didn't expect my arrival to bring you to tears."

She dropped the cloth, opened her eyes, and blinked until the stinging subsided.

Mr. Rutledge picked up the towel, dabbed at the tears streaming down her cheeks, and increased the temperature in the room with his radiant smile. "Tears of joy, I hope."

"But of course. There's nothing I like better than spending time with the man who wants to put me out of business."

He chuckled. "And I cherish the opportunity to share the holiday with the woman determined to bring me to my knees in an admission of defeat."

Why must he be so charming? Doing battle with him would be easier if he didn't have the ability to unsettle her with his ready laugh, blinding smile, and easy manner.

Will pushed himself from the blanket spread on the leaf-strewn ground and patted his stomach. "You ladies certainly outdid yourselves. I won't need to eat for a week."

Pearl laughed. "You say that now, my love, but I suspect you'll be the first to ask when supper's ready. You do like your meals."

"I like the cook." He dropped a kiss on her forehead.

Miles smiled. Will and Pearl had something special. Something he and Irene had never had. Something he wanted. His gaze wandered to Ellie, who swiped the back of a hand across her forehead and blew a breath over her face. The heat must be hard on her. Those not accustomed to temperatures that hovered around the century mark for days on end often suffered.

Unlike many who dressed too warmly their first summer, she'd chosen wisely. The dotted Swiss with its navy spots and the red bow at her throat were fitting for the day, but he preferred her in purple with the cluster of silk violets at her throat. The color suited her—regal and elegant.

Ellie was a beautiful woman, but she didn't seem to realize that. Unlike Irene, who'd fussed over her appearance, Ellie didn't seem overly concerned with hers. She sold fancy hair combs, ear-bobs, and the like, but she didn't indulge in such things herself, which he preferred.

The children were absorbed in a game of tag. Mother sat in the chair Will had brought along for her and dozed. Pearl began clearing the remnants of their picnic dinner, and Ellie jumped up to help.

Miles joined Will at the wagon and helped load it for the trip back to the farmhouse.

"I'm glad you decided to accept Pearl's invitation, my friend."

"Couldn't resist. Her fried chicken is the best in El Dorado Township."

"You came for the chicken, did you? I thought it was the company." Will inclined his head toward Ellie and grinned. "When are you going to wise up and go after what you want?"

"She's intent on—"

"Beating you in business? I know."

"On leaving."

Will put the last basket into the wagon. "Leaving? Yes, Pearl mentioned that. What's the story?"

Miles told Will about Grayson's offer. "How can I stop her? It's what she's always dreamed of."

"There's more to life than business. I'm not a rich man, but I have what matters most." Will held out a hand to Pearl, who stood with their three children gathered around her. "If you've seen what you want, don't let it get away."

Miles mulled over Will's comment all the way back to the house.

Tildy rushed up to Miles. "It's time for my lesson now, isn't it, Mr. Rutledge? *Please*, say it is. I've been real good and haven't pestered you, have I?"

"You've been very good. Let's get that new saddle and get this lesson underway."

The next hour was one of the best he'd ever spent. Tildy was an apt student—bright, eager, and teachable. Before he knew it, she was ready to go off with the Dupree children on her first ride. He hated to see the lesson end. Will was right. There was more to life than working, but could he convince Ellie of that before it was too late?

Miles returned to the paddock and reined in his mount.

"Remember everything I told you, and listen to Paul. He won't let you get into any trouble."

"I will." She rode over to Ellie, who stood in the shade of the barn. "Don't I look like a real Western girl, Mama? All I need is a cowboy hat like the sheriff wears."

"You look lovely, dear. Have a good time, but—"

"Be careful. I know."

Paul, the Duprees' eldest child, rode up and beckoned Tildy to follow him. She was off in a flurry of dust.

Miles closed the gate and watched them leave. "She'll be fine, Ellie. I've never seen anyone take to riding as quickly as she did. She's a natural, and my mare is a docile creature."

"I'm trusting you on this."

Nothing she said could have meant more to him. Now to see if he could get her to have a little fun of her own while Tildy was away. "I need to care for my horse, but how would you like a ride on the swing afterward? I could push you."

"I—I don't know. I haven't swung since I was Tildy's age."

"Did you like it?"

She nodded enthusiastically. "You might not believe it, but I was quite brave back then. I used to love to jump out. I would imagine I was a bird soaring over the countryside."

"Then it's high time you took flight again."

Miles made short work of grooming his horse, led Ellie to the swing, and pushed her. Once he got her so high that he could no longer reach her, she pumped.

He leaned against the trunk of the sturdy oak and savored the sight. When she extended the endpoint of her arc to where the seat bounced, she straightened her arms, threw her head back, and ceased pumping. How captivating she looked, with her skirts fluttering about her ankles and sheer pleasure curving her lovely mouth into a wide smile.

She gradually slowed and leaned forward, focused on the ground before her. He positioned himself far enough in front of her so he'd be ready to catch her when she made her flying leap. She let go of the ropes and hit the ground running—right into his arms.

Ellie pressed her palms against his chest and gave him one of her sweetest smiles, the kind that turned his knees to applesauce and gave him a hunger for more. Much more.

He angled his head and lowered it, anticipation surging through him. How he'd waited for this. Just before he reached her lips, he closed his eyes and kissed—

Her cheek?

Yes. She'd turned her head at the last minute.

"Mr. Rutledge, please."

"I thought you wanted it. You smiled."

She pushed away from him and took a step back. "If I did— and I may have—I didn't mean it as an invitation. I have to think about my future. I'm a mother with a daughter to provide for. I can't get involved. Please. I need to go inside." She headed to the farmhouse, pausing to look over her shoulder and cast him a glance that said more than all her words combined.

Ellie could protest all she wanted, but she was attracted to him, too. He was sure of that. And one day he'd kiss her and weaken her knees so that she'd cling to him, her resistance gone as she lost herself in the pleasure of the moment.

Elenora pulled Tildy's door closed and paused by her own bedroom. Much as she wanted to lose herself in slumber, her mind raced. She'd played all her favorite pieces, and yet not even her music had been able to soothe her.

Settling on the small sofa in her pillbox of a parlor, she gazed at Rutledge Mercantile, which was bathed in moonlight. The impressive structure reminded her of its owner. The building towered over those on either side, as he did most people in town. Large uniform gray blocks formed at the nearby quarry and two rows of evenly spaced windows presented a polished front reminiscent of his carefully tended appearance.

Any similarity might seem to end there, but she disagreed. The crazy quilt pattern of the rock sides brought to mind another aspect of Mr. Rutledge. While he worked to maintain an image of a man with his life in order, his private world was held together with much effort, in the same way the rocks were kept in place with plenty of mortar.

That day on the train when he'd told her about his daughter, he'd opened a window to his soul, however briefly. Pain had clouded his eyes and caused him to shudder, revealing how deeply he'd been affected by his tragic loss.

At the beginning of Tildy's riding lesson that afternoon, a flicker of sadness had passed over his face. Although his reaction was less intense than what she'd seen before, teaching her must have brought back memories of his daughter. He'd spoken May's name with great feeling, as though the very word itself was precious. Witnessing his agony had drained Elenora—and planted a desire to know what had happened to his family. If she found out, perhaps she'd understand him better.

His sadness had been fleeting, though. What followed as he'd focused on Tildy could only be described as happiness. No. Not happiness. Joy. He'd radiated it. And her daughter was the reason. Mr. Rutledge and Tildy had formed a special bond, although that bond would make it hard for Tildy when it came time to leave El Dorado.

But it couldn't be helped. Mr. Grayson's offer would

enable Tildy to have everything she needed. Well, maybe not quite everything. She would miss her friends here, but children were resilient. She'd meet new people in time. Best of all, Mr. Grayson could become the warm, loving grandfather she'd never had.

Elenora left her post at the window and settled on the sofa. Who was she fooling? Leaving El Dorado would be hard on her, too. The people here had accepted her. Many of them had gone out of their way to help her. Mr. Rutledge especially.

But she couldn't give him what he wanted. Pushing him away when he'd tried to kiss her after she'd jumped from the swing and ended up in his arms hadn't been easy, but she'd had no choice. Giving in to the temptation to feel his lips on hers would bring nothing but trouble. She must remain firm. Tildy's future depended on it.

Elenora wrapped her arms around her knees and stared at the candle's flickering flame. It sputtered, and a drop of wax plopped on her Bible. She blew on the spot until it hardened, removed it with her thumbnail, and clutched the leather-bound volume to her chest.

Pearl's suggestion came back to her. Perhaps if she were clearer about what she wanted, she would actually hear from the Lord. She could certainly use some guidance.

She dropped to her knees beside the sofa and whispered her petition. "Lord, You know I have difficulty sharing my struggles with You, but I come on behalf of my dear girl. I want to do what's best for her, but sometimes I'm not even sure what that is. I must not listen well, because I've never heard from You the way others do. If You would make Yourself known to me and give me direction, I'd be grateful."

Even though God seemed as distant as ever, perhaps He'd hear her plea this time, especially since she'd used everyday language and talked to Him like He was a caring friend the way Mr. Rutledge did.

Miles unlocked Rutledge Hall and stepped inside. "Whoa!" The place was hotter than Tiny's forge. The musicians at tonight's rehearsal would be mighty uncomfortable unless he got some airflow going. He left the door ajar and hurried to open the windows, a task he should have seen to hours before.

"Good evening, Mr. Rutledge."

Ellie was early. He raised the last window and turned to face her. "Evening."

They hadn't been alone since he'd attempted to kiss her. Because she'd assumed her businesslike manner, he had no way of knowing what she was thinking. That put him at a disadvantage, a place he didn't like to be. He'd wait for her to say something so he could gauge her mood.

He lifted his violin from its case and began tuning it. She did the same.

"Oh no!"

He spun around. "What is it?"

"I broke my E string."

"Do you have one?"

"Of course I do. I sell them, remember?"

Her competitive spirit was alive and well. "Just trying to be helpful."

"You've been helpful all right. Overly so, if you ask me."

"What's that supposed to mean?"

She threaded one end of the string through the tailpiece. "Nothing."

"When a woman says 'nothing,' she means something. Are

you talking about Tildy's riding lesson?"

"Not exactly."

Why couldn't she tell him what was bothering her instead of forcing him to pull it out of her? Perhaps if he acted as though it didn't matter, she'd say what was on her mind. That tactic had worked with Irene. "It'll be interesting to see what pieces Mr. Morton has selected for the fall concert."

She fed the other end of the string through the peg and gave it two turns. "I hope there's something by Handel. I'm fond of the Overture to Alcina. Do you have a preference?"

If he hadn't known her as well as he did, he might have believed she was totally engrossed in her task. One corner of her mouth twitched, though, which meant she was doing her utmost to keep her smile from escaping but having a hard time of it. "I prefer something that moves right along, such as Mozart's Serenade No. 13 in G Major."

"Since you're a *fiddle* player, I can understand your preference for lively music."

She was good. Irene would have given in by now—or lashed out at him—but Ellie had changed the rules and was teasing him instead. He rather enjoyed it. But if she didn't tell him what she'd meant by that comment about his helpfulness soon, he'd be forced to admit defeat and ask her again. "I like folk and classical music, but I understand not everyone is able to appreciate both. Perhaps those who don't embrace fiddling are afraid they might have fun."

Her hands stilled, and the note she'd just plucked faded. Several seconds went by before she spoke, and when she did her voice sounded as flat as her instrument. "I don't really have time for fun, Mr. Rutledge. And when I do make the attempt, it can lead to trouble, like it did the other day."

Finally. Now he knew what was bothering her. "You're

talking about when I pushed you on the swing, aren't you? Or what it led to."

"Nothing happened."

Judging by the flush on her cheeks, she knew that wasn't exactly true. "It could have." If things had worked out the way he'd planned, it would have. But she had a habit of thwarting him at every turn—in business and pleasure.

She clutched the violets at her throat. "No. It mustn't. Surely you can see that."

All he could see was how lovely she looked with the added splash of color on her pretty face and her dark eyes peeking at him through lowered lashes. He ought to be a gentleman and assure her nothing would happen, but he wouldn't give his word when he knew he might not be able to keep it. "I can see that you need some time. You also need to tighten that string, so I'll leave you to it."

"Yes. Leave me be. Please."

A steady stream of Musical Society members filled the stuffy room. While they tuned their instruments, Mr. Morton sorted through sheet music. Promptly at seven he raised his baton, and they ran through their scales. Once he'd had a few members make adjustments and was satisfied, he addressed the musicians.

"I've chosen the music for the fall concert." He read the names of three pieces, two of which Miles was familiar with, and then he paused. An expectant hush fell over everyone.

"The final selection will be Bach's Double Violin Concerto. I gave a good deal of thought to my choice for the two soloists. Most of you would agree that Miles Rutledge is an exemplary musician and won't be surprised that he'll take one of the spots. The second will go to our newest member, Mrs. Elenora Watkins, who is also exceptionally talented."

Ellie's bow clattered to the floor.

Chapter 20

Elenora reached for her bow and sat up so fast her head swam. No. Righting herself so quickly wasn't the reason. Mr. Morton's announcement had caused the world to spin. She'd best breathe deeply and steady herself, because she wasn't about to swoon in front of a roomful of men. And not just any men. Her fellow musicians, among them several violinists who might not be happy she'd garnered one of two solos.

A loud clap rang out, followed by several more, and then every one of the members was applauding for her and Mr. Rutledge. She dared not look at him. The others might be willing to show her support, but after their earlier exchange, he might not be in as generous a mood.

"Congratulations!" His rich voice held a note of surprise.

He held out his hand as one man would to another. She extended hers. Although his firm handshake was a perfectly acceptable gesture given the circumstances, heat raced to her cheeks with the speed of a runaway locomotive. His touch brought back memories of his near kiss at the Duprees'—memories she was trying hard to forget. "The same to you."

He leaned close. "We'll have to work together on this. Are you up for that?"

"Why wouldn't I be?"

He smiled. "Thought you might feel a need to prove that you're as good a violinist as I am."

She cast him a sidelong glance. "I don't have to prove that. I am."

The room quieted. Mr. Morton set them to work on the first selection and assigned both Mr. Rutledge and her to second violin. She did her utmost to play flawlessly, but she was unfamiliar with Schubert's symphony and missed a few notes the first time through, as did several others, including Mr. Rutledge.

Mr. Morton wanted them to get an introduction to the four works they were to perform, so he had them move on to the second. She relaxed. Her instructor in Omaha had helped her with Bach's Air from Suite No. 3 not long before she'd left for California. The gentle strains flowed from her fingertips, whereas Mr. Rutledge struggled. Each time he faltered, she fought the urge to smile.

"And now, gentlemen and Mrs. Watkins, we'll make Miles's evening and try our hands at the first movement of Mozart's *Eine kleine Nachtmusik*."

She ventured a glance at Mr. Rutledge. Sure enough, he looked as happy as Tildy did when a new wanted poster went up in the sheriff's office. Something told Elenora that Mr. Rutledge had played the serenade before, which she hadn't, although she'd heard it performed. If memory served her, the tempo was brisk. She scanned the sheet music on the stand. The first movement was allegro, which would keep her fingers busy. She'd need to keep her focus on her playing and not allow herself to be distracted by the man beside her.

Despite her good intentions, she was unable to ignore him. The music flowed from him as freely as words from Tildy. Elenora concentrated, but the further into the piece they got, the tighter her neck and shoulders became. She must stop this or—

She squeaked.

It took every ounce of willpower she had to forge ahead as if nothing had happened. How she made it to the end she didn't know, but it came at last. She'd never been as eager to lower her violin. Hopefully her fellow musicians would overlook her mistake.

Mr. Rutledge whispered in her ear. "Don't worry. Once you've had some practice, it'll come easier."

How dare he act as though he was a virtuoso when he'd fumbled his way through Bach's Air? With her mouth clamped shut to keep from spewing some spicy words, she took a number of shallow breaths, which did nothing to calm her. She parted her lips and filled her lungs three times before she could focus on Mr. Morton's instructions.

"I realize I'm rushing you tonight, but since it's unusually warm, my goal is to end our practice early."

It was beyond warm. It was downright hot. The temperature at the front of the mercantile had still registered ninety-five degrees when she'd checked it on her way to the rehearsal at a quarter of seven. Her undergarments stuck to her, and she could feel moisture on her forehead. Some of the men had been mopping their brows with their shirtsleeves, but a lady couldn't indulge in such behavior. Her only option was to pull out her lace-edged handkerchief, even though such an action would draw attention to her as the lone female. As damp as she was, she had no choice. She'd just have to endure any teasing that came her way. She dabbed her forehead.

"Miles. Mrs. Watkins. I'd like you two to come up front, and we'll have a go at the concerto. Shall we?"

She rose, and the viola player across the row did the same. He grabbed her stand and moved it into position. "Here you go, ma'am."

"Thank you." Perhaps there were advantages to being the only woman after all.

Mr. Rutledge took his place, and she stood facing him. The

next few minutes were her opportunity to redeem herself. She kept her eyes glued to the music in front of her and made no attempt to look at him while she played.

The accompaniment faded, and she realized the only sound was coming from her instrument. She ceased playing. Everyone was looking at her. A shiver rippled down her spine, and she came close to swaying.

"Mrs. Watkins?"

"Yes?" She gave Mr. Morton her full attention.

"It's customary for a musician to watch the conductor."

"I know—I mean, yes sir. I understand."

He started them at a point several measures before the one where she'd finally stopped playing. Why had it taken her so long to notice she was no longer accompanied? She couldn't think about that now. She must concentrate on the music, on Mr. Morton, but *not* on Mr. Rutledge. If she were to look at him, she'd think about other things. Things not at all related to the music. Things like how nice it had felt to be in his arms, and how close he'd come to ki—

She jerked her thoughts back to the piece, making sure to cast frequent glances at the conductor.

Mr. Morton lowered his baton a short time later, and she and the orchestra came to a discordant halt. He shook his head, stepped from his platform with his arms folded and brow furrowed, and crossed the stage until he stood between Mr. Rutledge and her. He spoke softly but with a firm tone.

"I chose you two because you have the ability to do a fine job. However, I'm at loss to understand what's going on. The concerto works because of the interplay between the two soloists. The violinists chase one another at times. At others they play in unison. It's a team effort, one that will require you to work out your differences, whatever those may be. I know we're just beginning to learn the piece, but I want you to put forth your best effort. And I want you to look at one another. You can't play this concerto without doing so. Have I made myself clear?"

Elenora trembled. "Yes, sir."

Mr. Morton returned to his platform, told them where to begin, and raised his baton.

She did her best to divide her attention between the music, Mr. Morton, and Mr. Rutledge, but the room began to spin. She couldn't hear the others. The phrase "Have I made myself clear?" echoed in her fuzzy mind. Mr. Morton, with his full face and spectacles, didn't look a thing like Pa, but he'd sounded exactly like him when he said that.

Her trembling intensified. Her body was wet and cold. Her knees were melted wax. She mustn't faint. If she did, her violin could be damaged.

She sank to the floor and sat in a crumpled heap, clutching her violin with one hand and her churning stomach with the other.

Miles shoved their music stands aside and dropped to his knees. "Ellie, what's wrong?"

She tilted her head and nearly toppled over. "I—I don't know. I feel s–s–sick."

He wrapped an arm around her and pressed a hand to her damp forehead.

A chorus of concerned voices peppered him with questions.

"She's burning up." A quick check of her pulse told him her heart was racing. He scooped her in his arms and rushed to the door. "Hank, run over to the house and tell Mother to meet me in the garden with water and a cloth. We've got to cool her down."

"I'm on my way."

Miles tried not to joggle Ellie too much as he descended the stairs and crossed the alley behind his shop, but she was as limp as a rag doll, bouncing in his arms with each step. He shoved his way through the tall hedges that formed a border around his yard and made for the shade of the large oak tree, where he lowered himself to the bench beneath it with her in his lap, and cradled her to his chest. She smelled of rose water and rosin, sweet and woodsy.

He stroked her moist brow, which felt cool to the touch. The color had drained from her face. All were signs of heat exhaustion such as he'd seen on the wagon train during his trek to California.

"Mr. Rutledge?" Under different circumstances he would've enjoyed hearing her say his name in that soft, breathy tone. As it was, he'd prefer her usual direct manner of speech.

"It'll be all right, Ellie. You got overheated, but we'll get you cooled down. I need to loosen your collar." He held her with one arm, removed the silk flowers pinned at her throat, and reached for her top button.

"No!" She swatted at him.

"It's too tight. You've got to get some air."

The front door slammed, and Ellie jumped. "Tildy! Sh—she can't see me like this. Put me down. Now. *Please.*"

He didn't want to let her go. She was in a sorry state. And he liked having her in his lap. Very much. But if he continued to hold her against her will, she'd hold that against him. He set her next to him. She leaned against his side, and he resisted the temptation to wrap his arm around her.

Tildy sped across the yard. "Mama, Sheriff Henderson said

you almost fainted. Are you all right?"

"I will be, sweetheart, as soon as Mr. Rutledge takes me inside. I got too warm, and I need you and Mrs. Rutledge to help me cool off." Ellie jumped to her feet, but she teetered, grabbed his shoulder, and sank back onto the bench beside him.

Tildy reached out to steady Ellie. "I think you'd better let him carry you."

"She has a good idea. You're none too steady on your feet."

Ellie pressed her palms together and rested her chin between her thumbs and forefingers, looking as though she were praying.

Lord, she needs me, but I can't force myself on her. Please, let her accept my help.

She gave him a weak smile. "I'm doing a little better. If you'll support me, I think I can walk."

"Certainly." He stood and helped her to her feet. She wrapped her arm around his waist, and he put his around her, pulling her to his side. She fit perfectly.

Tildy supported her other side, and together they got her to the front stoop.

Mother met them with a pitcher in one hand and a basin and cloth in the other. She set them on the entry hall table and rushed over. "Elenora, you poor girl. Come inside, and we'll take care of you."

"I'm sorry to be a burden. I won't impose on you any longer than necessary." Her voice was still weak, but her independent streak was as strong as ever.

"It's no trouble, dear. It does my old heart good to be there for a body in need, especially one who's become like a daughter to me."

Mother patted his arm, motioned him to step aside, and traded places with him. "Son, you can go take care of things at the hall while Tildy and I see to Elenora. We'll have her right as rain again in no time, and then we can all have some dessert and a nice chat."

She started toward the parlor but cast a glance at him over her shoulder and gave him one of her knowing smiles. Mother had known all along what he'd been slow to realize. Ellie belonged here in El Dorado—with him. He just had to keep her from leaving.

The way he saw it, his best tactic was to keep Grayson from finalizing his offer and spiriting her away. And the best way to do that was to prevent Ellie from being so successful that she was sure to impress him.

Starting tomorrow she would have to redouble her efforts because things at the mercantile were about to change.

Elenora nestled in the corner of the settee in Mr. Rutledge's parlor half an hour later, a helping of caramel pudding on the end table beside her.

"Don't you want to try the pudding, Mama? I did most of the work myself. The only thing Mrs. Rutledge did was turn it out after it cooled."

Elenora ate a bite of the creamy dessert and set her bowl aside. Although she was no longer unsteady, her stomach was still unsettled, and the rich dessert didn't sit well. "It's delicious, dearest."

Tildy smiled an appreciative smile. "Mrs. Rutledge is going to teach me how to make gingerbread for the bake-off at El Dorado Day."

"I hadn't heard about that. When is it?"

Mrs. Rutledge's spoon clinked in her empty dish. She set

the items on a side table and joined Elenora on the settee. "The celebration, which we hold on the first Saturday in August, commemorates the summer of '56 when Miles and two other merchants constructed the first of our fireproof buildings. There are games, competitions, and a barbeque."

"It sounds like fun."

Tildy squeezed between them, her eyes bright. "She said it's almost as much fun as Placerville's Fourth of July celebration. And she wants you to help her plan things."

"Me?" Elenora clapped a hand to her chest.

Mr. Rutledge entered. "Were you missing these?" He set the two violins down, reached inside his jacket, and produced the violets he'd removed earlier, which he handed to her with a flourish. "Flowers for a lovely lady."

"Thank you." She took them, and her fingers brushed his, causing her to feel light-headed again. Keeping her distance from him was vital, because his every touch made her skin tingle. Although pleasant, she couldn't allow herself to lose sight of her goal. She needed to remain focused if she wanted to secure the offer from Mr. Grayson.

"You must be feeling better. Your color's returned."

"I am."

He took his place in his armchair and dug into his pudding. "This is right tasty." He ate a few bites and pointed his spoon at Elenora. "I owe you an apology."

"I don't understand." Surely he wouldn't mention the intimate scene in the garden when she'd been in his lap. It had been improper of him to suggest he unfasten her top button, but she'd set him straight, so no harm had been done.

"I forgot to open the windows in the hall this afternoon so the place could air out. Mr. Morton rarely cancels practice early, but it was like a furnace in there."

"Oh, that. I should have known better than to work so hard in this heat and neglect to take in liquids. I'll be more careful in the future. Thank you for getting my violin—and the flowers."

"The men send their well wishes, and Mr. Morton said he was sorry if his surprise contributed in any way."

Tildy sprang from the settee and stood beside him. "Surprise? What kind of surprise?"

"Your mama and I were assigned a duet, which we'll perform at the fall concert."

"Congratulations to you both." Mrs. Rutledge beamed. "What piece?"

He informed her, and she nodded. "That will call for plenty of practice."

"Yes, a great deal. He told me he'd like us to run through the concerto at least three times a day."

Elenora was in the process of pinning on her spray and poked herself. She shook her finger. "Together?"

"Is that a problem?"

"We're both busy people. I don't see why we can't rehearse our parts separately during the week and leave the joint sessions for the rehearsals."

Mr. Rutledge scraped the last bit of pudding, cleaned his spoon, and pushed his empty bowl away. "I think his request has to do with tonight's performance. You didn't exactly—how shall I say this?—make the best impression on him."

Tildy chimed in. "What happened?"

"Your mama. . ." He chased his thumbs around each other.

Elenora held her breath. There'd be no end to Tildy's teasing if he told her about the embarrassing mistake.

"I think she was feeling poorly and that affected her playing."

"Did she squeak?"

His twinkling eyes met Elenora's, and she released a shaky

breath. She'd just have to endure the jests.

He smiled and pulled Tildy close. "Squeak? Why yes, as a matter of fact she did, but what violinist hasn't at one time or another. What I wonder, though, is if I can make a certain young lady squeak." He tickled her sides, and she squealed with laughter.

"D–d–don't! St–stop!" She tugged at his hands.

"Don't stop, you say? All right." He tickled her once more, and she dissolved in a fit of giggles.

Elenora's eyes stung, and she studied the braided rug at her feet. Jake hadn't been able to enjoy his daughter, and Tildy had missed out on far too many moments like this. He hadn't valued the gift he'd been given. Mr. Rutledge, on the other hand, must have been a doting father. Look how good he was with Tildy. Perhaps someday she'd have a father like him.

The ache in the pit of Elenora's stomach didn't help her queasiness. She did her best to be a good mother, but the task of raising a child on her own was a lonely one. Surely there were nice men in Marysville who would make decent husbands— when the time came that she had a healthy bank account and could consider such a self-indulgent option.

Tildy's laughter subsided. "I'm going to enter the bake-off at El Dorado Day, and Mama's going to help with planning."

"She's doing what?"

Mrs. Rutledge intervened. "I'm busy with Tildy these days and haven't time to plan the events the way I did before. I thought Elenora would be an ideal choice to take my place, seeing as how she's one of the merchants." She grabbed Elenora's hand and gave it a squeeze. "How about it, dear? Will you take over for me?"

"I can't say. I don't know what's involved."

"Miles organizes three competitions for the men. You'd do

the same for the women. Will and Pearl take care of the games for the children, and a group from church arranges the barbeque. The whole town takes part in the fun."

Judging by how close Mr. Rutledge's brows had drawn, biding her time before answering would be wise. She reached for her water glass.

"Since I'm the one in charge of the entire event, Mother, don't you think it would have been wiser to talk to me about this first—privately? I don't like being put on the spot like this."

Elenora spluttered, spraying water down her front. How could he, who'd done that very thing to her in regard to the saddle, rebuke his mother? She had half a mind to tell him what she thought about his show of male dominance.

On second thought, perhaps showing him would be better. She patted herself dry, turned away from Mr. Rutledge, and faced his mother. "I think the project would be quite enjoyable. I could get some of the women to work with me, but I think it would be more fun for us to devise competitions for the men, and ask the men do the same for us."

"*What?* You can't be serious. I'm not about to discuss bake-offs and such with my committee. That's women's territory. And I certainly don't want a bunch of women putting their pretty little heads together and conjuring up competitions no man in his right mind would enter. I'm certain the others would agree. Why, if you had your way, you'd probably put us in frilly aprons and have us chop onions just to watch us cry."

She counted to ten in her head before she trusted herself to answer and pasted on the sweetest smile she could muster. "I would never dream of doing anything to endanger your masculinity. In fact, I feel certain we could come up with several ways to emphasize your strengths. My concern is that you men lack a real understanding of what we women are capable of and would be hard-pressed to come up with three contests that would showcase our abilities. So, are you willing to trust us or not?"

He shifted and helped Tildy out of his lap. Seconds passed as he stared into Elenora's eyes, his own a deeper shade of blue than she'd ever seen. She didn't blink, didn't move, didn't breathe. Just when she thought she couldn't last one moment more, he slapped his leg. "All right. I'll do it."

"I'm happy to hear that." Elenora extended her hand.

He shook it and grinned. "This year's event may prove to be more interesting than those in the past. You women had better work hard to come up with the best ideas you can because we men certainly will."

Tildy returned to the settee and slumped between Mrs. Rutledge and Elenora, who patted her daughter's back. "What's wrong, sweetheart?"

"Mrs. Rutledge said there's always been a bake-off for the ladies and a shooting match for the men. But now you're changing everything, and I won't be able to enter my dessert."

"Oh dear. I didn't think of that. Perhaps. . ." She sent Mr. Rutledge a silent plea for understanding.

"I tell you what, Tildy girl. Since El Dorado Day wouldn't be complete without those traditional events, we won't consider them part of the new arrangement. We'll each think up two new competitions. How's that sound?"

She was at his side in an instant, hovering over him. "Thank you."

He chucked her under the chin. "Have to keep my little friend happy."

Tildy's grin mirrored his. "I am happy. . .but you could make me even happier."

Elenora tensed. She should say something. She opened her mouth to do just that, but no words came out.

Chapter 21

Tildy trailed a hand along the arm of Miles's chair. "If you married my mama, you'd be my new papa, and I'd be the happiest girl in the whole wide world."

He stole a glance at Ellie. She'd been pale before, but her face now rivaled his white dress shirt, and her eyes couldn't open any wider. Mother's mouth twitched as though she were stifling a laugh. And Tildy wore a smile wider than the American River, her eagerness evident in her shining eyes.

What a picture the three painted: astonishment, amusement, and anticipation. And each of them had her attention focused on him. The pressure he'd felt when he'd preformed the Vivaldi solo was nothing compared to this. No matter what he said, he'd be hard-pressed to please them all.

Lord, I could use a wagonload of wisdom.

He pulled Tildy onto his lap. She cuddled up to him, filling him with longing for what he'd lost and giving him an idea how to solve his dilemma. "I want to tell you a story. It's not a long one, but it's true. I had a little girl once. Her name was May. She was born in May, and"—he swallowed—"she died in May a year later. I loved her very much." His voice broke, but he cleared his throat and forced himself to continue. "I didn't think I'd ever be able to open my heart again, but you found your way into it, Tildy girl. If I were to have another daughter some day, I hope she'd be as special as you."

Her eyes glistened. "Oh Mr. Rutledge, that was a sad, sad story. I'm sorry God took your baby away. But she's with Jesus now, and He'll take good care of her for you. I know He will." She cupped his face in her hands, pulled him toward her, and planted a kiss on his forehead.

The tender gesture nearly undid him. He held her close and soaked in the sugar and spice that was Tildy. If only he could tell her how much he loved her, but Ellie would never forgive him if he did. He'd promised her he wouldn't hurt Tildy, and he'd keep that promise—not only for Tildy's sake but also, more importantly, for Ellie's.

Her choices had forced him to fight her in order to earn his living, but he wanted more than anything to bring some happiness into her life. And he'd like some in his, too. It was about time.

He sought her gaze. She dipped her head in an apparent attempt to avoid looking at him. Was she upset with him? He'd tried so hard not to say too much, but— Wait. Were those— She swiped a hand over her cheeks. Yes. She'd shed tears for his daughter. Apparently he'd said the right thing to hers after all.

But would Ellie be as sympathetic when she learned he was to blame for May's and Irene's deaths?

Elenora smoothed her skirt. One petticoat would suffice. Practicality outweighed propriety in this case. There was no way she wanted a repeat of last night. She was sure to hear plenty of comments about her heat exhaustion, since the unfortunate episode had taken place in front of the entire Musical Society. On the bright side though, those who wanted to find out every little detail were likely to come into the shop, and some might make a purchase.

She peeked in the looking glass above her bureau, patted

her chignon, and prepared to face the day. The idea of being the source of hushed conversations behind gloved hands didn't appeal to her, but Mrs. Rutledge had assured her those prone to tittle-tattle would soon tire of the tale and move on to something else.

Elenora smiled. Mrs. Rutledge had been so kind and caring last night. And to think that she considered her to be like a daughter. After all the years without a mother, hearing those words had been wonderful.

"Mama, I'm ready. Mrs. Rutledge is going to teach me to play my first song on the piano today."

"I hope you have a good time, sweetheart." Elenora gave Tildy a hug, and her daughter flitted out the door.

An hour later Elenora pressed her lips together and pasted a smile on her face. Mrs. Rutledge might have been wrong. There were those who found the scene at the rehearsal a tantalizing bit of news. Mrs. Pratt had been in the shop since it opened, bending one set of ears after another. Since the pile of goods she intended to purchase continued to grow the longer she stayed, Elenora fought the urge to show her the door. What one would endure for the sake of a sale.

Mrs. Pratt sidled up to Mrs. Barton. "Did you hear about Mr. Rutledge and Mrs. Watkins? She fainted at his feet at the rehearsal last night, and he flew to her side, scooped her in those strong arms of his, and rushed out of the building with her—like a knight in shining armor. My Stanley said he'd never seen Mr. Rutledge more attentive of a lady. Isn't that the most romantic thing you've ever heard? It sets my old heart to fluttering."

Mrs. Barton gave a polite smile. "From what I heard she suffered from heat exhaustion, was wise enough to sit before she swooned, and accepted aid from Mr. Rutledge, who was the first to reach her." The kindly woman turned toward Elenora. "How are you feeling today, Mrs. Watkins?"

Elenora smiled warmly. How nice of Mrs. Barton to correct the misinformation. "I'm fully restored, thank you. Mrs. Rutledge was a dear and saw to my needs after her son helped me to the house. I'm grateful to both of them."

Another fifteen minutes passed before Mrs. Pratt made her purchase and left. Elenora took advantage of a lull to straighten her shop. She'd stooped to put away some hatpins when she caught the strains of a tune—a folk tune. Who would be playing on Main Street in the middle of the workday?

She walked to the open door and listened. The sound came from the mercantile. Mr. Rutledge stood in the front of his shop with his violin—fiddle—tucked under his chin. Half a dozen people encircled him, three of them clapping with the beat.

Three quarters of an hour went by, and not a single customer entered her place. He'd had a steady stream at his, and every few minutes he'd played a different tune.

With cloth in hand, she went out front and wiped some prints from the plate glass window. Tommy Talbot sat on the railing in the shade of the tall trees in front of Richwood House talking with the owner of the boardinghouse. Mr. Roussin was a model of patience. He never seemed to tire of Tommy's knot tying or Timmy's cat's cradle games.

Tommy glanced up, saw her, and waved. She beckoned him, and he sprinted over. "Morning, Mrs. Watkins. Did you need something?"

He pushed his curtain of blond hair out of his eyes and tucked several wayward strands beneath his hatband. They stayed put but a moment before tumbling down. Both he and Timmy were in desperate need of a trim, but since Tildy said she thought their long locks made them look like rugged mountain men, they'd refused to let Abe touch their shaggy manes.

Elenora put her back to the mercantile and lowered her voice. "A number of people seem to be enjoying Mr. Rutledge's music. Do you know why he's performing for his customers today?"

"I ain't heard anybody talking about it, but I could mosey on over and find out."

"I'd like to know, but I don't think having you go into his place and ask would be the best way to go about getting the information. He doesn't think as highly of you and Timmy as I do. I did see Mrs. Roussin come out of his place a few minutes ago though. Since you're on good terms with her husband, I thought you might—"

"I hear you. I'll ask him to find out from her and let me know. I'll be back in three shakes of a rattler's tail." He sauntered down the walkway, twirling his short piece of rope at his side.

Elenora smiled. Anyone who saw Tommy would know he was up to something. He never *walked* anywhere.

Less than five minutes later he ambled across the street, peered over his shoulder, and slipped into her place. "Here's the story. He's got a contest going. Anyone who buys a whole dollar's worth of goods gets to name a fiddle tune. If he can't play it, the person gets to pick out a nickel's worth of candy and don't have to pay for it."

"My, my." Mr. Rutledge had come up with a clever idea. "I think I'll get my violin and perform classical pieces. The first one to name the composer will get an extra Tildy Token."

Tommy frowned. "Um, not to throw a block of ice in the bathwater, Mrs. Watkins, but I don't reckon folks would be able to do that. Leastways, not many of 'em. I don't know any of them fancy tunes like the Musical Society plays, and my ma don't neither."

"I see. Well then, let me think." She tapped a finger to her cheek. "I've got it! We'll see if we can stump him." She'd have some fun, and at the same time she could show Mr. Rutledge what a bright young man Tommy was.

Ten minutes later Elenora locked the door to her shop, crossed the street, and entered the mercantile. She stood back from the group gathered around Mr. Rutledge and studied him. When he played classical pieces, he rested his weight on the balls of his feet, swayed from side to side with grace, and had a serious expression on his face. His stance when he fiddled was entirely different. When he wasn't tapping one foot or bouncing on the balls of both feet, he was moving his upper body forward and back in time to the music. And throughout the entire performance a broad smile conveyed his immense pleasure. He was not only a talented musician. He was also a versatile one.

She hadn't been in his shop in weeks, so she cast furtive glances around the place. He had an impressive display of ready-made men's clothing on the far wall that hadn't been there before. He'd added to his fabric selection and replenished his supply of notions. And he had an array of merchandise in a case bearing a card that read "Golden Gifts," which, as she'd heard tell, were part of his new program to reward repeat customers.

While the clothing and expanded dry goods section were welcome changes, giving away staples such as soap flakes, harness oil, and moustache wax wouldn't do much to draw the townspeople in. They'd be more interested in earning a Tildy Token for purchasing the vest chains, watch charms, and handkerchief boxes she'd received in her latest shipment.

Tommy arrived. He conferred with Sammy, completed his purchase, and kept his back to Mr. Rutledge.

He finished the piece and grinned at Elenora. After he bid the customers farewell he joined her. "What brings you to the mercantile today? Couldn't find what you need at the shop across the street?"

"I'm broadening my horizons. A friend of mine said I might enjoy fiddle music, so I thought I'd see if that's true."

He chuckled. "A friend of yours? I see. And was this friend correct?"

She wouldn't give him the satisfaction of knowing how hard it had been to keep her foot from tapping. "Perhaps, but I've not heard enough to know yet."

"Spend a dollar, and you can challenge me to play a piece." He held up his violin. "If you stump me—"

"I get some candy, I know. But since I do my shopping on the *north* side of Main, I won't be able to test you."

Tommy spoke up, right on cue. "I can." He pointed to his parcel on the counter. "I'd like you to play Air from Suite No. 3 by Johann Sebastian Bach."

"You would, would you?" Mr. Rutledge glanced at Elenora. The tell-tale twitch of his moustache told her he knew very well why Tommy had chosen that particular piece, the one Mr. Rutledge had stumbled over at the Society's rehearsal. "Well, Timmy, I—"

"I'm Tommy."

Mr. Rutledge fixed his penetrating blue eyes on Tommy, but the young man didn't flinch. He drew himself to his full height, thrust out his chest, and met Mr. Rutledge's gaze. Elenora's own chest swelled with pride. Her protégé was performing admirably. Surely Mr. Rutledge would see that Tommy was no mere boy.

"As I was saying, Tommy, I believe you've been counseled by someone unfamiliar with the rules of the contest. You have to name a fiddle tune, not a classical piece."

Tommy smacked a hand to his forehead. "That's right. Mrs. Watkins is the one who's performed the composers' works for her customers." He paused to give his comment its full impact, just as she'd asked him to. Mr. Rutledge's half-smile confirmed that he was well aware of her attempt to best him at his own game and found it amusing.

She'd not coached Tommy beyond that point, so he improvised. "I reckon you thought she had a good idea, seeing as how you're using it yourself. 'Course, your fiddle music is more to my liking than what she plays. Do you know 'Camptown Races'?"

Mr. Rutledge actually grinned at Tommy, and Elenora savored the sweet taste of victory. Her obvious goal to beat Mr. Rutledge in his contest may have failed, but he was treating Tommy with more respect than usual. Had Mr. Rutledge overcome his distrust of Tommy and his brother? "She didn't tell you to pick that one, did she?"

Tommy glanced at Elenora. She waved a hand. "We've had our fun. You may tell him."

"She said I could pick my favorite, and that'd be it. Timmy and I like to race."

"I'm well aware of that. You should be grateful Mrs. Watkins is a forgiving person. There are those who believe you two should have received a more severe punishment."

She must intervene, or no telling what Tommy would say. He could be as outspoken as Tildy. "If you don't mind, I'd like to hear the tune Tommy chose."

Evidently Mr. Rutledge still had misgivings about the Talbot twins. Somehow, she'd find a way to convince him they weren't the troublemakers he believed them to be.

Elenora reached the cemetery at the top of Church Street. For some reason, once she'd seen Tildy and the Duprees off after church, she'd felt led to climb the hill and pay a visit to the Rutledge plot.

There were those who insisted God spoke to them. A still, small voice was what some called their encounters. Others reported actually having heard Him, as though He'd spoken audibly. That was poppycock as far as she was concerned. She'd never heard God tell her anything, even though she'd heeded Pearl's advice and asked Him to make Himself known to her. She was here because she felt the need to be, and nothing more.

She reached for the latch on the wrought-iron gate, jerked her hand away, and stuck her fingers in her mouth. How silly of her to forget that the black metal would be hot. It was a blistering summer day after all.

By wearing a lightweight lawn dress she hoped to avoid another incident of heat exhaustion. She didn't dare risk finding herself in Mr. Rutledge's strong arms again. Her pulse had skittered like a scared rabbit when he held her. She'd practically melted when he murmured words of reassurance in a tone as soft and soothing as a mother crooning to her newborn babe.

Or an adoring father to his beloved daughter.

What would it be like to rest in the arms of her heavenly Father and feel His love surround her? To know she was wanted, treasured even?

Using a stick to lift the latch, she let herself into the cemetery and scanned the well-tended grounds in search of the Rutledge plot. When she spotted a twelve-foot-tall marker with its slender marble obelisk mounted on a massive granite base, she was certain she'd found what she was after. Nestled beneath a towering cedar at the far end of the grove, the impressive monument towered over all the others. Mr. Rutledge had spared no expense. He'd obviously loved his father deeply.

She strolled down the path to the plot, her boots making

no sound on the hard-packed earth.

As she'd suspected, the pillar belonged to Mr. Rutledge's father. She read the inscription aloud: "Mark David Rutledge. Beloved Husband and Father. Died 1867. Aged 62 years, 7 months, 4 days. Born in New York." Above the words an etching of a hand pointed to a Bible.

Her gaze shifted to a pair of matching marble headstones to her left. She stepped over the low border surrounding the plot, knelt on a bed of leaves in front of the first marker, and clutched the sides of the cool slab. She blinked to clear moisture from her eyes and forced the words past the boulder lodged in her throat. "May Rose Rutledge. My Beloved Daughter. Born May 7, 1861. Died May 13, 1862." A single rosebud had been etched above them, a poem below.

> There's a void, a painful void,
> That nothing here can fill.
> You are home in Jesus' arms,
> And yet my heart aches still.

Even though she squeezed her eyes shut and took several rapid breaths, a tear trailed down her cheek. She swiped it with a sleeve, released her grip on the first stone, and moved to the next, one with no inscription or ornamentation except the showy script used for the name. "Irene Anne Rutledge. Died May 13, 1862. Aged 22 years, 2 months, 3 days."

He'd loved his daughter and made a public declaration of the depths of his grief, but his memorial to his wife gave no evidence of feeling. Why was that?

A squirrel scampered through several of the plots, stopped, and rummaged through a pile of leaves in search of acorns. Another of the bushy-tailed creatures darted over and chased the first up a nearby tree, scolding loudly all the way. Elenora smiled. How silly of the animals to fight over a single nut when the ground was littered with them.

Despite the heat, a rush of goose pimples swept over her. She'd been guilty of the same thing, doing battle with Mr. Rutledge on a daily basis. But in their case the competition was real. There were only so many customers in El Dorado, and if her business was to succeed, she had to solicit their patronage.

She took a seat on the hard concrete border, brushed crunchy brown leaves from her skirt, and studied the plot. It could use some attention. Those she'd passed were well tended, whereas this one was littered with debris and a healthy crop of weeds. Mr. Rutledge took such care of his garden, but for some reason he'd neglected his family members' resting place. Perhaps he hadn't noticed the decline.

Or he didn't visit the site.

Her visits to Mama's grave had brought her comfort. But if Mr. Rutledge hadn't dealt with his heartache and found healing, the place could serve as a reminder of things he'd rather forget. That was true in Pa's case. Once the graveside service for Mama was over, he'd never returned to the churchyard—or the church.

Elenora tugged on an obstinate thistle. Her efforts rewarded at last, she reached for a shriveled dandelion but stopped. As much as she longed to see the plot restored to rights, the task wasn't hers to perform.

The front door of the mercantile banged shut, and hurried footfalls heralded Tildy's approach. Her words rushed out between noisy puffs. "Mr. Rut. . .ledge, I have. . .something fun. . .to show you."

"Take a minute to catch your breath, Tildy girl." Miles rested a hand on her shoulder. "You've been racing around, haven't you? Those cheeks of yours are looking quite rosy this morning."

She nodded enthusiastically, setting her braids to bouncing.

"What did I tell you about exerting yourself when it's so hot? I don't want you to suffer from the heat the way your mama did."

A mischievous twinkle lit Tildy's bright blue eyes. "It wasn't so bad. You got to put your arm around her, and I think you liked it, didn't you?"

"I think, young lady, that you ask too many questions sometimes."

She grinned. "It's true. I know it 'cause Mama says the same kind of thing when she doesn't want to answer me. But I don't mind, because it won't be long before I can call you something else."

"You're right."

"I am?" Her eyes were as big as the boiler hole on the stove he'd ordered for Mrs. Barton.

"When you said my name a minute ago, you couldn't get it out in one breath. So. . .I'm going to let you call me Mr. R. I don't let anyone else do that. It will be your special name for me. How's that sound?"

She pursed her lips and folded her arms over her chest. "That's not what I meant. I want you to be my papa. I told Mama, but she said I should be happy that you're my friend."

"I believe, my young friend, that you had something you wanted me to see."

She perked up. "That's right. You have to come over to Mama's shop. She got something special just for you."

"For me?"

"Uh-huh. C'mon." She grabbed his hand and pulled him toward the door.

"Whoa up there. I'm not going—"

"You have to. *Please.*" She tugged harder.

"I'm not going out in public wearing my apron. I need my jacket."

She paced while he changed. He took a quick look in the mirror, let Sammy know where he'd be, and followed her across the street.

Ellie had propped her door wide open, so she didn't hear them enter. Huddled over a fashion plate in one of those women's magazines he refused to carry, she seemed totally absorbed in Miss Crowley's every word. An older gentleman at the back of the shop pulled out one of Ellie's woman-sized shovels, examined it, and grinned. There was something vaguely familiar about him.

Tildy slipped behind the counter and tugged on Ellie's sleeve. She leaned over so Tildy could whisper in her ear, looked up, and smiled. "I'll be with you shortly, Mr. Rutledge."

He popped a lemon drop in his mouth and wandered to the rear of the shop, where the gentleman studied each item intently.

The fellow saw him, ceased his perusal of the treadle sewing machine on display, and joined him. She must have ordered more machines since their Sacramento City trip because the two that had arrived shortly after their return had been snatched up within days. One of them sat in Mother's bedroom in a place of honor, and the grocer's wife had the other. If Ellie had replaced both, that meant she'd sold three already.

"Good morning. I've not had the pleasure. Grayson's the name. Bartholomew Grayson." He extended a hand.

Miles nearly swallowed the candy. He tucked it in his cheek and shook Grayson's hand. "Miles Rutledge."

For an older man, Grayson had a firm grip. He smelled of pipe tobacco and hair elixir. He'd obviously taken pains to see that his salt-and-pepper locks were in place. Evenly spaced grooves gave evidence of careful use of a comb. One gray brow rose. "You must be the owner of Rutledge Mercantile."

"I am. And you must be the proprietor Mrs. Watkins met in Sacramento City."

"The very same. I was hoping to meet you. When I stopped by your place earlier, you were out. You've got a fine establishment, Mr. Rutledge. I couldn't help but notice, though, that business seemed slow at your place while Mrs. Watkins has been wearing her bootheels down waiting on folks. Pardon me for being outspoken, but El Dorado's a mite small to support the two of you, isn't it? You must be feeling the pinch."

He wasn't about to let this Grayson fellow know how his business was faring. "I'm doing fine."

Grayson clapped a hand on Miles's shoulder. "Of course you are. You've been here fifteen years. She's just getting started, although she has quite a knack for attracting customers. Folks seem eager to collect those Tildy Tokens. Clever idea, don't you think?"

"She's innovative, I'll grant you that, but I've got my own program going."

"Your clerk mentioned it, but between you and me, I think your customers are going to see through it."

Miles forced himself to take a deep breath and think about what he was going to say before he opened his mouth. If Ellie knew what he was doing, she'd admire his restraint. "I'm unclear exactly what you mean, Mr. Grayson. Would you be kind enough to enlighten me?" He fought the urge to smile. That had come out far better than he'd expected. Perhaps there was hope for him yet.

"The young man said that for every dollar I spent, I'd earn a Gold Country Gem, which I could cash in on selected items." He pulled one of the collection cards from his jacket pocket with two of the ten squares bearing the image of a gold nugget from the rubber stamp Miles had ordered.

"I see three drawbacks to your ploy. The first is the fact that you're copying her idea. Second, I have to spend twice as much at your place to get a Gem as I do to get a Tildy Token. Mrs. Watkins gives one out every time a customer parts with four bits. You do know that, right?"

Just what did Ellie see in this nosy fellow? "You said there were three things."

"Drawbacks. Yes, I did. The third is your downfall. I looked at your selection of Golden Gifts, and what you're offering is fool's gold. Getting a tin of axle grease or a cake of lye soap when I've filled my card is about as exciting as a tooth extraction. But if I were to see a fancy carved briarwood pipe or a fine leather tobacco pouch, you'd get my attention."

"I can't afford to give away pricey items like that, not unless a person were willing to stockpile the cards."

Grayson gave him a light punch on his arm. "That's the point, young man. Give them a reason to keep coming back. That's what she's doing. I heard her say that when a customer has saved ten tokens she'll give the ten percent discount on anything, even that sewing machine." He held out a hand to two women now examining it. "The savings might be just what it takes to convince a reluctant husband to get one for his wife. Mrs. Watkins would lose a portion of her profit on that sale, sure, but she'd still make good money. And talk about loyalty. That woman would be her customer for life."

This man was peskier than a swarm of aphids. Miles assumed his most commanding look, the one he reserved for cantankerous vendors. "She wouldn't have to worry about being successful over the long term if you talk her into leaving, though, would she? But she wouldn't be able to prove she can survive on her own either, which is very important to her. If you knew her as well as I do, you'd realize that."

"I would have thought you'd be eager to see her go. Your life would be a whole lot easier without the competition."

"I don't want to see her rush into something and get hurt."

Grayson smiled. His smile wasn't the shifty variety Miles often encountered when he visited certain disreputable wholesalers down the hill. The older man's conveyed sincerity, much the way Abe's did. But there was something else. Something disturbing.

"Neither do I. But she's capable of far more than she can achieve, given her current circumstances." Grayson cast a glance at Ellie, who'd finished her conversation with the longtime spinster and was talking with Tildy. "I can offer her a secure future for herself and that darling girl of hers—among other things." The admiration in his eyes wasn't that of a father for his daughter. It was that of a man captivated by a woman—in this case one far too young for him.

Miles crushed what was left of the lemon drop between his teeth. "Has she—"

"No. We're still working out the details. You'll have to keep up the fight a little longer, son, because I don't see her easing up. She's got spirit."

He'd fight all right. And pray.

Chapter 22

Elenora bid Mr. Grayson farewell and turned to find Mr. Rutledge staring at her, a scowl on his face. She'd hoped he would like her new friend, but apparently that wasn't the case. Well, she didn't need his approval. The decision was hers to make when the time came.

"I'm sorry I had to keep you waiting, Mr. Rutledge. Tildy's rather eager for you to see something that just arrived." She glanced at the two women examining the remaining sewing machine in the back of her shop and lowered her voice. "Something we think you'll be unable to resist."

He rewarded her with his ready laugh, which was a decided improvement, and she caught the faint scent of lemon. "You mean you invited me here to *shop*? In case you haven't noticed, I have ample wares right across the street."

"But you don't have this." Tildy pointed to a row of silver items. "A comb. See? You use one all the time, and Mama found a pretty one with a rose on it."

He lifted a brow and a corner of his mouth simultaneously, coming too close to a sneer for Elenora's liking. But he'd be smiling soon, she was sure of it.

She opened the display case, reached in, and withdrew the elegant set. She removed the pocket comb from its silver sheath and placed both items on a pad before him. With a sweep of her hand, she presented them to him.

Several seconds passed while he stared at the beautiful implement without saying a word. Tildy pushed the black velvet square closer to him. He smiled at her. Although it wasn't his happy smile, the one that had melted Elenora's resistance on numerous occasions, he was making an effort.

"Pick it up, Mr. R. Please."

He grasped the comb between his thumb and forefinger and acted as though he were making a thorough inspection. His smile drooped at the corners, but he was quick to restore it and nod as though impressed—which he clearly was not. He laid it down, picked up the cover, and ran a finger over the single bloom in the center.

Tildy raced around the counter and slid to a stop beside him. "You have to turn it over."

"Whatever you say, Tildy girl." He did as she requested. When he beheld the leaf-wreathed oval on the other side, his mouth fell open and his hand shook so that Elenora was grateful he had a firm grip on the expensive item.

"He's likes it, Mama! Didn't I you tell he would?"

"El—" Color crept from his crisp clean collar up his neck until his cheeks were aflame. "El. . .egant. It's elegant, Mrs. Watkins."

"Elegant?" She had to admire him for coming up with a word to cover his blunder. Had he called her Ellie in front of Tildy, all their efforts to discourage her flights of fancy would have been for naught. Elenora couldn't fault him for his mistake though. The blame fell on her. She should never have allowed him to call her by the nickname he'd given her, even though she felt special every time he did. She smiled.

"Yes, quite elegant," he said. "Would you help me out by reading it?"

Tildy quickly complied. "It says—"

"I'd like your mama to do it, if you don't mind."

What was he up to? Perhaps this was his way of letting

her know that he found the flowing script she'd chosen too feminine. The jeweler who'd engraved it for her had tried to persuade her to use a simpler font. She ought to have listened to him.

"Here! Give it to me." She snatched the comb cover from his hand, spun it around so the words faced him, and shoved it in front of his eyes. "Anyone can tell what it says. It's as clear as the glass in my new front window." She said each word slowly and distinctly. "Miles. David. Rutledge."

"What did you say?"

"Miles—" She dropped the silver sheath, which hit the soft pad and bounced. Thankfully she caught it before it struck the counter, sparing the comb cover damage.

"What is it, Mama?"

"He. . . He teased me. He really could read it." What an exasperating man. He'd tricked her into saying his Christian name and, judging by the width of his grin, was quite pleased with himself.

"Mind if I try the comb out?"

"Be my guest." She held it out to him. Instead of taking the free end, he clasped it in such a way that he was practically holding her hand. The instant she was sure he had a grip on the comb, she let go.

He sauntered to the looking glass mounted on the wall near the hat display and made an elaborate show of grooming himself, tilting his head this way and that until satisfied with his efforts. When he turned to face her with every hair in place, as had been the case when he started his playful primping, he wore his happy smile. He held up the comb. "I'll take it!"

The women in the back of the shop tittered. Elenora had forgotten about her customers. They might think her quite forward if she were to carry out her original plan, which was to give Mr. Rutledge the gift as a thank-you for the generosity he'd shown Tildy. After all, this was the kind of present a woman would give her intended. But since she didn't want tongues to wag—and since he'd been so nettlesome—she'd accept his payment.

He withdrew a money clip from his pocket, laid a banknote on the counter, and slipped the comb inside its cover. With the set clutched in his raised hand, he winked at Tildy. "You were right, my little friend. This is special. I never expected to buy any of your mama's fancy things, but this one had my name on it."

"Mama was going to have the man put M. D. Rutledge, but I told her you like all your names, so she should use them instead. Are you glad she did?"

He aimed his words at Tildy but his grin at Elenora. "Very glad."

The women had finished their trial of the sewing machine. The nosy one, Mrs. Pratt, planted herself in his path and pointed a finger at him, a gesture so rude Elenora swallowed a gasp. "Shopping at your competitor's place, Mr. Rutledge? Now I've seen everything."

Miles paused before the mirror in the back room of his shop and checked his hair. He slid the comb set into his jacket pocket and gave it a pat. If anyone had told him he'd proudly carry something as showy as that, he wouldn't have believed it. But Ellie had a way of knowing exactly what would appeal to a person. Abe couldn't stop talking about that new razor of his, and every time Mr. Morton removed his new ebony baton with the ivory handle from its case, he practically caressed it.

Ellie could be a handful though. She'd bristled like a cornered dog and yanked the comb out of his hand yesterday because he asked her to read his name. And that was before she'd realized what he was up to. But dealing with her huff had been a small price to pay in order to have her say it. Even in her pique, hearing his first name on her lips was music to his ears. If only he could convince her to use it. But try as he might, she insisted on keeping things formal.

That wasn't entirely true. She no longer looked liked she'd chomped into a dill pickle when he called her Ellie—as long as he didn't count the near disaster in front of Tildy yesterday. He'd come close to doing irreparable damage. Too close. He'd managed to catch himself, though—and make Ellie smile.

But he had more important things to think about. That Grayson fellow was a problem. He must be seriously considering offering Ellie the partnership—likely a more permanent one than she realized—since he'd come all this way to see her. Judging by the warm reception she'd given him, she was prepared to accept it.

Not that Miles could blame her. Grayson wasn't a bad sort. He'd shown that he knew Ellie quite well, spice and all. And anyone could see he was enamored with Tildy. He was shrewd, too. Giving her that five-dollar gold piece so she could buy a Stetson from the mercantile had earned him her gratitude. And Miles had to admit it had been a clever—albeit wasted— attempt to establish some goodwill with him, too, since Ellie didn't carry the popular felt hat.

Unlike Tildy, who'd been over to buy her cowboy hat without delay, he preferred a dignified derby. He grabbed his, set it carefully on his head so as not to disturb his hair, and donned his jacket. Ellie hadn't said a word about Grayson at dinner yesterday. Since her place was empty, now would be a good time to try and find out when she planned to make her decision.

Miles crossed the street, stepped onto the walkway in front of Ellie's shop, and stopped. He hadn't noticed the hand-lettered sign in her window from the mercantile, but there, in youthful scrawl, were the words, "Mr. Rutledge shops here."

That wasn't Tildy's writing, and it certainly wasn't Ellie's, but he had a good idea who'd put the message there. He stormed though the open door.

"Ellie, are you aware what's in your window?"

She wheeled around. "My sign. And perhaps a cobweb or two. I have a hard time reaching the ceiling, even when I stand on one of the stools."

"Come with me, would you?"

She followed him outside, took one look at the placard propped against the glass, and burst out laughing.

"It's not funny."

"Oh, but it is. Quite."

"You know who's responsible, don't you?"

She leaned over, studied the sign, and straightened. "Their writing is similar, but my best guess is Timmy. However, I doubt it was his idea. Tommy is usually the instigator."

"Aha! So you admit it? They are troublemakers."

"I hardly think a harmless prank like this is reason to slap a label like that on them. Come to think of it, this isn't even a prank. Merely a statement of fact. You *did* shop here."

"That wasn't why you got the comb, was it? To entice me into making a purchase?"

She turned away. "Won't you come inside? We can talk there without being overheard."

He followed her and took a seat on one of the stools. She removed the small sign from the window, laid it on the closest display case, and took a seat on the stool next to his.

"Mr. Rutledge—"

"Miles. Please."

"—I didn't intend for you to *buy* the comb. It was to be a gift, a way of thanking you for all you've done for Tildy. But there were customers in the shop, and I knew if word got out that I'd given you something so. . .personal, the gossip mill would grind out new stories. After the gibes and innuendo I endured in the days following the incident at the rehearsal, I didn't want to go through that again."

She was right. A woman only gave a gift like that to her betrothed. But Ellie had planned to give him the comb. That could only mean one thing. She did have feelings for him. She might not be ready to admit it, but he could hope that one day she would.

Mrs. Sanders considered a trip to visit her sister in San Francisco cause for new dresses, and she wanted fabric for a special one. "She's going to take me to the symphony, so I've got my heart set on a silk gown."

Elenora pulled out several bolts in a dazzling array of colors and arranged a selection of coordinating notions with each.

The matronly woman examined them and settled on the navy. "I think it would have a slenderizing effect. But I'm not at all fond of having silver or pearl buttons with it. I think a row of those down the front of the bodice could draw attention to my, um, full figure. If you have navy ones, I'll take the silk as well as the fabric for the other two dresses."

Navy buttons? Oh dear. She'd sold the last of hers the day before. But wait. She knew just where to get some. Although she didn't relish the idea of traipsing into the mercantile after

Mr. Rutledge had accused her of buying the comb to trick him into making a purchase, she wasn't about to lose the sale. Since it was Tuesday morning, she'd be able to dash over while he was at Abe's, and Mr. Rutledge wouldn't have to know about her visit. She checked the watch pinned to her bodice. Ten minutes to eleven.

"I don't want to keep you, Mrs. Sanders. You could tend to your other business and stop back by for the parcel this afternoon if you'd like."

"I'll do that."

Elenora waited until Mr. Rutledge disappeared into the barbershop, the mercantile was empty, and few people were about before dashing across the street.

The bell on the door rang, and his young clerk looked up. "Good morning, Mrs. Watkins. What can I do for you?"

"I'm after navy dress buttons."

"I'll show you what we have."

Sammy completed the transaction and handed her the small parcel, which she tucked in her reticule. "I'd appreciate if you don't tell Mr. Rutledge I was here."

She returned to her shop, packaged Mrs. Sanders's order, and waited on a customer.

At noon she locked her shop and set out for Mr. Rutledge's house, but something on the door of the mercantile caught her eye. Had he put up a poster advertising El Dorado Day? She stepped onto the walkway and read the notice.

FOR THOSE THINGS NOT AVAILABLE IN HER OWN STORE,
MRS. WATKINS RUSHES THROUGH THE MERCANTILE DOOR.

Mr. Rutledge stepped from behind a nearby wagon. "Are you laughing now?"

She shook her head and smiled. "Sammy assured me he wouldn't say anything."

"He didn't, but Miss Crowley, Mr. Olds, and Mrs. Pratt did."

"But the poem was your idea, wasn't it?"

He grinned, and those beautiful blue eyes of his twinkled. "Shall we head up the hill? Mother's got something delicious cooking. I've been smelling it the past hour."

"Mrs. Watkins!" Tommy bolted down the street waving something in his hand. He arrived and drew in several noisy breaths while Elenora waited. "I was down at the post office. Mr. Willow said you've been waiting for this."

She took the envelope, glanced at the return address, and smiled. "Thank you, Tommy."

"Anytime." He doffed his hat and dashed off.

"It's from Marysville, isn't it?" Mr. Rutledge's good humor had faded as quickly as newsprint left in the summer sun.

Well, she wouldn't let his foul mood spoil hers. The letter was likely the one in which Mr. Grayson formalized his offer of an equal partnership.

Chapter 23

Will spread his final pitchfork full of straw in the milk cow's stall and hung the tool on the barn wall. He tossed his gloves on his worktable and beckoned Miles to follow him to the paddock. They stood by the gate and watched the children saddle their mounts. The sun lay low in the western sky. Not a single cloud could be seen in the azure expanse.

"Tildy has become quite an accomplished rider. You taught her well."

Miles rested a foot on the bottom rung of the slatted fence. "She's an apt student. Mother agrees. You should hear her boast about how much progress Tildy has made with her cooking and sewing. She's started piano lessons, and Mother said she has a natural bent for music. Doesn't surprise me. El—Mrs. Watkins definitely does."

"From what I hear, last night's rehearsal didn't go much better than the one the week before. Musically, that is." Will chuckled, causing the piece of straw tucked in the corner of his mouth to bobble. "According to Abe, you two sound more like a couple of calves bawling their lungs out in a hailstorm than the Society's top violinists performing a duet."

"I don't know what's going on. She does fine on the other pieces, but when we work on the duet, she seems flustered and makes a passel of mistakes."

"Have you tried switching parts?"

"Didn't help. She can't seem to feel the music. She's too uptight."

Will pointed the straw at Miles. "Sounds to me like you need to help her relax."

"That's about as likely as snow in August."

"You wouldn't say that if you'd seen her lately. After her practice Monday night, she joined the children in a game of Blind Man's Bluff."

"Practice? What practice?"

"Target practice." Will held the straw like a gun and pretended to sight down its length.

"*You're* teaching her?"

"You're jealous."

"Never!" Miles lowered his voice. "Just curious."

"You don't need to get in a lather about it. She goes to the back field by herself."

"Do you think that's safe?"

Will shrugged. "She's a grown woman. Besides, judging by the condition of the cans, she's become a fair shot. Your trouble is, you underestimate her. You'd better wise up, my friend, or she might best you." He gave Miles a playful punch in the arm and strode to the house in answer to Pearl's call.

There was truth to that statement. Ellie seemed determined to prove she was every bit as capable as he in all respects. First she'd opened her business across the street from his. Next she'd joined the Society and ended up playing a duet with him. Now she had the ladies in town convinced the El Dorado Day competitions should be a showdown between the sexes.

From what some husbands had overheard, the women had taken it on themselves to think up activities that would be more exciting and well received than those the men came up with. He'd better give some thought to the event and not spend so much time thinking about the captivating woman heading up the female contingent. A woman who was being tight-lipped about the contents of a certain letter.

Mr. Rutledge took Elenora's hand and bowed his head for the prayer, as he'd done many times. And yet today was different. She wanted to hold his hand, to feel his warmth, to—

"Did you. . .want something?" he asked.

She looked up to find three pairs of eyes on her.

"No. Why?"

"You, um, well, squeezed my hand. I thought perhaps you wanted me to include something in the prayer."

"I—I don't think so. I'm sure you'll say the right thing. I'm sorry."

Tildy giggled, and Mrs. Rutledge shushed her.

Elenora dipped her head so low her chin practically rested on her chest. How embarrassing. She'd better be more mindful of her movements, or Mr. Rutledge might wonder what was behind her unusual actions.

Ever since the letter with Mr. Grayson's official offer had come the week before and she'd seen Mr. Rutledge's less-than-enthusiastic reaction, she'd had a hard time keeping her mind on business. Her thoughts strayed to him far too often. She'd expected him to be happy for her. After all, he'd no longer have to deal with a competitor taking business from him. Instead, he'd been withdrawn and closemouthed.

As she considered Mr. Grayson's offer, she found herself comparing the two men. Both ran a successful mercantile. Both had offered her a partnership. Both had blue eyes. But the similarities ended there. Mr. Grayson was like a stream in the lazy days of summer, steady and predictable. Mr. Rutledge was like a river swollen by the spring runoff, powerful and subject to unexpected surges. Being with him made her feel fully alive. If she weren't careful, she'd be swept away by the flood of feelings threatening to erode her self-control.

Now was no time to weaken her resolve. She'd worked too hard to give up her dream. The opportunity Mr. Grayson had offered her was more than she could have hoped for. She couldn't give way to a temporary bout of loneliness and longing—no matter how much she enjoyed Mr. Rutledge's company.

He'd just finished the prayer when a bell tolled in the distance, loud and insistent. He charged out of the room without a single word.

"What is it?" Tildy asked.

Mrs. Rutledge looked stricken. "The fire bell."

Elenora stood in Mr. Rutledge's flower garden an hour later, shielded her eyes from the sun, and stared at the wisp of gray smoke rising into the sky east of town. Some poor family had lost their home. There might even have been loss of life.

Judging by the location, the fire had been at either the Talbots' place or the Blackstones'. A mother raising two sons on her own, or a man and wife with three small children, one a babe in arms. Heartbreaking either way.

The restlessness that had taken hold of Elenora at the sound of the clanging bell threatened to unnerve her as surely as the acrid smoke was threatening to suffocate the men battling the blaze. She must remain strong and hold out hope that Tommy and Timmy were all right, that none of those fighting the fire had been injured, and that news would come soon and put an end to the agony of not knowing.

"There you are, Elenora. I wondered where you'd gone." Mrs. Rutledge joined her and studied the dissipating smoke in the distance.

"I had to get out of the house. I didn't want Tildy to see me like this."

"You're worried about the twins, aren't you?"

"Yes, but it's more than that. I can't really explain it. It's as though I'm feeling someone else's pain." She shuddered.

Mrs. Rutledge wrapped an arm around her. "Why don't we head over to the bench and sit a spell? I've set Tildy to shelling peas, so she'll be fine for a few minutes."

Elenora sank onto the bench next to Mrs. Rutledge, grateful for the support it provided, as it had the day she'd nearly fainted from heat exhaustion. But even more comforting was the presence of the strong woman on whose shoulder her head rested.

Several minutes passed as they sat in silence. But it was no longer stifling.

Elenora sat up, cast a sidelong glance at Mrs. Rutledge, and started. Tears coursed down the older woman's cheeks. "Are you all right?"

Mrs. Rutledge pulled a handkerchief from her sleeve and dabbed at her eyes. "I will be once I know Miles is all right. Fires are so hard on him."

Had he lost a house at some point? Or perhaps his business? Mrs. Rutledge had said El Dorado Day was a celebration of the first fireproof buildings in town, the mercantile being one of them.

"He'd been to Sacramento City on one of his buying trips, leaving Irene here with May. When he got home, they were gone. They'd perished in a fire the night before." She stopped and looked toward the smoke-filled sky, as though summoning strength to finish the tragic tale.

"Irene had left May at her washerwoman's place. When she got back, the cottage was engulfed in flames. The woman stood out front paralyzed with fear, so Irene ran inside to get the baby. Sheriff Henderson arrived just as the roof collapsed. He rushed in and found them under a massive beam. Miles's only consolation was that the end came instantly."

Elenora's chest was so tight she could hardly breathe. A sob broke free, followed by two more before she could regain enough control to speak. "Poor Miles. That's awful." She wiped the moisture from her eyes and drew in several ragged breaths.

"I'd better see to Tildy." Mrs. Rutledge patted Elenora's hand and rose. "Thank you for being here—and for caring." She trudged to the house. Her stooped shoulders and halting steps tore at Elenora's heart.

She knew what she had to do. Although she'd not heard a voice, there was no doubt in her mind. She was to go to the church.

In no time she covered the short distance between Mr. Rutledge's house and the small sanctuary farther up the hill. A lone figure walked toward her, his face streaked with soot. With the jingle of spurs and ash-dusted Stetson, he had to be the sheriff.

They met at the churchyard.

"Mrs. Watkins, you're just the person I wanted to see."

Her hand flew to her throat. "No! Tell me it isn't so. Tommy and Timmy. They're not—"

"They're fine. No one was hurt, but the Blackstones lost their house. We managed to save the barn and chicken coop though."

"Thank the Lord—and everyone who worked so hard. But if it's not—" The reason for her visit to the church became clear.

"It's Mr. Rutledge, isn't it? His mother told me about the fire. . . and his family."

"Whenever there's a fire, he rushes to help. But he was almost frantic today because the Blackstones have a baby. He tried to go in after the little fellow. It took Tiny and me to restrain him. Once he saw the little one in his mama's arms, he was some better. We sent him to work with the men wetting down the barn."

Sheriff Henderson removed his hat and rubbed a sleeve across his grimy forehead. "He could use a friend, if you're so inclined. He's not far behind me."

The sheriff left, and Mr. Rutledge crested the hill. He plodded toward her with his head down, looking more careworn than she'd ever seen him. His white shirt appeared gray, and his collar had come unfastened on one side. He'd dashed off without his hat, and his hair was a mess. Despite his disheveled condition, he was a welcome sight.

Her feet carried her forward as though of their own accord. She reached him and offered her hand. He closed his around it. Wordlessly they continued down the street. When they reached the church, she tugged him toward it. He opened the door Mr. Parks insisted never be locked and followed her inside. She led him to the front pew.

Once seated he looked at their hands, still joined. He gave hers a squeeze, released it, and directed his attention at some point near his scuffed, water-stained boots. The scent of smoke clung to him, overpowering all else. He crushed something in his teeth. A lemon drop most likely. "Why did you come for me?"

"I thought you could use a friend."

"A friend?" He ran his thumbs and forefingers down the crisp creases in his trousers. "Are we friends, Ellie?"

The sadness in his voice pierced her heart. "Of course."

"Mother told you?"

"Some, yes. I'm so sorry. That must have been dreadful."

His upper body shook, as did his voice. "It was the darkest day of my life."

Her breath froze in her throat, and she waited for him to continue.

Seconds stretched into minutes as he fought for control. Clearly the fire had dredged up painful memories. How she longed to ease his burden.

She swiveled toward him. He'd squeezed his eyes shut so tightly the adorable cleft between his brows was a canyon. She reached up and rubbed a finger over it. His eyes flew open—wide, wary. . .and winsome. A woman could lose herself in their deep blue depths. Were those flecks gold or green? She lowered her hand and leaned in for a closer look.

He cupped the back of her head in his palm and pulled her to him.

His mouth found hers, and she offered no resistance. He needed solace, and she couldn't deny him. Not this time.

The tender kiss ended almost before it began. He pulled back until he could see her.

Certain her disappointment would show, she slammed her eyes shut.

He claimed her lips once again, soft but seeking. She slid her arms around him and surrendered to the sensations surging through her. Every nerve in her body was alert, savoring the smooth fabric of his frock coat, the silkiness of his moustache against her skin. . .and the tart taste of lemon.

All too soon he sat back, a crooked smile on his face.

She'd succeeded in helping him. "You feel better, don't you?"

He chuckled. "That was rather. . .unusual."

As wonderful as it was to hear him laugh, she wouldn't suffer in silence as she had when Jake said horrid things about her efforts to be a dutiful wife. "What's so funny?"

"That's the last thing I'd have expected you to do. Not that I'm complaining, you understand?" His smile held no malice.

"You weren't finding fault with me?"

He trailed a fingertip down her cheek. "Have I ever?"

"You've done nothing but since the day I set foot in El Dorado, Mr. Rutledge."

He grasped her hands. "Ellie, I think it's time you call me Miles."

"But that's not proper. We're not—"

"Yes we are. Friends that is. You said so yourself. So say it. Please."

"Why is it so important to you?"

"Because. . ." He pressed his lips together and gazed at the ceiling, as though debating how best to answer. When he looked into her eyes, his held warmth and sincerity. "Because I like it. That's why."

"It's a fine name. I like it, too. . .Miles."

Chapter 24

Someday you two are going to play this piece without destroying its beauty. Let's hope it happens in time for the concert." Mr. Morton returned to his platform, gazed at the ceiling, and muttered what sounded like a prayer.

Miles tucked his violin under his chin, tore his eyes from Ellie, who stood facing him, and watched the conductor.

"We'll begin with the third movement. Is everyone ready?"

She nodded. Miles lifted his bow in a salute.

Mr. Morton raised his baton, and the room grew quiet as the musicians got into position. On the downbeat they began.

Miles attempted to divide his attention between watching his fingers and the sheet music, and casting glimpses at Mr. Morton and Ellie. Try as he might though, his gaze tended to linger too long on his pretty partner. He scrambled to find his place in the score. Again.

This wouldn't do. He'd simply have to memorize the concerto so he could feast his eyes on her while he played. When she was swept away by the piece, she looked more beautiful than ever. The way she swayed in time with the music. Her slender fingers moving over the strings with such precision. The curve of her lips—

He lost his place entirely, and the orchestra stopped.

Mr. Morton stepped from his platform once again, beckoned Miles and Ellie to come close, and addressed them in a tone that reminded Miles of an exasperated schoolmarm. "Have you two been practicing every day as I asked?"

Ellie bobbed her head. "And I spend time each evening as well. I have the first movement memorized and am making good progress on the second."

Miles stifled a groan. Leave it to her to show him up.

"That's fine, Mrs. Watkins. But what's happening with you, Miles? It's not like you to lose your place."

"I practice. Just have a lot on my mind, I guess."

Ellie's mouth twitched. She, of all people, should be able to understand how difficult it had been for him to concentrate since the fire. It was bad enough she'd seen him struggle to hold himself together, but she'd as good as invited him to kiss her. For the past two days he'd been able to think of little else.

"Well, I need you to focus on your duet. The dialogue between your violins in this magnificent piece is intended to be fascinating—not frustrating."

"I'm afraid it's my fault, Mr. Morton."

She'd done nothing wrong, so why was she taking responsibility?

"The women and I have come up with some wonderful competitions for El Dorado Day, and I daresay Mr. Rutledge is preoccupied with those the men are planning for us." She tossed him one of her saucy smirks, the kind that used to annoy him but now only served to draw attention to her lovely lips.

The contests for the women had nothing to do with his inability to perform his part. He'd barely given them a thought. Perhaps this was her way of letting him know she planned to outshine him in that area as well. Not that he cared. Not anymore. If besting him in that made her happy, he was all for it. What mattered most was convincing her to stay in El Dorado.

The rest of the practice passed quickly. He managed to play his part without making too many more mistakes. Ellie put her violin away and dashed out without a word to anyone—even him—taking the sunshine with her.

Hank rested his cello on its side and made a beeline for Miles. "What's with you tonight? I've never heard you miss as many notes. Judging by the lost-puppy look on your face when she scooted out of here, I'd say she's the reason. Something happened after the fire, didn't it? You haven't been the same since."

"I'm fine."

"Can't fool me, Miles. I've known you too long. You told her about that day. That's it, isn't it?"

Miles laid his violin in its case, clicked the latches closed, and faced his friend. "She knows enough. But she's too smart to pry."

The windows, which he'd opened hours before to allow the room to cool, needed to be shut and the hall locked, but he had to get out of there. "Tell Mr. Morton I'll close up later, will you?"

"You can't hide from the past forever." Hank plunked a hand on Miles's shoulder. "One of these days you've got to stare it in the face, make your peace, and move on."

If his friend knew the ugly truth, he'd understand why revisiting that tragic time was impossible.

Mrs. Rutledge settled on a stool and addressed the group of women who'd filled Watkins General Merchandise. "I have to agree with Elenora. Showcasing our men's strengths is a sure way to guarantee that El Dorado Day will be a success."

One outspoken woman stepped forward. "Why should we go out of our way to make the men look good? I think it would be far more fun to see them struggle with tasks we're more suited for. I can just see my Harvey trying to sew on a button."

Jane Abbott fidgeted.

Elenora felt certain the young woman wanted to speak. "Miss Abbott, what are your thoughts?"

She cast Elenora a grateful smile. "Since Sammy hasn't asked permission to come courting yet, you might think I lack the experience to voice an opinion, but it would pain me to see any man shamed in front of the townspeople. I think Sammy would be more likely to show me respect if I did the same for him."

Elenora chose her words carefully. "We have no control over what the men do, but I know Mr. Rutledge has spent a great deal of time planning the competitions for us."

Mrs. Morton chuckled. "As taken as that man is with you, I doubt he'll want to see you publicly disgraced. My husband said he's never seen Mr. Rutledge fumble a piece the way he did last night. Seems he couldn't take his eyes off you."

Since reflecting on the heart-stopping kiss he'd given her would cause heat to flood her cheeks, Elenora chose to leave the comment untouched. "Perhaps we can accomplish both goals. I know one chore we women perform that requires considerable strength. I don't think a gentleman would feel his manliness was in jeopardy if we use it as one of our competitions, but you can be the judge."

She did her best to present the idea in a positive light, and the women quickly agreed that she'd come up with a clever contest. Talk turned to the second competition, and the room buzzed with several conversations. Elenora went behind the counter to jot down the suggestions.

A shrill scream rang out followed by a chorus of shrieks.

She wheeled around. Several women stood with their fingers pointed at the back of her shop. The unexpected sight made her skin crawl, but she did her best to remain calm. "It's a rattlesnake, isn't it?"

"Get it!" someone cried.

One woman swooned, and two others caught her.

Elenora reached underneath the counter, grabbed her revolver, and took aim at the poisonous creature slithering across the floor. "Cover your ears."

Her first two shots missed. The third met with success.

She resisted the urge to kick her toe on the floor. Surely with the amount of practice she'd had lately, she could do better than that. If someone tried to rob her and pulled a gun, she wouldn't have time to fire three shots. She laid her revolver on the shelf beneath her cash drawer and looked up.

Instead of the shaking heads and frowns she expected, the women's mouths gaped. Mrs. Olds was the first to regain her speech. "How did you do that? You hit a moving target no bigger around than a broom handle."

Mrs. Rutledge beamed. "In all my years I've never seen such a feat, Elenora. Not by a man, and certainly not by a woman. Wait until the men hear about this."

The door to her shop flew open. Miles burst in, his revolver drawn. Sheriff Henderson and several of the other businessmen crowded into her small shop, weapons at the ready.

Mrs. Rutledge rushed to her son's side. "It's all right. Elenora shot a rattlesnake."

The sheriff scanned the women's faces, clomped to where the creature lay, and squatted. He turned and gave Elenora the widest smile she'd ever seen him wear. "I heard three shots. That right?"

"It took me three, yes."

"You got it with *only* three shots? A snake so small its rattle only has two sections?" He stood. "Mrs. Watkins, what you did is amazing. I've half a mind to deputize you."

The straightforward lawman wasn't one to tease a woman.

The few words he'd managed to get out whenever he spoke to her had always been sincere. "You're too kind, Sheriff."

Several of the men—and two brave women—examined the disgusting reptile. The woman who'd fainted revived when smelling salts were waved beneath her nose. A good quarter hour went by before the shop cleared.

Elenora flopped onto one of the stools and stared at the damaged floorboards. Extending her lower lip, she blew out a breath, fluffing a few loose hairs. The smell of gunpowder lingered in the still air.

What had she been thinking to go for her gun when she could have grabbed one of her shovels or hoes instead? Then again, they were in the back of the shop where the snake was, whereas she'd been in the front. Surely no one could question her choice to use the weapon at her disposal. She couldn't very well have a rattlesnake loose in her shop, could she?

Even so, her landlord would be livid if he saw the damage she'd caused. Mr. Steele had been none too happy about the front of the shop, but that wasn't her fault. This was. Now she'd have to hire Mr. MacDougall to perform the repairs and bear the expense herself.

Footfalls on the walkway roused her from her ruminations. Miles tromped through the open door, bearing boards under one arm and a bucket of tools in the other. "Heard you had some work that needs to be done."

"As a matter of fact, I do. But I don't expect you to do it."

"That's what friends are for." He flashed her a warm smile that drew her attention to his mouth and sent heat racing to her cheeks. "So, are you going accept my help?"

"Yes, Miles, I am."

He ripped out the damaged sections of her floor, cut a length from one of the boards he'd brought, and wiggled it in place. Once he was satisfied with the fit, he produced a nail, set it with a tap, and pounded it in with two strikes of his hammer. My, but he was strong.

She grabbed a fistful of nails from his bucket and passed them to him one at a time until he finished. He rose, dusted his hands, and surveyed his handiwork. "Good as new."

"Thank you."

"You know, Ellie, we make a good team." He brushed her cheek with the back of his hand. "Have you given any more thought to accepting my offer of a partnership? I can't promise you everything Grayson can, but you wouldn't need to uproot Tildy if you were to stay put."

"I wanted to talk to you about that, and I guess now's as good a time as any."

His face fell. "From your serious tone it doesn't sound like this bodes well for me. Should I sit?"

"That's a good idea." She perched on one of the stools, and he took another. "In his last letter Mr. Grayson said I'm his first choice for partner. I know you don't share my opinion of him, but he's a kind and generous man. You haven't forgotten what he did for Tildy, have you?"

He gave a most ungentlemanly grunt. "How could I? Mother had to make padding to go inside the Stetson Tildy bought, and I had to punch holes in it and thread a leather chinstrap through them so she could keep the thing on her head. He could have given her something more practical—or at least found a hat that would fit her."

"You don't have to sound so upset about it."

"He plans to take you and Tildy away from here, and I don't like it."

He wanted her to stay and work with him, but how could she do that after everything that had taken place between them?

Besides, she couldn't pass up the opportunity of becoming half owner of a mercantile every bit as a successful as his, could she? Not unless he had a very good reason for her to turn it down. "Why?"

"Well, for one thing, you're helping plan El Dorado Day. And you're supposed to play a duet with me at the next concert."

Her hope dissolved as quickly as a spoonful of sugar in a cup of hot tea. If he had feelings for her—lasting feelings—surely he would have said so. "You needn't worry. I'll honor my commitments. I told him I need time to think things over. I'm to receive a letter from him in a few weeks with more information. Recommendations and such."

"Not that you value my opinion, but things aren't always what they seem. Take the Talbot twins for example. You seem convinced they're trustworthy, but what would you say if you found out they were responsible for the fire at the Blackstones' place?"

"That's a serious allegation. What evidence is there?"

"Hank found the charred remains of a cigar in the field where the fire started, and they were seen in the area not long before the blaze began."

Why must he assume the worst where they were concerned? Elenora gritted her teeth. *One. Two. Three.* "Cigar smoke is strong, and I've never smelled it on them. And as to being seen, they live out that way."

"My point exactly. Make sure you know who deserves your trust, Ellie. I don't want to see you get hurt." He grabbed his tools, stalked out of her shop, stormed across the street, and shut the door of the mercantile with such force she expected to hear the glass center shatter.

His concern was touching, but he was wrong about the Talbots—and Mr. Grayson. And somehow she'd prove it to him.

"Oh Mama! I'm so excited, I might pop. Do you think my gingerbread is as good as Mrs. Rutledge's? She said no one will be able to tell a difference, and hers has always taken a prize."

"It's delicious, dearest. I think you deserve a ribbon." Elenora glimpsed her reflection in the looking glass on her shop wall, the one where Miles had tried out his comb. Despite his initial reluctance, he must like it, because she'd seen him use it several times. Hopefully he'd like the competitions that morning as well. She'd done her best to come up with two that would show the men in a favorable light. Convincing the women they'd be well received hadn't been as difficult as she'd expected. They seemed to value her opinion.

She would miss El Dorado if she were to accept Mr. Grayson's offer. But the opportunity to work in a large mercantile alongside a man who valued her opinions and wanted her *because* she was a woman was tempting.

Tildy caught her eye in the mirror. "There's going to be a three-legged race. Constance is my partner. We've been practicing, and we're fast. I think we can beat some of the boys. And when we do, I'm gonna laugh at them."

"Gloating isn't kind, sweetheart. Do you think the Lord would be happy if you made fun of the boys because they lost?"

"No, I don't think He would, 'cause He's a man. He'd probably want the boys to win."

Elenora stifled a laugh, spun Tildy around, and fastened her hard-to-reach button. "He loves women as well as men. Mary and Martha were His friends. And Mary Magdalene, too."

"But if He loves us all the same, why are the men in charge of everything?"

"They're not. Look at me. I own my own business, and I'm in charge of the women's committee for El Dorado Day. And speaking of that, we'd best be on our way."

Tildy exercised caution as she carried her gingerbread to the grocery store. Elenora followed right behind and rejoiced inwardly when Mrs. Olds treated Tildy with the same respect she did an adult entrant.

"My gingerbread will be safe, won't it? You won't let anybody snitch any, will you?"

The grocer's wife chuckled. "I'll rap the knuckles of anyone who tries to snitch it, so you can join in the fun and trust that your entry will come to no harm."

Tildy rushed off. Elenora strolled along Main Street, visiting with one person after another.

Two wagons rumbled down the street and creaked to a stop in front of her shop. Tarpaulins covered the load in the back of each. Miles and several of the men on his committee rushed over. He said something to one of them and strode in her direction.

When he reached her, he gave her one of his most charming smiles. "Ellie, may we use your sewing machine in one of the competitions?"

"But you said the machines are a luxury and won't carry them in your shop. Why would you want to use one now?"

"You'll see. And if things go as planned, you'll have a buyer for it before the day's out."

She raised a brow. He was up to something. "You want to help me sell it? Why?"

"Mother loves hers. Says it saves her hours on every garment. She believes every woman who sews would benefit from owning one. I'm inclined to agree."

"Why, Miles Rutledge, I think you honestly mean that,

which makes this a red-letter day. Feel free to use the machine." She handed him the key to her shop.

Half an hour later the women on her committee stood in the middle of Church Street flanking her as she faced Miles and the men on his. The townspeople gathered around them.

Abe stood in the center of the assembly and mopped his shiny brow with a bright red bandanna. "Ladies and gents, seein' as how I've lived here in town since the early days, Miles invited me to serve as your master of ceremonies. So, without further ado, I hereby declare El Dorado Day officially begun. Because we've got a woman headin' up part of the festivities, we'll let her go first and tell you what she and her group have planned for us menfolk. Mrs. Watkins." He held out a hand toward her.

"Thank you. In keeping with tradition, we'll end with the shooting match. We have, however, come up with new contests that will allow you fine men of El Dorado to display your strength and prowess in two different manners. I promised Mr. Rutledge we wouldn't ask you to don aprons and slice onions, but we did determine one task commonly considered women's work that we believe you men would be as skilled at as we are— if not more so."

Several of the men glanced at one another and shrugged.

"The Talbot twins have hung rugs between trees. Very dirty rugs. My daughter and the Dupree children rubbed five full cups of sand from the riverbed into each one. Your job, gentlemen, will be to choose three teams of five. Each man will beat his team's rug for a full minute. At the end of the five minutes we'll collect the sand on the sheets spread beneath each rug, measure it, and determine the winning team."

While the townspeople processed the news, she stole a glance at Miles, and he smiled. With his experience beating rugs for his mother, he stood to do a fine job.

Abe got everyone's attention with a piercing whistle. "If I can get you to stop your yammerin', we'll hear about the second competition."

When all was quiet, she continued. "Our second contest is simple. Tommy and Timmy have laid out boards, nails, and hammers. Any man who wants to compete may do so. The winner will be the one who can hammer three nails flush with the wood using the fewest strokes. In the event of a tie we'll go by time, so you'll want to work quickly."

Her announcement was met with cheers and some good-natured ribbing as men boasted to one another about how well they would do. Although Mr. MacDougall was sure to win, if Elenora's assessment of the strength and skill of a certain shop-keeper were accurate, he would have some serious competition.

The townspeople trooped up the hill to the field beyond the church. Three Axminster rugs hung in readiness, an identi-cal rug beater lying in the center of the sheet underneath each of them. In no time the three teams were chosen, with Miles serving as captain of one.

Each team lined up twenty paces from its rug, Abe gave another of his shrill whistles, and the first men were off. One team put their largest man first, but the others led with their smallest. The air filled with the smack of beaters against the sturdy carpets and billowing clouds of dust as each competi-tor gave it his all. Cheers rang out from those rooting for their friends and loved ones.

Every man made a valiant effort, but by the time the fourth heat neared its conclusion, only an occasional puff could be seen. At the signal, the final member of each team grabbed the wooden handle of his beater and slammed the tear-shaped top into the rug. To Elenora's delight, Miles managed to fill the air with a fresh flurry of fine powder, something the other contenders couldn't do.

Before she could stop it, a squeal escaped. With all the excitement, she hoped no one had noticed, but his mother must have because she graced Elenora with a smile.

At the end of the five minutes, Abe called time. "All righty, ladies and gents, let's see which team couldn't be beat." He chuckled at his own play on words.

The Talbot twins made quite a show of collecting the dirt on each of the sheets and measuring it. How it thrilled Elenora's heart to see the young men being treated with respect. They'd worked tirelessly on her behalf and shown her such kindness.

The barber examined the cups of sandy soil. "We have a clear winner, folks. Miles's team got a full cup more'n the others. They'll get the blue ribbons. Tiny's team takes the red, and Mr. Morton's will be sportin' white."

Tildy and Constance pinned the ribbons to the men's jackets. When Miles received his, he said something to Tildy, and she laughed so loudly Elenora could hear her even though she was a good fifty feet away. Her dear girl had grown very close to Miles. Leaving El Dorado and her friends here would be far more difficult for her than Elenora had first thought. She'd have to pray for wisdom—and an extra measure of patience—because when Tildy wasn't happy, she had plenty to say about it.

When Mr. MacDougall took first place in the nail pounding competition and Miles second, no one seemed at all surprised. Apparently Miles's prowess with a hammer was a well-known fact.

Mrs. Rutledge sidled up to where Elenora stood at the edge of the crowd watching the girls present the ribbons. "I'm impressed. I didn't say anything before, but I couldn't have been happier to see the contests you championed. They certainly allowed Miles to shine. Does this mean you've forgiven him for withdrawing his offer when you arrived in town?"

"I do believe I have. I've come to see that his reluctance to accept me as his partner served a purpose. Had it not been for him, I don't know that I'd have found the courage to strike out on my own. I've enjoyed running my shop and doing things my way. Thanks to my hard work, I've been offered an opportunity beyond my wildest dreams."

Applause followed the presentation of the nail-pounding winners. Mrs. Rutledge waited until it died down and leaned close to Elenora. "Doing things our own way is all well and good, but don't be surprised if the Lord has other plans."

Other plans? It seemed He did at that. Once she received Mr. Grayson's credentials and had a clearer picture of exactly what he was offering, she'd be in a better place to determine what those plans might be. Perhaps God really did care about her hopes and dreams.

Chapter 25

Miles stood in the shade of the awning in front of Ellie's shop and waited for Abe to finish his preamble. Normally he found his friend's fondness for flapping his jaw entertaining, but today Miles wanted to get on with things. Ellie had obviously chosen competitions in which he was sure to excel. While he appreciated the recognition, what set his heart racing faster than a hound after a hare was the fact that she must care about him.

He'd given himself so many mental kicks for kissing her after the fire that his brain must be black and blue, but things had changed for the better since then. She'd dropped her guard. And the way she looked at him sometimes. . .

He ventured a glance at her. She seemed to be suppressing a smile. Only when she inclined her head toward Abe did Miles realize it had grown quiet.

Abe chuckled. "You'd best be careful how far you let your mind wander, Miles, or you'll be windin' your hair and combin' your watch. The womenfolk are waitin' to hear what we gents have planned for them."

Miles cleared his throat. "We entertained many ideas but settled on two contests we think everyone will enjoy. Some of us have come to realize the old ways of doing things are not always the best or most expedient, as the first competition will show."

Surely Ellie hadn't missed his message. A quick look at her revealed nothing. She'd assumed her businesswoman persona.

"My mother bought the first sewing machine Mrs. Watkins

sold, and I've seen how much time it saves. We men borrowed three machines to use today. The competitors will sew the four sides of a square to make a handkerchief. My mother, Mrs. Watkins, and Mrs. Olds have agreed to time the seamstress using her machine. The winner will be the one with the shortest time. Mother will demonstrate how easy the sewing machine is to operate, and we'll be ready to begin."

He stepped back to allow others a better vantage point. He'd never tell another soul, but after a short lesson from Mother, he'd sewn one of the squares himself. The machine was a marvel. Every woman who did her own sewing could make good use of one, which was exactly what he hoped the competition would prove. How shortsighted—and prideful—he'd been to scoff at Ellie's idea of selling the sewing machines.

His pride had driven a wedge between them, one he would have to keep chipping at if he were to overcome her resistance. Hopefully he wasn't too late.

One woman after another sat at a sewing machine, some appearing eager, others apprehensive, and a few doubtful. Without exception they left clutching a handkerchief and wearing a satisfied smile. One woman whispered to Ellie. Judging by the animated gesturing, Miles was sure the machine had been sold. He shouldn't be so happy to send business her way, but he wanted her to make a sale. To prove to herself she was a successful merchant in her own right. To stay in El Dorado.

As soon as the sewing competition ended and the ribbons had been awarded, the crowd gathered in front of the mercantile, where the men had helped him set up makeshift tables using planks, sawhorses, and some of Mother's old tablecloths.

He addressed the gathering. "Ladies, as everyone knows, I'm fond of flowers, as are many of you. Our second competition is to create a floral arrangement. I purchased a dozen cut glass vases. Those participating will be able to take home their creations. And here are the flowers."

He opened the door to his shop, and his committee carried out buckets laden with fragrant blooms of assorted varieties and colors. Their sweet perfume filled the air. From the way many women's eyes lit up, he knew this idea, one several of the men had thought silly, was anything but. Now to get Ellie to participate.

"Each contestant will have five minutes to arrange her bouquet. Our judge is none other than Mr. Parks, whom some of you know is the gardener responsible for the beautiful beds at the main church in Placerville. At the conclusion of the three rounds he'll determine the winners."

Women who provided arrangements for the church services filled the first eight slots. The second group of four contestants set their bouquets on a side table, where Mr. Olds labeled them, and stepped aside.

"Time for the final round." Miles shot a glance at his mother, and she nodded.

Before she could say anything Pearl spoke up. "Elenora, you must take a turn. Everyone's seen your shop and how beautiful your displays are."

"That's kind of you to say, but I've not had experience with fresh flowers. The ones I'm accustomed to are silk." She patted the spray at her throat.

Mother chimed in. "Mrs. Dupree is right. You've a knack for putting things together. There are still openings, and I think you should take one."

Miles held out a hand toward the four stations and gave Ellie what he hoped was his most encouraging smile. "And who will join Mrs. Watkins?"

Three other women were coaxed into competing and took

their places behind the other tables. Abe gave the signal, and they set to work plopping flowers in their vases willy-nilly.

Ellie, however, laid her selection of blooms on the table, arranging them by color. She tilted her head and scrunched her mouth in an adorable gesture so like Tildy's that Miles couldn't keep from grinning. She took the pruning shears to the stems, snipping them into varying lengths.

He glanced at his pocket watch. Nearly half the time had elapsed, but she showed no sign of rushing. With deft movements she arranged the tallest stems in the rear, adding the others in graduated groupings until she slipped in the final pink rose front and center. She brushed her cuttings into a tidy pile, lined up the shears flush with the edge of the table, and spun her vase to face front just as he called time.

If Ellie didn't end up with a blue ribbon, he'd be surprised. Her bouquet was by far the most artistically arranged, which was no surprise. She could make a display of rat traps into a thing of beauty.

Mr. Parks took his time examining each of the twelve entries. He paused in front of Ellie's and nodded. A good sign. He moved to the other end of the table, studied another arrangement, and smiled. Not good. He returned to stand before Ellie's and wiggled his moustache back and forth as though he were torn. Couldn't he see hers was the prettiest?

The minister smiled again and spun around. "Ladies, you're a talented group. In my mind you're all winners. However, I do have to choose three of you to receive ribbons. Third place goes to Miss Crowley."

Applause followed as Constance pinned the white ribbon on the older woman. Tildy held the red and waited for Mr. Parks to continue.

"The final two placements presented a challenge. Both are

beautifully arranged, but after some deliberation I made my decision."

Must he drag things out? He needed to announce the second-place winner so he could move on to Ellie.

"Second place goes to. . .Mrs. Watkins."

Ellie looked as stunned as Miles felt, although from what he could see, she wasn't disappointed. It didn't appear she'd expected her name to be called at all. She'd been whispering with Pearl, who gave her a gentle shove. She smiled, an open-mouthed version that conveyed disbelief.

Tildy beamed as she pinned the red ribbon on her mother. He fought the urge to scowl and clapped a little less enthusiastically than the others when Mrs. Morton received recognition for first place.

Miles attempted to reach Ellie, but she was swept away by a gaggle of gabby women eager for her to announce the winners of the bake-off—and one very excited girl. Tildy practically danced down the street to the grocer's place.

Ellie presided over the ceremony with poise and grace, complimenting each entrant and thanking everyone who'd helped her with even the smallest task. She'd been in El Dorado a few short months, and yet she had captured the hearts of the towns-people. She'd certainly captured his. Somehow he must convince her to stay, because if she were to leave, she'd take the sunshine with her.

Tildy sidled up to Miles, who leaned against a pillar opposite the grocer's place. "Did you see my ribbon, Mr. R? I got first place for sweet breads."

Elenora patted Tildy's shoulder in an effort to calm her

exuberant daughter. "He was there, dearest."

"Congratulations!" Miles made a show of admiring the blue ribbon pinned beneath Tildy's lace-edged collar. "I'm not surprised you won, Tildy girl. I've tasted your gingerbread, and I can't tell a difference between it and Mother's. In fact, I'm hoping to get a piece at the picnic when you and your mama join us."

"I'm afraid, Mr. Rutledge, that I made plans for Tildy and me to share our meal with the Duprees."

"Well, that works out fine. Will said they'll be eating with us."

Pearl hadn't mentioned that, but perhaps she hadn't known. Either that or she was as determined as Miles's mother to see that Elenora spent time with him.

Not that she minded. But she mustn't allow attraction to be a distraction. As fond as she was of him, she wasn't about to let a newfound friendship cloud her judgment when it came to making the decision about Mr. Grayson's offer.

"It's time, Miles." Sheriff Henderson formed his thumb and forefinger into the shape of a pistol and used it to point to the edge of town, where the shooting match would take place.

Miles excused himself, went into his shop, and emerged with his holster creating a bulge beneath his frock coat. The two men headed west on Main, stopped at a large field cleared of trees, and tromped through the bunchgrass.

"C'mon, Mama." Tildy raced after them.

Elenora strolled down the rutted road, careful not to stir up dust. Her lavender skirt bore enough of it all ready. Although not practical, the light color kept her cooler than her darker dresses. The last thing she needed was to swoon and end up in Miles's arms again. To do so would only serve to fuel a fire that mustn't be allowed to spread. A clear head was what she needed. That and a splash of cold water.

The citizens of El Dorado gathered at the south end of the

field. Two sets of uprights had been stuck in the ground at the north end, each pair supporting a crosspiece as high as her top button. Miles and the sheriff set five tin cans on each target at one-foot intervals. The setup reminded her of the range at Will and Pearl's place, where she'd spent many an evening practicing.

Apparently satisfied, Miles and Sheriff Henderson strode toward the boisterous crowd. The excitement in the air was palpable.

Miles stood by her side in his waistcoat, his frock coat discarded, with one hand resting on the handle of his revolver. Sheriff Henderson faced the gathering.

"Ladies and gentleman, it's my privilege to once again oversee the shooting match that has always been the highpoint of El Dorado Day. For the benefit of those new to town, I'll go over the rules." He smiled at Elenora and continued.

"Each man will get one practice round of five shots. For the actual competition there will be three cans and three shots. Anyone blasting all three cans off the board will be considered a winner and get a gold ribbon. Miles is the only one who's earned one every year. We'll see if he can keep up his winning streak. And now that we got the formalities out of the way, who are the first contenders?"

Tommy and Timmy stepped forward, and Miles muttered to Elenora. "What do they think they're doing? They're just boys."

She spoke in a heated whisper. "Those *young men* have every right to compete. They've proven themselves repeatedly, and yet you persist in thinking ill of them. They didn't start that fire, and I intend to prove it."

He refused to believe the Talbot twins were responsible, reliable, and hardworking. Miles would owe them an apology when she discovered the real culprit.

Sheriff Henderson allowed them to compete. The crack of Tommy's revolver signaled the start of the match. When the brothers had completed their practice rounds, they reloaded while Paul Dupree and his brother dashed to the targets to set up cans for the final round. Timmy got one, Tommy two. Not a bad showing, considering how old their guns were and the fact that the sheriff had them stand fifty feet from their targets.

Two-by-two the men competed. The acrid smell of gunpowder filled the air, so thick Elenora could almost taste it. When the last duo fired their final shots, only two men had earned a gold ribbon. From what the sheriff said, Miles would be the third. Having seen him shoot, she agreed. He was a true marksman.

"And now, ladies and gentlemen, the moment we've all been waiting for." Sheriff Henderson had never been as animated. "The question on everyone's mind is, 'Will Miles Rutledge earn his fifteenth gold ribbon in a row?' Come on up, Miles."

Miles approached the mark in front of the target on the left, took out his revolver, and put on a show for the crowd, pretending to polish the wooden handle on his crisp white shirtsleeve, blowing on the end of the barrel, and exercising the fingers of his right hand. His ready smile was firmly in place. Clearly he was enjoying himself.

"Sheriff, wait!"

Elenora turned to see who'd spoken, surprised to find the blacksmith pushing his way to the front, the large man with his dark brown hair and full beard reminding her of a grizzly. Despite his size, he'd proven to be a gentle giant. Surely he wasn't going to take issue with the sheriff.

"What's on your mind, Tiny?"

"I had me an idea. We seen lotsa men take aim today, and only two got all the cans. There's one here who's proven to be an excellent shot but hasn't taken a turn. I'm thinking we oughtta let her."

"*Her?*" Miles practically shouted the word. "Oh no! I'm not competing with a woman. I have my pride."

He certainly did. And he and his pride deserved to be challenged.

Tiny continued. "Mrs. Watkins done shot a scrawny little rattler in only three tries. I reckon she could take out some cans. What do ya say, Sheriff?"

"I. . . This is. . .highly unusual. What do the rest of you think?"

Mr. Olds stepped forward. "Miles competes with her every day. Why should today be any different? I say give her a chance."

A number of other men took turns voicing their support.

"Mrs. Watkins!" Timmy raced toward her. "Tommy's got your gun."

"He does?"

"You're gonna shoot, aren't ya?"

"She is." Miles approached her and whispered, "I'm sorry, Ellie. I hope you can forgive me for putting my foot in my mouth again."

He'd be sorry all right, because she'd do her utmost to hit every one of those cans. She'd have to stand twice as far away as she did at the Duprees' place, but she would have five practice shots to make adjustments in her aim. "Yes, Timmy, I'm going to shoot."

Tommy arrived with the walnut case containing her revolver tucked under his arm. "Here you are, Mrs. Watkins. You can do this. Just take your time, and you'll do swell."

Miles chuckled. "What do you have in there? Your cute little derringer?"

"I'm sorry to disappoint you, but it's a Smith & Wesson,

Model Number Two Army, .32 caliber, with a six-inch barrel."

His stunned silence was her reward. Tommy opened the box, and she removed her revolver. It's blued finish and varnished rosewood grips never ceased to impress her.

"Would you look at that?"

She couldn't identify the speaker, but the admiration of the men in the crowd was evident from the number of compliments about her gun being aimed her way. Their approval boosted her confidence, which had wilted rapidly when she realized the expectations placed on her. Hopefully she'd not disappoint the many who'd touted her ability.

Sheriff Henderson removed his hat, mopped his brow, and replaced his Stetson. "You two ready?"

Miles strode to the mark in front of his target. She sauntered to hers, doing her best to appear unruffled, although she feared her breakfast might reappear. She forced herself to ignore the wave of nausea. If she concentrated on the task at hand, she ought to be able to still the turbulence.

"Rutledge," a male voice called, "you gonna force a woman to stand as far away as you? Give her ten feet, why don't you?"

Several echoed the suggestion, and Miles motioned her forward. She was about to protest, when she caught Will's eye, and he inclined his head toward the target. He was right. It wouldn't do to disgrace Miles in front of the town. Should she hit all the cans, he could console himself with the fact that he'd given her an advantage. She stepped off the ten feet, stopped, and turned toward him.

"Ladies first."

Great. She had to take her practice shots in front of everyone before he took his. There would be no chance to study his form as she'd done before. Nothing like pressure. Oh well. She could do it.

Taking careful aim, she fired and missed. The shot had gone below the can, so she'd have to raise the end of the barrel next time.

Focus, Elenora. Don't think about anything but your next shot.

Blocking out the murmuring behind her, she listened for birdsong, leaves rustling, anything reminiscent of her quiet evenings spent on the back field of the Dupree farm. A hawk squawked. That wasn't exactly what she was after, but it would have to do.

She hit two of the five cans with her remaining four shots. Not impressive, but she'd gotten the feel of things on her last one. She was as ready as could be under the circumstances.

Miles took his practice shots, hitting a can with each one. He lifted one side of his mouth in a half smile and joined her at the stump where they'd left their ammunition.

Now to reload and prepare for the showdown. She tipped up the barrel of her revolver, removed the cylinder, and loaded it with five bullets from her box of fifty. He watched in stunned silence.

Everything in her ached to smirk, but she fought the almost overwhelming urge, speaking in her best customer voice instead. "Convenient, isn't it? When Sheriff Henderson explained the process involved in loading his Colt and told me about this gun, I knew it would be just the thing. I don't get black powder on my fingers, and since the cartridges are uniform, my accuracy is quite good."

"I'd heard there was a metal cartridge model available, but I've never seen one before. That's not exactly the type of gun I'd expect a woman to be packing."

"I've never done things quite the way you expect, have I, Miles? Why should I start now?" She grinned.

Moments later she stood on her mark, extended her arm,

and brought it down slowly. She pulled back the hammer, rested her left hand beneath her right just as he'd taught her, and adjusted her aim until she was certain she'd hit her target. Holding her breath, she put her finger on the trigger, squeezed it slowly, and squealed when she sent a can sailing. One down. Two to go.

Miles took his first shot. With seeming ease he hit his target. Both made their second shots as well.

She returned to her mark ready for the final shot, eyed the lone can atop the crosspiece, and got into position. Her hand trembled, and she lowered her weapon to her side. Now was no time to falter.

Despite the size of the crowd, she heard not a sound. The townspeople seemed to be holding a collective breath. She released hers, held her arm parallel to the ground, rested her right hand on her left, pulled back the hammer, inhaled, and—

"Wait, Mrs. Watkins! Wait!"

Chapter 26

W hat were those boys up to now? Miles clenched his teeth to keep from uttering words that would dig a deeper hole. If he said anything else against the twins, he'd be so far in he'd have to clutch the sides to heave himself out. Ellie believed they were innocent, and now was not the time to challenge her.

She lowered her revolver. "What is it?"

"We've got an idea." Tommy ran toward the target with his brother right behind.

They reached the lone can perched on the crosspiece in front of Ellie. Tommy rummaged in his jacket and produced the small section of rope he always carried. Timmy slipped a hand in his pocket, pulled out the loop of string he was never without, and yanked so hard it snapped in two. They huddled together, their backs to the crowd.

What did they think they were doing? And why didn't Hank put a stop to their shenanigans? They were distracting Ellie.

"Mrs. Watkins," Tommy called, "you can do it. Just aim for this." He held up the can with his rope coiled around it. He lifted up the end, to which they'd tied what looked to be an arrowhead. Yes. That must be it. Tildy had said Timmy had several.

"Would you look at that?" Tiny guffawed. "They done made a rattlesnake."

Laughter rang out. Ellie grinned at the two miscreants as though she couldn't be more pleased with them. Tommy set the can on the crosspiece, and the two rejoined the others watching the match.

Hank tromped to the boys, his spurs jangling. "I had half a mind to call you back, gentlemen, but now that I see what you were up to, I can't help but think you had a fine idea."

Gentlemen? A fine idea? It sounded like Hank's opinion of the twins had changed. Had he been listening to Ellie?

She beckoned to the sheriff, and he joined her. After a brief conversation Hank addressed the crowd.

"Ladies and gentlemen, Mrs. Watkins believes it's only fair for her to take her final shot from the fifty-foot line like we men do. I said that wasn't necessary, but she insists, so she'll be standing at the same mark as Miles."

Several people shouted their approval of her action. Apparently the townspeople wanted to see her show him up. If he were to miss his shot and she made hers without the benefit of her earlier advantage, he'd never hear the end of it.

Why did Ellie feel the need to best him in every arena? First it was business, then music, and now shooting. His life had been moving along just fine until the day she came into town and turned things upside down. She was downright exasperating. And stubborn. And she was leaving.

He felt as though someone had rammed the handle of his revolver into his gut. She couldn't leave. Ellie belonged here with him. He wanted her in his shop—and in his arms.

Hank waited until the noise died down before speaking. "Please be quiet so she can concentrate."

Ellie got into position and did everything Miles had taught her with an ease that came only from hours of practice. She pulled back the hammer and took aim, lifting the end of her barrel to compensate for the added distance, just as she'd done earlier.

She squeezed the trigger. The can flew into the air, along with two pieces of rope and shards from the shattered arrowhead.

"Well I never!"

"Look at that!"

"You did it, Mama!"

Shouts such as those abounded, and hats flew into the air. Miles hadn't seen such commotion since the monumental day in May the year before when news reached town that the Union Pacific and Central Pacific locomotives had met at Promontory Summit in Utah Territory.

Ellie lowered her revolver and cast him a sidelong glance, but no joy shone in her eyes. She didn't even turn around to acknowledge the adulation of the crowd but merely swept a hand toward his target.

Hank quieted everyone and told Miles to take his last shot. He fired, the report of his revolver ripping the air, and sent the tin can bouncing over the ground. The clanging ceased.

Silence followed, as thick and suffocating as the smoke from the explosion. Ellie approached him, her hand extended. He took it in his and gave it a firm shake, and only then did the assembly applaud.

"Congratulations, Miles. Your reputation is intact. I know you don't think I should have been allowed to participate, but one day I hope you'll realize women are as capable as men in many areas."

He might have won the match and maintained his record, but never in his life had a victory felt as hollow. Even though he'd tried hard to prove to Ellie that he'd changed, his pride had been his downfall. She'd accept Grayson's offer for sure now.

Elenora left the sheriff's office the following Monday and hustled across the street. The door to the mercantile stood open, with Miles the only person inside. She entered and marched to the case housing his display of smoking tobacco, pipes, and cigars.

"Morning, Ellie. Shooting with the men wasn't enough for you? You're not thinking of taking up pipe smoking now, are you?"

Although Miles's voice held a hint of laughter, she was in no mood for his teasing. "Do you sell cigars in tins?"

"Tins? No. The government just allowed cigars to be sold in them. Mine are still in wooden boxes. But you, of all people, would know that, so why are you asking?"

"After church yesterday I went for a walk out by the Blackstones' place and made an interesting discovery. I scoured the neighboring field for evidence of a campsite near the charred area where the remains of the cigar were found."

"So?"

How she'd looked forward to setting him straight. "I spotted an empty cigar tin and three stubs beside a campfire ring. No one in town has the tins for sale yet, so it had to come from somewhere else. Since Tommy and Timmy haven't been away from El Dorado in months, there's no way the cigars could have been theirs. I showed Sheriff Henderson what I found, and he says the fire must have been started by someone passing through, a vagrant perhaps."

The smoker was no vagrant. The description Sheriff Henderson had been given of the man who'd been seen in the area matched that of the outlaw who'd attempted to rob the stagecoach. He had long blond hair—like Tommy and Timmy—and he favored cigars. He'd pulled one from his pocket when she'd dangled her foot out the coach door.

Although she'd shared her suspicions with the sheriff, she wasn't about to tell Miles. He hadn't believed her when she told him she'd seen the outlaw's big black horse at Deadman Creek. Besides, from what Sheriff Henderson said, it sounded like the horrid man had moved on. A skinny, blond-haired man had robbed a grocer down in Fiddletown the week before.

Miles traced a knothole in the top of the display case. "They couldn't have started it then. I was wrong."

Elenora stared at him dumbstruck. Had Miles just admitted the Talbot twins were innocent?

"I was every bit the boor on Saturday that I've worked hard to prove I'm not. I believed the allegations against the Talbot twins and treated them accordingly." He lifted his firm chin and met her gaze. "But worse than that, I allowed my pride to get in the way during the shooting match, and I'm sorry. I wanted to tell you that night when I dropped by, but I'd, um, caught you at a bad time."

He certainly had. When she'd answered the knock on her back door, she'd opened it a scant three inches, unwilling to let anyone see her with her hair loose. But there he'd stood with her bouquet in his hands, and she'd had to open the door to take the vase from him. "I didn't mean to be so short with you. It's just that I was preparing to. . ." How could she explain herself without total disregard of propriety? Bathing was an intimate matter, one a lady didn't discuss with a gentleman.

"To do battle with the dust of the day?"

"Why, yes. That's it." For once he'd shown more tact than she knew he possessed. Apparently there was hope for him yet.

"I know I shouldn't say it, but you looked beautiful with your hair flowing over your shoulders. Standing with the lamplight behind you like it was, you looked like an angel."

A smile tickled the corners of her mouth. "No, you shouldn't say such a thing to a lady."

"But you'll forgive me. You always do. Just like you'll forgive me for misjudging Tommy and Timmy. Please, say you will." He reached for her hand and gave it a squeeze.

She shouldn't allow him such liberties, but the sincerity in his voice matched that in his eyes, and she couldn't bring herself to pull away. "Sometimes I count to three before I speak. It's what I do when I get exasperated with Tildy. You might find it helpful."

"Does that mean I'm forgiven?"

She dipped her chin and looked at him through her lashes. "I never stay angry with you for long."

"The storms do blow over quickly." He grinned. "What I wanted to say that night when I showed up at such an inopportune time was that you did a remarkable job at the shooting match."

"Hmm. That's not what I heard." She couldn't resist teasing him. "My recollection is of a certain gentleman who didn't believe a woman should be allowed to compete."

"He did say that, but he came around."

"That's true. He did. After the townspeople made him see the light."

Miles ran his thumb over the back of her hand. "The poor rascal is a mite slow at times, but he's willing to learn."

She studied his handsome face. His eyes were such a brilliant blue she could drown in their depths.

The back door to the mercantile opened. "Mr. R! I'm back."

He dropped her hand, and Elenora hoped she didn't look too guilty. She should have pulled away sooner, but his touch was warm and wonderful.

Tildy burst through the curtain and slid to a stop before them, her boots scraping on the smooth floorboards. "Mama? Why are *you* here?"

"I had a question for him."

Miles tugged Tildy's braid. "You ready to help me unload the rest of those toys, Tildy girl?"

"Mm-hmm. Guess what, Mama? A family with six children came in this morning. Since nobody else was around, Mr. R let me play salesclerk. I got to take one of every single new toy out of the crates in the back and show them to the boys and girls."

"Six children? My goodness."

Miles chuckled. "The shop was noisier than usual. But we won't be seeing them again. They were on their way to Placerville where their father has a job waiting at one of the mines."

Tildy rushed to add more information. "They all had red hair, and their names started with *M*. The boys were Marshall, Merritt, and Monroe. The girls were Mamie, Millie, and Mina. Isn't Mina pretty? Lots prettier than my plain old Matilda."

Elenora caressed Tildy's cheek. "Matilda is a fine name, but Tildy does suit you."

"Mrs. R still won't use it."

"Mrs. R? Does she let you call her that now?"

"I told her Mrs. Rutledge takes too long say, and she said I could call her Nana if I wanted, but Mr. R said that wouldn't work."

"Really?" Elenora did her best not to appear overly interested, but she couldn't wait for Tildy to explain.

Miles answered. "I told her some people might choose to use terms reserved for relatives for those who aren't, but I don't hold to that practice. I've never let the Dupree children call me uncle, even though Will considers me a brother."

"Well said, Mr. Rutledge." He'd not only apologized. He was supporting her efforts to keep Tildy from becoming more attached to those in El Dorado than she already was.

The warmth in his smile could have melted all the blocks of ice in the soda works. "I do listen—and learn."

"So I see."

His clerk emerged from the back room.

"Sammy, can you keep an eye on things? Tildy and I are going to unpack those toys, and then I have an errand to run."

"Sure thing, Mr. Rutledge."

Miles walked Elenora to the door. "Once Tildy and I finish, I need to pay a visit to two young men. I owe them an apology. So I'll see you at dinner."

"Thank you—for everything."

She crossed the street to her shop with a light step and a song in her heart. Her life had certainly taken a turn for the better recently. And from all accounts, even greater things were in store. Perhaps God did care about her after all.

No! It couldn't be true. Elenora strangled the spray of violets at her throat. Dr. Lyle must be wrong. He *had* to be wrong. Tildy might have coughed a few times in the night, but that didn't mean she had a dreaded disease.

Elenora clutched the display case nearest Miles. "I don't understand, Doctor. Why do you think she has measles? Couldn't it be something like influenza? I know that's still serious, but. . ."

"Your daughter has symptoms that could be attributed to both. A fever, red eyes, a sore throat, and a cough. But I have reason to suspect measles. I understand a family with six redheaded children visited the mercantile over a week ago and that she spent a good deal of time with them."

Miles fixed her with a probing gaze. "You remember, don't you? Tildy was excited because their names all began with *M*."

Of course she remembered. Tildy had talked about them all

through supper that night. "What do they have to do with it?"

Dr. Lyle's eyes filled with compassion. "There's no easy way to say this. I received a telegram from my colleague in Placerville who is tending the children. The three youngest have the measles. Has your daughter had them before, Mrs. Watkins?"

Despite the heat, a chill crawled over her, leaving goose-flesh in its wake. She hung her head, shook it from side to side slowly, and trembled.

Miles rested a hand on her shoulder, and she took hold of it, grateful for his support. He cared for Tildy. So did Mrs. Rutledge. "When will we know? What do we do?"

"I hope I'm wrong, but we must prepare ourselves for the possibility. The disease is highly contagious. I'm putting the Rutledge place under quarantine until we know if we're dealing with the measles. Only those who've had the disease can enter, and the fewer the better. Miles and his mother have had them. Have you?"

"I—" She couldn't answer. If she did, Dr. Lyle might keep her from Tildy. "I'll bring her here and be her nurse. There's no sense inconveniencing anyone else."

Miles took her other hand in his and turned her toward him. "You haven't had them, have you? No. Don't look away. Tell me the truth."

Her throat grew tight, and she blinked to clear her vision, sending tears streaming down her face. They felt cool on her warm cheeks. Her voice came out faint and squeaky. "It doesn't matter. I know what this means. She's all I have. I can't lose her. I need to take care of her."

Dr. Lyle plunked his black bag on the display case. "Children generally fare quite well. She'll be uncomfortable for a few days, but I expect a full recovery. I'm more concerned about you. The disease is more dangerous for an adult. I can't let you take the risk of continued exposure."

Miles released her hands, produced a fresh handkerchief, and wiped her face with gentle strokes. "Mother nursed me through my case of the measles. She'll do the same for Tildy. I'll help all I can. She'll be fine. You'll see."

"I don't care about myself. I need to be with my daughter. Surely you understand."

"She needs you to stay well." Miles spoke with the same level of intensity he'd used when he told her about losing Irene and May. "You've got to do everything you can to take care of yourself."

Dr. Lyle's tone was equally serious. "Miles is right. We'll keep you informed, but you're not to enter his house until the danger of contagion has passed. I'm sorry to have to be so firm, but it's for your own good."

No, Lord! How can this be happening? My precious girl is sick, and they won't let me see her. I thought You cared.

Chapter 27

Elenora sank onto Tildy's bed, picked up her daughter's new doll, and rocked it, crooning the lullaby her dear girl had loved when she was little. How empty the place was without her.

Three long days had passed, but Elenora had yet to hear if they were facing measles or something else. If she didn't find out soon, she'd go mad. Or she'd go up the hill to Miles's place and see for herself how Tildy was doing—quarantine or no quarantine. A mother shouldn't be kept from her child like this.

For the tenth time that morning, Elenora's eyes grew moist. She blinked away the tears. Keep busy. That's what Mama had said was the best way to ward off worry. Her advice was worth heeding.

Several minutes later Elenora returned the emerald-green silk to the shelf. Her fabric display had never looked better. The swatch she'd draped over the front of the bolt was the same length as those flowing from all the others. There, in an artful arrangement of eye-catching colors, was a sight sure to capture the attention of any woman in search of calico or chiffon, linen or lawn, poplin or pongee.

Aside from one stranger, not a single customer had entered her shop since the measles scare had swept through town. She'd scrubbed every inch of the place, rearranged every item, and dusted every surface. But what good did it do when no one ventured inside? Not that she could blame them for staying home. The townspeople didn't want an epidemic. They'd even cancelled the church service that morning.

She'd opened the door to her stifling shop to get a breeze through it, noticed a few more tasks she could tend to, and busied herself seeing to them. The Lord might be angry with her for doing a few chores on the Sabbath, but she had to do something to keep her mind off things.

Elenora spied a cobweb clinging to the wall above the top shelf. She dragged a stool over, climbed up, and stretched to swipe the feather duster over the wispy strands.

"For the love of licorice, Ellie. What *are* you doing?"

Miles! How wonderful to hear the sound of his voice, even though it was raised in rebuke. She clutched the shelf and turned ever so slowly on her perilous perch. "I'm cleaning."

"How many times do I have to tell you to ask if you need help? It's too dangerous for you up there like that. Here." He wrapped his hands around her waist and lowered her to the ground.

She longed to rest her head on his broad chest, inhale the pleasant scent of sandalwood that was Miles, and soak the front of his jacket with the tears she'd struggled to keep in check ever since Dr. Lyle's visit.

Miles released her and paced. His face was drawn.

"You didn't come here to wear out my floorboards. It's measles, isn't it?"

He ceased his pacing and reached a hand toward her cheek, pulling it back before he made contact. "I shouldn't even be here."

"You had to tell me."

"I've been in the sickroom." He looked toward the ceiling as if he were lifting a prayer to the heavens. Hopefully God heard his, because He certainly hadn't been answering hers.

"How is she?"

His anguished gaze met hers. "I won't lie to you, Ellie. I

took one look at her this morning, and I knew. She's got a rash on her face, and she's coughing. The hardest part is seeing her lying there so listless. I miss her chatter."

"I do, too. Dreadfully. And I'm worried about her. I know she's in good hands, but I wish they were mine."

"I should go. Will you be all right?"

"I'm fine." She gave him the brightest smile she could produce.

"You're a strong woman, but this is enough to test anyone. There are so few people out that I'm only opening the mercantile an hour each morning. Do you have enough to get by? I could loan you—"

"I'll manage, but thank you anyway." Under no circumstances would she accept Miles's money. And she certainly wouldn't tell him how lean her bank account had grown.

"The Lord's there for you. Don't forget that. I'll be off then."

He might believe that, but God seemed more distant than ever. "If you have a minute, I'd like to get something."

She returned with Tildy's doll, kissed its forehead, and handed it to Miles. "Would you please give this to Tildy and tell her I love her very much?"

He took the doll and left, and her knees threatened to buckle. She sank onto the stool from which he'd lifted her. Was she to lose everything that mattered to her?

Elenora sat in her tiny kitchen and picked at her slice of pie. Even the sweet taste of the peaches combined with the nutty goodness of the pecans couldn't tempt her. Ever since she'd seen Miles that morning, she'd felt hollow, empty, totally alone. Nothing could fill the void. Not her music, the book she'd tried to read, or the dessert the hotel owner had sent over.

Tildy had the measles. She could lose her daughter to the dreaded disease. Although Dr. Lyle and Miles assured her Tildy stood an excellent chance of making a full recovery, Elenora couldn't help but worry. Most people survived influenza, but a severe case of it had claimed Mama and her newborn son and left Pa forever changed. People died of measles, too.

Elenora left the dessert half-eaten, trudged to her postage-stamp-sized parlor, and knelt by the sofa. She'd prayed several times a day since Tildy had taken ill. Lifting her daughter to the Lord was far easier than praying for herself.

"Lord, I don't know what to do. My dear girl's at Miles's place with a life-threatening disease, and I'm stuck here. I feel so helpless. I thought I could handle anything on my own, but this problem is too big for me. You're the only One who can take care of us now. Help me. *Please.*"

Tears streamed down her face and splashed on her bodice. There was no stopping them. She crawled onto the sofa and wrapped her arms around her knees. She choked out the words, "Hold me, Lord," curled into a ball, and wept. When her outpouring subsided, she gave way to exhaustion and drifted to sleep.

Hours later Elenora woke to find that the sun had set. She gazed at the waning moon peeking between the curtains she'd not yet closed. The milky wedge bathed the room with soft light. Lying on her side as she was, she imagined God smiling down on her—a bright wide smile—as she snuggled in His great big lap.

Warmth filled her, chasing away the chilly fingers of fear that had threatened to squeeze the life out of her. "Oh Lord, You are here, aren't You? And You do care about me."

After she'd lain in the moonlight for some time reveling in

the unexpected feeling of connection, she rose, stretched her weary limbs, and went to the window. She pressed her cheek against the smooth glass, her hands splayed on either side. She closed her eyes and sighed. "Thank You, Father."

The next morning Elenora awoke to find she was still wearing her day dress, having crawled into bed exhausted after her sweet fellowship with the Lord. After changing and performing her toilette, she fixed herself breakfast as usual, but something was different. *She* was different. The change wasn't huge, but something had happened deep inside where her dearest dreams dwelt. Her worries and cares didn't seem as heavy.

She savored the soothing scent of peppermint as she stirred her tea. God had smiled on her last night. She didn't know what the future would bring, but she could trust the One who held her in His arms.

A plan took shape in her mind. Staying here fretting did no good. She'd never been one to shy away from problems, and she wouldn't do so now.

Twenty minutes later, she dried the last dish, grabbed her violin, and ventured into the brilliant sunshine. Although the thermometer on the mercantile registered in the upper eighties already, she wouldn't let the heat deter her. Now that she'd grown accustomed to the hot, dry days of a California summer, she preferred them to the humidity she'd dealt with in Omaha.

Her heels tapped a steady beat on the walkway. With each step her spirits lifted. Taking action suited her far better than moping around her place.

She reached the barbershop and rapped on the doorframe

so as not to startle Abe, who sat in his barber chair behind a newspaper. "Good morning."

He cast his paper aside and hopped up. "Well Ellie-nora, this is a pleasant surprise. I didn't expect to see the likes of you here. What brings you in this mornin'?"

She pulled her violin case from behind her. "I've come for a lesson, if you have the time."

He gave her an ear-to-ear grin. "You have, have you? Things've been so quiet 'round here lately you could hear hair grow, so I reckon now's as good a time as any. What did you have in mind?"

Two hours later Elenora put her violin back in its case. "Thank you, Abe. I appreciate your help—and your company. I was going mad cooped up in my rooms."

"I'm right sorry about this measles business. That girl of yours is a tough one, though. That spunk of hers will pull her through, you'll see."

She had half a mind to hug the older gentleman. His warm, friendly manner appealed to her and made her wonder what life would have been like if Pa hadn't become so irascible and impossible to please after Mama died. Working with him ought to have been a joy instead of a challenge. If Mr. Grayson lived up to her first impression, he could be the mentor and champion she'd never had. He didn't have Abe's propensity for homespun speech she found so endearing, but he exuded the same friendliness and charm.

The barber walked her to the door. "I've been bendin' the good Lord's ear on her behalf. Yours, too. Take care of yourself, young lady."

She left his place, marched up Main, and turned onto Church Street. With each step her resolve strengthened. Miles was sure to be angry, but she'd just have to deal with him, because no one was going to stand in her way.

When she reached his house, as clean and white as his stiffly starched shirts, she slowed. A green shade hung at a window on the upper floor. That room must be the one in which Tildy fought her battle.

To keep from making any noise, Elenora skirted the graveled path leading to the front door, careful not to tread on any of Miles's flowers. Since the shutters at the mercantile were open, he must be there. The sound of cupboard doors closing gave evidence of Mrs. Rutledge's whereabouts.

Now was a good time to enact her plan, since it appeared Tildy was alone. Elenora removed her boots, set them on the porch, and opened the door with the speed of a sleepy snail. Bless Miles for keeping the hinges well oiled.

Dishes rattled in the kitchen, and she used the noise to cover her dash to the tri-level staircase. The steps were covered with an Oriental-patterned runner, so she'd be able to slip upstairs without anyone noticing.

Several tense moments later she reached the top. The door at the upper landing was ajar. She tiptoed to it and peered inside. The sight caused her mouth to fall open.

Even in the low light caused by the blinds, she could see Tildy asleep in a canopy bed with a pale pink top, which was set against the far wall. A quilt featuring dark pink and red flowers in forest- green baskets on a white background lay across the foot. Ruffled side curtains, drawn back at each of the bedposts, puddled on the floor in soft folds. Pink curtains the color of the bed draperies framed the windows. Never in all her years had Elenora seen a room as beautiful. Tildy must feel like a princess.

What was Miles doing with a room like this? His daughter had only been a year old when she was taken from him. A quick glance to the right revealed a crib tucked in the corner. Lying atop the coverlet was a Grenier papier mâché doll, most likely the one he'd bought on his fateful trip to Sacramento City and had never been able to give her. He'd lost his beloved daughter and experienced agony only a bereaved parent could understand. Was she to endure such pain, too?

Elenora's eyes grew moist, and she blinked back the tears. For Tildy's sake she must be strong. *Lord, uphold us in these dark days, and if it be Your will, heal my daughter.*

Elenora darted to Tildy's bedside, gazed at her precious girl's face covered with angry red spots, and pressed a kiss to her forehead. She felt warm, so Elenora laid her violin and reticule on the corner of the bed and pulled back the blanket.

She looked up and froze. She'd been so glad to see Tildy, she hadn't noticed the rocking chair on the left side of the bed where Miles sat with his head lolled to the side as he dozed.

Only once before had she seen him unshaven—the morning after he'd spent the night watching over her shop. He'd looked tired then, but his previous fatigue paled in comparison. In addition to the stubble on his chin, his hair was mussed and he had dark smudges beneath his eyes. He'd removed his waistcoat and rolled up his shirtsleeves, revealing muscular forearms. It was improper to see a man in such a state, but try as she might, she couldn't take her eyes off him.

Miles had obviously sacrificed sleep to see that Tildy received the best of care. Drawn by an irresistible urge, Elenora went to him. She reached out to brush a wayward lock of hair off his forehead.

He grabbed her wrist and spoke in a gruff whisper. "What are you doing here?"

"I—" The flash of anger in his eyes silenced her.

"Come with me."

He pulled her after him into the hallway and backed her against the railing, giving her no way to escape. "Do you have any idea what you've done? Tildy's at the height of contagion."

She found her voice. "I know the risk I'm taking. I've thought long and hard, and then I prayed. God heard me, Miles."

His expression softened. "Of course He did. But surely He didn't send you here?"

The thickness in her throat made speaking a tremendous effort. Her voice faltered, but she didn't let that stop her. "I came of my own free will. My pa wasn't there when my mama and little brother passed from this world, and I saw what that did to him. I knew I couldn't live with myself if I didn't do everything possible to take care of my little girl. If I get sick, so be it. But if I were to sacrifice my well-being for hers and something happened. . ."

A flood of tears poured forth in a torrent.

Miles pulled Ellie into his arms and rubbed her back as she sobbed into his shirtfront. He should be furious with her, but the childlike wonder in her voice when she said the Lord had heard her prayer had caused Miles's anger to fade. It had dissolved completely when she gave him her reason for defying the doctor's orders.

She'd obviously reached the limit of her endurance and had nowhere else to turn. Miles wanted to hold her and never let her go.

All too soon she broke free and turned away. "May I use your handkerchief?" She reached a hand behind her back, and he filled it with the freshly laundered square. After mopping her face, she lifted penitent eyes to him. "How angry are you?"

"I'm not."

She dropped the handkerchief and groped for it, catching it just before it hit the floor. "You were. I saw it."

"I was, but I'm not now. Mother said she told you about the fire and how Irene had left May with her washerwoman, but there's more to the story. What you don't know is that I'm to blame for what happened that night."

Puzzlement pinched her face. "How can that be? You weren't even there."

"Exactly. Irene and I had words. As you know, I have a tendency to speak before I think. She'd been out socializing four nights that week, and I accused her of being a negligent mother. She tried to tell me how trapped she felt being stuck at home all day with a baby, but I didn't listen. All I could think about was how little May and I mattered to her. Instead of trying to understand what my wife was telling me, I said I needed to take a buying trip. I left the next morning—without saying goodbye. If I hadn't stormed off. . ."

He didn't dare look at Ellie's face, for he was sure to see disgust or disapproval there. He deserved that, but he wasn't sure he was strong enough to endure her disappointment in him.

She took his hand and said his name with such feeling that a ray of hope penetrated his parched soul. He lifted his head, and the compassion and caring in her warm brown eyes were unmistakable. He released the breath he'd been holding, and the viselike tightness that had taken hold of him eased.

"Jake and I had our troubles, too. Every couple does. But you aren't to blame for the fire. It was an accident." She squeezed his hand and released it. "Thank you for trusting me with this."

"I wasn't there, and I've had to live with that knowledge every day of my life. I can't change what happened. I see that now, and I understand why you're here."

"Then you'll let me stay? I have a surprise for Tildy, one I think she'll like."

A knock sounded on the front door. Following a call from the kitchen, Dr. Lyle let himself in. He crossed the entry, grasped the railing, and stopped. "Mrs. Watkins! What on earth are you doing here? I strictly forbid it."

Miles put a hand at the small of her back to show his support. "She knows the risk, but she needs to be with her daughter."

"Oh, she'll be with her all right, because I can't allow her to leave the house now and run the risk of her exposing anyone else."

Mother bustled into the entry. "That's not a problem, Doctor. We have a guest room."

"You know you may well end up with two patients on your hands."

"Miles and I are ready for that, aren't we, son?"

Meddlesome though she might be, Mother had her moments. And this was definitely one of them. "We are. *If* Mrs. Watkins takes ill—which she may not—we'll care for her as diligently as we've been caring for Tildy."

Ellie had remained quiet throughout the exchange, which wasn't like her. She darted her eyes from one of them to the other. "I never intended to stay. I thought I'd take her to our place."

Dr. Lyle began his climb. "As sick as she is, I don't want her moved. You'll have to remain here until I lift the quarantine."

"But I can't stay here. It wouldn't be proper."

"You should have thought of that before you disregarded my directive."

"Elenora, dear, you needn't concern yourself." Mother smiled at her. "I'm a more-than-adequate chaperone. It isn't as though this is a house party. Your daughter has a dreaded disease. Dr. Lyle will simply tell anyone who asks that you're here to nurse her back to health, won't you, Doctor?" She shifted her smile his way.

He threw up his hands in defeat, and Miles stifled a grin. He liked the idea of having Ellie here. Perhaps he'd finally have the opportunity to show her how much he'd changed and figure out a way to convince her to remain in El Dorado.

Chapter 28

"Play it again, Mama. *Please*."

Poor Ellie. She might wish she'd never learned how to fiddle if Tildy kept this up. Miles still couldn't believe Ellie had asked Abe for lessons and had surprised Tildy with a lively rendition of "Pop Goes the Weasel" when Dr. Lyle left after their heated meeting.

But Ellie was a devoted mother. Ever since the day she'd learned of the possibility of the measles, she'd thought of nothing but her daughter. She hadn't mentioned her shop but once or twice, and then only in passing. Her entire focus had been on getting Tildy well.

"Sweetheart, I'd love to, but I need to rest." She sank into the rocker beside Tildy's bed. Ellie had spent hour after hour over the past nine days making up stories for Tildy about a girl who saved a town from an outlaw, playing cat's cradle with her, and fiddling.

Ellie had welcomed Miles's instruction and added several numbers to her repertoire, including "Turkey in the Straw" and "Old Dan Tucker." Although she was still tight, she'd made considerable progress. Sadly, her interest in their upcoming duet had waned, which showed in her performance during the few practices they'd squeezed in while Mother sat with Tildy.

"Your poor mama has been at your bedside day and night. I think it's time you gave her a break. Dr. Lyle said you could get up now if you take it easy, so how about you and I play a game of checkers? I'll even let the two of you into my study—as long as your organized mama promises to turn a blind eye to the piles on my, um, less-than-tidy desk."

Ellie didn't smile at his teasing. In fact she looked as though she hadn't heard him.

"C'mon, Mama. Mr. R's been promising me a visit to his special room. He said it's his haven, and he only lets Mrs. R in there to clean once a month."

He set up the game on the table in the center of the room. Tildy trooped in wearing her dressing gown and house slippers. Ellie chose his wingback leather armchair, where she rested her head against the side and closed her eyes. She looked exhausted. A nap would do her good. Since Tildy was much improved and the blazing red spots had faded, she was no longer in danger from a draft, so he opened the windows to create some airflow.

Midway into the third game a hoarse cough from Ellie caught his attention. He turned and found her huddled under a coverlet. She appeared to be shivering, which made no sense. It had to be in the eighties. He pressed a hand to her forehead. *Fever.*

"Tildy, would you pull back your mama's bedcovers? She needs to lie down."

"What's wrong?"

He did his best to keep the panic out of his voice. "I'm not sure, but she doesn't seem to be feeling well." Dr. Lyle would make the official diagnosis, but Miles had learned a great deal about measles the past few days and knew the symptoms. Tildy had coughed some and run a low-grade fever, but she'd never complained of cold or trembled the way Ellie was. Although he'd known this was a possibility, he'd prayed fervently that she could be spared the discomfort Tildy had endured.

"I'm going to pick you up, Ellie." He scooped her in his arms, carried her to the guestroom, and laid her on the bed.

She roused and shook her head. "You have to go. It's not proper for—"

"Shh." He pressed a finger to her lips. "You need to lie still. I'll get Mother for you, and then I'll go for Dr. Lyle."

"No!" She grabbed his hand and searched the room frantically, her eyes coming to rest on Tildy. "Sw—sweetheart, would you get Mrs. R?"

"Yes, Mama." Tildy hurried off. She shouldn't exert herself, but it seemed Ellie wanted her out of the way.

"Miles." Her voice was soft but insistent. He leaned close. "I know it's the measles. And I'm afraid I'm going to get worse before I get better. Promise me that if anything happens to me you won't send Tildy back to my pa. I want you to take her."

Of all the things Ellie had ever said to him, this was by far the most amazing. He didn't know what to say. Not that he could get any words out. She'd rendered him speechless.

Dr. Lyle removed his stethoscope and put it back in its case. If he didn't say something soon, Miles was afraid he might shake the man.

"I'd hoped to see some improvement."

"It can't be that bad. She doesn't have nearly as many spots as Tildy did."

"Unfortunately, a mild eruption often portends a more severe case, which is what we're seeing here."

Mother rested a hand on Miles's back. "What can we do, Doctor?"

"Continue bathing her with cool cloths and offering her plenty of liquids. I suggest barley or rice water, or you can pour hot water over apples and make apple-tea. Give her five grains of Dover's powder in a little syrup for the cough, and apply a mustard plaster morning and evening until she stops complaining of chest pain."

"Much of what she says is gibberish." This troubled Miles more than anything else. He had decisions to make, and he needed Ellie's input. So much had happened the past four days.

Dr. Lyle closed his black leather bag. "That's the fever talking. I don't have to tell you how critical the next couple of days will be. One of you needs to be with her at all times. Call me if her condition changes—no matter the hour. Otherwise, I'll see you tomorrow."

Miles pressed a fist to his mouth to hide his trembling chin. Ellie would make it. She had to. Tildy needed her. And so did he.

Mother saw Dr. Lyle out.

"Lord, hold Ellie in Your arms." Miles dropped to his knees beside the bed and caressed her cheek, her speckled skin warm to the touch. "You're the Great Physician. If it be Your will, please bring her through this. I'll do whatever You ask of me, even if means stepping aside so she can pursue her dream."

He clutched her hand and continued to kneel, his head bowed and his heart heavy. A touch on his shoulder roused him.

"My old knees ache seeing you like that. Why don't you take a seat?"

He did as Mother asked. Strains from the piano below let him know Tildy was occupied. Praise the Lord, she was on the mend. Other than being even thinner than before, she looked like herself again. Mother's tempting fare would soon restore her to full health. Now to get Ellie better.

"Elenora's a fighter, son. You know that better than anyone. She'll pull through. You'll see."

"She's strong. But she's going to have surprises in store. When she sees what I've done, she'll be more than ready to take

Grayson up on his offer."

"You had no choice. She'll understand."

He hoped Mother was right. But when Ellie emerged from her fever and found her merchandise in the mercantile, no doubt she'd have some heated words for him.

Elenora woke and found Miles asleep in the rocking chair next to her bed. Judging by the amount of light sneaking in around a green blind that had been hung in the window, morning was making its appearance. For the first time since he'd carried her to the bed, she felt hungry. She had vague recollections of being held up to drink some rather unpleasant concoctions. What she'd give for a cup of peppermint tea and some toast.

She wriggled until she'd untangled her nightdress from around her legs, propped herself against the pillows, and pulled the sheet to her chin. Someone had removed her hair from its chignon and plaited it. She arranged the braid over one shoulder, pinched her cheeks to give them a little color, and moistened her parched lips with the tip of her tongue.

Miles looked dreadful. Much worse than he had when she'd surprised him the day she sneaked into his house. From the looks of things, he'd not shaved in days. His hair had the tousled appearance that came from raking one's hands through it. And although the idea seemed incomprehensible, she had the distinct feeling he hadn't changed his shirt in some time.

If he were in such a state, what a sorry sight she must be. And here she'd been primping when her face was likely swollen and covered in a riot of unseemly red blotches. What a silly goose she could be at times. A giggle began deep inside, growing until she could no longer contain it. She burst into a fit of laughter mingled with coughing.

His eyes flew open, and he was at her side in an instant, running his hands over her face as though he had every right to touch her. He pressed his lips to her forehead and each of her cheeks, soft and slow. She closed her eyes and savored the sensations surging through her. Miles's kisses made her feel alive—and cherished.

When he sat up, his face was aglow. "Praise God! The fever's broken. You're going to be all right, Ellie." He leaped up, his hands raised to the ceiling, looking completely overcome.

Her thinking must still be fuzzy. He hadn't been kissing her. He'd merely been checking her temperature. If she'd had the strength, she'd have smacked a palm to her forehead. She contented herself by watching him roam around the room singing praises to God for seeing her through the dark days of the disease.

Miles did care about her, and that warmed her to the tips of her toes.

Her stomach rumbled. "If you don't mind, Miles, I could use something to eat."

He grabbed the doorframe, leaned out, and hollered, "Mother! Tildy! She's awake, and she's asking for food."

Mrs. Rutledge and Tildy clomped up the stairs and carried on in much the same way Miles had. When they finally contained themselves, Mrs. Rutledge shooed Miles and Tildy from the room and helped Elenora with her toilette. Although it felt strange to accept the older woman's ministrations, the sponge bath and fresh nightdress were welcome.

The bed creaked when Mrs. Rutledge settled on it. She brushed Elenora's hair and plaited it afresh, chatting all the while about this and that.

Elenora's questions couldn't wait. "How many days have I been in bed?"

"You came down with measles at the end of Tildy's two weeks, and you've been sick five days."

"How sick?"

Mrs. Rutledge tied a thread on the end of Elenora's braid. "I suppose it won't hurt to tell you now that you've turned the corner, but yours was one of the worst cases of measles Dr. Lyle has ever treated. He'd done all he could and told us to pray. Day and night we sat by you and did just that. And God's seen fit to give you back to us."

"Miles sat with me?"

"I spelled him as often as he'd let me, but aside from meals and an occasional catnap, he was planted in that rocking chair. And you needn't get that worried look on your face, my dear. Everything was proper. The door was open whenever he was with you, Tildy and I were here in the house the entire time, and I took care of your personal needs."

Elenora pressed her hands to her cheeks. "My face. How bad is it?"

"I always know a woman is on the mend when she starts thinking about her appearance. You were a far sight sicker than Tildy, but you don't have nearly as many spots as she did."

"That's the third time you've called her Tildy."

She busied herself at the bureau, but Elenora could see Mrs. Rutledge's reflection in the looking glass. She swiped at a tear with the back of her hand and continued as if nothing were amiss. "We've spent a good deal of time together, and I figure if the name is that important to her, I can use it. I know you don't want her to call me Nana, but that chatty girl is as dear to me as my own flesh and blood."

When she turned around, a smile lit her face. The strong

resemblance between mother and son struck Elenora. Why had it taken her so long to see what a kind heart was hidden beneath that seemingly gruff exterior?

"Miles said you're hungry. I'll fix you a boiled egg, tea, and dry toast and send Tildy to keep you company."

Tildy entertained Elenora while she awaited her breakfast, filling her in on the latest news in town. "Mr. Olds has rock candy in his shop now, clear and straw-colored. And Sheriff Henderson nailed up a new wanted poster for an outlaw named Dead-Eye Dan. That sounds as creepy as Deadman Creek, doesn't it?"

Elenora smiled. "You are certainly yourself again, aren't you, sweetheart?"

She ate her breakfast with an audience of three. When she finished the simple meal, which tasted like manna from heaven, Mrs. Rutledge took the dirty dishes and ushered Tildy from the room. Miles remained, sitting in the rocker, chasing his thumbs around one another. He'd changed, shaved, and smelled much better, as did she.

After a good three minutes of silence, Elenora could stand it no more. "What's troubling you?"

He ceased his fidgeting and scraped his teeth over his lower lip. "I did something you might not approve of. I had my reasons, and I hope you'll not be too sore at me."

"No! If you let Tildy call you—"

"Ellie, trust me. I wouldn't go against your wishes like that. It's about your shop."

"My shop? Why, I hadn't even thought about it. So tell me. What did you do?"

He grimaced. "That greedy landlord of yours blew into town and stirred up trouble."

"Oh dear. I'm late with the rent."

"I took care of that, but I couldn't talk Steele out of—" He pounded a fist into his other hand. "There's no easy way to say this. He found a man willing to pay even more per month than the exorbitant amount he's been charging you. And he evicted you."

"Evicted me?" The scoundrel! *One. Two. Three.* She scrambled for a semblance of control. "Well, I'm not too surprised. He made it clear he didn't like renting to a woman. When do I have to be out?"

"I moved your things day before yesterday. Your personal items are in Tildy's room. I cleared some cases in my shop and put your wares in them. But don't worry. Sammy's keeping your funds separate."

"You moved my *personal* things?"

Color crept up his neck. "Not your intimate things. Tildy packed those."

"I don't know what to say. I mean other than thank you. I'll pay you back, of course."

"Don't even think about that right now. You've got more important matters to deal with, such as getting well. And your offer from Grayson. He sent you another letter." Miles held up a bulging envelope sealed with red wax the same shade as the older gentleman's cravat.

"Since I'm not supposed to read, would you do it for me?"

"Are you sure you want me to?"

"I can't ask Tildy. I've not told her about this yet. Would you please begin with his letter and save those from the others for last?" She'd waited weeks for this packet, and she wasn't about to wait another minute. She shifted until she was comfortable and nodded.

Miles picked up Mr. Grayson's letter. "It's dated September first, which is four days ago.

"My dear Mrs. Watkins,

I must apologize for the delay in getting this missive to you. My attorney was involved with a case and was unable to draft his recommendation until the trial concluded. I've included his letter as well as those from my banker and minister. All three gentlemen are more than willing to entertain questions from you, should you desire to make further inquiries.

I'm sure you're eager to hear the details of my offer, so I'll enumerate them."

Miles stopped. "I really don't think I'm the best person to be reading this."

"I disagree. I can think of no one more qualified to give me an assessment of his offer."

"I suppose that's true, but. . ."

Once she'd convinced him to keep reading, she listened intently. Joy bubbled inside her. Mr. Grayson's credentials were exemplary, and his plan exceeded her expectations.

Miles hesitated. "There's a postscript."

"Go ahead. Please."

He grasped the sheets of parchment so tightly they crinkled and read the addendum.

"P.S. I don't share this information to solicit sympathy, but I want to be honest with you. A recent visit to my doctor revealed that the shortness of breath I've experienced recently is due to a weak heart. By following his instructions to the letter, he said I might have a couple of good years left. If you were to accept my offer, you could inherit my business sooner than I'd originally thought—and bring me considerable happiness in my last days on earth."

At her request, Miles read the sterling recommendations Mr. Grayson had included. She sank into the pillows feeling light-headed. The past hour had been unreal. She'd returned from a trip through the Valley of the Shadow of Death and learned that Miles had gone to battle for her against her former landlord and ended up moving her wares into the mercantile. And now Mr. Grayson had offered her his business on a silver platter, but the poor man had serious health issues. She'd need some time to sort everything out.

Miles folded the letters, wiggled them into the envelope, and crossed the room, where he set it on the bureau. He rested his hands on the edge and stood with his back to her saying nothing.

"What do you think?"

He returned to the rocking chair and drummed his fingers on the arms. When he lifted his head, she was struck by how exhausted he looked. Weariness had carved crevices in his brow and stolen the sparkle from his eyes. He'd done so much for her, and yet she'd been so busy thinking of herself she hadn't thanked him properly. "Miles, I—"

"I'm sorry I kept you waiting. I can find no fault with him or his offer based on what I read. This is everything you wanted. . . and more—aside from the postscript, of course."

"Then you don't think me foolish to consider it?"

"You came all the way out here from Omaha with less incentive than that. My proposal wasn't nearly as attractive. But are you willing to be more to him than a business partner? It seems clear that's what he has in mind."

She laughed. "You said something like that once before, and I told you I view this as a business arrangement, which I feel certain Mr. Grayson does, too. I've never given him any reason to think otherwise. He's kind and generous, but he's old enough to be my father, as you pointed out. I don't foresee a proposal coming my way."

Miles made a strange sound, a cross between a grunt and a chuckle. "You might be surprised. Once a determined man chooses a course of action, he tends to follow it."

She smoothed the bedsheet, allowing herself time to form her reply. A dizzying procession of thoughts paraded through her muddled mind. One struck her with such force that she lay against the pillows, drawing deep breaths until she slowed her racing heart. "The concert! It's only eight days away. We have to practice."

"Mr. Morton understands the situation. If you don't feel up to it—"

"I'll just have to do everything in my power to recover quickly, because I'm going to perform with you. Nothing will keep me from that."

For the first time since she'd awakened that morning, Miles gave her one of his heart-stopping smiles.

Chapter 29

Mrs. Sanders handed Miles a black serge sun umbrella with a curved wooden handle. "I had something a little fancier in mind, Mr. Rutledge. My sister is coming from San Francisco and is used to nice things."

He smiled. She was the first customer who'd come in since Ellie had recovered sufficiently to work in the mercantile, and he relished the opportunity to show her that, like Grayson, he could appreciate her ability to meet women's needs.

Since Mrs. Sanders was hard of hearing, Miles had an excuse to raise his voice. He made sure to speak loudly enough so Ellie could hear him in the back room, where she sat at the desk going over the record of sales he and Sammy had made on her behalf during the two weeks she'd convalesced.

"Mrs. Watkins has a parasol you might like. Let me show you."

The matronly woman accompanied him to another display case, where he removed a showy contraption that was sure to please, one he and Ellie had discussed that very morning. Good thing he'd listened. "This satin model is trimmed with Spanish lace and has a heavy silk lining. As you can see, it comes in three colors, which Mrs. Watkins informs me are cardinal, myrtle green, and plum. And notice how the silver handle has a floral pattern."

"Ooh. How lovely. Hortense is sure to be impressed. It must be rather dear, but my sister is worth the added expense."

He leaned over to whisper the price, which was ten times that of the model he'd first shown her. No doubt she'd prefer Ellie's frilly version. Women seemed to have a greater appreciation of fine things than he did, although he now used his sterling silver comb with pride. Every time he pulled the engraved case out of his pocket, he marveled at the thought Ellie had put into the gift.

The older woman lifted her hooked nose in the air. "Mrs. Watkins does have good taste, doesn't she? I'll take the green one."

He completed the sale and handed Mrs. Sanders her parcel. She went her way, leaving the shop empty. Since things had been slow during the measles scare, he'd given Sammy time off to help Mr. Abbott bring in his crops. Hopefully his clerk would get up the nerve to ask permission to court Abbott's daughter while he was there.

Sammy had the right idea. A man needed a woman in his life. The right one could make all the difference. Miles glanced at the curtain behind which Ellie sat. What a fool he'd been to turn her away the day she'd arrived in town. She wasn't at all like Irene. He'd been so afraid of making another mistake, he'd done just that. Unless his final attempt to convince Ellie to accept his offer succeeded, she'd be packing her things the day after tomorrow and heading to Marysville.

The bell on the door clanged, and a tall man in a ragged linen duster entered. "I see you got ready-made clothing. I want a complete outfit, including one of them there Stetsons and a fancy coat like that one." He jabbed a finger at the black model on the dressmaker's dummy.

"Ah, yes. The rifle coat is an excellent piece of workmanship." After a month with scanty sales, an eager customer was welcome.

Elenora stared at the numbers she'd tallied. Whether she liked it or not, Mr. Steele's eviction had given her no choice but to accept Mr. Grayson's offer. There were no other buildings for rent in town, and she couldn't work beside Miles feeling the way she did. Being so close to him and not being able to tell him would be tortuous. If only he'd say something. . . But he hadn't.

Her stomach revolted at the thought of leaving El Dorado. She rose from the desk and walked around the back room of Miles's shop, admiring the floor-to-ceiling shelves now filled with his replenishment stock, thanks to her efforts to get the items out of the crates. If she had more time, she'd get his paperwork in order, too, but after paying him back, she'd have just enough money to cover her hotel bill and get her and Tildy set up in Marysville. She couldn't put off her departure any longer.

Tonight's concert would be her farewell to a place, a people, and a man she'd grown to love. She'd rest on the Sabbath and break the news to Tildy as gently as possible after the service. First thing Monday morning she'd pack her wares and embark on her new adventure—just in time to get Tildy enrolled in a new school term.

Elenora pressed a hand to her stomach. Perhaps by then the queasiness would cease. God had provided for her, and she wasn't going to let her topsy-turvy emotions rule. Hadn't Pa always said that following one's heart was foolhardy and to trust one's head in matters of import? He might have been wrong about many things, but she could see the logic in that bit of advice.

Now to let Miles know she was ready to run her errand. She'd heard him talking with one man, but that was all. She slipped through the curtain as a lanky man with short blond hair came out of the changing closet wearing a whole new outfit.

Miles saw her and smiled. "If you want to run to the bank now, I'll be fine."

"I'll get my things and be on my way then." She nodded a polite greeting at the customer, who leered at her. He focused with one eye. The other was turned to the floor, unmoving.

Cold fingers of dread gripped her. Somehow she managed to keep from visibly trembling.

This horrid man had held up the stagecoach the day she and Tildy had arrived in El Dorado. She was sure of it. He must be Dead-Eye Dan, the outlaw Tildy had read about on the wanted poster. They were in danger, but Miles didn't know it. She'd have to act quickly.

Elenora forced herself to walk to the back room at a relaxed pace. She didn't want to alarm Miles prematurely or let the outlaw know she'd realized who he was. Once there she grabbed the back of the desk chair and whispered a prayer. "Please protect us, Lord, and be with me now. I can't do this without You."

Her hands shook as she shuffled some papers at the desk. She grabbed her reticule, along with the lavender envelope she used for her deposits, and headed out front. It seemed Dead-Eye had made his final selection. His attention was on Miles.

She went behind the counter, her eyes never leaving the men, and reached under the cash drawer until her hand came to rest on Miles's revolver. Good. The Colt was right where he'd told her he kept it—loaded and ready. She put her handbag and deposit on the shelf beside it.

The outlaw, now fully dressed in the new finery, strapped on his pistol belt. Her heart sank. It was worse than she'd thought. Dead-Eye carried not one but two guns. He shoved the first into his holster and slipped the second into the waistband of the new trousers.

The men came to the counter. Miles folded the wanted man's old garments and carried on a casual conversation. Not until the bell on the door rang and Pearl Dupree entered the shop did Dead-Eye make his first move. He looked directly at Elenora, patted the gun on the side away from Miles, and spoke in a low growl. "If you love this man of yours, you'd best get rid of that lady and lock the door."

"He's not—" She'd come so close to correcting his mistake but caught herself in time. Her ploy would seem even more believable if the outlaw thought she and Miles were married.

"Go nice and slow-like. You say anything out of line, and your feller will be ready for the undertaker."

Elenora heard Miles's sharp intake of breath, but she dared not look at him. He'd obviously attempted something, because the outlaw muttered another menacing threat. Her mind raced. She could use her friend to deliver a message—if she were careful how she worded it.

"Good morning, Mrs. Dupree. I'm sorry, but we're going to have to close the shop today. Mr. Rutledge is feeling poorly. I'm sorry for the inconvenience. Would you be so kind as to tell Mr. Henderson we won't be able to make it to our fiddling practice? I'd appreciate it. And now, if you'll excuse me, I need to lock up and see to my husband."

Pearl's eyes widened for an instant, and she glanced at Miles. "Yes of course. I do hope you'll be feeling better soon, Mr. Rutledge. Take good care of him, Mrs. Rutledge."

Pearl ambled in the direction of Sheriff Henderson's office looking unhurried and serene, and Elenora breathed a sigh of relief.

She locked the door, turned, and gulped. The outlaw had pulled his gun and had it trained on Miles.

"Now missy, your man here was kind enough to let it slip that you was on your way to the bank. I don't reckon you'll be needin' to make that trip today. I'll take care of it for you. Be a good girl, and hand over the money."

She went behind the counter, got the deposit, and held it out to Dead-Eye with a trembling hand. She looked directly at Miles for the first time and witnessed his horror as his eyes came to rest on her lavender envelope.

"No, Ellie!" He received an elbow in his side for his outburst.

Dead-Eye raised his gun to Miles's temple. "Leave her be, or your pretty wife will find out how much damage one of these can do. That ain't something you want her to see, now is it?"

"I'm sorry, M—miles."

Dead-Eye snatched the envelope out of her hand. He tried to slip it in the inside breast pocket of the trail coat with his free hand while maintaining eye contact, but he was forced to look down to locate its whereabouts in the new garment.

In that brief instant Miles inclined his head ever so slightly in the direction of his revolver. She gave him the barest hint of a nod in return.

"Well now, that's a right nice turn of things. I come in for some new togs and to clean out your till, and I get a bonus for my work." The outlaw patted the bulging pocket. "Now, Ellie girl, open that there drawer and give me everything in it, or your man's buzzard bait."

She pulled out the currency and slapped it on the counter in front of him. With hands now shaking violently, she scooped up the coins. They slipped through her fingers and rolled across the floor. "Oh no! I'm sorry."

"Dumb fool woman! Don't stand there gawkin'. Get down and pick 'em up, every last one. And be quick about it. I got places to go."

Dead-Eye's finger was on the trigger. Her vision swam, and the blood pounded in her ears, but she mustn't lose her head now. She scrambled around on her hands and knees. When she'd gathered a handful of coins, she dropped them on the counter. They clattered on the varnished wood surface.

She hadn't fired Miles's Colt in months, but he'd been right about the range during a holdup. No way would she miss at this distance, even with a trembling trigger finger.

The next few seconds seemed like hours. She tossed a few more coins on the counter.

While Dead-Eye scraped them into his hand, she grabbed Miles's gun, pulled back the hammer, stood, and pointed the revolver at the outlaw. In the same instant Miles smashed his clasped hands down on Dead-Eye's arm.

The outlaw's gun went off.

Glass shattered

His revolver hit the floor.

Miles kicked the weapon out of the way.

The outlaw went for his other gun, but Miles grabbed Dead-Eye's hands, pinned them behind his back, and shoved him forward. "Move it, mister! We'll deal with you out back."

Elenora kept the revolver aimed at the outlaw as she walked along beside the two men.

Dead-Eye let out with a raucous laugh. "Ain't this a sight. A girlie with a gun. You even know how to use that thing?"

"I killed the last intruder that came in my shop," she said without hesitation, her voice firm. "Unless you want to suffer the same fate, you'd better do what my husband says."

"And don't even think of trying anything," Miles snarled. "If you value your life, you'll go nice and easy. She's a crack shot." He shoved Dead-Eye forward.

When she was past the counter, Elenora got in position behind the outlaw. She had the gun trained on him, her finger poised and ready to slip before the trigger and squeeze it if need be.

They made it out the back door and onto South Street

without any trouble, but without warning Dead-Eye rammed his heel into Miles's shin.

Miles groaned and dropped to his knees.

The outlaw tore the gun from Elenora's hands.

Two shots rang out.

Dead-Eye fell on top of Miles.

Elenora screamed and rushed to Miles. With strength born of necessity, she dragged the outlaw off him and beheld a sight that caused her deeper agony than anything she'd ever seen.

Miles, the man she loved, lay motionless in the dusty street, the front of his white apron drenched with blood.

She threw herself on top of him. "No! Dear Lord, no! Not Miles. Please, not Miles."

Chapter 30

"Mrs. Watkins." Sheriff Henderson placed a hand on her shoulder. "Come now, Elenora, let the poor man up." He helped her stand. "Miles is fine. Look."

He unfolded himself and got to his feet.

"You're not dead!" She was in his arms in an instant, clinging to him and shaking violently. "Miles! Oh Miles, I was so scared."

"It's all right now. I'm fit as a fiddle." He crushed her to him, his heart drumming against her ear.

The sheriff cleared his throat. "I know this has been a shock and all, but I've got a dead man to deal with and will need to ask you two some questions."

She ended the embrace. For several seconds she stared at Miles with her mouth agape, still as a statue. She'd thrown herself at him in full view of the sheriff and several others. She'd even called him by his first name. And yet he didn't say a word, smile, or give her any indication of his feelings.

How could she have misread things so badly? She'd been so sure he cared about her as much as she did him.

Somehow she managed to regain her speech and did her best not to come across as a hysterical female, even though she must have sounded like one when she'd forgotten herself moments before. "That awful man shot you. I heard the shots, and you both fell."

"He got off a shot that missed me mere seconds before Hank shot him. He knocked me backward when he fell on me."

"The sheriff shot him? But I didn't see anyone else."

"He and the others were behind the shrubs in my yard." He motioned to the men who'd emerged from the hedge across the alley from the mercantile. "You were so focused on the outlaw, you didn't notice them. But I did. I dropped after the scoundrel kicked me so I could give them a clear shot."

"I'm sorry I let him get your gun, but he took me by surprise."

"If it hadn't been mine, it would've been his. Don't discount yourself. You were remarkable." His eyes shone.

Miles *was* pleased with her. Really, truly pleased with her. And that knowledge pleased her to no end.

"Mama! Mr. R!" Tildy flung herself at them. "You're all right."

"Miles!" Mrs. Rutledge stopped short when she saw his bloodstained front. "Merciful heaven. Are you all right, son?"

"I'm fine."

"They told us you and Elenora were in trouble and to stay inside, but we heard the shots and the scream."

"I know it looks bad, but this fellow missed me." He nodded toward the outlaw, who lay facedown on the street.

"Do you have any idea who he was?" Sheriff Henderson asked.

"None," Miles said, "but whoever he was, he died wearing some of the finest clothes Rutledge Mercantile has to offer. That's what he'd come in for. That and all the money he could get his hands on."

"I think he was Dead-Eye Dan, Sheriff," Elenora volunteered. "Tildy saw his name on a wanted poster, and when I noticed that his right eye roamed, I made the connection. I'd be willing to testify he's the same man who held up the stagecoach the day Tildy and I arrived in town."

"Oh, Mama. He would've shot us that day if hadn't been for the Talbot twins, wouldn't he?"

"Yes, dear. I believe he would have, but the Lord used them to protect us."

Sheriff Henderson shook his head. "We won't be able to put a stop to Tommy and Timmy's boasting when they hear who they ran out of town. Dead-Eye Dan was wanted for three murders up in Placer County. I'll send a telegram, and they'll have someone here to identify him right off."

Miles laid his violin in its case on the table in his parlor. Ellie had managed to make it through their duet, although after two weeks with little practice, she was rusty. "Are you sure you feel up to performing tonight?"

She put her instrument away and sank onto the settee. "My first morning back might have been more draining than I'd expected, but I'm not about to let that man rob me of anything else. I've looked forward to this concert for months."

Tildy plopped down beside Ellie. "But the sheriff said he wouldn't have made off with too much money, just the new clothes from Mr. R's shop."

Miles chuckled. "That's because your mama put one big bill at the front of her deposit, but all that was behind it were outdated fliers. That was some shrewd planning if you ask me."

Ellie rewarded him with a smile. She'd been amazing. When he'd taught her to shoot, he never expected the life she'd save would be his.

"Oh Mama, you were so brave. I wish I could've been there to see you take on an outlaw."

"I'm glad you weren't. I had enough on my mind without

having to worry about you."

"Would you have shot him?"

Now that the excitement was over, there would be no end to Tildy's questions. Poor Ellie would be answering them for weeks.

"I don't like to think about it, but yes. If I hadn't been afraid I'd miss and shoot Mr. Rutledge by mistake, I think I would have. I've never been as scared in all my life as I was when that awful man put a gun to his head."

Miles settled into his armchair. "And I've never been as proud as I was when your mama figured out how to get Mrs. Dupree to help us. The sheriff said she got the entire town to come to our rescue. There were men on roofs, up trees, and behind my shrubs."

Tildy scrunched her face. "What did Mrs. Dupree do?"

"When she came in the shop, the outlaw ordered your mama to get her out fast, so she told Mrs. Dupree I was sick and asked her to let the sheriff know we'd not be at fiddle practice." And she'd referred to him as her husband.

If only that were true, but she still insisted she was leaving the day after tomorrow, even though she'd thrown herself at him and shrieked his name at the top of her lungs—his *first* name. She'd clung to him, and he'd wanted to hold her and never let go, but she'd pushed away just as she had after the wall of her shop had collapsed. And she'd kept her distance ever since.

He'd promised the Lord he would let her go if that's what she wanted, but honoring his promise could turn out to be far more difficult than he'd expected.

"I was glad Pearl understood what I was trying to say and that you figured out some of the men who'd come to help us would be out back and led us there. That was clever."

"Not as clever as you telling that outlaw you'd killed the

last intruder in your shop. If he'd known you meant a snake. . ." Miles laughed.

"I know Sheriff Henderson shot Dead-Eye Dan, Mama, but I still think you should get the reward. But there's one good thing. I won't be in trouble for reading wanted posters now, will I?"

Ellie cupped Tildy's face in her hands. "You can read them to your heart's content, sweetheart, and I won't say a thing about it."

Miles rubbed his ear as if to clear it. "I can't believe what I'm hearing. You've changed."

"Oh, I do hope so."

She had. She'd overcome one obstacle after another and grown stronger in the process, and yet at the same time she'd softened into someone who didn't take life as seriously. Her faith had deepened, and she'd welcomed the townspeople into her heart. She was a wonderful mother, a good friend, and a successful businesswoman.

But it wasn't enough. Ellie wanted more, and she was going elsewhere to find it. He'd known Grayson was trouble the minute he'd laid eyes on him.

Miles had one thing to offer Ellie the older man didn't, though. Would it be enough?

Elenora stood before the mirror in the guest room of Miles's house and smoothed the skirt of the satin gown Mrs. Rutledge had made for her. The dress was several shades lighter than the two wide strips of dark purple velvet running the length of the bodice on either side of the buttons. Hopefully people would focus on the stunning creation and not her pale complexion.

Battling the measles for two weeks had taken its toll. Her

face was as white as the one on Tildy's porcelain doll. Elenora felt as fragile as the ceramic creation. When she'd seen Miles flat on his back in the alley behind his shop with bright red blood covering his chest, she'd been so sure she'd lost him. At that moment she'd come face-to-face with the truth. She loved him with every fiber of her being.

But he didn't love her. If he did, surely he would have said something by now. After her display that morning, he had to know how she felt. As it was, she'd spent the rest of the day struggling to remain outwardly calm, while inside her heart was breaking. If she were prone to tears, she'd have exhausted her supply of handkerchiefs by now.

She joined Mrs. Rutledge and Tildy in the parlor.

"You look pretty, Mama."

"So do you."

"Watch me." Tildy spun so Elenora could admire her peach chiffon gown from every angle. "Did you notice my skirt goes all the way down to my boot tops? I feel so grown up."

Mrs. Rutledge patted Tildy's shoulder. "You'll be ten in a few weeks, so I thought a young lady like you should have a longer skirt."

"She's right, Tildy. You aren't my little girl any longer. You're growing up."

"You've changed, too, my dear, in many ways." Mrs. Rutledge adjusted the ribbon flowers on either side of Elenora's collar. "You've let God work in your life, and it shows. And you've shown El Dorado what a difference one woman can make. You'll make us all proud tonight."

"Thank you. I appreciate the encouragement—and the beautiful dress. I feel more confident knowing I look my best. I need to be going now. I'll see you both in a few minutes."

Elenora shuddered when she reached the place on South

Street where the shooting had taken place. God had kept Miles from harm. But she must bid him farewell.

She mounted the stairs to Rutledge Hall, her violin case in hand. Tonight was her debut performance. Sadly it would also be her last.

The spacious room grew quiet when the curtains opened half an hour later, and Mr. Morton addressed the audience. "Ladies and gentlemen, it's my distinct pleasure to welcome you to the Mud Springs Musical Society's fall concert. Please join me in acknowledging our gracious benefactor, Miles Rutledge, whose generous contributions help make the Society the fine institution it is."

Miles stepped forward. "I want to thank you for your support as Mrs. Watkins and Tildy battled the measles. God graciously spared them, and there were no other cases in town. And then this morning you rallied around Mrs. Watkins and me as we dealt with another threat. The Lord used you to minister to us in our time of need, and I'm grateful for all you've done. I hope you enjoy the concert."

Abe introduced the first selection. "We'll be starting off with a lively piece that warms our fingers up nicely, the final movement of Mozart's *Eine kleine Nachtmusik*, which my German friends tell me means a little smooth music at night."

They began, and Elenora was transported to another place with no measles, no murderers, and no man expecting her in Marysville—a peaceful place where her soul took wings.

A violinist announced the next number. She did her best to focus on it and not to think about her impending move.

When the applause died down, Sheriff Henderson rose to introduce the third selection, and she gulped. Despite her attempts to keep her feelings under control, her eyes stung and her throat grew tight. Somehow she made it through the piece.

Before she knew it, Miles informed the audience that she was to join in him in a duet of the closing number, Bach's Double Concerto for Two Violins and Orchestra. She stood and moved into position.

Lord, You know my heart. Please be with me as I play.

She and Miles faced each other, their violins in position, their bows poised above the strings. Mr. Morton lifted his baton. Moments later the room was flooded with the beauty of Bach's creation.

Everyone but Miles faded from view. She played for him alone. The music became the words she longed to share. She couldn't tell him how much she loved him, but she would do her utmost to show him.

Never in all the months they'd practiced had the piece sounded like this. Their transitions as lead were seamless, the sequences where one violin seemed to chase the other exquisite, and the sections during which they accompanied each other a perfectly balanced duet. She thrilled at the intimate dialogue between their instruments.

When the concerto ended Miles took her hand, and she curtsied. The appreciative audience jumped to their feet and filled the room to the rafters with their thunderous applause.

After his bow, he put up a hand to silence them. "Ladies and gentlemen, I'm sure you'd like to offer your congratulations to Mrs. Watkins on her fine performance, but I've waited all day for a few minutes alone with her. So if you'll excuse us. . ."

He handed his violin to Abe, and Hank took hers. Every pair of eyes followed Miles and her as he escorted her to the door, where Tommy and Timmy flanked it.

What was Miles doing taking her out of the hall like this? Why didn't someone say something? Why didn't he?

"Is everything ready, gentlemen?" he asked the twins.

"Yes siree, Mr. Rutledge. And we'll take care of the other, too."

Tommy handed Miles a lit lantern, and he led the way to the street below. He released her hand and put his at the small of her back.

"Where are we going?" Could it be he had something special planned after all? Or perhaps he simply hoped for a farewell kiss.

"I have something to show you."

She half expected him to take her into his garden where they'd sat on the bench beneath the large oak tree, but he turned toward Main Street instead. "What is it?"

"Have patience, Ellie."

Patience? She'd waited all afternoon and evening, and he'd said nothing. Once they'd finished their practice, he'd insisted she stay at his house and rest while he oversaw the repairs to the door of his shop. If she hadn't been so tired, she'd have protested, but she needed that nap.

And now he wanted to *show* her something when all she really wanted was to *hear* something? Something that would give her a reason to remain in El Dorado.

They rounded the corner, and he guided her down the walkway toward the mercantile. The glow of the lantern revealed two half-barrels filled with plants, one on either side of the door. They drew closer, and she squinted. "Are those. . .violets? They're lovely."

"Mr. Parks let me have some from his flower beds at the main church."

"These planters weren't here this morning." She stooped and fingered the tiny blossoms. The light bounced off the door, which had been covered by a tarpaulin earlier. "How on earth did you get the glass replaced so quickly? It took me a good ten days to get the sheet for my door."

"I've had it on order for a while. Why don't you read the wording and see what you think? Out loud, please."

He sounded eager. Did her opinion mean that much to him? "Rutledge Mercantile. Purveyor of Fine Goods. Established 1855. Miles and—"

"Don't stop now."

Her voice shook. "Miles and Elenora Rutledge, Proprietors." She tore her gaze from the door and faced him. "Miles!"

"Ellie."

"This glass. It's been here for hours. Anyone who walked by would have seen it. That means they know, don't they?"

"They do." He squatted and reached behind one of the planters, smiling when he found what he was after.

He stood, opened the small box, and held it out to her. There, nestled in a bed of black velvet, was a ring. She couldn't take her eyes off it.

"I know it's customary for a gentleman to offer his betrothed a diamond or pearl engagement ring, but you know my propensity for flying in the face of convention. I got you an amethyst instead, a deep purple stone the same shade as the flowers you wore the day I met you. The day I made the biggest mistake of my life. One I want to rectify."

He set down the lantern, knelt, and took the ring from the box. "Ellie, I love you. I know I don't deserve you and that I can be a bit hardheaded at times, but I hope you're willing to overlook my failings. Will you do me the honor of marrying me?"

"You love me? I spent this entire day thinking you wanted me to leave. Why didn't you tell me?"

"Um, Ellie, if you're going to turn me down—"

"Turn you down? That's preposterous. I didn't want to leave. I wanted you to ask me to stay."

His brow furrowed. "I'm asking, but you're not answering. And I worked hard to say things well this time."

She dropped to her knees and cradled his face in her hands. "Yes, Miles. Yes, yes, *yes*!"

He slid the ring on her finger, pulled her into his arms, and leaned toward her.

"We're on Main Street. Anyone could see us."

"Tommy and Timmy are ensuring our privacy, so no more arguments. I've waited a long time for this."

His lips met hers. She buried her hands in his hair, drawing him closer. The heady sweetness of the kiss caused her to lose all track of time and space. Nothing existed beyond the two of them. She'd never felt such a connection to a man.

When at length he released her, she gazed into his eyes. "I love you, too. I didn't know for sure until this morning, mere minutes before I thought I'd lost you. But you. . ." She glanced at the door. "You must have known for some time."

"I started falling in love with you when your shop was damaged and you bandaged my hands. But when we sat in the church after the fire and you let me kiss you, I was sure. I'd tried before, and you'd always managed to waylay me. But that day when I needed you most, you were there for me."

She stood and ran a finger over the letters of her name, which were outlined in gold just the way she'd always envisioned them. "Why did you use our first names and not our initials?"

He rose and draped an arm around her. "Because I want the world to know my partner is a woman—a wonderful, capable, amazing woman."

"You might not think me quite so wonderful when you hear what I have planned for the mercantile. You know I'll have my say."

"I look forward to your ideas. Grayson isn't the only one who sees the value in your way of doing things."

She inhaled sharply. "Mr. Grayson. I'd forgotten about him. I'll have to send him a telegram right away. But I know he'll understand. He told me the day he came to El Dorado that if anything—or *anyone*—enticed me to remain here, he'd make his offer to a woman who owns a shop down in Jackson. I don't think it will come as a surprise to him when I tell him what I've decided."

"Now that I've convinced you to stay, how long do I have to wait before I can make you my bride?"

"Hmm." She tapped a finger on her cheek. "Since Tildy will pop if we set the date too far in the future, what do you say to a wedding a week from tomorrow when Mr. Parks is due next?"

His face lit up. "Only eight days, and you'll be mine to kiss anytime I want?"

She gave him a coquettish smile. "You don't have to wait. You can give me another kiss right now if you'd like."

And he did.

Award-winning novelist **Keli Gwyn** is a California native who lives in a Gold Rush–era town at the foot of the majestic Sierra Nevada Mountains. Her stories transport readers to the 1800s, where she brings historic towns to life, peoples them with colorful characters, and adds a hint of humor. She fuels her creativity with Taco Bell and sweet tea. When she's not writing, she enjoys spending time with her husband and two skittish kitties.

A Bride
Sews with Love
in Needles,
California

by Erica Vetsch

Dedication

In memory of the brave men and women of the Great War who served in the US and abroad. And to the memory of the thousands of Harvey Girls who provided hospitality and service to soldiers and passengers of the AT & SF railroad.

Acknowledgments

The author would like to thank Mary Ann Bucher and Faye Ricter of the Dodge County, Minnesota Historical Society for their assistance with the history of World War One veterans of Dodge County. It was at the DCHS Museum that the idea for this story was born after seeing a vintage WW1 Red Cross signature quilt. Very special thanks go out to my sister-in-law, Linda Ambrose, for all her help in creating our own Red Cross signature quilt, embroidered with the names of over 300 Dodge County WW1 Veterans. Both quilts are on display at the DCHS Museum in Mantorville, Minnesota.

Chapter 1

"There is nothing so stubborn and exasperating as a headstrong Irish daughter."

"You only bring up my Irish half when I'm suggesting something you don't like. If I please you, you claim my Norwegian side." Meghan set her jaw, determined to stand up to Papa.

"How do I know this isn't just another one of your wild schemes? Like the mail-order candy or the door-to-door sewing notions? Remember how those ended? Flying high only to fall to earth with a thud after a few weeks." His huge boots clomped as he paced the sitting room floor, drowning out the sound of rain pattering against the windowpane as a late spring storm blew through. "You always start out with the best of intentions, child, but you don't think things through. Always you think you can whip the world, but you take on too much and come crashing down."

"It won't be like that. I was a child then. I didn't know what I was doing." Meghan Thorson poked the logs in the fireplace, sending a shower of sparks racing up the flue. "I won't be trying to start my own business. I'll be working for one of the most reputable companies in the country. And it's only for six months, not forever. If I don't like it, I can come home then. But I will like it. You'll see. You're the one who has been saying I need to find something to occupy my time, something that would help the war effort and keep me out of your hair. This job will definitely keep me out of your way. Needles is more than fifteen hundred miles from here."

Papa stopped pacing, stroked his reddish-blond beard, and studied her with somber blue eyes. "And how long will it be before I get a letter saying you hate it out there and you're coming home?"

"You won't get such a letter from me."

"Couldn't you find something closer to home? I thought you would get a job here in Mantorville, or even over in Rochester. California is too far away."

Mama's knitting needles clicked, a sound as familiar to Meghan as her own breathing. "You hoped it would be in Rochester so you could have an excuse to drive your new motorcar over there." She barely looked up from the sock she knitted. Socks, socks, and more socks. American soldiers in the trenches in France needed socks, and Mama's knitting needles never stopped.

I pray over every pair as if they were going to Lars himself. They are all my sons in that way, all those soldiers. And I know their mamas are praying for them as well. Mamas of soldiers knit and pray.

"I don't want a job close to home. I want to stand on my own two feet, do something bigger, travel, and"—she spread her hands—"I don't know how to explain it. I just know I need to do this. I knew it as soon as I saw the advertisement in the *Tribune*."

Mama sighed. "She needs to go. She's gone in her heart already." *Click, click, click.* "I'm surprised we were able to keep our little sparrow in the nest this long. She's always desired to fly. This is her chance." A faraway look invaded Mama's expression, softening her face in the firelight.

But Papa was not softened. "Mary Kate, I thought you would have agreed with me that Meghan should stay here. With us. She's too young to leave home." He thrust his hands into his pockets and stood square before Mama's chair. "She is barely more than a child. Not old enough to go so far away from home."

Mama's red lashes flicked upward from her yarn, showing eyes so green they seemed to glitter—the same eyes she'd passed on to Meghan, along with her red hair and freckles—and according to Papa, her Irish stubbornness.

"Look at her. She's twenty years old. When I was eighteen, I set out on a wonderful adventure. I sailed away from Ireland to America. And I met a handsome Norseman on the boat who swept me off my feet and carried me away to his new home in Minnesota." She grinned. "By the time I was twenty, I was already a mama to Lars."

Papa's brow scrunched. "That's different."

"Is it? I think it is very much the same. Let her have her adventure, Per. She's young, and there is so much strife in the world right now, so little for a young woman to be excited about. Who knows, perhaps she'll find a strapping, brave young man to call her own like I did."

Jabbing the poker into the coals, Meghan protested. "Mama, that's not why I'm going. Working for The Harvey Company means I will get to see more of America than this little corner. I'll get to meet lots of people and have a steady job that pays well. I want to be busy just now. I want to feel like I'm doing something important. Serving people, especially soldiers, in the restaurant will be my way of helping with the cause. The woman who interviewed me for the position said hundreds of soldiers pass through their eating establishments on their way to the war."

Papa made a gruff sound in his throat. "But it's so far away. If I had known you were going to apply at The Harvey Company while we were there, I never would've taken you with me to Chicago."

Meghan left her spot beside the fireplace and stood on tiptoe to kiss his cheek above his full beard. "Well, I'm glad you did take me. Seeing Chicago was a real treat, and so was getting this job. The interview nearly scared me out of my shoes, but I lived through it, and they hired me. Please, Papa, give me your blessing. It's only for six months."

He enfolded her in a bear hug, resting his chin on top of her head. "The women in my life will be the death of me."

She squeezed his waist and pulled back to look up into his face. "You know I wouldn't be going if I didn't think this was what God wanted me to do. It feels right."

His eyes narrowed. "Be careful how you throw that around, child. Many a foolish thing has been done in the name of God. And many a thing we *want* to do has been justified by calling it the will of God."

She bit her lower lip. Was she being headstrong and impulsive? It wouldn't be the first time. But she wanted this so badly. And it did feel right.

He tweaked her nose and let her go. "When do you have to leave?"

Meghan whirled and pounced on the letter that had come that day. "I'm to report to the offices in Chicago in three days. They'll provide the uniforms, the training, and the transportation to my new job."

"You will be homesick within the week," Papa predicted, crossing his arms once more. "You've never been away from home, and you love Minnesota. Your Irish and Norwegian heritage has given you a need to be surrounded by green, growing things. The desert won't feed your soul the way the fields and forests of this land do."

"I will miss you and Mama, but seeing different places and meeting new people is part of the fun. It wouldn't be much of an adventure if where I'm going turns out to be exactly like here."

"And you are sure you will be safe? You'll have someone to look after you?" The doubt-clouds returned to his eyes.

She rushed to reassure him. "All the girls must live in a dormitory, and there is a strict curfew, and there are lots of rules. Your little girl will be just fine."

"Will she?" Papa's mouth twisted, rueful and wry. "Lots of rules and my Meghan have never gotten along too well."

Mama chuckled and loosened more yarn from her skein. "That's a plain truth. How will you do following rules and behaving yourself?"

"I can do it," Meghan boasted. "I'll be the best Harvey Girl that company has ever seen. By the time my contract is up, they'll be begging me to stay."

"Needles, California, coming up!" The dapper conductor, brass buttons gleaming in two bright rows down his navy suit, rocked his way along the aisle as passengers stirred and began removing belongings from the overhead racks.

Meghan turned her attention to the window, eager to get a glimpse of the town that would be her home for at least the next six months, but she was on the wrong side of the train.

Empty wasteland swept by, punctuated by clumps of cactus and scrub. Jagged, rocky peaks and rounded piles of sand thrust upward into the sky, and occasional sparse green patches showed where someone was trying to scratch out a living in this inhospitable landscape. They had crossed over the muddy Colorado River which flowed sullenly, as if the heat had sapped its energy and the sand had choked its will to move.

"I knew we'd be living in the desert, but I didn't realize how stark it would be."

"It doesn't look much like Illinois. It's terribly hot, and it's only May. What must it be like here in July?" Natalie Daviot, a Springfield native, dabbed her temples again and nudged Meghan's arm. "Are you nervous? I sure am."

Meghan shook her head automatically, paused for a moment, and crumbled, nodding. Though they'd only known each other a few short days, she and Natalie had become instant friends. Neither had ever been away from home before, and they'd grasped onto each other like a lifeline in the huge, bustling depot in Chicago where they had been met by someone from the Fred Harvey Company to begin their employment as Harvey Girls.

Meghan was grateful to have Natalie with her, because instead of the customary four weeks of training in one of the Kansas Harvey House Restaurants that they'd been told to expect, they'd been whisked away on the train to fill vacant spots in Needles, California, that had suddenly opened up. They'd had no time to become acclimated, to make new friends, or to get their bearings. Instead, they'd had a brief orientation meeting, been measured for uniforms, and been all but tossed onto a southwest-bound train.

"Okay, so we're nervous." She sat up straight and squared her shoulders, lifting her chin to a confident angle. "But we won't show it. We're capable, independent, intelligent women employed by the Fred Harvey Company." Which sounded so much more impressive than she felt. And yet, the glow of accomplishment and pride at being hired by such a prestigious company remained. The company's high standards were well-known, and the pay was better than anything she could've expected to earn back in Mantorville. Not to mention the bonus pay Harvey Girls received for working in Needles during the summer. For the next six months, she was a Harvey Girl, subject to the company rules and expectations, and the recipient of the respect her new black-and-white uniform would command.

Natalie fanned herself with a folded newspaper. The air in the car had grown progressively warmer until someone had finally relented and opened a window. The trade-off for air circulation was the smoke and soot from the engine blowing in the window and coating everything with smuts and smudges. Still, it was better than suffocating.

"I'd be pleased to help you with your bags, ma'am." A gravelly voice had them both looking up. A scruffy man in a battered cowboy hat stood in the aisle. Sunshine had tanned his skin to leather and etched deep lines around his eyes and mouth. Those eyes lit with admiration as he looked at Natalie, and though Meghan couldn't blame him for staring at her friend's blond loveliness, she couldn't help but feel a prick in her heart. Her own wavy, red hair and pale, freckled skin never drew that kind of admiration. What would it be like to have men falling over themselves to assist her? What would it be like to be classically beautiful and capture every man's eye when she walked into a room? Not that she really wanted to be the center of attention like that any more than Natalie did. But it would be nice to know she *could*.

"That's most kind, thank you, but I'm sure we can manage." Natalie showed not the slightest interest in him, just as she had ignored the advances of every man they'd encountered on the journey. The hopeful stranger touched the brim of his hat and turned away.

Natalie leaned her head against the seatback and closed her eyes. Her profile reminded Meghan of the cameo Papa had given Mama as a wedding gift, delicate, regal, beautiful.

The sadness in her new friend's eyes seemed only to add to her beauty. It made Meghan want to protect Natalie, to reassure her that everything would be all right. Was it simple homesickness, or did Natalie carry other burdens?

The train slowed and lurched to a stop, causing all the standing passengers to grab seatbacks to steady themselves. The conductor opened the door, and like a gopher trying to squeeze out of a too-small hole, folks crowded through. Not until the car had half-emptied did the girls file out of their seats and reach for their bags in the overhead racks. Meghan searched their seating area for any stray belongings.

"I need to see about my trunk." Natalie dug her luggage ticket out of her bag.

"The conductor will direct us." Meghan gripped the handle of her case, her only piece of luggage. With the company providing room, board, and uniforms, she had chosen to pack light. If she needed anything in the future, she could purchase it once she got paid. The thought of earning her own money, being able to buy the things she wanted, made her squeeze her hands together and bite her lower lip. No more asking Papa every time she wanted something from the mercantile. Twenty-five dollars a month, plus tips, room, board, uniforms, and travel vouchers. And a bonus on top. That was nearly as much as her brother made as a soldier on the front lines in France, and she wouldn't even be risking her life in a placid little railroad town like Needles.

She followed Natalie toward the end of the car. When they reached the door, the smart little conductor greeted them with a broad smile and a quick pattering tone that fascinated Meghan. He never seemed to pause for breath, and the words blurred together into one long sentence. "You the two new Harvey Girls I was told to expect? You look the type. This here's the back of the hotel, but you can reach the lobby through the center doors. You want to see Mr. Stock, the hotel manager, or Mrs. Gregory, the head waitress. Someone will direct you. But you'd do well to wait until after all these passengers are fed and back aboard the train before you bother them. Passengers have first priority, and the hotel staff will be busy for the next thirty minutes or so. If you have other bags, you can walk along to the baggage car. One of the bellhops will be gathering the hotel guests' luggage, and he'll see that yours gets to your room. That will fill some of the time. Good luck, and I'll probably be seeing you." He flashed a quick smile before hurrying to help other passengers disembark.

Meghan stepped down onto the sidewalk and got her first glimpse of the El Garces, the jewel in the desert crown of Fred Harvey establishments along the Atchison, Topeka & Santa Fe Railroad line. The heat hit her full force as she emerged into the sunshine, but she couldn't take her eyes off the imposing concrete structure throwing back the sun's rays from its blazing white exterior. She screwed up her eyes and shaded her brow with her hand.

"More pillars than the Parthenon." Though the building was impressive, she wouldn't really call it beautiful. Large, imposing, and a trifle daunting, but not particularly appealing. Majestic palms stood in little patches of emerald grass along the sidewalk. Surely the grass must take daily watering to keep it so green in this dry heat. Two stories high, the hotel stretched out before her to either side like a royal palace. Pairs of pillars marched across the hotel on both floors, supporting wide porches that must help shade the rooms and keep them cool. Or as cool as one could be in the desert. Iron-railed balconies cantilevered from the second-floor loggia in graceful scallops.

Beyond the hotel and spreading out on either side, lay

the town of Needles—a straggly conglomeration of wooden, adobe, and brick buildings popping up between clumps of grayish-green brush and yucca. Electricity and telephone lines crisscrossed limply over the streets, and a jumble of automobiles and wagons lined the roads. Everything seemed to shimmer in the heat, and the few folks on the sidewalks moved slowly. Most curiously, Indians stood before the hotel with baskets, pottery, and blankets for sale, their faces solemn, patient, and long-suffering. Was it the heat or their nature that made them so stoic?

Meghan tightened her grip on her valise handle and headed toward the front of the train and the baggage car. The sooner they tracked down Natalie's trunk, the sooner they could get into the shade. She had expected to be battling a damp, sweaty feeling, but a dry breeze evaporated any perspiration instantly. She moistened her lips, only to find them dry a moment later.

They had to wait in line at the baggage car as cart after cart of luggage and US Mail and supplies for the hotel came out first. Finally, one of the workers was free. Natalie turned over her trunk ticket to the dark-skinned man with flashing, white teeth. "Shore enough, ma'am. I'll get your luggage over to the hotel with the rest. One of the bellhops will take it to your room." He accepted the nickel Natalie placed in his large, big-knuckled hand.

"Let's get out of this sunshine. I'm wilting." Natalie tilted her head so her hat-brim would shade her face. Meghan's own hat, a small sailor-style, offered little protection. Heat prickled her fair skin. Her face would probably be as red as an apple by the time they got inside. If she wasn't careful, she'd walk around with a red, peeling nose for the next six months. Sunshine always deepened the despised freckles covering her face. Not all the lemon juice in the world would lighten them if she spent much time out of doors here.

A large sign emblazoned in white letters near the lobby doors directed the way to the lunch counter, and another on the other side pointed the way to the dining room.

Natalie put her hand on Meghan's arm and stopped her in a thin patch of shade cast by a straggly tree. "We might as well wait a few minutes here. The conductor said the head waitress won't be able to meet with us until all the passengers have been served anyway."

Meghan didn't mind delaying their meeting with the woman who would have charge of their lives for the next six months, though she refused to acknowledge any hesitancy. Instead, she gave free rein to her curiosity and let her eyes take in her surroundings from the relative coolness of the shade. Her sense of adventure crowded out her anxiety, and she tried to see everything at once. "Someone on the train said there was a park across the street from the front of the hotel. Santa Fe Park? The company put it in when they built the hotel. He said there were trees there. It will be nice to have a place to sit in some shade every once in a while."

"I have a feeling even the shade here in the summer would bake a lizard." Natalie turned her face toward the hot breeze, lifting her bangs and closing her eyes.

Eventually passengers began trickling out of the hotel and boarding the westbound train. On the other side of the passenger train, a freight train sat roasting. From a car near the front of the freight train, a pair of men lethargically lowered a ramp, banging it off the hard-packed dirt. A man emerged from the dark, square opening, leading a horse. He handed the animal over to another worker and disappeared. In moments, a string of animals stood in the sunshine, and the workers removed the ramp and closed the doors. The poor animals must be positively wilting, stuck in that boxcar. She hoped they had a nice, shady place to go to, one with water and a breeze.

A man in a straw cowboy hat strolled by, capturing her attention. His shoulders stretched the fabric of a faded blue shirt, and well-worn jeans covered his long legs. Battered boots scuffed the concrete, and his steps were so slow and measured, she wondered if he'd ever hurried in his life. He barely glanced at her, touching his finger to his hat brim and dipping his chin. Something about his face intrigued her, but she couldn't quite put her finger on what it was. He continued on toward the hotel doors, and Meghan shook her head when she realized she had wandered out of the shade to stare after him.

She returned to Natalie's side, staying out of the way of the travelers boarding the train. One of the passengers, a woman with two small children, dropped a bag and spilled the contents across the hot concrete. Meghan handed her valise to Natalie and hurried over to help the poor mother as the engine whistled and the train puffed smoke, signaling its imminent departure.

"Thank you. Thank you," the woman said again and again as she grappled the baby, who started to cry, and the toddler who wanted to get too close to the train wheels.

"Hurry. Climb aboard." Meghan stuffed a toy dog, a string of wooden spools, and a crocheted blanket into the bag.

The conductor came trotting toward them and lifted the toddler. "Whoopsie-daisy! All aboard!" He handed the woman up into the train and scooped the child onto his arm, a cheery smile on his face. Inexorably, the wheels began to move. Swinging his set of steps aboard, the conductor hopped onto the platform with a wave.

Meghan stepped back a pace as the train picked up speed. Movement to her left caught her eye, and she noticed the string of horses being led down the wide sidewalk toward them. The train whistle pierced the air in a quick blast, and Meghan raised her hand to wave at the conductor who leaned out from the train saluting her.

His expression changed from cheery to alarmed, and he pointed behind her, his shout drowned out by another whistle blast. She turned and froze. One of the horses had broken free of its handler and bore down on her at a gallop. A rope trailed from its halter, and with a wild, panicked neigh, the animal leaped a stack of flour sacks in its way and raced toward her. She gathered her skirts to leap out of the way of the juggernaut, but she was too late to escape a collision. The horse brushed her shoulder, sending her spinning. The impact threw her toward the train. She staggered, let go of her skirts, and cast out her hands to brace her fall.

Lord, help me!

The prayer screamed through her head, but she couldn't make a sound. The cars whizzed by, gaining momentum as she flailed, teetering on the edge of balance. Her throat squeezed shut, and she knew she was falling toward the iron wheels.

At the last moment, strong hands yanked her back. She collided with a solid wall of chambray and muscle. Arms came around her, absorbing the violence of her headlong sprawl.

Caleb McBride had just finished folding the shipping papers and tucking them into his shirt when a shout and a loud neigh grabbed his attention. One of the horses he'd come to pick up had broken free from the string and now barreled up the sidewalk straight toward an empty-headed woman who didn't even have the sense to get out of the way of an oncoming horse. He tried to sprint her way, but the instant his left foot hit the ground, a shaft of pain and weakness shot from his heel to his hip, and the limb almost buckled beneath him. He gritted his teeth and forced himself forward, praying no one saw his hitching gait. Thankfully, at the last instant, the horse veered away from the woman, only grazing her. She staggered, her arms windmilling, but she was flailing the wrong direction, toward the moving train instead of away from it.

He reached her as she staggered only inches from the side of a car. His fingers closed on the fabric of her shirt, near her waist, and spun her away from the cars and into his arms. This time as the pain shot up his leg, it buckled beneath him and down they went, scrunching his shoulder into the sidewalk. She landed atop him, shoving the air from his lungs.

"Meghan, are you all right?" Another woman, silhouetted by the sun dazzling his eyes, bent over them.

So the woman in his arms was named Meghan. She didn't respond at once, and he feared that in saving her from the train, he might've hurt her. Then she stirred and struggled, sinking her elbow into his diaphragm.

"Oof!" The sound shot out of him. He looked up into the most striking pair of green eyes he'd ever seen. Green as new grass, and only inches from his face. Freckles peppered her nose and cheeks, and her little mouth gaped as if gasping for the air she'd knocked out of him. He vaguely remembered nodding to her on his way to the freight depot.

"I'm so sorry." She scrambled off him in a flurry of limbs and skirts. Her hat sat askew, dragging her fiery curls out of their pins. He caught a glimpse of shapely legs in black stockings and white lacy edging of a petticoat. With a flick, she tugged her skirts into place so they fell just above her pretty ankles.

Massaging his middle, he tried to ignore the pain radiating up his left leg. Carefully, he rolled to his right side and pushed himself to his feet. "Are you hurt?" Her near-miss sent weak ripples through him. If she'd been killed, it would've been his fault. Those horses were his responsibility, even if he hadn't been the one leading them through the train yard.

"I'm fine, I think, thanks to you." Her voice quivered, and her hand shook a bit as she righted her hat. "I thought I was a goner."

"You almost were."

"Whose horse was that?" The other woman spoke up, full of indignation. "Whoever it was should be held accountable, letting an animal like that run loose on the sidewalks." Her blue eyes snapped fire and a hint of color tinted her cheeks.

Caleb stooped to pick up his hat and rubbed his hand on the back of his neck. "It wasn't done on purpose, I assure you, miss. I apologize for the accident, and I'm glad no one was injured."

A bit of the heat went out of the blond woman's expression, and she took a shuddering breath. "Are you saying the horse was yours?"

"That's right. The train whistle must've spooked him into bolting." Something he'd have to make sure he trained out of the animal in the next few weeks. He took a couple of steps back, and the redhead's eyes widened.

"You've hurt yourself. Did you twist your ankle? You're limping." She reached for his arm, and he stepped away again, angry with himself.

"I'm fine. No harm done."

He glanced up the track and breathed a sigh of relief. Someone had managed to capture the escaped horse and now led it back toward the hotel. He couldn't afford to lose any horses, nor could he count on the goodwill of the people of Needles if the animal found its way onto the streets. Hot pain raced up his calf and behind his knee, but he set his jaw and whacked at some of the dust covering his pants and shirt. He leaned all his weight on his right foot and tried to ignore the messages from his left boot.

The girls gathered their scattered belongings and brushed themselves off. He studied them from under the brim of his hat, the blond with the arched brows and even features and the redhead with windblown hair and color now so high it nearly obliterated her freckles. Not as immediately pretty as the blond, but a face one would remember. Especially those eyes.

"I'm sorry, Mr. McBride, he bolted on me." The man leading the rest of the horses drew near. He took a greasy kerchief from his pocket and wiped his face. "I couldn't hold him."

"That's all right, Al. No harm done, as it turns out. They caught the runaway and are bringing him back now." He motioned up the line.

The fugitive animal arrived at the same time as Mrs. Gregory in full sail, her white uniform more blinding than the sunshine glaring off the hotel, appeared. She stomped the ground with nearly as much force as the gelding had, and she blew and sputtered more, too. A formidable woman, Mrs. Gregory. If she kept a list of people she disliked—and Caleb figured she probably did—his name would reside at the top. In capital letters. And maybe underlined. Her eyes glittered, and she looked loaded for bear. Dread settled in his chest.

"Are you Miss Thorson and Miss Daviot? I've been expecting you inside. What are you doing out here with this—this person?" She pulled herself up to her full height, which was tall enough to look him square in the eye, and she tilted her head to stare down her skinny nose. With a scornful snort she turned to the girls. "What on earth happened to you two? Harvey Girls do not appear disheveled, ever, and Harvey Girls do not loiter outside the hotel, especially not with the likes of him." Her mouth pinched like she'd just drained the vinegar barrel.

He stuck his hands into his back pockets. "And a good day to you, too, Mrs. Gregory. I hope you're feeling well? You look a mite liverish. Perhaps you should stop in to see Doc Bates. I'm sure he has something for biliousness." He smiled at her just to get her goat.

"Mr. McBride, take your filthy animals away. The hotel sidewalk is no place for horses." She made shooing motions toward the girls to get them moving and muttered a constant stream of indignant complaints as she headed toward the hotel. The girls picked up their bags. The blond hurried after her, but the redhead—Meghan—lingered for a moment.

"Thank you, sir. That was very brave of you to come to my rescue."

Her words twisted the ever-present knife in his gut. *Brave.* He swallowed and nodded.

"This way." Mrs. Gregory's command sliced the air. Meghan lifted her valise, holding her hat on and tripping along with the light steps of a schoolgirl.

She thought he was brave. A shame that she'd soon be told otherwise.

Chapter 2

Following in the head waitress's wake, Meghan barely had time to note the EL GARCES carved over the entryway or the floor-level fountain splashing gaily in the open-air courtyard. In the lobby, arrangements of wicker chairs and sofas clustered in cozy groups, and potted palms rose majestically, splashes of green against the white walls. Ceiling fans spun slowly, and she soaked in the relative coolness. The hotel's designers had known what they were doing. Thick concrete and high ceilings, ceramic tiles and splashing fountains all combined to thwart the oven outside.

"Don't straggle." The head waitress, identifiable as much by her commanding manner as by the all-white uniform they'd been told to expect, turned at the base of the staircase and stopped, crossing her arms and pinching her lips. A handsome woman with bold features, dark eyes, and hair streaked with gray, she reminded Meghan of her Aunt Penelope. All starch on the outside but soft as pudding on the inside. You just had to crack the outer shell to get to the real woman.

"I'm sorry. I was admiring the beautiful lobby." Meghan shifted her case to her other hand and brushed a strand of hair off her face. "How many guestrooms are there?" Perhaps the woman was just hard to get to know at first. Or really busy. Running the restaurant and lunch counter and overseeing all the wait staff couldn't be easy.

"Sixty. Please try to remember you are not a tourist." Icy frost blew through the woman's voice. "This way."

Meghan shot a look at Natalie, whose eyes widened. Her shoulders lifted slightly in a shrug, and she followed their new boss up the stairs. Meghan took one last glance at the newsstand and front desk and mounted the staircase, her footsteps sounding loud on the tile.

On the second floor, they traveled down a long hallway punctuated with doors. "These are rooms for the paying guests. The staff is housed at the end."

Meghan hustled to keep up, her bag hampering her. They turned a corner and entered a narrower hall. "Are there a lot of girls working here?"

"You two make twenty. The minimum I need to run a successful establishment. I asked them to send me at least six experienced servers and they sent me you two, green as tadpoles. Not only did they short me, but they didn't even take the time to train you properly. Now I'll have to take over the task." She let her glance flick over Meghan. "Look at your hair and dress. How am I supposed to turn you into a credit to the company? You"—she motioned to Natalie—"you at least show some promise. Have you ever worked in a restaurant before?"

"No, ma'am. This is my first job."

"Heaven help me. And what about you? I don't suppose you have any experience either?"

Meghan tamped down her ire and smiled. "No, but look on the bright side. We won't have any bad habits that you'll have to correct. We're like clean slates, all ready to be trained in the way you see best."

This didn't seem to impress the starchy woman.

"You two will share a room, the second on the right. You're expected to keep your room clean and tidy. Inspections are frequent and unannounced. Your uniforms are in the closet. Kansas City sent along your sizes. You are responsible for sending them to and retrieving them from the laundry downstairs." The tall woman checked the timepiece on her lapel as she stopped before a white door. "Be downstairs in uniform and ready to work in thirty minutes." She opened the door to their room, stepped back, and turned on her heel to head back the way they'd come.

"Excuse me." Meghan almost shouted. She was tired, disheveled, and suddenly fed up with being condescended to. She let her suitcase thump to the floor. The woman stopped, keeping her back to the girls.

"What?"

"Do you have a name?"

"You may call me Mrs. Gregory."

Meghan gave in to impulse. She jogged down the hall and circled around Mrs. Gregory to stand in front of her. "How do you do?" She stuck out her hand. "My name is Meghan Thorson, and it's a pleasure to meet you. I look forward to working with you for the next six months."

Mrs. Gregory sniffed so hard her nostrils sucked inward. "Miss Thorson, I suggest you turn your attentions to preparing yourself for work. No doubt it will take every single one of the now"—a quick check of her watch—"twenty-eight minutes you have left."

She left Meghan standing, hand outstretched, in the middle of the hallway. Meghan blew her bangs off her forehead and grimaced, letting her hand fall. So much for thawing out the old girl. She headed back to her room, scooping up her suitcase by the door.

"You shouldn't have twisted her tail like that." Natalie opened the closet door, took out a black uniform, and held it up. "At least the laundry is right here in the building. It shouldn't take much time to get uniforms back."

"I wonder where the laundry is here. In the basement? And can you imagine how hot it must be working there?" Meghan sat on the side of one of the beds, testing the springs. "I'm surprised they don't have laundry facilities at every hotel. I meant to ask during that whirlwind orientation why they only had two laundry centers. Seems odd to ship everything to Needles or to Kansas then ship them all back again."

"They must find it easier to keep everything consolidated. At least we won't have to worry about running out of clean dresses and having to wait for them to arrive on the next train." Natalie removed a snowy apron from a hanger and laid it on the other bed.

"This is a nice room. Look at all this space." Meghan ran her hand along the curved white metal footboard of her bed and scuffed her feet on the colorful rug. "I wonder where the bathroom is on this floor."

"I think you'd best stop wondering and start getting ready."

"Before Mrs. Gregory comes back and breathes fire all over me." Hauling herself up off the bed, she removed her hat pins and hat and shook out her curls. "Do you think she's that starchy with everyone, or did she just take a dislike to me?"

"You have to admit, the conditions in which she first found you were less than desirable, sprawled all over a strange man on the sidewalk out front. And you didn't do yourself any favors out in the hall pointing out her lack of manners in not introducing herself."

"I couldn't exactly help what happened outside. I'm only fortunate someone was there to help me, otherwise. . . ." She shuddered. "I know I shouldn't have been rude to her in the hall, but I couldn't stand it anymore. She looked like she wouldn't wipe her feet on me if I was a rug." Meghan dug in her bag for her hairbrush. She'd show Mrs. Gregory she could be the perfect Harvey Girl. Not that she had any idea just what that entailed, but she was a bright girl and she could learn.

"Look at this." Meghan peered at a framed piece of paper by the mirror as she jerked her brush through her hair. "Take a gander at this list."

— EMPLOYEES ARE REQUESTED NOT TO SCRATCH MATCHES, DRIVE NAILS OR TACKS, OR IN ANY OTHER WAY MAR THE WALLS OF THEIR ROOMS.

— NO RUBBISH OF ANY KIND MUST BE THROWN IN THE TOILETS.

— BATHTUBS MUST BE THOROUGHLY CLEANED BY EMPLOYEES AFTER USING.

— LOUD TALKING AND LAUGHING IN ROOMS AND HALLS SHOULD BE AVOIDED.

— EMPLOYEES MUST BE IN THEIR ROOMS BY 11:00 O'CLOCK P.M. UNLESS GIVEN SPECIAL PERMISSION BY MANAGER TO REMAIN LONGER.

— ROOMS MUST BE KEPT IN TIDY CONDITION AND WEARING APPAREL MUST BE KEPT IN ITS PROPER PLACE.

— CLOTHING OF ALL EMPLOYEES MUST BE NEAT AND CLEAN AT ALL TIMES.

— EXPECTORATING ON THE FLOORS IS POSITIVELY FORBIDDEN.

— THE PURPOSE OF THE ABOVE RULES IS TO BRING ABOUT A TIDY AND HOMELIKE CONDITION IN YOUR ROOMS AND WE REQUEST YOUR COOPERATION SO THAT THE DESIRED RESULTS WILL BE BROUGHT ABOUT.

FRED HARVEY

"I feel like I just joined the army. Are we supposed to salute

Mrs. Gregory or the hotel manager when they come by?" Meghan wrinkled her nose.

"I doubt we have to salute, though a bit of deference and respect would surely be in order. We'll get into the swing of things soon enough. The rules will become second nature and we won't even have to think about them." Natalie continued dressing. "Fred Harvey might have passed away, but his son, Ford, is following all the guidelines set down by his father."

"I'm not complaining. I know the company has to have rules. I just didn't think they'd be posted in our bedroom." Meghan finished tidying her hair, checking for stray curls. "At least we've got running water in the basin here." She turned the tap and ran her hand under the cool water before dipping a pristine towel into the liquid. A sigh escaped her lips as she wiped her hot, soot-streaked face. A bath would be wonderful about now.

"The clock's ticking, Meghan." Natalie took the cloth from her hand and gave Meghan a friendly nudge toward the closet. "You've made enough of a first impression on Mrs. Gregory for one day. Don't add 'late' to the list."

Meghan heaved a playful sigh and quickly removed her travel-stained dress, took a sketchy basin-bath, and donned the black uniform. The snowy apron was so starched it almost crackled. She slipped her arms through the armholes and tied the bow in the small of her back. Twisting and turning before the mirror on the dresser, she checked to see that every button and fold was in its proper place.

"Do you suppose the laundry here does the ironing and starching for us?" Ironing was the bane of Meghan's existence, and she didn't look forward to trying to keep half a dozen uniforms pressed and crisp.

"We can only hope." With one last check in the mirror,

Natalie turned around. "How do I look?"

Meghan studied her while hopping on one foot trying to get one of her new black shoes on. They were the latest style, with laces down the front that were purely ornamental. A tight, elastic gusset on the inside of the top allowed just enough movement so they could be slipped on. The trouble was, the elastic did such a good job she could hardly get her foot into the shoe.

"You look perfect. Like the quintessential Harvey Girl." She finally managed to get the boot on and straightened. "How about me?"

Natalie eyed her critically. "Neat and tidy. Let's get downstairs. If I'm not at least five minutes early, I feel late."

They found their way to the first floor, through the lobby, and past the tinkling, floor-level fountain that sent diamonds of droplets into the air. Meghan wanted to linger and watch the cool water for a moment, but Mrs. Gregory's clock ticked in the back of her mind. When they inquired as to where to find the head waitress, the man behind the front desk directed them toward the door marked LUNCHROOM.

Three horseshoe-shaped counters, each with twenty-five stools, filled the room. Meghan stopped in the doorway to admire the glass-fronted refrigeration case full of the day's menu items. "Can you believe they have a refrigerator right in the lunchroom?"

"We'll look at it later. Come on." Natalie took her elbow and urged her toward the far end of the lunchroom where several Harvey Girls stood at one of the counters. As they arrived, Mrs. Gregory emerged through a set of batwing doors, holding some files. Meghan glanced at the clock. Five minutes to spare.

The woman's dark eyes raked over them from head to toe, her nostrils thinned and pinched, and she turned away. Meghan let out a sigh. They must look all right, or the head waitress surely would've said something, audience or not listening on.

"Girls." Mrs. Gregory clapped her hands to get their attention. "This is Miss Daviot and Miss Thorson." She opened one of the file folders and consulted the pages inside. "Miss Daviot, you will be serving in the dining room, first as the drinks girl, and when I feel you've made satisfactory progress, you will be given charge of your own tables. Only the most well-mannered and accomplished waitresses are allowed to serve in my dining room. I have a feeling you will fit in well there."

The head waitress flipped open the other folder. "Miss Thorson." Her voice was as dry as the desert outside the lunchroom windows. "You appear to be more suited for the lunchroom. I've already encountered your ready tongue. See that you hold to the standard and keep your conversation with customers to a minimum. We are to serve them with a smile, get them in and out as quickly as possible, and not bore them with mindless chatter, understood?"

Heat charged into Meghan's face, and she bit the inside of her cheek. Hard. In that instant, she vowed to prove to Mrs. Gregory that she was the best Harvey Girl ever to don the uniform. Her service would be above reproach, her appearance impeccable at all times, and her customers would rave about the way she took care of them. Mrs. Gregory would have no choice but to recant her initial assessment and beg Meghan to work in the formal dining room.

"Yes, Mrs. Gregory. I understand perfectly." Keeping her voice modulated cost her quite a bit of effort, but she even managed to put on a pleasant smile.

"Good. Dining room girls, I want the linens changed and the tables set. Then there is the silver to polish and the stations to clean. Come, Miss Daviot. Miss Plunkett, you take charge of the lunchroom. You all know what to do. Miss Thorson, do as Miss Plunkett tells you until I can get back here to show you how to do things right."

More than half the girls, including Natalie, followed Mrs. Gregory through the double doors that led to the dining room, leaving a handful at the counter.

"Whew, what'd you do to Gregsie?" An extremely short girl of about twenty-five stuck out her hand. "I'm Jennifer, by the way. Miss Plunkett when Gregsie's around." She had laughing pale blue eyes and straight, light brown hair pulled back from her round face.

"Gregsie?"

"Mrs. Gregory, but you'd best not let her hear you calling her that. Trust me, that's one of the nicer nicknames she has around here."

Several of the waitresses giggled. One tall girl with a long, narrow nose and a dimple in her chin paused as she passed Meghan. She cast a look over her shoulder toward the dining room door and bent to whisper, "I heard one of the busboys call her 'Iron Drawers' the other day."

Jennifer snickered and then put on a stern expression. "She'd better never hear you repeating that one either or you'll find yourself on report."

The tall girl shrugged. "I'm on report half the time the way it is. My employee record must be about the size of the dictionary by now."

"This is Barbara. Miss Charteris. She takes care of the soda fountain just through those doors." Jennifer pointed to a pair of saloon-style half doors. "She started out in the dining room, got shifted to the lunchroom, and now she's relegated to the soda fountain. Which she needs to get back to, since it's always open." Jennifer tilted her head toward the doors.

Barbara snapped to attention, gave a smart salute, and

disappeared, leaving the doors flopping in her wake.

"She's a good egg, but she doesn't pay close enough attention sometimes. And Mrs. Gregory isn't as bad as she seems at first. She runs a tight ship, she's good at her job, and she's got more prickles than a beaver-tail cactus, but she's loyal to her girls. Just do as you're told, follow the rules, and she'll be your staunchest ally. Buck the rules, and you'll be her favorite target."

Meghan renewed her vow to be the best Harvey Girl on the line. She'd have Mrs. Gregory eating out of her hand in no time.

Caleb nudged his mount to go a bit faster, conscious of the growing heat and ready to be home. The barn and corrals shimmered ahead. The string of horses he led plodded along in the heat, tired from their long, hot journey and ready to stop. He checked over his shoulder to see that the men he'd hired to bring the rest of the horses were still keeping up.

Buildings grew closer. He led the string of horses into the corral and dismounted. His left leg ached from his knee clear to the ends of his toes, but he refused to give in to the pain. He had no one to blame except for himself, running toward the train like he had. Still, if he hadn't, that girl might've fallen under the wheels and been killed or at least badly injured. A little pain wasn't too much to bear to save a life, right? Especially since he was used to the pain.

The girl—Meghan—he let his mind try out her name for the hundredth time since he'd left town. Meghan what? It had been a long time since he'd held a pretty girl in his arms. More than three years now. Ever since Patricia threw him out like yesterday's stall bedding.

The familiar ache, as familiar as the one in his leg, squeezed his chest. He needed to get his mind off the girl at the hotel. He'd learned his lesson, had it burned into his memory. Only a fool repeated his mistakes expecting a different outcome.

The hired men, Carlos and Diego, led their strings of horses into the corral. They swung out of the saddles, their boots making puffs of dust.

"Just unsaddle your mounts and leave the saddles on the top rail." He hooked a stirrup over the saddle horn and pulled on the latigo strap. Grasping the blanket and saddle together, he hoisted it onto the corral fence and looped the cinches up out of the dirt. He then turned to study the horses, untying the lead rope and feeding it through the halter rings to free each animal. "Turn 'em loose, but don't take off the halters."

Fifteen new horses joined the twenty already in the big corral. All browns or bays, not a pinto, gray, or buckskin in the lot. Just as his supplier promised, just as his customer ordered.

"*Señor*, what you going to do with so many horses out here?" One of the men shoved back his hat and scratched his head. "You don't got no pasture. How you goin' to feed them?"

"Barn's full of hay and grain. And there's plenty of water." Caleb jerked his thumb toward the muddy river a hundred yards past the corral fence. His first, backbreaking job when he took up residence on this hard-scrabble piece of roasted earth was to install an irrigation pipe and pump from the river to the corrals. House water came from a well sunk deep and a cistern, though the cistern was almost always bone dry with less than six inches of rain falling in a whole year out here. Nothing like the Vermont woods of his boyhood, that was for sure, or even the Kentucky horse farm where he'd worked upon escaping Vermont. Still, he didn't own this land, nor even rent it. His employer took care of all that, and Caleb had few complaints.

If only the stark landscape didn't look quite so much like

the barren dryness he felt inside.

Shrugging aside these notions, he reached into his pocket for his wallet and pulled out some money for each of the men. "Thanks for helping me get them here from town. If you'll give me a minute, I'll drive you back."

"*Gracias.*"

Caleb made sure the water troughs were full and opened two bales of hay for the new arrivals. They would settle in with the herd that had been here for a fortnight already. Most of the horses stood dozing under the shade shelter he'd erected. Siesta time. Work was for morning and evening when the temperatures were more manageable. Funny how quickly he'd adapted to the rhythm of life here in the high desert.

When these basic chores were done, he headed toward the dilapidated building he called a garage. Inside, he flipped the tarp off his brand-new truck. The pale blue paint gleamed, and the highly varnished wood shone. A 1918 Chevy, fresh from the dealership in Barstow. His chest swelled, and he admitted satisfaction when Carlos and Diego sucked in their breaths and made approving noises. The six hundred dollars the truck had cost him had been worth every penny. The larger of the two men, Diego, ran his hand along the door and with a guilty start jerked back.

"She is beautiful, señor."

"Climb in."

Diego piled into the back while Carlos took the passenger seat.

They headed back to town at a zippy twenty-five miles an hour, creating a dust plume that hung in the air behind them in a brown-yellow haze.

"What you do with so many horses, señor?"

"They're army mounts. For the cavalry. The army is paying me to break them, and when they're ready, I ship them to Fort

Riley up in Kansas. From there they head to Europe and the war."

Carlos tugged his weedy moustache. "A shame to send so many fine horses to war."

It was a shame. Caleb loved horses—loved working with them, caring for them, just being around such noble beasts. To think of animals he'd befriended and come to know heading into the perils of battle sat heavily on his shoulders. And yet, a well-trained mount could save a man's life. Could save many lives. Officers rode horses, couriers rode horses. Command and communication relied on swift, brave, intelligent mounts, well trained and reliable. Often horses could go where automobiles and cannons could not.

"You going to work alone? That's a lot of horses to manage by yourself."

"I have a hired man." The outline of Needles showed to the northwest. Hired man. At least as much of a hired man as he could afford full time.

Joshua Hualga waited for him on the front porch when Caleb returned to his ranch. A full-blooded Mojave Indian, Joshua, at eighteen, reminded Caleb of a forest white-tail from back home in Vermont—lean and graceful. His big, dark eyes were reminiscent of a deer, too, watchful and shy.

His father, Cairook Hualga, in contrast, reminded Caleb of a black bear, with thick, muscled arms and shoulders. His figure was made even more imposing by the fact that he had followed the ways of the Mojave and tattooed his chin. Black lines scored his jaw, chin, and cheeks like cactus needles, poking upward toward his eyes.

Cairook tilted his big head and scrutinized his son as if the boy were a stranger. "Are you sure this is what you want? He has no experience with horses. He prefers to be indoors reading rather than hunting or growing crops." Cairook rubbed his finger down his cheek and over his tattoo. "I don't know what kind of Mojave he hopes to be. He won't even get his tattoo."

Joshua said nothing, but his fingers tightened on the porch rail.

"If it doesn't work out, send him home." The big man picked up his walking stick from where it leaned against the porch rail and wheeled away. He did not look back at his son.

Joshua's narrow shoulders sagged, and he tucked his hands into his pants' pockets.

Caleb slowly made his way up the steps to the porch and sagged into one of the two straight-backed chairs, grateful to get the weight off his aching leg for a moment. He motioned to the other chair.

With a sigh, the boy joined him, easing his lanky frame into the rocker with a fluidity Caleb envied. "Why did you ask me to come here? There are plenty of boys on the reservation who would be better suited to working on your ranch. I don't know anything about horses."

"You're smart, and you can learn. That's why I wanted to hire you. That, and you want to get off that reservation so badly it's eating you alive. You're hungry for something that you can't find there, and maybe working for me is the first step to finding what it is that you need to fill you up."

Joshua's head came up, and his glance collided with Caleb's. Caleb knew that look of longing, for he'd felt it himself, many times. A desire to be more than he was, to break free of the bonds holding him back and fly as high as his dreams.

"How'd you come to be called Joshua? That's not a Mojave name."

"The boarding school gave white names to every student. They allowed us to pick our own from a list. I chose Joshua."

"For the biblical character? Caleb and Joshua worked pretty well together in the Old Testament, if I remember correctly."

He shook his head. "For the Joshua tree. A Joshua tree stands alone in the desert. Like me. My tribe is like the brush that grows at the river's edge, so close their limbs get tangled, unable to grow upright unless they are supported by those around them. And they all look the same, blending one into the other. If one of those bushes grows alone, the wind blows it over and rips it out of the earth, sending it tumbling away. But the Joshua tree stands without help, alone and proud." The boy's spine straightened, and his youthful jawline tightened as he spoke.

Caleb caught himself reaching down to rub his lower leg and stopped his hand. He pondered the boy's analogy, admiring his way with words and identifying with him more than ever. Caleb, too, stood alone like a Joshua tree while the town of Needles grew up entwined and enmeshed like riverbank brush. "That can get pretty lonely, standing by yourself. Sometimes you don't realize how much you miss things until they're gone."

"I am fine alone. I've always been alone, even when I am in the middle of my family."

"You have a big family?"

"I have four younger brothers, all just like my father. Father is proud of them, proud of the way they are like him. I think he does not know what to do with me. We were strangers even before I was sent to the mission school, but since I came home, it is worse. I think he was as relieved when you asked if I could come work for you as I was."

Caleb crossed his legs, took off his hat, and hooked it over his boot toe. "Dads and sons don't always see eye to eye, but maybe if you give it some time, things will get better."

"Did you get along with your father? Did things get better?"

A hollow feeling pressed against Caleb's breastbone. "I haven't seen my father in almost ten years. He wasn't glad to see me then, and he was happy to see me leave."

"Then I don't think you are one to give me advice on how to deal with my father." Sober judgment coated Joshua's expression.

Caleb forced himself to his feet. "You're right. When it comes to dealing with parents, I don't have a leg to stand on."

Meghan flopped onto the bed and immediately bounced up to check her uniform. She was so tired she'd forgotten she mustn't muss the dress or apron. As she removed her apron, Natalie slipped into the room and closed the door, leaning back against the white panels and closing her eyes.

"I'm so tired I can't even think."

"Me too, and we didn't even serve any customers yet." Meghan unbuttoned her black dress and peeled it off, enjoying the relative coolness of the evening air coming through the window. "I had no idea we'd spend so much time polishing. If I never see another piece of silverware or a coffee urn again, it will be too soon."

Natalie straightened and began preparing for bed, albeit slowly. "But tomorrow we have to get up and do it all over again, and this time we'll be polishing and cleaning in between serving six different sit-down meals."

Meghan fought with her shoes. The elastic had all but embedded itself into her ankle, and her toes cried out to be free. "Ah, that feels so good." She peeled off her stockings and wriggled her toes, crimping them into the rug a few times before padding over to the cool tile.

"How many miles do you think we put on our feet today?" Natalie flipped a nightgown over her head and tugged it into place.

"About a million. Last thing before I came upstairs, Mrs. Gregory told me we have to have the menus memorized before tomorrow." Picking up the stiff pages from the counterpane, she perused them before giving them to Natalie. She struggled into a nightgown and dunked her washcloth into the basin to cool her face. "We can quiz each other."

Half an hour later, yawning and with her head full of unfamiliar words like Albondigas soup and Chicken Lucrecio, Meghan turned out the lights and crawled into bed. Tired as she was, the instant her head hit the pillow, her mind snapped awake.

Unfamiliar night sounds filtered through the window. A dog barked, and footsteps sounded in the hall. A moment later their door eased open. Meghan sat up, clutching the sheets to her chest. "Who is it?"

"Just me. Jennifer. It's my night to do a bed check. Sorry to disturb you. G'nite, and see you in the morning."

Bed check. Meghan eased back onto the pillow while Natalie mumbled and turned over in her bed, causing the springs to creak.

As her mind hopped and skipped from one impression to another, she remembered her mother's wise words. "If ever you can't sleep, spend the time praying. Your heart and mind will calm, and you will put your burdens into the hands of the One who cares more for you than anyone else ever could."

The thought and worry always on her heart and mind these days was her brother, Lars. He must've reached France by now.

The last word they'd had, before she left home, was a postcard mailed from New York. A postcard printed by the army with general words and places for him to fill in blanks. "The weather here is _____ and I am in good health. I arrived safely and they are feeding us well. I especially like the _____ the mess cooks fix for us." The army mailed the cards once the troop transport ship reached England. Though the blanks had been filled in by Lars himself, and the postcard was addressed in his own hand, it wasn't as if it really contained his words and thoughts. If only they would receive a letter from him.

Even now he might be engaged in battle against the Kaiser and the German army. Was he in one of those dreadful trenches? Did he have his gas mask with him? Would she ever see him again?

Realizing her hands had fisted at her sides and her stomach had begun to ache in a familiar way, she forced herself to relax and pray, asking for God's protection on Lars and all the American and Allied soldiers fighting in this Great War.

And for a fleeting instant, the face of the man who had rescued her today flitted across her mind. How soon before he signed up and headed off to war?

Chapter 3

No, no, no. Every pat of butter must have fork marks. The diner must be assured that his food was handled appropriately. The butter must always be cold enough to hold crisp fork marks." Mrs. Gregory pursed her lips and showed Meghan how to put butter on a plate *The Harvey Way*. "Never use your fingers or a knife to put butter on a plate."

Nothing escaped the head waitress's scrutiny, and nothing Meghan did seemed to please her. After less than an hour of her tutelage, Meghan had no doubts as to why the busboys called Mrs. Gregory Iron Drawers. And *The Harvey Way* covered everything from how to sweep the floor to how to fill salt shakers. Meghan's head swam with all the directions, methods, and instructions coming her way.

"When you take the beverage orders, use the cup code. That way the girl coming behind you will know what the customer wants without you having to tell her. See?" Mrs. Gregory flipped the coffee cup over and rested it in the saucer. "An upturned cup in the saucer means the customer wants coffee. For milk, flip the cup and put it next to the saucer. Iced tea; rest the cup against the saucer." She went through the three positions for the three variations of hot tea: black, green, or orange pekoe.

Meghan bit her tongue and concentrated, trying to ignore the "in-way-over-her-head" feeling rising up her windpipe every time she relaxed her guard. She would not fail. She would not be sent home. She would not disappoint her papa again. Amen.

"Bread is baked here at the hotel and not sliced until the

customer orders it. Every slice must be three-eighths of an inch thick, no more, no less."

Was she supposed to carry a ruler in her pocket to measure? What would happen if she accidentally served a customer a slice of bread that was a whole half an inch thick? Chaos? Rioting in the streets? Meghan stifled a giggle and kept her face composed.

Girls bustled around them behind the counters preparing for the first customers of the day. The hands on the wall clock climbed relentlessly toward the time when the train was due. Miss Ralston hurried up with a piece of paper and waited until Mrs. Gregory had finished slicing off a perfectly-proportioned piece of bread.

"Mrs. Gregory, here are the numbers." She handed the paper over, stepped back, shot Meghan a sympathetic glance, and hurried through the doors to the soda fountain.

The head waitress glanced at the page. "Hmm, Miss Thorson, tell the chef we're expecting fifty-one for the lunch-room and twenty-nine in the dining room."

Meghan hustled off to the kitchen where pots steamed and the smell of fresh bread drifted through the brick archway that separated the cavernous kitchen from the bakery. High transom-like windows let in sunshine and let hot air escape, and cooks in white shirts, aprons, and trench caps stirred, sliced, and sautéed. The chef, recognizable by his tall, white hat, expertly flipped a skillet of browning potato chunks. The smell of bacon and sausage cooking made her mouth water. Too nervous to eat this morning in the midst of all the chattering, confident Harvey Girls, she'd only nibbled a slice of toast and sipped a glass of milk.

She relayed the message from Mrs. Gregory, and the chef's friendly smile and nod emboldened her to ask, "Is that a lot of people or about average?"

"Zat is more zan before ze war. Now we have soldiers on nearly every train. And zey have big appetites." He turned and spoke to one of the cooks in rapid French before returning to his skillet.

Meghan returned to the lunchroom where activity had picked up in anticipation of serving breakfast to eighty passengers in under thirty minutes in order to keep to the train's schedule.

"Miss Thorson, come here. You have too much to learn to be gawping and standing idle."

She got a firm grip on her temper and side-stepped a girl carrying an armload of stacked plates. Mrs. Gregory tapped her foot.

"When you are not serving customers, you will be caring for your equipment and your station. Also, the coffee urns. These are the most visible symbol of Harvey hospitality." Pride swelled her voice. "They must be spotless at all times." She waved her hand at the immense silver urns anchoring the end of each of the long counters. "I will now show you the proper way to make the coffee."

Meghan wanted to protest that she'd been making coffee for a long time and how hard could it be, but she bit her tongue and followed in the head waitress's wake.

"No less than eight ounces of freshly ground—not too fine, mind you—coffee per gallon. The customers will ask what brand we use, so be sure to tell them we use only Chase & Sanborn, and we never reheat and serve old coffee. Every two hours you will empty each urn, rinse them with scalding water, and brew fresh coffee."

Blinking, Meghan knew her mouth had fallen open. "Every two hours? Isn't that wasteful? What do you do with the old coffee if you don't reheat it?"

Mrs. Gregory rolled her eyes. "We are not some border-town cantina or lowbrow slum restaurant. This is a Harvey establishment. Old coffee is thrown away. On the rare occasions when the chef needs cold coffee for a dessert, some of the brew is reserved, but that is the exception rather than the rule." The head waitress had more starch in her voice than in all the aprons in the room.

"Don't any of the Harvey hotels practice hooverizing?" In this time of voluntary rationing so every soldier on the Allied front could have the best possible diet, such waste was criminal. How did the hotel handle the Meatless Mondays or Wheatless Wednesdays? If Mrs. Gregory wouldn't even reheat coffee, Meghan doubted she would serve cornbread squares in place of dinner rolls or rye instead of white bread cut exactly three-eighths of an inch thick.

A drawstring-bag pucker tightened Mrs. Gregory's lips, and an icy snowdrift invaded her eyes. "Lest you think us unpatriotic, Miss Thorson, perhaps you should get your facts before you judge. The Harvey Company has a contract with the government to serve soldiers on their way to Europe. The military has granted us the concession, and they have approved our menus and practices. The food we serve and the methods we employ are fully in keeping with our agreement with the War Department and have the approval of Herbert Hoover himself as the head of the US Food Administration. We—the company and the staff at this hotel—are very patriotic and fully behind the war effort."

Meghan wiped the incredulous expression off her face. Mrs. Gregory took a deep breath, the color fading from her cheeks. "My own son has recently enlisted and left for Europe only a week ago." The cords in her narrow neck stood out as she raised her chin. "I'm very proud of him, and as the mother of a soldier,

I can assure you, my patriotism is without equal." She turned, but not before Meghan caught the glimmer of tears.

Well, the old duck did have a heart. Meghan's conscience chided her. No wonder she was a bit prickly with her son heading off to war that very week. A feeling of kinship swept over Meghan. They both had loved ones fighting for the cause.

A bell sounded near the lobby door. "The train's been sighted. Places, girls!" All emotion vanished from Mrs. Gregory's face and voice, and she once again became a martinet, ruling the establishment with her steely will.

Though her head spun from the speed at which she was expected to move, her first customers were so friendly and gracious, Meghan discovered partway through serving her first meal as a Harvey Girl that she was having the time of her life. She remembered the majority of the menu and even managed to navigate the mysterious cup code with only a couple of mistakes.

Perhaps part of her lightheartedness came from the customers themselves. Every last passenger this morning was dressed in the olive-brown uniform of the US Army. Straight from training camp in central California and headed to Europe. Fresh-faced, young, exuberant, reminding her of her brother.

"Say, I sure wish the train wasn't leaving so soon. Never expected the scenery to be so nice here in the desert." A sun-burned recruit with white-blond hair held out his coffee cup. "Wouldn't mind staying around for a while."

Meghan poured his coffee, holding the handle of the pot in her right hand and using a white towel in her left to support the spout, just as Mrs. Gregory had shown her. "I bet you say that to all the girls."

Jenny passed behind her with two steaming plates. "He said it to me, not three minutes ago."

The sunburn deepened, and Meghan laughed. "Not that it isn't nice to hear." As she moved on, his buddies elbowed and kidded him.

One dark-eyed boy grabbed her attention, not through anything he said, but because he was so somber and quiet in the midst of this boisterous crowd. He cupped his coffee mug, staring into space and not touching his food.

"Is there anything I can get you, sir? Can I warm up your coffee?"

He blinked, as if just returning from a faraway land. "Pardon?"

"Would you like more coffee?"

"Um, sure." He held out his cup.

"Where are you from?"

"Monterey."

She did a quick gallop around her knowledge of California geography. "That's on the coast, right?"

"Yep. Grew up within sight of the sea. My whole family is there." His voice vibrated with homesickness, and her throat constricted.

"I bet they miss you already, and they're looking forward to the day when you come home. Do you have a big family?"

He dug in his shirt pocket and pulled out a photograph. "I'm the oldest of ten kids."

"That *is* a big family." She admired the somber faces, picking him out and scanning the family all the way from the father down to the baby on the mother's lap. "I only have one sibling, a brother who is already over there."

"I've never been away from home before. I don't know how they're going to manage without me. Pa has a bad back and can't work too much, so I've been running the store."

Meghan studied the picture a moment longer before returning it to him. "I imagine your younger brothers will help out, and you can send pay home, right?"

"Miss Thorson, you are neglecting your duties." Mrs. Gregory's hand gripped Meghan's shoulder, slowly turning her around and guiding her toward waiting customers. Though she wanted to shrug off that commanding clamp, Meghan allowed herself to be drawn away. She glanced back at the homesick soldier and gave what she hoped would be an encouraging smile.

Meghan poured enough coffee to float a transport ship, smiling and chatting briefly with each man but ever aware of Mrs. Gregory's stern gaze following her around the horseshoe-shaped counter.

In what seemed an incredibly short amount of time, the room cleared and the noise died down. With barely a pause to draw a deep breath, the Harvey Girls went about the task of cleaning their stations in preparation for the next train. Meghan leaned against the counter and wiped her brow, eyeing her station.

"You're standing idle again, Miss Thorson. Start wiping down the counters and chairs. And Miss Thorson." Mrs. Gregory's skin stretched over her cheekbones as she pursed her lips into the now-familiar pucker. "While we do endeavor to be friendly and cheerful with the customers, chatting up young men while you are supposed to be working will not be tolerated. Your job is to present a friendly face and superb service, not a shoulder to cry on, an ear to gossip into, or a flirtatious manner to titillate or lead on."

"But Mrs. Gregory, I wasn't—"

"And you are never to argue with the head waitress. Is that understood?"

Meghan's cheeks burned. Though none of the workers

around her had so much as paused, she knew every ear in the room had heard the dressing-down.

"Yes, ma'am. I understand."

"Good, now get to work. The next customers will be arriving soon."

Caleb made his way through the maze of greenish-brown woolen uniforms filing into the lunchroom at midday. Why had he come? Sure, he had an appointment in town this afternoon, but he could've steered clear of the El Garces. He hadn't needed to come in early, and he certainly didn't need to have his lunch at the hotel.

And yet, here he was.

It was that girl. The redhead he'd rescued yesterday. All night she had haunted his dreams, her brilliant green eyes, her saucy walk, and most of all the beautiful sound of her voice as she called him brave. Over and over in his dreams he'd rescued her at the last moment, savoring the sense of accomplishment, her gratitude, and the feel of her in his arms.

Shaking his head, he chided himself for the millionth time. Most likely she didn't even remember him, or worse, she'd talked to someone and gotten the whole story. By now she knew this town wouldn't wipe their muddy feet on him.

And yet, here he was.

He'd just peek into the dining room and see if she was there. Glancing down, he checked that his clothes were presentable. White shirt, cloth vest, dark brown pants. His boots were worn, but he'd polished them the best he could. No dust or dirt. He'd even scrubbed under his fingernails, all the while telling himself he was sprucing up for his appointment, not on the off chance that he might run into a certain Harvey Girl.

Mr. Stock, immaculate in his dark suit, stood in the dining room doorway, smiling at the customers filing inside. The manager stiffened for a moment, his smile slipping when he caught sight of Caleb, but he quickly recovered, returning to the consummate hospitality professional. "Will you be dining with us today, Mr. McBride?"

"I thought I might."

"Dining room or lunchroom?"

Caleb looked into the paneled dining room with its snowy tablecloths and quiet austerity. Men dressed in business suits, ladies in traveling attire. In contrast, across the lobby, the soldiers filing into the lunchroom jostled and joked, talking loudly. He'd be more comfortable in the dining room away from all the military men, but where was the girl? The blond woman who had been with Meghan yesterday crossed the dining room, weaving between the tables with a tray of china cups. Caleb stood awkwardly, undecided.

At that moment, someone behind him laughed loudly, and he turned toward the sound. He glimpsed Meghan's face through the throng in the lunchroom doorway, and a strange jerky feeling landed in his chest. "Lunchroom."

"An excellent choice."

Caleb joined the line filing into the lunchroom and, once inside, scanned the room to locate Meghan before choosing a spot at her counter. Soldiers filled most of the chairs. Half a dozen girls in black dresses and white aprons bustled, conversations buzzed, and the sounds of cutlery and glassware chimed.

Meghan carried two silver coffeepots. She went to one of the tall urns near the wall and filled them. His eye was drawn to the perfect white bow nestled in the small of her back and the way her hair lay in smooth waves under a white, lacy headband.

Nothing like the disheveled creature he'd held in his arms only the day before.

Then she turned around, the vivid green of her eyes evident, even at ten paces. He hadn't over-imagined the color. If anything, they were more emerald than he remembered.

"What can I get you to drink?"

He dragged his gaze away from Meghan and noticed the short waitress in front of him for the first time.

"Coffee." The word came out before he realized it, and he almost took it back. He loathed the taste of coffee.

She turned his cup over and placed it in the saucer. "Cream and sugar are right here. Would you like a menu, or would you prefer me to tell you what the chef's prepared today?"

"Um, a menu, please."

He pretended to peruse the stiff card. Meghan started at the far end of the counter pouring coffee and smiling and chatting with the soldiers. Their faces lit up, and they joked and teased. A pretty flush crept up her cheeks at the joshing of one fellow, and a whole new feeling hit Caleb's gut, something so foreign and unexpected, he couldn't identify it at first.

Before he could make sense of that bit of absurdity, she stood before him.

"Hello. If it isn't my rescuer. I was hoping I'd see you again soon." She poured the fragrant brew into his cup. He never minded the smell of coffee, it was the taste he couldn't stand.

"I wanted to thank you properly for saving me from harm yesterday."

Her eyes shone, and color filled in the space between her freckles.

"You thanked me at the time." Clearly no one had gotten to her yet with their low opinion of him, or she wouldn't be greeting him with a smile. He didn't know whether to be relieved or uncomfortable. If she didn't know now, it was only a matter of time until she did. Would she hop on the town's bandwagon, or would she decide for herself what kind of man he was? How quickly would she take back the notion that she thought him brave?

"Actually"—she poured another cup of coffee for the next customer—"I can't thank you properly until I know your name. I'm Meghan Thorson. And you are?"

"Caleb McBride."

"Caleb. That's a good strong name. It means bold, right?"

He sipped the hot coffee, trying not to screw up his face at the taste. How foolish could a man get? Ordering a drink he didn't even like, just because a pretty girl was pouring it. He must have holes in his head. He reached for the sugar bowl.

"That's right."

"And are you? Bold, I mean?"

"Miss Thorson, there are customers waiting." Mrs. Gregory spoke over Caleb's shoulder. "We've already discussed this once. I shouldn't have to tell you again."

"Yes, Mrs. Gregory." Meghan glanced one last time Caleb's way and continued up the counter.

"Mr. McBride, I would prefer if you didn't detain my girls. They have work to do."

Frost feathered the back of his neck at her icy tone.

"Gentlemen," she addressed the men in uniform on either side of him, "if there is anything we can do for you, please, let us know. Nothing is too big or too small for our men in uniform. Just ask. The Harvey Company is behind American *soldiers* one hundred percent." Leveling a flat stare at Caleb and treading heavily on the word *soldiers*, she made it clear she didn't include him in the admiration of The Harvey Company. She swept on to the next group of recruits, and he forced his jaw to relax.

The man on Caleb's right elbowed him. "You signed up yet?" His voice carried painfully far, and several men swiveled their heads his way.

He should've eaten in the dining room. Scratch that, he shouldn't have come to the hotel at all.

"No." Caleb kept his eyes on the menu.

"You're a likely looking lad. Why aren't you in uniform? You ain't a German sympathizer now, are you?" Though he said it in jest, his loud tone drew even more attention. Men lowered their coffee cups, knives, and forks, staring.

The muscles in Caleb's upper back and neck tightened, and his mouth went dry. Meghan's eyebrows rose, and her lips parted. Of all the eyes in the room, he was especially aware of hers.

"No. I'm no friend of the Kaiser's."

"Well, why ain't you upped yet?"

"That's my business." He dug in his pocket for a coin, laid it with a snap on the counter, and stood. His appetite had fled.

Doctor Malcolm Bates pushed his spectacles up onto his forehead and pinched the bridge of his nose. This latest missive from his younger brother had him worried. A military surgeon stationed at Fort Riley, Captain Paul Bates wasn't one to cry wolf. Nor was Doc one to run around yelling that the sky was falling. But there was a definite thread of worry in the missive, a faint bell clanging in the background that didn't bode well. He picked up the letter and resumed reading.

Mac, I've never seen anything like it. A small group of men showed up at the infirmary complaining of fever, sore throat, and headache. At first I assumed it was a mild illness traveling through the camp. But I soon came to the conclusion—or rather had it forced upon me—that I'm dealing with something altogether different. Soldiers are succumbing to this sickness in shocking numbers. Strong young men in the morning, and by nightfall, they're dead. I can only pray it runs its course quickly.

Many strange things are at work here. The contagion passes swiftly from one man to the next. Having the soldiers crammed into the barracks as they are contributes to the communication of the sickness, but this particular malady seems more virulent than anything I've met up with. Worse than a cold or the measles or standard influenza. On top of that, the men who should be best suited to fight off a bout of sickness are the first to fall prey. Strong, healthy, young. This thing shouldn't be attacking with such vigor.

The speed with which the sickness strikes is astounding. And the violence. These men are literally drowning. Fluid builds up in the lungs so fast the body can't siphon it away. The feet and hands start to go black as circulation diminishes, the fever rages, pain in the joints and muscles, and a cough that tears apart the pulmonary tissue. The patients who reach the stage of expectorating blood have, without exception, died.

Lest you think I am exaggerating, I went from eighteen cases the first morning to more than one hundred by that same evening. And more are crowding in every hour.

I'm sorry, I didn't mean to go on like this, but I will admit, this sickness is disturbing. We saw some cases of influenza last year that were particularly strong, but this strain defies description. It feels good to be able to talk things over with you, to voice my fears. You have always been a good friend to me, despite the twenty years separating us. You've mentored my medical career every step of the way, and I find myself longing for your counsel.

Your little practice out there in the desert is looking more and more appealing. After this war is over, I hope to join you there.

Until that day, I remain faithfully yours,
Paul

Doc folded the letter, glancing at the photograph on his desk. He and Paul smiling into the camera on Paul's graduation day. And how proud he'd been when Paul had chosen to follow in his big brother's footsteps and pursue a medical career. Paul was the only person on this planet who called him Mac, short for Malcolm. He'd just been plain old Doc for so long to the people of Needles, he'd taken to thinking of himself by that name.

Shrugging into his white coat, he stuffed the letter into a pocket and scanned his appointments for the afternoon. Or should he say appointment, since he had only one penciled in.

Caleb McBride. 2 p.m.

One of his favorite patients. And one of his most stubborn.

The bell on the front door chimed.

One of his most prompt, as well.

He stepped into the hallway. The first floor of his home housed his office, his examination room, his sick ward, and his waiting room with the kitchen out back. His private apartments took up the second floor. Nothing like living close to one's work.

Caleb removed his hat and hung it on the rack beside the door.

"Afternoon, Doc."

"Come on in."

As was his habit, he allowed the patient to enter the examination room ahead of him to give himself some time to look things over.

Caleb didn't perch on the examination table. Instead, he chose one of the chairs along the wall that Doc used for anxious parents who brought in a sick child. Caleb spun the chair around, straddled it, and crossed his arms along the back. Resting his chin on his arms, he looked Doc over.

"Haven't seen you out at the river lately."

"I've had to forgo my fishing pleasure lately. A touch of tonsillitis made its way through the elementary school. Not to mention the chicken pox which landed on quite a few of the youngsters. A common spring malady, though this was later than usual, but now they're all on the mend." He settled into his customary chair and tipped it back against the wall, hooking his heels on the rungs. "Things should settle down this summer, and you'll find me on your riverbank in the mornings again."

They talked of the fish they'd pulled out of the muddy waters of the Colorado River, the ones that got away, and the ones they were sure still lurked under the ripples.

"That record-breaking pikeminnow is only a single cast away." Doc rubbed his chin.

"You're a true addict." Caleb grinned and straightened, wrapping his fingers around the curved back of the chair. "One thing I always appreciate about you, Doc, is that you never seem to be in a hurry, always have time to chew the fat before talking anything medical."

He shrugged. "That's because I'd like to think we were more than just doctor and patient. I'd like to think we were friends who had more in common than just medical diagnoses and treatments, needs, and services."

And also because treating the patient was about more than

prescribing medicine or sewing up wounds. He gleaned more from these little chats than most of his patients realized, the astute Caleb McBride included.

"Truth is, you're about the only friend I've got in this town. Nice to see a friendly face every once in a while. Might as well get to the medical part though. I can't take up your whole afternoon." The young man pushed himself off the chair and replaced it along the wall.

"This just a regular check-up? Or is something else bothering you."

"Nothing serious; I just need a new pair of boots." He steadied himself with one hand against the exam table and stuck his foot out. A gap had opened along the inside of the left toe as the upper came apart from the sole, and the sole itself had worn paper thin. The right wasn't in much better shape. "They don't fit as well as they used to either, so I figured I was better off getting a new pair than trying to fix these."

"Those look fairly hard used for a man who is supposed to limit his physical activities." Doc raised his eyebrow.

Caleb shrugged. "Work won't do itself."

"Peel them off and we'll have a look."

Doc fussed with some papers on the small desk in the corner. Caleb sat on the exam table and pulled off his left boot—with considerable effort and a grimace—and rolled up his pant leg.

"How's the pain these days?" More sorting of papers, pretending he didn't know how difficult it was for Caleb to be open about what he considered a shameful flaw.

Another shrug as he stripped off his sock. "You want them both bare?"

"Please."

He slid his other boot off easily, took off the sock, and stuck it into the boot top.

Doc kept his face neutral, though the sight always jarred him. Caleb's right leg was strong, muscular, and robust, everything a young man's leg should be. The left was enough to make one want to wince and look away—though he would never do that to any patient, especially Caleb.

Wizened, atrophied, and shrunken, his left leg bore more resemblance to the leg of a ninety-year-old than a man in the prime of life. The foot, especially, drew attention—smaller, with an odd buckle in the middle. Infantile paralysis—polio—was a cruel disease.

Caleb stared hard at the wall over Doc's shoulder, gripping the edges of the exam table as if he feared it would throw him off at any second.

Gently, Doc took the withered foot into his hands. Cool flesh. To be expected. Polio-afflicted limbs were often cool to the touch. He wrapped his fingers around Caleb's healthy right foot. Warm, almost hot.

"I need you to be honest with me if I'm going to treat you effectively. How is the pain?"

Caleb shrugged again, but Doc waited for a real answer.

"It bothers me now and again. I can tell when I've done too much."

"Which is pretty much every day? How about when you're resting?"

"Some cramps, especially at night." He lifted his foot out of Doc's hand. "I know what you're going to say, but forget it."

"I'm going to say it anyway. If you'd wear the brace, it would help. You need the support along the back of your leg and your heel."

"I'm not walking around like a freak. People take one look at leg braces and assume you have the intelligence of a turnip. Their eyes slide over you, and they start doling out the pity, or the contempt." Caleb muttered the words, his shoulders hunched, arms straight, palms jammed into the tabletop. "I just need a new pair of boots."

Doc sighed. "You're a stubborn man."

"I prefer to think of it as strong-minded."

"I bet you do." He chuckled. "We can't just send the measurements from the last pair. Your leg has changed some. That's why this pair of boots doesn't fit as well. I'll need to make a new mold. Wait here while I mix up the plaster."

Returning to the exam room with a tray of supplies, Doc noted that Caleb had replaced his right sock and boot.

Using cotton strips dipped in a tray of wet plaster of Paris mixture, he wrapped the limb in several layers. "Is it too warm?"

Caleb shook his head. "How long will it take?"

"Don't you remember last time? It will take about forty-five minutes to set up hard enough so I can cut it off."

"I meant how long until the new boots come?"

"A month, give or take. It's not like walking into Claypool's and plucking shoes off a shelf."

"I suppose."

He wrapped the last white strip, smoothing it with his fingertips. "There. Now we wait a bit. You want some coffee? Oh wait, I forgot. You don't like coffee. Water?"

"I'm fine. Just came from the hotel."

"That's unusual. One of those Harvey Girls catch your eye? Maybe that redhead you rescued?"

His eyes widened, and a dull flush rose from his collar. "You heard about that?"

"You forget, Needles is a small, isolated community, and I am one of its oldest and most-respected residents. I hear things. So, you didn't answer my question. Are you sparking one of the waitresses? As a rule you steer clear of the El Garces."

"Which is a rule I should've remembered before I had lunch there. Lotsa soldier boys down there today." Though he kept his tone offhand, Doc knew it had to bother him.

When Caleb had first come to town, Doc had signed his draft notice certifying him as 4F, physically unfit for military duty. As the only person who knew about Caleb's malady, the two had formed a bond that extended beyond doctor and patient or casual friend. Caleb trusted Doc never to reveal his deepest secret, though often Doc had longed to do just that, to fight back against the prejudice and wrong judgments hurled at Caleb by some of the folks in this town by telling them the truth. Mrs. Gregory had taken a particular dislike to Caleb, putting out the word around town that Caleb was too cowardly to fight in the war, but not above profiting off it at the same time by breaking horses for the cavalry. Doc ached to set her and the rest of the town straight.

But Caleb would hate him for that. He'd rather suffer in silence and protect his pride than reveal the truth about his leg.

"Do you know the Hualga family?" Caleb changed the subject.

Doc went to the sink in the corner to wash his hands. "I do some work over on the reservation from time to time, so I've met the family. Why?"

"The oldest boy, Joshua, is working for me now."

"I don't know him too well. He's been away at school for the past several years. He's working with the horses? He didn't strike me as the horseman type." He began tidying up his equipment.

"From what I can tell, he'd rather be reading books than cleaning up after horses. But I think he'd rather work for me than stay home. He doesn't get along with his pa." Caleb rubbed the back of his neck. "I know what that's like."

Doc quit fussing with his instruments and sat down.

Befriending and doctoring Caleb called for perception and patience. He revealed things about himself only slowly. Admitting he hadn't gotten along with his father was a big step of trust.

"Fathers and sons don't always see eye-to-eye."

A rueful smile brushed the corner of Caleb's mouth. "My father couldn't stand the notion of having a crippled son." He went silent for a moment. A shudder went through him, and his eyes took on a faraway, painful look. "I was only five when the polio hit. Living in Vermont. A whole slew of kids went down with it. Worst pain I've ever felt." He jerked his thumb at his casted foot. "What's going on in there now isn't a shade to waking up in knots, feeling like your muscles were being ripped off your bones, but not able to move. My brain screamed at my leg to run away from all that pain, but it was like my leg couldn't hear it. Even now, the communication isn't too good, though it's better than it was."

He took a deep breath, his brows lowering, still introspective. "My folks sent me to a hospital for polio kids somewhere near Albany, New York. I was there for two years. They came to see me once in all that two years, and my pa barely looked at me. When the hospital had done all they could for me, they shipped me home. My pa took one look at my leg brace and crippled foot and never spoke another word to me. Within a week I was in another hospital, this one for freaks and crazy people. People nobody wanted. My ma used to come and visit a couple times a year, but never my pa. He was too ashamed of me."

That explained so much. No wonder he refused to wear a brace or tell anyone about his leg.

He seemed to have realized how much of himself he'd revealed, and the shutters closed. His face molded into the familiar mask of remoteness he used on the citizens of Needles, and he crossed his arms, leaning his back against the wall.

"How about we play some checkers while that finishes setting up?" Doc rose. "I think last time you beat me. Time for some revenge."

As he headed to the office to get the game board and pieces, Doc filed away what he'd learned. As surely as Caleb wore a plaster cast on his leg, he also wore a cast on his battered heart. What would it take to peel back and chip away that brittle covering and get to the man, the emotions, and the heart underneath?

Chapter 4

Meghan pulled off her shoes and stockings, hiked her skirts to her knees, and dipped her toes into the soothing basin of cool water. "Fourteen hours."

"What?" Natalie's muffled voice came from the pillows. She'd come in, removed her uniform, and sprawled face-down on the coverlet in her shift.

"That's how long it's been since I sat down. The alarm went off at five. It is now seven o'clock in the evening. I've poured a million cups of coffee, my face hurts from smiling, and my feet have gone on strike." She put on her best "Mrs. Gregory" tone. " 'A Harvey Girl must never be seen sitting down while in uniform.' We were so rushed with that special train, I even ate my lunch standing up in the kitchen."

Natalie rolled over with a groan. Her hair straggled from its pins where she'd dragged her lace headband off. "I had no idea being a Harvey Girl would be so much work. You'd think after two weeks working seven days a week, I'd have gotten used to it by now. I can't even move."

Glancing at the clock on the dresser, Meghan scowled and wiggled her toes. "Move is just what we'll have to do if we're going to make it to the Red Cross meeting."

Another groan. "I forgot about the meeting. Go without me."

"Oh no, I'm not facing Mrs. Gregory all by myself. You know she doesn't like me. After all her picking and poking this last fortnight, I'm beginning to wonder if all of the apostles and prophets rolled together could please her. I doubt even a biblical saint could live up to her exacting standards. What's a poor Irish-Norwegian lass like myself supposed to do?" Meghan lifted one foot and rotated her ankle as all the commands, orders, corrections, and opinions she'd received from Mrs. Gregory washed through her memory.

Her vow to be the best Harvey Girl the company had ever seen had taken a beating over the past two weeks. At the moment she was tempted to settle for just being good enough to be ignored by the head waitress.

Hold on there, girl. When did you surrender your courage? You're no coward, ready to duck and run for cover. You're a Celtic-Viking lass, and you'll fight to the bitter end.

She straightened her stiff shoulders. "I'll tell you what I'm going to do. I'm going to go to that meeting tonight and dazzle the picky head waitress. I'm going to show the dragon-lady that I'm the best little Red Cross worker and pledge-gatherer she's ever seen, and then perhaps the dragon-lady will come to appreciate my talents and abilities and might even deign to speak nicely to me every so often. I ain't licked yet."

The bedsprings creaked as Natalie pushed herself upright and braced herself on her palms. "You say that every day. That you're going to be the best Harvey Girl the company has ever seen. But if tonight goes like the past fortnight, you'll get down to the meeting, Mrs. Gregory will say something you object to, and you'll spout off something that will get you further into trouble."

Meghan giggled, shrugging and wrinkling her nose. "How is it that you know me so well, when we've only been friends for less than a month?"

A head-splitting yawn preempted any immediate attempt at speech. Natalie flopped back onto the bed. "It must be my astute powers of observation. That, or you really stink at hiding your emotions. Promise me you won't ever try to hustle a game of poker, all right? You'd be fleeced like a sheep in a heartbeat."

Promptly at eight o'clock, dressed in an ivory muslin gown she hoped wouldn't be too warm and with exhaustion still pulling at her limbs, Meghan followed Natalie into the large, screened veranda at the end of the hotel's first floor. Ceiling fans circulated the air, but even at 8 p.m. the mid-May heat of the day lingered. Tables had been pushed to the sides of the room and rows of chairs stood in their place. Most of the Harvey Girls were already there. Several women clustered in small groups, as well as a handful of men in shirtsleeves.

Mrs. Gregory stood with a pair of older ladies at the head of the table. All three wore Red Cross armbands and nearly identical expressions of officialdom.

Natalie made for the closest empty chair and subsided into it as if her bones had turned to jelly. Meghan dropped down beside her, her feet throbbing from being thrust back into her shoes. She leaned over to whisper. "I sure hope this doesn't go on very long. I'm liable to put my head right on the table and go to sleep."

"I won't be able to wake you, because I'll be passed out right beside you," Natalie whispered back. Though she smiled, dark circles hovered under her eyes, and her skin looked thin and translucent. She looked every bit as tired as Meghan felt. Maybe even more. As the days had gone by, she had become more dear to Meghan, but she'd also grown more remote, more self-contained. When Meghan asked her about it, she shrugged and said it was nothing. Maybe she was just a touch homesick, but it was nothing to worry about, she was working through it.

Meghan squeezed Natalie's elbow and tried to coax a smile. "I'm sure it will get better. We'll get used to the work and the heat, and we won't be so tired."

"I hope so." She fingered her necklace, a gold chain she wore beneath her uniform during the day since Harvey Girls were forbidden from wearing jewelry at work.

Meghan scanned the room, seeing familiar faces. Things had been so busy she'd had to make friends on the fly. Hopefully, she'd be able to deepen some of those friendships over the coming months, but for now, she was glad she had Natalie. This place would be intolerable without her new best friend.

Mrs. Gregory called the meeting to order. "Ladies and gentlemen, thank you all for coming."

"Like we had a choice." Meghan rubbed her hands on her lips and spoke *sotto voce*.

"Behave yourself," Natalie murmured, stifling a yawn.

"Tonight we're launching a new campaign to raise funds and gather materials to help the war effort. While we appreciate all this community has done to help up to now, the needs of our soldiers are fast outgrowing the efforts we've made in the past. We've got to do more." A fervent light gleamed in her eyes.

"I cannot impress upon you strongly enough how important our efforts are. Every pound of scrap metal, every bushel basket of peach pits, every truckload of rubber ensures the safety and well-being of our soldiers and brings the end of this terrible war closer."

She held up a poster of a Red Cross worker cradling a battle-torn soldier in her arms. Emblazoned across the top were the words IF I FAIL, HE DIES. The Red Cross nurse on the battlefield held one arm out, imploring a Red Cross volunteer sitting at a desk for help. A ripple went through the crowd, shoulders straightening, backs stiffening, resolve almost audible.

Meghan blinked and stared at the poster, all levity gone. The boy in that picture was a perfect rendition of her brother. The face, the coloring, the build, everything. He could've posed for that painting. Her throat closed, and her mind raced.

"What is it?" Natalie nudged her. "You're not sleeping with your eyes open, are you?"

Meghan shook her head, unable to look anywhere but at that soldier. The combination of serving all those fresh-faced, brave young men in the lunchroom and seeing the perfect image of her brother on that poster. . .

"It is with great pleasure and honor that I introduce our speaker this evening. Mr. Leonard Gibson, a Red Cross volunteer who has seen firsthand the atrocities the Kaiser has committed, and an impassioned speaker who is currently crossing this country speaking at Red Cross events to raise awareness of the needs of our boys over there. Organizing volunteers and calling upon citizens to rise up and do something for the cause." Her eyes glowed, and color suffused her cheeks.

Meghan had to admire her fervor, and she couldn't help but be drawn in as the room burst into applause. Bowing slightly, Mrs. Gregory turned the podium over to a balding man with a florid, jowly face. Mr. Gibson bounced on his toes, gripped the edges of the stand, and launched into his speech.

"I have come to bring you news from the front. I have come to carry messages of great need and suffering from our brave soldiers. And with your help, I will return to the battlefield with evidence of your love and support, with supplies and hope and all your prayers and best wishes for our boys.

"The war goes hard for us. The need is great. We need ambulances, medical supplies, food, clothing. And most of all we need funds. Funds to buy these things here and ship them to Europe, funds to purchase supplies there, funds to get our Red Cross nurses and doctors and volunteers to where they are most needed."

The entire room seemed to hold its breath, and Meghan

found herself leaning forward, her hands clutched in her lap. She saw herself wearing the white armband emblazoned with the red cross, standing shoulder to shoulder with her fellow Americans, a vast army of volunteers contributing to the war effort, contributing to saving the lives of the valiant young men who sacrificed family, home, and even their very lives in order to preserve freedom, not only for America but for the Allied countries. If serving soldiers in the lunchroom could be a worthy calling to help the cause, how much more would additional volunteering and service be?

The speaker drew vivid pictures of the courageous men battling pitiful conditions. He told of how the Red Cross was in the best position to help those in need, but not without the help of volunteers. Meghan lived every word, stirred up inside and ready to answer the call. The longer Mr. Gibson talked, the more impassioned he became, drawing his listeners along with him until electricity fairly crackled in the air around them.

"I ask, nay, I demand! I demand that the citizens of Needles rise up and come to our aid. Anyone who would do less than his or her best, would sacrifice less than these brave men, is a coward to be shunned and shamed. Won't you join us in the fight? Won't you stand with us against the evil forces of the Kaiser? Or will you be one to turn a blind eye, to ignore our pleas, to leave our brave young men to face the enemy alone?"

He smacked the pulpit with all the fervor of a revival preacher, his face glowing with sweat and emotion.

Every last person in the room surged to their feet, cheering and clapping. Some women wiped tears, and Meghan's heart threatened to burst out of her chest. Even Natalie seemed to have regained some of her vigor, for her eyes shone, and she dabbed her eyes with a lacy hanky.

Mrs. Gregory stepped up to the podium, shaking Mr.

Gibson's hand. They stood there together a full minute as the applause continued. Finally, she made damping motions, encouraging everyone to take their seats.

"Thank you, Mr. Gibson, for that rousing account. I am sure you will find the citizens of Needles and the employees of The Harvey Company to be most patriotic. By the time you return, we will have proven this through our efforts. Now, before we conclude our meeting tonight, I want to take this time to assign each of you who is willing—and who wouldn't be willing after such a stirring call to arms?—to a particular task. I have several here that I've come up with, and Mr. Gibson will be available to talk with you if you would like to hear more ways we can help. For now, I will list a few." She consulted a piece of paper.

"There are several things we're collecting. Used kitchen grease. Peach pits. Rubber. Scrap metal. Yarn." The paper fluttered as she spread her arms wide. "There are dozens of drives we might put on. In addition, we'll be collecting funds door-to-door, including encouraging folks to buy more war bonds, and we'll have several knitting bees to make socks. I believe Trudy Rivers has a new knitting machine we can use."

Mr. Gibson stepped forward again. "I challenge you each to sign the pledge sheets. Put your name down and how much you think you can raise for the war effort. Be sure to include in your sum the amount you yourself will be contributing. Every bit helps."

Conversations buzzed, the excitement still high in the room. All around Meghan, folks chattered, passing the sign-up lists and jotting their names down. But none of the activities seemed big enough or grand enough to match the zeal in Meghan's heart. Each time she glanced at that poster, now hanging from the front of the podium, each time she thought of those stories Mr. Gibson had told and imagined the bravery with which those soldiers were fighting, she wanted to do something substantial and tangible to help them.

She left Natalie dithering between signing up to roll bandages or to collect peach pits to be used in the making of gas masks and sought out Mr. Gibson. She had to wait for her turn as he was surrounded by eager faces.

"What they really need there on the front are more ambulances. A single ambulance can be the saving of dozens of lives. If only the cost wasn't so steep. One thousand dollars to purchase and ship an ambulance from the US to France. Most groups of this size, communities of this size, aren't up to committing that kind of money." He tucked his thumbs behind his suspenders and bounced on his toes. "Still, if we pool together a lot of little efforts, I'm sure it will make a difference."

"A thousand dollars?" One girl's jaw dropped. "We'd have to collect dimes from now until forever to come up with that kind of money. Especially as we'll be asking folks for bandaging materials, yarn, grease, iron, rubber, and about anything else that isn't nailed down. We've already been through rationing and buying war bonds. I don't think the folks of Needles could raise that kind of money."

Meghan stepped forward. "I'll raise the thousand dollars."

Conversations slowed. Mr. Gibson's eyebrows arched, and he plunked down off his toes, landing hard on his heels.

"Young lady, I admire your spunk, but perhaps you should attempt a more modest monetary goal."

Nothing less would do. One thousand dollars, one ambulance. "I can do it." The hot coals of zeal burned bright in her chest. No sum was too big, no obstacle too immense. She could and would get an ambulance to France. She would prove her courage and her value. And no one, not Mrs. Gregory or her father, or anyone would be able to deny what she had accomplished.

She stepped up to the pledge sheet and boldly wrote her name with a flourish. Beside it, she wrote the sum: One Thousand.

"A lofty goal, Miss Thorson." Mrs. Gregory's voice pricked like a pin. "I hope you have a plan for raising such a significant amount of money in only a few months. The Red Cross takes these lists very seriously. They plan ahead based upon the pledges made by citizens. I'd hate for them to fall short because you bit off more than you could chew."

Meghan's glance flicked to the paper and a splash of uncertainty damped a bit of her enthusiasm. Then the crowd parted a bit and her gaze fell on the poster: If I FAIL, HE DIES.

And she mustn't fail. Not for his sake, nor for her own.

Now if only she had a plan.

Chapter 5

A week later Meghan felt like she was the only one not contributing to the war effort. Every idea she had failed to stand up under much scrutiny or was already being done by someone else. She considered the calendar on the bedroom wall.

"Mr. Gibson said he will return October 15th, and between now and then, I've got to come up with a way to raise one thousand dollars." She tapped her front teeth with her fingernail, racking her brain.

Natalie finished pinning up her hair. "I wish you hadn't made such a pledge. If you'd shown more sense, not let yourself get caught up in the fever in that room, you wouldn't be worrying so much now. You're spending every waking minute trying to come up with a way to raise the money, and it's affecting your work, your appetite, even your sleep. You tossed and turned for hours last night."

The thousand dollars had consumed her. To fail would be not only to humiliate herself in front of Mrs. Gregory, but to let down her brother and men like him. Men such as she served every day on their way to war. How could she do that to them? Not to mention what Papa would say about what he would call another one of her harebrained schemes.

She couldn't fail. She'd have to come up with a way, and that was that.

"Are you ready?"

After three weeks of steady work, Meghan and Natalie had finally earned a half day off. With the arrival of two more new girls, Mrs. Gregory had enough staff to allow them their one afternoon off each week, and Meghan could hardly wait to get out of the hotel and explore the town.

Only she wished their half day was in the morning when it was still marginally cool, but they were low in the pecking order and their days off were assigned accordingly. She took a deep breath that seemed to bake her lungs in her chest. The afternoon sun roasted everything in sight. Only the palm trees seemed indifferent to the swelter.

They passed through the front doors of the hotel and crossed into Santa Fe Park. Though it had been created ten years before when the new hotel had been erected, the trees looked small, stunted, and brittle. Nothing like the lush, greenness of Minnesota. Her eyes longed to see a blue spruce or red maple. The ground crunched under their shoes, parched and hard as terracotta tiles.

"Where should we go?"

"Jenny said Claypool's is the best store."

They meandered slowly. As they walked along the wide street, railroad track after railroad track stretched by on their left, shimmering in the heat. A hot wind blew against their faces, and Meghan scanned the eastern landscape.

"There's the river. Jenny said sometimes the girls take a trip out there to swim. Wouldn't that feel nice, to sink into the water? There's not a soul out here on the street right now."

"And there's the sign for Claypool's." Natalie fanned herself with her handkerchief. "Nobody is silly enough to be walking around in this heat. We should've stayed at the hotel and taken a nap."

"I don't care how hot it is. I'm tired of the hotel. It feels good to get outside for a change. Back home, unless it was a blizzard, I never stayed indoors."

"I could use a blizzard right now." Natalie dabbed at her throat and temples, her brows coming together. "It's unbearable out here."

"I tell you what, as a reward for coming out with me, we'll stop and get some ice cream at the drugstore on the way home."

"I'm going to hold you to that, though we could've gotten ice cream at the soda fountain in the hotel."

Meghan frowned a little, but let Natalie's comment slide. The heat made everyone a touch irritable, even the normally even-keeled Natalie.

They stepped into Claypool's, and once out of the sunshine, the temperature dropped to almost tolerable.

"Afternoon." The clerk barely looked up from his newspaper.

The store stocked everything from groceries to clothing items on two floors. Ceiling fans stirred sluggish air, and the place looked dead. Meghan began to wonder if Natalie wasn't right, that they should've stayed at the hotel. Still, they were here. They might as well look around. She just might find some inspiration for her Red Cross pledge idea.

Nothing caught her eye. Housewares she skipped by quickly, in no mood to look at coffeepots or gravy boats. She saw too many of those every day. The book department slowed her down some as she ran her fingers along the spines. Not much time to read right now and less when she figured out what her Red Cross project would be and got it into full swing.

"Help you with anything?" The clerk scratched his ribs and yawned. "You from the hotel?"

"Yes. We're Harvey Girls."

"Figured. Seen enough of them. They having a social up there this Friday? Been awhile since they had one."

"I believe Mrs. Gregory is planning something, not for this

Friday but for next. A Dime-A-Dance to raise money for the local Red Cross chapter."

"Good. Always like those Harvey socials. I'll bring the wife. She'll enjoy it."

Natalie stopped to study a bin of yarn balls, and Meghan found herself in the fabric and notions section of the store. Bolts of cotton, muslin, denim, and twill, patterned, striped, plaid, and plain. She missed her sewing machine at home. Working the treadle, feeding pieces of cloth through, turning bits into a finished garment or quilt.

Her hand stilled on a bolt of bright red cloth. A single thread of an idea wisped through her mind. She grasped it and tugged gently. Sewing. Maybe she could use her love of sewing.

Suddenly, full-blown, the idea surged into her head.

"I've got it!"

Natalie dropped a skein of yarn, and the sales clerk jerked.

"I've got it." She grabbed Natalie's hands and swung them. "Why didn't I think of it before? I'm going to make a quilt. A signature quilt. I'll sell space on the blocks for folks to have their signatures embroidered, and I'll sell advertising space to the businesses in town, and when it's done, I'll raffle it off." She hugged Natalie, who stood like a wax doll, blinking her long lashes.

Stirring herself, Natalie's brow wrinkled. "A quilt? Are you sure? That's an awfully big project to take on. Not just the sewing but the embroidering and the selling of names? And how are you going to afford the fabric and such? Or find a sewing machine? You'll be so tired."

The idea had taken such a hold in Meghan's mind, she didn't want to hear anything dampening. For the first time in a week, she felt like she could breathe freely.

"As my grandma is fond of saying, 'No one ever died of

tired.' I'll figure it out." She turned to the clerk. "Do you have a piece of paper I could use? I need to do some figuring."

The man produced a scrap of brown store paper and a stubby pencil, and Meghan went to work.

"The women in my mama's auxiliary at home in Mantorville made a quilt like this last year. I don't know why I didn't think of it before. A white quilt with red crosses and red names embroidered in the corners of the squares. They had four names per square, and fifty-six squares. Plus some room on the end of each row for a business name or a big donor. . ." The pencil scratched as she slashed out a sketch of the quilt as a whole, a single quilt block, and some rough estimates of cloth, batting, and thread. "I would need at least two hundred twenty-four names to fill the blocks, and with seven staggered rows of eight squares each, that leaves seven half-blocks on alternating ends to be filled with company names."

"Meghan, please, think about this before you jump in boots and all." Natalie tugged on Meghan's sleeve. "I'm sure it isn't too late for you to amend your pledge to something more manageable. You could knit socks with me. Just stop and think, please?"

She looked up from her scribbling, her mind racing so fast she had to concentrate on what Natalie said. "I've done nothing but think about this for the past week. I made the pledge, and it is up to me to see it through. I've been quilting since I was a little girl. Just imagine. In a few months, I'll have a whole thousand dollars to turn over to Mr. Gibson, and he can buy an ambulance to help our wounded soldiers. I don't care how hard I have to work. The end result will be worth it."

"What if you don't raise enough money?"

"I will. I have to." She turned back to her paper. "If I get two dollars for every signature, plus maybe ten dollars to have a business name on the quilt. . ." More scratching. "Then I can raffle the quilt or auction it off. Didn't Mrs. Gregory say something about having an auction on the night Mr. Gibson comes back?" A glow burned in her chest. This would work. She could do it. She just needed to get started.

"Where are you going to get the money for the fabric and such?" Natalie crossed her arms and tapped her foot.

Meghan narrowed her eyes and her thoughts raced. The idea was so big, so perfect, she couldn't wait to get started, and it bothered her that Natalie wasn't as excited as she about it. Instead of joining in her enthusiasm, Natalie insisted on pointing out all the roadblocks. Meghan turned to the clerk. "Do you own this fine establishment?"

He chuckled and scratched his ribs. "No, ma'am. You want to talk to William Claypool."

"And where would I find him?"

"Back there in the office." He pointed them to the rear of the store.

Twenty minutes later, Meghan clutched a scrip for fabric and thread as well as a ten-dollar donation to get Claypool's name embroidered in one of the half-blocks on the quilt. She put a superior little skip into her step as she showed Natalie the paper and the cash.

"He was most kind."

"You got him to donate the fabric and some money? How?" Natalie's eyes narrowed. Her hand went to her hip, and a schoolmarmish pucker drew in her mouth.

"You act like I robbed the man. I simply told him what I wanted; explained how, as a leading citizen of Needles, I was sure he would want to be at the forefront of any civic cause; and he did the rest."

She would not mention her nervous stumbling, how she'd

invoked the name of the Red Cross several times, and—her conscience gave a little shiver—pandered just a wee bit to the man's pride. Flattery often got you what plain speaking couldn't.

"Miss Thorson." Mr. Claypool stuck his head out of the office doorway. "Thank you for your patronage. I look forward to seeing the end result. Mr. Weeks, be sure you give them just what they ask for."

The clerk snapped to attention like he'd been poked in the ribs. "Yes, sir."

He unrolled bolts of cloth onto the cutting table and with an enormous pair of shears, snipped off lengths of white and red fabric. Natalie found skeins of embroidery thread to match, and Meghan selected a suitable length of fiber batting.

"I'll have these delivered to the hotel for you." Mr. Weeks tucked his pencil behind his ear after totting up the total.

"Thank you." Meghan hesitated at the door. No time like the present to get started. "By the way, would you like to make a two-dollar donation and have your name on the quilt? I'm sure, as someone so familiar in the community, you would want be an example for your friends and neighbors." She smiled. This was exactly the phrase she'd used on Mr. Claypool. "I imagine folks around here would notice if a name as prominent as yours didn't appear on the quilt."

His hand was already diving into his pocket. "Best put my name and my wife's on there, too. She'd be put out if she got left off."

Meghan and Natalie headed to the drugstore, and Meghan couldn't help but put her chin in the air a bit. "Fourteen dollars *and* free materials."

Natalie rolled her eyes. "Only nine hundred eighty-six dollars and one whole quilt to piece, embroider, and auction off left to go."

Caleb handed Joshua the metal bucket and length of pipe. The bucket had a rusted out hole in it anyway and couldn't be any less useful. It would do for what he had in mind.

"When I give you the signal, you go to whacking on it."

"Why? You've got that horse eating out of your hand. He's perfectly trained and bridle-wise. We've done nothing but school horses for the past month, and each one is as gentle as a lamb. Why upset them?" Joshua set his jaw, an expression Caleb was all too familiar with. Nothing seemed to happen on this place without an argument from his hired man. No, not quite a man, or he'd quit arguing all the time and do what his boss said. He was a hard worker, Caleb would grant him that, it was just that he expected to be informed of the reason behind every chore before he'd stir a step.

"You're a smart lad. I'll leave you to work it out." He headed toward his mount. Grit filtered through the seam in his boot, working its way through his sock and abrading his skin. Those new boots couldn't come soon enough. Sunshine baked everything around him, whitening the sky and making him squint, even under the broad brim of his hat.

The bay stood quietly in the morning sunshine, one hind leg tucked up, resting. A level-headed, hardworking, honest mount, typical of the animals sent to him by the US Cavalry's horse buyer for the Southwest. Major Alexander had a good eye for horses and a firsthand knowledge of what was needed in a military mount.

Caleb gathered the reins and jumped, landing on his stomach across the saddle and scrambling upright. Once mounted, he slipped his right foot easily into the stirrup, but he had to guide his left leg into position. He couldn't mount any other way, not with his bum foot. The maneuver might not be pretty, but it was effective. Settling aboard, he couldn't help but miss the deep seat on his favorite saddle. This flat, cavalry saddle was what the officers at Fort Riley and overseas would be using, so he trained with it, but he didn't like it as well. Being forced to put more weight on his left leg than he otherwise would caused the muscles to radiate weakness, but he gritted his teeth, balanced himself, and gripped with his knees.

Shaking up the reins, he put the horse into a slow walk, then trot, then canter, circling the big corral. When the horse had fallen into a rhythm, he lifted his hand to signal Joshua. As the horse approached the boy, Joshua did justice to his job and banged the bucket with vigor almost under the animal's nose.

The horse jerked his head up and bolted, skidding sideways and seeking to escape the cacophony. He added a few bucks, just for good measure. Caleb hung on to the swerving animal, keeping a tight rein and finally, on the far side of the corral, bringing him back under control. He let the horse stand for a moment, trembling and sweating. With soft words and a few pats on the neck, Caleb soothed his mount.

"Easy, boy. You're all right." Squeezing his knees, he asked the horse to walk out.

With much head-tossing and sidestepping, he obeyed, but when they got near Joshua and the racket began again, he fought the bit and skidded backward.

"Whoa." Caleb brought him to a halt, calmed him, and tried again. This time, though the horse hastened his pace, he kept going in the circle. By the fifth time, the animal continued on without changing course, though he kept an eye on Joshua.

Finally, Caleb dismounted and motioned the boy to come

over. "Here, unsaddle him and walk him out a bit to cool him down, and then give him a drink."

Joshua set the bucket and pipe on the ground near the gate. He rubbed his hands on the back of his jeans and took the reins. "I figured it out."

"Did you?"

"You're sending these horses into battle where there will be lots of loud, sudden noises. You're getting them used to it so they don't bolt into trouble."

"I knew you were a smart boy. And having you here makes it so much easier. I was stacking up buckets and cans and knocking them over as I rode by, but this is a lot more effective."

Joshua shrugged. "I should've seen it right away. But banging on a bucket is a long ways from cannon fire. How're you going to get them ready for that?"

Caleb opened the gate so Joshua could lead the horse out. "I guess we could always blow something up and see how they react."

Joshua stopped. "You can't—" He grinned ruefully when he realized Caleb was teasing.

"All right, we can't blow up anything, but we'll do the best we can. The bucket, a shotgun, a nice big smoky fire. We'll put them through their paces as best we can, then when we turn them over to the military, they can take it from there. If we've already conditioned them not to jump at loud noises or get spooked over a little fire and smoke, they'll be well on their way to making cavalry mounts."

The boy nodded and led the horse away.

Caleb headed toward the water trough, dragging his hat off and dunking his head into the cool water. Straightening quickly, he flung droplets into an arc over his head. Rivulets ran down his face and neck, soaking his shirt but already beginning to evaporate. He swiped his forearm across his brow and resettled his hat. Time for some rest.

Because Joshua had his back turned fifty yards away, Caleb went ahead and gave in to the ache in his ankle and limped over to the shade of the front porch. Dropping down into one of the chairs, he dug his fingertips into his left calf above the boot and kneaded. On days like today, when the ache persisted no matter if he was resting or working, wearing his brace seemed more and more attractive.

And yet, he knew he wouldn't. Not even when he was alone. If he didn't use his leg, it would atrophy worse. And if anyone saw him in the brace, he'd be the object of pity, and that was something he refused to stomach.

The new boots would help. The note from Doc Bates said they would arrive in a month or so, about the time for him to take a string of horses in to meet the train.

Thinking of Doc Bates made his insides squirm. He'd never meant to reveal anything about his past, especially not his father, but something about Doc's patience and acceptance made Caleb want to spill everything. Up to and including all about Patricia.

His mind balked. Not Patricia. Never Patricia. He never wanted that name to pass his lips again. He certainly didn't want to blab about it to Doc.

Which reminded him, he'd best stop letting his mind wander to Meghan, too. He had more than enough evidence that his future held no place for a woman in it, and he was foolish to even daydream about a girl like Meghan. If she ever found out he was crippled, she'd run as far and as fast as Patricia had. So he had to make sure she didn't find out, and the surest way to do that was to stay away from her.

This Friday, when he went to town, he'd go to the station

and deliver the horses, and head home. The hotel, the lunchroom, and Meghan Thorson were strictly off limits.

"You're sure he won't mind us cutting through his property?" Meghan held her hat on her head as the hotel car bounced and jounced along the rutted road. Girls laughed and jostled, talked and sang all around her, but all Meghan's thoughts were on Caleb McBride. The minute the excursion to the river had been voiced, she knew she would go along. Cajoling Natalie to join her had been the most difficult part.

"He won't care. We probably won't even see him. We didn't last time. Anyway, Doc comes out here to fish all the time, and he said Caleb wouldn't care if we picnicked by the river." Jenny turned in her seat and waved to the automobile behind them. Sunlight flashed off the windscreen and paintwork, as well as the twin rails of the railroad tracks parallel to the road.

"I wonder what came over Mrs. Gregory to up and give the whole lot of us the afternoon off."

Natalie, a picnic basket balanced on her knees, dodged Jenny's elbow. "She said the three-thirty had engine trouble and wouldn't be coming through today, so we might as well have the time off, though she did promise at least half of us would have to help with the breakfast prep when we got back."

Jenny shrugged. "Who cares? A whole afternoon to paddle in the river, lay about in the shade, and be lazy. Look, there's the turnoff."

They bumped over the railroad tracks and followed a narrow drive toward the smudge of green bushes that marked the riverbank.

A plain, single-storied house came into view, drab and gray, with a rusty tin roof. A wide porch shaded the front of the structure, and miles of corral posts and rails wove in and around the house. Open-sided shade shelters stood at various angles, and horses dozed, lazily swishing their tails, heads down, standing still. Trying not to be obvious, Meghan took in as much as she could as the car bumped through the farmyard.

She tapped Jenny on the shoulder. "Shouldn't we stop and at least let him know we're here?"

"There's someone." Jenny pointed toward a low outbuilding. Meghan craned her neck, but the figure emerging from the building wasn't Caleb. Blue-black hair and a slouching, lean look. Too young to be Caleb. She quelled her disappointment.

The driver, one of the porters from the hotel, honked the horn. Jenny waved wildly, half rising from her seat. The young man waved back, and the car bounced on.

The road dipped down into a cut with sandy walls rising on either side. Brushy trees and scrub bushes clung to the earth walls, obscuring their view of the house and corrals a few hundred yards away. A sandy spit of beach opened before them, and everyone piled out of the cars. Girls in high spirits continued to talk and tease as they unloaded blankets and baskets and belongings. Meghan took out her handkerchief to wipe the dust and grit from her face while she surveyed the beach. The river slapped against the bank in lazy, breeze-induced waves. Her spirits lifted at the sight of the water, and she couldn't resist walking right down to the edge and trailing her fingers in the lukewarm liquid. The picnic area was in a small cove carved out of the sand, like sitting in a bowl. From here, they couldn't see the house or very far up or downstream.

"I'm going wading." Jenny plopped down on the sand and tugged at her shoelaces. Her stockings followed, and she lifted her hem and strode into the water. "Ah, heavenly. I've been wanting to do this for weeks."

Several of the girls followed, but Meghan, mindful of her fair skin, headed back to the safety of the shade.

Natalie joined her on a blanket, drawing her legs up and wrapping her arms around her knees. She covered a yawn. "I could stretch out right here and sleep the afternoon away. That's what I was going to do before you talked me into coming out here."

Slight guilt skipped through Meghan's heart, but she bumped shoulders with Natalie. "It's cooler by the river than upstairs in our room. At least there's a breeze."

Natalie nodded, stretched out on her side, and pillowed her head on her arm. "Wake me up when it's time to go."

The girls laughed and splashed. Another carload, this time of railroad men, joined the party, swelling the numbers to nearly twenty. Flirting and boisterous jesting became the rule of the day.

Meghan rose and tugged Jenny away from a brawny switchman. "What are they doing here? What would Mrs. Gregory say? We're forbidden to mix with the railroaders."

Jenny shrugged. "Who cares? Mrs. Gregory isn't here. She said we could come to the river. If other people show up at the same time, we can't be blamed, can we? Don't worry so much."

When the men began splashing the girls, accompanied by shouts and screams, Meghan wandered upstream and around the jutting bank to get away from the noise. Natalie must be exhausted to slumber in spite of the activity.

A hundred yards upstream, she found a patch of shade under a twisted juniper tree that hung over the water. Lifting her hem, she divested herself of shoes and stockings and poked her toes into the water. Her eyes closed, and a deep sigh relaxed her. Meghan loved being around people, but after awhile, she needed to be alone to let her soul fill up again. She sniffed the warm desert air, inhaling scents of water, mud, and tangy juniper. Sand trickled through her fingers as she breathed a prayer of thanks for this time alone.

The ground thudded, and her eyes popped open. Coming toward her on her left, a horse and rider flew along the shallow edge of the river, sending up sheets of water. She yanked her feet back as the rider pulled the horse up a few yards away.

Though his hat shaded his face, she knew him instantly.

"Mr. McBride." She tugged the hem of her skirt down as far as it would go, though it didn't cover her bare feet and ankles. Deciding to stand, she pushed herself up and brushed the sand from her dress.

He nudged his horse out of the water and slid to the ground, his eyes wide. "What are you doing out here? Are you lost?"

She wet her lips and tried a laugh, but feared it didn't sound natural. He was more handsome than she remembered. His worn shirt stretched across his shoulders, and he'd rolled up the sleeves to reveal muscular forearms. He had the long legs and lean waist of a natural horseman, and his face would turn any girl's head for another look.

"I'm not lost. There are a few of us from the hotel and rail yard having a picnic just around the bend." She motioned toward the south. "You don't mind, do you? I asked Jenny if we shouldn't stop at the house and ask permission, but she said you wouldn't care." Her hands twisted in front of her, and she was very conscious of her bare feet.

He looped his arm over the saddle and leaned into the horse, putting all his weight on one foot. "I don't mind. You just surprised me, that's all. I wasn't expecting anyone along this stretch." He patted the horse's rusty-brown neck. "I was just taking the edge off this fellow. He had a long, tedious afternoon in the corral learning to respond to voice commands, and I thought he needed some of the cobwebs blown out with a good run along the river."

She edged forward and brushed the animal's velvety nose. He whiffed her fingertips and submitted to a few pats before tossing his head and sidestepping away. "He's a beauty, Mr. McBride."

"Smart and capable. He'll be a good mount. And call me Caleb." A smile quirked his lips. "How come you're up here by yourself and not with the rest of the picnickers?"

"It was getting pretty loud. I just wanted some time away from all the people and noise."

A shadow passed over his face, and he backed up a step. "I don't mean to intrude. I'll leave you alone then."

Her hand shot out and touched his arm, warm, masculine, with a dusting of blond-brown hair. "Please. I'd like you to stay." Heat at her boldness crept into her cheeks, but she looked him in the eyes.

He tilted his head, studying her for a moment, then, as if making up his mind, he tied the reins to a juniper branch and lowered himself to the sand.

Meghan sat beside him, a few feet of sand between. "Have you always lived in Needles?"

He shook his head, plucking a stem of long, dry grass from a clump under the juniper and breaking it into small pieces. Tossing them into the water, one by one, he watched them bob and drift. "No, I've only lived here a few months. I hail from Vermont originally. I live here because of the horses. The army rented the place because it was a good location along the railway."

"What do you do with the horses?"

"Work them, condition them, train them." Another inch

of grass stalk voyaged southward. "Then I ship them east so the army can feed them to the war machine." His face hardened. "This stupid, endless, murderous war."

"You don't approve of the war?" Her eyes widened. Was he a German sympathizer?

"Should anyone really approve of war?" His glance flicked toward her and then back to the river. The horse lowered his head to drink, making the bit jingle.

"Well, no, but when it becomes necessary, it is our duty as citizens to stand up and fight the oppression of our allies. We cannot let the Kaiser overrun sovereign nations on a whim. He must be stopped, and it is the duty of every American citizen to do what they can to help reach that goal." Her shoulders straightened, and her back stiffened.

He laughed. "You sound like a recruitment poster."

Heat flooded her face, and a pebble of pride lodged in her throat. "And you, sir, sound like. . .like. . ." She faded to a stop.

"Now, don't take offense. I didn't mean anything by it. Of course I think everyone should do their part to help America win the war. I save my paper, grease, and peach pits, just like everyone else."

Steering away from the topic of war, she asked, "Do you miss Vermont?"

"I miss the green, and sometimes when it's hot enough to melt rocks out here, I miss the snow."

"Not your family?"

Again his face hardened, and she knew she'd touched another nerve. "I have no family to speak of."

"Not anyone?" She couldn't comprehend what that must feel like. What would her life be like without having her parents and her brother; her aunts, uncles, cousins, even her grandparents back in the old countries?

"Nobody who claims me, nobody I lay claim to." He shrugged and threw the rest of the grass into the water.

The isolation in his voice tugged at her. "That must be lonely."

He shrugged again. "Loneliness isn't the worst hurt a man can endure." Pushing himself upright, he stumbled and grabbed onto a low-hanging branch to steady himself. Stepping out of the shade, he judged the angle of the sun. "You'd best get back to the others. I imagine they'll have eaten all the food by now. Anyway, I doubt your lady-boss would approve of you wandering off by yourself and keeping company with the likes of me."

Meghan gathered her shoes and stockings. This whole conversation had been so unsatisfactory somehow, and she wasn't ready to let it go. Everything about this man intrigued her—his face and form, his mind, and above all, the bewildering sense of strength and vulnerability that tangled around him.

"Will I see you again?"

"I don't go to town much. In case you hadn't noticed, Needles doesn't take too kindly to strangers. It's like an island in the desert here. If you work for the hotel or the railroad, you can come from anywhere and be accepted, but if you come for any other reason, you're measured by a different stick."

The thought of not seeing him left an empty place in her heart. He was a puzzle she needed to figure out, and somewhere inside him was a wound she felt compelled to heal.

"There's a social coming up on Friday to raise war funds. A dance at the hotel. I'd love it if you would come. The whole town is going to be there. Perhaps, if you came, the people of Needles would get to know you better and begin to accept you."

He chuckled and shook his head, loosening his horse's reins from the tree. "A dance? At the hotel? I don't think so. But thanks for the invitation. I'd best be getting back to the house before Joshua thinks I drowned in the river."

Swinging the horse around so the animal stood between them, he gave a one-legged hop and swung into the saddle. Touching his hat brim, he sent the horse flying along the water's edge once more in the direction from which he had come.

Meghan stood there watching him ride out of sight, wondering what it was about him that so intrigued her.

Chapter 6

"It's going to feel good to be dressed up for once and not in that uniform, don't you think?" Meghan laid her primrose gown out on the bed and studied it. Organza, with barely off-the-shoulder sleeves of ruffled lace, the dress had been her graduation gift from her parents.

Natalie nodded without looking up, twirling a curl around her finger and reading a letter she'd received that day.

Meghan tried again. "You're going to look lovely. I wish I could wear pink, but alas, as a redhead, that is one color that is definitely off limits. My hair turns bright orange, and I look like I got sunburned. Redheads have to be so careful about the colors they wear. You, on the other hand, look stylish no matter what." She sighed and picked up her own letter from home. "Mama wants to know if I can come home for a visit anytime soon or if I have to wait the whole six months. She says the mill is doing fine. The crops are growing well, and Papa is practically living at the mill. Lars sent another letter. I wish he'd write to *me*. I sent him my address. Still, I suppose when you're a soldier, it's all you can do to get one letter written from time to time, and he knows Mama will send along any news. He's probably somewhere in France; that's all we know. So much of his letter was redacted, it's impossible to tell just where he is for sure."

"Hmm."

Meghan set her letter aside and went to the mirror to brush her hair. "A whole evening of dancing. Isn't that wonderful? I haven't danced since last fall, and that was a barn dance put on

443

by the local farmers' association. Tonight won't be anything like that. Did you see the decorations? All those banners and bunting. Flags everywhere. I hardly recognized the loggia. I'll tell you something, Mrs. Gregory might be a tartar when it comes to following the company rules, but she sure knows how to get things done. She's more organized than an accountant and more vigilant than a Victorian governess. How many dances do you think there will be? And how many partners? Too bad that train full of soldiers pulled out. If they were here, I bet we'd be danced off our feet most of the night. Though it would seem wrong to take dimes from the very soldiers we're trying to raise money for, wouldn't it?"

No response.

Meghan turned from fussing with her hair. "Natalie?"

Tears streamed down Natalie's cheeks, and she let the pages of her letter fall to her lap. Her hands came up to cover her face. Silent sobs shook her shoulders.

Meghan dropped the hairbrush and knelt by the chair. "What is it? Are you all right?"

She shook her head, still trembling. A small, keening sound escaped her throat, full of pain and fear.

"Did you get bad news from home? You've been so quiet since you got that letter, and here I am babbling on like a silly nitwit." She rubbed small circles on Natalie's back, chastising herself for not paying better attention.

After a moment, the worst of the storm passed, and Natalie's muscles eased. Slowly, she lowered her hands, revealing tear-stained skin and drowning eyes. "I know I shouldn't, but I have to tell someone." Her voice rasped, sob-roughened. "Can you keep a secret? I mean, never-tell-a-soul-not-even-if-your-life-depended-on-it keep a secret?"

Sitting back on her heels, Meghan studied her. "What is it?

Are you in trouble? Is something wrong at home? You can tell me, and you know I'd never repeat it."

Natalie took a shuddering breath and gripped the letter in her lap. "I have someone at home who is very ill. Her medical bills are so large I had to leave home to find work. I tried to find a job near her, but nothing I was qualified for paid enough to make much difference. Then I saw the advertisement for becoming a Harvey Girl. I applied, and I volunteered to come to Needles because of the bonus pay."

Meghan chewed her lower lip and took Natalie's hands, squeezing them. She'd taken the Harvey job more as a lark, an adventure, a desire to see more of the world than Mantorville, Minnesota, and to do something bigger and more challenging than helping out in the family business and waiting for someone to come along to marry her. And here was Natalie, far from home where she was needed, trying to earn enough money to help with a relative's medical care. And she'd never said a word, never complained, carrying the burden all alone.

"I'm sorry you've got an ill relative, but why is it a secret? Lots of the girls here send money home to help out. There's no shame in that. Is this relative's condition worse?"

Natalie swallowed and freed one of her hands to wipe her cheeks. She pressed her lips together, as if battling with herself. Finally, she whispered, "The sick woman is my mother-in-law."

"It's an honorable thing for you to help your mother—What? Mother-*in-law*?" Meghan lost her balance and toppled onto her backside. She braced herself on her palms, sprawled in an unladylike heap. "Mother-in-law as in. . . ?" She gulped. "But that would mean. . . You're a widow?" A frown tugged at her forehead as she grappled with this notion.

"No, I'm not a widow. At least I pray I'm not." Her eyes closed, and a wave of pain contorted her features. "My husband is a soldier. By now he's in Europe."

"You're married?" Her voice squeaked.

"Shhh! Not so loud." Natalie made a damping motion. "Do you want the whole hotel to hear you?"

"I'm sorry." Meghan lowered her voice and straightened her limbs until she could wrap her arms around her updrawn knees. "It just caught me so off-guard. Married. No wonder you want to keep it a secret. Have you been married long? How did your husband feel about you leaving your family to take this job?"

"Derek has no idea I've left home. Things happened so fast. We were already engaged when America entered the war, and we decided to marry before he enlisted." A shiver rippled through her slight frame. "He wanted me to have his pension if anything happened to him. He left for training, and while he was gone, his mother had a stroke. I had left my job as a store clerk when we got married, and they hired someone else in my place. In any case I knew that salary would never cover hospital and doctor bills. When I saw the Harvey ad, I jumped at it. Derek got leave to come home and visit his mother for a few days before he shipped out, and we, his parents and I, decided we wouldn't tell him I was leaving for California. He had enough to worry about. He returned to his unit the day before I met you in Chicago to come here."

"Oh, Natalie." Meghan pressed her fingertips to her lips.

"I know. I'm breaking all kinds of rules. If Mrs. Gregory found out, she'd have me on the first eastbound train. But she can't know. I can't lose this job. My salary and Derek's army pay are supporting all of us. My father-in-law is elderly, and it's all he can do to take care of his wife. He can't work. I have to stay here, at least until Derek comes home again." Her blue eyes swam with tears and worry. "You won't tell, will you?"

"Of course not. I'm only sorry you didn't tell me sooner.

Here I've been blathering about silly things like dances and dresses and such, and you've been worrying about your mother-in-law and your—it seems so strange to say it—your husband. No wonder you look so pale and drawn all the time. And you've the appetite of a finch, down to skin and bones."

"Sometimes I think I'll go mad with worry, but I'm so thankful for this job. It keeps me busy; I can't worry too much while I'm working, and I'm making far more money than I could at home, and I send almost all of it back there. I only wish I didn't have to lie to Mrs. Gregory or to Derek. If he knew, he'd be crazy with worry. He's always been protective of me, since we were kids. One of the last things he said to me before he left was how glad he was that I was safe with his parents. That he rested easier knowing we were together and taking care of each other."

"How do you keep it secret from your husband?"

"I write letters to him and send them home to Springfield. His father sends them on for me. When one of Derek's letters arrives there for me, they pass it along here. We can only hope no one from home writes to him, at least until after I've made enough to cover the medical bills and Genevieve is doing better." Natalie glanced at the clock. "We'd better hurry and dress. I wish I didn't have to go to this social. The last thing I feel like doing tonight is dancing with strangers."

"Maybe we can work something out so you don't have to. There's always the refreshment table, though after a day of serving food, you probably don't want to do that either."

"Actually, if it meant I could get out of dancing, I'd serve punch until sunup."

A half hour later, they walked out onto the loggia. This wide, covered seating area on the second floor was reserved for hotel guests and provided an excellent place to view the rugged desert hills surrounding the town. Festive lanterns illuminated the open area reserved for dancing, and a long table held a punch bowl and a variety of cookies and cakes prepared by the bakery that day. A small cluster of musicians optimistically calling themselves the Needles City Orchestra tuned up, and Harvey Girls fluttered around like brightly colored flowers with nary a black dress or starched apron to be seen. More guests drifted up the stairs, local men and women in their Sunday best. Meghan spied Mr. Weeks from the department store and waggled her fingers his direction. He had a smiling woman on his arm whom Meghan took to be his wife.

Mrs. Gregory sailed across the floor in a dark blue dress with black beading along the bodice and down the front of the skirt, clapping her hands for attention. She'd powdered her face and wore a bit of lip rouge, which made her look a bit softer, especially under the light of the paper lanterns.

"Ladies and gentlemen, thank you all for coming. I'd like to give you a few instructions as to how this social will work. First, note the donation box on the end of the refreshment table. All proceeds go to support the Red Cross, and we ask you to be generous. As many of you know, this is a dime-a-dance social. So all the ladies, if you will pick up dance cards from Miss Ralston"—she waved to Jenny standing by the conductor— "and gentlemen, you are free to either pay each lady for a dance or you can settle up at the end of the evening. We want you all to have a good time and to dance a lot. Remember, every dime you donate is a blow against the Kaiser." She fisted her hand and swung it upward in a little arc as if bopping the German leader in the nose.

Meghan, her mind still ruminating on Natalie's surprising disclosure, waited her turn to pick up a dance card. All the while, she scanned the room. Boys of sixteen or seventeen huddled together, eyeing the girls. Middle-aged men in suits, most with their wives on their arms, talked in small bunches. Conspicuous by their absence were young men. Every man between eighteen and thirty-five, it seemed, was gone from the town of Needles.

Except one.

Though he'd said he wouldn't come, she spent a few moments imagining what it would be like if he had. Would he ask her to dance? What would he look like all dressed up? And why, out of all the young men in town, hadn't he enlisted? She supposed his work for the army was important, but someone older could train horses, couldn't they? Someone who wasn't able to enlist? She'd wanted to ask him when they sat on the riverbank, but something wouldn't let her voice the words. As if she was afraid of the answer. His jibes about the war had set up a faint echo of doubt in the back of her mind, but she quelled it whenever it whispered.

She remembered the strong feel of his arms around her when he'd rescued her, his face only inches from her own, the scents of sunshine and soap and hard-working male surrounding her. At the lunch counter, in the midst of all those soldiers, he'd looked closed off, almost wounded. She had a feeling there was so much more to Caleb McBride than anyone here knew, and she longed to discover more about him. Many times a day, and even more often at night as she lay in bed waiting for sleep to claim her, her thoughts strayed to the horseman, and though she watched the door of the lunchroom for him every day, hoping he would come in, true to his word, he stayed away.

"May I have the pleasure?" A young man with a cowlick stood at her elbow.

"Of course." She smiled at him, offered him her dance card, and read the name when he returned it to her. "Of course, Lawrence. I'd be delighted." She allowed him to swing her into a waltz, joining the twirling figures already dancing.

Her dance partner was so nervous, he stared at his feet and counted the steps under his breath. Perhaps a bit of conversation would help him relax. "Are you a student at the high school?"

He looked up, stumbled, and righted himself. "Um, no. Not anymore. I graduated last month. Just turned eighteen." His narrow chest swelled a bit, and he dared another glance at her face. "Just enlisted, too. Gonna go kill me some Germans."

A lump formed in Meghan's throat at the eager light in the boy's eyes. He was so young, on the cusp of manhood, eager to go to war. How soon before battle jaded his fresh, smiling eyes or snuffed out his life altogether.

She smiled her warmest smile at him. "I'm proud of you. Everyone must do their duty. We'll all be here praying for your safe return."

Natalie stayed by the refreshment table, serving punch and cakes. When Meghan stopped by after the third dance, Natalie smiled and winked. "Mrs. Gregory approved my overseeing the refreshments." A bit of color had come back into her pale cheeks, and her eyes looked less tense. Perhaps sharing her secret with someone really had eased some of her burden.

Meghan danced and chatted and got to know the people of Needles. They were friendly and accepting of the Harvey Girls. Most of the men worked in some way for the railroad, and they considered the waitresses part of the Santa Fe Railroad family. She enjoyed herself and added quite a few dimes to the donation box. She even added a few names to her quilt list, thanks to Mr. Weeks spreading the word. But the night lacked a certain luster.

Then at half past eight, Caleb McBride emerged at the head of the stairs. Impossible to miss his entrance, because a murmur went through the crowd and Mrs. Gregory sucked in a sharp breath. Meghan, dancing with the man who owned the drugstore, tripped a bit and had to right herself, leaning on her partner's guiding arm.

Caleb looked fine all dressed up. Better than fine. He took her breath right away.

Caleb resisted the urge to turn around and go back down the steps. He was all kinds of a fool. In spite of repeated warnings to himself to steer clear of the hotel, this dance, and Meghan Thorson, here he was, dressed like a strutting turkey and acting like a besotted beagle pup.

He scanned the crowd, aware of the eyes turned his way but trying to ignore them as he sought out the one person he'd come to see. There she was, dancing with the druggist. What was his name? Cooper? Hooper? Didn't matter. Caleb never went into the drugstore anyway. Come to think of it, he hardly went anywhere in Needles anymore. Feed store, Claypool's for groceries once a month, Doc Bates's, and to church where he sat in the back, kept to himself, and ducked out the minute the music for the final hymn started.

And now here he was at the El Garces. Second time this month. He was definitely loco.

The song ended, and Meghan slipped from her partner's arms and allowed him to lead her off the dance floor. The druggist's touch on her elbow made Caleb's gut churn, and he forced himself not to go over and yank the man's hand away from her. Surprised at the strength of his reaction, he reminded himself he had no claim at all on Meghan, and moreover, he didn't want to have one. But if that was the case, why was he here? Why was he doing this to himself? He was like a starving, penniless man standing outside a bakery window, salivating over what he couldn't taste. Coming here was a mistake. He could still get out of here. It wasn't too late.

Then she looked right at him, and her smile smote him in the chest like the kick of a mule. She excused herself from her partner and walked toward him. He hadn't counted on talking to her, hadn't thought beyond just getting to see her. He'd figured by now Mrs. Gregory would've spilled out all her dislike of him to Meghan, and Meghan would disdain him like the rest of the town. Just getting a glimpse of her would've been enough. But here she was, coming at him all friendly, like he was a welcome guest.

That yellow dress was sure something. Pretty as a spring sunrise. And her smile. He couldn't look away. She acted like he was the only one in the room and she couldn't wait to talk to him. Unlike every other person here. He hadn't missed the pinched lips, the whispers, the pulling aside of skirts as he passed.

Her green eyes sparkled in the glow of the paper lanterns and lightbulbs strung along the balconies as she stopped before him and held out her hand. "Caleb, I'm so glad you came." Her smile warmed him, and he couldn't help but notice how burnished her coppery hair looked and how a rosy tint graced her cheeks.

"Evening. After your reminder down at the river that everyone should do his part, I figured I should come and lend my support to the cause." His voice rasped like he'd swallowed a fistful of horseshoe nails. When their fingers touched, warmth zipped up his arm, and he had to remind himself to let go.

"I'd been hoping to see you in the lunchroom, but I suppose you're busy with your horses. How is the training going?"

"Fine." She'd been watching for him at the hotel. That thought shot him through with golden arrows, and he cautioned himself, though it seemed to do precious little good. Her friendly reception was like water to his parched insides.

She flicked open a lacy, yellow fan and stirred the air, but she wasn't using it as a flirting tool like some girls did. No lowering her chin or batting her eyes. Instead, she looked right at him, her lips parted, eyes such a deep green he wanted to sink into them and forget to come back to reality. "I hope the work won't keep you away indefinitely. With so many strangers and travelers coming through, it's nice to see a familiar face once in a while."

He dragged his mind away from how creamy-smooth her skin looked and how several delicate russet curls wisped at the nape of her neck. "I'll be sure to stop by next time I'm in town."

Now where had that come from? Hadn't he just told himself he wasn't going to—?

"The orchestra is about ready for another song." She consulted her dance card.

And he could dance about as well as a peg-legged duck on ice. How was he going to get out of this? Why hadn't he thought how awkward it would be coming to a dance and not being able to take a turn around the floor?

Because he'd been too busy thinking about how lonely his life was and about how pleasant it was when a pretty girl noticed him. Not just noticed him, but was nice to him. Treated him with respect instead of like something she needed to scrape off her shoe.

She glanced at him expectantly, and he noted the three men waiting nearby, eager to claim her for a dance.

"I'm not much for dancing. If I pay the dime, will you sit out this dance with me?"

A small furrow appeared between her brows, and questions invaded her eyes, but she nodded. "Of course. Would you like some punch?"

He cupped her elbow, savoring the whisper-softness of her skin, and led her to the refreshment table. The three men hoping for a dance faded away, and he made sure his face bore not a trace of smugness.

"You remember Natalie?" Meghan accepted a cup of lemonade.

"I do. A pleasure, ma'am." He reached up to touch the brim of his hat before he remembered he'd left it downstairs at the hatcheck. Back home they'd call it the coat check, but the need for coats was so rare here, he didn't even own one anymore.

Natalie handed him a crystal punch cup. His fingers were way too big to fit them into the tiny handle, so he wrapped his fist around the whole cup instead. "Lots of folks here tonight." A sip. Tart coolness slid down his throat.

Music started up and couples swung out onto the floor. A few dowdy matrons sat on benches along the balcony rails, and a few older men clustered at the far end of the loggia, smoking cigars. He was the only man over twenty and under forty in sight. The old biddies glared at him, especially Mrs. Gregory.

Caleb tried to cut her some slack. After all, she was a widow woman who had just sent her only son off to war. She had to be scared and probably mad at circumstances and life. For all he knew, she was maybe even mad at God. Lotta good that would do. Caleb had been known to get mad at God himself from time to time. Didn't change anything, except to make himself miserable.

With a grimace he drained his cup and gave it back to Natalie.

Meghan sipped her punch, watching the dancers and only occasionally glancing up at him. What was wrong with him? He'd thought of not much else than being with her over the past month, and now, when he had the opportunity, he couldn't think of a thing to say.

She set her cup on the table. "It's so warm up here. Would you like to go down to the lobby? I know it isn't much cooler, but the sound of the fountain always refreshes me. I think I've earned a break."

The tightness in his chest relaxed as they made their way down the stairs and away from all the prying eyes. Concentrating on concealing his limp and thankful she wasn't in a hurry, he even grew bold enough to put his hand on the small of her back—the same place her apron bow usually rested—to guide her through the deserted foyer to the edge of the fountain. Moonlight tinted everything bluish-white and cast deeper shadows under the balconies and loggia. Over their heads, the music drifted down like rain.

Water splashed from the marble tower in the middle of the pool and rippled the surface of the water. He skirted potted palms and ferns scattered around the edges of the open space and guided her past a row of empty wicker rocking chairs. White pillars stood at attention around them like silent sentinels. The only electric light came from wall sconces along the perimeter of the atrium, creating an almost magical mix of lamplight and starlight.

"It's so peaceful here in the evenings. Though most nights I'm too tired to enjoy it. And Mrs. Gregory doesn't really like to see us lounging in the public areas. She says the guests don't pay good money to run into the hired help in the lobby."

"She runs a pretty tight ship, doesn't she?"

Meghan shrugged. "I suppose so, though from what I understand, that's what the company requires. Everything here has a proper procedure, and it's Mrs. Gregory's job to see that we follow it. She has high expectations, and at first I thought they were impossible, but you know what? Now that I've been here for a few weeks, I find myself able to meet those expectations and standards without too much effort. And I love the work, especially serving the soldiers. They're so brave and manly in their uniforms."

He pressed his lips together and let his hand fall away from her back. Every conversation always seemed to wind its way back to the war. His gut tightened, and he shoved his hands into his trouser pockets.

She knelt and scooped up a handful of water, letting the droplets trickle through her fingers. "And they're always so nice and full of fun. It's heartbreaking to think that some of them won't be coming home. That's why we must do all we can, like tonight's appeal for funds, to see that our soldiers have the best of everything. That's why I'm working on a project, a rather ambitious project, to raise one thousand dollars to purchase an ambulance to send to Europe to help our boys. I know it's a lot to take on, but after hearing the speech that Mr. Gibson from the Red Cross gave, and knowing how badly our soldiers need help, I couldn't do any less." She was so eager and innocent. How soon before she realized that life couldn't be conquered just because you wanted to conquer it? Someone needed to educate her before she got hurt.

"A thousand dollars? Where are you going to get that kind of money? I'd be surprised if tonight's dance netted you more than twenty-five after you take out the money for the refreshments and such." No one in their right mind would try to raise that kind of money, not here in Needles where most folks made less than a thousand dollars in a whole year.

"Oh, I expect to see it accomplished. The cause is too great for me to fail, and anyway, I gave my word." She linked her arm through his and did a happy little hop. "Mrs. Gregory is going to be so surprised. And Mr. Gibson. He came to the organizational meeting to get us all started on service projects, and he'll be back in a few months to see how we've done.

Everyone chose a project and how much they thought they could raise."

"And you put yourself down for a thousand dollars. What are you going to sell to raise that? The Statue of Liberty?" He jerked his thumb at a war poster someone had fastened to one of the columns. Lady Liberty stood with outstretched hands, imploring America to send her sons to protect her and her Allies. The words came out harsher than he had meant, and she let her hand fall away from his arm.

Those incredible eyes blinked, and her arched brows drew together in puzzlement. "No, nothing like that. I'm making a quilt. A Red Cross signature quilt, and I'll sell space for folks to have their name embroidered on it."

"That's crazy. Who would want to pay to have their name put on a blanket?" The notion baffled him.

Her spine stiffened, and her chin came up. "Patriotic Americans, that's who. People who realize what an honor it is to sacrifice a little of our comfort here so that those men fighting for our freedoms, who have sacrificed much more than we ever could, can have proper medical treatment, food, and clothing. I'm not trying to squeeze Needles to death. I have a plan to go door-to-door in the neighborhoods, visit all the local businesses, and I got permission to have a donation jar on the front desk. That way travelers who are so inclined can donate and print their name on one of the slips I'll leave there. Dozens of people come through here every day, people with enough money to travel. Surely some will contribute. Not all the money has to come from the citizens of Needles. I've thought it all out. I'm not stupid, you know." Her voice vibrated with fervor, and her green eyes glowed with the conviction of her cause. He couldn't help but notice her beauty as she stood before him all zealous and eager in the starlight.

"Someone ought to take your photograph like that. Or paint you for a recruitment poster. You'd sell a million war bonds and have soldiers enlisting in droves."

Relaxing, she gave him a soft tap on the arm. "Don't be silly. Not with this red hair and freckles. I'm no great American beauty, not like Natalie." A touch of something wistful crept into her voice. As if she knew without a doubt the truth of her words and longed to be different.

His voice went gruff on him. "Natalie's all right, but she's not to every man's taste. Some men like fiery redheads who believe in things so strongly they can almost stir a dedicated cynic to action."

She raised luminous eyes to him, and he found himself stepping closer, drawn to her fire and innocent, untouched air. Her sweet lips parted, and a slight breeze fluttered the lace on the neckline of her dress. His fingers found hers, entwining, slowly drawing her closer. Time seemed to stand still as he drowned in her eyes, in her goodness, drawn to her fire and courage. He had a feeling this girl held the power to heal some of the broken places in his heart, the starved, atrophied, dead places he'd locked away.

Her breath came in shallow gasps, as if she, too, were caught in a maelstrom of unfamiliar feelings. It was all so sudden, and she was so sweet and passionate and fresh. He wanted to crush her to him, to stave off the loneliness that stalked him.

It had been so long since he'd allowed himself to feel anything but anger and shame. Even longer since he'd let himself care how someone else thought of him. Warning bells clanged in his head as his mouth went dry. She wore a beguiling perfume that wrapped around him, muffling the doubts. The last time he'd let his defenses down, had allowed someone into his heart, she'd used that power to crush him. And here he was on the verge of making the same mistake again.

He drew her nearer. His lips hovered over hers, a mere breath away. She wasn't resisting, but then again, she was so innocent, she probably didn't know of the raging hunger sweeping over him, the need to kiss her and see if she tasted as sweet as she looked. The warning bells got louder. He had to stop before he got hurt, or before he was so deeply ensnared he couldn't escape.

"What on earth are you doing?" Mrs. Gregory's scalded-cat screech jerked them apart. "Miss Thorson." Like an avenging angel, the head waitress strode across the courtyard, hands fisted at her sides.

Meghan backed away from him a couple of steps. "Mrs. Gregory, I—we—"

"Your behavior is scandalous. Bad enough for you to be caught dallying with a man right in the hotel, but this man!" She raised her bony forefinger to pierce the air before Caleb's nose. "I won't stand for it. If you want to keep your job, Miss Thorson, you'll get yourself upstairs to that dance this instant." Cold, terrible wrath poured from her eyes.

"We weren't doing anything wrong. Is it wrong to get a little air? We're here in plain sight. We were talking about raising money for the Red Cross. Mr. McBride is very interested in helping out the war effort in any way he can, I'm sure. Why else would he come to the dance?"

Her defensive tone hurt Caleb. Why should she have to explain herself to a woman who deserved no explanation? He winced when she invoked the name of the Red Cross, which she seemed to hold sacred.

Mrs. Gregory snorted. "Why indeed? He's shown not the slightest interest in the war or our efforts until now. In fact, until you arrived in Needles, he never came to the hotel, not even to eat. He's like a stray dog slinking around. A yellow-bellied cur at that. And if you know what's good for you, you'll stop encouraging him. It's disgraceful, and I won't have it. Get yourself upstairs now. And when this dance is finished, you and I are going to have a frank discussion about your behavior and your choice of companions."

Caleb stepped between her and Meghan. "Mrs. Gregory, nothing happened. If you want to be angry, be angry with me, not Meghan."

"Don't tell me what to do. I am constantly reminding Meghan not to be too familiar with the young male customers. I should've known it from the first day she arrived. This is the second time I've found the two of you in a rather compromising situation. The first could've been explained away as an accident, but there is nothing accidental about this." She flicked her hand at them. "You, Miss Thorson, are supposed to be upstairs earning money for the Red Cross. Not only are you in violation of the conduct rules for a Harvey Girl, you are stealing from the war effort by your absence at the dance."

Meghan's reddened face paled, and her eyes widened.

"I paid for a dance, Mrs. Gregory," Caleb cut in.

"That may be, however, three dances have come and gone since you two scuttled off."

Taking a deep breath to keep from saying something he would regret, something that might make the situation worse for Meghan, Caleb stepped back. "Mrs. Gregory, I apologize for your distress, though there is no need to take your ire at me out on Meghan. She isn't at fault here." He dug in his pocket and withdrew a dollar. "Here you go, Meghan. Put that in the kitty. It will more than cover the time you spent with me."

He had to press the folded bill into her palm. "Go on upstairs. And thank you for telling me about your project. I'm sure it will be a success."

A *harrumph* from Mrs. Gregory. "We don't need money from the likes of you, Mr. McBride. The Red Cross in Needles will not take a coward's cash. You won't assuage your conscience in this manner, or for so paltry a sum. I may not be able to ban you from this hotel, but I can make sure you stay away from my girls. I won't have their reputations sullied, not by your amorous advances nor by being associated with a yellow coward like you."

Meghan stood frozen, her expression shifting from guilt to confusion. Soon the confusion would give way to disgust, the same disgust dripping from Mrs. Gregory's every word once Meghan had a talk with the head waitress. A sense of fatalism gripped him. Why even bother to fight back, to declare he wasn't evading military service? She'd only ask why he didn't enlist, and he'd rather be boiled in oil than ever let Mrs. Gregory know of his leg. He'd been a first-class fool to come here, to think that anything had or would change. In the eyes of this town, he was and always would be a coward.

Meghan climbed the stairs to the party and dropped the well-creased dollar into the collection box. Natalie drew her behind the refreshment table, her pale blue eyes full of questions.

"Where did you get off to? Mrs. Gregory is searching for you, and she looks fierce."

"I know. She found me." Meghan couldn't keep the tremor out of her voice. She'd just come within a small cat's whisker of kissing Caleb McBride.

"What happened? Where were you?"

"Downstairs in the courtyard by the fountain."

Natalie searched Meghan's face and jumped to the correct conclusion. "And you weren't alone, were you? You went down there with Mr. McBride. Meghan, what were you thinking?"

"I wasn't thinking. But nothing happened. We just walked a little and talked. It's not illegal to talk to someone, is it?"

Mrs. Gregory emerged at the top of the stairs. Her piercing eyes found Meghan, but she was prevented from marching over as someone stopped her to talk. The current waltz ended, and the band began to pack their instruments. A smattering of applause rippled from the guests, and several of the musicians bowed and nodded. The dancers seemed loath to leave, however, and they lingered in little groups, visited the punch table one last time, and strolled under the colorful lights.

Filling yet another punch cup, Natalie handed it across the table. She kept her voice low. "It isn't illegal to talk to someone, but it is risky, especially the likes of Mr. McBride. After you left, Mr. Weeks and his wife mentioned to me that Mr. McBride isn't well thought of here in town. Some folks say he's a coward who won't enlist. They say he's making a mint off the war by selling horses to the army. What kind of a man would try to make a profit off a war he's too afraid to fight in? Everyone's shocked to see him here at all. He usually stays away from town, and he never accepts hospitality, not that it sounds like anyone's offering him any these days. Folks say he's a recluse."

The need to defend him coursed through Meghan. "He's not like that. Surely he has an exemption to the draft, since he's in agriculture? He works for the army."

Natalie shook her head. "Mr. Weeks says since he doesn't grow crops or raise animals for food, he shouldn't be exempt. And lots of men enlist anyway, even if they could claim an exemption."

"Girls."

Meghan jumped as Mrs. Gregory's hand came down on her shoulder. "I can see, Miss Daviot, that you are filling Miss

Thorson in on a few facts. You would do well to heed her warnings, Miss Thorson. Mr. McBride is not a suitable companion for any young lady, much less a Harvey Girl. You mustn't allow your head to be turned. Caleb McBride is a coward and an opportunist. He allows others to fight for his freedom while at the same time pocketing a profit at their expense. Surely you don't want to be linked with such a man?"

Meghan's cheeks grew hot as she realized that several partygoers had stopped talking to listen in. Heads nodded and tilted toward one another, and a couple of hands went up to shield whispers.

"Of course you wouldn't," Mrs. Gregory answered for her. "You may not appreciate it just now, but I truly do have your best interests at heart."

Chapter 7

Meghan called at the front desk for her mail and Natalie's. "Here you are, Miss." The desk clerk's gray moustache twitched. "Something to enjoy on your afternoon off?"

She scanned the envelopes. One from Mama, and a small, square envelope addressed to her in a hand she didn't know. For Natalie, a nice thick one from Indiana.

"Thank you, Mr. Johns." Flashing him a quick smile, she headed out the main doors to the park in front of the hotel where Natalie was already spreading a blanket under one of the trees. A picnic basket rested beside the trunk, and Meghan anticipated a quiet afternoon of reading and not thinking about work. The thin shade cast by the trees in Santa Fe Park did little to lower the heat, but at least today there was a breeze. Short of going downstairs to sit in the walk-in refrigerator—something Mrs. Gregory forbid the girls to do, more's the pity—the park was the coolest place they could find to spend their afternoon off.

Natalie eased down onto the blanket and looked up when Meghan arrived. "Anything?"

"Here you go." She tossed the letter. "It's a fat one, too."

Settling herself, Meghan slit open the letter from Mama, eager for news from home. She could almost hear Mama's Irish lilt as a blanket of homesickness settled around her shoulders.

Your papa is forever polishing that motorcar. He
takes any excuse to get it out onto the road. The Ladies'
Aid purchased a knitting machine to assist in making

stockings and hats for our soldiers. It works fairly well,
I suppose, but I prefer my old knitting needles.

Word of the Ladies' Aid reminded Meghan that she needed to get busy on her quilt. Over the last three weeks, she'd managed the cutting and begun the piecing, but she still needed folks to donate to get their names on the quilt. A lot of folks.

She finished Mama's letter and unfolded the brief note she'd included from Lars. She glanced at the date. Written almost six weeks ago.

Hey, Megsie, The familiar term made her throat tighten. Nobody but Lars called her Megsie.

> *Ma tells me you've moved out west and taken a job in a hotel. You're a Harvey Girl? Don't they have a lot of rules? How are you holding up? Remember when you took it upon yourself to campaign for class president, even though the teacher said you couldn't since you were a girl? Bless me if you didn't convince her to change the rules and then went out and won that election. You never were one for following the crowd. I figured you'd have taken over the Ladies' Aid or the Red Cross by now. I can't imagine you handing out menus and filling coffee cups. You're too much of a crusader. I'm surprised General Pershing hasn't knocked on your door and asked you to run the Expeditionary Forces for him. I've been telling my buddies here that if they'd just put you in charge of the War Department, we'd all be home by Mother's Day.*

She chuckled. Her brother had teased her ever since that day in the seventh grade when she'd challenged convention and gotten a whole class to change their minds about who could run for class president. Her folks had both said she would get herself in trouble with her crusading someday, but Lars was always proud of her for dreaming big and taking up causes others tried to ignore. What would he say about her signature quilt?

He closed with the plea to keep sending letters.

> *They're what keep me going these days, Megsie. Don't let on to the folks, because they don't need the worry, but conditions here are horrible. We're stuck in these trenches day after day, up to our knees in mud most of the time, and always and forever dreading the order to go "over the top" and into the path of enemy fire. I keep my gas mask with me all the time, and my rifle, but we all know that when it's your time, you won't have time to grab either one. Twice now I've been nearly buried alive when a mortar shell hit our trench. I've lost so many friends. Some days it's all I can do to hang on. Pray for me, Megsie. And write often.*
>
> *Love, Lars*

She glanced up, blinking hard. Her poor brother. Mortar shells and mustard gas and mud. How she wished she could do more to help him and all the boys over there. Pouring coffee and sewing quilts seemed so feeble in the light of what they faced every day.

Natalie was lost in her own letter, so Meghan picked up her other piece of mail. Turning the card over, she frowned. No return address and no stamp. Hand delivered? Slowly, she stuck her fingernail under the flap and ran it along the edge.

A single sheet of plain white paper. Her gaze dropped to the signature, and her heart started bumping. She swallowed and raced through the lines.

Miss Thorson,

 I apologize for any difficulty I might've caused you last Friday evening. Now that you know the regard in which I am held in this town, I am sure you want no further dealings with me. I wish you all the best with your project. You even inspired me, and I'm beyond inspiration these days.

     Sincerely,
     Caleb McBride

She read the lines again, remembering his face in the moonlight, the stoic mask that fell over his features when Mrs. Gregory found them. And all the questions flooded back. Why hadn't he enlisted? Was he really just out to make a profit off this war? Comparing Lars's letter with all she'd heard said about Caleb set up quaking doubts. Perhaps Mrs. Gregory was right. And the head waitress wasn't the only one who held such beliefs. The temperature of the party had gone down several notches when Caleb arrived at the dance.

And yet, Meghan couldn't deny the pull of attraction she felt toward Caleb. Something about him drew her, and it wasn't just his handsome features. There was something inside him, something wounded and sheltered and guarded that she longed to uncover, bring to the light, and heal.

She shook her head for being so fanciful. Lars would tease her about her penchant for helping lame dogs cross the road and taking up lost causes.

Natalie folded her letter and used her cuff to swipe at her eyes.

"Is everything all right at home?"

"Yes, thank the Lord. My mother-in-law is doing better. She's starting to talk again, though slowly, and she's learning to do more with her left hand. The doctor is sending his nurse every day still to bathe her and change the linens, but the money I send home is covering that expense with a little left over for them to buy food. The church is also helping out, bringing meals and supplies."

"Any word from Derek?"

She nodded, and whether it was from the heat or something Derek had put into his letter, her cheeks pinked. "He's fine. Misses us all. He says he can't wait to come home and take a walk with me down by the creek. When we were first courting, we'd stand on the bridge and drop leaves into the water and make a wish, then hurry to the other side of the bridge to see which one came out first. A silly game, but so fun." Her eyes took on a dreamy, faraway look. "If we were together now on that bridge, neither of us would have to make a wish, because our most important wish would've already come true."

Meghan tamped down the surprising envy that oozed out of some hidden place inside. What would it be like to have someone's fondest wish be just to be with you? Unbidden, Caleb's face rose to her mind. *Stop being silly. He would never feel that way about you, and you shouldn't feel that way about him.*

Footsteps on the gravel path caught her attention. Jenny Ralston, skirts gripped in one hand and the other gripping her lace headband, ran toward them.

"Did you hear?" She flopped down onto the grass beside Meghan and Natalie, panting.

"Did we hear what, and you'd better not let Mrs. Gregory catch you sprawling on the grass in your uniform." Meghan nudged her shoulder. "You should've heard the bawling out she gave Sarah Jane yesterday for having a coffee stain that was no bigger than a pin head on her apron. Imagine what she'd be like if she found a grass stain."

"She won't have time to notice, not with the news she just got."

"It must be something to have you running in this heat." Natalie tucked her letter back into its envelope and leaned back against a tree trunk, letting her eyes fall shut. A trickle of worry coasted down Meghan's spine. Natalie looked paler and more drawn every day. She was still tired at night, and she didn't eat enough.

"Natalie, what say we go back inside and sneak down to the cold store and cool off? It's hot enough, I'm thinking of going wading in the fountain."

"I'm not getting caught doing either. I need this job too much." Natalie spoke without opening her eyes, her voice just above a murmur.

Though she'd only been playing, a prickle of guilt feathered across Meghan's conscience. "I know, Nat, and I won't do anything to jeopardize either of our jobs."

Jenny grabbed Meghan's arm. "Are you even listening to me? This is the biggest news to hit Needles since the railroad came to town. Mrs. Gregory just got word that a *celebrity train* will be coming through on a Red Cross appeal trip. And guess who will be on it?"

"Woodrow Wilson." Meghan couldn't resist teasing Jenny, though the words "celebrity train" sent her mind spinning and her heart racing.

"Better." Jenny's eyes grew round.

"Better than the president?"

"That's right. The celebrity train will carry none other than Charlie Chaplin and Mary Pickford!" Jenny stacked her hands under her cheek, tilted her head, and batted her eyes. "Can you imagine? Charlie Chaplin and Mary Pickford, right here in little old Needles. And they're dining at the hotel. Mrs. Gregory is about fit to be tied. She's been such a grump since her son enlisted—not that she was exactly cozy before he left, but at least she was bearable—but when she got this news, she actually smiled. A real smile all the way up to her eyes and everything. I hardly recognized the old girl."

Movie stars coming to the hotel. Meghan bit her lower lip. Her mother loved the cinema, and together, she and Meghan had cajoled Papa into taking them over to Rochester whenever a new Mary Pickford film came to the theater. And Charlie Chaplin? Maybe President Wilson and the Kaiser were more famous than Charlie Chaplin, but only maybe.

"When?"

"One week." Jenny stood and smoothed her apron, checking for spots. "That's why I came out here. Mrs. Gregory sent me to fetch you. No more time off until after the movie star train has come and gone. She says we're really going to concentrate on the polishing."

Meghan groaned. "We already do concentrate on the polishing. If I rub those coffee urns any harder, they're going to wear right through."

Jenny held out her hand and pulled Meghan to her feet. "C'mon. She'll be out here in search of us in a minute."

Meghan and Natalie hurried to their room to change, Meghan with alacrity, Natalie lethargic.

"If I wasn't so excited, I'd gripe about missing our afternoon off." Meghan threw her letters onto the dresser and reached for her uniform, but thought better of leaving Caleb's note out in plain sight and tucked it into her top bureau drawer. She lifted her dress off the hanger and shook it out, studying it for flaws. "I hadn't counted on having to wear this again today."

Natalie moved slowly, putting away her letters. "I'd counted on a nap this afternoon. I'm so tired. This heat just saps the life out of me."

"Sounds like no one will get any afternoon naps this week."

The lunchroom, blessedly free of customers at the moment, was in a complete uproar. Harvey Girls bustled and chattered and laughed, and Meghan paused in the doorway. She hadn't realized it, but she really loved her job here at the hotel. They were a team, a well-trained and organized team, serving shoulder-to-shoulder to serve customers and represent the company.

"Girls." Mrs. Gregory clapped her hands, her signal for all work to cease and everyone to pay attention. Meghan had begun to hear those claps in her dreams. Skirts rustled and cutlery clanked as they hurried to gather around the head waitress.

"Girls, I'm sure you've all heard the news. Now, before you get all scatterbrained and giddy, let me assure you, I will not tolerate laxity, shirking, or silliness. You are professionals, and you will behave accordingly. Tonight, after the last train pulls out, we will start with the crown molding in both the dining room and the lunchroom and work our way down, cleaning every inch of every surface."

Meghan joined in the groan that rippled through the group. As if they didn't clean and polish nearly every waking minute already.

"I know." Mrs. Gregory made damping motions with her hands. "However, there will be a reward at the end. I will be watching each of you this coming week. The Harvey Girl who works the hardest, does the best job serving customers, keeping her station clean, and acts as the best possible representative of the company, will be given the honor of serving our distinguished guests when they arrive. Every girl, even the lunchroom staff, will be considered when I make my decision."

Meghan's mind fizzed and popped. A glimmer of hope that perhaps, if she worked hard enough, she could actually meet Mary Pickford and Charlie Chaplin, rose in her chest. And perhaps in the doing, she'd get off Mrs. Gregory's naughty list. They hadn't gotten off to a great start together, and since being found strolling in the moonlight with Caleb McBride, Meghan had the feeling Mrs. Gregory had been looking for any reason to fire Meghan and send her packing.

This was her chance. And she wasn't going to waste it. Her confidence in her abilities as a waitress had grown since that first day, and though Mrs. Gregory still found reasons to criticize, Meghan knew she was good at her job. Perhaps good enough to be moved to the dining room. Perhaps good enough to serve Mr. Chaplin and Miss Pickford.

Tiredness fell away, and she dove into the work. She had seven days until the train arrived. Seven days to prepare and prove herself.

The housekeeping staff, the kitchen crew, the busboys, and the groundskeepers joined in the task. Mr. Stock and Mrs. Gregory conferred often, compared notes, and critiqued. Meghan plastered a smile on her face, spoke only pleasant words, and worked until she could barely move.

One of her assigned chores was to remove the glass globes from the light fixtures and hand them down to Natalie who took each one while also holding onto the ladder for Meghan.

"Don't you dare drop one of these. That would be the end. Can you imagine the tizzy Mrs. Gregory would be in if one of the light bulbs was left bare?" She passed a frosted shade down while studying the whorls and twists of brass that made up the fixture itself. "There, that's the last. Now I just need the polish and a rag, and I'll have these lights shining like the King's scepter in no time."

The ladder wobbled, and Meghan clutched the top. "Whoa. Natalie?"

Natalie had abandoned her post of ladder-steadier and leaned against the lunch counter, pressing her hand to her forehead. Hurrying down as fast as prudence dictated, Meghan joined her friend.

"What is it? Are you ill?"

Keeping her eyes closed, Natalie took deep breaths. Her pulse jumped in her throat, and a faint sheen of perspiration clustered at her hairline. At last she opened her eyes and swallowed. "Sorry."

"What happened? Do you need to sit down?" Meghan tried to guide her to a lunch counter stool.

"I'm fine." Natalie resisted gently. "It was just a dizzy spell. The heat and working so hard got to me, and I imagine craning my neck gave me a spot of vertigo."

Her face was still the color of fresh milk, and her hand trembled as she smoothed her hair.

"Are you sure? Maybe you should take a break."

"No. I'm better now." She lifted the box of globes. "I'll just get these to soaking in hot water, and I'll be back."

"Let me take them." Meghan reached for the box, but Natalie swung it away.

"Nonsense. I'm fine. You have polishing to do." She disappeared into the dish room, setting the doors flopping in her wake.

Frowning, Meghan picked up the bottle of brass polish and the cleaning rag and ascended the ladder. The high ceilings of the hotel, helpful in keeping things cool, meant she had quite a climb, especially with no one holding the ladder. And in order to reach the highest points of the light fixture, she would have to stand on the next to last rung.

With a few wobbles, she finally got settled. The pungent smell of the polish wrinkled her nose, but she ignored it and began on the many nooks and crannies. Her arms, raised above her head as they were, began to ache, and a knot formed between her shoulder blades, but she refused to slow down. This very morning, Mrs. Gregory had praised the way she'd dusted and polished the ceiling fans. Meghan had every intention of garnering praise once more for her work on the lights. Sweat beaded on her forehead and trickled from her temples.

Shifting her balance carefully, she tilted the bottle of polish again onto a clean spot on the rag. Below her, Jenny and Sarah Jane attacked the swivel chairs bolted to the floor. Their scrub brushes swished, and not a particle of dust or dirt remained in their wake, not even around the bolt heads. The boots and shoes of hundreds of customers had kicked the stool supports and rested on the rails, but Mrs. Gregory insisted that the seating areas must be as perfect as when they were first installed.

Meghan hummed the popular tune "There's A Long, Long Trail A Winding." As she scrubbed, the humming became singing.

> Nights are growing very lonely,
> Days are very long;
> I'm a-growing weary only
> List'ning for your song.
> Old remembrances are thronging
> Thru my memory.
> Till it seems the world is full of dreams
> Just to call you back to me.

By the time she reached the chorus, she realized she wasn't singing alone any longer. Jenny and Sarah Jane had joined in, as well as Natalie, now holding the ladder once more.

A BRIDE SEWS WITH LOVE IN
NEEDLES, CALIFORNIA

There's a long, long trail a-winding
Into the land of my dreams,
Where the nightingales are singing
And a white moon beams:
There's a long, long night of waiting
Until my dreams all come true;
Till the day when I'll be going down
That long, long trail with you.

Natalie brushed a tear from her cheek and her lips trembled in a smile. Meghan's heart swelled to think of how happy Natalie would be when Derek came home from the war, safe and sound.

All night long I hear you calling,
Calling sweet and low;
Seem to hear your footsteps falling,
Ev'rywhere I go.
Tho' the road between us stretches
Many a weary mile.
I forget that you're not with me yet,
When I think I see you smile.

They finished with the chorus once more, and when they'd done so, applause from the kitchen and lobby doorways had them laughing. The hotel and kitchen staff grinned and waved, lots of white hats and aprons in evidence. One laundress clapped around a huge armload of bed sheets, her cheeks red and her hair straggling out of her mobcap. A couple of the busboys whistled and stomped before Mr. Stock, smothering a smile, sent them on their way back to work.

Meghan finished wiping the last brass curlicue and crevice

and made her way down the ladder. The singing had somehow brought them all together, made them forget how tired they were, and lightened the burdens, if only for a moment. Natalie squeezed Meghan's arm.

"Thank you."

"For what?" Meghan capped the polish and wrapped the rag around the bottle.

"For just being you. I think we all benefitted from the singing. It was fun."

"Miss Thorson."

The prunes-and-persimmons tones of Mrs. Gregory's voice pierced the camaraderie.

"Yes, ma'am?"

"You have the brass polish. The counter rails are not going to polish themselves. I expect them to be finished today."

All the fun went out of the room, and once more heads bent and scrub brushes scratched.

"Yes, ma'am." Though she wanted to stalk over to the head waitress and poke her cheek to see if she was even human, or at the least roll her eyes and sigh, Meghan refrained. If she wanted to be chosen, she couldn't afford to give in to impulses. The restraint nearly killed her.

Think of Mary Pickford. Think of Charlie Chaplin. Think of anything except grabbing Jenny's scrub bucket and anointing Mrs. Gregory with its contents.

Gathering her skirts and apron so she wouldn't be kneeling on them, she began at the far corner. Three horseshoe-shaped lunch counters, each one possessing a continuous brass footrail for customers to rest their shoes on. Over a hundred feet of brass rail and brackets to polish. She raised her head like a gopher above the countertop to check the clock over the kitchen door. Only an hour until the next train arrived. She'd have to break off the polishing and make sure the light fixtures were reassembled. No way would she get the rails done today, not with two more trains expected and all her regular work to do as well.

Mrs. Gregory's foot tapped on the tiles. "Miss Thorson, is there a problem?"

Meghan returned to rubbing, jettisoning the idea of being finished before lights-out tonight. "No, ma'am. I'll get it done."

"See that you do."

By the eve of the celebrity train arrival, Meghan's muscles ached and her patience had worn paper thin. Mrs. Gregory drove everyone hard, but it seemed to her—and Natalie when consulted—that she was especially hard on Meghan.

Barely holding on to her determination not to complain, Meghan worked longer hours, did more tasks, and served more customers than any other Harvey Girl in the hotel. She rose extra early each morning to press her uniform and all her aprons in case she needed to make a hasty change during the day. She even pressed Natalie's, giving her roommate a little more time to sleep. Though it didn't seem to do much good. Natalie looked paler and tighter-drawn every day.

When the last train pulled out that night and the finishing touches had been put on every work station, Mrs. Gregory called all the girls together.

Meghan met Jenny's eyes and smiled, blowing a wisp of hair off her forehead. They'd done it. Not a thing remained on the list on the head waitress's ubiquitous clipboard. Both the lunchroom and dining room smelled of soap and polish, and every surface, from the woodwork to the marble to the brass and silver shone as if it had just come out of the box. Jenny shrugged and bit her lower lip. They'd all worked hard. Now it was up to Mrs. Gregory to choose who would have the honor of serving their special guests.

"You've all done amazing work this week. You are to be commended. I know some of what I asked you to do seemed unreasonable and overly picky, but you've all responded well. I couldn't be happier with the results."

Meghan gripped her hands together until they ached. Surely, after all her work, she would be chosen. No one had stayed later than she, arrived earlier, done more.

"Now to the awarding of the positions." Mrs. Gregory consulted the clipboard she had clasped before her. "Serving the drinks is Miss Ralston."

A quiver went through Meghan. Jenny beamed, her smile lighting up her face. Barbara threw her arm around her much shorter roommate and squeezed her shoulders, a broad grin making her glasses slide on her nose.

"And the waitress for the main table will be. . ."

Meghan held her breath.

"Miss Daviot."

Disappointment crashed through Meghan's chest, and her heart took an elevator to her heels. Natalie? Girls congratulated Natalie while Meghan stood rooted to the spot. Shaking herself, she smiled and hugged her roommate and friend. She was happy for her. She was! But it would be silly to deny being sad for herself.

Mrs. Gregory read the list of girls who would also be working in the dining room. "You six, plus Miss Ralston and Miss Daviot, are the best of the best. There will be nearly one hundred guests on the Red Cross train, and sixty-five of those will be eating in the formal dining room. The overflow will be dining in the lunchroom. You should all get your rest tonight.

I expect everything to go smoothly tomorrow and for each girl to do her job as she has been trained." She sent a pointed look at several of the girls who hadn't been chosen, and that piercing gaze rested longest on Meghan.

Meghan's chin came up. So, she hadn't been chosen. Fine. She'd show Mrs. Gregory she'd made a mistake. Meghan's customers would be the best served, most contented, most taken care of customers the El Garces Lunchroom had ever seen. Natalie and Jenny might be serving cinema royalty, but Meghan's customers would be treated better than royalty. She smiled politely to Mrs. Gregory, as if the decision to leave her off the dining room serving roster met with Meghan's complete approval.

Once back in their room, Natalie tried to apologize. "I wish it was you, Meghan. You deserved it. You worked the hardest, and everyone knows it."

Meghan hung up her dress and slipped into her housecoat. She shrugged and began unpinning her hair. "We all worked hard, and Mrs. Gregory had the final choosing. It's all right."

"But it isn't fair."

"If there's one thing this war and Mrs. Gregory are teaching me, it's that life isn't fair."

"You're taking this better than I thought you would."

"Am I? I'm disappointed, but it isn't the end of the world. I keep reminding myself that others have it far worse than I do." Meghan smiled at her reflection in the dresser mirror. Mocking green eyes stared back at her, rueful, a bit embarrassed. Though she tried to brush it off as no big deal, she knew better, and inside, her heart was bruised. She'd made no bones about how much she wanted to be chosen to serve the movie stars. And she hadn't made it. Hadn't made Mrs. Gregory's cut. Now everyone knew that in spite of her best efforts, she hadn't been good enough. And Mrs. Gregory's choice had little to do with Meghan's work over the past week. From the first, the head waitress had been biased against her, and all because of Caleb McBride. Caleb, who had taken Mrs. Gregory at her word and steered clear of the hotel since the night of the dance. Three weeks, and Meghan hadn't seen so much as a glimpse of him.

And yet he'd occupied her thoughts. How often she'd thought of him while scrubbing and polishing this week. His memory had the power to make her forget the celebrity train. The look on his face when Mrs. Gregory had accused him of being a draft-dodging coward seared her mind, and she knew she should forget about him, but when she was falling asleep, in that blessed twilight between wakefulness and slumber, another memory dominated her thoughts. Caleb McBride, his face so close to hers she imagined she could see her reflection in his eyes, his lips hovering over hers a breath away.

She set her hairbrush down and turned away from the now dreamy-eyed girl in the mirror. *Get a hold of yourself, you ninny. He's brought you nothing but trouble, and he's shirking his military duty. Quit mooning about him and pull yourself together.* "I'm happy for you, Natalie. I really am. You're going to do a wonderful job, and just imagine what you'll have to tell Derek when he comes home."

Natalie sank into the rocker and put her face in her hands, her shoulders shaking. "I only hope he can forgive me for lying to him."

Chapter 8

Caleb climbed out of his truck in front of the Feed and Seed and used his sleeve to wipe the dust off the hood ornament. With the roads so sandy and gritty out here, keeping the automobile clean was impossible, but he couldn't resist buffing the silver radiator cap shaped like a running horse. He'd poured over a catalog for a week trying to make up his mind whether to get the ornament or not, finally deciding to purchase it after squaring it with his conscience to give the equivalent amount in the offering plate the next week.

Joshua joined him, hands jammed in his pockets. "You want to load the feed first?"

"Sure are a lot of people in town." Wagons and motorcars lined the street, and peering through the window of the feed store, he spied quite a crowd at the counter. Not wanting to face all those disapproving eyes, he turned and studied the substantial bulk of the El Garces three blocks up the street. Hard to miss, since it was by far the largest building in Needles. That and the fact that his thoughts had strayed there again and again all week, in spite of the finality he'd tried to include in his note to Meghan. "We'll head over to Doc's first and then come back to the feed store." He started across the street.

"Wonder what everyone's doing in town on a Friday. Most folks wait till Saturday." Joshua sidestepped a group of teenage boys who laughed and shoved each other. He didn't move fast enough, and one of them knocked into him.

"Dirty Indian. Go back to the reservation."

Joshua tensed, his hands fisting. His face turned to stone except for his eyes which glowed hot. The town boys formed a half-circle with Joshua at the center.

Caleb stepped up onto the sidewalk once more. "Maybe you boys should move along."

"Maybe you should mind your own business, coward. You're too scared to fight the Huns, you'd best not mess with the likes of us." A cocky youngster threw out his chest, raised his fists, and danced, throwing a few playful jabs that just missed Caleb's chin. His compatriots laughed, egging him on.

"Go ahead. Smack his mug, Pierce. Show him what this town thinks of cowards."

"We should tar and feather him. Him and his dirty Indian friend."

"Enough." Caleb kept his voice even, but he sidled closer to Joshua so he could keep all of the young thugs in view. "You've had your fun, now move along. We don't want any trouble."

"Trouble? We haven't even started yet." The leader, Pierce, reared back to spit, his mouth twisting and his lips puckering. At the same time, he tried one more jab, this time aiming for Joshua.

Like a snake striking, Caleb grabbed the boy's fist and twisted his arm up and behind his back. "I said that's enough. Now, you and your friends back off and leave us be. I'm sure you have better things to do with your time, and I have better things to do than teach you all a lesson in manners."

The boys, eyes wide, backed up a step. Giving Pierce a push, Caleb sent him toward his friends. "Now get."

The boys slunk away, but regrouped half a block up the street and turned back to jeer. The smallest boy made a rude gesture before they took flight, running toward the hotel.

"Jerks. Punk wood for brains." Joshua stared after them, his muscles taut.

"Forget about it. Let's go over to Doc's."

Caleb started up the street, aware that several folks had witnessed the confrontation and were eying him unfavorably. You'd think he would be used to it by now, but it still stung. And with each new war report from the front, animosity and fear grew. Every time the list of casualties for the county was printed, his neighbors' eyes got harder, their lips thinner, their tolerance shorter. What had started out as dislike had begun to feel a lot like outright hatred.

They reached Doc's and Joshua stopped at the bottom of the porch steps. "Why do we have to come here? I'm not sick, and you aren't sick. Are you?"

"No, I'm not sick. I just have to see the doc for a minute."

"I'll wait out here. Don't know why I had to come to town today anyway."

"Stop your griping. You've met Doc before. He doesn't care if you're Indian, Chinese, or ancient Babylonian. It's too hot to hang around out here."

Caleb knew pricking Joshua's pride was the quickest way to get him to do what Caleb wanted. Often it was the only way.

Doc greeted him with a smile, looking over his half-moon glasses and setting aside the magazine he'd been reading. "I hoped you'd come to town today. Saved me a trip out to your place. Your order arrived yesterday."

His glance went past Caleb. "You brought reinforcements today, eh?"

Joshua stood by the door shifting his weight, his hand on the knob.

"Doc, you remember Joshua Hualga. He's working for me this summer."

"Ah, of course. I hardly recognize you. You've grown some since I last saw you." He came forward and held out his hand.

"Come in, come in."

Joshua released the doorknob and eased his hand forward. "Sir."

"Caleb, why don't you head into the examination room, and Joshua, let me get you some cake. One of the neighbor ladies dropped it off, and there's no way I can eat it all by myself. And we'll get you some milk. You look as if you could use some to put some meat on those bones."

Caleb smiled at the wary look on Joshua's face and jerked his head to tell the boy to go with Doc. No sense fighting it. Doc was kind of like a flash flood. Barreling downstream and not much you could do to stop it.

Wiping his hands on a towel, Doc joined Caleb in the exam room. He opened a corner cupboard and withdrew a box. "Here, try these on."

Caleb sat on the ladder-back chair next to the doc's desk and tugged off his tattered boot. "Sure hope they fit. This pair has had it."

"That boy, Joshua, he's kind of prickly. Doesn't look much like his father, does he? Cairook's a big, broad man. Joshua could pass for a streetlamp."

Grunting, Caleb nodded. "He's skinny, but he's a hard worker. Surprised his back isn't bowed with the size of the chip he's carrying on his shoulder."

"Oh, really? Remind you of anyone?" Doc cocked a gray eyebrow, and his moustache twitched.

"Yeah, yeah." Caleb shrugged and rolled his eyes, unable to stop a smile at Doc's ribbing. He opened the box and withdrew the butter-soft leather boots. Rusty-brown, calf-high, they had the look of cavalry-issue footgear.

"Put on the right one first. Then we'll deal with the left. The manufacturer sent me some insoles so we can customize them further." Doc reached into the box and pulled out some leather of varying thicknesses while Caleb slid his right foot into the new boot and stamped it on. Perfect.

"Feels good. Hope we don't need to do too much to the other one. Joshua can eat you out of house and home faster than a swarm of locust."

"He can have all the cake he wants. I'm not much of a fan of fruitcake, and Mrs. Bennington brought a whopper. Payment for a bottle of cough syrup."

"Guess you do a lot of barter these days, eh?" Searching the inside of the left boot, Caleb felt the rigid staves along the sides of the upper as well as the thick back wall. His stomach muscles tightened, and his palms slicked with sweat. *Please let these work, Lord.*

His arrow prayer surprised him a bit. Lately, he'd been working up quite a bout of frustration against God, and prayer wasn't on the top of his to-do list. Oh, he went through the motions, attending church, praying before meals and before bedtime, but he knew his heart wasn't in it. He and God had a few things to work out between them, but not until he was ready.

Working his mangled leg into the boot hurt, but he refused to stop until he'd pushed his toes all the way to the bottom. Snug, firm, and molded to every buckle and bend of his foot. He stood, keeping his weight on his right foot, gradually shifting so his left took more.

"How's it feel?"

He took a few steps. The upper gripped the back of his calf, supporting it and giving him some added stability. "Nice." Better than his last pair had been, even brand-new.

"Does it pinch anywhere?" Doc went through several checks, and when he was satisfied, he sat back, smiling. "It's not as good as a brace would be, but better than nothing."

"Thanks, Doc. These will be just fine. How much do I owe you?"

"The bill's in my office. Why don't you join Joshua in the kitchen and have some cake while I fetch it?"

Caleb found Joshua at the table reading. The boy looked up with a start, his hand around his milk glass and the other holding open the pages of a book.

"Any cake left?"

Doc entered, holding an envelope. Joshua quickly closed the book and pushed it away a few inches, leaning back with a bored expression. But Caleb knew better. Joshua, in the six weeks or so that he'd been living with Caleb, had blown through every book Caleb had in the house and had read several of them over again.

Doc hadn't missed it either. "Are you interested in medicine?" He picked up the book and turned it to look at the spine.

Joshua shrugged. "Interested in a lot of things. Not that it will do me much good."

"And why not?"

The boy rubbed his skin. "Don't you see this?"

"A fine example of healthy, human epidermis."

"It's Indian skin, and nobody can see past it. Doesn't matter if I'm interested in medicine and science. Doesn't matter that I was tops in my class at the mission school. Any college would take one look at me and send me packing. No way I'd get into a medical school."

The yearning in Joshua's voice caught Caleb's attention. It was the first time he could recall Joshua mentioning any specific desire he had beyond getting out from under the authority of his father and away from the reservation.

Doc poured himself some milk from the glass bottle. "Not with an attitude like that, I assure you."

"This attitude comes from years of experience, Doc. Ask Caleb. I can't even walk down the street here without running into some bucket-head who wants to remind me how low in the pecking order I am in this town."

"What you do is up to you, not someone else. If you want to be a doctor, you're the only one standing in your way. Don't use the color of your skin as your excuse not to try."

"Tell that to the marines." But the yearning in his voice and the spark of hope in his eyes belied his words. "I wouldn't even know where to start."

Doc pushed the book toward him. "Start here. Read it, study it, and when you're done, come get another one. If after a summer of learning medical terminology, anatomy and physiology, therapeutics, and diagnoses you still want a career in medicine, we'll see what to do next."

Joshua took the book, cradling it against his lean stomach, a determined tilt to his chin.

"Hey, Doc." Caleb took a slice of fruitcake. "Why're so many people in town today?"

"Don't you know? There's a movie star train due to pull into the station"—Doc slid his watch from his vest pocket—"in just under an hour."

"Movie star? Like who?"

"Charlie Chaplin and Mary Pickford, if the posters at the El Garces and over at Claypool's are to be believed. They're gathering money for the Red Cross from San Francisco to New York. Lots of bigwigs on the train and folks flocking to each stop. I thought I might go myself." He flicked a glance at Caleb. "I thought that might be why you'd come to town today. Surprised you didn't know about it. Folks have talked of little else for the past week."

"I haven't been to town for a while."

"Since the hotel dance? Didn't I see you there, and in the company of a certain titian-haired maiden?"

Caleb refused to be pushed off-center, but it was a fight. Doc saw way too much. Joshua looked up from his book, his dark eyebrows climbing. Caleb remained still.

Doc drained his glass and wiped his moustache. "Tell you what, how about we all head over there? I've a hankering to see me a genuine, for-real, in-the-flesh movie star." He put a funny drawl in his voice and winked at Joshua. "Don't you want to see one, Joshua?"

So Caleb found himself on the platform at the El Garces with several hundred of Needles's finest, watching for the eastbound train. Red, white, and blue bunting hung from every porch rail, and streamers floated in the lazy breeze. Caleb remained on the edge of the crowd, glad that everyone's attention was directed elsewhere. Maybe he and Joshua could get a peek at the movie stars and get out of the throng unnoticed.

Behind him, the doors to the lunchroom stood open, and from his position, he had a good view of the interior. Half a dozen Harvey Girls bustled behind the counters, disappearing through the kitchen doorways, setting the doors to flopping. Sidling a few feet closer and craning his neck, he spied Meghan filling a coffeepot. Nearly every stool was full, and she didn't see him, being focused on her customers.

His heart started the familiar crazy bumping it always did when she was near, and he tugged his hat down lower on his brow, turning away and leaning against the wall, taking the weight off his left foot and feigning boredom. Joshua joined him. Doc had disappeared into the crowd.

"What do you think they're like?" Joshua held the medical book tight to his chest behind his crossed arms.

"Just like us, I guess. Probably better dressed though."

"I've never been to a movie before. Seen the posters out front of the theater, but never been inside. Have you?"

"Couple of times."

"What's it like?"

Caleb shrugged. "Depends on who they have playing the piano. There's a piano down front and someone plays music to go along with the film. First time I went, the piano was so out of tune it sounded like a bloated cow, and the player must've been deaf, because he just kept banging away. Next time was much better. Music was good and sounded like it fit the picture."

A ripple went through the crowd and someone yelled, "Here she comes!"

Hissing, clanking, rocking, the eastbound chugged down the track, belching smoke and steam. Bunting hung from every roof edge and rail, mirroring the decking-out the hotel had received. As the train slowed to a stop so that the last car was opposite the main hotel doors, the crowd surged forward.

A small, dark-haired man emerged onto the railed platform smiling broadly and waving to the crowd. A cheer went up.

"Is that him?" Joshua had to shout to be heard.

"I guess so. I thought he'd be taller."

Charlie Chaplin himself. The little man turned back to the door and held out his hand. A woman emerged, her shoulders draped in a fox stole. Furs in this heat? She must've felt it too, for she let the fur slip from her shoulders and tossed it playfully back through the door into the car. The crowd cheered and clapped.

"Guess that's Mary Pickford."

"She's pretty."

Caleb shrugged. Pretty enough, he supposed, but nowhere near as beautiful as a certain waitress had been with the moonlight on her skin and the fire of her cause in her eyes.

The crowd swelled as the patrons of the lunchroom and dining room came out onto the sidewalk.

"Might be a good time to get some chow." Joshua straightened. "I don't care much for speeches from people I don't know."

Caleb checked around the corner. Not a customer remained in the lunchroom. One of the passengers must've had the same idea as Joshua about beating the crowd, because he climbed down from the train about midway up the line, skirted the throng, and walked to the lunchroom doors.

He was greeted by Mr. Stock, the guy in charge of the hotel. They held a quiet conversation as if Mr. Stock knew the man. Stock practically tugged his forelock and bowed as they spoke. The hotel manager's eyebrows rose at something the passenger said, and he gestured to the dining room, but when the man said something and shook his head, Stock nodded and stepped back so the man could go into the lunchroom.

"Let's get in and get out before the speechifying is done and the whole town moves in." Joshua nudged Caleb's arm.

This is a mistake. Why is it you vow never to come back to this place, and yet, you're always here?

At the doorway to the lunchroom, Mr. Stock stopped them. "Mr. McBride, you may go in, but I have to insist the boy stay outside."

Joshua gave a low figures-everywhere-I-go-people-treat-me-the-same-way grunt and hunched his shoulders.

Caleb went cold inside in spite of the heat. "Excuse me? Why would you want him to stay outside? He won't welsh on the meal. I'm paying his tab."

Mr. Stock's nose twitched like a rat's. "I'm sorry, sir. Hotel policy. Especially in light of the distinguished guests we have dining with us today."

"What hotel policy?" He knew what Mr. Stock was driving

at, but he wanted to hear the man say it.

The skinny manager's Adam's apple lurched, and he dug a handkerchief from his pocket to mop his brow.

"Really, Mr. McBride, now is not the time or the place. Can't you see we have important guests today? I would rather not discuss hotel admittance policies at this time."

"I bet you don't, but I need to hear it, just so we're clear. I wouldn't want there to be any misunderstandings."

Lowering his voice along with his eyebrows, Mr. Stock leaned close to Caleb. "It is against the policies of the El Garces to allow Indians into the public areas."

"Since when?" Caleb raised his voice, not caring who heard. "The whole interior is decorated from top to bottom in Indian designs. You invite members of the Mohave tribe to stand out on the sidewalk all dressed up in their Indian finery and hawk their wares to the tourists and travelers, but you won't let them inside to eat at the lunch counter?"

The man who had left the train and entered the lunchroom ahead of them showed up at Mr. Stock's shoulder while the hotelier made damping motions with his hand and looked back toward the crowd and the train.

"Is there a problem here?" The man, though not big, had a commanding presence that certainly brought Stock up short.

"No, sir, not at all."

"Actually, there is a bit of a problem." Caleb put his hands on his hips.

"Forget it. It won't make any difference. I'm used to it." Joshua tugged on Caleb's elbow. "I'll wait outside for you."

"No way. If they won't serve you, they don't serve me."

The stranger's eyes widened. "What's this? Are you refusing admittance to these gentlemen?"

Stock looked like he wished one of the palm trees would

crash right down on top of him and knock him out. He swiped at his brow with the sweat-soaked hanky again. "I just thought, with the prestigious guests—"

"Every guest at a Harvey House is a prestigious guest." The man nodded toward Caleb and Joshua. "My name is Ford. I'd be honored if you'd be my guests for lunch today. I hope you don't mind eating at the lunch counter. I'd rather bypass the hoopla of the dining room."

Caleb made sure he showed no triumph as they walked past the wilted Mr. Stock, but he would have been lying if he said he didn't feel at least a little bit of satisfaction.

They took their seats, one on each side of the man called Ford. Whether it was his first name or his last name, Caleb didn't know, but whoever he was, he had some clout.

The kitchen doors flopped, and Meghan came to a stop before them. "Hello, and welcome to the Harvey House lunch-room at the El Garces." Her smile lit on each of them, but when it got to Caleb's it wobbled just a fraction. "What can I bring you to drink? We've got freshly brewed coffee, or, if you'd like something cooler, there's iced tea, or I could squeeze you some orange juice."

She looked cool and fresh and every bit as beautiful as he remembered, but questions lurked in her green eyes, and he sensed her withdrawal from him. Mrs. Gregory's warnings must've penetrated even Meghan's idealistic heart.

But you'd never know it by the service she gave him. Everything was perfect, from the shine on the silverware to the easy way she set the plates before him. And it wasn't just him. When the speeches outside finished, diners crowded into the lunchroom until not a seat remained empty. The noise level rose, and the batwing doors into the kitchen were in constant motion with uniformed girls coming and going.

Meghan fairly flew, carrying, pouring, serving, chatting. And she never needed to write down an order. With a smile and a nod, she listened, answered questions, made recommendations, and hustled without ever seeming hurried.

Ford examined each item of his place setting as if he were preparing to buy it instead of just eat off it, and his eyes searched every part of the lunchroom like Pinkerton. Lifting his coffee cup, he inhaled the steam rising from the dark liquid and took a sip, savoring the brew. Caleb watched him but made no comment. The train brought folks from all over the country through Needles, and there were bound to be a few odd socks in the mix from time to time. If this fellow wanted to parse and examine every morsel and mouthful, that was his business. At least he'd smoothed things over with Mr. Stock. Joshua ate as if he'd never heard of fruitcake, much less eaten three pieces an hour ago at Doc's.

At the end of the meal, the Ford fellow sat back, patted his lips with his napkin, and neatly folded it beside his plate. "Miss, I must commend you on your service. I've never received better. Are you perchance filling in here at the lunch counter? I would think someone of your caliber would be in the dining room serving the distinguished guests."

Meghan paused, a smile curving her mouth. "No, sir, this is my customary position. And as far as I'm concerned, every guest of the Fred Harvey Company is a distinguished guest. But I do thank you for your compliment."

Ford followed her movements, a satisfied look in his eye.

Joshua couldn't keep still, watching everybody and everything, curious as a cat. Meghan treated him as well as everyone else, smiling, serving quickly, and when it came time for dessert, she chose the largest piece of chocolate cake from the refrigerator cabinet and placed it before Joshua.

"A growing boy deserves a nice big piece. They're all supposed to be cut exactly the same, but somehow this one came out a little larger." Her nose wrinkled, and Caleb found himself staring at her freckles.

"Can I get you anything else, Mr. McBride?"

He swallowed and shook his head. "No, thank you, Meghan." Her use of his last name pricked him. When they'd been together at the dance, she'd called him Caleb.

"Very well. Have a nice day, and thank you for dining at the El Garces." Her skirt belled out as she turned toward the coffee urns near the kitchen door.

He swallowed and tore his eyes away from the gentle sway of her hips and the narrow span of her waist.

"Do you know her?" Ford crossed his knife and fork on his plate.

"We've met." He pressed his lips together at the memory of their first cataclysmic encounter, and his heart quickened at the thought of how close he'd come to kissing her in the moonlight during the dance.

"What's her name?"

He cleared his throat and his head. "Meghan. Meghan Thorson. She's been here. . .must be a couple of months now."

Ford stroked his moustache, his intelligent eyes following her every move. "Interesting."

A stab of what Caleb had to admit was jealousy pierced his gut. This geezer was old enough to be Meghan's father and here he was watching her like a hawk eyeing a mouse.

"Do you know the head waitress?" Ford dug in his pocket for his watch, flipped open the cover and compared the time-piece with the clock on the far wall.

"Mrs. Gregory. We've met." He rubbed his cheekbone. "I imagine she wouldn't be too pleased to see me and Joshua in here. She can be a bit sticky. Do you know her?"

"I've not had the pleasure, yet. She's new since my last trip through Needles. Promoted from housekeeping, from what I understand."

"Where is it you're from?"

"Kansas City. But I'm through here quite often, though with the war on, my travels have been more eastward than westward recently. What about you? That isn't a Southwest accent I'm hearing."

"Vermont, actually, though I haven't lived there in some years. Lived in Kentucky for a while, and moved here for a job with the army."

His eyebrows rose. "You're a soldier? My son, Frederick, is an aviator."

Why'd he mention the army? It only brought uncomfortable questions he didn't want to answer, but there was something about this man that made him feel more at ease than he'd felt in weeks. "I'm not a soldier. I train horses for the cavalry. Bring 'em in by train from the west coast, season them a bit, and ship them to Fort Riley to finish their training."

"Well done. We need men like you. You're doing good work, though I suspect you don't get quite the glowing accolades as those with more high profile jobs. The current circus-on-the-rails that I'm traveling with, they're doing good work, too, raising funds and such, but it does get to be quite the extravaganza. I prefer less ostentatious means of helping the cause."

Caleb's chest swelled. If only other folks thought like this man, his time in Needles wouldn't be so difficult.

Ford tucked his watch away. "Now, I must see Mr. Stock before it's time for the train to pull out. I enjoyed dining with you, and I suspect, after this, any time you want to bring the boy in with you to eat, there won't be any trouble."

With a brisk handshake, he rounded the lunch counter and disappeared toward the lobby. Caleb drained his water glass while Joshua polished off the last crumbs of his cake. Meghan appeared to clear their spaces, and when she picked up Ford's plate, a bill fluttered to the counter. She blinked.

"Ten dollars?" She searched the lunchroom. "He must've dropped this by mistake, or perhaps he thought he was putting a dollar bill under his plate, though that would be far too big a tip in any case. Do you see him? Which way did he go?"

"He headed toward the lobby. Said he had to see Stock before the train left." Caleb stood and dug in his pocket. "That was a fine meal, Meghan, and well served. Thank you." He left as big a tip as he dared, though it couldn't compare to ten dollars.

Her eyes collided with his, and he read all those questions and doubts she must be harboring about him. A pretty flush tinted her cheeks, and his heart bumped hard against his ribs. How he wished she'd heard what Ford had said about his job being vital to the war effort, even if it wasn't worthy of a medal or a headline.

"I need to find that gentleman and return his money to him."

"We'll help you look. He's bound to be around here some-where. I'd like to thank him again for a little service he did me and Joshua." He stood and waited for Meghan to round the end of the lunch counter. "He's probably at the front desk."

Caleb identified Ford's voice before he actually saw him. Meghan, continuing on her way toward the dining room, stopped when Caleb touched her arm. Caleb raised himself up on his good leg to scan over the people.

"There he is." They crossed the tile floor near the foun-tain. Caleb almost paused in the spot where he'd nearly kissed Meghan before pressing on with a stern warning to himself to forget such foolishness. They wove through passengers now exiting the lunchroom and dining room and working their way toward the train. The man they sought stood near one of the pillars conversing with the hotel manager and the head waitress.

"Maybe we'd best hang back until they're done. Mrs. Gregory sees us together, she's liable to pitch a fit."

"Mr. Stock, I trust there will be no more unpleasantness with our guests. The El Garces will not refuse service to any paying customer. Is that understood?"

"Yes, Mr. Harvey."

Meghan gave a small gasp, and her fingertips came up to cover her lips. "Mr. Harvey?" She whispered, seemingly half to him and half to herself. Her green eyes widened.

Caleb put his lips close to her ear. "He said his name was Ford."

She clutched his arm. "Ford Harvey. Son of Fred Harvey, the founder of the company. I served Ford Harvey?"

"And Mrs. Gregory," Ford Harvey continued. "I have to wonder why the young woman who served my meal is being wasted in the lunchroom. She was as attentive to detail, as personable and professional a Harvey Girl as I have ever seen and certainly deserves to be moved up to the dining room. I hate to think of one of the girls missing out on the larger tips offered in the dining room if she deserves to be there."

"But, Mr. Harvey, she's only been here a short while, and there have been. . .some issues."

"Would you care to explain these issues?"

Meghan's eyes closed. Caleb wanted to draw her away, but he wanted to hear what Mrs. Gregory had to say as well. They certainly weren't having a private conversation, not out here in the crowded lobby where anyone could hear.

"She's been seen several times in the company of a

rather undesirable man in the Needles community, and she's impertinent."

A small groan escaped Meghan, and she clutched Caleb's arm. "Let's get out of here."

"Right."

Their movement must've caught Mr. Ford Harvey's eye. "Excuse me. Miss Thorson, Mr. McBride."

They turned, and Caleb wondered if his face looked as guilty as Meghan's. "Sir?"

Mrs. Gregory's mouth pinched, and her eyes glittered. Mr. Stock looked like he wanted to sink beneath the floor and never return. Copious amounts of sweat leaked from his forehead, and his handkerchief swiped continually.

"I've just been having a word with Mr. Stock and Mrs. Gregory. I don't anticipate any further difficulties for either of you here at the El Garces. Miss Thorson, you will be moved to the dining room immediately, and Mr. McBride, you are always welcome here. You and your friend." He flicked a finger to where Joshua hovered behind them. "I'll be back through this way soon. I imagine I'll find everything as it should be." Though he smiled, there was no real warmth in it, and his tone was such that Caleb had no doubt he expected to be obeyed.

He left, and Mrs. Gregory's face went from white as a blister to red as a bloodstone. "What have you been telling him, Miss Thorson? It's shameful of you to take your complaints to Mr. Harvey instead of coming to discuss them with me first."

"Here now." Caleb stepped forward. "She didn't know who he was any more than I did. And she didn't complain about you. Not a word." Though he might've mentioned something about her difficult personality.

Mr. Stock wrung his hands. "The damage has been done. Rehashing it won't help. I wanted to warn you, Mrs. Gregory, but he forbade me from saying anything about his being here. And you were in the dining room the whole time. I can't imagine why he didn't want to dine with Mr. Chaplin and Miss Pickford." He mopped his forehead again.

"It seems trouble follows you wherever you happen to be, Miss Thorson." Mrs. Gregory's back stiffened. "I will move you to the dining room as he requested, but if you so much as spill a drop of coffee into a saucer, I'll fire you." Her eyes bored into Meghan before switching to Caleb. "And if you persist in hanging around here panting after one of my waitresses, I'll set the sheriff after you."

She wheeled and marched away.

Mr. Stock took a deep breath. "We must make some allowances for her. She's under a great deal of stress. She hasn't heard from her son since he arrived in Europe, and she's been so busy with all the preparations for the celebrity train. Mr. McBride, I hope you won't think me churlish, but it might be best for all of us if she doesn't find you here when she returns."

Caleb nodded, wishing he could stay and spend more time with Meghan, but knowing, as he'd known all along, that his being with her would only cause her trouble and himself pain. He wouldn't wait around to be thrown out. A man had his pride, after all.

"I'm sorry my presence seems to get you into difficulties."

Meghan shrugged. The train whistle sounded, and she glanced over his shoulder to where Mr. Chaplin and Miss Pickford stood in the doorway to the dining room. "I don't have any problem getting into trouble. Like Mrs. Gregory said. It follows me to wherever I happen to be."

"That might be true, but I don't want you to face censure because of me. I'll stay away from the hotel. That will make Mrs. Gregory happy—or at least as happy as a woman of her disposition can be." He hadn't realized how much he had looked forward to seeing Meghan when he came to town. A hole tore open in his chest. Still, it was for the best.

She turned those wide, green eyes on him. "Will I see you again?" Her pretty, pink lips parted, and his breath hitched, but he forced himself to take a firm grip on his resolve.

"No. It's for the best." Settling his hat on his head, he touched the brim and walked out into the sunshine, careful to make sure he didn't show even a trace of a limp.

Chapter 9

Doc washed his hands and wiped them on the roller towel beside the sink. One last patient waited in his front parlor before he could escape to the river for a little sunset fishing. A small practice might not be very exciting out here in the California desert, but it sure gave him plenty of time to stalk record-breaking pikeminnows.

"Miss?"

The pretty blond perched on the edge of one of his wingchairs jumped. One of the girls from the hotel. He remembered seeing her in the dining room. Wedgewood blue eyes fringed with pale lashes met his. Her pale pink dress hung on her slight frame.

"Won't you come in?" He studied her as she rose and entered the examination room. Slight, pale, with dark smudges under those pretty eyes. She had the bone structure of a bird, and her skin was so translucent he could see the blue lines of her veins on the backs of her hands and at her temples.

He motioned toward the chair beside his desk and took his own seat, leaning back, propping his elbows on the arms of his chair, and steepling his fingers under his nose. "What brings you in to see me today?"

She swallowed, staring at her hands in her lap. A single tear splashed onto her thumb. "I don't know where to start," she whispered.

"How about we start with your name?"

"Natalie Daviot."

"There, that wasn't so hard, was it?" He smiled, but she didn't look up. "And how old are you, Natalie?"

"Twenty-two."

Older than she looked. He'd have wagered she wasn't a day over seventeen.

"Are you feeling ill, Miss Daviot?"

The cuff of her dress seemed to fascinate her. She plucked at the lace edging, smoothing it and scrunching it by turns. "I'm just so tired. I thought I'd pick up once I got used to the work, but I'm dragging around like a hound dog's chew toy."

Doc scratched the word *fatigue* on his notepad. "You're a Harvey Girl at the hotel, correct?"

"Yes."

"For how long now?"

"Almost three months."

"From what I've seen, Harvey Girls work very hard. Lots of time on your feet and lots of lifting and carrying. Fatigue after all those long shifts is natural. Any other symptoms?"

She shook her head. "I had a little stomach bug a few weeks ago that hung on for a while, but that's gone now."

Sitting on the very edge of the chair, she looked ready to take wing at any moment. And she had yet to meet his eyes since coming into the exam room. Her slender shoulders bowed, and she wore an unmistakable air of guilt. He began putting all the pieces together and formed a preliminary diagnosis.

"I'm going to have to ask you some fairly pointed and personal questions, I'm afraid, if we're going to figure out what's going on with you."

She took a deep breath as if fortifying herself. "Doctor, I'm afraid I know what it might be, but I really don't want it to be." This time her chin came up and she blinked, sending a fresh pair of tears tracking down her cheeks.

He raised his eyebrows and laid his pencil down before digging in his pocket for a clean handkerchief.

"Are you in trouble?" He kept his tone as kind and nonjudgmental as he could.

She nodded, dabbing at her eyes. "But not the way you think."

"Oh?"

"I think I'm having a baby."

Which confirmed his initial thoughts based upon her symptoms. Poor girl. She had a hard road ahead of her. This wasn't the first time he'd been called upon to make such a diagnosis, and it was never a happy occasion. He wouldn't wish being an unwed mother on anyone, and this fragile girl seemed less able to bear it than most. With as much tact and understanding as possible, he asked a few pertinent questions.

"I'll need to examine you to make sure, but from what you've told me, I suspect you're right. What about the father? Is there any chance he will marry you?" Doc ran his hand down his face. He'd have to get his address book from the desk in his study. That's where he kept his contact information for the girls' home over in Barstow. Marjorie Banks ran the place, and she'd take good care of Miss Daviot during her confinement, and if the girl so desired, she'd find a home for the child.

"But I *am* married." She reached for the back of her neck and slid her finger under a chain, tugging it out from the collar of her dress. A circlet of gold dangled from the links. "My husband is a soldier. I didn't tell anyone about my marriage because if they found out, I'd have to leave my job. The Harvey Company only hires single girls who can live in the dormitories to be Harvey Girls. And I need the money."

The story she spilled out had him shaking his head, both in sadness and admiration. Her husband had answered his country's call to serve, her mother-in-law had suffered an apoplectic attack, her father-in-law was frail, and she'd taken a high-paying job halfway across the country in order to help out. He listened to every word, knowing she needed to talk as much as she needed a diagnosis. What a burden for her to carry. Her pent-up emotions rushed out, and a torrent of tears followed.

"I'll be back. Don't go anywhere."

He went to the kitchen and got a glass of water. Returning to the exam room, he pressed it into her hand. She'd stopped crying, but her chin quivered, and the occasional hiccup jarred her.

"Sip on this. It will help."

"Thank you."

He resumed his seat and put his forearms on his knees, leaning toward her. "Miss Daviot, or should I say Mrs. Daviot? When you're ready, I'd like to get the examination out of the way so we can confirm your suspicions. Then we'll talk about what to do."

Fifteen minutes later, he went to the kitchen to brew some tea, leaving Natalie in the exam room to gather herself and come to terms with his findings. When the tea had steeped, he put everything on a tray and carried it to his study. They'd both be more comfortable there than in the exam room.

She eased into one of his wingchairs and sipped her tea, some color returning to her face.

"I'm sure you can give in your notice without saying why you're leaving. Your husband's family will be glad to see you. You can be with them by the end of the week."

Her eyebrows rose. "I can't go back yet. My mother-in-law's doctor bills aren't paid, and she still needs the district nurse visits. And with the added expense of a baby next year, I need every penny for as long as I can earn."

"But, my dear, you can't conceal your condition forever, and you should be at home with your family."

"I can serve my family best by staying here as long as possible. Every dollar I earn pays for past bills and future expenses." She let her hand drop to her abdomen. As frail and delicate as she was, a determined light gleamed in her eyes. "Working won't hurt the baby, will it?"

Disquieted by her determination, Doc turned his cup in its saucer. "I'd like it better if you could spend more time with your feet up. An unborn child places quite a burden on its mother, and with your demanding job, you'll have to expect that the fatigue will continue."

She sighed. "Is there anything else I can do?"

He rattled off his standard expectant-mother spiel. "Drink plenty of fluids, especially milk. I will caution you against becoming overtired. You have a rather taxing job, and you're not yet used to the climate out here. Dehydration comes on quickly."

Her lower lip disappeared, and she nodded.

"Avoid heavy lifting. I know you sometimes have to carry loaded trays, but try to minimize that. Make extra trips if you have to. That's better than carrying too much at once. What part of the restaurant do you work in?"

"I'm a waitress in the dining room."

"Perhaps you could get yourself transferred to the soda fountain instead. That would be much easier on you. No heavy lifting, no walking miles between tables and the kitchen."

For the first time, a smile curved her pretty mouth. "I could probably do that. I know my roommate, Meghan, just got moved up to the dining room. Mrs. Gregory will be looking to move the girls around to make room for her. I can volunteer for the soda fountain, and Barbara can move to Meghan's spot in the lunchroom. That will be perfect."

"I want to go on record here as saying it would be better in the long run if you were to go home to your family. It would be best all around if you came clean to Mrs. Gregory about your marriage and your coming child."

"I wish I could. And I know I won't be able to hide it forever, but I have to stay as long as I can. If there was any hope of me getting a job at home that would come close to the wages I get here, I'd do it in a heartbeat, but there just isn't. And no one would hire me in my present condition anyway. I need this job, and I plan to stay until they kick me out." Again that determined blue light gleamed in her eyes.

"Then I'm going to caution you. You're going to be tempted at some point to bind yourself up to conceal the fact that you are with child. Don't do it. That's the worst possible thing you could do to your growing baby and your own internal organs. Loosen your apron and let out your dresses to conceal your shape, but don't, under any circumstances, bind yourself. You can do irreparable harm."

She set her teacup down, and the slender column of her throat moved as she swallowed. "I understand. And I can rely on your reticence? You won't tell anyone?"

"You can trust me."

He showed her out, but a heaviness he couldn't dispel hung over him. Nothing good would come from her hiding her condition. It put him in mind of Caleb, also hiding a medical issue. She would be condemned for revealing hers, while his would exonerate him. Hers was a reason to celebrate, and yet she couldn't risk it for fear of losing her job. His was a reason to commiserate, and yet he wouldn't reveal the truth for fear of losing his pride.

But secrets had a way of coming out. He could only hope to minimize the consequences when they did.

"What did the doctor say?" Meghan gathered her sewing supplies into the basket she'd rounded up for the purpose. Blocks of red and white fabric, red embroidery thread, white quilting thread, red yarn for tying the quilt. She mentally checked off her list.

Natalie unpinned her hat and set it on the dresser. "He said to drink plenty of fluids and to get as much rest as I can. There's nothing whatever wrong with me."

"So he thinks it's just taking you some time to get accustomed to the climate and the work?"

A soft smile, as if she were privy to an inside joke, quirked her lips. "Time will solve all my problems. He said for me not to worry so much, but I don't know that I can help it, not with Derek on the front lines like he is."

Meghan nodded. "I think about Lars every day. I can't imagine what you must be going through. A brother isn't the same as a husband."

Natalie shook her head. "It's hard on everyone. Think of Mrs. Gregory with her son gone. She mentioned that she hadn't heard from him since receiving his disembarkation card. I know she worries something terrible. Parents miss their sons, siblings miss their brothers, wives miss their husbands, and children miss their fathers. I don't know that you can rank people's pain as more or less dear. We're all in this together."

"We'd best get downstairs together before Mrs. Gregory comes hunting us."

"Has she gotten over the shock of Mr. Harvey's visit?"

Grimacing, Meghan hefted the basket handle over her arm. "I try to make allowances for her. I mean, like you said, her son has shipped out and she hasn't had word from him in a while, and she is in a position full of responsibility looking after all us girls and the restaurant and all, but I am in danger of getting frostbite every time she walks by me these days. She said I'm supposed to start in the dining room on Monday. She still hasn't figured out how she's going to shuffle everyone around."

Natalie closed the door behind them, and they headed to the Red Cross meeting. "How is the quilt coming along?"

"Okay. I need to get out and about to get more signatures. Though I did manage one rather big coup." A burst of excited warmth spread through Meghan as she remembered.

"Oh?"

"I ran to the celebrity train just before it pulled out, and I managed to get donations and signatures from both Charlie Chaplin and Mary Pickford, and. . ." She paused and wrinkled her nose. "Mr. Ford Harvey made a donation to have his signature put on the quilt, too." She squeezed Natalie's arm. "Isn't that great? More people will want the quilt knowing three famous people donated to have their names embroidered on it."

"That's wonderful. I imagine folks will be eager to put their names on the quilt alongside Mr. Chaplin's and Miss Pickford's."

"I only wish I had been able to canvass the crowd while the train was here. Folks were in a very enthusiastic, supportive mood. I would've been able to get a bunch of donations, I bet."

They reached the bottom of the staircase and turned toward the screened porch. The sound of chattering women reached them through the open doorway.

"Do you want some help with the quilt, or should I go over to the knitting machine?"

"You go make socks. I want to do the quilt myself." She couldn't explain it, but she wanted this project to be all hers. Having help would somehow diminish the effort she was making, or make the project somehow less impressive. Meghan scouted out an empty table. She began laying out her supplies, creating neat stacks of red and white squares and rectangles. When she had laid out all the fabric and threads, a shadow fell across the table.

"How is your project coming along?" Mrs. Gregory, still in her white uniform, stood beside the table with her hands on her hips. "Are you sure you don't want me to assign you some helpers?"

Meghan read the challenge in her eyes and tone, and her chin shot up. "That's quite all right, Mrs. Gregory. I've got everything under control here."

One of the laundresses entered the room, spotted Meghan, and raised her eyebrows in a silent question. Meghan stood and motioned the woman over.

"Mrs. Lassiter."

"Are you ready? I found a couple of boys to bring it in." Mrs. Lassiter twisted her work-reddened hands in her apron, darting looks from the corner of her eye at Mrs. Gregory.

"What's this?" the head waitress demanded.

"I am ready. You can put it right here by my table. And thank you." Meghan put her hand on the laundress's arm for a moment before turning to Mrs. Gregory. "I've arranged for a sewing machine to be brought in from the laundry area. Using a machine will speed up the piecing of the quilt."

Mrs. Gregory's mouth puckered. "Do you know how to use a sewing machine? I can't have someone inexperienced messing around with company property."

"I can use a sewing machine. My mother has had one for years, and she taught me to sew when I was a child. The machine will come to no harm." Meghan did her best to sound appeasing and reasonable, but waves of disapproval flowed from her supervisor, and the woman's lips pressed so hard together, they disappeared.

Two of the bellboys carried in the treadle sewing machine, its tabletop scratched and the gilded scrollwork on the black machine almost worn off.

Mrs. Gregory inspected the battered machine. "Oh, it's the old treadle. You can't do much harm there. I was afraid you wanted to use one of the new electric ones. Very well. Carry on." She turned on her heel and marched away to check on one of the other stations.

Meghan settled in to work, pinning, sewing, snipping threads. She'd have a mountain of ironing to do on all the seams, but that could be done later. For now, she wanted to finish the piecing she'd begun by hand so she could start the embroidering.

All around her, Red Cross volunteers chatted and worked. Some cut bandage materials, others rolled them up. Some, like Natalie, knitted scarves and caps, others turned cranks on two of the knitting machines that created socks lightning fast. At another table, women sorted through the buckets of peach, cherry, and apricot pits saved over from the kitchen for the making of gas mask charcoal. One of the girls had brought in a phonograph. Songs like "Pack up Your Troubles in Your Old Kit Bag," "It's a Long Way to Tipperary," "Keep the Home Fires Burning," and "Just a Baby's Prayer at Twilight (For Her Daddy Over There)" reminded them all of why they were working so hard and who they were working for.

Several of the ladies stopped by to see what Meghan was up to, and though many offered to help, she refused. She couldn't wait to hand the money over to the Red Cross, knowing she'd accomplished the entire task by herself.

Natalie drifted over after a while. "How are you coming along?"

"Fine. How's the knitting going?" She barely looked up from her sewing.

"The knitting's fine, but I thought I might give you a little warning."

The treadle stilled. "What?"

"I know how much this quilt project means to you, both the actual assembly of the quilt and the money you are hoping to raise before Mr. Gibson returns, but you're not making any friends here. A lot of these women would like to help you, but you've rebuffed every offer. You're coming across as selfish and standoffish."

"I'm not being selfish. There's plenty for everyone to do. I don't need any help. Anyone else would just be in the way." Meghan snipped a thread and finger-pressed the seams of a completed block.

"Maybe it's not about you needing their help as much as it's about them needing to help you."

"You're not making sense." Meghan laughed. "Anyway, after I finish this last block, I've gone as far as I can with the sewing. Now I just need to gather the names and collect the donations. I'll embroider the squares before I put them together." With a final snip, the square was done.

Sighing, Natalie shook her head. "I've been talking to Mrs. Gregory." She helped Meghan gather and stack the pieced quilt blocks and pick up stray threads.

"What about?"

"Since you're moving to the dining room day after tomorrow, she needs to do some shuffling of positions. I volunteered to work at the soda fountain."

"You what?" Meghan dropped her scissors onto the table with a clatter that had conversations pausing and heads turning. She lowered her voice. "But I was so looking forward to finally working with you. Now you're moving to the soda fountain? You won't get nearly the tips there. That's one thing that Barbara is always complaining about, the paltry tips people leave when they order a soda or an ice cream cone."

"I know, but I've been so tired lately, and the doctor said I should find a way to conserve my strength. Working the soda fountain will do just that, and Barbara can move to the lunchroom to take your vacant position. See? It all works out."

"Mrs. Gregory went along with that?"

"She did. I mentioned that I wasn't acclimating to the heat too well and that I'd been to see the doctor. She was actually very nice about it. I understand they had a girl pass away from heatstroke a couple of years ago, and she takes that kind of thing very seriously." Natalie shrugged. "I think somewhere under all that starch and protocol lurks a lonely, hurt woman who just wants a friend."

"And I think you're a very nice girl, Natalie Daviot. You see the good in everybody."

Jenny passed their table, her arms full of bandage rolls. "Hey, ladies, how's it going? We're just about done with bandages for the day."

Natalie took the rolls, one-by-one, out of Jenny's arms and lined them up on the end of Meghan's table. When she finished, she pressed her hands to her lower back. "I'm beat. I think I'll go lie down before we have to go back on duty."

"I'm about done, too. I'll be up to our room to drop off all this stuff before I head into town to go door-to-door for signatures." She mounded fabric into her basket. "When I have a good list going, I can get started on the embroidery."

Natalie gave a small wave and left the sunroom. Hopefully, she'd get some good rest in spite of the heat.

"Your quilt's an awfully big project." Jenny leaned against

the table. "Are you sure you can get enough donations just from town?"

"If I have to, I'll drive around the county and up toward Bullhead City. I'm sure Mr. Stock would let me borrow the hotel's automobile."

"You can drive?" Wonder and admiration colored Jenny's tone, and her eyes widened. "You can drive an auto?"

Meghan nodded. "My father has an Oldsmobile. He taught me to drive."

A mischievous glint came into Jenny's eyes. "Then you'll be able to drive out toward the river, right?"

"I imagine so."

"Then you could take some of us girls swimming." Jenny grinned. "We wouldn't have to wait for one of the bellboys to drive us out to Mr. McBride's place."

At the mention of Caleb's name, Meghan's heart bobbed. She was so conflicted about him. On the one hand, he was kind and interesting and intriguing. Something in him called out to her, as if he had some secret, hidden hurt that she could ease for him. And yet, from other sources she'd heard nothing good. He was a coward, a profiteer. How could she be drawn to him and repelled at the same time? Which was true, or was it all true? All she knew was that she couldn't stop thinking about him. And yet, he'd made it clear they wouldn't be seeing one another again.

Jenny must've sensed something, because she pounced. "Speaking of Caleb, isn't he handsome? All the girls think so. Don't you? Mrs. Gregory has warned us all against him. To hear her talk, you'd think he was the Kaiser's brother or had the typhoid or something. Though there wasn't much danger of any of us girls coming under his influence, at least not until you came along. He never used to come in here, hardly even came to town, but he's been in the hotel a bunch of times since you showed up. I heard Mrs. Gregory a couple of days ago telling the bellhops and maids to let her know if he came into the hotel again. She said he'd been 'sniffing around' one of her girls, and she wasn't going to stand for it. I figured she must mean you, since you're the one he heads for when he comes to town." Jenny blinked innocent eyes that invited Meghan to share a confidence.

Meghan's cheeks betrayed her, growing hot. "Sniffing around" had such bad connotations, she felt she had to put Jenny right.

"He's done nothing of the sort. I've served him a couple of times in the hotel, and I saw him at the dime-a-dance. That's all."

Jenny raised one eyebrow and crossed her arms. "Uh-huh. Tell that to the horse marines. Caleb McBride has given the cold shoulder to this town ever since he arrived. I bet he wasn't in Needles more than a handful of times ever, but in the last couple of months, he's been hanging around town and coming to the hotel. He never came to any of the Harvey Girl Friday Night Socials, and he sure never ate in the lunchroom before your arrival. And not only did he come to the dance, but the minute he arrived, he snatched you away for a stroll under the stars. Folks are talking. Small town and all, everyone knows everyone else's business."

Snatching up her basket, Meghan propped it on her hip. "Well, people should mind their own business instead of poking their noses in where they don't belong."

Jenny blinked at her tone, but she persisted. "Then there *is* something going on with you two?"

"Of course there isn't. I barely know the man. Anyway, Harvey Girls aren't supposed to court. I signed a contract."

"Fiddlesticks. What do contracts have to do with courting? Do you know how many Harvey Girls have gotten married the day after their contract expires? Half the girls working here are being courted by railroad men. The joke is that The Fred Harvey Company is actually a matchmaking service for the Atchison, Topeka & Santa Fe." She linked arms with Meghan. "Anyway, enough about that. If you can get the hotel car, let's get up another swimming party or two, okay?"

Meghan let Jenny prattle on as they headed upstairs, but she gave no firm assurances. With Mrs. Gregory expanding her web of informants, she had a feeling that if she wanted to make a success of her move into the dining room, she'd best steer clear of Caleb McBride's property.

Chapter 10

Meghan wove between the square tables for eight, raising her tray of desserts carefully over her head so as to clear the patrons but not hit the low-hanging chandeliers. Her first week as a dining room waitress had gone well. At least Mrs. Gregory hadn't said anything to her about any mistakes. And the dining room supervisor seemed satisfied with her performance.

She had fallen into the rhythm of the new work. One blessing of being a senior waitress meant she no longer had to polish coffee urns in between train departures. The dining room urns were kept in the kitchen, not out on the counter for all the diners to admire. Everything in the dining room lent a more sober atmosphere, from the rich paneling and coffered ceilings to the linen tablecloths and ornate chandeliers. Though speed was appreciated and necessary, one must never give the appearance of rushing.

"Two queen's puddings and two Muscatine ices." She set the plates before each person, working counterclockwise around the table. "Will any of you be having coffee with your dessert?" Holding the now empty tray low before her, she gave her most encouraging smile.

Heading back to the kitchen, she scanned the room. Close to capacity. Though she enjoyed the patrons in the dining room, she missed the camaraderie and informality of the lunch counter. Most of the soldiers passing through had vouchers for the lunchrooms, part of the deal worked out between the company and the military. The dining room was reserved for more well-to-do travelers and those looking for a little peace and quiet after the clattering bustle of the train.

"Coffee to table six."

The drinks waitress, Sandra, nodded and lifted her tray where a silver coffee pot rested in solitary splendor. The maître d' showed two gentlemen to one of her tables for two under a window, and Meghan's breath caught. The first man was a stranger who walked with all the military precision she'd expect from an officer in uniform, but the man who took the chair opposite him was familiar from her thoughts and dreams.

Sandra nudged her. "What are you waiting for? Go take their drinks order and give them their menus."

Meghan walked across the dining room as if in a trance. What was he doing here? He'd made it clear he wanted nothing to do with her. Yet, here he was again.

She put on her best smile. "Good afternoon, gentlemen. Welcome to the Harvey restaurant. Today's specials are Viennaise chicken with homemade noodles and beef tenderloin stroganoff. I can also recommend the fried chicken Castañeda. It's excellent. While you're considering the menu, may I take your drink order? We have coffee, hot tea, iced tea, water, freshly squeezed orange juice, tomato juice, and lemonade."

The man in uniform set his hat on the window ledge. He had pale blue eyes, sandy hair, and a sharply defined nose. "A hot day like today, lemonade sounds good. How about you, McBride? Something cool before we talk business?"

"Make it two lemonades." Caleb kept his attention on the printed menu.

Meghan arranged the cups according to the code to let Sandra know what the gentlemen had ordered and stepped away.

"Miss Thorson." The dining room supervisor crossed the

room and spoke softly into her ear. "Please inform Mrs. Gregory that Mr. McBride is in the hotel."

"What?"

"We are under orders to inform the head waitress when Mr. McBride patronizes our establishment. Go and tell her, then return here to take their orders."

Dread coursed through her. "Why does she want to know? Surely she won't throw him out? He's done nothing wrong."

"Ours is not to question the demands of Mrs. Gregory. Go find her and get back here quickly."

"Please, send someone else."

"There is no one else. Go." She made a shooing motion before stepping around a potted fern to man her station beside the kitchen door.

Meghan blew out a breath, trying to tamp down the nasty feeling that she might be betraying Caleb somehow by telling Mrs. Gregory that he was dining in the restaurant. The clock was ticking. She had to find her and get back to the table to take their orders in a timely manner. Maybe that was her out. If she couldn't find Mrs. Gregory quickly, she'd have to abandon the task to get back to work.

Unfortunately, she spotted the head waitress across the lobby standing in the doorway of the lunchroom. "Mrs. Gregory."

"What do you want? Aren't you supposed to be waiting tables? What are you doing traipsing around the hotel?"

Meghan swallowed and grabbed hold of her temper. "I was sent to inform you that Mr. McBride is dining with us today."

Her eyebrows rose and her face hardened. "Really?"

"Yes, ma'am." Meghan turned to go.

"Wait."

"I must get back. I have customers."

"Is he alone?"

518

"No, Mrs. Gregory. He's with an army officer. A major, I believe."

"Fine. Return to your station. I'm sure your customers are wondering where you've gotten to."

Meghan gritted her teeth. Shooed away as if she were the one dawdling. Her footfalls sounded loudly on the tile floor.

She returned to the busy hush of the dining room and approached Caleb's table. "Have we decided?"

The gentlemen placed their orders, and she went to the kitchen to report to the chef. On the far side of the blistering hot kitchen, Harvey Girls bustled through the flopping doors to the lunch counters. They chatted with the sous chefs and busboys, cheerful and busy. The dining room staff proceeded with pleasant but serious expressions. No jocularity, the ultimate in professional service behavior.

She missed the lunchroom.

Carrying the first course to Caleb's table, she couldn't help but overhear part of their conversation. Her curiosity surged, and she slowed her pace to linger without being too obvious.

"I'm going to have to have at least one more carload of hay. What I can get around here is so thin and light, it hardly puts any meat on their bones. And half a carload of grain. When can I expect the next shipment of horses?" Caleb leaned back, staring somewhere over the major's shoulder and giving no indication that he knew Meghan or even realized she was there.

She set their salads before them, noted both needed refills on lemonade, and motioned to Sandra. Unable to think of a reason to hover, she moved away. Unbidden, she looked back over her shoulder and caught Caleb watching her leave. Their gazes meshed, and a stab of guilt pierced her. Why had Mrs. Gregory wanted to know he was in the hotel?

When they'd finished their salads, Meghan cleared their

plates and served the main courses. She couldn't help but notice the strong backs of Caleb's hands, the way his muscles played beneath his white shirt, and the crisp springiness of his sun-bleached hair. She had to force herself not to touch his shoulder to test the warmth of his skin.

The major picked up his fork. "I've made the rounds of several ranches in central California and purchased fifty new mounts. They'll be coming on the train in just over a week. I'll send several handlers along with them. They'll deliver them to your place so you don't have to come into town."

Meghan bit her lip. If he didn't have to come to town for horses, when would she see him again? She served her other customers, but Caleb's table received more than its fair share of her attention, for she couldn't stay away. With each course she caught snippets of their conversation, adding to what she knew about Caleb. The major's commendation of Caleb's training warmed her through with pride.

"The last group you sent to Fort Riley, the commandant was especially pleased. They were certainly in tiptop shape, and very well trained, ready for learning battle maneuvers. He wanted me to pass along his thanks."

"Fifty head is the most I can handle out at the ranch. I wish I had a better place. It's pretty stark out there. Without getting feed hauled in, I couldn't even support fifty."

"We'll drive out there after the meal and we can go over any equipment you might need."

"Gentlemen, your dessert." She set the plates before them and opened her mouth to offer coffee, but she stopped as a large woman she recognized from their Red Cross meetings stormed into the dining room.

"There you are. I heard you were in town again." Red-rimmed eyes blazed, and a quivering chin jutted high. With hard steps, she marched across the floor. She wore black, unusual in the high desert heat. She even had a black hat with weepers trailing down her back.

The maître d' flapped behind her ineffectually, with small cries of "Madame Babineax, please."

Coming to a halt before Caleb, she clutched her purse. Both he and the major rose, placing their napkins on the table. Meghan, frozen by the righteous indignation in the woman's pose, stood slack-jawed, a sense of foreboding wrapping around her like a cloak, the dessert tray forgotten in her hands.

"Excuse me, ma'am?" The major bowed. "How may we be of assistance to you?"

"I don't want to talk to you. It's this yellow coward I want to address." She scrabbled in her purse and pulled out a large white chicken feather. "My son is dead. Killed in France, while you sit here dining in comfort without a worry in the world. But no more. This entire town is going to know you for the coward you are. I hereby bestow upon you the Order of the White Feather."

A gasp went up from the diners. Meghan's skin prickled as Caleb went white under his tan. The woman tucked the feather into his shirt pocket and slapped it hard.

"Any man who would refuse to enlist, then calmly sit in the nicest restaurant in town plotting how to profit off the very war he is too cowardly to fight in, well, that man deserves a chicken feather and much worse. You should be thankful I didn't bring tar with me. The people of this community are patriotic and proud, and we know a flat-out coward when we see one. You, sir, are a coward." Her face quivered with emotion, her eyes blazing.

Caleb said nothing, his lips pressed into a thin line.

The major couldn't hold his tongue, however. "Madam, please. You are mistaken. You judge him unfairly. Why, this man—"

"Sir, please. Let it go." Caleb shook his head.

"But, you can't let her go on thinking—"

"Please." There was a hard edge to his voice, and his eyes went steely.

A lump formed in Meghan's throat. He wasn't even denying it. In spite of all the evidence to the contrary, she'd held on to a shred of hope that the whispers and accusations of his cowardice weren't true. And yet, when faced with this humiliating debacle, being called out in front of the town and this fine army officer, he put up no resistance. He just stood there mute, letting his accuser win.

He *was* a coward.

Blinking back tears of disappointment, she turned away. She couldn't bear to look at him, so shameful and weak. How had she ever imagined him to be fascinating and interesting? Mrs. Gregory was right.

He deserved that chicken feather.

"Why didn't you explain to that woman? Why just stand there and take it?"

Major Alexander's questions hung in the air as they bounced along the rutted road leading to Caleb's place along the river. Caleb turned the wheel to avoid a rock.

"Aren't you going to answer me? You had every right to throw that feather back at her." The major's mustache jerked. "A distasteful custom if there ever was one, handing out chicken feathers to those deemed too cowardly to enlist. Started over in Britain, Admiral Fitzgerald rousing the press and then silly girls continuing it to spur young men to enlist. Ridiculous."

Caleb glanced down at the tip of the feather protruding

from his shirt pocket still. A writhing ball of humiliation twisted in the pit of his stomach. Bad enough to be humiliated in front of the major and the entire complement of customers in the restaurant, but to have Meghan witness his disgrace. The horror in her eyes, the confusion at first, and then the distaste. It gnawed at him like a hungry pack rat. He'd known the instant she went from incredulous to disillusioned. All the light had gone out of her, and she'd turned away from him just as the rest of the town had. She'd held out longer than most, but in the end, things had gone just the way he had expected from the first.

"What are you going to do with it? You should've thrown it away or left it at the table. Why keep it?"

He grunted. "Believe I'll hang on to it. The way this town is riled up against me, I figure in a week or two I'll have enough to make a fan. It gets powerfully hot here most days. I could use a fan."

"McBride, I don't know how you can joke. I checked up on you, and I'm very sorry about your. . .well, your infirmity, shall we say." He cleared his throat and stared out the windscreen, as uncomfortable as everyone was who learned about Caleb's foot. Not knowing what to say, not knowing where to look. And unconsciously treating him differently than normal men. Some behaved as if he were a freak, something to be ashamed of, like his father had. Others seemed to consider that it was his mind that was twisted and warped, that a weak foot meant a weak intellect. And then there were those like the major, who tried to bluff, to act as if the notion didn't bother them, but subtly, they behaved as if Caleb were fragile. They were so embarrassed by the whole notion, they walked on eggshells, trying not to let him know they were uncomfortable.

"Fifty horses will really stretch us. Is there any money to

hire another wrangler or two?" Caleb changed the subject, freeing both himself and the major from awkwardness.

The major grabbed onto the new topic, relief coloring his voice. "I'm afraid there isn't at the moment. The truth is, this war has made the higher-ups have to rethink their strategies. This newfangled tank, airplanes, trench warfare. The mounted cavalry is becoming obsolete. The War Department is putting more money into mechanizing our troops than it is into acquiring and training horses. We've only got about six of these operations like yours going across the country. At the start of our involvement, we had close to fifty."

Caleb pondered this as the house and barn came into view. If the war went on long enough, he'd be out of a job. He could leave the Needles area. When he'd first been approached about taking on the job of training horses for the cavalry, the idea had appealed, even though they'd sent him to this inhospitable region—both the climate and the people as it turned out. He'd thought of little else than doing what he'd been hired to do, knowing that when the war ended, he would shake the dust of this town off his boots and not look back.

But that was before he met Meghan. Before she erupted into his life and made his heart spin wild dreams. Dreams where he had someone special who loved him, in spite of his flaws. Someone who knew the real him, the real Caleb who lived inside his less-than-perfect shell. Someone who would believe in him in spite of what everyone else thought or said.

He pulled to a stop before the porch and killed the motor and his foolish thoughts. Joshua came out, letting the screen door slap closed behind him. His brows arrowed toward each other, and distrustful lines formed on his forehead. Joshua hated strangers. Like a dog who had been beaten, he would circle warily, sniffing things out before he formed a judgment as to whether to trust the newcomer. Caleb had a fair idea of how the boy felt.

The major hopped from the truck, shading his eyes and surveying the property with as close a scrutiny as if he were a prospective cash buyer. He was silent for a long time.

"You should be proud of yourself. I can't imagine how you turn out such fine horses on such a barren spit of land." His piercing blue eyes met Caleb's. "Only the best trainers are still in business. Those near fifty other trainers I mentioned before? One by one they've been shut down as demand decreased. But we let them go in order of their abilities as much as for their geographical locations."

Joshua's dark expression lightened a bit, and Caleb shrugged and nodded. Again he wished the townsfolk could hear the major's praise, though precious little good it would do.

The boy clomped down the wooden steps and pointed to Caleb's pocket. "What's that?"

"Nothing."

"It doesn't look like nothing. It looks like a chicken feather."

"Your keen powers of observation are staggering. Yes, it's a chicken feather."

"Why do you have it in your pocket?"

The fiery shafts of humiliation returned, and Caleb swallowed hard. "Did you finish the chores while I was gone?"

"Yeah, but that sorrel mare's getting worse. I think she's got a case of the wobbles."

"I'll check on her."

"He staying to supper?"

" 'He' is Major Alexander to you, and no, I'll run him back to town before then. Major, this is Joshua Hualga, my assistant. Joshua, this is Major Alexander, the man who buys the horses we train."

The major sized up the boy, stuck out his hand, and gave Joshua's reluctant hand a brisk shake. "Good to meet you. You're doing good work here. McBride's horses are consistently the best turned-out mounts coming into Fort Riley. You should be proud."

"Yes sir." Joshua tucked his hands into his back pockets and lost a little of his wariness.

"I'd be interested in seeing your training methods, McBride."

The major had a reputation as a fine horseman, and his experienced eye missed nothing. He ran his hands down fore-legs, stood back and watched the animals both on the long line and under saddle, and gave some practical advice on what to do with one little bay with a tendency to bite.

They finally worked their way around to the last pen and the sorrel mare Joshua had mentioned, alone in the small pen. Joshua climbed the fence and dropped lightly into the corral. The mare turned her head to look at him but stayed under the shade shelter. Her legs splayed at odd angles, her stance wide as if bracing herself on a rolling ship deck.

"Hmm, I think your wrangler's diagnosis of the wobbles might be correct." The major tapped his trim moustache.

"Lead her around, Josh." Caleb folded his arms on the top rail. He lifted his lame foot to rest it on the bottom rail and missed the slat. Lurching, he let out a surprised grumble, mentally smacked himself for being so careless, and looked down at his boot as he lifted it again to make sure he got it placed right.

The major had clearly noticed Caleb's stumble, but he turned his attention back to the horse as if nothing had happened.

Caleb studied the mare. "At first I thought she got into some loco weed, but now I think it's more serious."

The mare swayed and lurched, keeping her head low and walking as if she couldn't quite feel the ground.

"She's worse under saddle." He pushed his hat back and swiped at the sweat on his forehead. "I haven't put a saddle on her in a week, hoping she'd come out of it, but I think she must've injured her back somehow."

The major climbed the fence and slowly approached Joshua and the horse. He ran his hand under her mane, patting and murmuring. "See if she'll back up for you, Joshua." He kept his tone low and soothing.

Though Joshua pulled back on her halter, and even put his hand on her chest, all the while commanding her to back up, the mare stood still. Her brown eyes appeared bewildered, as if begging them to help her, to tell her what had gone wrong.

"That's enough, son." Concentrating, Major Alexander started at the withers and pressed along the mare's spinal column. Bone by bone, he worked his way toward her hips. Just back of where the saddle would sit, he pressed and the mare's head came up, her eyes widened, and she skittered away from him with a neigh. Joshua hung on as she slewed around, her legs going in all directions.

Somberly, the major joined Caleb. "There's a back injury there all right. Maybe a tumor, maybe a compression fracture, but something." He fisted his hand and banged it on the top rail. "A shame. I remember purchasing this mare near Santa Barbara. Big and rangy, and certainly up to carrying an officer through the French mud."

"Nice temperament, too." A weight settled in Caleb's gut.

"Best to get it done soon. Especially if it's a tumor. She's in a bit of pain now, but that will get worse."

Joshua released his hold on the halter and loped over. "What are we going to do?"

"Nothing for it. We'll have to put her down."

The boy gnawed his lower lip, staring at the mare. "Are you

sure?" He blinked rapidly. From the bright sunshine or tears? Joshua presented such a tough face to the world. This was the first crack Caleb had been able to detect in his armor. Well, that and the hunger in his voice when he talked about studying medicine.

The major put his hand on Joshua's shoulder. The boy tensed, but he didn't shrug it away. "I'm afraid so. Maybe someday a veterinarian will invent a surgical procedure to help a horse with the wobbles, but for now the only thing we can do is put her down."

Joshua nodded. When the major dropped his hand, the boy tucked his hands into his pockets and moved a few steps away.

"I'll take care of it when I get back from town. You don't have to be here." Caleb gripped the top rail, pushing back until his arms were straight and lowering his head to stare at the ground for a moment. He hated the thought of Joshua being anywhere around when he put the mare down. An idea struck him. "In fact, if you want to, you can take Major Alexander to the depot."

Joshua's head swiveled. "Really?" His eyebrows rose. The truck was Caleb's pride and joy, and though they'd had some driving lessons, Joshua hadn't been allowed off the ranch while behind the wheel.

"I think you're ready for a trip to town." Perhaps a little reward would distract Joshua from the sadness of losing the mare.

Normally stoic features softened, and white teeth flashed. "I'd like that."

"Straight there and straight back, but don't hurry. I'd rather you got there slowly and in one piece, and I'm sure the major would, too."

As they disappeared down the long, dusty lane, Caleb pulled

the feather from his pocket. Though he'd joked with the major about keeping it, he had no desire to hang on to the offensive object. The wind fluttered it, and he opened his fingers.

The feather floated, skittered, dropped to the ground, and was borne away on the hot breeze. Just like his hopes and dreams of being with Meghan.

Chapter 11

"I sure wish we had mornings off instead of afternoons." Meghan tied a voile scarf over the top of her hat and under her chin. Digging for her gloves, she glanced at Natalie. "Are you sure you want to come with me? You could take a nap. I'll admit you look a little better since you've been working at the soda fountain, but you still don't look any too robust."

Natalie shook her head. "It's much too hot to try to sleep. At least in the automobile there will be a breeze."

Meghan threw her bag on the seat and went around to the front of the car to turn the crank. Getting permission to use the hotel's transportation hadn't been easy. She'd had to prove her driving skills not only to Mr. Stock, but to Mrs. Gregory as well. Only the fact that she wanted to go door to door appealing for Red Cross money swayed them in the end. The engine sputtered to life, and she hurried around to slip behind the wheel.

"Where are we going first?" Natalie raised her voice to be heard above the rattling.

With one hand on the wheel, Meghan dug in her bag for the map Mr. Weeks from Claypool's Department Store had drawn for her. "We'll drive north along the river for about ten miles and stop at places along the way back toward town, then, if we still have time, we can swing south and hit a few places in that direction." Though one place on the map she intended to give a wide berth. No way would she stop at Caleb McBride's. Having his name on the quilt would mean sure disaster when it came time to auction it off. In fact, if folks knew he'd contributed, she likely wouldn't get another signature at all.

That white feather. Why hadn't he stood up for himself, given his reason for not enlisting? At least had the fortitude to. . .what? What did one expect from a coward? It was like asking a lemon tree to produce apples.

Why? Why couldn't she get him out of her head? Even with concerted effort she couldn't eradicate him. He'd said he wanted nothing to do with her, she knew she wanted nothing to do with him, and yet, he occupied far too many of her thoughts and dreams.

Natalie trailed her hand out the window, cupping the breeze. She laid her head back on the seat and closed her eyes. At least the road was fairly smooth, though the dust they raised coated everything. Perhaps Meghan should've taken Mr. Stock up on his offer of driving goggles.

Flat, sandy desert stretched out on both sides of the road, though on their right, a greenish-gray smudge marked the brush that grew along the riverbank. When she'd reached the farthest noted point on Mr. Week's map, she turned in along a narrow, rutted path toward a house in the distance.

"How'd it go at this one?" Natalie poured some water from the jug they'd brought with them onto her handkerchief and dabbed her throat and swiped the back of her neck. Her cheeks bore pink blotches, and the hair at her temples clung to her skin. The car roasted in the sunshine.

Taking the jug, Meghan let some of the lukewarm water trickle into her mouth. She wrinkled her nose, both at the tepid fluid and the reception at the house. "Pass. She's got no money and too many mouths to feed."

At most of the houses along the road the answer was the same with varying degrees of animosity. Some were apologetic, some antagonistic, and in all, she garnered only two donations. Four dollars. With each stop, the temperature rose and Meghan's spirits fell.

"Don't be discouraged. It's four more dollars than you had before." Natalie shifted on the seat and pulled her blouse away from her skin. "Maybe we should call it quits for today. It's hot enough to melt rocks. It's got to be well over a hundred degrees, and there's no shade out here."

A dull headache had started at the base of Meghan's skull. "I'm not ready to give up yet. There's still the south road. Things might be better there."

Natalie passed her the water jug. "There's not much left. Maybe we should be done."

"No." She shook her head, surprised when a wave of dizziness washed over her. "I can drop you off at the hotel if you want, but I can't afford to wait another week to go out again. I don't have many afternoons off between now and when the quilt needs to be done." Lifting the water jug, weakness made her arms tremble, and water sloshed onto her chin and ran down her neck. The momentary coolness jarred her, and she blinked. Almost immediately, evaporation set in, leaving her parched.

She gripped the steering wheel and pointed the nose of the car south. The clock was ticking. They only had a couple more hours before they had to have the car back to the hotel. She pressed on the gas pedal. "When we get done, I'm going to go hide in the basement refrigerator, and I don't care if Mrs. Gregory finds me. If we weren't so rushed for time, I'd do it now."

"Before we hide in the cold store, I think we should stop for some ice cream at the soda fountain. I'd love to get a cold-food headache and shiver a little bit." Natalie consulted the map. "There are six places marked on here."

"So five more stops."

"Six."

"No, five. I'm not stopping at Caleb's place."

"Are you sure? How will he feel if he knows you stopped everywhere else but not his place?"

She shrugged, concentrating on keeping the car in the center of the road. "He said he didn't want to see me anymore, and the feeling is mutual."

"What?"

She squinted. Heat waves shimmered on the horizon, obliterating the distance. The road worsened, bouncing and jouncing them, kicking them from rut to rut. "He won't be hurt if we don't call. He'll be relieved."

None of the first four houses produced any subscriptions. The last one she wanted to visit lay on the far side of Caleb's property. Was it even worth it to go that far? She checked her timepiece against the map. They could make it there and back to town in time if they hurried.

She blinked, trying to clear her eyes. Black spots encroached at the edge of her vision. She shook her head. What was wrong with her? Was she getting sick?

"Meghan?" Natalie gripped the door with one hand and braced her other hand on the dashboard.

She sounded as if she were standing at the end of a long hallway, miles from Meghan. "Huh?"

"There's something wrong with the car. Look." She took her hand off the dash to point at the hood. Steam leaked around the edges and through the vents in the black metal. Slowly, Meghan pulled to the side of the road and the car bumped to a stop. She turned off the motor, though it took her a couple of tries to find the ignition. Wobbly didn't begin to describe how she felt. Maybe it was something she ate?

"I shink. . ." She tried again. "I think we overheated the car." Why did her head feel like it had been stuffed with pillow ticking?

"Meghan." Natalie grabbed her shoulder and shook her. Waves of nausea sloshed through her middle, and the black spots in her vision grew bigger and closer together.

"Meghan, what's wrong?" Natalie's voice got slower and farther away as darkness claimed her.

Caleb leaned forward in the saddle, relishing the breeze pressing against his chest and fluttering his shirt. Though it was a bit on the early side for his evening ride out into the desert, he'd been so restless at the house he thought he might go crazy. Joshua's mother had come by for a visit, and he'd wanted to give the mother and son privacy. With him in the house, Mrs. Hualga wouldn't say a word.

His mount, a sturdy sorrel with plenty of stamina and very little speed, cantered over the hard-packed sand at a steady pace.

"You'd be better off on a bridle path back east, teaching youngsters at some riding school, old boy." Caleb patted the gelding's sweating shoulder. But in another week or so, he and his corral mates would be on a train headed to Fort Riley and the next stop on their journey to the war zone.

Pulling his mount back to a trot and then a walk, Caleb removed his hat and swiped at the sweat on his forehead. The ground sloped upward away from the river, and clumps of dusty brush dotted the landscape. The temperature hovered somewhere in the midnineties, down a dozen degrees from that afternoon, but still scorching. As they topped out on the rise, he made out the dark, wavering smudge of Needles in the distance.

From here, he could see just how isolated the town was, a small dot on the map, an island in a sea of sand and cactus. Insulated. They protected their own, and they were none too accepting of strangers. If one hadn't been born in Needles, or one didn't work for the railroad in some capacity, inclusion and acceptance into the community was a fairytale wish.

A tumbleweed bounced across the road, and the placid sorrel merely flicked his ears and studied it, never breaking stride. Caleb watched it roll and spin until it disappeared down the far side of a sandbank. He was so much like that tumbleweed. Needles hadn't embraced him, and as soon as the war was over or the need for horse-trainers for the cavalry ended, he'd brush the dust of this town off his boots, climb aboard the train, and head somewhere else. No ties, no roots. . .he shook his head. . . no home.

No Meghan. He'd seen the look of disappointment, of embarrassment, when that woman had handed him that feather. Though Meghan had held out and taken his part longer than he'd thought she would, in the end the opinions and accusations of the people of Needles had drawn her away.

As he had known they would. He'd been a fool to think otherwise. And he'd rather she turned away from him for a reason that wasn't true than to have her know about his shameful secret and reject him because of it. He'd lived through that once with Patricia. He didn't know if he could live through it again.

Enough feeling sorry for himself. Things were as they were, and there was nothing he could or would do about them. He was alone by choice and inclination. Even if the town of Needles had embraced him like a long-lost son, he'd still want to move on, to be alone. It was safer, for his heart and his peace of mind.

On the verge of turning back to the house, something caught his attention out of the corner of his eye. Squinting against the sun and cupping his hands at his temples, he strained to see. A dark object wavered on the road ahead. Big, like an automobile, but no dust plume followed it. Who would be stopping out here in the desert in the late afternoon? It was hot enough to fry a stove lid over easy.

Curious, he heeled the sorrel into a lope. As he approached, the heat waves resolved themselves into a dusty black car at the side of the road. Car trouble? A lost tourist? This road saw about as much traffic as the vegetable tray at a pie social. Only one more ranch lay beyond his, and Wilbur Frame was even more of a recluse than Caleb tried to be, always pottering among the rocks, prospecting for who knew what. Except for Joshua's mother and Major Alexander, Doc was the only person who ever drove this far out of town. This car was much too big to be Doc's battered old runabout, and Joshua's family didn't have a vehicle.

Someone huddled beside the car, and uneasiness tightened the back of his neck. Something was definitely wrong. He jabbed the sorrel in the ribs, wishing now he'd chosen a more fleet-footed mount.

The mass beside the car resolved itself into two people as one of them stood and shaded her—it was definitely a her— eyes. When she spied him, she waved her arm, beckoning him before kneeling beside the other figure once more.

The car was big, and as he approached, he recognized it as belonging to the El Garces. The kneeling girl was Natalie Daviot. A flash of red hair from the prone figure had his heart clogging his throat. He pulled his horse up a few paces away and swung from the saddle.

"What's wrong? What are you doing out here?"

Natalie, her normally pale face raspberry red in the heat, looked up. "The car overheated then Meghan passed out, and I don't know what to do." She fanned Meghan's face with her hand.

"Where's your water?" He unclipped one of his canteens from his saddle and unscrewed the cap. Kneeling beside Natalie, he touched Meghan's skin. Paper-dry, and her pulse leaped under her jaw.

"We ran out." She pointed to the empty jug on the running board. Her movements were slow, as if the heat had taken all of her energy and will.

"That's all you brought with you?" Cupping the back of Meghan's head, he raised her up, gently bringing the canteen to her lips. "How long have you been out here, and what on earth possessed you to head out into the desert by yourselves without enough water to wet a handkerchief?"

Meghan's eyes rolled, and she sputtered as the water hit her tongue. Mumbles that became words leaked from her dry lips. Her eyelashes fluttered, revealing her green eyes clouded and disoriented. "Lars. Hold on, Lars. I'll get that ambulance. I love you, Lars." She went limp once more.

Lars? Who was Lars? A shaft of jealousy ripped through him. He'd been a double-fool. No way a girl as pretty and lively as Meghan would be unattached, and he'd never asked her, partially for fear of what she would answer. He chose to hide his disappointment behind anger.

"What are you doing out here with no water?" His barking tone made Natalie jump.

"We were gathering subscriptions for the Red Cross. Is she going to die?" Her eyes reddened but no tears leaked out. She was probably too dehydrated. And she had no idea of the danger they had put themselves in.

"I've got to get Meghan back to the house, and I need your help. Get my horse." He lowered Meghan's head once more and tipped the contents of the canteen over her hair and splashed her face and throat. Natalie drew his horse close. He wanted to curse his weak leg as he contemplated the logistics of getting Meghan onto the horse and mounting behind her.

But it had to be done. If he didn't get her temperature down, she was going to die.

"Unhook that other canteen." He tucked his hand behind Meghan's shoulders and scooped behind her knees with his other. Lurching to his feet, he stumbled against the side of the car. Heat from the blistering metal shot through his thin shirt, and he jerked away. "Help me get her into the saddle."

Between them, they managed to get her situated, though she was no help at all. She lolled and sagged, unconscious and unresponsive. Using the running board as a mounting block, he scrambled up behind her, wrapping his arms around her waist and leaning her back against his chest.

Though he hated to leave Natalie behind, he had no choice. His horse couldn't carry three, and he had to get Meghan to help as soon as possible. "Don't leave the car. Stay in the shade and make sure you drink the entire contents of that canteen. I'll send someone back for you as soon as I can. Don't stir a step, you hear me?"

"Just take care of her. I'll be fine."

The ride to his house, though less than two miles, seemed to take forever. Thankful for the sturdy sorrel who seemed not to notice his double burden, Caleb prayed as he hadn't prayed in a long time.

Please, Lord, don't take her. She's so young and full of life. She hasn't hardly even started to live, and she's got such big plans. Please, Lord, don't take her.

His prayer muscles were as atrophied as his left leg. Though he had long ago asked Jesus to be his Savior, he had a hard time not resenting the fact that God had chosen to send infantile paralysis his way and cut him off from the love of a family. Since Patricia's rejection and the move to Needles, there were some parts of his heart that were as dry as the desert around him. His spiritual life had been gathering dust.

A wavy blur appeared in the distance, resolving itself into house, sheds, corrals, and garage as he approached. Thankfully, Mrs. Hualga and Joshua still sat on the front porch. He rode straight to the nearest corral and swung down. Meghan toppled off into his arms.

Joshua pounded across the dirt yard. "What happened? What's Meghan doing out here?"

"Get the truck out of the garage. The hotel car broke down on the road and there's another girl out there. I need you to drive out and get her. Ask your mother to come here and help me with Meghan." He hitched her higher into his arms. "And open the corral gate."

Not bothering to hide his limp, he crossed the corral to the sunshade and lowered Meghan, clothes and all, into the water trough. Getting her cooled off was his first priority. Her hair floated in the water like red seaweed, and her face was deathly pale.

Mrs. Hualga stooped beside him and put her hand on Meghan's chest. "Her heart is racing."

"What else can we do?" He looked up into her brown, impassive face, so like Joshua's.

"Keep her there. I will be back." She padded toward the house.

The truck sputtered to life and rattled out of the garage.

"There's another girl, not as bad off as Meghan, but she's

going to need help, too." Caleb called after Mrs. Hualga, who raised her hand in acknowledgment but kept walking.

Something nudged him between the shoulder blades, and he turned on his knee. His horse clopped over and stuck his muzzle into the trough. Caleb grabbed the reins and pulled him away. After running in the heat like he had, the last thing he needed was a bellyful of water. He should be walked until he was cooled off, rubbed down, and brushed. But there wasn't time. Meghan came first.

"Lars?" she whispered.

"Can you hear me?" He cupped the back of her head, wiping her cheeks and forehead with his wet fingers. "Meghan?"

No response. Even her lips were white. Her freckles stood out, and her skin was as silky as a baby's. His suntanned, work-roughened hand seemed so coarse in comparison. But she was so still. So deathly still.

Who was Lars?

Mrs. Hualga returned. "Bring her to the house."

He lifted Meghan, streaming water and still unconscious, into his arms. He jerked his chin toward his horse. "Please tie those reins to the fence. I'll take care of him when I get her inside."

His leg radiated weakness, and afraid he would stumble and drop her, he shuffled his foot along the ground, not daring to lift it lest it buckle under him. He'd done too much today, taxed his twisted limb too far. Soon it would be a knot of cramps and twitches. If Mrs. Hualga noticed his halting gait, she said nothing. He got Meghan into the house and into his bedroom. Mrs. Hualga had pulled back the thin blanket, and Caleb lay Meghan on the sheet. Joshua's mother bustled in and elbowed him out of the way.

"What can I do?"

"See to the horse. Then bring water and newspaper and thermometer. You have ice?"

"I do." An old-fashioned icebox that went through ice at a ridiculous rate. He usually bought a block of ice when he went into town for groceries, then raced like a madman back home to get it into the insulated compartment in the top of the icebox before it turned to water. Thankfully, he'd gotten groceries the day before. There should be at least half a block left. A block tended to last about three days, and after that, he made do with powdered milk and canned vegetables and fruit until his next trip to town.

"Bring broken ice."

He tended to his horse, stripping the saddle and bridle and haltering the animal. Tying him to the fence in the shade, he left a single bucket, a quarter full of water where the horse could reach it. When Joshua returned, he'd send him out to finish the job. He swung by the tool shed for a hammer.

Working the pump in the kitchen, he filled a pitcher and a bucket with water. The box of medicaments on the linen closet shelf gave up the thermometer. Outside his bedroom, he tapped on the door. "Here's what you wanted. I'll bring the ice as soon as I can."

Please, Lord, don't take her. Why isn't she waking up? Why was she so stupid as to be careening around the desert in that car? It was that quilt. That stupid signature quilt. She was like Don Quixote, charging around, heedless of danger.

He hefted the dripping block of ice out of the icebox and set it on a kitchen towel. Wrapping it tightly, he picked up his hammer and smashed away until he'd reduced the block to manageable chunks.

"I've got the ice." He tapped on the bedroom door once more. A rattling rumble came through the open front door down the hall. Joshua returning with Natalie. Mrs. Hualga called for Caleb to enter. She straightened from the bed, studying the thermometer she'd just removed from Meghan's mouth.

"What does it say?"

She shook her head. "It's bad."

He studied the glass tube. The mercury hovered near the one hundred and four degree mark. His mouth went dry.

"Newspaper?" Mrs. Hualga took the ice bowl from him.

"I forgot it. I'll be right back." Meghan lay swathed in wet sheets. Her bare arms and lower legs stuck out, and her lashes fanned her cheeks. She was so still, he had to concentrate for a moment to make sure she was breathing.

"Go get the newspaper." Mrs. Hualga's sharp voice uprooted his feet.

Joshua and Natalie came up the front steps, the boy with his arm around the young woman's waist. Caleb snatched the newspaper off the front hall table. "Bring her in here. We can treat them together."

Natalie's face was still an alarming shade of red, and more worrisome, she wasn't sweating a bit. Mrs. Hualga tut-tutted, sent the men from the room, and took over.

Caleb leaned against the wall and took his weight off his left leg. "Thank you for bringing Miss Daviot." He scrubbed his hand down his cheek. "I pray they'll both be all right."

"Ma's dealt with heat sickness before." Joshua stuck his hands into his back pockets, shifting his weight. "Anything I can do?"

For a moment Caleb couldn't think. His entire being was focused on Meghan. "I left my horse tied up in the corral. He should be cooled out enough to turn in with the other horses. Then I want you to drive to town and get the doc. Stop by the hotel and let someone know where the girls are and that we'll bring them and the car back as soon as we can."

The bedroom door opened once more. "Come, I need you." Mrs. Hualga grabbed his arm and pulled him inside.

Natalie lay beside Meghan, draped in damp sheets. She gave a weak smile and raised her fingers an inch off the bed. Meghan didn't stir.

"More water." Mrs. Hualga was a woman of few words. She held up the bucket. "And towels."

As Caleb manned the pump in the kitchen, the truck rattled out of the drive once more. Joshua might be prickly and defensive, but he was a young man who could be counted upon in an emergency. What would he have done today without the Hualgas? Balancing a stack of towels in one hand and the bucket of water in the other, he limped down the hall.

She took the towels and bucket and pushed him into the chair beside the bed. "Here." He found himself clutching the newspaper. Did she expect him to read it?

Rolling her eyes, she folded it in half. "Fan." She moved the air over Meghan's face, and then dipped a cloth in water to moisten her skin. "Water, then fan."

Natalie raised her head from the pillow, but Mrs. Hualga pressed her small, brown hand against Natalie's shoulder.

"Lie still." She bustled out and returned with a drinking glass. Ice clinked, water poured. "Drink."

Caleb dipped the edge of a towel in the bucket of water at his feet and trickled it over Meghan's arm. Mrs. Hualga took a section of the newspaper and began fanning Natalie.

After an eternity, a groan escaped Meghan's cracked lips, and she stirred. "My head."

"Shhh." He clasped her fingers and gently pressed them into the mattress. "You have to be still."

Her lashes fluttered, and confused, pained green eyes

appeared. "Caleb?" She blinked, squinting. "Where am I?"

"You're at my house. Your car broke down in the desert."

She stiffened. "Natalie?"

"Easy. She's right beside you. Joshua's gone for the doctor."

Mrs. Hualga nudged his elbow. "Make her drink." She held out a glass of water. "All of it. Then more, but slow."

He pressed the glass to Meghan's lips, letting sips of water trickle inside her mouth. Slowly, aware of her headache, he eased wet strands of hair off her cheek and temple. On the far side of the bed, Mrs. Hualga tucked a towel-wrapped bundle of ice behind Natalie's neck. She quickly fashioned two more bundles and slipped them under Natalie's arms.

"Here, like that." Thrusting a bundle at Caleb, she pointed to Meghan's neck and arms. "Keep fanning."

The color subsided from Natalie's face and returned to Meghan's over the next half-hour. Pulses slowed, breathing became more regular, and the knots in Caleb's muscles began to relax. Perhaps they were out of danger.

Meghan didn't mention Lars again. In fact, she said nothing, just lay on the bed, drinking when told and not opening her eyes.

Footsteps clomped on the front porch, and Doc Bates came into the bedroom. "What have you girls been doing to yourselves?" He adjusted his glasses and set his medical bag on the edge of the bed. Opening the bag, he rummaged, making glass clink. Gripping his thermometer, he rounded the footboard and went to Natalie, his brow wrinkled. "Open."

Resentment jabbed his ribs that the doc would automatically go first to Natalie.

"Doc, it's Meghan who was passed out. Don't you think you should check her first?"

Meghan clasped his hand. "Don't. I'm all right."

He leaned close to her ear. "But you were worse off than Natalie was. Your temperature threatened to blow the end of the thermometer right off."

"But then you helped me." Her voice still sounded too weak and slow for his liking. Meghan was a firebrand, a crusader, and righter of wrongs. She was full of life and movement and color. To see her so still and unresponsive had jarred him more than he'd realized. Her fingers entwined with his as her eyes closed.

Doc read the thermometer, shook it down, and stuck it back in Natalie's mouth. "Joshua should be here soon. I came in my own car, and I believe he was going to stop at the hotel. Caleb, step outside so I can do a thorough examination of both these young ladies." Doc took his stethoscope from his bag. He looped it around his neck and lifted Natalie's wrist to check her pulse. "I think, thanks to the good nursing they received from Mrs. Hualga, that they're both going to be just fine."

Caleb leaned against the hallway wall, as drained as a leaky bucket.

Joshua joined him there. "I stopped by the hotel on the way out of town. That French chef fellow sent a block of ice, and Mr. Stock said not to rush back. Make sure the ladies are going to be fine first."

"What did Mrs. Gregory say?"

"I didn't see her, thankfully."

"Probably just as well. What did you do with the ice?"

"Stuck it in the icebox."

"Great. Let's bust it up and make some more cold packs in case Doc needs them. And I could use a cold drink. How about you?" He clapped Joshua on the shoulder and followed him to the kitchen.

Twenty minutes later, Doc and Mrs. Hualga joined them. "Ah, iced tea, just what I need." Doc rubbed his hands together.

Caleb poured. "What's the verdict?"

"They'll be back to their old selves in no time. For now, they need rest, fluids, and no more gallivanting around the desert in the middle of a summer afternoon. What on earth were they doing out there?"

"It's that ridiculous quilt." Caleb rubbed his fingers down his glass. "They were looking for donations for a signature quilt Meghan's making to raise funds for the war effort."

Doc pursed his lips. "A worthy cause, though I'd think they'd be more sensible about their timing. Not even a Gila monster would stir in this heat."

"It might be a worthy cause, but if they'd have died out there in the desert—" He broke off. Now that they were out of danger, the enormity of their folly smote him. Someone needed to explain to them, to Meghan in particular, how stupid they'd been.

Meghan dozed and woke, dozed and woke over the next couple of hours. Doc checked on her, as did Mrs. Hualga, dousing her skin with water, forcing her to drink, taking her temperature. Natalie lay beside her, sleeping peacefully. If only Meghan could drift into a deep slumber and forget the pounding in her head. She ran all the metaphors for headache she could think of through her mind, but none seemed adequate to describe the pain in her skull. At last, some strength returned, and she forced herself to sit up and reach for her dress draped on the foot of the bed.

"You should lie still." Natalie rolled over and sat up slowly.

"So should you." Fumbling with the buttons, she squeezed her eyes shut for a moment. "My head is killing me, and lying there thinking about it isn't helping." Nor was thinking about how little she'd accomplished in the way of procuring donations and signatures for her quilt. The one thousand-dollar goal seemed further away than ever.

"We should be thankful God sent Caleb McBride to rescue us. You could've died out there."

"We both could've." Meghan didn't know how she felt about Caleb's rescue. Part of her got all warm and swimmy thinking of him bearing her away on his horse—if Natalie's recounting could be believed—like some gallant, brave knight of old. Another part of her cringed and skittered about. After what she'd witnessed in town with him refusing to stand up for himself, to give an accounting of why he hadn't enlisted, she couldn't help but be disgusted. How could a man be so brave and yet cowardly at the same time?

A tap sounded on the door, and Natalie finished buttoning up her blouse before opening it. Caleb stood in the doorway, his weight shifted on one leg as it often was. Meghan's stomach muscles tightened, and she looked away.

"Are you sure you two should be up?" He stepped inside, his boots rasping unevenly on the floor.

Natalie balled up the sheets they'd been wrapped in and gathered soggy towels. "I'm fine, but I think Meghan should stay in bed."

"We should get back to town. Mrs. Gregory will be having a fit already. And Mr. Stock must be wondering where his car is."

Caleb took the bedclothes from Natalie and dumped them into a basket beside the dresser. "Don't worry about these. I'll tend to them. There's iced tea in the kitchen. Do you want me to bring you some?"

"No, I'd like to go out and say thank you to the doctor and to that young man who came to get me out on the road. What is his name?"

"Joshua. Joshua Hualga."

Natalie disappeared, and Meghan became acutely aware that she and Caleb were alone in his bedroom. She bent and picked up her shoe, her head throbbing and a bit of dizziness swirling at her temples.

He cleared his throat. "Don't worry about rushing back to town. Joshua told Mr. Stock where you were when he fetched Doc out here. As for the car, Joshua and I will drive out there and refill the radiator once the sun goes down, and we'll see that it gets back to the hotel."

She nodded, her insides swooping. "Natalie tells me you came to my rescue again. Thank you. That's twice you've saved my life."

Shrugging, he leaned against the dresser. "How are you feeling?"

"Better. Thanks to you and Joshua's mother." Weakness flowed through her arms, and her shoe weighed a ton. She forced herself to tug it on and planted her foot on the floor to work her toes all the way inside.

"It was a close-run thing. You were babbling and passing out. You scared about ten years off my life."

She'd scared herself. "I'm sorry. The car overheated, and I guess we did, too."

He rubbed his palm against the back of his neck. "What were you doing out there in the first place? You could've been killed."

"I know. Good thing you came along. We were near to roasting." She tried to keep her tone light, to push away the fear of nearly dying. "It's hot enough to bake a lizard."

His brows slanted downward, and his mouth hardened. "This is no joking matter. As much trouble as you are always in, you need a full-time keeper."

Jamming her foot into her other shoe, she straightened. "I do not." She pressed her fingertips to her temple, regretting her loud tone.

"Yes, you do. You're always leaping before you look, expecting others to pull you out of your troubles and save your neck. When are you going to grow up and realize the world is a dangerous place?"

"I've said I'm sorry. What more do you want?"

He crossed the room and grabbed her by the shoulders, lifting her up and giving her a shake that, while not rough, awakened a new wave of agony in her head. "I want you to promise me you'll never be so foolish again. I want you to stop taking risks. You're so busy tilting at windmills and charging fortifications, you don't stop to think of the danger you put yourself in. And this time it wasn't just you. You could've killed Natalie, too, and what for? For a blanket? Because you want to get in good with the Red Cross and Mrs. Gregory and make a big name for yourself by raising a thousand dollars, you're willing to put yourself and your friend in jeopardy."

Stung by his harsh tone, she spit back. "How dare you speak to me about taking risks? At least I'm not afraid. You won't enlist. You won't even speak up for yourself when someone calls you a coward. You just stand there and take it."

Anger sparked in his eyes, and something else, pain, a deep hurt that had her regretting her harsh words even as they flew from her lips. That is, until he spoke again, wounding her, accusing her.

"You don't know what you're talking about. You rarely do. Instead of getting the facts, you jump to conclusions and leap into the fray. My reasons for not enlisting are my own. I'm entitled to my secrets, just as you are yours. You've kept things from me."

"What secrets have I kept from you?" Surely he wasn't talking about Natalie's marriage. He couldn't know about that, and why would he care if he did?

"What about Lars?" He curled his lip.

Meghan blinked. "What about him?"

"You said you loved him."

"Of course I love him." She bunched her forehead. "Are you sure you aren't the one who had too much sun?" When had she talked to Caleb about Lars? As a rule she didn't say much about him, but she didn't exactly make a secret of having a brother "over there."

"And I bet he's a soldier."

She squared her shoulders and lifted her chin. "He is. He enlisted right away. While I long for him to come home, and I'm afraid for his safety, I'm so proud of him, of his courage, I could burst. He's the reason I'm raising the money for the ambulance. And I don't care what it costs me. If he can be brave and sacrifice, so can I. He's a real man who knows his obligation to his country and those he loves. He'd never shirk his duty. He's no coward."

"Like me, you mean. Why don't you come out and say it? A man like me would never be worthy of a girl like you." A look of tortured anguish twisted Caleb's face, so near her own. His fingers tightened on her arms, and as if he couldn't help himself, his lips came down and claimed hers, hard and insistent, as if his frustration had finally outpaced his normal, tight control.

She forgot about her headache. She forgot about being angry. She forgot about everything. The kiss started out fierce and angry, but in a split-second it changed to something else altogether. His lips were wonderfully warm, his skin raspy as his whiskers brushed against her cheek. He smelled of sunshine and horses and hot desert air. Her hands crept up his shirtfront and edged around his neck. His hands spanned her waist as if to steady himself, and then found their way around her, bringing her tight up against him.

This is wrong. This can't be happening. Stop it! Like a scream, the thoughts echoed in her head.

Balling her fists, she shoved against him, breaking the kiss.

Immediately he pulled away, letting go of her waist and stepping back. His chest heaved, and his eyes glowed hot.

Her own breath came in gasps, and hot shame swirled in her ears and up her cheeks. What kind of woman was she to allow a man who insulted her one moment to kiss her senseless the next? "How dare you? You want me to say right out what I think? All right, I will. Caleb McBride, you disgust me. You avoid going to war when every able-bodied man in the country is answering the call. You hide out here on this barren spit of land training horses to go into battle. Horses that will show more courage in one day of wartime service than you will your whole life. And you take money from the same government you are afraid to fight for. It's despicable. You, sir, are a coward, and I wish I had a whole fistful of white feathers, because you would deserve them all." Her hand rose and smacked his cheekbone. "Don't ever come near me again."

Cupping his offended cheek he stepped back another pace, stumbling and knocking his shoulder against the doorjamb. His face had gone white under his tan, and a bleak, cold remoteness had replaced the heat in his eyes. "Don't worry. I won't. A person can only take so much sanctimonious claptrap, and I get enough from Mrs. Gregory and the rest of this two-bit town. When you get back to Needles, be sure to congratulate your head waitress. She'll be so proud to know you've turned out just like her."

He left her, and she sagged back onto the bed, holding her

face in her hands. Her head threatened to split in two. And why shouldn't it? Her heart was already shattered.

Caleb avoided the kitchen and headed to the back porch. What had he been thinking? His cheek stung from the impact of her hand, and his pride stung from the acidic accusations she'd hurled at him. In spite of all his warnings to himself, he'd allowed himself to spin dreams about Meghan Thorson, about how she would be different from every other woman he'd ever met. About how she might be the one to heal those broken places in his heart and love him in spite of his faults and flaws, his infirmities and insecurities. About how together they could be the family he'd always longed for. And he'd allowed those dreams to override his common sense to the point that he'd actually kissed her. Not just a peck either.

His chest still lurched in breaths of hot summer air, and weakness raced along his limbs. For an instant, for a suspended moment in time, everything had been perfect. Anger had fallen away. They'd stopped being adversaries and melded together in a giving and taking that had started a firestorm of longing raging in his heart and opened realms of possibilities he'd only dreamed of before.

But it had all come crashing down, as it always did when he dared to risk his heart.

She hated him. She thought him a coward. She was so enamored of soldiers and the Red Cross and her cause, she would never see him as anything but a yellow dog.

Not to mention this Lars fellow, whom she admitted outright that she loved. Lars the brave soldier who had enlisted the moment the call went out. Who was probably at this very moment covering himself with glory on a European battlefield.

He leaned against the weathered siding and smashed his heel backward into the gray boards. Pain shot up his leg, but he didn't care, bashing his foot into the wall again and again. He gripped handfuls of hair, gulping in breaths and striving for some semblance of control.

Why? Why, God? Why did You destine me to be a cripple? Why can't I be whole so I can prove I'm no coward? Why can't I be a real man and win the love of a woman? Why won't You let me be worthy?

Sinking to the porch floor, he rested his crossed arms on his good knee and let his useless foot sprawl on the boards, pressing his forehead into his wrists. He never should've kissed her, and yet, he hadn't been able to resist the need to claim her, if only for a moment. And though he might regret a lot of things in his life, he knew he'd never regret giving in to that overwhelming impulse. It changed everything, and yet it changed nothing.

She loathed him. And who could blame her? He loathed himself.

Chapter 12

"Miss Thorson, nicely done with table seven. The customers were demanding, but you've managed to satisfy them all very well." Mrs. Gregory stopped beside Meghan clutching her ever-present clipboard. "I'm glad to see you've finally settled into your job."

"Thank you, Mrs. Gregory." Meghan didn't know whether to laugh or cry. From the moment she'd arrived in Needles, she'd longed for any kind word of approval from the head waitress. Now that she'd gotten it, it seemed a hollow victory indeed.

Nothing felt right inside or out. Lethargy and listlessness stalked her. All her normal drive and verve had deserted her, and she went through the motions of her job automatically. The only thing that brought her any joy at all was the quilt project and even that had become burdensome.

She cleared empty plates and removed centerpieces to replace the tablecloths with new, snowy linen before the next train arrived. Sweat trickled between her shoulder blades. She'd asked a long-time Needles resident when the heat wave would break, and he'd laughed in her face. Maybe around Christmas. She shook her head, realizing Mrs. Gregory was still speaking.

"As soon as you finish setting the tables, go sit down and have some ice water with the others. We can't have you passing out from the heat again."

Though brusque, Mrs. Gregory's voice held a hint of concern, another new facet. She'd been particularly solicitous ever since Doc Bates had returned the girls to the hotel with several admonishments to both them and Mrs. Gregory about all the staff taking care in the heat. He'd ordered Meghan and Natalie to bed for the rest of that day and the next, and to half days of work over the weekend before allowing them to return to normal duties.

Meghan let the batwing doors flop behind her as she carried an armful of table linens to the hamper in the corner of the kitchen. A thermometer beside the back door showed the temperature to be hovering near one hundred five. She resisted the urge to cover up the mercury and numbers. Knowing just how hot it was made things worse.

A mountain of tablecloths and napkins spilled over the edge of the hamper, and with a sigh, Meghan added hers, shoving at the pile to make it stay. Tugging, she pulled the balky cart away from the wall and wheeled it toward the laundry room. The only sound in the darkened laundry was the squeak of the wheels and her footsteps gritting on the tile. In deference to the heat, the laundry staff now only worked at night when the temperature dipped into the eighties.

When she returned with an empty cart, the dining room girls were seated around a plain work table in the kitchen drinking iced tea. Nobody talked much, conserving their energy for the customers to come. The kitchen staff continued to work around them, though without the customary bustle and noise. The chef had altered the menu to suit the temperatures, and most of the dishes were served cold.

Mrs. Gregory motioned to the empty chair beside herself. "Sit down. We've got awhile before the two-thirty rolls in."

Plopping down, Meghan reached for a pitcher and glass. Ice clinked, and when she raised the glass to her lips, the cold tea tasted so good, she almost sighed.

The head waitress looked up from her clipboard. "I'm glad

we have a few moments to visit before getting back to work. I wanted to ask you how your quilt project was coming along."

The quilt. For the past week, ever since her disastrous trip into the desert and the fight with Caleb, Meghan had thrown herself into gathering names and embroidering the quilt. She'd even unbent so far as to allow Natalie to help with the sewing. It was as if she had to make a success of the quilt just to prove to herself that Caleb's accusations had been wrong.

"Better now that more donations are rolling in. Mr. Claypool put up a notice in his store along with a sign-up sheet and collection box. And one of the schoolteachers sent home a letter to all the parents at the school. The children made it part of their back-to-school first week activities." Their involvement in the project had greatly encouraged Meghan. She only needed a handful of new signatures and donations to fill the quilt.

"That's good. As the chairperson of the Needles chapter of the Red Cross, I'm responsible to see that pledges are filled. I had my doubts as to your ability to finish the quilt and raise the funds you've promised, but you've made great progress. You're sure you'll have it done?"

"Yes, especially with Natalie's help. Thank you for allowing her to work on it at the soda fountain when she doesn't have any customers." This concession had baffled and pleased Meghan when Mrs. Gregory had offered. "I know the money we raise is going for such a good cause. I haven't heard from my brother in a while, but his last letter spoke so highly of the Red Cross workers over there. He said knowing that medical care is close by gives him and his comrades courage to face the enemy."

Mrs. Gregory patted her pocket, crinkling some paper inside. "I finally heard from Jasper this week. He's working with the quartermaster's department on rations and supplies for the troops. Isn't that wonderful?" The lines in her brow softened, and her lips quivered, losing a bit of their perpetual pucker.

"Wonderful." And it was, for Mrs. Gregory. She knew her son wasn't on the front lines, wasn't in a trench somewhere waiting for the horrifying word to go "over the top." Wondering if the next breath he took might bring with it mustard gas or phosgene. Wondering if he'd die by bullet or mortar shell or sickness.

Her heart constricted. No word had come from Lars in over a month. Mother's last letter had been full of worry and bits of news she'd gathered from the papers, things she couldn't talk about with Meghan's father. Papa insisted that Lars would be fine. He wouldn't hear any talk to the contrary. But Mama was worried about Papa, too. He'd grown quieter, withdrawn, sitting each evening brooding on the front porch until the mosquitoes drove him inside.

Mrs. Gregory leaned close and patted Meghan's arm. "I have to say, you're a different girl since you had your heat sickness. You've finally lost your impetuosity. You've become levelheaded and devoted to your work in a new way. I asked Miss Daviot if she could account for your new, sober outlook, but she said she didn't know. I have an idea that you've finally come to your senses about that Caleb McBride. If that's the case, I can only say how thankful I am. You're much better off devoting your time and attention to your job and to the support of our soldiers. A man who won't don the uniform and serve his country isn't worthy of your notice."

Every girl around the table listened in and didn't even pretend not to. Heat that had nothing to do with the outside temperature sloshed through Meghan's middle and made its way into her cheeks.

"You are over your fascination with Caleb McBride, aren't you?" The head waitress's eyes pinpointed Meghan.

Her skin prickled, and she didn't imagine that several of the girls leaned in. Dryness invaded her mouth, and she raised her glass, both to drink and to stall for time. Images of Caleb flashed before her eyes, just as they did every night before she went to sleep. His handsome face, his wounded eyes, his gentle care of her.

She blinked, reminding herself to consider the masked look he'd worn when presented with a chicken feather, the anger and fear in his eyes when he'd yelled at her, and the almost loathing twist to his features when she'd slapped his face for kissing her.

And that kiss. The more she told herself to forget it, the more it came to mind. Powerful, earth-shaking, life-changing.

"Well?" Mrs. Gregory's eyebrows drew together at Meghan's hesitation.

She swallowed. "Yes, ma'am. I'm over Caleb McBride."

Later that evening, Meghan leaned against the door and dragged her lace headband off her hair. Closing her eyes, she let her muscles relax.

"Another long shift?" Natalie's rocker creaked.

Meghan dragged herself upright and tossed the headband on the dresser. "Seventy-five for supper. Everyone's temper is frayed to the breaking point with the heat, and one of the girls dropped an entire tray of dirty dishes in the dining room right in the middle of service. China and silverware went everywhere." She slipped out of her shoes and hiked her skirts to unclip her stockings. Rolling them off, she sighed, wiggling her toes against the tile floor. "I thought we'd never get it cleaned up. How about you? How'd the soda fountain go?"

"The usual rush just before the train left. Lots of soldiers.

Seems they all wanted some ice cream to take with them. Mr. Stock even came in to help me when the line started snaking out the door." She poked her needle in and out of a quilt block, drawing the red embroidery thread along the penciled-in name. "Between times, I worked on the names. There's only one quilt square left to embroider after this one."

"Really?" A bit of tiredness slipped from Meghan's muscles and she hurried over to inspect the block Natalie held up for her inspection.

"Yes. And it works out perfectly. The only names left are yours, mine, Doc Bates, and. . .one more."

"I can't." Meghan's lips grew stiff and her stomach muscles tightened. "I won't."

"You have to."

"It will ruin the whole project. You've heard what people have said. If I put his name on it, no one will bid for it. I'll fall well short of the thousand dollars I need for the ambulance, and I'll be stuck with the quilt."

"A month ago, you thought his name belonged on the quilt."

"A month ago, I didn't know what he was really like. A month ago, he was a brave hero who had rescued me from falling under a train, a fascinating, handsome man I thought was courageous."

Natalie shook her head. "Nothing has changed. All those things are still true. If you could've seen him riding to our rescue out there in the desert and the tender way he cared for you, you'd know what a kind, gentle man he is." She shrugged. "You can't hold his harsh words against him. He was upset, scared that you might die. If you hadn't run away from his house, you two might've been able to patch things up instead of letting things fester. Trust me, I know. Derek can fly off the handle quicker than you can wink, but his temper never lasts. I'm sure if you and Caleb could just talk things out, you'd change your mind about him."

"That's where you're wrong. He isn't brave and heroic. He's a coward. He won't stand up for himself, won't give anyone a reason behind his actions, and he thinks I'm a brainless flutter-budget who leaps before she looks and always expects someone to rescue her. He thinks I don't care about the consequences as long as I get my way, that I have no grasp of reality, and that I need a keeper." Her ire rose as she recounted his accusations. "You should've heard him."

A snort escaped Natalie's lips. "I did. So did Dr. Bates and the Hualgas. We couldn't help it. You were shouting at each other."

Mortification spilled through her. She sagged onto her bed. They'd heard it all? No way was she asking if they'd heard the slap. Or if they guessed at the kiss. That stupid kiss. Why did her mind insist on returning to it, returning to the iron-hard grip of his hands on her arms, of the heat that had rushed through her—heat she would go to her grave vowing was anger and not attraction—or the way her heart had leaped like a wild thing in her chest when his lips had touched hers?

"Meghan, I don't want you to take this the wrong way, but Caleb does have a point."

"What?" Her spine stiffened.

"Wait. Before you get all defensive, hear me out." Natalie let her handwork fall to her lap and folded her hands over her waist. "You do tend to leap before you look. You see every obstacle as a challenge to be conquered, and you don't know the meaning of the phrase 'can't be done.' Whether it's raising a thousand dollars for an ambulance, becoming the best Harvey Girl on the line, or proving to Mrs. Gregory that you deserve to be promoted, you won't back down. Sometimes this courage and drive are assets for you, and sometimes they lead you to behave heedlessly." Her eyes were filled with warmth and friendship. "The only battle you're not willing to fight anymore is for Caleb. What happened to proving the whole town wrong and standing with him?"

"Even someone as hardheaded and obstinate as I am can recognize a losing battle when she gets hit over the head with it. I was wrong about him. He won't stand up for himself. I can't respect that, and I won't keep hurling myself against that wall."

A bit of starch invaded Natalie's tone, and she shoved the unfinished quilt block into her work bag. "You need to broaden your definition of courage. Caleb McBride isn't weak and cowardly. Everything I know about him, everything I've seen, supports the idea that he's a hardworking, honest, generous man who just wants to do his job and be left alone. If he chooses not to answer a foolish woman who tries to humiliate him in public, I think that shows remarkable self-restraint. He's got the courage to remain true to whatever convictions or reasons he has for not enlisting. Dr. Bates believes in him, and so did that nice Army major who came through. Joshua tries not to show how much he likes and respects Caleb, but he can't help it. The only people who take up against him are the women of Mrs. Gregory's set who are too silly for words. And you. If you could see how you've drooped around here the past week like a battered ragdoll, you'd be ashamed of yourself."

Meghan scowled. "I have not drooped around. I've come to my senses. I can't accomplish my goals when I'm distracted by the likes of Caleb McBride. People tried to warn me about him, but I was too headstrong to listen. You and Caleb have accused me of being impetuous, but when I finally listen to reason and decide to be sensible, you say I'm being silly."

"I think you're being unfair to Caleb and to yourself, and you won't be happy until you resolve your differences." She stood up and pressed her hands to the small of her back, arching and stretching. Her uniform lay across the bed, and she only wore her shift, which stretched tight across her middle.

Meghan's eyes widened. "Natalie?"

"What?"

She pointed to her roommate's waist, clearly outlined by the arch of her back. A suspicious bump pressed against the fabric. "Are you. . . ?" She blinked. "Is that. . . ?"

Natalie glanced down, and her back relaxed. Her hands went to her belly. Sinking down into the rocker, with pink suffusing her face, she let her head fall back, closing her eyes.

Mind chaotic, Meghan knelt beside the chair. "Natalie Daviot, are you pregnant?" Her voice came out with a low intensity that made the air between them vibrate. She shook Natalie's arm. "Are you?"

Her lips pressed together, and her eyelashes fell. A swallow lurched her throat. "Yes."

"Oh, Natalie." Meghan threw her arms around her and hugged her close. Natalie held herself stiffly. "That's wonderful." She pulled back to study Natalie's crumpled face. "Isn't it?"

"How can you say that? With Derek in France and my mother-in-law ill? I'm already hiding the fact that I'm married. This"—she pointed to her stomach—"isn't something I can hide forever. I'll be fired, sent home, and not only will I not have the money from this job, but I won't be able to get another job, and I'll have a baby to support." Her lips trembled, and a heavy sigh heaved out of her chest. "This baby is a disaster."

Meghan grabbed Natalie's hands and shook them. "Stop it. My mama says babies are a blessing, a gift from God." At Natalie's rolled eyes, Meghan tried again. "I know it won't be easy, but if you think of this baby as a little part of Derek. . ." She stopped. If Derek didn't come home, Natalie would at least have his son or daughter. "You're going to be a wonderful mother, and Derek will be so happy when he finds out. Just imagine how proud he's going to be when he holds his child for the first time."

For a moment, a soft, maternal glow invaded Natalie's eyes, but the clouds soon re-gathered there. "But what about Mrs. Gregory? What about my job?"

Meghan's mind raced. "I'm not saying it will be easy, but you've managed so far, and I'll help you. With your uniform on, nobody would guess. I only noticed because you're in your shift. How far along are you, and how much time do you think we have before it becomes really obvious?"

Natalie's blush intensified. "It must've happened right before Derek shipped out. If I had known about the baby, I never would've applied for this job. I'm about four months along."

Meghan's mind whirled. "Good, then we have some time. Our contracts with the company end in mid-November. If we can keep it to ourselves until then, you can finish out your contract, get your bonus for working through a Needles summer, and go home to your family. By that time, maybe Derek will be home."

"You're still a dreamer. The war won't end so soon."

"Well, whichever comes first, the end of the war or the end of our contracts, we'll do our level-best to keep the baby a secret."

Chapter 13

Doc Bates leaned back in his office chair and let the newspaper fall to his desk. Hundreds of soldiers and civilians falling prey to the Spanish Lady, the worst strain of influenza the world had ever seen. Though officials were reluctant to call it such, he had no qualms about naming it an epidemic. From what he could gather in the papers, the big cities were being hit the hardest, Philadelphia, Boston, New York, Minneapolis, but the illness had also spread into rural areas. Nobody was safe.

He picked up the Red Cross literature he'd received that day. Encourage folks to stay home, not to congregate together in large groups, to wear masks, disinfect, clean, wash their hands often. Mrs. Gregory had contacted him about speaking at the next Red Cross meeting. A rueful chuckle escaped his lips. He'd be speaking at a gathering, flying in the face of his own recommendation to steer clear of large groups. Still, word needed to get out somehow, and this was the best way.

A train whistle pierced the evening air. He wiped his forehead with his handkerchief and shrugged out of his waistcoat. Flicking on the desk lamp against the growing dusk, he checked the clock. Those poor folks, trapped on the train in this swelter, and the poor Harvey Girls serving them a meal. Who had an appetite in this kind of heat? And who wanted to be rushed through a meal in order to keep to the AT&SF schedule?

But the train waited for no one.

He hoped Natalie and Meghan were taking it a bit easier. It had been a week since their car broke down in the desert. Once a person had fallen prey to heatstroke, one tended to always have a sensitivity to the heat. Natalie especially worried him. At Caleb's house, she'd been too quick to get up and dressed, and he'd surmised she feared someone discovering her secret. By her calculations, she was about four months along in her pregnancy, and slight as she was, her waist must be thickening. Bounding out of bed and back to her normal routine too quickly could spell disaster. He'd have to call in there and see about scheduling another appointment so he could keep a close eye on her.

Then there was Meghan. A little dynamo most of the time, she hadn't rebounded as quickly as he'd liked. She hadn't met his eyes the entire trip back to town, and no wonder. Everyone in the house had been able to hear the argument she'd had with Caleb, from the opening salvo to the final crack of the slap she must've planted on Caleb's cheek.

Though it was the moment of silence between the fighting and the slap that intrigued him.

When he'd gone into the hotel midweek to check on the girls, he'd been surprised that all the life seemed to have drained out of Meghan. She still worked efficiently, but her smile was automatic, and the sparkle had gone from her eyes. She no longer looked as if life were a grand adventure.

Frankly, he wanted to knock some sense into both Caleb and Meghan. Caleb for being so stubborn and prideful keeping his leg a secret and Meghan for not seeing the caliber of man who stood before her and for listening to harping old gossips with nothing better to do than judge and meddle.

They were making each other miserable, which was a sure sign that they cared for one another. One couldn't be in the same room with them for long without seeing the sparks flying. Before she arrived, Caleb's trips to town had been few and far between. Since her arrival, Doc had practically tripped over him at least once a week.

Not to mention the anguished look on Caleb's face when she lay on the edge of consciousness in his bed and the gentle way he had brushed her hair off her face and smoothed her skin with a damp towel when she'd been delirious from the heat. Caleb had no idea how much he'd revealed in his expression and his actions. If Meghan had been able to comprehend it, she would've known in an instant that he loved her.

And Caleb was fighting it with all he had in him. Of course, with Caleb, Doc expected nothing less. He was too proud and stubborn for his own good. By his own admission, his father had rejected him when he'd contracted infantile paralysis, and Doc had a sneaking suspicion that another similar hurt lurked somewhere in Caleb's past. From the way Caleb was fighting his attraction to Meghan, Doc suspected it had to do with a girl who had let him down.

He hoped Meghan wouldn't do the same. A man could only take so much.

Maybe he'd head out to Caleb's this evening. On the pretense of doing a little night fishing on the river, maybe he could induce Caleb to open up a bit. And a chance to dabble his feet in the river or even wade in up to his neck seemed like a good idea.

Footsteps on the front porch drew his attention. The bell buzzed, and then buzzed again. He was halfway across the foyer when a fist pounded the door. His heart rate picked up.

"Yes?" He swung the oak and glass door open.

Jeremy Peterson, a bellhop at the hotel stood there panting, sweat dripping from his temples. "There's trouble at the hotel." He gasped, pressing one pudgy hand to his chest while gripping the doorframe with the other. "Mrs. Gregory sent me to fetch you."

"What trouble? Is it Miss Daviot or Miss Thorson?" He knew he should've insisted they take the whole week off to recover, especially Natalie.

Jeremy's brow crinkled. "Who? No, they're fine. It's the train. More than a hundred soldiers, and they're all sicker than a foundered mule." He lowered his voice and leaned in. "Mrs. Gregory says it's the influenza."

Doc's heart tripped, and a hollow feeling grew under his breastbone. Lifting his bag from the table beside the door, he made a mental list of everything he would need and where he might procure supplies. "Go roust the druggist and Mr. Weeks or Mr. Claypool from the store. We're going to need help. You said a hundred soldiers?"

"Yep. They started feeling sick right after the stop in Barstow."

"Let's get going then. Tell the pharmacist I'm going to need every bottle of aspirin and rubbing alcohol he's got, as well as whatever he has on hand for coughing, too."

Braking to a stop in front of the hotel, Doc hopped from the car and grabbed his bag. His worst fears had come to life, and now it was up to him to meet the challenge. At least he had some idea what to expect from his brother's letters. But the prospect of a hundred sick soldiers made his insides quake.

A wild-eyed baggage man met him at the door. "Shore glad you got here, Doc." His eyes rolled, showing a lot of white in his black face. "Miz Gregory is shouting at everyone, and Mr. Stock is trying to figure out what to do with all the people. We's all so scared." He looked over his shoulder toward the lobby as if he expected the influenza to reach out and grab him. "I been posted at the door to keep folks out."

Doc brushed past him with a nod. He had too much to do to palaver.

He stopped short just inside the door. Every chair, bench, and several yards of floor in the lobby were occupied by groaning soldiers. A sea of brown uniforms and miserable faces greeted him. Mrs. Gregory rushed up to him. "Thank heavens you're here. What should we do?"

A soldier lying on the floor by the front desk rolled to his side and vomited across the tiles. Several more coughed, their bodies wracked with spasms. Overwhelmed at the sight of so many ill young men, Doc closed his eyes for a moment, bracing himself.

Dear Lord, give us all strength. Guide me through this.

He opened his eyes. "I want these men in beds as soon as possible. If there are any soldiers who aren't ill, put them to carrying men up to the rooms. Send the busboys and bellhops to fetch basins, pans, buckets, whatever they can find. Gather the rest of the staff for a brief meeting."

Mrs. Gregory hastened to do his bidding, proving once again what a capable lieutenant she made, but how unsuited for command she was. Why hadn't she thought to get these men to beds? Though to be fair, the sheer numbers of ill men paralyzed him.

Meghan wove through the soldiers, her face pale, eyes wide. She clasped a stack of towels to her middle. "Doc." She took his elbow and drew him into a corner. "Natalie is going to want to help, and she shouldn't. We have to get her out of here."

He raised his eyebrows. "You know?"

"Yes, she told me. What are we going to do?"

He thought fast. "Tell her to pack a bag and get to my house. She can stay there until this is over. If Mrs. Gregory asks, we'll tell her Natalie is specialing a patient for me. Which she will be doing, taking care of herself."

Lines of strain eased out of Meghan's face. "That's perfect. I'll tell her."

Busboys and waitresses began assisting soldiers to their feet. One of the handymen took a door off its hinges to use as an improvised stretcher. Mr. Stock roped in burly railroad men to help with the moving.

Doc commandeered the south wing of the hotel, turning it into a makeshift hospital. "Move any hotel guests into the north wing. I have a feeling they won't want to stay in any case. Close the dining room and lunch counter for the time being."

When Mrs. Gregory protested that train passengers had to be fed, he said, "Have the cooks prepare boxed lunches. Once folks hear we've got influenza in the hotel, I doubt they will object to staying on the train. I'm going to need the Harvey Girls to nurse sick patients. I can't spare any for serving coffee and sandwiches."

When every soldier had been placed in a room, Doc called the hotel staff together. They met on the second floor loggia. A stiff, hot breeze ruffled aprons and lacy headbands. "There's no pretending this is going to be easy. At latest count, seventy-three of the one hundred soldiers are in the beginning stages of the Spanish Influenza. From what I've read and what my brother, an army physician, has told me, this disease moves fast."

He clasped his hands behind his back. "Mr. Stock, I'm putting you in charge of keeping us supplied with clean basins, hot and cold water, and clean linens. You'll also need to see about moving in more beds. I'm sure these cases won't be the last we'll see. The laundry will need to be going day and night. We must have clean bed linens, and we're going to go through a mountain of washcloths and towels."

The thin, sallow manager nodded. "It shall be done."

"Each waitress will have at least four patients. We've put the men four to a room, with one girl in charge of each room. There isn't a lot you can do, but keeping the patients as cool and comfortable as possible is your first priority. Try to get them to drink, and above all, keep the room clean. We have a limited supply of medicines, and we've wired for more to be sent." He nodded toward Miss Ralston.

"I asked Miss Ralston to break into the Red Cross supplies you've been preparing to send to Europe." He withdrew a gauze mask from the box she offered. "Wear this at all times. This illness is very aggressive and will seek any way it can to infect you. Wash your hands often, and turn your head away if your patient is sneezing or coughing."

He looked out over his allies in the coming war. Some scared, some eager, all unprepared for what was to come, even as he felt himself unprepared. Young, strong, healthy, the exact types who were most vulnerable to this strain of the disease. How many would succumb to the illness over the coming days? How many would survive?

Meghan swallowed hard, tied her gauze mask over the lower half of her face, and opened the door to room twenty four. Two double beds, both occupied by soldiers still in uniform on top of the covers. She braced herself. Unaccustomed to illness, she wasn't sure what she should do. One of the men lay on his side, coughing hard enough to rattle the bedsprings.

His bedmate lay with his arm flung up over his eyes, groaning softly. The others lay with fever-bright cheeks, coughing or sneezing, moving their legs and arms restlessly. The fan overhead clanked softly, stirring the heavy afternoon air.

Meghan bent over the first man. "Is there anything I can do for you?" She touched his arm, shocked at the heat radiating from his skin.

"Water." His voice rasped.

Relieved at so simple a request, she hurried to the hallway. Mr. Stock had set up a table there with pitchers of ice water and ranks of glasses. A dishpan sat on the floor to receive used glasses, and stacks of towels, washcloths, and sheets stood ready for use.

Mrs. Gregory went by with her clipboard. "I'll be in to get the names of your soldiers in a minute. Be sure to catalog their belongings and put them into separate laundry bags with a tag."

Meghan nodded, but her heart beat hard under her ribs. She'd have to help them all out of their uniforms and get them properly to bed. Quelling the blush that wanted to soar into her face, she reminded herself not to be silly. Though she'd never performed such personal tasks for men, and strangers at that, she knew her duty and she would do it.

You're a nurse and they are ill. You'll do what you need to do, and you won't be silly about it. You can blush for a whole day after all this is over, but for now, pull yourself together and get on with the job.

She pressed the glass to the young soldier's lips. He drained the contents and let his head fall back as if he couldn't keep it up an instant longer. His eyes closed, and his chest rose and fell rapidly.

Meghan went to the far side of the bed to the soldier with his arm over his eyes. "Sir, I need to get you out of your uniform. Can you sit up?" The mask muffled her voice and made the air taste and smell like cotton, but she was thankful for it.

He lowered his arm, revealing startlingly dark eyes in his pale face. Even more alarming, the whites of his eyes were no longer white, but red. And the pain in his expression reached out and grabbed Meghan by the throat.

"Please, leave me alone," he whispered.

"I wish I could. Just let me get you settled and you can go back to sleep." She reached for the buttons on the front of his tunic. "Are you thirsty?"

"No." He gave a token protest, pushing softly at her hands before resigning himself. The most difficult part was getting him to sit up so she could remove his blouse. Mindful of Mrs. Gregory's orders, she bundled his belongings into a hotel laundry bag and tagged them.

"What's your name, soldier?"

"Patrick Newton."

Each of the other three did their best to help her, and the last boy blushed hard and insisted she leave the room for a moment, that he could get himself undressed. When she returned, she found him under the light sheet, his eyes focused on the ceiling.

Patrick, Wesley, George, and Harold. All army privates, all from California, all very ill.

"Here, let's put this over your eyes." She folded a damp cloth and set it on Patrick's brow. "It will cool you off and cut the light." She'd drawn the shade, but his headache was so fierce, even the smallest bit of light seemed to stab his brain cruelly.

Wesley's fever soared, and she sponged him, wringing the cloth over and over, wiping his face and neck and arms.

This is what Caleb did for you.

She forced that thought away. Thinking about Caleb was useless, and she needed to focus on her patients.

George coughed and coughed until she feared he would tear his lungs apart, and Harold lost the contents of his stomach over and over again, leaning over the side of the bed, his head over a bucket. Meghan moved from one to the next in a continual round, seeking to help, her alarm at the speed and severity of this sickness mounting.

Doc came in. "How are they doing?"

She shrugged. "I don't seem to be doing very much for them." Helplessness swept over her. "I'm sponging them off and trying to make them as comfortable as I can, but what else should I be doing?"

"That's about all you can do." He bent over Wesley and placed his stethoscope on the rapidly moving chest. With his other hand, he popped a thermometer into Wesley's mouth. "Get some of the hotel stationery out of the desk, one page for each man, and put their names on the top. I'm going to have you chart their conditions. If you notice any changes, make a note on their paper. Do it every time. If you don't, things are going to blur together. You won't remember when you gave them medicine or when they last had something to drink or when their breathing changed."

He took the vital signs of each man, and she carefully recorded them along with the time.

"I'll send someone in with a couple of bottles of cough syrup and some aspirins. Be sure to mark when you give each man the medicine. And keep the aspirin bottle in your pocket at all times. It's too precious to mislay. In about an hour someone will bring you some chicken broth. Don't be alarmed if they don't want any." He stuffed his stethoscope into his pocket and inclined his head toward the door.

Once in the hallway, he rolled his head as if loosening tight neck muscles. "I want you to watch their breathing and their skin. If they can't fight off the sickness, the next step is petechia, hemorrhages under the skin. The one boy, Patrick, already has bleeding in his eyes. After the small bleeds start, my brother, who has seen quite a bit of this, says the lungs will begin to fill with fluid, causing pneumonia. When that happens, their breathing is going to become much thicker, and might even sound bubbly. Prop them up with extra pillows. If they request anything, try to give it to them. If anything worries you, send someone to find me. There will be a bellhop posted in the hall to run errands and track me down if you need me."

She nodded. The weight of responsibility settled on her, but she refused to bow under it. She could do this. "How are the others faring?"

"Another ten soldiers from the train have come down ill. How are you feeling?"

"I'm fine." She forced some strength into her voice.

"You should still be resting after your heatstroke. You both came back to work too early." He rubbed his hands down his face, disturbing the mask. "You did get Natalie away all right?"

"Yes. She protested, but I threatened to come and find you. She gave in because she knows it's for the best."

"Did Mrs. Gregory give you any trouble?"

"No, she barely seemed to hear me because she was so busy getting sick men into beds."

"It's going to be a long night, and with the way things are going, I expect we'll be seeing more patients. The flu is bound to spread to the town, despite our best efforts. The hotel had townsfolk in it when the sick soldiers arrived, and they carried the sickness to their homes. I've put the police chief wise, and he's going to send his constables around town to check on folks. Those who are the most ill or who don't have anyone to care for them will be brought here."

"What about the trains?"

"For now, they'll stop and refuel, but no passengers will be allowed to get off unless they're sick or live in Needles. The AT&SF will try to keep their schedule, but they'll inform passengers that there won't be any meals or lodging in Needles until we give them the all-clear."

Mrs. Gregory marched past them carrying two buckets,

and Meghan nodded to the doctor. "I'd best get back to my patients."

She lost all track of time. Her hands grew red and puckered from wringing out cool cloths, and her back ached from bending over the beds. Her apron bore stains she'd have been chastised for had she worn them into the dining room, and her shoes pinched, her feet swollen and hot.

Harold finally stopped retching and lay still. George's cough grew worse, and he gasped for breath, his face turning purple with each prolonged spasm. When Patrick's breathing changed for the worse, the hairs on Meghan's arms lifted. She sent the bellboy for more pillows and with his help, got Patrick propped up. It seemed to do little good. And most alarming, Wesley's nose began to bleed. She sent for Doc Bates.

His hair seemed to have gone grayer, and new lines had appeared on his kind face. He lifted the sheets and checked his patients' feet. Patrick's and Wesley's were both an odd bluish color.

She wiped the trickle of blood off Wesley's upper lip once more. His eyes moved behind his eyelids, but his lashes remained closed.

"So fast." Doc's murmur was barely audible over the labored breathing in the room. "My brother said it moved fast, but I've never seen anything like this. Yesterday morning, these boys were hale and hearty."

Meghan wrung out yet another cloth and swapped it for the one on Harold's brow. "Tell me these are the worst, that the other soldiers are faring better."

Doc's breath puffed out his mask, and he shook his head. "I wish I could. Step out in the hallway with me for a moment."

Once in the hall, he tugged down his mask. "Jeremy, watch this room while Miss Thorson takes a break."

The bellhop put down the tray of glasses he carried and nodded. Meghan dropped onto a bench and leaned back. Red streaks of light showed through the filmy curtains on the balcony doors, harbingers of sundown. She'd spent all night and all day in the room and beyond noting times of medication, the hours had blurred together. Had it really been more than twenty-four hours since the train had arrived full of sick soldiers?

Doc sat next to her, pinching the bridge of his nose. "We've already lost two of them, and a score more are critical. The one that's bleeding from the nose. . ."

"Wesley." A lump formed in her throat.

"Don't be surprised if he starts coughing blood soon."

"What's happening to them? This isn't like any flu I've ever heard of."

"Smarter doctors than I seem to think it's a reaction by the body's immune system. The flu is a respiratory disease, and when it attacks, the immune system attacks back. Fluids build up in the lungs, and the patient begins to drown. They cough so hard trying to expel the fluids they end up damaging their lung tissue and bleeding into their lungs. They ultimately die of pneumonia. You saw the blue feet on a couple of those boys? The body is starving the limbs of oxygen in an effort to keep the internal organs alive. Once the illness reaches this stage, death is almost certain."

He heaved out a sigh. "You need to go downstairs and get something to eat. It's going to be another long night, and you will need all your strength. When you've eaten, take a few minutes to walk along the platform and stretch your legs. Jeremy will watch over your patients."

With leaden legs and a heavy heart, Meghan dragged downstairs toward the kitchen. Mrs. Gregory sat at one of the tables, her face in her hands, her shoulders shaking. She raised her head when Meghan entered.

"Miss Thorson." She straightened and smoothed her hair, swiping at her eyes and gathering her composure. "Did you need something?"

Meghan noted her blotchy cheeks and the extra starch in her voice that repelled any comment about her appearance. "Doc sent me downstairs to have something to eat and to get a little fresh air."

"Fine. Chef's got sandwiches and cake in the cooler. I'd best go see that the laundry is keeping up." She pushed away from the table and marched away, her heels tapping briskly.

A yellow piece of paper and an envelope fluttered behind her as she passed, and Meghan stooped to pick it up. A telegram. Without really meaning to, her eyes scanned the brief missive.

WHILE ADVANCING AGAINST THE ENEMY, PRIVATE JASPER GREGORY WAS STRUCK BY SHELL FRAGMENTS IN THE TORSO AND LEG. PRIVATE GREGORY IS RECUPERATING AT THE ARMY FIELD HOSPITAL NEAR THE CITY OF ARRAS. HIS CONDITION IS CONSIDERED CRITICAL. AS SOON AS POSSIBLE, HE WILL BE EVACUATED TO BRITAIN THEN TO THE UNITED STATES.

Meghan's hand shook. Mrs. Gregory's son was supposed to be safe behind the lines working for the quartermaster, not advancing against the Germans on the Western Front. She folded the telegram and replaced it in the envelope, unsure what to do. Poor Mrs. Gregory. Her son was all she had.

Her thoughts went to her brother, Lars, praying he was still alive, praying her parents wouldn't receive a telegram like this. She sank onto a chair and put her face in her hands. Her appetite had fled. Hot tears flooded her eyes, for Mrs. Gregory who held people at arm's length even in her most sorrow-filled moments, for the soldiers on the front lines, and for the poor soldiers upstairs fighting for their lives. She blinked hard, forcing down her fear and despondency, knowing that if she gave in to her tears now, she'd be useless.

"Ma'am?" The whisper barely penetrated the big empty kitchen.

She turned. Joshua Hualga opened the batwing door wider.

"Joshua, what are you doing here?"

"I've been all over this hotel looking for you." He stuck his hands in his pockets and hunched his shoulders. "What's going on upstairs? Why isn't the restaurant open?"

"Does Caleb know you're here?" She braced her hands on the table and stood.

"No, and I figure he'd skin me alive if he did know. He let me borrow the truck to go visit my family on the reservation, but I figured somebody better come talk to you."

"Why? Is something wrong with Caleb?" She cast a quick glance over her shoulder. "You're not supposed to be in the hotel. Let's get outside before someone sees you."

His face hardened. "Because I'm an Indian? We went all through that with the man who owns the hotel. I have as much right to be here as anyone."

"Oh, my stars and garters, boy." She grabbed his arm, exasperated and tired. "I don't care if you're Indian, Greek, or the King of the Cannibal Islands, you can't be in the hotel. It's under quarantine." She hustled him out of the kitchen, through the dining room and foyer, and out onto the railroad platform. "Some passengers came in yesterday who weren't feeling well. They're staying here until they get better, and Doc put the hotel into quarantine as a precaution." She downplayed the severity of the situation, not wanting to scare him.

"Doc's here? Does he need help?" Light leaped into Joshua's eyes and he took a step back toward the lobby doors.

She put her hand on his chest. "Doc's got plenty of help. Now go home."

"No, ma'am, not till you've heard me out. I risked my job to come find you, and I intend to say what I've got to say before I go back and own up to what I've done." His jaw stuck out, and his eyes glittered in the dusk. "You were pretty harsh on Caleb when you were out to his place, and it cut him up pretty deep. He's been like a badger with a boil all week. He was sweet on you, and he thought you were woman enough to stand up to the opinions of this town and take his part. He's so disappointed in you, he can hardly think straight."

"He's disappointed in me?" She gaped. "I'm not the one who earned herself a white feather. I'm not the one who's so afraid that he won't enlist."

Joshua snorted and scowled. "You're talking through your hat. Caleb isn't afraid of anything or anyone. Spend just a minute and think back on what he's done. He threw himself practically under a train to rescue you the first day you met. He hired me when he knew lots of folks in this town wouldn't spit on an Indian if he was on fire. He stood up to Mr. Stock when he would've thrown me out of the hotel for being Indian. He faces down bullies and gossips every time he sets foot in this two-bit burg. He even braved a dance here at the hotel, one hosted by a bunch of cow-faced old gossips who'd like nothing better than to roast him on a spit, just because he wanted to spend more time with you. You don't know what courage looks like if you think it can only be found in uniform."

Stung by the vehemence in his tone and the fire in his eyes, she fought back. "Then why won't he enlist? Why won't he stand up for himself?"

"His reasons are his own, I reckon, and when he's ready he'll tell you. Until then, you should have faith in him. Caleb McBride holds everything in, even his temper, when most men would've punched someone or struck back somehow. He's patient and careful and private, and he tries not to let anything show. He must care for you an awful lot to be so hurt by you turning against him. The whole town has turned against him, and he hasn't cared a cup of sand what they thought, but you're different. He let himself care, reached out to you a little, and you bit him like a rattler."

Before she could respond, Mrs. Gregory called out. "You there, boy. Get away from here. Miss Thorson, you're needed upstairs."

"Think on what I said." Joshua stepped back. "And tell Doc that I'd be happy to help out with the sick if he needs me."

Meghan returned to the hotel under the watchful eye of the head waitress.

"What did *he* want?" Mrs. Gregory's voice was loaded with animosity.

Mindful of the terrible news the head waitress had just received, Meghan softened her reply. "He offered to help with the sick if we needed him."

"Did you tell him we had the influenza here?"

"No, just that some passengers had fallen ill and Doc quarantined the hotel as a precaution against the illness spreading to the town."

"Fine. Good. Hopefully he'll stay away. You do need to get back upstairs. We've lost two more soldiers, and a couple of the hotel staff aren't feeling too well." The lines had deepened around the head waitress's mouth, and her eyelids were still pink.

Meghan nodded. "You dropped this in the kitchen." She

handed over the yellow envelope, giving no indication she knew the contents. When Mrs. Gregory was ready, she'd let people know of her son's condition. Until then, Meghan would guard her privacy.

With her chin held high, Mrs. Gregory took the envelope, but the storm clouds of fear gathering in her eyes belied her outward calm.

Meghan returned to room twenty-four and relieved the bellboy. Her patients clung to life by tenuous threads, and she settled in for a long night of nursing care and thinking over what Joshua had said.

Chapter 14

"You did what?" Caleb let his saddle *thunk* to the ground and wiped his forehead. After a day of dust and wind and heat and stubborn horses, his fuse was short. All he wanted to do was get the weight off his leg and drink about a gallon of cool water.

"I went to see Meghan last night." Joshua tucked his hands into his back pockets and stared at Caleb from under his hat brim, defiance in every line of his thin body.

"I thought you were visiting your parents."

"I did. But afterward I stopped in town. That's why I was so late getting back. I'd have told you then, but you'd already gone to bed. And this morning you were in too bad a mood."

"You had no call to see Meghan." The initial explosion of surprise in Caleb's chest grew and rippled outward into anger.

"Didn't I? You've been hissing and snapping around here like a cornered Gila monster all week, ever since she smacked your face. You're miserable, and you're taking it out on me. Somebody had to do something about what's wrong between you two."

"I have not been a Gila monster, and how I feel has nothing to do with Meghan Thorson. There's nothing wrong between us."

"Then why haven't you gone to town and talked to her?"

"I've been busy, and there's nothing to say."

"That hasn't stopped you all summer. How many trips to town did you make just so you could see her? You're eating your heart out for her, and you're too stubborn to admit it."

"Is that what you told her?" He jerked his hat off and

thwacked his thigh, lifting his face to the sun. "Somebody save me from interfering friends and gabbity employees." Curiosity ate at him, and he couldn't help asking, "What else did you tell her, and what did she say?"

Joshua mopped his face and grimaced. He rolled his neck and shoulders and blinked against the glare. "I told her you were more courageous than anyone I had ever met and that she was a fool to let other people define courage for her."

He stilled, leaning against the corral rails. Pleasantly surprised, he didn't know what to say, so he busied himself by coiling and recoiling his rope.

Joshua continued. "I have eyes in my head. I told her to remember all the courageous things you've done that you didn't have to do. About how you do things without thinking about the cost to yourself and that you held onto your temper better than anyone I knew. I just wish you'd tell her the real reason you haven't enlisted."

The rope dropped from his hands. "What do you mean?"

Joshua shrugged. "I told you I have eyes. Why don't you tell her about your leg?"

Cold swept through him. "What about my leg?"

"Can we go sit down in the shade to talk about this? I'm weak as a cat today. Guess staying out late last night didn't agree with me." Joshua turned and headed for the porch.

Snatching up his rope, Caleb made sure the corral gate was latched before following him. When they were both seated in the ladder-back chairs on the porch, he stared hard at his employee. "What do you know about my leg?"

Joshua let his head rest against the top slat and closed his eyes. "I know that you limp on it when you think nobody's looking. I know it pains you, especially after a long day. I figure that's why you've gone to see Doc a few times this summer, and

I know that your boots are special made. So what's wrong with it anyway?"

A lifetime of silence on the issue clamped Caleb's lips shut. He got up and went into the kitchen, pouring two glasses of water before returning to the porch. Joshua cracked one eyelid and accepted his glass, drinking it in small sips. Caleb returned to his chair and drained the contents of his water glass.

"You done stalling?"

He glared at Joshua, but the gesture was lost on his hired hand. He had his eyes closed again.

"I had. . ." He could hardly bear to say the words, he loathed them so much. "I had infantile paralysis when I was a kid." He braced himself for a reaction.

Joshua let out a long breath through his nose and raised his eyelids. "That's rough. I've been reading those books from Doc. I guess it's a blessing you can walk at all. But why hide it? It's not like getting sick was your fault."

The words jammed in his throat. It was so hard to explain, how his damaged leg made him feel less than a man, how he'd been judged and found wanting by the very people who were supposed to love him, who should've loved him, infirmity and all.

"I don't like to talk about it. This bum leg has cost me too much. When people know about it, they treat me like I don't have any brains, that my head must be as withered as my foot."

"People like who? Doc knows about it and he treats you just fine. I imagine that major who came to buy the horses must've known something about it, and he looked you in the eye and commended your work."

"They're the exceptions, trust me."

"So who treated you bad because of your leg? Nobody else in town knows, or word would've spread and they'd have laid off all the coward nonsense." Joshua was like a crow picking corn off a cob, peck, peck, peck.

"My father stuck me in an asylum for crippled kids and never spoke to me again." Caleb sucked in a breath and barely avoided putting his hand on his chest. How could a wound so old still hurt like it had just happened?

A phantom smile crossed Joshua's face. "Your dad and mine sound a lot alike. Mine barely speaks to me and was only too glad to see me leave the reservation to work for you. He doesn't know what to do with me. I had the audacity to be different."

Caleb remained silent, leaning forward and bracing his forearms on his thighs, rolling his empty glass between his palms.

"You should tell Meghan at least. She deserves to know. Then she can quit thinking you're a coward. I bet she'd pin the ears back on any of those nosy biddies in town who wanted to run you down. She's a sure enough go-getter and smacker-downer when she gets the bit between her teeth. She'd fire up so quick in your defense, she might burn down the town with her words alone."

"I doubt that." Her outraged face swam in his memory, her hand lifted to strike his face.

"I have a feeling that once you had Meghan on your side, she'd take a bullet for you."

"But if she knew about my leg, she wouldn't *be* on my side. I can live with her thinking I'm a coward because it isn't true. I can't stomach her turning away from me because I have a crippled leg."

"What makes you think she'd bail out on you?"

"Bitter experience."

Joshua raised his eyebrows and took a sip of his water. With the back of his sleeve he mopped his forehead once more. "How so?"

"Nothing to be gained by talking about it." If there was one wound he didn't want exposed, it was his failure with Patricia.

"Nothing to be lost either." Joshua sighed and closed his eyes. "Man, I feel like the dog's dinner."

"I'd best go start supper." He braced his hands on the arms of the rocker and rose.

A grimace twisted the boy's features. "None for me. I'm going to go to bed."

Caleb stopped halfway to the door. Not hungry? That wasn't like Joshua. He reversed direction and laid his hand on the boy's forehead. Heat radiated from his skin.

"You're burning up."

"I think I might've done something stupid."

"What do you mean?"

"When I went to see Meghan. . .the hotel was under quarantine. I went inside anyway, slipped past the bellhop they had manning the front doors."

"Quarantine? For what?"

"Meghan didn't say, but it must be pretty serious if they locked down the hotel and closed the restaurants. From the little bit I saw, I'd venture to say there are a lot of soldiers in the hotel. One of those troop trains. Now I'm thinking going inside wasn't such a great idea. I feel terrible."

Sick soldiers. It didn't take a genius to guess that the Spanish Flu had invaded Needles. The papers had been full of the epidemic for weeks, especially in the military camps.

And Joshua had come into contact with the sickness.

"Let's get you to bed. Maybe it's just a touch of heat or something. If you don't perk up after a good night's rest, I'm taking you to town."

Meghan stood in the hallway, her shoulders bowed, tears stinging her eyes and throat, trying to hold on to her self-control. Within a half hour of each other, Wesley and Patrick had succumbed to the dreadful illness. A pair of hotel porters bore Wesley away on a stretcher, just as they had Patrick only a little while before. George and Harold clung to life, racked with coughing and fever, but still alive.

Patrick had slipped away quietly, his labored breathing becoming more and more shallow, until he'd sighed his last. His face lost its tension, and all movement ceased. Meghan called for the doctor to confirm her fears, and when he'd completed his cursory examination, he'd pulled the sheet over Patrick's face and summoned men to carry the body away.

Wesley had left this world hard. At the end, he'd turned dark, purplish blue, fighting for air, clutching her hand, his eyes pleading with her to help him. Finally, he'd coughed up a great cloud of blood and passed away, his hand growing limp and his eyes unfocused.

Nothing had prepared her for the speed, and in Wesley's case, the violence of death. One moment they'd been alive, and the next, dead. She leaned against the wall, trying to summon the courage to return to the sick room. She'd need to strip the bed and disinfect every surface. George and Harold needed her.

And yet, her stomach quivered at the thought of going back in there. She hadn't known those men at all, but they had been under her care. Had she failed them somehow?

"Miss Thorson?"

Mrs. Gregory pushed a laundry cart down the hallway. She stopped beside Meghan. "I heard you lost another one." She adjusted her mask. "So fast. They've been here less than three days and we've already lost seventeen men."

"Are there any new cases?"

"Nine hotel workers, including Mr. Stock. And a handful of

folks from town. They were in the hotel when the train pulled in. And a couple of railroad men have come in, part of the group that helped us transfer patients from the train to the hotel." She shook her head.

A creepy, crawling feeling skittered across Meghan's skin. Such slight contact was enough to catch the illness? Her mask seemed less than adequate to shield her from something so pervasive. And she couldn't get the image of Wesley, drowning in his own blood, out of her mind.

"Do you have any bedclothes that need to go to the laundry?" Mrs. Gregory jarred her back to the present.

"I do. I'll get them." Forcing herself away from the wall, she slipped into room twenty-four. A quick check told her nothing had changed in either George or Harold's conditions. Early morning light seeped in around the edges of the window blind. While the rising sun of a new day usually filled Meghan with optimism and energy, today it just filled her with dread.

With hasty jerks, she tugged the sheets loose from the empty bed, trying and failing to ignore the bright red splotches staining the once-white fabric. Taking the pillows as well, she balled everything together and carried them to the hamper.

Mrs. Gregory gathered fresh bedding from the table a few doors down and brought it back. "We're running out of clean pillows, but Doc insists we not reuse them until they've been washed and dried and sprayed with bleach. The next westbound train is supposed to have more pillows, sheets, towels, and other supplies."

"What do I do about the mattress? Blood soaked through the sheets."

"We'll spray it with that new Lysol stuff the hardware store sent over, flip the mattress, and hope for the best."

"Meghan." Doc's voice called from the head of the stairs.

"I have a new patient for you." Doc and Caleb held Joshua up between them. "Hurry and get that bed made."

Meghan wasn't sure which jarred her most, the sight of Caleb standing in the hotel or Joshua, hanging limp, his arms stretched across the shoulders of his boss and the doctor. She stood rooted to the floor. The last time she'd seen Caleb, she'd practically thrown herself at him then slapped his face. Her shocking behavior still had the power to send shame shivering down her spine.

"Miss Thorson?" Mrs. Gregory shoved the stack of sheets into Meghan's hands. "You heard the doctor. Get to work."

Out of habit, she leaped to obey the head waitress, her mind spinning. Joshua had come to the hotel to see her. If he hadn't, surely he wouldn't have fallen ill. Together, she and Mrs. Gregory got the mattress sprayed and flipped. Meghan snapped open sheets, tucked in edges, shoved pillows into slips, and folded a clean blanket across the bottom of the bed. Mrs. Gregory worked on the other side, mirroring Meghan's work.

A wry twinkle lit Mrs. Gregory's eyes. "We'd have made decent chambermaids, wouldn't we?"

Doc and Caleb shuffled through the door with Joshua and lay him on the bed.

He moaned and squeezed his eyes shut. "Why don't you leave me alone?" The words came out slurred but discernible.

Doc stuck a thermometer under Joshua's tongue and lifted his wrist to check his pulse. "Caleb, you'll get him undressed in a minute, and you can stay and help Meghan since you've already been exposed to the sickness. Mrs. Gregory will give you a mask, and Meghan can show you what to do for Joshua."

George and Harold slept on, and Meghan took a moment to feel their foreheads and straighten the sheets. The water pitcher on the bedside table held only a half a glass, so she picked it up. "I'll step out while you get him settled."

When she returned with fresh water and a stack of cloths, Joshua lay under the sheets, undressed down to his small clothes and restless. Caleb had donned a mask, his eyes watchful and serious, and his skin tanned against the stark white of the cotton gauze. She looked away, unable to meet his gaze for long.

Doc had gone, leaving them alone.

"What should I do for him?" Caleb stood beside the bed, his hands in his pockets, his weight resting on one leg.

She checked the notepaper on the desk to decipher Doc's scrawl, trying to put some distance between her chaotic thoughts and what needed to be done. Temperature 103.9. Pulse 126. Aspirin and cool cloth treatment for fever and aches. Encourage fluid intake.

"There's a basin of water on the bedside table. Wet this cloth." She handed him one of the clean washcloths. "And bathe his face and chest and arms. If that doesn't help lower his temperature, we'll use alcohol. Until the next train comes, there's not much ice left, so we'll use what we have sparingly."

Harold groaned and turned his head on the pillow. A spasm of coughing caught him, and Meghan hastened to his side to help prop him up until it passed. She held a cloth under his chin as he coughed, praying he wouldn't bring up any blood. After a minute or two the coughing ceased, the redness subsided from his face, and he fell back limp on the pillow once more. She smoothed the hair on his forehead and offered him a drink.

"Shhh, just rest. You're going to be fine." His skin felt paper-dry, and his fever-bright eyes disappeared behind his eyelids once more. She wrung out a cloth and passed it over his face and neck.

"What else can I do?" Caleb pulled the chair from the desk

and dragged it to Joshua's bedside. She couldn't miss the helpless note to his voice. It resonated with her own feelings of trying to hold back a sea surge. All her efforts were futile in the face of such a rushing, relentless foe determined to take what it wanted.

She withdrew the precious bottle of aspirin tablets from her apron pocket, her only real weapon in the fight. "Try to get him to take two of these. If he can't swallow them, we'll crush them up and give them to him by spoon in some water."

"Is that all?"

"I'm afraid so. Keep them comfortable, write down everything you do for them and when, and pray."

Pray. Pray. Pray. How many prayers had she uttered for the men under her care in the last three days? She closed her eyes to compose yet another imploring, beseeching plea.

When she opened her eyes, Caleb stared at her above his mask. "When was the last time you slept?" He squeezed water from the cloth and pressed it against Joshua's forehead. She handed him a half glass of water and the two tablets.

"Here, kid. You have to swallow these then you can rest."

Thankfully, Joshua opened his mouth for the pills and swallowed them down. A chill rippled through his lean frame, and Meghan tugged the sheet a little higher around his bare chest.

"You didn't answer my question. When was the last time you slept?"

Blinking hard against the grittiness in her eyes, she shook her head. "I've dozed in the rocker at night."

"Why don't you rest for a while? If all we can do is change wet cloths and watch them, I can do that."

"You're sure?" The thought of sleep beckoned like a powerful dream.

"I'll wake you if anything happens."

She eased down into the rocker in the corner of the room and let her head rest against the high back. As disturbing as having Caleb here made her feel, she had to admit not being alone was comforting. Weariness tugged at her limbs and eyelids, and sleep claimed her.

"Meghan." Something shook her, but she ignored it. "Meg—" The sound broke off, caught in a maelstrom of coughing.

Her weighty lashes parted. Cotton-wool filled her head, and pillow-ticking coated her mouth.

"Meghan. Are you awake?" The hand shook her shoulder again.

Caleb's voice. She blinked, sitting upright.

"Meghan, I'm so sorry." More coughing. He put his hand to his chest, his mask puffing in and out with the jagged coughing. Fever brightened his cheeks and eyes. "I think it's got me. So fast. I felt fine awhile ago—" More coughing obliterated his words.

Dread surged through her, yanking her to her feet. She put her hands on his shoulders and then felt his forehead. Heat seared her skin. "Oh, Caleb."

"I'm sorry." Another racking spasm of coughing grabbed him, and he yanked down the mask, gasping for air.

"You need to lie down." She turned him to the double bed where Joshua lay. "I'll send someone for Doc."

The last bit of sleepiness drained from her as she hurried down the hall. Where was that bellboy? The clock at the head of the stairs told her she'd slept for almost four hours. From the open doorways of the rooms she passed the sounds of coughing and sneezing, wheezing and moaning emanated. She checked each room for Doc's reassuring presence, but couldn't find him.

She finally ran into him downstairs in the kitchen, seated at a table, his head pillowed on his crossed arms, snoring softly. Poor man. Should she wake him? What could he do, really? She settled for leaving him a note.

Caleb is sick now. I've put him to bed with aspirin and liquids. I'll wake you if things look bad for him.

She hurried back to the sickroom. Caleb had undressed and climbed into bed next to Joshua. He coughed, holding his chest. Red suffused his face, and he fell back against the pillow gasping. "Feels like I'm being stabbed." His voice rasped.

Dosing him with aspirin, bathing his face and neck with cool water, encouraging him to drink. All things she'd done a hundred times for her patients and yet, this was Caleb. Just being near him set her nerves to jangling, jerked her thoughts in every direction, and made her wonder if she was coming down with the flu herself. Her breath hitched in her throat, her heart beat erratically, and heat warmed her through. How could he have this effect on her when she'd done everything she could to put him from her mind?

"Check on Joshua." He grabbed her hand, his eyes bright and insistent.

"I will. Lie still. If you try to talk, the coughing will get worse."

She checked on all her patients. Resting her hand on each brow, she tried to determine if their fevers had abated any. George stirred and rolled to his side, his breath slow and even. A spark of hope for him lit in her chest. For the first time, he appeared to be resting naturally.

Harold's head tossed on his pillow, his cheeks still red. She pressed a fresh cloth to his brow and consulted her notes and the clock. Time for more medicine. Every ministration came by rote, all her thoughts on Caleb.

"Meghan," he called.

A quick check on the sleeping Joshua, and then she rounded the bed to Caleb's side. He reached for her hand.

"What can I do?"

"Sit." His throat lurched, as if he fought against a cough. "I need to tell you something." He gave in to the cough, his chest heaving, the bed lurching with each racking spasm.

She moved to sit beside him, holding his shoulders as he curled in a half sit-up against the tearing coughs. "Don't talk. It will be all right."

"Don't leave." The worry in his eyes pulled at her heart. "Promise me you'll take care of Joshua."

Her fingers moved of their own accord, smoothing back the hair on his forehead and letting her finger slide down his cheek. The beginnings of a beard prickled her fingertips. "I'll take care of you all. Rest now."

His lashes lowered, but his grip on her hand remained tight.

Caleb wandered in a strange land. In moments of lucidity, he knew he was very sick, but between times, he drifted and dreamed. His bones ached deep in the marrow, and his joints radiated pain. Sharp-clawed beasts tore at his chest with every breath, and his head throbbed with every heartbeat. He staggered across a parched desert wasteland in search of water to quench his raging thirst, tripping, falling, fighting the thorns and sliding sand, the scorching heat and wind. In the distance, standing beside a waterfall, surrounded by trees and grass and cool mist, Meghan stood with her hands outstretched, a ring of yellow flowers gracing her hair. Her lips stretched in a beckoning smile, and she waved him on, but no matter how many sand dunes he stumbled over or cactus thickets he forced his way through, he could never narrow the distance between them. In time, her image began to waver and fade, and he clawed his way up yet another slippery slope, calling to her, begging her not to leave him. The wind sucked his words away, and she disappeared from view.

"He's so restless." Meghan mopped Caleb once more, holding down his arm when he tried to swat her away. "Half the time he's fighting me, and the other half, he's squeezing my hand so hard, it goes numb."

Doc Bates bent over Joshua on the other side of the bed, listening to his breathing while he waited for a thermometer reading. He straightened, his back cracking. "I sent word to Mr. and Mrs. Hualga at the reservation to tend the horses until Caleb and Joshua can go home. I told them under no circumstances to come here. They wouldn't be allowed into the hotel anyway, and I don't want them taking the sickness back to the reservation. I have enough patients as it is." He held the thermometer up to the light.

"How is he doing?"

"No better, no worse." He pressed his hands to the small of his back and kneaded. "I want you to get some rest. Mrs. Gregory is working out a schedule so we can spell everyone."

She wanted to protest that she couldn't leave her patients, but she was too tired. "What about you? Who's going to spell you?"

He rubbed his eyes, pinching the bridge of his nose. "There's a doctor coming from Flagstaff on the next train. As soon as he gets here, I'm going to fall into bed."

Meghan checked the clock, though the temperature in the room told her it had to be nearly noon. Four days since the train had come bringing the sick soldiers. Caleb stirred again, a soft moan escaping his lips. She smoothed the hair off his brow.

"At least we haven't lost anyone in the last few hours." Doc removed the thermometer from Joshua's mouth and squinted at the glass tube. Shaking it down, he swabbed it with alcohol before slipping it into its metal case and returning it to his pocket. After jotting a few notes, he swiped his wrist across his forehead. "Keep a close watch. From what I've been able to observe, the first sign of a patient heading toward real complications from this sickness is a bluish tinge to their extremities. From now on, I want you to check your patients' feet and check them often. I'll add it to the patient notes." When he'd finished writing out his instructions, he turned to leave and staggered, grabbing the edge of a dresser to steady himself.

Meghan rounded the bed to his side to grasp his elbow. "Are you all right? You're not feeling ill, are you?" Worry tightened her throat.

"No, just tired to the bone, like everyone else." He smiled and patted her hand. "You get some rest just as soon as someone comes to take your place."

She crossed her arms at her waist and bowed her head, leaning against the dresser. Sandpaper coated the insides of her eyelids, and her hands and shoulders ached from wringing out wet cloths. The room, in spite of her best efforts to keep it clean and fresh, smelled of sickness and heat. Lead weights pulled at her limbs, and sand dunes of tiredness invaded her head.

George shifted, drawing her attention. His eyes opened, and he stared at her. "Water?" His voice was weak as a whisper. She gave him a drink and went to check his patient notes to see when he could have more medicine.

Check all extremities for discoloration at least once an hour.

Doc's note swam before her vision, and she blinked, focusing once more.

She blew out a breath and went to George first, girding herself for the task. "George, I need to have a look at your feet. I'll get you tucked back in as soon as I can." He nodded and closed his eyes.

Tugging the bottom sheet out from the end of the mattress, she laid it back, exposing first George's feet then Harold's. Pink, and warm to the touch. Satisfied, she retucked the sheet and made a note of the time and condition.

Moving to the beds where Caleb and Joshua lay side by side, she took a deep breath and turned up the bottom of the sheet. Her hand stopped in midair, hovering, trembling, and the sheet dropped from her numb fingers.

Her breath clogged her throat. With her mouth hanging lax and her mind clanging and clamoring, she shook her head, blinking away what must be an exhaustion-induced hallucination. Her eyes roved to Joshua then back to Caleb.

Dizziness overtook her, and she clutched the footboard, closing her eyes against the nausea and vertigo. Realization smashed through her surprise. Her heart cried for Caleb, breaking into small pieces for all the wounds he'd suffered in silence, for the way he guarded his secret, never telling the truth about why he wasn't a soldier.

Many of the disjointed puzzle pieces, the things about Caleb that seemed to be in conflict, fell into place. The withered, buckled, wizened calf and foot explained so much, and yet filled her mind with questions. A tear splashed onto his twisted foot, and she reached out to brush it away. His skin was cool to the touch, and she swallowed against the lump in her throat.

Shame and guilt pounded hard on the heels of understanding.

Of all the wounding insults the people of Needles had inflicted, hers had been the most grievous. For she had given him hope and offered friendship and more before snatching it away, giving in to the pressures of those around her, siding with the ignorant and judgmental. Every accusation she'd hurled at him smacked her in the face.

After a quick check of Joshua's straight, strong limbs, she re-tucked the sheet, covering Caleb's secret and vowing to herself never to mention it to anyone. She was finished betraying Caleb's trust.

"Meghan?" he mumbled.

With a guilty start, she sought his face. His eyes remained closed, but he frowned, his hand grasping the air at his side.

She returned to her chair beside him and took his hand, rubbing the back of it with her thumb. His fingers closed around hers, fever-hot and rough, but his body relaxed a fraction, as if her touch brought him comfort.

He was the bravest man she'd ever known, and she'd called him a coward. He bore his burden in silence, never using it as an excuse, never giving in or giving up. He supported himself, even contributing to the war effort in spite of his leg. How did he manage to even walk without a limp? How had she and everyone else in this town missed the signs?

Her mind cast back to the clues she should've seen. How he usually stood with his weight on one leg. The strange way he mounted his horse. The fact that he'd come to the Dime-A-Dance but refused to dance. She'd taken his slow, even steps as a sign of his easygoing temperament, but now she could see he had to have been measuring his strides, concentrating on not letting his limp show.

And the chicken feather. Humiliated in front of a crowded dining room, in front of that army major, in front of her. Every word that bombastic virago had said to him pierced Meghan's heart. He'd bravely stood before that silly woman, taken her insults without firing back, and refused to fight. At the time, she'd thought he'd lost all dignity, but in truth, he'd preserved his honor, even if he was the only one who knew it.

Doc entered the room, his brows knit and furrows on his forehead. "I thought I'd just relieve you for a few moments and check your patients' feet myself, all right? Why don't you go get some fresh air on the balcony?" He took her elbow to lift her out of her chair.

Meghan tugged away, shaking her head. She kept hold of Caleb's hand on the white sheet. "You don't have to bother. I checked them already." Another tear leaked out of her eye, and she swiped it away.

The doctor slumped, hanging his head. "Then you know." A huge sigh heaved his white coat front. "If I hadn't been so tired, I never would've made that slip up." His hands balled at his sides. "Caleb is going to kill me when he finds out."

Swallowing against the lump in her throat, Meghan took a steadying breath. "Then we won't tell him, but I have to know what happened to him? Why is his leg like that?"

Doc sighed and scrubbed his eyes with the heels of his hands. "Let's go out into the hall where we can talk and not disturb anyone."

She followed him out of the room, blinking at the sunlight pouring in the hallway windows. With the blinds drawn and curtains pulled in the sickroom, she felt like a burrowing owl coming out at the wrong time of day.

Doc leaned against a windowsill, checking up and down the hall to make sure they were alone. "What you saw there is the result of poliomyelitis, otherwise known as infantile paralysis."

Meghan bit her lower lip. Poor Caleb. "Is it painful?"

"The initial illness certainly is. I'm told it's like the worst cramp or charley horse you can imagine. The muscles seize up and lock, and the nerves become confused. The body refuses to obey signals from the brain. The most severe cases result in permanent paralysis, atrophied muscles, and in some cases the bones get twisted and malformed because of the muscles pulling on them. Caleb was very young when he contracted the disease, and his legs didn't grow evenly afterward. The pain eventually subsides, but it can come back. Caleb's leg aches and is weak, especially when he overdoes the work, which is pretty much every day."

"Why didn't he ever tell anyone? Why let everyone think him a coward and profiteer? He has a perfectly legitimate reason not to enlist. In fact, the army wouldn't take him."

"Because he's proud and stubborn, that's why. He doesn't want any pity." Doc rubbed the back of his neck. "I suppose, now that you're his nurse, I can tell you a little of his history, the little bit he's shared with me, but it must go no further. We must guard his privacy in this matter."

Hearing how Caleb's family had turned against him when he'd contracted the disease broke her heart afresh. No wonder he'd said he had no family that claimed him. How could anyone turn their back on their own child? It wasn't as if he'd gotten ill on purpose. But to put him into an asylum, to refuse to even visit him. Fresh tears stung her eyes.

Doc waited as a busboy pushed a laundry cart down the hall before continuing. "He's so sensitive about people judging him because of his leg, he refuses to tell anyone. He won't wear a brace, even though it would help him, and he won't slow down. His leg gives him quite a bit of pain these days, but he keeps on. And I have a suspicion that somewhere in the not-too-distant past, a girl disappointed him, but he backs away from talking about it."

Meghan crumpled, leaning against the balcony railing. "And I haven't helped matters at all. Joshua was right when he said I'd let Caleb down."

"I've watched you two together. I had high hopes that you two might make a match of it. You care for him very much, don't you?"

"I did." She pressed her lips together. "I do. And I thought he cared for me."

"I think he still does."

"No, not after what I said to him. He'll never forgive me. He let himself be vulnerable, let himself show some emotion, and what did I do? I smacked his face and called him a coward."

"So that's it? One little setback in your relationship and you're going to quit on him?" Doc's voice flicked like a lash. "Who's the coward now?"

Meghan's backbone stiffened, and her hands fisted. "I'm no coward. It's just. . ."

"Just what? Caleb has had nothing but a raw deal for about as long as he can remember. But if you stand by him, you two can do anything. I've never seen anyone so willing to take on a challenge as you. Whether it's becoming a first-rate Harvey Girl—oh yes, I've heard from several sources what a fine waitress you've become, a credit to the company—or sewing that quilt and raising money with it, or being the best nurse we've got in the hotel right now. You never back down from a challenge, so why start now? If Caleb means anything to you, if you care for him at all, then get in there and fight for him. Fight first for his life, and then, when he's better, fight for his heart."

In spite of her exhaustion, the flame of ambition flared in Meghan's heart, the quickening of her pulse, the explosion of ideas, the call to the crusade.

"Do you think he'll forgive me? Do you think he'll have me?"

"You'll never know if you don't try." Doc stood, yawned, and checked his watch. "You'd best get back to your patients. Until Caleb is better, don't broach the subject. Between the two of us, we should be able to care for him without letting on that you know. I'm here if you need me."

He headed down the hall to check on more patients, and Meghan took a deep breath, girding her mind and heart for the battle of her life.

Chapter 15

The week passed in a blur for Meghan. For days, she left Caleb's side only to eat or change into a clean dress. Caleb's fever soared, his chest racked with coughs, and he writhed as if trying to escape his own aching body. The only time he lay still was when Meghan held his hand and bathed his face and neck with cool, damp cloths. She prayed long and often for both him and Joshua, dozing in the rocker, starting awake every time one of her patients moaned or moved, and refusing to budge, even when Mrs. Gregory offered to send someone to replace her.

On the fifth day, Caleb's fever finally broke. Meghan, so tired she could hardly raise her arm, touched his forehead. Cool and slightly moist as a fine sheen of sweat appeared on his brow. Tears of thankfulness sprang to her scratchy eyes, and she bit her lip, sending up a prayer of thanksgiving. For the first time in what seemed forever, Caleb looked at her with clear eyes.

"Meghan? How's Joshua?" His voice croaked from dryness and lack of use.

Meghan pushed him gently back against the pillows when he tried to sit up. "Shh, he's fine. We moved him to the other bed." She poured a glass of water and held it to his cracked lips. "His fever broke two days ago, and he's resting comfortably, though he's so hungry all the time, I can barely keep him fed."

He lay back with a sigh. "The soldiers?"

"A special train with army doctors arrived. They loaded all the recovering soldiers onto litters and put them on the east-bound. They're at an army base by now, recuperating."

"And the town?" His eyelashes fluttered, as if he had to work to focus. After nearly a week of delirium and fever, he'd lost weight, and no doubt would take weeks to recover fully. But her heart still soared. Once the fever broke, if he took care, he should be on the road to recovery.

"There have been a lot of cases, but most are being treated in their own homes now that the soldiers are gone and Doc can take the time to visit house to house." She straightened the covers, careful to keep from looking toward the foot of the bed. "You and Joshua are the last patients in the hotel. The trains are running again, and the dining room and lunchroom are operating once more, though all the waitresses wear their masks while they serve."

"What about my horses?" He struggled up to his elbows. "And how long have I been sick?"

She pressed her palms against his shoulders, conscious of warm, male muscles and solid bone. "Lie still. Your horses are fine. Joshua's parents are looking after them. You've been very ill, and it's going to take awhile before you regain your strength. I'm going to send down to the kitchen for some broth and hot tea." As she made to move away from the bed, he grasped her hand.

"Have you been here the whole time?"

Shrugging, she withdrew her fingers from his. "Mostly. Doc spelled me sometimes. Now, you rest. You need to build up your strength."

He was asleep again before he'd finished half the broth, but this time it was a peaceful slumber. Meghan drifted to sleep watching the steady rise and fall of his chest.

Doc gently shook her awake. "I see we've made some improvement since this morning."

Blinking and shaking her head, she chased the muzziness

from her brain. "Yes, his fever broke just before noon. He's been sleeping ever since."

Caleb's eyes opened. "I'm awake now."

Lifting Caleb's wrist, Doc stared at his watch. "How are you feeling?"

"Like last week's leftovers." He coughed, holding his chest and scrunching his eyes.

"That's to be expected. The cough will most likely hang on for a while. We'll try to get you propped up a little more now to help you clear your lungs. Don't want you developing pneumonia after all the fine nursing you've had."

After satisfying himself as to his patient's welfare, Doc sent a no-nonsense look Meghan's way. "Okay, young lady, I've humored you because it really did seem as if Caleb rested more comfortably when you were nearby, but now that he's on the mend, I'm putting my foot down. You're going to return to your room and go to bed. Natalie came back to the hotel yesterday, and she'll look after you."

Now that Caleb and Joshua were both out of danger, she longed to fall headfirst into her pillow and not resurface for a week, but she couldn't just abandon her post. "Who will take care of my patients?"

"I will. I'll get them shifted to my house where I can see to them myself. Mrs. Gregory wants her hotel back, and I quite agree. It appears the worst of the epidemic is over for the time being, so I can more than take care of two convalescent patients in my own home. Now get." He shooed her toward the door. "Natalie's waiting for you."

Meghan stumbled along the hallway toward the staff quarters, dragging at her apron strings and yawning. For more than ten days, she'd survived on catnaps and quick meals. She hadn't slept in her own bed for such a long time, everything seemed strange as she opened the bedroom door.

"There you are. How are Caleb and Joshua?" Natalie rose from the corner chair and laid aside her handwork. Tired as she was, Meghan noticed Natalie's thickened waist. She wouldn't be able to hide her condition much longer.

"Caleb's fever broke at last. Doc is going to take both of them to his house. He's ordered me to bed." Boat anchors tugged at her eyelids, and she couldn't stop yawning as she slipped out of her black dress.

"I'm glad he did. If you'll forgive me for saying so, you look like you've been dragged through a knothole backward." Natalie turned back the sheets and went to draw the drapes. "You sleep. We'll talk later."

Meghan fell into bed and fathoms deep into sleep.

"You can stop pretending now, Doc." Caleb eased down onto the mattress and let Doc help him swing his legs up off the floor. Tiredness seeped from every pore, and he didn't protest when Doc pulled the sheet up for him.

"Pretending?" Doc felt Caleb's brow.

"That she didn't see my leg."

"You need to rest. The move from the hotel to my place took a lot out of you."

"You're doing it again."

"What?"

"Changing the subject."

"Why can't you lie back and go to sleep like Joshua? He isn't giving me half as much trouble as you." Doc lowered the window shade. "We can talk about this later, when you're stronger."

In spite of his weariness, Caleb pushed himself upright.

His arms trembled, and the room swam. "Doc, I need to know the truth. How did she react? Was she repulsed?" He hauled in a staggering breath, his chest muscles aching from so many days of coughing. "Of course she was repulsed. Forget it. I don't know why I even asked." Arms buckling, he flopped back onto the pillows.

"If you must know the truth, then, yes, she did see your leg, several times in fact, and not once did I get the impression she was repulsed. Sorry and sad that you had to suffer? Yes, but most of all, I got the impression that Meghan was remorseful. She feels bad about how she and the town have treated you. Poor girl."

"Poor girl?" Caleb scowled.

"That's right. She feels bad, and so do I about you contracting polio and suffering long-term consequences, but you are the one who set the rules for this game. You chose to keep your infirmity a secret. You chose to let this town believe a lie. You chose to let Meghan believe a lie. I can only guess you wanted to protect your pride. You built a wall around yourself and rejected the people of this town before they got a chance to reject you. But Meghan got in, didn't she? She snuck around or over that wall, and when she got too close, you chased her away because you were afraid. Instead of telling her the truth, you used the lie to fend her off." Doc rubbed his hands down his face. "That girl cares for you a great deal. She told me so, but what does it matter if you're too afraid to accept her? In that respect, the town of Needles has it right. You *are* a coward."

Caleb's hands fisted on the sheet, and waves of weakness flowed over him. His one ally in this town, and he'd been betrayed. His mind swam with crashing thoughts, and he clamped his lips together to keep from saying all the words that crowded into his throat.

Doc shook his head. "I'm sorry. You're in no condition to deal with all this right now. I should've held my tongue." Lines deepened on his face, and sadness invaded his eyes. "It's just that I see how good you and Meghan could be together. She'd never let something like a bum leg come between you. I hope, if she comes to visit, you can finally be honest with each other."

He closed the door behind himself, leaving Caleb alone.

She won't come. And I don't want her to. Doc's bald statements reverberated in Caleb's head. *Doc doesn't know what it's like. He's a whole man. Nobody would pity him or reject him. When you aren't whole, all you have is your pride. If I gave that up, what would I have? A man had to have his pride, didn't he? And if he couldn't be proud of his abilities, then at least he could be proud knowing he had right on his side when others accused him of dodging the draft.*

"Pride goeth before destruction, and a haughty spirit before a fall."

Caleb's eyelids fluttered open. Where had that come from? As a man who had spent the past twenty years living in mortal terror of falling, the Bible verse hit hard at his very core.

If you let go of your pride, you'll have nothing, Caleb McBride. You'll be nothing, a nobody, just like you were when your father looked right through you as a kid. He clutched the sheet, trying to find a hold as the walls around his heart began to quake.

"If you let go of your pride, you'll have Me. I am your Father, and I know you. I always see you. I'm just waiting for you to finally see Me."

But what can I bring to You that You will accept, if I have nothing left of myself, nothing that makes me worthy of Your love? Had all his striving been for nothing? Bits of rubble fell from the barricade he'd erected around his pride.

"The sacrifices of God are a broken spirit: a broken and a

contrite heart, O God, Thou wilt not despise.

"There is nothing you can bring to make yourself worthy. I am the One who makes you worthy. Your worth isn't determined by your physical body or your intellect or your pride. Your worth isn't determined by how others see you or by how you see yourself. Your worth is established because I died for you. Because I have called you worthy. You are Mine. Abandon your pride, humble yourself."

A rock-hard lump formed in Caleb's throat as his soul wrestled with the truth he had known from a child but constantly fought against. If he abandoned his pride, he would be vulnerable. He would have to be open about his leg, about his life. He couldn't hide anymore.

And that meant facing the people of Needles.

Even worse, it meant facing Meghan.

"I thought you were over this nonsense." Mrs. Gregory snapped open a tablecloth and let it float onto the dining room table. "I thought you had come to your senses and finally seen Caleb McBride for what he is. You told me you were finished with him."

"It isn't nonsense, and I was wrong. I judged him unfairly, and so have you and the rest of the town. He's a fine, upstanding man, and he deserves to have his name on the quilt alongside everyone else." Meghan rolled a cart of china and cutlery across the floor and began setting the places. Her first shift back and the fireworks were already beginning. She tried to remind herself about the stress Mrs. Gregory was under, the worry that dogged her steps as she waited to hear about her son's fate, but the injustice of her claims made it difficult.

Meghan could tell, in spite of the mask covering the lower half of Mrs. Gregory's face, that the head waitress's mouth was pinched in a persimmon pucker. The next tablecloth snapped open with more force. "I won't have it, and what's more, the people of this town won't have it. If you persist and include Caleb McBride's name on that quilt, I assure you no one will bid on it."

"That's not fair. He's done nothing to deserve this treatment." Meghan's indignation burned hot and bright in her chest, all the more because of her guilt in the matter. But she wouldn't back down. It was too important. "If you really knew him, you'd see that." How could Meghan convince her without betraying Caleb's secret?

"Poppycock. I've known him longer than you have, young lady, and I have to insist that you stop this. Against all initial indications, you've become a valued member of this serving crew and one of the best waitresses I've ever trained. I would hate to see you throw it all away on a wastrel like Caleb McBride. If you persist in seeing him and in putting his name on that quilt—making him the equal of everyone in this town who has sacrificed and prayed and labored for the cause when he's nothing but a coward with no sense of duty, I will be forced to make an adjustment that I don't want to make." She straightened the chairs at the table. All around them girls bustled in and out of the kitchen and dish room and linen store preparing for the incoming train passengers. Though they continued with their work, they couldn't help but overhear. The longer Mrs. Gregory talked, the louder her voice grew.

Meghan adjusted her mask, gulping. Sent home in disgrace to face her father with yet another failed escapade. She couldn't let that happen. He'd never let her do anything ever again. "You'd dismiss me?"

"I would." Mrs. Gregory pulled herself up to her full height, several inches taller than Meghan. She crossed her arms at her waist, formidable and every inch the boss.

"You can't fire me for putting Caleb's name on the quilt. I donated the money in his name. If you fired me for that, I would be forced to go to Mr. Ford Harvey himself." Her knees quaked as she played her ace card.

All work in the dining room had ceased, and the girls didn't even pretend not to be listening anymore. Even Natalie poked her head around the corner of the soda fountain door.

Mrs. Gregory's eyes blazed and her face hardened, but it was the chilling calm, the razor edge to her voice that froze Meghan to the core. "The quilt is yours, and you can certainly choose which names you put on it, and I would not fire you for that. I would, however, fire you for having an improper relationship with a man while in the employ of the Harvey Company. You don't deny that you've been seen in Caleb McBride's company upon several occasions. I myself caught you consorting alone and unchaperoned the night of the benefit dance. You've been out to his property more than once, and when he fell ill here in the hotel, you refused to leave his side. Those are just the times I know about. Consorting with men, especially men of Caleb McBride's type, is forbidden. I've warned you before, and I'm warning you now. If his name goes on the quilt and you choose to make public your feelings for him, I will dismiss you from the company."

Meghan gasped. "I've never had an improper relationship with a man in my life."

"I know what I know." Her hands settled on her hips. "Now, unless you wish to have your employment terminated for insubordination, I suggest you finish setting these tables and learn to hold your tongue." She glanced at the clock over the doorway and clapped her hands, raising her voice to encompass all the wait staff. "The train will arrive in less than ten minutes.

I expect a flawless service, girls."

Meghan slapped plates and cutlery on the table, ignoring the curious, sympathetic, and speculative glances being sent her way. Now she knew how Caleb felt, being falsely accused. At least Caleb had the sense to keep his mouth shut.

"It's the right thing to do." Meghan picked at the seam holding the binding to the quilt. Her heart thudded in her chest, and her mind raced. Was she making the biggest error of her life or redeeming her biggest mistake?

Natalie ran the iron over the bib of an apron. "I know it is, but what about Mrs. Gregory? She was very clear."

"But she's wrong, and I've given in for too long. It isn't that I don't feel for her. Her son is fighting for his life, all shot up in some foreign hospital. But that doesn't mean she should be allowed to bully people. Your husband and my brother are on the front lines, and we're not slapping down ultimatums and threatening people with unfounded accusations." She freed the corner of the quilt block and picked up her embroidery thread. The need to hurry made her fumble-fingered.

"Mr. Gibson will be here this afternoon for the rally tonight. What are you going to tell him if no one bids on your quilt? How are you going to explain the shortfall in your pledge?"

She shrugged, though a heavy hand pressed her shoulders at the thought. "I'll give him the money I raised from the signatures, and I'll tell him the truth. I made the quilt in good faith, and if no one bids on it, then I will have to admit defeat in that quarter." She swallowed the bitter lump in her throat and jerked her chin up. "But I don't care. I'll be victorious in a more important battle. The battle of right and wrong." Her needle poked in and out of the white fabric.

"What about the ambulance? What about Lars and Derek and the other soldiers? You've been on a crusade all summer long, and you're so close to your goal. Not to mention what will happen if you go through with this. Mrs. Gregory will fire you quicker than you can say American Red Cross. Then where will you be?"

"I'll be on the side of right." Meghan set her mouth and drew the red embroidery thread through the cloth to form a capital *C*.

With a sigh, Natalie set the iron upright and hung the apron on a hanger. "You're the most stubborn person I've ever met. I'm going out for a bit. Do you need anything from Claypool's?"

"No. I have to finish this, and then I'm on duty in the dining room until the rally starts."

"I'll be back before then." She picked up a basket and held it in front of her. For the past week, she'd been carrying things with her to shield her middle from speculative eyes. How long before someone noticed and started whispering? "I hope you know what you're doing."

"So do I."

Caleb pushed his good foot on the boards and set the rocker into motion, studying the view from Doc's front porch. For the first time in nearly three weeks, he felt almost normal, and he sighed, flexing his hands and rolling his shoulders. Tomorrow, he and Joshua would head home. It was time to get back to the horses. The Hualgas had urged them both to stay in town until they were fully recovered, and Caleb knew the horses were well looked after, but a man needed to shoulder his own responsibilities. He'd been laid up long enough. Besides which, if he went home, he'd stop hoping and expecting Meghan to walk over from the hotel. In spite of Doc's prediction that he'd see her again, she'd stayed away, causing doubt and uncertainty and all the old feelings to come crowding back. His chest pinched. *Stop thinking about her.*

Forcing his mind away from Meghan, he considered his other dilemma. How to make known to the people of Needles why he hadn't enlisted. It wasn't as if he could just put an advertisement in the newspaper, could he?

He picked up the copy of the *Desert Star* from the side table and scanned the front page. The entire top half under the masthead was devoted to tonight's Red Cross rally at the El Garces Hotel. Below the fold, more news from the war front about the desperate fighting. But this time there was cause for hope. Only days before, the Allied troops had broken through the German fortifications at the Hindenburg line. Surely, with such a huge victory, the end of the war must be drawing near.

"Here." Joshua edged open the screen door, carefully balancing a tray. Ice clinked in a pitcher of lemonade. "It's going to be tart. I stirred in the last of the sugar, but it wasn't much."

Caleb sipped the pale yellow liquid and winced. "Whew."

"Yeah, but at least it's cold."

"You up to going back to the ranch tomorrow?" He set the glass down.

"I'm ready." Joshua took the other chair, stretching his legs out before him and resting his glass against his lean stomach.

"Doc said half days to start with for both of us. Last thing we want is a relapse."

"At least all this laying around has given me a chance to read." Joshua withdrew a slim volume from his hip pocket. *Diseases of the Pancreas* in gold letters on a clothbound cover. "I think I've read just about every medical book Doc has."

"You've made up your mind to go to medical school then?"

He nodded. "Doc says I can do it, and that he'll help me. He's already started putting out some feelers. Maybe I can start at the new year."

A small figure in black and white hurried toward them, and for a moment, Caleb's heart leaped, but as the woman drew near, his pulse subsided. No red hair, no flashing green eyes. Not Meghan. Caleb laid aside the newspaper and pushed himself to his feet as Miss Daviot turned in at the gate. He cleared his throat and frowned toward Joshua, who snapped his book shut and scrambled to his feet.

She mounted the steps, and Joshua offered her his chair. "Ma'am. I'll get another glass."

Wiping her brow, she took the chair and set her basket on her lap. "Thank you, Joshua. Mr. McBride."

"Caleb, please." He resumed his seat. "What can we do for you? Doc's not here. He walked up the street to the Sawyer place. A couple of their little ones had the influenza pretty bad, and he wanted to check on their progress now that they're on the mend."

"Actually, it's you I wanted to see." A flush decorated her cheeks, though he couldn't tell if it was from the heat or some other reason. "It's about Meghan."

His heart did a hiccup, and his mouth went dry. In spite of the tartness, he swigged a mouthful of the lemonade, screwing up his eyes as the sourness bit deep. "What about her?"

"She's about to commit Red Cross membership and career suicide. Since you're the cause, I thought you should know the sacrifice she's willing to make for you."

"What?"

"It's this quilt. She informed Mrs. Gregory this morning

that she intended to put your name on it. Mrs. Gregory told her in no uncertain terms that if she did, not a soul in town would bid for it. Meghan was hoping to raise several hundred dollars from auctioning the quilt in order to reach her pledge of one thousand dollars to purchase a Red Cross ambulance. If no one bids, she will be humiliated in front of the town, disgraced before the Red Cross, and even worse, Mrs. Gregory said she will fire Meghan."

A squirming ball of worms took up residence in Caleb's gut. Sick, clammy weakness washed over him. "She can't fire Meghan for something like that."

"She says she'll fire her for breaking the company's rules against fraternizing with gentlemen while in the Harvey employ. In short, Meghan will lose her job because she has fallen in love with you."

Caleb blinked, as stunned as if she'd hit him with a base-ball bat. He said the first thing that popped into his mind. "Meghan's not in love with me."

The screen door creaked, and Joshua emerged with another glass. Right behind him came Doc. Their snorts of derision mingled, and Joshua rolled his eyes.

Doc sauntered to the porch rail and leaned against it. "I came in through the back, and just in time, too."

Joshua sank, cross-legged onto the planks and leaned against a post. "How come everybody in town knows Meghan's in love with you except you?"

"Then where has she been the last couple weeks? Stands to reason if a girl loved a fellow, she'd come and see him, wouldn't she?" Caleb set his glass on the table and leaned forward, bracing his forearms on his thighs.

"She slept straight through the first day, and on my orders." Doc poked his chest with his thumb. "I told her to stick to her room and do no work at all for the next couple of days to recover from all that nursing."

Natalie toyed with the handle on her basket. "And ever since then, she's been either working flat stick in the dining room, or she's been sewing like crazy to get the quilt finished on time. As it is, she didn't have time to quilt it. Just ended up tying it with red yarn. Meghan's barely had a moment to herself. And if Mrs. Gregory found she'd snuck out to see you, she'd have been fired on the spot, quilt or no quilt. Her not coming to see you doesn't mean she doesn't love you. Perhaps it means she's trying to protect you from more of this town's scorn raining down on you." Her eyes narrowed, as if she were wondering if he were good enough for her friend, and he wasn't exactly coming up to scratch. "If she didn't love you, why would she risk her job and being humiliated in front of the whole town?"

"We've all tried to tell you." Joshua drew his knees up. "That girl is in love with you, and even a blind mule with his head in bucket could see you're in love with her. The question is, what are you going to do about it?"

"What about this Lars fellow she said she loved?" Caleb grasped at another straw.

Natalie rolled her eyes. "Lars is her brother. Of course she loves him."

Shocked relief made his face go slack. Her brother?

"Well," Joshua asked, "what are you going to do?"

Their eyes bored into him, and he wanted to squirm like a first grader caught putting a frog in the teacher's desk. And yet, Meghan loved him? Was willing to stand up to an entire town on his behalf, even knowing he was a cripple?

"Well?" Doc prodded.

"My truck is still at the hotel, isn't it?"

"Right where you left it when you brought Joshua in. Why?"

"I need it if I'm going to get out to the ranch."

"What?" All three spoke in unison. Joshua's mouth flopped open, and disapproval invaded Doc's eyes. Natalie bit her lower lip and shook her head.

"I need to go home."

Natalie's mouth dropped open, and a look of pure disappointed disgust locked Joshua's features. Doc shook his head and pulled his hands from his pants' pockets. "I don't want you driving out into the desert by yourself. I'll take you." His voice sounded leaden with defeat.

Caleb stood, bracing himself for what was to come and praying he had the courage to see it through.

Chapter 16

Meghan hurried to change out of her uniform and into the new dress she'd ordered from the Sears Roebuck catalog just for tonight's occasion. A beautiful green voile with lace trim, it was as up to the minute as the wide-brimmed hat she'd ordered to go with it. The satin sash on the dress and the ribbons on the hat matched perfectly. As she donned it, she felt she was gearing up as a knight to go into battle.

She set the hat at a cheeky angle and winked at her reflection to give herself courage. "We who are about to die salute you." She snapped a salute, picked up the carefully folded quilt, and went to meet her fate.

Citizens of Needles trooped upstairs for the festivities. Jenny Ralston had delivered the news that Mr. Gibson had arrived and that Mrs. Gregory had fallen over herself to make him welcome. With no evening train scheduled, the entire hotel staff had been pressed into service preparing the north loggia with lights and bunting, tables and streamers.

It seemed as if the entire city had turned out, as if to celebrate after laboring under the threat and burden of influenza for so long. Perhaps a little light gaiety would offset some of the sorrows.

Meghan skirted clusters of chatting guests, her quilt tucked under her arm. All around the perimeter of the room, auction items had been set out. Jars of jam, baskets, lace collars, breads and cakes, needlepoint pillows. A small card marked the place where her quilt should go, the last item, and the supposed highlight of the auction.

Feeling the eyes watching her, noting the stilling of conversation, Meghan laid the quilt out on the table, draping it to show off the red crosses on the white fields. From the curious craning of necks and the way people crowded around when she stepped back, Meghan could only surmise that word had gotten around about her confrontation with Mrs. Gregory.

Someone linked her arm, and Meghan turned. Natalie squeezed her elbow, her cheeks bright and her blue eyes brilliant. "You did it then?"

Meghan couldn't speak, so she nodded. Mrs. Gregory sailed into their sphere of vision, parted the onlookers and reached for the quilt. Shaking out its folds, she scanned name after name until she came to the bottom right corner.

Caleb McBride.

In the same square as Doctor Bates's, Mr. & Mrs. Weeks's, Natalie's, and Meghan's.

There could be no mistaking Meghan's intent. Where every other square bore four names, one in each corner, this square bore six. Meghan had embroidered Caleb's name just under hers.

They would rise or fall together.

And from the glare in Mrs. Gregory's eyes, it would be a spectacular fall.

She and Natalie found seats near the quilt and not too near the front. "I want to be able to make an escape if they come after me with torches and pitchforks." Meghan tried to make a joke, but it fell flat.

"Doc should be here soon." Natalie fussed with her handkerchief, twisting it into a knotted mess.

"Did you see him? Did he say how Caleb was?" All week her thoughts had centered on Caleb, praying he was recovering, hoping Doc would come to the hotel, eyeing the calendar waiting for her next half day off so she could at least go to Caleb and apologize face-to-face.

"Shh, they're starting."

This time it was the mayor of Needles who made the introductions as people settled into their seats. Jenny Ralston slid into the chair next to Meghan and bumped shoulders.

"Did you do it?" Her whisper carried at least three rows back.

"Shh. Yes."

"Girl, you are either really brave or really stupid."

At the moment, Meghan felt more the latter than the former.

Mr. Gibson stood and moved to the podium as applause rippled through the group. His florid face glistened in the evening heat. Someone grunted behind her and nudged her chair. Meghan glanced over her shoulder. A black-clad matron leaned forward. "How could you?"

In an instant Meghan recognized her. She was the woman who had given Caleb the white chicken feather. A shiver raced across Meghan's shoulders, and she turned to face the front. She knotted her fingers in her lap, pressing her knees together to stop them from quivering.

"Ladies and gentlemen, thank you so much for coming out tonight. I hope you've brought your generosity as well. We have a fine lineup of items for the auction." Mr. Gibson yielded the podium to the auctioneer for the night, Mr. Stock.

The hotel manager, thinner than ever after his bout with the flu, smiled and held up the first item, a hand-crocheted dresser scarf. "What's my bid for this fine piece?"

The bidding began sluggishly, and Meghan kept her eyes on her hands. As the auctioneer worked his way around the perimeter of the balcony, the tension in the room grew. Or was it just the tension in her own middle?

Jenny bid for a couple of small items, but neither Natalie or Meghan raised their hands. Finally, Mr. Stock approached the quilt. Meghan raised her chin and took a deep breath. The way Mr. Stock tugged at his collar, he acted as if Mrs. Gregory herself were holding the leash. He darted a glance at the head waitress as if to ask what to do.

Mr. Gibson stepped in. "I'm so pleased with this fine quilt. When Miss Thorson declared her intention of tackling such a large project by herself, I had my doubts." He lifted the quilt and motioned for a man on the end of a row to come help him hold it up for all to see. "Look at this. Every square filled. I see some familiar names here. Mrs. Gregory, Mr. Stock, Mr. Claypool." He nodded in the direction of Needles's most prominent businessman. "And some very famous names as well. Charlie Chaplin and Mary Pickford? And the distinguished Mr. Ford Harvey. Surely such wonderful additions to the quilt add greatly to its value. I can't wait to see how much money such a beautiful item will bring in. Proceed, Mr. Stock."

A ripple went through the room and through Meghan's body. Though she tried to take deep breaths, all her air crowded into the tops of her lungs and didn't satisfy her need for oxygen at all. This was it. Her final, glorious stand at the El Garces Hotel.

Mr. Stock cleared his throat. Meghan dared a look at some of the faces in the crowd. The hard eyes and pinched lips boded no good.

"What's my opening bid for this quilt?" His voice squeaked a bit, and he modulated it.

Silence.

"Shall we open the bidding at one hundred dollars?"

Nothing.

Heat rushed into Meghan's cheeks. Several women smirked

and crossed their arms. Mrs. Gregory's lips flattened.

"Shall we say, fifty?" A hint of pleading tinged the question.

The night breeze riffled the palm leaves just over the balcony rail, the only sound in the room. Hot tears burned the backs of Meghan's eyes, but she blinked hard, refusing to let on how much she hurt inside. If Caleb could bear this town's disapproval and scorn, she could, too. Natalie reached over and patted her arm.

Mr. Gibson frowned and tugged at his moustache. "Not a single bid? For this fine quilt?" His frown deepened, and he sought Meghan's face.

"Five hundred." A deep voice from near the staircase had every head turning.

Meghan's heart jumped right up to her throat and stayed there. That was the voice that filled her dreams, a voice she would know anywhere.

Her eyes met Caleb's, and her mouth went dry. Intense, locked on hers, and challenging her to rise to the occasion. She could only see him from the waist up as the people seated between them blocked her view. It was all she could do not to run straight to him, to throw her arms around his neck and beg his forgiveness for judging him so unfairly, to express her thankfulness that he'd come tonight, and above all, her shock at him bidding on the quilt.

Step, *clank,* step, *clank.* He came toward her.

A murmur started in the back—gasps, grunts, questioning tones.

Step, *clank,* step, *clank.*

The tears she had fought now won the war and tumbled over her lashes as he came into full view.

He was wearing his leg brace, the one Doc said he refused to ever wear again. Wide buckles held it to his thigh, knee, and ankle, and a steel frame ran down each side and under his boot. He ignored the reactions around him, making a beeline for Meghan. Jenny scooted out of her chair and into an empty one in the row ahead, turning to stare along with everyone else.

Without taking his eyes from Meghan, he spoke again. "I believe the bid was five hundred dollars, Mr. Stock."

He held his hand out to Meghan. Her own shot out to grasp his fingers.

"You don't have to do this." Her whisper strangled on all the emotions running through her as she took in his features. Paler and thinner, he still looked wonderful to her.

"I want to."

Mrs. Gregory snapped upright out of her chair. "Miss Thorson—"

"Six hundred dollars."

The balcony deck seemed to sway beneath Meghan's chair. Heads swiveled again, and Mrs. Gregory gasped.

A man stepped out of the shadows, hands in his pockets. A man Meghan recognized, and from her pale expression and slack jaw, a man Mrs. Gregory recognized as well.

"Sorry. You don't mind if I bid, too?" His lips twitched beneath his moustache.

Mr. Stock sagged against the edge of the table and mopped his brow. His Adam's apple lurched. When he'd finally composed himself, he managed to utter, "The bid is six hundred. Will you raise to seven, Mr. McBride?"

"No, thank you. I believe six hundred is enough. I wouldn't want to bid against my good friend, Mr. Harvey." He flashed a quick smile and nodded at Mr. Harvey. Meghan's heart swelled until she thought it might burst.

"Sold to Mr. Harvey for six hundred dollars." Mr. Stock drew in a deep breath. "I'd like to thank you all for coming. That concludes our auction for this evening, ladies and gentlemen. There are refreshments laid on in the dining room downstairs. If you will all make your way down there, and don't forget to pick up your auction purchases and pay for them before you go downstairs."

Everyone remained still for a moment, and then the room burst into movement and voices. Meghan hardly dared believe in the warmth surrounding her heart and mind, all caused by the tender glow in Caleb's eyes. She swallowed and twisted her fingers through his. He squeezed her hand and winked at her.

"Caleb."

Someone jostled her, and he steadied her, holding her elbow. She tried again. "Caleb, I—"

Before she could say another word, Mr. Gibson descended on them.

"My dear, so happy. Delighted. The quilt is wonderful. Six hundred dollars." Mr. Gibson shook her hand hard enough to rattle her teeth. "Mr. Harvey has agreed that I should take the quilt with me on my travels. He thinks—and I quite agree— that having it to display as I speak would certainly inspire other Red Cross groups to make their own signature quilts. You'll have an impact on not just this group, but many others as well." He clasped her shoulder, beaming.

Reluctantly she withdrew her hand from Caleb's and fumbled with her handbag, withdrawing a receipt. "I don't want to forget. If you give this to Mr. Stock, he will get you the money from the signature subscriptions. It amounted to almost five hundred dollars, and I thought it best to keep the money in the hotel safe. That, along with Mr. Harvey's generous bid on the quilt should be enough for that ambulance."

"Splendid, splendid. I shall chase down Mr. Stock forthwith." He drifted away, beaming and accepting congratulations.

Mrs. Gregory took his place. Her cheeks blazed with color. "Miss Thorson, what is the meaning of this?" She raked her gaze over Caleb's leg brace. "What sort of charade are you trying to pull?" She turned to Meghan. "And how dare you go behind my back and summon the head of the company." Her face went from red to dull purple.

Doc Bates, hitherto unnoticed by Meghan, tapped Mrs. Gregory on the shoulder. "Perhaps you'd like to sit down somewhere? You look a trifle flushed. I'm sure we can have a reasonable discussion without any unnecessary accusations."

"I quite agree." Mr. Harvey's voice dropped onto the conversation like a blanket smothering a fire. "Might I suggest the principle parties wait here until the rest of the guests have drifted down to the food?"

Natalie rose, but before she could leave, Meghan grabbed her hand. "Please, stay."

And so, in a very short time, only a few people remained under the bunting and paper lanterns: Meghan, Caleb, Natalie, Doc Bates, Mr. Harvey, Mrs. Gregory, and Mr. Stock, who came puffing up the stairs after seeing the reception was well underway. Caleb took possession of Meghan's hand once more.

Mrs. Gregory fired first. "Mr. Harvey, you should be advised that I'm firing Miss Thorson. In spite of multiple warnings by myself and others, she has persistently defied me in regards to seeing Mr. McBride. As you know, it is against company policy for Harvey Girls to have romantic liaisons while in the company's employ." She glared at Meghan and Caleb's linked fingers. "On more than one occasion I've found Miss Thorson in Mr. McBride's company including finding them in an embrace right here in the hotel."

Caleb's fingers tightened on Meghan's, and heat crept up her cheeks. That magical night by the fountain was forever burned in her mind and on her heart. If Mrs. Gregory hadn't interrupted, they very well might've shared their first kiss under a felicitous moon rather than that anger-prompted kiss that ended in a disastrous slap.

Mrs. Gregory wasn't finished. "I'm also appalled that she would bother you with this situation. Contacting the head of the company?" She rolled her eyes. "Insubordination, failure to follow the chain of command, improper behavior with a member of the opposite gender, and now this."

"But I didn't—" Meghan's protest was cut off by Mr. Stock clearing his throat.

"Mrs. Gregory, I was the one who notified Mr. Harvey. I received a bulletin that he was traveling on the westbound that came in at noon today, and I asked if he could stay over to deal with one or two things that were likely to crop up tonight." He tugged at his collar and rubbed his hand down the front of his white jacket. "You see, I heard you were planning action against Miss Thorson, and while I can appreciate your sympathies, what with your son off to war and all, I felt perhaps you were allowing personal prejudices to cloud your otherwise impeccable judgment."

Groping for a chair, Mrs. Gregory plopped down. Her face took on the hue of ashes, and Meghan's chest squeezed. She sent Mr. Stock a grateful look. Imagine the fussy, standoffish hotel manager going out on a limb for her like that.

Mrs. Gregory seemed to rally a bit. "Well, that doesn't excuse her behavior, consorting with the likes of this charlatan and coward, and openly defying me when I ordered her not to include his name on that quilt." She was like a cornered animal, spitting and snarling, and trembling with fear.

"Perhaps I can shed some light on this subject. With your permission, Caleb?" Doc Bates raised one eyebrow.

"No, Doc, I best do it myself." Caleb's thumb brushed the back of Meghan's hand, and an uprush of love for him welled through her. She squeezed back.

"I know it looks fishy, me wearing this brace, but the truth is, I should've worn it more often up to now. But I was too proud. I didn't want anyone pitying me. I could take disdain, anger, even disgust, but I couldn't stomach pity." His other hand strayed to the leather wrap around his thigh. "When I was a kid, I came down with polio. My leg"—he patted the steel brace— "isn't as strong as it should be. I would've liked nothing better than to enlist and go defend my country alongside fine soldiers like your son. But the army wouldn't take me."

"So," Doc butted in, "he's helping the war effort in another way. He trains horses for the military. They hired him, they ship the horses to him, and he turns them into cavalry mounts. He won't brag on himself, so I will. He's found ways around his—infirmity—to turn out some of the best mounts the army has ever seen. When Major Alexander was here to look over the operation, he was very impressed. Caleb is one of the best trainers the army has."

Mrs. Gregory's eyebrows bunched, and she glared, first at Caleb, then his brace, then at Doc. "Why didn't he say so in the first place? Why let us think he was a coward?"

"I didn't think it was any of your business. I've never asked you about your childhood illnesses or your past. I wanted to be judged for what I am—a man, a horse trainer, a good citizen, a patriot—not for what I'm not." He squared his shoulders. "And, because I want to be honest, I have to admit it had a lot to do with pride. I was ashamed of my leg, and I didn't want people to know about it. The pain of being shunned as a coward was nothing to the pain of being shunned as a cripple. But it's time to put that behind me. I am what I am. Folks can take it or leave it, but I'm not hiding it anymore." He shot Meghan a look that sent sparkles all through her veins. His eyes held a promise that soon they'd be alone.

Meghan swallowed against the lump in her throat. She was so proud of him she thought she might break right down and cry.

"As to firing Meghan. . .I hope you'll rethink that. I know, and she does too, that Harvey Girls aren't supposed to keep company with men, but I want you all here to know that we've never been out on a date together. Every time we've seen each other, it's either been here at the hotel or in the company of others, like when she came with the other girls out to my place to picnic at the river. And the time circumstances forced her into my company when her car broke down in the desert. We had a proper chaperone all the time, and Doc can vouch for that."

Mr. Harvey shook his head, easing his hands into his pants' pockets. "I don't think Miss Thorson needs to worry about being dismissed. I'm sure, now that Mrs. Gregory has heard the facts of the matter, she'll be more than willing to reverse her decision—about a lot of things. War and epidemics bring about special circumstances, and we need to be flexible and understanding with one another."

Meghan looked down, away from the shock and hurt and bewilderment on Mrs. Gregory's face. She had to feel as if the ground had fallen away from beneath her. "Thank you, Mr. Harvey. In any case, my contract is finished soon, and I don't believe I'll be staying on. I've learned so much the past few months, and I'm grateful for the job, but I think—I hope— there are some changes coming in my future that will make staying on at the El Garces impossible."

"I have something to say." Natalie rose from her chair. Her

pale, hollow cheeks and wide blue eyes made her look so vulnerable. "I'm so proud of Caleb for what he did here tonight, braving the scorn of this town to stand up in public for Meghan by sharing his deepest secret. It's given me the courage to face you all with my own secret."

"Oh, Natalie, no," Meghan whispered.

"I have to. I can't lie anymore. It's dishonoring to God, to Derek, to Meghan and Dr. Bates whom I asked to keep my secret and lie for me." She folded her hands in front of herself. "Mr. Harvey, Mrs. Gregory. I wasn't truthful when I applied for this position. The truth is that I'm married. My husband, Derek, is fighting in France. I took the job because we needed the money to provide care for my mother-in-law. But I shouldn't have lied. I should've trusted God to provide for our needs."

"Married?" Mrs. Gregory put her hand to her throat.

"And I'm expecting." Rosy tint ebbed and flowed in Natalie's cheeks. "I should've come to you the minute Dr. Bates confirmed it, but I was too afraid. But no longer." She lifted the chain from around her neck and removed her wedding ring from the gold links, slipping it onto her finger and raising her chin. "I was afraid to trust God to meet our needs. His way never includes lying and deception. Caleb and Meghan have given me the courage to trust Him to take care of me and my baby."

Meghan turned to her and hugged her. "I'm so proud of you. But I'm sorry, too. I'm going to miss you so much."

Mrs. Gregory seemed at a loss for words. She blinked, looking from one face to another as if she didn't recognize anyone. Mr. Stock took the head waitress's elbow and led her toward the stairs murmuring something about getting her something to drink.

"Miss, or should I say Mrs. Daviot? That was a very brave

thing you did. I'm sure we can come to a reasonable agreement about your employment." Mr. Harvey smoothed his moustache. Natalie nodded and gave a tremulous smile.

Doc took her elbow. "How about we go get some punch and cake and find a place to sit down?"

He escorted Natalie away, leaving Caleb, Meghan, and Mr. Harvey.

"Sir, thank you for all you did for me today. Thank you for bidding on the quilt. I hope you won't be too harsh with Mrs. Gregory. She's under so much pressure. Her son has been wounded and she's waiting to hear how he's faring." Meghan bit her lip.

"She's been a longtime faithful employee. I'm sure we can resolve things." He smiled. "Though I am not happy to hear that one of my best waitresses is planning on abandoning us at the end of her contract. How much time do you have left?"

"About six weeks. I should be home with my family before Thanksgiving."

His moustache twitched. "If I read the signs right, Mr. McBride might have something to say about that." Sketching a small wave, he sauntered toward the stairs and the murmur of conversation drifting up from the reception below.

Meghan found herself alone with Caleb at last. Shyness swept over her, surprising her. He released her hand.

Clink, step, *clink*, step, he walked over to the balcony rail and turned, leaning back against it. She moved to stand before him. His finger under her chin raised her face.

"Well, Meghan Thorson, it seems we have a few things to talk about."

She nodded.

"First, I want to apologize. I had no call to lay into you like I did when you were out at my place. I had no business kissing you against your will—"

"It wasn't against my will." The words tumbled out of her mouth before she could stop them.

He grinned and reached for her, cupping her shoulders and drawing her to him. "Is that so? Then maybe you won't mind this one too much. I've been wanting to kiss you all night." His lips came down on hers, familiar and yet so fresh and new and strange. Everything she remembered about their first kiss came rushing back before being drowned by feelings she'd never felt before. Stars burst behind her eyelids as she melted into him. His arms came around her, giving her an anchor in the storm of emotions and happiness and exhilaration. For the first time, she felt as if this was the real, unguarded, Caleb, free from his fears and his past, free to love and be loved. She murmured his name against his lips.

"Caleb."

A growl came from his throat, and he deepened the kiss as if he wanted to devour her. His fingers tunneled in her hair, dislodging her hat, and she clung to him as the world spun around her.

She loved him. With all her heart. She wanted her love to help heal him completely, to help him forget the pain of the past and reach toward a brighter future, together.

He lifted his lips from hers and peppered her face with kisses. "I know we have so much to talk about, but I could stand here with you in my arms forever."

Turning her face, she rested her cheek against his chest. His chin came down on top of her head, his arms still around her. She sighed. There was nowhere on earth she'd rather be. His heart thudded under her ear, in time with her own.

"I love you, Meghan. I've tried to fight it. I've tried to hold you at arms' length, but I just can't anymore. I think I fell in love the first time I looked into your eyes. You knocked the wind out of me, literally."

She hugged him tighter and looked up into his face. "I love you, too, Caleb McBride. And I'm so sorry for everything. I wish I had been true to my first instinct about you instead of letting Mrs. Gregory and her friends sway me. I let what they *said* override how you acted. You were courteous, brave, self-sacrificing, understanding, caring—"

"Whoa, whoa, whoa, I'm no saint. God had to have a pretty stern talk with me about my pride and about the anger and bitterness I was carrying around about this town. We haven't really started to work on how I feel about my family yet." He grimaced. "Nor the jealousy I felt toward someone named Lars that you claimed to love." Giving her a little shake, he kissed the tip of her nose. "That was naughty of you."

"I do love Lars." She put on her most innocent expression. "But not the same way I love you."

"My leg doesn't matter?"

"Not to my love for you. Not one single bit. I love you."

"You're sure, because it isn't going away."

"I certainly hope it isn't." She noted the tired lines around his eyes. "Let's sit down. You're still recovering from the flu."

Once seated side-by-side on the folding chairs, Caleb took her hands. "Thank you for taking such good care of Joshua and me when we were sick. I was scared that I would die before I got to tell you how I felt about you. Then, when I knew you had seen my leg and you didn't come to see me at Doc's place, I thought maybe you were so repulsed you couldn't bear it." He swallowed hard, his vulnerability blazing in his eyes. "That happened to me before, a woman I thought I loved and was going to marry found out about my leg and she couldn't handle it. She broke things off. That's when I left Kentucky and headed out here. The desert seemed to mirror how I felt inside. I didn't intend to keep my leg a secret here, but somehow, when someone asked me why I hadn't enlisted, I just couldn't make myself say the words." He shook his head. "I could've kept you from a lot of trouble if I'd just have been honest up front."

She stroked his cheek, reveling in the freedom to touch him and not be rejected. "No recriminations. The past is the past and we can't change it. Our job is to do the right thing here and now."

"I guess the right thing then is to ask you if you will marry me. I'd get down on one knee, but. . ." He waved toward his brace. "I might not be able to get up again."

He'd taken her breath away. "This will do me just fine. And if you're asking, I'm accepting. Yes, Caleb McBride, I will marry you. But I warn you. I don't do anything by halves. I'm going to love you with everything I have."

He leaned in and kissed her again, this time with a hunger and power she hadn't anticipated but reveled in. Ending the kiss, he put his forehead against hers. "I'm counting on it."

When he'd caught his breath, he asked, "What about your job? Harvey Girls aren't supposed to be engaged."

"I think it will be okay. I know a guy." She gave him a saucy grin. "Though I suppose we should be circumspect for the next few weeks. I don't want to flout Mrs. Gregory's authority completely. If they let me stay on, I'll be respectful, though it won't be easy."

He laughed. "Now why doesn't that surprise me?" He kissed her again. "I don't think I will ever get tired of that. Who would've thought the beautiful redhead with the amazing green eyes—the girl I rescued from falling under a train—would be the one to take on this town on my behalf? Not only that, but she stormed the walls and barriers I had put up around my heart. She snuck in when I wasn't looking and healed parts of me I didn't even realize were broken. How could I not love her?"

"And the man labeled a coward took on that same town on my behalf." She rested her head on his shoulder. "And he sacrificed his privacy, exposed his most vulnerable secret in order to stand up for me. How could I not love him?"

His chest heaved in a sigh. "I suppose we should head downstairs to the reception. We have to face the town sometime."

"A shame. I'd love to stay right here in your arms forever, just you and me."

"We'll do it together." He rose and offered his hand. "You and me."

Epilogue

Two days before Meghan's contract ended, she stood in the dining room, tears streaming down her face, reading the headline of the *Desert Star*. Caleb stood beside her as people cried and hugged and yelled.

The Armistice had been signed. The war was over. Lars would come home. Derek would return to Natalie and his family to await the birth of their baby. All of America's doughboys would come home.

Harvey Girl rules notwithstanding, Meghan dropped the paper and flung herself into Caleb's arms. "It's over. It's over. It's over," she chanted happily into his ear, squeezing his neck.

He held her tight as chaos reigned around them. Mrs. Gregory sat at a table and openly sobbed. Word had come the day after the auction that her son would recover from his wounds, but he had lost his right arm below the elbow. Broken, the head waitress had apologized to Meghan and Caleb, developing a whole new respect for what Caleb endured every day.

Joshua burst into the dining room. "Did you hear? Did you hear?"

"Yes. Isn't it wonderful?" Meghan reached out and drew Joshua into their hug.

"It won't change any of our plans, will it?" he asked when he'd extricated himself. "We're still going to Minnesota, right?"

"Right. On the Saturday afternoon train. You, Caleb, Doc Bates, and me. You're going to love Minnesota. I wish we were going in the springtime, but you'll get to see snow."

"I can't wait. I still can't believe he got me into college. Who would've guessed that Doc Bates had gone to medical school with Charlie Mayo?"

"Doc's going to miss you when he comes back here. He says you're underfoot all the time asking questions and trying to learn everything before you even start school."

Joshua grinned, so confident and excited, no longer the hunch-shouldered, resentful, haunted boy he'd been when Meghan first met him. His parents had given their consent to his leaving with them, and his father had even managed a rough hug of good-bye.

"Well, since you delivered the last batch of horses to the train, there hasn't been anything to do at the ranch." Joshua shrugged. "I'm going to go find Doc. He's probably heard the news by now."

That evening, Meghan and Caleb walked beside the fountain in the open-air lobby, holding hands. "It's going to be a long road ahead, isn't it? The world is going to have to find its way back to peace."

Caleb nodded. "But we'll do it. Time will heal the wounds, dull the hurt." They walked slowly to the musical accompaniment of the splashing water and the *clink* of Caleb's leg brace. He didn't wear it all the time, but by day's end, he usually had it on. She never mentioned it unless he did, still finding her way with how much he wanted to share about his leg and how he was feeling about it. Time would help with that, too.

"I'm just glad it's all over. Healing can't start until the fighting ends."

"That was certainly true for us, wasn't it? You're a little firebrand when you get riled up." He brushed his fingers along her temple, his eyes soft.

"Papa would say it was my Celtic heritage that makes me

volatile, and Mama says it's my Viking blood."

He wrapped his arms around her and rested his chin on her hair. "Whatever it is, I'm glad it's mine."

"Me too, Caleb. Me too."

Even though **Erica Vetsch** has set aside her career teaching history to high school students in order to homeschool her own children, her love of history hasn't faded. Erica's favorite books are historical novels and history books, and one of her greatest thrills is stumbling across some obscure historical factoid that makes her imagination leap. She's continually amazed at how God has allowed her to use her passion for history, romance, and daydreaming to craft historical romances that entertain readers and glorify Him. Whenever she's not following flights of fancy in her fictional world, Erica is the company bookkeeper for her family's lumber business, a mother of two terrific teens, wife to a man who is her total opposite and yet her soul mate, and an avid museum patron.